SUMMER OF THE VIGILANTES

CHRISTOPHER POOLE

authorHOUSE®

AuthorHouse™
1663 Liberty Drive
Bloomington, IN 47403
www.authorhouse.com
Phone: 1-800-839-8640

Published by AuthorHouse 12/16/2011

ISBN: 978-1-4259-5744-5 (sc)

Library of Congress Control Number: 2006907345

For Mom and Dad.
Without you, I'm nothing.

"The world is a dangerous place, not because of those who do evil, but because of those who look on and do nothing." ~Albert Einstein

CONTENTS

Picnic In the Bowery

The single, echoing gunshot; the woman's shrill cry of terror; the squishy 'thud' of the mugger falling to the pavement with a bloody hole in his forehead, his open switchblade clattering beside him. Gary Parker was intimately familiar with each of these noises, and he knew that none of them would draw unwanted attention here in the Bowery, the neighborhood being the seedy, derelict locale that Luc Sante had described as 'the capital of dissipation', 'the forum of the slums', and 'the last stop on the way down'. Serving as the boundary between Chinatown and the Lower East Side, running from Chatham Square in the south to Astor Place in the north, the notorious expanse of Manhattan degradation known as the Bowery was a regular stomping ground for violent criminals, and it was the hunt for that very species that had brought Gary into the dark, enshrouding fold of the predators' domain. The promise of bagging a big one always excited him. Of course, there had been nothing extraordinary about the mugger. The mugger had been little more than a distraction; a squirrel with which to amuse himself while he waited for the bear to crash into view.

"You all right, ma'am?" Gary, reholstering his Beretta 96 handgun, asked the woman whom he had just saved from the mugger. "Do you need a doctor?"

The woman – a plump, middle-aged specimen in chunky heels and an unflattering floral print – screamed again, then turned and bolted down the street, leaving her handbag lying in the dirt.

How do you like that? Gary thought. *Not even so much as a thank you. Sometimes I wonder why I bother doing this job.*

Many people would have argued readily that Gary's 'job' wasn't actually a job. Many people would have rushed to call him an outlaw, a rogue, and even a murderer. Gary preferred the term 'vigilante'.

Stifling a yawn, and rubbing the left of his two tired eyes, Gary took an uncomfortable seat atop a fire hydrant and looked across the street to a decrepit two-story building, its broken windows boarded up, its forlorn exterior crumbling visibly. It was the abandoned shell of a former flophouse, condemned to demolition like so many of its recently leveled brethren, but remained standing a full two years after its death sentence had been pronounced, looming over the street like a ruined monolith, haunting all passersby with conjurings of its despondent phantoms. Gary had visited this flophouse many times, as it had proven itself a favorite stop-off for fugitive sociopaths, and the sight of the dying giant – for 'twas surely a living thing – always stirred within him a deep blue feeling of melancholy.

I used to like to walk the straight and narrow line.
I used to think that everything was fine.
Sometimes I'd sit and gaze for days through sleepless dreams,
All alone and trapped in time.

Tommy Shaw's lyrics to the Styx song 'Crystal Ball' danced through his head with the wispy, ephemeral grace of ghosts riding the breeze, and it wasn't until he was snapped out of his haunting trance by the spontaneous barking of a dog three yards over that he realized he had pulled his metal flask automatically from within his jacket and had partially unscrewed the cap. Embarrassed, he scowled to himself, and hurled the flask fifteen feet into a garbage can. Two points.

Not gonna get me tonight, thought Gary. *Not gonna get me ever again.*

A series of three helpless, agonized shrieks pierced the relative silence, and Gary leapt reflexively to his feet and raced across the street and around the corner to the perceived origin of the ungodly noise, already horribly certain of what he would find.

From the sound of things, the young woman had experienced a quick death, and in that respect, she might actually have been lucky, as her mutilated corpse was truly a grotesque sight to behold, sprawled as it was over the curb like a piece of discarded litter, blood flowing steadily in rivers from six deep knife wounds in her neck, chest, and belly, and pooling in the gutter before trickling down a nearby storm drain.

Fuck! Gary cursed to himself, spinning around to punch a lamppost in frustration and regret. *Fuck, fuck, fuck! He did it right under my nose! I was just around the corner! Why was I over there? Why couldn't I have been over* here? *Why did I have to be so fucking nearby?*

A high-pitched, psychotic chortle lilted around from the front of the dilapidated building, followed immediately by the gleeful slamming of a door, and Gary began walking, his teeth set, and his darkened eyes devoid of any of the mercy or compassion that a less experienced, more principled man might have allowed.

If the flophouse's exterior resembled a disintegrating fortress, the inside of the forsaken building looked like a bombed-out bunker, and in the absence of an electrical light source, Gary had to pick his way carefully through the scattered wreckage of broken cots, shattered glass, and ragged clothes as he ventured ever further inside this den of iniquity, stepping across the dust-blanketed floor with quiet care, doing his best to ignore the rancid stench of rotting meat still emanating from what had used to be the kitchen.

Where are you, you son of a bitch? he wondered.

There were plenty of shadows and dark corners in which his quarry could hide, but the same advantage was afforded to Gary, and he doubted that the dragon of this dungeon had yet sensed the encroaching knight in its midst. Gary's mode of stealth was spoiled, however, when he happened to put his right foot down upon a roving rat, which squeaked indignantly and scurried back over to its established territory. He barely had time to wonder if this would draw any unwanted attention before he was struck hard in the side and cast to the floor beneath the impact of a firm, bony shoulder.

"Well, well, as I live and breathe!" trilled the voice of a lunatic. "A plainclothes cop coming after little ol' me! I'm really moving up in the world! Can SWAT teams be far behind?"

"I'm not a cop," said Gary, rising to his feet, brushing a thick layer of dust from his jacket. "I'm the boogeyman. A highly skilled, exhaustively trained warrior whose one ambition for the evening is to wring the last breath of life from your miserable body."

"Oooooh, you're creeeeepy!" giggled the unseen killer. "What's your name, sailor?"

"Gary Parker," said Gary. "I'm thirty years old, and a Taurus. I like classic TV, long walks on the beach, and men who cry."

The killer's ensuing fit of hysterics made it seem as if he was moving rapidly about the room.

"Well, hi there, Gary," the killer chuckled. "My name is Casey Munroe. I'm single and not looking, but I do like to tie up young women, fuck them with foreign objects, then stab them over and over again with really big knives! So, now that the introductions are out of the way, why don't we have ourselves a ball?"

Gary was forced to jump back and cover his eyes with his forearm as a wall of hot, orange flame shot up right in front of him, as if Casey Munroe had just set fire to a trail of kerosene. Mere seconds later, that same adversary came bursting through the very fire itself, swinging a wooden baseball bat at Gary's head.

By the light of the raging fire, Gary could now make out the appearance of his enemy. Munroe was a lightweight, sinewy man in a dirty t-shirt and jeans, with an unruly mop of dyed purple hair atop his pimply scalp. A long, crescent-shaped scar festooned the right side of his gaunt face, arcing from the outer corner of his eyebrow to the tip of his chin, and a peculiar muscle tic threw a small, involuntary spasm continuously through his left shoulder. Along with the utterly crazy look in his eyes, Gary thought, he looked like a rabid, drunken jackal.

Gary bent his body backwards to avoid the first swing from the bat, smoothly sidestepped the second, then grabbed it on the third, yanked it towards himself, and kicked Munroe in the gut, sending him flailing backwards into the fire. Munroe screamed in panic and began rolling desperately around on the floor while Gary watched.

"Now, you see, you weren't listening, Casey, old son," said Gary, smacking the end of the bat repeatedly into the palm of his left hand while he waited for his enemy to extinguish himself. "I told you, I'm no cop. I'm a vigilante, and not a very forgiving one at that. You see, I used to live in London, where I worked as an assassin for the British government. And before you make any cracks about flying Aston Martins or steel-rimmed bowler hats, let me assure you that I wasn't James Bond. No tuxedos or martinis or adoring Russian contortionists for me. No, the particular branch for which I worked was quite shadowy, and its existence was unknown not only to the populace at large, but also to most of the politicians and bureaucrats controlling the government. An elite, highly exclusive little corner of the Secret Service which deployed masterfully skilled, perpetually dangerous combatants like me in its own, personal piece of the never-ending war against enemies of the state."

Munroe groaned as he rolled limply over onto his back, the last of the ravenous flames having been smothered by his frantic maneuvers, though he'd obviously been badly burnt.

"And it's true that I was unquestionably loyal and obedient to my superiors, Casey, but that's what they taught us," Gary continued, dropping the heavy bat down onto the hapless murderer's stomach. "After all, if you don't do as you're told in that business, what fucking good are you? Sure, things were always a little bit under the level, but it's not as if any of it wasn't official government business. I was just doing my job. I really don't think I deserved to have my family slaughtered, but that's what happened, old chum. I failed to see a job through, and one of my more vengeful enemies doubled back on me and murdered my fiancée and the unborn child she was carrying."

The trip down memory lane clearly not improving his mood, Gary was sweaty and red-faced as he advanced on the incapacitated Munroe, knelt down, and seized him by the front of his blackened t-shirt.

"I can see you're in a great deal of pain," Gary growled, "so I won't go on and on about my interminable plunges into depression, despair, and alcoholism that followed. Suffice to say that I've been in New York for six years now, ripping the guts out of douchebags like you, because odds are it was someone's fiancée you just perforated out there. And I'm not alone, either. I head up a group of nine other uniquely talented individuals, all just as devoted as I am to the fighting of crime and the prevalence of justice. We're vigilantes, Casey. We're unaffiliated with, unsanctioned by, and unknown to any official police force or government agency, and that means we don't have to take any shit. We don't need to worry about search warrants, or Miranda rights, or probable cause, or anything else that ties the hands of better men than you or me. We're illegal, clandestine, and completely under the radar, and we're making scum like you disappear."

Five minutes later, Casey Munroe was standing precariously upright atop the rickety banister of the high, narrow mezzanine that overlooked the flophouse's first floor. His ankles were bound together, his wrists were tied behind his back, and a third length of rope, secured to one of the sturdier beams above, ended in a noose strung tightly around his neck. He stood perfectly still upon the slender rail of rotting wood, mad as a rabid dog but certainly not ignorant enough to believe he could survive a plunge from the makeshift balance beam. Gary enjoyed a much more secure position, leaning casually against the wall in an old, wobbly chair directly opposite the delicately placed killer.

"So, friend Casey," said Gary, his air of utter nonchalance adding insult to injury, "I've explained to you the reason why you've ended up in this position, which is a damn sight more than you do for *your* victims. The police can't catch you, and even if they did, they probably wouldn't be able to hold you. You're clearly off your nut, so just about any attorney worth his law school tuition would be able to have you installed in a nice, comfy, minimum security hospital, where you'd live out the rest of your days in taxpayer-sponsored tranquility, watching cable TV and feeding the ducks. And we, the Vigilantes, find such a proposition completely unacceptable."

"You can't kill me, asshole!" Munroe spat. "I'll be back! I'll be back to getcha!"

"You've killed a lot of people, Casey," said Gary. "Do you have anything to say about that?"

"Fuck you!"

"Wrong answer."

Still seated, Gary thrust out his right leg and kicked the banister, hard. The wood splintered, and Casey Munroe had just enough time for one good scream before he literally reached the end of his rope.

The sober expression on his face indicating neither satisfaction nor remorse, Gary rose from his chair, walked the length of the mezzanine to the old wooden staircase, and began descending, not paying an ounce of attention to the figure hanging from the ceiling, suddenly limp and lifeless, swinging from side to side like a windsock. Then the cellular phone in his pocket came alive to the tune of the *Cheers* theme song (he hadn't lied about his penchant for classic TV), and he answered it with his usual jocularity that belied his inner demons.

"Gary Parker's Wax Museum, Buffalo Farm, and House of Pancakes," he announced, his tone lighter than before. "What can I do for you?"

"Gary, are you still in the Bowery area?" asked the female voice on the other end of the line.

"Yeah."

"Well, we've finally got a trace on the Bayside Butcher. He's gone to ground inside a burned-out old tenement house down there."

"Then may God have mercy on his soul," said Gary, snapping the clamshell phone shut and re-pocketing it as he made for the lonely flophouse's exit, understanding and accepting that his night's work was far from finished, "because *I* certainly won't."

GAMBLING MAN

The White Stallion – planted in the very center of the busiest section of Manhattan's East Village, next to a cappuccino-and-poetry parlor, and directly across from a store that promised discreet sales of adult videos and erotic costumes – was one of the most popular nightclubs in the area. Open seven nights a week, the Stallion – where the stenches of sweat, cheap perfume and cologne, and cigarette smoke hung pregnant in the air, as offensive to the nose and tongue as was the deafening roar of the pounding, droning dance music to the ears – was jam-packed regularly with a diverse customer base, from the irresponsible, thrill-seeking youngsters drinking and puking their brain cells away, to the older crowd sacrificing their paychecks on the altar of alcoholism and cheating on their spouses with the loitering prostitutes, or the dancing strippers who were cleared to be taken behind the red curtain of the VIP room.

This evening was no exception.

"Six more beers for table five," said Lindsey, setting the plastic tray, laden with empty glasses, down on the bar.

"They must be havin' a contest over there," said Hal, the bartender, moving immediately to fill the order. "Maybe the last one to pass out pays the tab. Hey, you all right, Lindsey? You look kinda pale."

"I'm fine," said Lindsey, taking a few deep breaths and fanning herself with her hand. "Just a little hot in here, I guess."

"Y'oughta get a job someplace else, y'know," said Hal, filling the glasses with a speed and efficiency that came with years of practice. "This is no kinda place for a nice young girl like you."

Lindsey agreed, and she had been scouring Manhattan for another waitressing job for weeks now, with no results. She couldn't understand it. She was young, attractive, agreeable, and hard-working, yet not even Friendly's would take her on. Aware, as every young woman must be in the twenty-first century, of all of her potentially marketable talents and attributes, she had even applied for a job at Hooters, but that venture, too, had ended in disappointment. Apparently the unreliable economy was putting a crush on *everybody*, including well-endowed young waitresses.

Hal finished pouring the beers, and Lindsey hefted the tray and delivered it, reluctantly and with feigned friendliness, to the bingers at table five, each of whom took their turn at slapping or pinching her ass, to which she responded with the hospitable tolerance upon which the management insisted, gritting her teeth in a forced smile and saying things like, 'Hey, you, don't prod the produce!', and, 'Look, but don't touch!', in a precious, indulgent voice, when she really wanted to kick each and every one of the misogynist pigs in their overstimulated loins and cool them off by dumping their own beers over their stupid, pointed heads.

"Waitress!" another voice, this one emanating from the booth in the nearby corner, belted out the familiar call to duty, reminding Lindsey for the millionth time how she loathed being in the service industry. "Waitress! Over here!"

Lindsey sighed, forced her standard smile, and turned to answer the command.

The man in the booth was somewhere in his mid-twenties, and if he were standing, he would have been about six feet tall. His head was shaved smooth, and his eyes were concealed behind a pair of dark sunglasses. He wore an expensive leather jacket, open to reveal his bare chest, a pair of blue jeans with holes in the knees, and a pair of black leather gloves on his conspicuously large hands.

"Good evening, sir," said Lindsey, approaching the man's booth and turning over a new page on her notepad. "What can I get for you?"

The man didn't order a drink, but quickly produced a hypodermic needle and jabbed it into Lindsey's thigh. Lindsey gasped in surprise and recalled, immediately, with a sort of dreamy horror, the newspaper article she had read the other day about gang members going around stabbing randomly selected people with HIV-contaminated needles. Was that what this was? Lindsey didn't know, but suddenly she wasn't feeling very well.

"What...what did you...do...?"

Her legs buckled, and she slumped weakly to the floor, like a helium-filled balloon in a deepfreeze. The shaven-headed man smirked with satisfaction, then produced a ballpoint pen and a handwritten list, and ran his eyes down the list until he came to the third entry.

Age 20-25. Between 5' and 5.5' tall. Caucasian. Fair-skinned. Blond hair, shoulder-length or longer. Blue eyes, pouty lips, white teeth. Bubbly personality. Approximate measurements: 36-24-36.

The man read through the criteria three times, all the while shooting appraising glances at the unconscious waitress on the floor, knowing that Mr. Kubritz wouldn't be happy if he made a mistake. Finally, after satisfying himself that he had made a good choice, the man used the pen to place a large, decisive checkmark next to the list's third entry, then slipped both the pen and the list back into his pocket. He bent down and hoisted Lindsey over his shoulder like a sack of laundry, then made for the exit, but was stopped at the door by Hal, who had witnessed the whole thing and now brandished the double-barreled shotgun he kept hidden behind the bar.

"I dunno who you are, slimeball, but you better just set that girl down and walk on outta here before I blow your freakin' head off," Hal threatened.

The shaven-headed man didn't back down. Instead he just smirked, gripped the end of the gun with his free hand, and, with no apparent effort, squeezed and crushed both the barrels. Little slivers of metal rained down upon the floor.

"Ain't your night, Pops," he said to the astonished Hal.

The man shoved Hal hard in the chest, sending him crashing backwards over a table, and walked briskly through the exit, Lindsey's head bouncing continuously against the small of his back with each step he took. As for the Stallion's mass of inebriated urbanites, they were so caught up in their dancing and their drinking and their orgies that, when the police questioned them later about the waitress' disappearance, there was not one, solitary soul who could give eyewitness testimony as to what had happened.

The rusty bell clanged like a fire alarm, and the rough-around-the-edges crowd of rowdy, money-clutching, badly-groomed spectators roared – some with disappointment, but most with vindication – as the bloodied, black-and-blue face of CraterHead Montgomery collided with the ham-sized fist of an incredibly muscular black man, seven feet tall and built like a battleship. A dull, squishy 'thwack' reverberated off the crumbling walls of the condemned gymnasium, and CraterHead crashed down onto the mat of the small boxing ring, his eyes glazed over and gazing stupidly up at the cracked ceiling.

"Our winner, and still champion," declared the stocky, bald fight promoter – also filling the quite unnecessary position of referee – as he pushed his way through the elastic ropes and into the ring, "the massively muscled, the pleasurably powerful, the indestructible Checkmate Charlie!"

Those in the teeming crowd who had bet their weekly paychecks on the forty-five-year-old powerhouse whooped wildly and jumped up and down, pumping their fists triumphantly into the air.

"Next fight in ten minutes, folks!" the promoter announced. "Place your bets now!"

While the gratified spectators dispersed, and two heavyset hoods dragged the unconscious form of CraterHead Montgomery from the ring, Charlie clapped his big hand down on the promoter's shoulder and pulled him aside.

"I'm not doin' anymore fights tonight," he said. "We agreed on three, and I've done three."

"But you're so good for business, Chuck, ol' boy," said the promoter. "This is the biggest turnout we've had in weeks!"

"Has it ever occurred to you that I might have other things to do with my valuable time?" Charlie asked.

"Aw, don't be like that, Chucky," said the promoter. "Look, I'll give you an extra five hundred if you stay on for one more. Deal?"

Charlie sighed like a steam engine, then nodded. The promoter beamed with satisfaction, and wasted no time in going off to recruit another combatant, while Charlie climbed out of the ring and lumbered over to one of the locker rooms in the back. He had been doing this for some time now, participating in underground brawls for a little extra money. It was a profitable bit of moonlighting for a man who did not find it quite beyond his capabilities to benchpress a Volkswagen Beetle, but being the reigning champion of a circuit of illegal club fights came not without certain annoyances, one of which was the promoter's consistent demands for more and more appearances.

After tonight, I'll take a week or so off, thought Charlie, pushing open the locker room door and stomping over to the cracked, dirty sink. *It's about time he realized I'm not some kind of show horse.*

Charlie twisted the sink's squeaky cold water tap, causing it to noisily vomit out a tobacco-colored stream of rusty water, which he pooled in his hands and splashed onto his bruised face. He then dried his face with a dirty flannel, and looked in the cracked, filth-smeared mirror to examine the eye upon which CraterHead had landed a direct punch. It was bright red, and stinging like hell, but there didn't seem to be any damage.

Peeling his sweat-soaked tanktop from his prodigious frame, Charlie threw it onto the cot and walked over to the small shower – almost too small to accommodate his girth – but when he pulled the plastic curtain aside, he found that someone had beaten him to it.

The man called H.J. Haberdash leaned against the shower's scummy, mildew-covered wall, his arms crossed angrily over his chest, a scowl darkening his refined features, which included a full head of distinguished white hair, a bushy white mustache bristling beneath his patrician nose, and a monocle jammed into his right eye. As was typical of his taste in working clothes, he sported a three-piece, single breasted, classic cut business suit, navy blue with a black-and-white necktie, a gold pocket watch that had been in his family for three generations, and a pair of immaculately polished black leather shoes.

"That was very naughty of you, Mr. Checkmate," said Haberdash, stepping out of the shower. "I thought we'd agreed that you'd throw the fight with Mr. CraterHead this evening."

"I don't throw fights," said Charlie.

"Mr. Kubritz had a substantial amount of money riding on your opponent," said Haberdash. "He's hardly going to be pleased with this outcome."

"Tell him to bet on me next time," Charlie replied.

"I don't care for your insolence," said Haberdash. "I promised Mr. Kubritz a highly satisfactory result, and, because of you, I have failed to deliver. Of course, after spending any productive amount of time in Mr. Kubritz's employ, one learns quickly the necessity of redeeming oneself urgently after committing a blunder. So I'm going to take you back to base with me, and let him place the blame upon the man to whom it rightfully belongs."

Charlie felt the cold kiss of a double-barreled shotgun being pressed into the small of his bare back, and he turned his head slowly to see the weapon in the hands of Haberdash's flunky, his stubby finger curled around the trigger, his squinty eyes betraying a psychopathic eagerness to pull it.

"I trust you won't make any trouble," Haberdash said, haughtily, relaxing his guard while he polished his monocle fastidiously with a monogrammed handkerchief. "I will not hesitate to tell my man to shoot if I sense any forthcoming irksomeness."

"You guys are kidding, right?" said Charlie, almost stupefied by Haberdash's bubbling surplus of undue self-confidence. "I'm on one of those hidden camera shows, aren't I? All right, I give. Where's the little red light?"

"My friend, you have a most irritating habit of making light to your betters," said the arrogant Haberdash. "You would do well to remember your place in this world. You are an ox; a strong but unsophisticated beast of burden, inconsequential and certainly expendable. Taking into consideration your extraordinary brawn, Mr. Kubritz may see fit to spare you punishment in exchange for the utilization of your talents, but don't press your luck with me. I have little patience for punk niggers who don't know their chains have been cut off."

Well, thought Charlie, *that settles that, then.*

With surprising speed, Charlie whipped his muscled arm around behind his back, seized the barrels of the shotgun, yanked the weapon from the flunky's hands, and smashed the butt end into the tile wall like a club, breaking open the weapon and sending the twin shells clattering to the floor. Before either enemy could react to the surprising maneuver, Charlie spun around to deliver a vicious backhand to the flunky, resulting in the thug's bone-rattling collision with the far wall. Then he wrapped his thick fingers around Haberdash's lapels.

"Punk nigger? Rolls off your tongue real easy, don't it?" said Charlie, lowering his face and pulling Haberdash up onto his tiptoes until he stood nose to nose with the well-dressed enforcer. "You must've been usin' that language for a long time. Maybe since childhood. Why, if I'd ever said somethin' like that when I was a kid, my mother would've washed my mouth out with soap."

Still holding Haberdash by his jacket with one hand, Charlie reached into the shower with his other hand, seized the well-used bar of soap – decorated with dark hairs extracted from who-knew-how-many people's nether regions – and stuffed it forcefully into Haberdash's mouth, jamming it in with the heel of his palm while the smaller man foamed and gagged. When the bar was firmly inserted, the big Vigilante hoisted Haberdash to his full height and punched him on the jaw. Haberdash spun around twice and crashed facedown in the shower, where he remained, coughing and sputtering.

"Punk nigger, huh?" said Charlie, availing himself once again of his tanktop as he headed for the door. "Looks to me like only one of us has a master to run back to."

Then he was gone, and Haberdash clambered to his knees and clawed at the inside of his mouth with both hands, scraping out as much of the soap as he could, but he barely had time to remove the slimy remnants of the bar before the door opened again, this time revealing a shaven-headed man sporting sunglasses, black gloves, blue jeans, and an open leather jacket. He took one look at Haberdash, groveling pathetically on the grimy floor, and shook his head, slowly, with a chilling half smile.

"This doesn't bode well for you at all," he said.

Haberdash bowed his head, and groaned.

"Ralph, they're still following us," Margaret hissed to her husband, as the elderly couple picked up their pace. "That's two blocks now."

"I know," said Ralph. "Just keep walking. Don't look back. We're almost home."

Despite her husband's advice, Margaret couldn't help but look back once more at the trio of youngsters shadowing them persistently, the eerie glow of the interspersed street lights illuminating their gang colors and twisted grins.

"They're going to hurt us, Ralph, I just know it," she said, the tremor of panic in her voice becoming more pronounced. "What do you suppose they want?"

"Just keep walking," said Ralph, forging straight ahead.

Ralph tried to sound brave for his wife, and advocate the most reasonable course of action, but he, too, was troubled. A dark, virtually abandoned stretch of street in a rather notorious neighborhood, with no police in sight, and three young toughs, doubtless ill-intentioned, bearing down on them from behind. He just hoped, as he wrapped his raincoat tightly around himself for security, that Maggie couldn't sense how frightened he was.

Then the wind blew out of him, and a hard, sharp pain flooded through his midsection as an iron crowbar – clutched in the fist of a fourth punk who had stepped suddenly out in front of them from an alley on their left – struck him in the stomach, and he crashed to the pavement, gasping. The punk seized Ralph under his arms and dragged him back into the alley, and, an instant later, the other three, who had spent the past ten minutes in relaxed pursuit of the couple, arrived, and pushed Margaret into the alley after him.

"Nice night for a walk, huh?" said the punk with the crowbar. "Not on Red Cobra turf, though. Ya wanna use our street, there's a toll that's gotta be paid."

"What's the toll for two old farts out past their bedtime?" asked the punk with the eyepatch and length of bicycle chain.

"A pint each oughta do it," said the third punk, flicking open a switchblade and twirling it, fancily.

"Or we could just kill 'em both," suggested the fourth punk, pulling a handgun from his waistband. "I mean, it ain't like we ain't makin' this up as we go."

"That might not be such a bad idea," the Cobra with the crowbar acknowledged. "We ain't killed anyone in almost a week. The Hunters are gonna think we're goin' soft if we don't off somebody soon. What do you think, y'old scag?"

"No! Please! Please don't hurt us!" Margaret begged, tearfully.

"Then it's decided," said the Cobra with the crowbar. "We kill 'em. Straight execution style so they know who did it. Bullet to the head. Go to it."

The Cobra with the handgun grinned sadistically, extended his arm to aim the weapon at Ralph's forehead, and raised his thumb to cock it, and, in that instant, a razor-pointed shuriken throwing star flew in from nowhere, and, with a quick 'whiiiizzz', severed the thumb from the Cobra's hand. The kid screamed as he watched his thumb drop to the ground – followed immediately by his gun – and twitch spasmodically in the dirt like a writhing inchworm whose back end has just been stepped on.

"The lady said 'please'," said a dangerous, sinister voice from behind the startled group.

The four Cobras – and Ralph and Margaret – turned and were astonished to see a lithe, shadowy figure standing at the other end of the alley, his head held high, his back ramrod straight, his fists clenched at his sides, and his feet spaced broadly apart, like some elemental titan drawing pure energy from the earth beneath.

"Who the fuck is that?" one of the Cobras asked no one in particular.

"The thumb was a warning," said the newcomer. "If you do not surrender this instant, then I make no promise that all, if any, of you will leave this place alive."

"Fuck, I dunno who you are, man, but you are dead!" declared the Cobra with the crowbar. "Y'hear me? You're dead!"

Roaring furiously, the Cobra charged at the stranger, raising the crowbar over his head in preparation for a head-breaking swing. The swing never connected, however, as the stranger fell backwards onto his hands, thrust his feet up into the air to kick the weapon away, then brought his legs together like a pair of scissors against either side of the Cobra's ribcage. The Cobra screamed in pain as his ribs cracked, and he dropped to his knees. The stranger then delivered a hard knee to the Cobra's face, and the punk sprawled off to one side, blood oozing from his nose and mouth. The entire fluid chain of movements had taken less than four seconds.

The Cobra brandishing the bicycle chain, as skilled with his weapon of choice as Indiana Jones with his bullwhip, was next to charge the new enemy, but he was dispatched just as easily by the stranger. With one graceful move that carried him up and to the right of the chain's arc of destruction, the stranger leapt into the air, clapped one hand down onto the Cobra's left shoulder, and somersaulted over his head. The next second, the *katana* was unsheathed and in his hand, and the Cobra fell flat on his face, a bloody gash running the full length of his spinal cord.

Without a word of warning or a growl of ceremony, the thumbless Cobra seized his gun with his other, unmutilated hand, leveled it at the stranger, and curled his finger around the trigger. The stranger had, of course, seen the move coming a mile away, and, in the two seconds' time that it took the young thug to effectively aim the gun, the stranger tore a three-pronged *sai* from his belt and hurled it with perfect precision. Just as the dark combatant had planned, the center prong flew directly into the barrel of the gun, jamming it a millisecond before the Cobra pulled the trigger. It was with a degree of satisfaction that the stranger watched the gun explode in the punk's face, sending the misguided youth screaming to the ground, his hands clapped over his eyes.

The fourth and final Cobra stood nonplussed as his wide eyes darted from one of his fallen comrades to the other, all eating asphalt and moaning in agony, and he was sure – he was *certain* – that the stranger could hear the thunderous, uncontrolled pounding of his heart as he waited patiently for the young thug to make the next move.

"I give up!" he relinquished at last, dropping his knife to the pavement with a clatter and thrusting his hands straight up into the air. "You win! Just don't kill me, man!"

The stranger stepped forward, allowing himself to be illuminated, for the first time, by the harsh neon light of the pink Chuck's Chicken sign above. He was about five-and-one-half feet tall, and was dressed from head to toe in a bodysuit of black spandex; his face was hidden behind a black stocking mask, through which only his cool, almond-shaped eyes were visible.

"In realizing that knowing when to quit often puts you in the lead, you have proven wiser than your friends," said the stranger. "Or are you just the backsliding coward that hangs to the rear during every battle, so that you may see which side merits your sympathy? No matter. Either way, you have lost, and, as the loser, you must accept my terms."

Before the frightened kid could ask what those terms were, the stranger once again unsheathed his *katana*, and, with unmatchable speed, cut a shallow 'V' into the youth's forehead. The Cobra cried out, his exclamation born more of surprise than pain, as twin trickles of blood ran down into his face.

"Show that to your friends," said the stranger. "Show it to your enemies as well. Tell all of your loathsome kind that this street no longer 'belongs' to any of you, and that people like this gentleman and his wife are free to come and go as they please, without fear of persecution. Is that quite clear?"

The Cobra nodded, eagerly.

"Now, get out of my sight," said the stranger.

The humbled Cobra wasted no time in running past his triumphant enemy, but when he reached the alley's exit, he seemed to grow suddenly bold again.

"This ain't over, y'know!" he shouted. "S'long as big boss Kubritz rules this town, there's always gonna be a piece for guys like us!"

The stranger whirled to face the Cobra once again, a threatening glare in his steely eyes, and the punk quickly departed. Then the stranger turned to Ralph and Margaret, still on the ground and understandably apprehensive about this mystery man's intentions towards them.

"Are you all right?" he asked them.

"Erm…uh…yes," Margaret stammered, somewhat breathlessly. "Yes, I think so. Thank you."

"Not at all," he said. "Now, you'll excuse me if I hurry off, but the piece of human filth I was pursuing was already three blocks ahead of me when I stopped to teach these boys a lesson in manners, and I badly need to make up for lost time."

The elderly couple didn't have time to say anything more before the stranger leapt up to grab the bottom rung of the fire escape suspended above, and, with the speed and agility of a cat, swung himself up onto the set of metal steps and ascended once again to the rooftops from whence he had come, making not a sound. Within five seconds, he had disappeared completely from view.

Her name was Marla Hennessy, fifteen-year-old daughter of wealthy philanthropist, politician, and man-about-town David Hennessy. In the normal course of events, she'd probably have been trussed up in an overpriced evening gown, accompanying her father reluctantly to one of his boring and tedious social extravaganzas; such as it was, she was instead trussed up in ropes and tied to a chair, as she had been for the past four days and nights, ever since her kidnappers had abducted her from outside of her private school on Monday afternoon. As the two men hadn't bothered to blindfold her at all, she knew that she was being held inside the deserted two-story building that had served, up until late last year, as the home of the computer laboratories of TekTronics, Inc., which, having gained over time the status of being one of the foremost pioneers in its field, had ultimately outgrown the facility. Unfortunately, the police didn't seem to be as apprised of this fact, and Marla wondered forlornly if she would ever see the light of day again.

Her kidnappers were a pair of ne'er-do-well brothers looking to cash in on Marla's father's financial prosperity. Indeed they seemed determined to take him for nearly every penny he had in exchange for the safe return of his only child, then buy a couple of islands in the South Pacific and live out the rest of their lives there in luxury. The elder brother was called Luca, and was clearly the brains of the operation. He spent most of his time guarding Marla, and kept a semiautomatic handgun in his shoulder holster. The younger brother, Maury, was somewhat on the jittery side, as if he were waiting constantly for someone to sneak up behind him, and he kept leering unashamedly at Marla, the look in his eyes making it frighteningly clear what he would have liked to do to her.

"Y'know, it's too bad she's worth so much undamaged," said Maury, pacing back and forth in front of her. "We could really have some fun with her."

Marla swallowed nervously, and, for the hundredth time since her abduction, wished she wasn't still wearing her disheveled Catholic school uniform. She knew as well as anybody the erotic button the white blouse, plaid skirt, white knee socks, and black patent leather shoes pushed on a man's libido, and she was sure that her being tied up and gagged was only serving to arouse Maury further.

"Keep it in your pants," Luca commanded. "I'm not gonna risk losin' the score of a lifetime just because you have a hard-on for teenagers."

"Oh, right," said Maury, rolling his eyes. "Like you wouldn't like to stick it up the tight, little bitch."

"Whether or not I'd like to stick it up the tight, little bitch is completely irrelevant," said Luca. "This is about money, plain and simple. If you can't keep your priorities straight, go somewhere and jerk off."

"I'll bet she's wearin' the cutest little panties under there..."

"Go! Now!"

Maury shot his elder sibling a dirty look, then plunged his hands into his pockets, turned, and stormed out of the room.

Arrogant bastard, Maury fumed to himself. *He thinks he's better than me.*

Scowling, Maury stomped down the deserted, dimly-lit corridor, to the room that he had made his own over the course of the past week. As he went, he entertained fantasies about beating Luca's face to a bloody pulp. Then he imagined what Marla would look like on her knees in front of him, her soft, manicured hands tied behind her back, her pretty little head bobbing up and down as she pleasured him with that rosebud mouth. He pictured himself seizing Marla by her long, chestnut hair, and bending her firm young body backwards like a pretzel as he thrust himself all the way up inside of her. Shit, he was horny. Just looking at her in that chair, bound and gagged, her clothes and hair disheveled, her legs parted, was enough to make him crash his coconuts. Imagine what actually touching her would be like...

Badly in need of relief, Maury reached his room, planning to pop his favorite Jenna Jameson DVD into the player and recline on his cot with a cold beer. As he opened the door, however, a hand leapt out of the room like a striking snake, grabbed him by the front of his shirt, and yanked him inside. Maury flew backwards against his cot and heard the door slam shut again before he even had the chance to look up and identify his assailant. Then the gun was in his face.

"Where's the girl?" asked Gary Parker, looking down on the kidnapper, anger in his eyes.

"Who the hell are you? How the hell did you get in here?" sputtered Maury.

Gary snarled, and struck Maury on the side of the head with the butt of his weapon, drawing blood and evoking a howl of pain from the kidnapper.

"I asked you a question, shit-for-brains," said Gary. "Where's the girl?"

"You can't treat me like this!" protested Maury. "You gotta read me my rights! I have the right to remain silent, and I wanna lawyer!"

Gary dealt Maury another blow, this time across the jaw. Maury yelled as blood spouted from his mouth and a tooth landed on the floor in front of him.

"That's brutality!" Maury lisped. "What the hell kinda cop are you?"

"I'm not a cop," said Gary. "The difference between me and a cop is that I get results. I don't give a shit about your rights, and if you don't tell me where the girl is right now, I'm going to blow your motherfucking head off."

Maury gulped.

"My brother is a small-thinking idiot who follows his dick around like a divining rod," said Luca, coming around to stand in front of Marla, "but he is right about one thing. You're a really cute kid."

Marla shuddered as Luca stroked the side of her face with the barrel of his gun.

"Maury has no imagination or depth, though," Luca continued. "He just likes what he thinks he's supposed to like; the tits, the ass, that kinda stuff. But me, I notice things; little details that make each woman unique.

And I've been noticing you. I've been noticing that your left eye is just a little bit darker green than your right. I've been noticing the three freckles on your right cheek that form a perfect triangle. And I've been noticing the way your lips..."

Luca trailed off for a few moments, as if sinking deeply into thought. Then he ran his tongue over his upper lip, and fixed his gaze with Marla's.

"Would you like me to take that stinky gag out of your mouth?" he asked, at last.

Afraid of what Luca was planning to replace it with, Marla shook her head rapidly, but Luca pulled the gag out anyway, then placed the barrel of his gun gently against her lips.

"Kiss it," he ordered.

A fat tear rolled down Marla's cheek as she parted her trembling lips and allowed the deadly phallus to be inserted into her mouth, afraid of what Luca would do to her if she disobeyed.

"That's right," cooed Luca, relishing the sight of the pink lips wrapped around the cylindrical barrel. "That's right. Caress it with your tongue. Suck it a little bit. Good girl."

Marla wept with terror and shame as she fellated the weapon. The metallic taste filled her mouth as Luca forced it progressively closer to the back of her throat until it was just short of triggering her gag reflex. Then she heard a very loud 'bang', and squealed with horror, as she thought that Luca had just discharged the gun and her spirit was now leaving her body in slow motion. Then a big glob of thick, red blood splattered down onto her white blouse, and, daring to look up, she saw that half of Luca's head had disappeared.

The kidnapper's body remained standing for exactly four seconds, then tumbled forward, the bloody remains of the head landing in Marla's lap. With the obstruction that Luca had posed now gone, Marla could see a grim-faced man standing in the doorway at the far end of the room, holding a smoking handgun.

The sudden relief of having the gun removed from her mouth, combined with the horror of Luca's exploded brains resting in her lap, and the arrival of a violent newcomer whose intentions towards her were unknown, was all too much for Marla's fragile emotional state, and she began screaming and crying as loudly as she could, wrestling against her bonds, stomping her feet, and squeezing her eyes shut, as if it would make the whole nightmare go away. Indeed she was so involved with her venting that she only vaguely felt the hated ropes being cut away, and the reassuring arm being draped across her heaving shoulders.

"It's all right, sweetheart," said Gary, wiping Marla's face gently with his sleeve. "I'm one of the good guys. You're safe now."

After a few more sniffs, sobs, and gulps of air, Marla dared to open her eyes and face the newcomer. This close, he didn't look as frightening as he had standing in the doorway. The cold, heartless grimace he had worn then was gone now, replaced by a concerned, perhaps even friendly expression. He appeared to be a bit younger than she had first thought, and though his face was home to a number of small scars and bruises, and his eyes betrayed a deep-seated anger and bitterness, none of that could completely disguise his boyish nature.

"I dropped an anonymous tip to the police a couple of minutes ago, so they should be here very shortly," said Gary. "Just wait here for them. I've taken care of the other guy as well, so you won't have to worry about him either."

"Can't...can't you stay?" asked Marla.

" 'Fraid not," said Gary, holstering his Beretta 96 and turning to leave.

"My father is a wealthy man," said Marla. "He'll want to reward you."

Gary glanced over his shoulder at the girl and smiled, slyly. "If you really want to reward me," he said, "don't give my description to the police. In fact, don't even let on that you saw anything. Say you were blindfolded the whole time."

"You want me to lie to the police?"

Gary sighed, then tore off half his right shirt sleeve, walked back to Marla, and tied the sleeve over the girl's eyes.

"There," he said. "Now you won't have to tell them."

That was the last Marla heard from him. She didn't even hear his footsteps as he walked out.

Norman Kubritz was a *big* man in every sense of the word. Tipping the scales at five hundred and ten pounds, he wore the finest tailor-made clothes to accommodate his ponderous belly and grotesque layers of fat. His neck wobbled like a turkey's, he spread out like a melting snowman when he sat down, and every inch of his massive body seemed to jiggle when he walked. Adding to the ridiculousness of his appearance was the giant bald spot atop his ill-proportioned head – he appeared to be wearing a flesh-colored skullcap – the bristly, black beard surrounding his circular mouth, and the ever-present expensive Montecristo cigar clenched between his big, yellow teeth. If he had been any other man,

Norman Kubritz's appearance would have evoked no end of laughter and ridicule from anyone who laid eyes upon him. But no one ever made fun of Norman Kubritz, because Norman Kubritz was the most powerful and feared gangster on the east coast, and had maintained that lofty position for the past thirty years.

He was a fearless and resolute man of iron, to be sure. If he had one (and only one) weakness, it was his psychological addiction to gambling. While to most people gambling is just a one-time indulgence exercised during vacations to Las Vegas or Miami Beach, to Kubritz it was a religion and a way of life. He depended upon it with an almost obsessive-compulsive fervor, and he gambled constantly with his friends and colleagues, wagering obscene portions of his ill-obtained fortune on all manner of frivolous eventualities. Indeed Kubritz laid down money on everything, from how many executions he would have to arrange during the coming week, to how many times he would have to visit the bathroom during a single twenty-four hour day.

Given this love of gambling, it was only natural that the front for Kubritz's base of operations would become a lavish casino in the center of Manhattan's grandiose Theater District. Called 'Fives & Lives', the first floor of the multilevel complex included a large gambling facility, where one could play roulette, craps, slot machines, or any number of card games amidst golden tapestries, charming wood carvings and exotic alabaster sculptures, dancing fountains, and a sea of plush, red carpeting. In another large area on the same floor, for those who were looking for less risky but equally satisfying pleasures, was one of the world's largest and most comprehensive collections of arcade video games and pinball machines. The room was practically a museum devoted to the golden age of interactive electronic entertainment, and, alongside the games, boasted several pieces of related paraphernalia, including the very first *Pac-Man* arcade machine ever constructed, and, hanging in a glass case, one of the red-and-blue jumpsuits that Bob Hoskins had worn in the *Super Mario Bros.* movie. The rarest item in the whole place was likely the *I Dream of Jeannie* pinball machine, inspired by the TV sitcom of the same name. As far as Kubritz's extensive research led him to believe, it was the last of its kind in the world. He had last heard of a duplicate in a small toys-and-games museum in South Carolina in 1999, and had subsequently hired a reliable arsonist to burn the place to the ground.

The third large area on the first floor, dubbed 'the rec center', boasted still more to do, with a heated swimming pool, a go-kart track, an area for bumper cars, a twelve-lane bowling alley, a food court, several pool tables, and nightly rounds of bingo with fabulous prizes to be won.

On the second floor, accessible by elevator, escalator, or a good old-fashioned solid oak staircase, was the pub, stocked with ample supply of every alcoholic beverage from *Dom Perignon* to Bud Lite, and the restaurant, which served the very best of French, German, Italian, Asian, Mexican, and American cuisine, while bands and orchestras played, and lovers held each other close on the dance floor.

Such was the lair of one of the most powerful criminals in the world. The seemingly legitimate cover not only protected him from the city's public officials and law enforcement authorities, all of whom knew that Kubritz was dirty but found themselves lacking in sufficient proof, but it also served as a very excellent source of income; every dollar dropped in Kubritz's casino went straight towards funding his dark and sinister enterprises.

The restaurant was where Kubritz was now, reclining in a wooden chair that creaked and groaned beneath his weight, and taking puff after relaxed, indulgent puff on his Montecristo cigar. On the table in front of him was a half-empty glass of champagne, and a china plate that had been scraped immaculately clean. Sitting across from him, on the other side of the table, was an Arab man sporting a charcoal gray business suit, a blue-and-white checkered turban, and a neatly trimmed beard that jutted only slightly outwards from his chin. The Arab's name was Malik, and he was one of Kubritz's dearest friends and most frequent gambling partners. As an arms dealer and career terrorist, Malik had lived in Afghanistan for most of his life, and, aside from being an associate of Kubritz's for the past fifteen years, had worked closely with the Taliban. When that despotic regime had finally fallen to the Americans, however, Malik thought it prudent to uproot himself and find a new place of business. And since the United States of America had been the nation responsible for his expulsion from his old country, he saw no cause for hesitation in adopting that same nation as his new country, delightfully ironic as it was.

"My countrymen are right about you Westerners, friend Norman," said Malik, grinning as he looked around at the rich surroundings of Kubritz's establishment. "You are drowning in your own disgusting decadence."

"And by 'decadent', you of course mean 'prosperous and bountiful'," Kubritz countered, also grinning, enjoying the usual banter with his friend. "Don't feel bad, Malik. It's not your fault that we're the most industrious people on Earth, and your people are the most abominable race of bloodthirsty heathens ever to walk the planet, contributing nothing to global civilization but a few gallons of pirated oil and the promise of a hideous death to anyone who doesn't wear a rag wrapped around his head."

Malik chuckled, and rapped the tabletop three times with his hairy knuckles, displaying his appreciation for the verbal jab. He reached for the open bottle of *Dom Perignon* '59 and charged both his and Kubritz's glasses.

"Permit me to propose a toast," he said, raising his bubbling glass. "To the scum of the earth. There's a reason that decent people call men like you and me the lowest of the low, friend Norman. Because we're the very foundation of humanity. As long as we're around, the rest of the human race has nowhere to go but up."

Kubritz chuckled, exhaling wisps of cigar smoke from his gaping nostrils, and clinked his glass against Malik's. After draining his glass, Malik wiped a hand across his mouth, and spoke again.

"As always, it has been a pleasure visiting with you, friend Norman," he said, "but the primary reason I came tonight was to check your progress on the arrangement we made."

"But of course," said Kubritz, heaving himself to his feet with some effort. "Let us adjourn to my private offices."

Kubritz's private offices were on the casino's third and highest floor, sealed off from the public, accessible exclusively by an elevator that could be activated only with a scan of Kubritz's right eye. There was one other elevator for use by Kubritz's most trusted and loyal lieutenants, but they still could not access the offices without Kubritz's case-by-case permission and clearance. Instead, they were deposited in a secure lobby where they awaited an audience with their employer. These were necessary measures, for although Kubritz placed a great deal of trust and faith with his best men, he knew that this business bred treachery and duplicity, and he had to be prepared for the eventuality that even his closest allies might someday turn on him. If such ever came to pass, Kubritz would have the comfort of knowing that they would be unable to access the thousands of incriminating secrets kept within the confines of the offices.

Stepping off the elevator, Kubritz invited Malik into his primary office – a large, windowless room with red carpeting on the floor, elegant cedar wood paneling on the walls, and just the right amount of soft lighting that served to illuminate, yet wasn't hard on the eyes. A potted palm tree sat in the corner by the door. The room's centerpiece was a huge mahogany desk, partnered with a big padded chair sturdy enough to support Kubritz's weight. A boastful five-by-seven-foot portrait of

Kubritz grinning nastily and smoking his trademark Montecristo graced the wall behind it.

Kubritz waved a pudgy hand at a leather couch, inviting Malik to sit down, while he walked behind his desk, took a seat in his own chair, and tapped a few keys on his computer's keyboard. The monitor was linked directly to the surveillance camera mounted on the wall in the private lobby, and, as he had hoped, he saw a shaven-headed man sporting dark sunglasses, blue jeans, black gloves, and an open leather jacket sprawling casually on the couch. Kubritz pressed the button on his desk that would unlock the lobby's only door and allow the man access into the office.

"I don't believe you two have met," said Kubritz, taking another puff on his cigar. "Malik, this is one of my most loyal and reliable employees. He's been working for me for about five years now. My, how the time flies. Anyway, he's been playing an integral role in that little arrangement of ours."

"The name's KnuckleDuster," said the shaven-headed man, extending his gloved hand to Malik, who, when taking it in his own to shake, was surprised by the severe lack of warmth in the extremity.

"An odd name," Malik observed. "Why do they call you that?"

KnuckleDuster smiled out of the left corner of his mouth, and proceeded to answer Malik's question by squeezing the Arab's hand. Hard. Very hard.

"Ow! Ow! Ooooooooowww!" Malik cried as he sank to his knees, helpless to do anything as he felt the bones in his hand cracking. "Norman...Norman, what the hell...?"

"All right, son, that's enough," said Kubritz, amused in spite of himself. "Play nice."

Obediently, KnuckleDuster released Malik, who cried out in pain again as he tried to move his swelling fingers.

"My hand!" he shouted. "You broke my hand, you son of a bitch!"

"I'll send for the house doctor before you leave," said Kubritz. "Try not to move it in the meantime. It'll hurt like hell."

"What the hell is going on here, Norman?" asked Malik, angrily. "I certainly hope that you're not planning to re-evaluate our relationship! Remember that I have a lot of special information on you, and I've made sure that it will all come out into the open if anything happens to me!"

"Please, Malik," said Kubritz, puffing calmly on his cigar. "There's nothing devious going on here. No double-crosses. I value your friendship far too highly for that. Forgive me if I indulge myself in rather... unconventional ways. I'll be honest with you now. KnuckleDuster, show our guest your hand."

Without hesitation, the young man called KnuckleDuster pulled the black glove from his right hand, and Malik was startled at the sight of a hand that looked skeletal, stripped of all flesh and muscle; the Arab did a double-take when he realized that the hand was constructed not of bone, but metal, giving it the appearance of belonging rightfully to a psychotic cyborg or evil android in a late-night movie on the Sci-Fi Channel. KnuckleDuster proceeded to roll up the sleeve of his jacket to reveal that his entire forearm, all the way up to the elbow, was in much the same condition, fashioned entirely of metal 'bones'.

"*Ebn el metanaka!*" Malik swore in his own language.

"His left is much the same," said Kubritz, blowing a smoke ring that encircled a bouquet of red and white roses on his desk and lingered there for well over a minute. "Two bionic arms that give him the strength to rend steel as if it were cardboard."

Kubritz went on to explain how the aptly named KnuckleDuster had become endowed with his artificial appendages. It turned out that KnuckleDuster had once been a young, ambitious thug called Kenny, who did freelance enforcer work for smalltime mobsters. The reputation he had garnered from many a job well done eventually won him a permanent position of employment with a Russian racketeer called Alyusha Davidov. Kenny did sterling work for Davidov for a year and a half, but was less than discreet in his pursuit of the mobster's seventeen-year-old daughter, and said mobster inevitably caught his young employee with his pants down.

"You had such promise!" Davidov had hissed, genuine disappointment in his voice, as he dragged the naked Kenny out of the bedroom and down to the basement. "But you had to go and let your dick do your thinking for you!"

Davidov had personally cut both of Kenny's arms off at the elbows with a chainsaw, then dumped him in an alley and left him to bleed to death, and he surely would have if Norman Kubritz hadn't passed the bloody, dismembered figure in his limousine and recognized him as a fellow who could one day prove useful.

Kubritz had rushed the lad to the nearest hospital just in time for the doctors to save his life, and, after Kenny had recovered and become lucid once more, Kubritz had pitched his proposal.

"I will give you back what you have lost, and allow you to take your revenge against Davidov," he had said, "and, in return, you will work exclusively for me for the rest of your life. As long as you are useful to me, you will be treated well. When you are no longer useful, you will be granted a painless and merciful execution by lethal injection, as are all of my closest lieutenants who can no longer be kept around."

To have his arms restored? To destroy Davidov? To work for a high roller like Kubritz? The pros definitely outweighed the cons. Kenny had agreed, and Kubritz had had him flown immediately to a private clinic in Switzerland, where the most advanced techniques of bioengineering and neurotechnology had been applied to endow Kenny with a pair of super strong, bionic arms that could be moved and manipulated by the brain just as naturally and as easily as the flesh-and-blood articles.

"After he had spent a sufficient amount of time in physical therapy, I brought him back to the States, and he wasted no time in using his new appendages to crush Alyusha Davidov's neck to the size of a soda straw," said Kubritz, allowing himself a faint smile. "Ah, what it must be like to be young and impetuous, eh? And since that time, KnuckleDuster has been one of my most valued employees."

"Sorry about the hand," KnuckleDuster said to Malik, in such a way that made it clear that he wasn't sorry at all. "I guess I like showing off."

Malik glowered, remaining silent as he cradled his injured hand against his chest.

"You shouldn't be angry with KnuckleDuster over a trifling incident like this," said Kubritz, finally stubbing out his cigar in a twenty-four karat gold ashtray resting on his desk. "After all, he's the one who's been diligently gathering up your...requests."

"I picked up number three tonight," said KnuckleDuster. "Just what you wanted. Blond, busty, a real sperm trap. Plus, she's a waitress, so she's used to taking orders. I deposited her with the other two."

"You're progressing very nicely, Norman," said Malik, instantly cheering up a bit. "That leaves only two more to go. And don't forget the other conditions to which you agreed."

"Certainly not," said Kubritz. "Everything will be in the offing very shortly."

"I also brought you a visitor, Mr. K," said KnuckleDuster. "Be back in a second."

KnuckleDuster disappeared from the office for a moment, then returned, dragging behind him a man of mature years, sporting a soiled navy blue business suit, a monocle, and thick ropes around his wrists and ankles.

"Call me psychic," said KnuckleDuster, dropping the exhausted form of H.J. Haberdash to the floor, traces of white foam still clinging to his lips, "but I don't think your boy won tonight."

Kubritz's eyes narrowed as he looked down from his desk at Haberdash, who trembled like a man brought before God after a lifetime of rape, theft, and murder.

"You disappoint me, old man," said Kubritz. "I had considerable millions riding on this evening's fight."

"It...it wasn't my fault!" stammered Haberdash, groping desperately for an excuse, while knowing full well that none would be enough to save him. "It was *him*! He refused to see reason! He was completely uncooperative! I was going to bring him to you, but he...he got away."

"I will deal with him in due course," said Kubritz, heaving himself to his feet and seizing a sledgehammer from the corner. "Right now, I will deal with you."

"You want me to do it, Mr. K?" asked KnuckleDuster, a hopeful tone in his voice.

"No, I'll do it," said Kubritz. "Every crime lord needs to stay a little hands-on. It is unwise to allow oneself to become exclusively managerial. You just hold him."

"No! Please, no, for the sake of all my years of loyal service to you!" pleaded Haberdash, as KnuckleDuster pulled him to his bound feet, then bent him over so that his head was resting on the top of Kubritz's desk.

"You'll ruin your desk, Norman," Malik pointed out.

"I'll buy a new one."

Kubritz raised the sledgehammer high into the air, then brought it crashing down upon the screaming Haberdash's head, which exploded like a ripe watermelon at a Gallagher concert, splattering red blood and spongy bits of brain tissue onto the clothes of Kubritz and his two associates. The blow, having been cushioned by Haberdash's head, left only a small, spider web pattern of cracks in the desk's hard surface.

"Such talent and experience is wasted," sighed Kubritz, almost as if he regretted the necessity of smashing his henchman's head to smithereens.

"Theatrics, Norman," said Malik. "Hollow, meaningless theatrics. It would have been much less trouble, and much more sanitary, to have simply shot the man."

"But not nearly as much fun," said Kubritz, "and since Haberdash's incompetence tonight has cost me a pot in the upper seven figures, I wanted to get my money's worth."

As is the case every year in the northeastern United States, winter had been a complete and total bitch. This most recent of past winters had endured for a full stretch of nearly eight months, with the sun appearing sporadically and infrequently between late October and mid-May. Even within the urban confines of one of the largest cities on Earth, where the constant pollution tended to keep the air at least tolerably warm, the denizens of New York had been blasted back to the Ice Age by the raw, biting cold, made a hundred times worse by the perpetual wind chill that seemed to keep the mercury level hovering consistently between zero and negative ten degrees.

Statistics had shown an all-time low in the use of public transportation; not only because it had been far too cold to stand out in the open waiting for a bus or a taxi, clutching one's laughably inadequate winter coat around oneself while one's extremities lost all sense of feeling, and the icy wind stripped three layers of skin from one's face; and not only because the interiors of the subway stations had become coated with frost, crowded constantly with shivering people trying to get out of the wind, and serving as a new winter residence for the throngs of homeless who knew they would be unable to survive even one night exposed to the elements in the parks; but also because the miserable weather had declared its own brand of biological warfare upon the metropolis, weakening people's immune systems, and forcing them together into small, closed, heated areas. Hundreds of thousands of people were stricken with horrific head and chest colds and various strains of the flu, rendering them totally incapable of traveling anywhere apart from the short distances between their bedrooms and bathrooms. But it had snowed so frequently, and accumulated so quickly past inches and into feet as the frozen water swirled down from the gray skies in one traffic-halting blizzard after another, that traveling the streets would have been far too much trouble anyway.

It had been two weeks now since Mother Nature's kinder, more maternal side had returned decidedly for the long term, melting away the dirty slush and snow and welcoming back the lush parade of colors that the warm weather brought to even a filthy, polluted, totally urbanized setting like Manhattan. This long overdue change in climate was the reason for Gary Parker's good mood of late, for, infected as his soul was with coolness and cynicism after years of sending people to their deaths, his heart still remained powerless to put up a defense against the infectious magic of a warm, spring day. Of course, the new season had its cons as well. The warmth was bringing out the criminals and miscreants after the savage winter that had forced them into hibernation, the drivers on the streets were far from thrilled about having to share the avenues with cyclists, joggers, and pedestrians again, and the hundreds of thousands of pigeons dwelling on rooftops and behind department store signs had gone back to crapping on everybody's cars. With the brutality of the past winter still fresh in the populace's collective memory, however, these were but minor annoyances, and no one had trouble mustering up the ability to cope. As for Gary, he was just happy to see hot dogs again.

As a bachelor with very little talent – and very little interest in improving said talent – in the art of cuisine preparation, Gary had always been a true connoisseur of junk food. He had several favorite dishes that could be classified within that smallest compartment of the dietary food pyramid, many of them going beyond the orthodox, including chocolate-covered potato chips and cheese milkshakes, but one of the all-time high scorers on his list had to be the classic New York hot dog, which Gary had discovered when he had moved to the great city just over six years ago. Oh, sure, hot dogs were available in England, but vacuum-packed inside of colorful plastic packages emblazoned with a cartoonish picture of a wiener dressed in a silly costume, striking a comic pose next to the list of ingredients that had gone into the thin, little dogs at the factory. There was simply no comparison between those mundane fingers of processed meat and the bold, beefy miracle that was a New York frankfurter smothered in mustard, relish, mayo, and chopped onions and peppers. Though it was only nine o'clock in the morning, Gary was hard-pressed to think of a more tempting breakfast, so he jovially ordered one from the first street vendor he happened across.

Each New York hot dog was a new adventure, Gary had found. He could only guess at what the tubes of mystery meat contained. Anything from dirt to sheep intestines to pieces of rat could have been part of the constitution of those cigar-shaped appetizers swimming tantalizingly in a bucket of grease, oil, and fat. Oh, how was it possible that a food could be so disgusting, yet at the same time so compelling? Even the staleness of the bun, the newly hatched flies diving into the condiments, and the filthy sweatiness of the vendor's hands as he prepared the whole mess possessed a certain eloquence. The vendor even sneezed on it for good measure before handing it over to Gary, and Gary thought that was just wonderful.

Handing a five dollar bill to the vendor and telling him to keep the change, Gary took his first big bite and relished – if you'll pardon the expression – the mix of taste sensations in his mouth. Each of his thousands of taste buds, whether in charge of sweet or sour, salty or bitter, were pulling their fair share of duty this morning.

Gary wiped his mouth on his sleeve, then thrust his free hand into his pocket and produced two quarters, dropped them into a newspaper box, and claimed for himself a copy of the day's edition of *The New York Minute*, one of the Big Apple's most popular metropolitan newspapers. The front page was dominated by the boldfaced headline, 'Marla Hennessy Rescued!', complimented by a large, color photograph of the kidnap victim in question. He scanned the accompanying article for any mention of the mysterious individual who had taken it upon himself to defeat the kidnappers and free the girl, and was gratified to find none.

"We can only guess that the kidnappers were involved with some very nasty customers who chose this time for a confrontation, and just didn't bother with the girl," read a quote from a policeman who had arrived on the scene. "I don't think we'll ever know the full details of what went on here."

Simultaneously traversing the crowded sidewalk and chomping on his hot dog, Gary continued to read the paper, flipping over to page two, which featured an article concerning an elderly couple being saved from a group of gang members by 'an Asian man in black pajamas'.

Gary allowed himself a chuckle as he sucked a glob of mustard from his finger and arrived, at last, at the entrance to the subway station that had been his destination all along, where he descended the flight of concrete steps into the underground, folding and tucking the newspaper under his arm, and swallowing his last mouthful of hot dog in a manner similar to that of a lesser animal wolfing down a gobbet of meat. As always, the station was busy with throngs of morning commuters, and it was easy for Gary to jump discreetly over the turnstile and off of the platform when no one was looking.

Disappearing into the darkness of the tunnel, Gary followed the tracks – careful as always not to touch the deadly third rail that carried the thousands of volts of electricity necessary to power the trains – with an air of mundane routine like that of a man walking to work, or to the corner to drop a letter in a federal mailbox. When he had walked approximately five hundred yards, well out of sight of any person not insanely intent on being run down by a train, his eyes searched for and found the patch of stone wall that was only slightly lighter in color than its surroundings. He pushed against this patch of wall with his back, and, after a small, token exertion of effort, actually pushed it open to reveal that it was, in fact, a heavy door.

Pushing the door closed behind him, he emerged in a narrow, dimly-lit corridor lined with tiny surveillance cameras, invisible laser tripwires, and automated guns that would fire stun blasts and fast-acting tranquilizer darts at any unauthorized invaders in the highly unlikely event that anyone should ever discover the secret area. Each of the ten Vigilantes identified themselves regularly as authorized personnel by pressing their right thumbprint against a wall-mounted panel just inside the door, thereby deactivating the security measures until they reached the far end of the corridor. Once the far door was open – this also requiring a thumbprint scan – the security measures surged back online.

Behind this second door was the well-furnished base of operations the Vigilantes affectionately called the Rat Hole, formerly one of the many subway stations that had been taken out of operation and abandoned over the years. Though Gary and the other founding members of the group had discovered the forgotten station in a state of squalor and disrepair, no expense had been spared by the Vigilantes to transform it into an admirable, thoroughly functional base of operations, equipped with the most advanced crime-fighting technology, as well as a complete utility package that included electricity, heating, air conditioning, cable TV, and hot and cold running water.

A lounge, furnished with all the comforts of home, occupied a large part of the Rat Hole's square footage. There was carpeting on the floor and paint on the walls, and placed about the room were several items of furniture, including a variety of couches, chairs, and tables. A widescreen TV dominated one corner of the lounge, and various other conveniences, including a stocked refrigerator and a microwave, were situated about the room. Because of its size and comfort, this room often served as the Vigilantes' venue for meetings, but, should the need have ever arisen, a smaller conference room, containing an oak table large enough to seat the ten of them, could be accessed through a glass door off to the side.

The laboratory was almost as large as the lounge, and was home to sprawling banks of computers taking up entire walls, and several PCs, all Internet-ready. This was also the room that housed an impressive assortment of chemicals and materials – some organic and some synthetic, some noxious and some not – as well as the tools and resources for testing them, and applying their properties towards practical use. A bookcase stuffed with volumes on chemistry, biology, technology, criminology, physics, engineering, and modern weaponry stood in the corner. Accessible through a door at the back of the lab was a small workshop, always messy with countless pieces of disassembled weapons and machines. A sign hanging from the doorknob read 'Keep Out, Zeke'.

If one is to be successful in a hands-on war against the despicable species of criminal that regularly prowls the streets of New York, then it is essential that one keeps oneself fit, and the Vigilantes achieved this, in part, by keeping and maintaining a modest but sufficient gymnasium where they could lift weights, punch bags, jump ropes, run laps, or hang from rings suspended from the ceiling. While the daily and nightly battles in which the Vigilantes engaged usually proved to be ample workout sessions in themselves, it would never do to fall out of practice.

The final section of the Rat Hole – apart from the luxuriously-sized bathroom – was the infirmary, which had proven to be an essential facility on many, many occasions, especially when visiting a hospital would have elicited unwelcome questions from the doctors. Having seen more than its fair share of gushing blood, broken limbs, and mangled bodies, the infirmary was stocked with the most advanced tools and medicines for patching up the very worst of wounds. Medicines being her field of expertise, and her reason for membership with the Vigilantes, Leeza – an ill-tempered, seventy-five-year-old physician reared in Nazi Germany – ruled over the infirmary as her own kingdom, making sure that everything was neat and in order at all times, and sometimes even going for days without sleep as she obsessively researched and set about acquiring the latest in healing medicines and technology.

As Gary arrived in the Rat Hole's lounge, he was met by the familiar sight of his colleagues indulging themselves in a well-earned break, some yawning and looking forward to collapsing into their beds at home, and others fresher and preparing to take on the duties of the daylight hours. Keeping the public's best interest constantly in mind, none of the Vigilantes ever considered themselves officially off-duty. Like police officers or firefighters, they could be called to action at any time during the twenty-four hour day, and they were expected to tend appropriately to any business that happened to spring up during their free time. In order to make it possible for the ten individuals to lead normal, reasonably well-balanced lives, however, the regular watches and patrols alternated in shifts.

Surveying the lounge, Gary could see that nearly everyone was gathered in that room, busying themselves with one thing or another. Carla – a reformed cat burglar, thirty years of age – was curled up in a recliner, her long, attractive legs folded beneath her as she paged through a paperback copy of Dan Brown's *Angels & Demons*. Peg, the group's neurotic, pill-popping, emotionally unbalanced scientist and chemist, was scribbling unintelligible notes in a spiral-bound notebook, and Carolyn, the Vigilantes' weapons quartermaster, was poking a box-shaped object repeatedly with a screwdriver. The enormous Charlie had evidently decided to catch forty winks, as his massive frame was sprawled out on the leather couch, and deep, rumbling snores that sounded like the warning growls of a protective mother tiger were thundering up from his steadily rising and falling chest. Buzz, the psychologist, blind since his birth fifty-five years ago, was sitting quietly in the corner, using his sensitive fingertips to read the braille edition of the same newspaper Gary had purchased just minutes ago, and the thin, high-cheekboned Leeza was sitting straight-backed in front of the TV, watching a Josef Stalin documentary on the History Channel. Finally, there was the sixty-five-year-old redneck Zeke, slouching in his own battered, beer-stained armchair, unashamedly ogling an action centerfold from the latest issue of *Hustler*, and chain-smoking his favorite Marlboros; the only justification for his membership was his infallible photographic memory. The only members absent from the colorful troupe were William, the sixteen-year-old computer prodigy who was at school this time of day, and Sushi, the thirty-five-year-old ninja, whom Gary guessed was busy sweating it up in the gym. (The ninja generally asked for very little, but he absolutely insisted on private and uninterrupted use of the Rat Hole's gym for two solid hours each day.)

"Hero worship, Eva?" Gary asked the German woman, simultaneously poking fun at her choice of programming and observing the Vigilantes' long-standing tradition of teasing Leeza about her background with the name taken from Adolf Hitler's mistress.

Leeza snorted, and tilted her rigid nose just a bit higher into the air, refusing to dignify the jibe with a response. Gary chuckled, threw his newspaper down onto a nearby coffee table, and addressed the room.

"All right, guys," he said, walking over to an overhead projector. "After giving the subject due thought and consideration, I've hit upon our next major project. Somebody wake Charlie up. Zeke, go get Sushi out of the gym."

"No way in hell, boss," said Zeke. "You know what he's like when he's trainin'. He gets way too deep into it. Last time I tried to interrupt him, he damn near snapped my neck 'fore he realized I wasn't a samurai or whatever these crazy Japs like to fight."

"Fine, then you can fill him in later," said Gary, pulling down a rolled-up, white screen in front of the wall and setting a plastic sheet onto the surface of the projector. "Now, where the heck's my laser pointer?"

"I modified it for you, Gary," said Carolyn, producing the small object from her pocket and tossing it to Gary, who caught it. "Don't press the second button unless you want to burn a hole through someone's chest."

"Y'know, you've got a dangerous mind, lady," said Gary. "And for some reason, that arouses me."

"This had better be good," rumbled Charlie, rubbing his eyes as he rose from the couch like a mountain pulling itself free from the earth. "After weeks of trying, I was finally beginning to have a vivid dream about Halle Berry and Tyra Banks being tender with each other."

"I don't understand why men are so obsessed with the idea of two women making love," said Carla. "What's the appeal, anyway?"

"Ask yourself this," said Zeke. "What's better than a candy bar?"

"I don't know," said Carla.

"Two candy bars," Zeke grinned, lecherously. "And there's your answer."

"Disgusting," said Leeza, contemptuously.

"Actually, it's a bit more complex than that," said Buzz, adding his psychological expertise to the discussion. "Some of the eroticism, as Zeke says, does come from the sight of two perceived sex objects pleasuring each other, but a much larger bulk comes from the universal fetish of voyeurism. You see, up until quite recently in human history, the male of the species was the only one to pursue and initiate sex, while the female was exalted on a pedestal of purity and chastity. Even the very notion of a woman's lust was offensive to the moral sensibilities of society. This repression of the female libido helped contribute to the eternal divide between the intimacies of men and women. Consequently, men still view womanhood as a sort of secret sorority, and find it highly arousing to think about the members of that sorority indulging in each other's forbidden fruits of passion. Add to that the fact that men prefer to think of women as being inherently naughty, and constantly in heat, and therefore always on the prowl for a sensitive and sympathetic outlet, and..."

"Could we just move on?" asked Peg, conspicuously uncomfortable with the whole discussion.

"Yes, there's a time and place for everything," said Gary, flicking on his laser pointer. "Crimefighting now, shameful fantasies later."

Gary pressed the projector's ON switch, causing a crude drawing of what could have been a person to appear on the unrolled screen. The person had one big circle for a body, a small circle for a head, and mere sticks for arms and legs, and on the round body, Gary had drawn a sloppy-looking necktie and a set of ill-proportioned buttons going up and down both sides of the belly. The face bore a scowl, and an oval-shaped object extended from the clenched teeth, a wisp of what must have been smoke rising from its tip.

"Who the hell is that supposed to be?" asked Carla.

"Norman Kubritz," answered Gary, circling the drawing with the red dot of his pointer. "Crime boss, multibillionaire, and all-round fat bastard. He controls most, if not all of the organized crime in this part of the country. You all know him because we've all been beaten and thrashed within an inch of our lives trying to stop his unending criminal escapades. But this time we're going to scramble right to the top of the tree and take out Kubritz himself."

"Now *that's* an ambitious idea," said Charlie, folding his muscled arms across his broad chest.

"We're completely capable of pulling it off," Gary insisted. "The city's crime rate will plummet into the basement, at least temporarily, and I need hardly bring up the obvious financial benefits."

Each of the Vigilantes nodded at this. After all, they were, in a sense, pirates. Serving as the innocent man's last line of defense in a city transformed into a veritable jungle of terror, sadism, and violence was a fulltime job, and the Vigilantes found themselves compelled to confiscate the money and possessions of their vanquished adversaries in order to maintain and refurnish their operations, as well as pay their own individual salaries and living expenses. For people who lived by this 'packrat' method, Norman Kubritz was a solid gold lottery ticket with diamond embossments, attached to a fifty dollar bill with a platinum paper clip.

"Of course, it won't be easy to get to him," Gary continued. "He surrounds himself with some of the best talent in the criminal industry. In order to reach our boy, we'll have to take them out first."

"Shouldn't be a problem," said Carla. "We've always won before, no matter how big our enemy was."

"But Kubritz is *big*," said Peg, perpetually nervous.

"Well, y'all know what they say," said Zeke. "The bigger they are, the more ass there is to kick."

William stumbled out of the classroom in a daze, gloomy with the knowledge of how spectacularly he had failed the algebra test; the algebra test for which he and his classmates had had a week to study; the algebra test which had been nothing more than a cumulative review of the formulas and problem-solving procedures that the teacher had been pounding into the students' heads for the past month, and that William should have been able to summon up in his sleep. Yet he could envision, even now, as he stared down at the green and white tiles in the hallway floor, the big, red 'F' that would soon be decorating the top of his test, accompanied by the scrawled note reading 'See me after class!'

William knew his work with the Vigilantes was to blame. He knew that, if not for the Vigilantes, his grades wouldn't be slipping so dramatically and his parents and teachers wouldn't be nagging him so incessantly. The very reason that he hadn't had the time to study for the algebra test was because his Vigilante work seemed to consistently eclipse the time and effort he would have otherwise devoted to his schoolwork. (He had also been extremely tired after spending the better part of the previous night hacking into the old TekTronics building's security system in order to help Gary rescue the Hennessy girl.) This, for William, posed a conflict. He was very proud of the work he was doing with the Vigilantes, and it felt great to put his phenomenal – if he did say so himself – computer skills to good, constructive use. It was more gratifying than anything he got out of school. On the other hand, the time for considering colleges was fast approaching, and William did need to keep a sharp eye on his academic performance. But, did he really need to go to college? With his enviable talent, perhaps he could get a high-paying job with just his high school diploma in tow. After all, Bill Gates had never finished college. Or maybe he could just stay with the Vigilantes throughout his career. The work was exciting and rewarding, and he had come to think of them as family. Yes, that would certainly be the ideal job, but it wasn't something upon which he could fully depend.

William's ponderings on his future were interrupted by the outstretched leg that tripped him, and the peals of sadistic laughter that filled his ears as he crashed to the floor.

"And the dork falls for it again!" crowed the culprit, a tall jock named Jason. "Get it? He *fell* for it!"

The two boys flanking Jason – William recognized them as a couple of hyenas called Randy and Kyle – increased the volume of their obnoxious laughter, displaying their appreciation for this extraordinary example of sophisticated wit. William just groaned as he gathered his books and got to his feet. He was used to this sort of thing. It happened all the time. He was an easy target for pea-brained bullies like Jason and his friends. After all, though he was a crimefighting Vigilante, he was also a short, physically unimpressive kid with glasses and a reputation for being a total nerd.

"What's the matter, Willy?" asked the chortling Jason. "Don't you have anything to say?"

William hated being called Willy!

"I would," said William, "but I hate conducting conversations using only monosyllabic words."

"Will you listen to this geek?" snickered Jason. "What normal human being uses big words like that?"

"Yeah, he sure is a freak," Randy concurred.

"Just get out of my way," said William, attempting to push his way past the bullies.

"Whoa, whoa, where do you think you're going?" asked Jason, pushing his hand against William's chest. "You don't go until we say you can go."

William suppressed a heavy sigh. For how many more years of his life would he have to endure these humiliating indignities that deflated his self-esteem and made him feel like less of a man? He was sixteen! He was too old to allow himself to be victimized like this. He should be standing up like a man, making the challengers pay for their insolence. But, as always, William's mind overcame his primal rage, and he realized that taking on just one of the bullies – never mind all three – would be suicide. So he resigned himself to endure the remainder of Jason's attention span, and it was then that a female voice rang out from behind the wall of bullies.

"Jason, what are you doing?" asked the girl, a frown shadowing her face, her hands placed moodily on her hips.

"Just keepin' myself amused between classes, Rachel," Jason grinned, turning to face the girl.

"I told you, I don't like you picking on people," said Rachel, stepping closer. "It's mean."

"Aw, come on, Rachel, I was just havin' a little fun," said Jason.

"Well, find a new hobby," Rachel insisted. "If you keep being a jerk to everybody, I won't go to the dance with you next Friday."

Jason scowled, said, 'Hrmph', and turned back to William.

"See ya around, twerp," he said, shoving William in the chest.

William tumbled backwards, landing on the floor once again, and Jason and his cohorts snickered, and stalked off. The girl called Rachel rolled her eyes in visible disgust and moved to help William to his feet.

This wasn't the first time William had seen Rachel. She had been in a few of his classes in the past, and they had exchanged a few words on occasion, and nearly every time he saw her he had to cover his groin area discreetly with a textbook. Indeed William ranked her as one of the most beautiful girls he had ever seen. With her pretty face, long, blond hair, shapely legs, creamy skin, and pair of perky, well-developed breasts that just cried out to be squeezed, she was the very picture of what a fertile teenage girl should be.

That was another cruelty of nature that William found to be

exceedingly unfair. He had never had a date in his life, while all the attractive girls saved themselves for bastards like Jason. William might not have been as tall or as strong as Jason, but that didn't mean his manly desires were any the less. Having the same urges, did he not have the same right to the premium fruit of the opposite gender? Just because he didn't necessarily boast all the physical appeal of a Brad Pitt or a Tom Cruise didn't mean that he was willing to settle for tablescraps and leftovers.

"I'm sorry those guys were being such jerks," said Rachel, picking up William's algebra textbook for him. "Please don't think that I'm like that."

"Why would I think that?" asked William, avoiding the girl's eyes.

"Just because my boyfriend is an asshole sometimes, I'm afraid people might assume that I am, too," she said.

"Then why don't you break up with him?" asked William, letting his personal frustration pour forth into his words.

"To be honest, I've thought about it a few times," said Rachel, taking a step closer to William. "I guess it would all depend on whether I could find someone better."

Rachel let this hang in the air for a few seconds as she eyed William, thoughtfully. Then she touched him on the shoulder. William could feel his forehead moistening with perspiration as he took a reflexive step back.

"Uh...yeah," he said. "Well, thanks. I really have to go now. I'm five minutes late to get crucified by my biology teacher."

"Wait," said Rachel.

William halted obediently while Rachel produced a pen, and, taking hold of William's right arm, wrote her phone number on the back of his hand. William stared at his new 'tattoo' in awe, and Rachel smiled, flirtatiously.

"Call me," she winked.

With that, she turned and walked down the hall, leaving William standing as still as a statue, his eyes popping out of his head, his jaw just inches from touching the floor.

Maria sighed as she climbed bashfully out of her blue-gray jumpsuit and entered the shower room with the rest of the group. Five years. That was what the judge had said, and that was the portion of her irretrievable youth that she would lose inside the walls of Bayview Correctional

Facility. Oh, sure, she'd probably make parole in three, but that was little consolation to her now, as she'd been locked away for only six days.

Maria was afraid to fraternize with the other women, as she had no way of knowing what evil sins they had perpetrated in their past lives. Many could have been killers. That was why she made a point of keeping to herself as she showered, and yelped in surprise when she felt someone tap her on the shoulder.

"Hi there," said a middle-aged, heavyset woman with dark brown hair. "You're new, aren't you?"

"Uh...y-yes," Maria stammered.

"Thought so," said the woman. "I can always spot the newbies just by looking for the scared expressions. Don't worry. It's not like a men's prison around here. With a few exceptions, we tend to look after our own. The name's Brenda. What's yours?"

"M-Maria," she answered, still stammering nervously.

"What are you in for, Maria?" asked Brenda.

"F-five years," she said. "I was...I was selling pot. You know...to try and get a little extra money."

"Wow, that's small-time," said Brenda. "Me, I'm here for the long haul. Killed my old man to collect on the insurance. A lot of good it's doing me now, right?"

Maria didn't have time to form a response to this unsettling confession before the only door opened again and another line of inmates was marched in. There were only six in this group, but many of the women who had been showering near Maria, including Brenda, began moving hastily to the other side of the room like a group of cattle being herded across a field.

"Where's everybody going?" asked Maria.

"Y'know what I just said about things being relatively okay around here, with some exceptions? Well, here comes the mother of all exceptions now," said Brenda, nodding subtly towards the third woman in the line.

Maria looked at the inmate indicated by Brenda, and gasped as a chill ran immediately down her spine. What she saw was a tall black woman, about six feet in height, and muscular, with long, sinewy arms and legs. Complete with a tough, flat belly, and large, jutting breasts, her intimidating figure was not unlike that of some mythical earth goddess given human form. Her black hair was cropped close to her scalp in a neat crewcut, and her hate-filled eyes were as dark as her skin.

"Her name's Janet," Brenda whispered. "Meanest bitch I've ever met. If you're smart, you'll come over here with the rest of us."

Brenda took off speed-walking for the safe refuge of her grouped peers, but Maria didn't have time to follow suit before she felt a hand seize her by the hair and spin her around.

"Who's the newbie?" Janet smirked, towering a full two heads over the frightened Maria.

Maria looked to Brenda for help, but the other woman just shook her head and turned away. She was on her own now.

"I asked you a question, you little white bitch," Janet snarled, with a faint trace of a British accent.

"M-M-Maria," she said, back to stammering.

Janet nodded, her hands on her hips, looking Maria up and down appraisingly, and finally brought her eyes to rest on her breasts, which Maria's arms leapt up reflexively to cover. Janet frowned, and slapped Maria across the face with such force that the smaller woman stumbled backwards and nearly slipped on the wet floor.

"Do that again and I'll break those arms!" Janet threatened.

Maria trembled with fear and stood very still as the taller woman continued examining her.

"You know, you're not bad-looking," Janet mused, at last. "Better than some of the cows we get in here, at any rate. Why don't you come over here with me?"

A wicked smirk playing about her face, Janet grasped Maria's right wrist and led her firmly over to an isolated showerhead in an empty corner of the room. Once they were both underneath the showerhead, Janet reached for the nearest bar of soap and rubbed it with her hands until she had a decent lather worked up.

"Turn around," she commanded.

Trembling, Maria obeyed, and Janet began to run her soapy hands up and down the smaller woman's back. Maria shuddered as Janet massaged the soap firmly into her shoulder blades.

"Mmm, you're very dirty," said Janet. "In fact, I don't think you know how dirty you are."

Maria gasped as Janet seized her buttocks and squeezed hard, letting rivers of soap trickle down the backs of her legs.

"Now, turn around again and face me," Janet ordered.

The last thing Maria wanted to do was stand face to face with this dreadful woman, but she knew there would be dire consequences if she disobeyed. Working up another lather, Janet clasped Maria's face, gently and with boths hands, and smeared the soap across her cheeks.

"Don't worry, love, I won't get it in your eyes," Janet cooed, like a mother washing a child.

Next came the part Maria had been dreading. A mound of soap in each hand, Janet clasped Maria's breasts and kneaded them like lumps of dough, being sure to run her thumbs continuously over the nipples. All Maria could do was gasp with pain and embarrassment, and she didn't think it could get any worse than this until Janet gave her next order.

"Now, bend over," she commanded.

Maria hesitated, so Janet gripped her by the back of her neck and bent her over so far that her chin nearly touched the floor.

"Flexible," Janet observed, as she went to work. "I'll remember that."

Maria wanted to scream. She wanted to cry. Hot tears of agony squeezed themselves out of her eyes as testament to the shame she felt for what this horrible woman was doing to her. The other inmates in the shower room pretended not to notice what was going on, but afforded her looks of real pity out of their peripheral vision.

Finally, Janet was finished. She stood Maria up again and moved her underneath the showerhead, where she gently rinsed the lather off for her. Then she patted her on the head, and smiled.

"You're definitely clean now," she said. "Both inside and out."

Maria hung her head in shame, and wished she could die. But the ordeal wasn't over yet.

"Now it's my turn," said Janet. "*You* have to wash *me*."

Maria's mouth fell open as Janet pushed the well-used bar of soap into her hand.

"Do it exactly the way I showed you," she said, "and don't forget the important parts."

While such an appointment instills nothing but trepidation and feelings of imminent doom in most people, a visit to the dentist was always enjoyable for the male patients of Dr. Victoria Broker, DMD. Being one of those lucky women blessed with both beauty and brains, she had an above average IQ, and a slender, alluring figure, well-suited to the low necklines and short skirts she always wore, complimented by black stockings and high-heeled shoes. She kept her eyebrows plucked thin, her lips painted dark red, and her ebony hair tied up in a bun. If she possessed one physical flaw, it was the astigmatism in her right eye, but most men were of the opinion that the stylish pair of glasses perched eloquently astride the bridge of her upturned nose only served to heighten her sex appeal.

Yes, she was beautiful and intelligent, but her bedside manner left something to be desired. In her general demeanor, she was a cool, arrogant, aloof woman who focused first and foremost on her career, and kept her emotional distance from anyone whom she deemed a threat to her ongoing success, especially horny, amorous men looking for a wealthy woman to support them while they struggled with careers in writing or poorly conceived entrepreneurial ventures. With an indifferent frown behind her sanitary mask, she spoke hardly a word to the patients in her chair as she corrected whatever was wrong with their teeth, then sent them on their way with an expensive bill to pay. This unyielding attitude, combined with the way she dressed – she believed sexually flattering clothes on a woman to be a display of empowerment – precipitated many a male fantasy of the doctor in a dominant role, towering over them while she visited upon them varying degrees of exquisite pain.

Dr. Broker's appeal was not lost on KnuckleDuster, but, as he lay back in the reclining chair, with the dentist's trained fingers concluding their work, he made certain to keep his mind on business.

"Thanks for seeing me without an appointment, doc," said KnuckleDuster, poking his tongue against his reinstalled tooth, and feeling just a slight twinge of pain that was as far beneath his notice as any other ever since his encounter with Alyusha Davidov's chainsaw. "It was a real emergency."

"For a knocked-out tooth, it was remarkably sound," Dr. Broker commented. "It's almost as if it was pulled out."

KnuckleDuster had to give the good doctor points for her excellent perception. He had indeed yanked that tooth himself, with his own super strong fingers, as an excuse for getting close to her. Now, while Dr. Broker discarded her rubber gloves and piloted her castor-equipped chair over to the counter to write something down, KnuckleDuster made his move.

Maneuvering quickly, KnuckleDuster pounced from the chair, seized Dr. Broker by the back of her neck, and threw her to the floor. She landed on her back with a crash, her arms and legs flailing, dental tools clattering around her. Holding her down with one foot on her torso, KnuckleDuster reached for the tank of nitrous oxide gas used to sedate patients, and the doctor didn't even have time to get out a full scream before the rubber mask was clamped over her nose and mouth and the tank's valve had been thrown fully open.

Once Dr. Broker had succumbed to the effects of the gas and collapsed into a sound sleep, KnuckleDuster closed the valve and tossed the tank aside. He then reached into his jacket pocket and produced the list. The fourth entry read:

Age 30-35. Between 6' and 6.5' tall. Caucasian. Fair-skinned. Dark brown/black hair, shoulder-length or just above. Eye color: Any. Slim, petite, but shapely. Arrogant and frosty. Approximate measurements: 34-20-32.

KnuckleDuster nodded his head approvingly as he read the criteria to himself, and wasn't altogether surprised to see a single drop of blood splatter onto the paper. His newly repaired tooth still had some healing to do.

Stealing a wad of gauze from a convenient box on the counter, KnuckleDuster stuffed it inside his mouth, then hefted the unconscious Dr. Broker over his shoulder and skulked out the office's back exit.

"And therein lies your problem, my dear Malik," said Norman Kubritz, opening the elevator doors with a retinal scan and inviting the well-dressed Arab to enter the large, metal box ahead of him. "Your political loyalties are your weakness, and they will be your downfall. How do you expect your enterprise to flourish if you deal exclusively with Islamic militants?"

"Islamic militants are the world's most feared enemy," Malik retorted, stepping into the elevator car, his right hand in a cast as a result of his earlier handshake with KnuckleDuster.

"For the time being, yes," said Kubritz, entering the car himself and pressing the button marked with a 'B'. "But there was a time when the communists enjoyed that lofty status, and look what has become of them. Once contenders for world domination, they have been wiped out almost completely because of their failure to adapt and modernize. Your people are just as ignorant and stubborn, Malik. They might be a thorn in humanity's side for now, but they will never strike a decisive victory against the civilized world unless they modernize."

"My weapons are very modern," said Malik. "Guns, rockets, tanks, jetpacks..."

"And what do they do with these weapons, Malik? Murder a few low-ranking American soldiers? Blow up a handful of Israeli civilians in a bus shelter? They're misguided, visionless monkey boys, the lot of them. If you want to stay in business for the coming decades, you would do well to diversify your customer base."

"I am devoted to the cause of my people, Norman," said Malik. "A callow Westerner like you, a man who stands for nothing and believes in nothing but his own immediate pleasure, could never understand that." Kubritz chuckled, exhaling thick clouds of cigar smoke into the confined space of the elevator car.

"Well, that's enough talk of business for now," he said. "As you're not going to be in New York much longer…"

"Only until our arrangement has been settled," Malik interrupted.

"…I wanted to give you a rare treat," Kubritz finished.

A soft 'ding' sounded, and the elevator doors slid open to reveal a very large, well-lit, concrete basement resembling an empty parking garage. Kubritz clapped his chubby hands together twice, and, almost immediately, a small, balding man, wearing a suit that hung on him like a tent, skittered into view.

"Phillips, my guest and I are ready to begin the festivities," said Kubritz.

"Of course, Mr. Kubritz," said Phillips, in a sniveling, nasal voice. "Very good, Mr. Kubritz."

With that, Phillips speed-walked out of sight again. Kubritz offered Malik a cigar, and Malik had just enough time to take one and accept his friend's kind offer of a light before Phillips returned, pushing two large chairs on castors ahead of him.

"Have a seat," Kubritz said to Malik, taking the biggest, sturdiest chair for himself.

In the time it took Malik to bend his knees and plant his backside in the seat, the speedy Phillips had departed and returned once again, this time with a castor-equipped table laden with snack foods. Bowls of potato chips, pretzels, and popcorn were laid out like the components of a Thanksgiving banquet, and the centerpiece was a chilled bottle of white wine.

"*Cheval Blanc '89*, sirs," cackled Phillips, pouring the wine into two glasses. "Matured to its full potential."

"The fact that you seem to drink extravagant wines in the same way that lowlier men drink Coca-Cola is wholly reflective of your excessive, unhealthy lifestyle, you decadent Western dog," Malik smiled, as he raised his glass to toast his host.

"Have some potato chips, my friend," said Kubritz, passing the bowl to Malik. "They're the new egg-and-sausage flavor."

Cheval Blanc *and potato chips*, thought Malik. *And he calls* me *a barbarian.*

Kubritz drained his glass, took one more long drag on his cigar, then placed it aside in a golden ashtray – of which he seemed to have an abundant supply scattered throughout the casino – and addressed his eager servant once again.

"Highly satisfactory, Phillips, as always. Now, send in the girls."

Phillips bowed low, then hurried over to one of the thick, steel pillars that prevented the casino above from falling into the basement, and pressed an inset button. Immediately a metal door at the far end of the large room slid open electronically and spat out two young, attractive women that couldn't have been much older than twenty-five. One was a fiery redhead and the other was a platinum blond, and they were both completely naked and drenched in oil. They looked very timid and frightened, yet their troubled eyes conveyed a certain vacancy, as if nothing around them really mattered.

"Go on, you two! Get moving!" commanded Phillips, pushing them, like stubborn livestock, into the center of the room.

"Well, I must confess I like the looks of things thus far, Norman," said Malik, still smoking his cigar. "What happens next?"

"I've organized a little gambling event for our enjoyment," Kubritz explained. "For the past several months, these women have been locked away in tiny, cramped cells, in pure, utter darkness. They have been allowed no comforts, little human contact, and only a requisite minimum of food and water. Aside from that, their spirits have been broken via long, endless hours of mental, emotional, and physical torture. We will now watch them engage in a brutal, animalistic fight to the death. The duel will not end until one has killed the other. Because this is purely recreational, we will both wager a trifling five million dollars on the outcome. And since you are my guest, you may have your choice. Which of the two do you like to win?"

Kubritz never failed to impress Malik with his sensational gift for entertainment. Why, this would be riotous fun! Truth be told, Malik was even somewhat embarrassed that he hadn't come up with such a capital idea himself, considering he hailed from a part of the world where women were treated with only slightly more dignity and respect than a lump of camel feces stuck to the bottom of one's sandal.

Malik took his time studying both the girls, puffing thoughtfully on his cigar. The blond was taller than the redhead, and perhaps just a bit more muscular, but she seemed to lack the innate ferocity and savage killer instinct that Malik could feel emanating from the other girl. Besides, even the most conventional and elementary knowledge of women insisted that the redhead of the species was the fiercest.

"I'll take red," said Malik, at last.

"Very well," said Kubritz. "Then I shall back the blond. Well, what the devil are you waiting for, Phillips? Give them the command and let's get this show started!"

Phillips produced a metal triangle, and, holding it ceremoniously in the air at arm's length, struck it with a tiny percussion stick, causing a single 'ding' to ring loud and clear throughout the empty basement. Then the girls leapt for each other's throats.

"Interesting," mused Malik. "These women feel no affection or loyalty for you, yet are willing to kill or be killed for your amusement."

"Conditioning, my dear Malik," Kubritz grinned, tapping his fat forefinger against the side of his fat nose. "Conditioning of the most earnest quality. They couldn't rebel against my orders if they wanted to."

Malik raised his eyebrows, conveying his admiration, then went back to watching the fight, which had begun decidedly in the blond's favor. She was delivering a series of punches to the redhead's face, driving her backwards and keeping her off balance. When she decided to finish the attack with a kick to the gut, however, the redhead caught her outstretched ankle and twisted hard, evoking a shriek of pain from the blond. She then twirled around twice and released the blond, as if throwing the hammer at the Olympics, causing the fairer girl to fly into the nearby wall face first. A sickening 'crunch' indicated the breaking of the blond's nose.

The redhead rushed up to kick the blond while she was still down, but the blond leapt to her feet unexpectedly quickly and drove her fist into the redhead's belly. The redhead expelled a 'whoof' of air and doubled over in pain, but was brought right back up again by an uppercut that sent her flying off her feet. She crashed onto her back on the hard, concrete floor, and the blond, hobbling a bit to save further torment to her twisted ankle, was on her in seconds.

"Good move!" Kubritz shouted, approvingly, spitting out pieces of chewed pretzels.

Droplets of oil flying in all directions as if from a sizzling skillet, the two girls wrestled back and forth, grinding against each other's bodies, exchanging places as one combatant and then the other took the top position. It was the redhead who managed to break away first, biting savagely down on the blond's left nipple, drawing blood, and refusing to let go until the blond rolled off of her.

The redhead spat out the piece of nipple that had come away in her teeth, then lunged at the blond with her head down, intent on butting her in the stomach. The blond moved to the side to avoid the attack, clasped the redhead by her shoulders once she had passed, and delivered a hard knee to the small of her back. The redhead straightened up and arched her back in pain, helpless to resist as the blond pulled her down onto the floor once again.

"Would you like some popcorn, dear fellow?" Kubritz asked Malik, offering him the bowl.

"Homestyle or movie theater?" Malik inquired.

"Homestyle."

"All right, then."

The redhead landed on her back again, and rolled away just in time to avoid having her collarbone stomped on, but she only had time to clamber to her knees before the blond brought both clenched fists down hard upon her breasts. The redhead howled in agony and collapsed again.

"Bravo!" Kubritz applauded. "Phillips, let her finish her off."

Being careful to keep his distance from the fray, Phillips threw a six-inch combat knife into the center of the action. The blond snatched it up and knelt over her fallen opponent, gripping the knife's handle with both hands as she prepared to plunge it into the redhead's heart.

The redhead's animal instincts, functioning in the absence of her ability to think on a human level, screamed at her that death was imminent and that something needed to be done about it within the next two seconds. So, ignoring the pain that wracked her body, the redhead thrust both her feet into the air, kicking the blond backwards and sending the knife clattering away across the concrete floor. She then leapt astride her surprised opponent and began raining blow after closed-fisted blow down upon her already bruised face. The blond clawed at the redhead's body with her long fingernails, but was not successful in dislodging her assailant.

Finally, the blond stopped resisting, and it was then that the redhead climbed off her, flipped her over onto her belly, grasped her head in both hands, and, with one sharp yank, snapped the blond's neck and rendered the writhing body motionless.

Her breath coming ragged and heavy, her battered, bloody body trembling, the redhead remained on her knees for a few seconds, then collapsed onto her side and began crying, loudly. Kubritz snapped his fingers, and Phillips scurried over to the unmoving blond. He kicked her over onto her back with his foot, saw that her eyes and mouth were agape, then pressed his index and middle fingers onto her neck's pulse point and felt nothing.

"She's dead all right," he declared. "The redhead wins."

"How very satisfying," said Malik. "You just can't seem to keep up with me, Norman."

"You'll be the ruin of me yet, Malik," said Kubritz, playing the good sport. "Come upstairs and I'll write you the check right now."

"What should I do with the other one, Mr. Kubritz?" Phillips inquired.

"What's her condition?" Kubritz asked.

"Her physical wounds will heal," said Phillips, "but I think this last ordeal has finally destroyed her mind. She'll never be worth so much as a dime to anybody ever again."

"Then do to her what you would do to any other poor, suffering animal," said Kubritz, turning his back on the scene and draping a comradely arm over Malik's shoulders as they walked back to the elevator together. "And clean the rest of that food up afterwards."

As the dismissal bell rang to herald the end of the school day, and the hundreds of highly-strung students craving a breath of fresh air, a bit of sunshine on their faces, and some social time with their friends away from the hated world of stuffy teachers, boring classes, and dreary science projects galloped out of the high school building's doors to embrace the weekend that had been all too sluggish in arriving, William merely shuffled along on autopilot, his gait casual, his mind focused intently on the same thing that had kept him preoccupied all day.

'I guess it would all depend on whether I could find someone better', Rachel's words kept running through his mind like a broken record. *She told me to call her. She was flirting with me, and she wants me to call her.*

William still couldn't quite bring himself to believe that this wasn't some sort of enormous misunderstanding. After all, nothing like this had ever happened to him – or indeed, any boy *like* him – before. Why would a flawlessly beautiful girl like Rachel, who could have had her pick of any boy in school, be at all interested in a pale, skinny, four-eyed computer nerd like him? It was inconceivable that she could be attracted to him physically, yet she certainly didn't know him well enough to have become enamored with his character or personality.

Or maybe she did. Maybe she had been watching him for some time now, and was only just coming forward with her true feelings. After all, there had to be some logical explanation for the earlier encounter in the hallway, made poignant by the girl's soft hand on his shoulder and the look of sincere adoration in her sparkling blue eyes.

William was so engrossed in thought, his brain working so hard to decipher the puzzle, that he didn't see the hand that shoved him.

William cried out in surprise and sprawled forwards into a mud puddle, his books flying everywhere, his glasses taking a blow that bent the frames. Standing over his fallen form like a trio of jackals who had just downed a wildebeest, Jason and his two followers laughed their silly heads off.

"There's no girl to stick up for you this time, you little fag," said Jason. "You're gonna have to fight this battle on your own."

William's face reddened, and a snarl of rage took control of his features. Growling with frustration, he scrambled to his feet, mud dripping from his clothes, the fingers of his right hand curling into a fist.

You've taken enough from these people! declared his last remnants of dignity. *Stand up for yourself for once in your life, you weak piece of shit! Show them you're a man!*

Having to reach slightly upwards in order to do so, William swung his fist at Jason's chin. The effort was admirable, but he was not accustomed to fighting, and the swing was far too clumsy, missing its mark by several inches. Consequently, the next sensation he felt was the shattering pain of his testicles seemingly breaking into thousands of pieces as Jason kicked him hard in the crotch. His breath caught in his throat, and his watering eyes bulged like a frog's as he collapsed to the ground once again.

"You actually thought you could take a shot at me, you little shithead?" Jason scowled. "You actually thought you even had the right to try? Get this through your head, dickbreath! You're nothing! You're not even worth the dogshit on the bottom of my shoe! You're a little bug who doesn't know when he's been squashed!"

Doubled over in agony, William was helpless to retaliate as Jason snatched the bent glasses from his face, threw them to the ground, and stomped on them. A heart-rending 'crunch' indicated the destruction of William's artificial twenty-twenty vision as Jason ground the broken lenses beneath his heel.

"That's for showing me up in front of my girlfriend!" the bully declared. "Now, you just stay sitting in that mud until we leave, or I'm gonna come back and nail you again!"

With that, Jason and his two cohorts turned and laughed their way off of school property. William watched them go through blurred vision, his teeth and fists clenched. He was furious! Furious at the bullies, of course, but even more furious with himself. Why the hell was he such a wimp? Why should he have to take this sort of abuse lying down? This was unacceptable! Approaching the threshold of manhood, he should have been able to defend himself in some way! He should have been able to stand up for himself as a human being, assert his strength, and maintain his dignity and self-respect! Yet here he was, sitting timidly in a mud puddle, waiting for his tormentors to disappear. Oh, how he longed to strike back and get even! Oh, how his embittered heart ached for vengeance against his hated enemy! Oh, if only there was something he could do to even the odds and really hurt the bastard!

The idea came to William in a flash, as if a lightning bolt of sheer genius had infused his brain with a new super power of inspiration. For several seconds, he simply stared ahead into space, infatuated with the notion that had just entered his mind. Then he looked down at his clenched, trembling fist, and saw the blurred, faded remnants of Rachel's phone number, and his enraged, indignant scowl slowly gave way to a cunning, devilish half-smile as he realized with glee the grand opportunity with which providence had blessed him.

In the time that William had known Jason, the larger boy had taken William's dignity, self-respect, and God-given right to walk tall as a man, so, in return, William would take Jason's girlfriend. He would take for himself that source of pride and joy that was valued so highly by all men. In the most victorious of all victories, he would win for himself the affections of his enemy's queen, shaming his enemy with emasculation almost unequaled. He would waste no time. He would call Rachel this very evening and devote the entire weekend towards wooing and entertaining her. After the good first impression he had so obviously made upon her, he knew he could do it! Ah, the idea was so delicious that William had to actually lick his lips. He might not have been able to defeat Jason in a test of physical strength, but, by heaven, he could wage an emotional war against the pea-brained brute that would make him rue the day he had ever chosen the slight-physiqued but strong-resolved teenager as his victim!

"And now she's talkin' 'bout the magic bein' gone," Zeke said to Buzz, as the pair of them entered the Rat Hole's empty conference room. "And she's angry a lot these days. She's always had such a sweet disposition, but now the woman is findin' everything wrong with our marriage. Damned if I can put my finger on what's eatin' at her."

"Well, I appreciate you feeling you can come to me with your problems, Zeke," said Buzz, finding a chair with his cane and lowering himself down into it.

"Well, you're the only head-shrinker who'll give me free advice," said Zeke. "Everyone else wants 'bout a thousand bucks an hour. It's a material world we're livin' in, Buzz, ol' boy; a material world."

"Tell me about Molly and yourself," said Buzz. "Exactly how long have the two of you been married?"

"Thirty-nine years, eight months, an' twenty-two days," Zeke rattled off. "Y'know, that's one o' the things Molly always loved about me. Thanks to my photographic memory, I never forget our anniversary."

"Quite."

"Or her birthday."

"I'm sure."

"Or Christmas."

"Do people forget Christmas?"

"Well, I reckon I would if I didn't have this gosh-danged photographic memory."

"So, you've been married for nearly forty years," said Buzz. "That's a long time to spend with one partner."

"Wait a minute, Shades," said Zeke, employing the nickname with which he had christened Buzz some time ago. "Are you suggestin' that Molly is getting bored with me?"

"Perish the thought," said Buzz. "I'm sure that your wife still loves you very much. Whether she loves her present life, however, is another matter entirely."

"Whadda ya mean? Molly and I have a great life together. Why, our trailer is the biggest, fanciest one on the lot, thanks to the money I rake in doin' this work. All our kids are doin' all right. Our youngest boy just left home last year. He's gone down to Louisiana to sell houseboats to the swamp folk. Marvelous state, Louisiana, if you don't mind the skeeters an' all them crazy Cajuns."

"So, your children are grown and gone, pursuing lives of their own. What does Molly do with her time now?"

Zeke opened his mouth to answer, then realized he had to close it again and give the question some thought.

"Well, I guess I don't rightly know," he admitted. "She don't have to work, 'cause I provide for both of us. And she don't have to lift a finger 'round the trailer till I get home with my manly cravings for beefy pot roast, mashed 'taters, and deep-fried turkey legs so meaty you could kill a water buffalo by smackin' him upside the head with one. She's one hell of a cook, my Molly is."

"I see," said Buzz, thoughtfully. "Well, from what you're telling me, it sounds like Molly might be suffering from the old empty nest syndrome. Having devoted her life to caring for her family, she now finds herself at a complete loss as to what to do with her time and energy now that that family is gone. She's entered a new stage in her life, Zeke, and she's bored out of her mind."

"Well, I can't have that," said Zeke, decisively. "What can I do to make her feel better?"

Buzz scratched his chin and cleared his throat. Then he asked a question which he hoped wouldn't make his friend feel too uncomfortable.

"Tell me, Zeke. Do you and Molly still have…relations?"

"Well, we have the kids, o' course," Zeke answered. "And that's about it, 'cept for a couple o' cousins who could belong to either one of us. Hell knows I can never keep 'em straight. Molly's mother died just five months ago. It was 'bout freakin' time, if you ask me. The grouchy old trout just kept hangin' on and hangin' on and hangin' on…"

"No, no, you misunderstand me," said Buzz. "I mean sexual relations."

"Well, most of our boys are very active when it comes to that sort of thing," said Zeke. "I guess they must get their virility from their old man, eh? Well, 'cept for Leroy, but there's always been somethin' a little peculiar 'bout him. Mind you, he's my boy, and I love him, no matter how passionate he is 'bout interior decoratin'. Then there are the three girls. They're pretty into it as well, always hangin' offa their boyfriends whenever I see 'em. I tell ya, Buzzer, girls didn't act like that when we were that age."

"No, Zeke," Buzz sighed, wearily, and rubbed his right temple. "What I mean is, do you and Molly ever engage in sexual intercourse?"

"Wait a minute," said Zeke, the true subject at hand finally dawning on him. "Are you talkin' 'bout Mr. Johnson's trip to the fish market?"

"Er…well, okay," said Buzz. "If you prefer."

"Well, sometimes we do," said Zeke. "Can't say I rightly remember the last time we did. Photographic memory doesn't help a whole lot with that particular department, eh? But ya'll know how it is. After forty-seven years, eight months, an' twenty-two days, a man starts to slow down. It ain't natural to be carryin' on like a couple o' jackrabbits at our age. So maybe I do come home drunk an' collapse on the floor sometimes. Maybe I do keep my eyes glued to *The Brady Bunch* when we're in bed together. Maybe I do fake a headache every now an' then.

I'm only flesh an' blood. I mighta been a wild animal in my youth, but... aw, let's face it, Buzz. I jus' ain't a stallion anymore."

"That's all right, Zeke," said Buzz. "It's natural for a man's libido to cool off in his autumn years. And I'm sure Molly doesn't expect you, nor want you, to turn your home into the Playboy Mansion. But, from what I'm gathering, she feels neglected by you. Perhaps she feels that she's no longer attractive to you, or that you view her as nothing more than the worn-out mother of your genetic legacy. I think there's a real danger, Zeke, that she believes you've fallen out of love with her."

"But that jus' ain't true!" protested Zeke, jumping to his feet. "I love Molly with all my heart! Why, she's the best thing that's ever happened to me! Did I ever tell ya how we met? I was drunk an' wanderin' around in the woods when I got caught in a steel bear trap. There I am, totally helpless, an' this hungry coyote starts bearin' down on me, snarlin' and foamin' like a hound o' hell! Then Molly appears, holdin' a double-barreled shotgun, lookin' like a beautiful angel sent from heaven, an' before ya had time to blink, she aims that gun and blasts that coyote's head clean off! It was beautiful! Why, I reckon it was the nicest thing anyone's ever done for me!"

"And that's what you need to tell her, Zeke," said Buzz, insistently. "You need to express yourself to Molly with the same enthusiasm for your relationship that you've displayed here. Make sure she realizes, on no uncertain terms, how much she means to you."

"I will," declared Zeke, decisively. "Damn all and sundry, I will! Thanks for the pep talk, Shades."

With that, Zeke turned and marched out of the conference room like a man on a mission, slapping his right fist determinedly into his left palm.

Janet, by her very nature, was a creature of the night, most comfortable when shrouded in the cloak of darkness that provides protection and safe harbor for all things that share a sinister kinship with the devil. During her times as a free woman, she would prowl the shadowy back alleys and forbidding city rooftops like an uninhibited black cat, stalking her prey in the manner of a vampire, leaping from the inky darkness, straying from it reluctantly, just long enough to grab an unsuspecting victim and pull them back into the shadows as quickly and as noiselessly as a snake striking at a field mouse. And would her victim be killed, or merely humiliated? Sexually violated, or relieved of their valuables and then thrown as a sack of human garbage into the nearest gutter? Frankly, it all depended upon Janet's mood.

Even in her present state of incarceration, Janet thrived in the night, after the guards had locked down the cells and called for lights out. Although she could not leave the confines of her six-by-eight-foot cell during this time, she remained active, putting herself through a strict and vigorous string of exercises to keep herself fit and strong, and taking what little sleep she required during the daylight hours. Janet was on the inside for now, but she knew she'd be out again sooner or later – she'd always managed it before – and she didn't want to be flabby and out of shape when she hit those streets again.

Janet always exercised in the nude, allowing her body to breathe far more effectively than her prison jumpsuit would permit, and this only served to embolden the image of raw power that she already conveyed. Indeed, she could have been an X-rated PowerAde commercial, grunting with exertion and determination, her teeth clenched tightly, torrents of sweat running down into her narrowed eyes as she achieved her five hundredth push-up, her almost masculine shoulders heaving with the effort, her ample breasts hanging from her chest like fleshy pendulums, brushing against the floor.

Her push-up regimen completed, Janet sat back on her haunches for one full minute, her long, bony toes supporting her nearly all by themselves, and inhaled and exhaled several times, steadily and deeply. Then, perspiration dripping from her glistening body to form small puddles on the floor, she stood and moved over to the corner, where a severely battered punching bag hung from the ceiling by a chain.

Both fists clenched, Janet began attacking the bag, and each punch she visited upon the object was accompanied by a resounding 'thwack'. The punches continued, followed by a series of kicks, each of which was strong enough to shatter a man's ribcage. The blows kept increasing in speed until Janet's limbs were blurs of lethal movement, plowing into the bag with speed sufficient to render the consecutive, independent 'thwack' sounds a continuous, uninterrupted roll of thunder. Finally, with a savage roar, she diverted her right fist from its collision course with the bag and punched the wall instead. A loud 'crack' echoed throughout the cell block, and inside Janet's cell, little, flaking bits of concrete flurried to the floor, dislodged from the section of wall she had struck. The effect was quite similar to that of a pair of brass cymbals being clashed together after a long drum roll.

"Keep it down over there! Some of us are trying to sleep!" hollered an inmate who was too naïve to know that one did not speak to Janet that way if one wished to remain on a diet of solid foods.

Janet made a mental note to beat the woman senseless the next time she was in the yard, then proceeded with the next stage of her routine, lying down on her back on the cold floor, elevating her legs atop her cot, and folding her arms across her chest in preparation to begin the sit-ups. She had performed no more than twenty of these before her sharp ears detected the sound of approaching footsteps, and, seconds later, a man in a guard's uniform appeared outside her cell.

"Excellent form," said the newcomer, his observation carrying more than one meaning.

"Take a picture," Janet suggested, continuing her sit-ups. "It'll last longer."

"Why should I settle for a picture when I plan to have *you*?" asked the newcomer.

"I'm not allowed conjugal visits," said Janet, still not breaking her stride. "Not after what happened last time."

"I have good news for you, my caged canary," said the man in the guard's uniform. "You have been pardoned by one of the highest authorities in the land, and I have orders to escort you from this facility immediately."

Janet halted her sit-ups, rose gracefully to her feet, and approached the bars, her hands on her hips.

"Yeah fuckin' right," she sneered. "Do you have any idea what I'm in here for?"

"Mr. Kubritz is well aware of your history, and that is precisely why he is so interested in meeting you," said the man in the guard's uniform.

"Wait a minute, wait a minute," said Janet. "Kubritz? As in *Norman* Kubritz?"

"I did say one of the highest authorities in the land, didn't I?"

"You're not a real guard, are you?"

KnuckleDuster chuckled humorlessly, his eyes gleaming behind his sunglasses. "I have a pair of handcuffs here, and an armored van parked outside," he said. "To any security that spots us, we'll look like nothing more than a guard taking a prisoner away for transfer. If you'll just put your clothes back on, we'll get this show on the road."

Janet needed all of five seconds to consider the offer. Hell, freedom was better than incarceration any day of the week, and her curiosity about what Norman Kubritz's interest in her could possibly be was peaked. So she slid back into her blue-gray jumpsuit, while KnuckleDuster, who could have bent the cell bars with his extraordinary hands, settled for the more conventional method of unlocking the door with a stolen key.

"Lead on, my new best friend," said Janet, stepping out of the cell and allowing KnuckleDuster to cuff her hands behind her back. "Lead on."

One of the most cunning and cold-blooded professional assassins working the international circuit, the man called Henry Hugo was a snappy dresser and a flamboyant homosexual. He was tall, thin, and pale-skinned, with long, skinny arms and legs, cutting quite an Ichabod Crane figure. His hair was bright blond, highlighted by darker streaks of gold, and flowed about his shoulders in a quasi-feminine style. His ears were pierced three times each, expensive stones decorating the lobes. His eyes were pale blue, his cheekbones were high, and his lips were deep red and ghoulishly thin. His gaudy taste in fashion leaned towards pastel leisure suits, his favorite being the powder blue ensemble he wore now, along with the matching fedora, the numerous rings bejeweling his bony fingers, and the immaculately shined Donnell leather shoes on his feet. He was, without a doubt, a most curious specter who arrested the attention of anyone who laid eyes upon him, even in a place like Fives & Lives.

"It's absolutely marvelous to see you again, dear Norman," said Henry Hugo, in his high-pitched voice, as he made himself at home on the leather couch in Kubritz's main office. "It's been simply too long since you and I got together for a little chit-chat."

Kubritz grimaced. He was repulsed by homosexuals in general and Henry Hugo in particular, and if the man had not been such an undisputed master of his craft, Kubritz would have killed him without hesitation for his insolence in keeping up the pretense that they were, in some way, friends.

"What has it been now?" Hugo mused. "Three years since I last did a job for you? You're not being unfaithful to me with another hitman, are you?"

Kubritz shuddered at the word 'unfaithful'. It was as if Hugo was convinced Kubritz had a crush on him.

"Not at all, Henry," said Kubritz, congenially, foregoing his beloved Montecristo cigar during this meeting, lest Hugo should interpret it as some sort of suggestive phallic gesture. "I just didn't want to waste your valuable time with the petty, relatively unimportant executions that I've been able to delegate to my fulltime employees. As I look towards the near future, however, I feel that I shall be in need of your enviable expertise. There is a group of people of unique talent whose disposal I shall soon require, and I daresay your rare skills will prove absolutely essential."

"You sure do know how to flatter a girl, Normie," said Hugo, producing a gunmetal cigarette case and Zippo lighter from his jacket pocket. "It's always nice to know where one stands with one's colleagues."

We are not *colleagues,* Kubritz wanted to say. *I am one of the most powerful men on the face of the planet, and you are a loathsome freak of nature with absolutely no right to the wealth you command. I made my fortune with hard work – sweat, blood, and intricate planning – while you prance around the world with your popgun, content with taking orders from men like myself who are a thousand times your equal. We are* not *colleagues, Mr. Hugo!*

"You mentioned over the phone that I would have the opportunity to kill someone upon my arrival here," said Hugo, exhaling a wisp of cigarette smoke through a set of unnaturally white teeth, both his arms flung over the back of the couch, his legs propped up on the mahogany coffee table. "I'm just itching to get started. I haven't had occasion to fire a single shot in nearly two weeks, and Li'l Dick is absolutely dying to blow his load."

Grinning ridiculously, Hugo opened the left side of his jacket and pulled Li'l Dick from his shoulder holster. It was a Heckler & Koch Elite handgun, and embossed in gold lettering on both sides of the pearl handle were the words 'HH Loves LD'.

"For all his good qualities, he's a naughty little boy," said Hugo, running his fingers suggestively along the barrel of the weapon. "If Daddy neglects him for too long, he gets bitchy."

Kubritz managed to suppress a shudder of revulsion, and maintained his sociable front.

"Indeed I did make that promise," he said. "My staff have informed me that there is an unwelcome guest in the casino. Unless I'm gravely mistaken, he should be joining us very soon."

Detective Jim McAdams, looking like a tourist in his Bermuda shorts, Florida Marlins baseball cap, and 'I Love New York' t-shirt, kissed the pair of dice for luck and threw them down towards the end of the craps table, sending them tumbling and rolling, performing their customary dance of suspense and luck upon which so much often hinged. The dice had performed extremely well for McAdams over the course of the past fifteen minutes, but the little cubes were fickle, and this time they scowled at McAdams and stuck out their sadistic tongues at his attempt to exploit them for easy money, and the detective sighed as his winnings disappeared, and the 'fan club' that had been crowding around him and cheering him on dispersed and waited for the next lucky streak to emerge.

Losing money under any circumstances was unpleasant, but Jim McAdams hadn't come to Fives & Lives for the recreational gambling. Disguised as an unassuming vacationer, the detective had orders to infiltrate Norman Kubritz's inner sanctum and collect incriminating evidence sufficient to finally jail the man. No one was certain that any evidence recovered would hold up in court, having been obtained without a search warrant, but the city was at its wit's end trying to flush Kubritz's dirty deeds out into the open for all to see, and this latest strategy seemed as likely as any to succeed.

Taking his leave of the craps table, McAdams strolled over to the large, oak staircase and ascended to the restaurant, which seemed nearly as crowded as the casino below. Directly to his right, past a middle-aged man chomping on a hamburger and a young woman enjoying a bowl of lobster bisque, was the elevator.

Remaining as inconspicuous as possible, McAdams approached the elevator. There was no button to press to make the doors open, but there was a tiny hole in the wall, no larger than the head of a pin, at eye level to the right of the elevator. McAdams knew what that was for, and, thanks to the reluctant cooperation of Kubritz's optician, he was prepared.

McAdams moved in close to the wall and pressed his right eye against the hole. There was a flash of red, accompanied by a soft 'pleep' as the scanner read the special contact lens in McAdams' eye and identified him as Norman Kubritz. Then the elevator doors slid open, revealing an interior as lavish as that of the rest of the building, boasting cedar wood paneling on the walls, a layer of plush, red carpet on the floor, and a rousing chorus of 'Macho Man' playing through an eloquent sound system.

McAdams reached the third floor in a flash, and the elevator's doors slid open automatically with a quiet hum, revealing Kubritz's web of private offices. McAdams could only imagine the thousands of dirty secrets stored on this level of the fun-filled resort, and he guessed that any one of them would be enough to put Kubritz away for life. The ambitious detective had only just stepped out of the elevator, however, when both of his knees were blown out from under him and the walls and carpet became stained with splatterings of his own blood. Howling in agony, he crashed onto his belly and looked around through blurred, teary vision, for the man who had fired those two shots. He didn't have to look for long.

"I'm sorry, sir, but this area is strictly employees only," said Henry Hugo, leaning casually against the wall, twirling his Heckler & Koch Elite in his right hand like a boastful cowboy. "If you're looking for the restroom...well, never mind. I can see you've already pissed yourself."

"Who...who are you?" McAdams gasped through clenched teeth, clawing at the carpet with his fingernails, as if he could somehow drag himself to safety.

"Like the tattoo between my shoulder blades says, honey, I'm a killer queen," said Hugo. "And that means something extra special for you. Remember what happened to Ned Beatty in *Deliverance*?"

McAdams' eyes widened with horror. "No!" he screamed. "Not that! Please!"

"You know, that's something I could never understand about you straighties," said Hugo. "You're all ready, willing, and I daresay almost eager to take a bullet in the line of duty, but you run screaming in terror from the very notion of having another man's cock inside of you. It's a fate worse than death, isn't it? Even now you wouldn't trade places with a homo like me, and I'm the one who's going to survive to gaze in wonder at another dawn."

McAdams writhed in agony and continued clawing his way along the carpet. If he could stall for just a little more time and manage to remain conscious, perhaps he'd be able to devise a plan for survival.

"Aw, don't worry, I'm just yanking on your chain," said the sadistic Hugo, still twirling his gun. "I'm not going to break down your backdoor. Contrary to popular belief, we of the queer persuasion are not whisked to the peak of sexual excitement by every man upon whom we lay eyes. Personally, I think you're rather a Plain Jane. Besides, I'm not in the mood. I just got off a long flight and I'm feeling a little jetlagged, so I'm just going to let Li'l Dick have his way with you instead."

Hugo covered the distance between the crawling detective and himself in two strides of his long legs, and pressed the barrel of his gun against his victim's forehead.

"Don't worry, sweetie," said Hugo. "He'll be gentle."

McAdams didn't have time to throw out one more desperate plea for mercy before Hugo pulled the trigger a final time, sending a bullet through the detective's brain. McAdams convulsed violently enough to hurl himself onto his back, and his dead eyes fixed in a shocked stare as he gaped up at the ceiling, blood soaking into the expensive carpet beneath and around him.

"Excellent work," said Kubritz, revealing himself. "Though this does mean that I'm going to have to get the carpet cleaners back in."

"If you want a clean kill, hire the Boston Strangler," said Hugo, reholstering his gun with one more stylish twirl. "Me, I shoot people."

Kubritz nodded, and handed Hugo a bundle of ten one hundred dollar bills.

"He was small potatoes," the corpulent crime boss said. "I could have killed him myself.

Your real money will come later, when you eliminate the more formidable targets I have chosen for you."

Hugo tucked the bundle of cash into a pocket on the inside of his coat, and followed Kubritz back into the main office. Once inside, Hugo reclaimed his seat on the leather couch, and Kubritz went behind his desk to check his computer monitor's link to the camera in the private lobby.

"Ah, good," he said. "My next guest has arrived."

Kubritz jabbed the button that would release the occupants of the lobby, and, mere seconds later, the office door swung open. KnuckleDuster, back in his comfortable outfit of blue jeans and open leather jacket, entered, followed by Janet, who had swapped her prison togs for a tight, black leather top that strained to contain her breasts and left her shoulders and midriff bare, an equally tight pair of black leather pants that made Olivia Newton-John's outfit from *Grease*'s final number look baggy by comparison, and a pair of black stiletto heels that completed the stunning picture of a dominant, sadistic, and altogether very nasty woman. Despite his general distaste for the Negro race, Kubritz couldn't help but feel aroused, and he was thankful, for modesty's sake, that he was standing behind his desk. Henry Hugo, on the other hand, didn't give

Janet a second glance. He looked at KnuckleDuster instead.

"Long time, no see, KnuckleHead," he said, cheerily. "By the way, I love the bare chest. I'm very into the bare chest."

"Quit ogling me, you flamin' fag," said KnuckleDuster, contemptuously.

"Meow!" said Hugo. "Kitty has claws."

"Claws that could cave in your skull with one punch!" KnuckleDuster snarled, tearing the glove from his right hand and shaking his metal fist threateningly at Hugo.

"Boys, boys!" said Kubritz. "Manners, please. Let us not forget that there is a lady present."

"I'm no lady, but thanks for the compliment," said Janet, her hands on her hips as she took in her lustrous surroundings. "This is quite a nice operation you have going, by the way."

"Why, thank you," said Kubritz. "One tries, after all. Won't you sit down? Henry, you lazy slug, stop sprawling all over the couch!"

Hugo moved reluctantly over to make room for Janet, while Kubritz advanced on her with a wooden box – decorated with ornate, colorful carvings of exotic flowers – cradled in his fat hands, and lifted the lid to reveal a luxurious quantity of Montecristo cigars. KnuckleDuster couldn't help but be surprised. In his experience, the boss never shared his cigars with anybody, and a twinge of jealousy wriggled its way under his skin. Why should this total stranger be offered a cigar when he, KnuckleDuster, had served Kubritz loyally and well for years, and still had yet to receive this highly exclusive gesture of fellowship?

Janet took a cigar from the box and permitted Kubritz to light it for her. She took a long draw from it, then began puffing like a pro, exhaling plump plumes of smoke from her nostrils.

"Okay, what's the story?" she said, at last.

"What do you mean?" asked Kubritz, innocently.

"What the fuck do you think I mean? Why the early release? Don't tell me you want to give me a job as a dealer at one of your tables."

"Ah, a woman who enjoys getting straight down to business," said Kubritz. "I admire that. All right, then. I'll waste no words."

Kubritz paused just long enough to light a cigar of his own – he still didn't offer one to anyone else in the room – then got down to brass tacks.

"I understand that you are a longtime acquaintance of one Gary Parker," he said, little eruptions of cigar smoke punctuating his every word. "Is this correct?"

"Sure it is," said Janet. "Gary and I go way back."

"How much do you know of his present circumstances?" Kubritz asked.

"Well, it's been a few years since we've seen each other," said Janet, reclining against the back of the couch, blowing smoke rings reflectively at the ceiling. "But, last I heard, he and a bunch of other losers had banded together to form some kind of outlaw anti-crime unit. That's Gary for you; habitual do-gooder."

"Precisely," said Kubritz. "And it is because of your relationship with Parker that I wish to hire your services."

"Say what?" said Janet, sitting up and fixing Kubritz with an inquisitive but impatient look.

"Before too many more nights have fallen, I aim to have killed Parker and each of his nine colleagues," said Kubritz, his cigar smoke lending him a devilish quality as it encircled his visage. "My sources tell me that you know more about Parker than just about anyone else. Combine that with your underworld reputation for being one of the most dangerous killers around, in spite of your gender, and I doubt that I could find a better assassin to send after this fellow."

Janet took one more puff on her cigar, then threw it into the wastebasket on the far side of the room, where it began to smolder.

"I'm no one's lackey," she said, decisively, rising to her feet. "If you have dirty work to unload, give it to James Dean or Elton John here. Meanwhile, I'll be walking. Maybe we'll bump into each other again someday and we can do lunch."

With that, Janet began walking towards the door, and KnuckleDuster moved over to Kubritz's desk and picked up a gunmetal briefcase.

"I understand," Kubritz called after her. "You're an independent woman with plans of your own. I respect that. But perhaps what my assistant has to show you will change your mind."

Janet stopped, and the shaven-headed killer drew level with her and opened the briefcase, revealing row upon row of bundled one hundred dollar bills.

"There's a hundred thousand there, and that's just the down payment," said Kubritz. "You can take that now, and earn ten times that amount later on. If you decide to accept my little proposal, of course."

A lustful look came into Janet's eyes as she regarded the money. If she had been living in a cartoon, her eyeballs would have transformed into dollar signs, accompanied by a loud 'cha-ching!' As much as she hated the idea of being subordinate to anybody...aw, what the hell. If she was going to kill Gary anyway, she might as well get paid for it.

Like Janet, Sushi was a solitary creature of nocturne, most comfortable when swathed in the all-enshrouding blanket of the night. It was during the hours of darkness that his finely-honed *ninjutsu* skills – a near perfect mastery of the art of stealth and invisibility chief among them – were at their most effective, allowing him to go almost anywhere unnoticed. As silent and as light on his feet as a cat, and moving with the liquid grace of a snake, Sushi stalked his prey from the shadows, darting from one dark patch to the next, taking in views of the urban jungle from both streets and rooftops, taking cover behind such unlikely shelters as lampposts and fire hydrants.

The Vigilantes' watchword was 'teamwork', and Sushi was usually willing to go along with that, but nothing could beat the thrill of a solo hunt, with no one upon whom to depend but himself, and nothing upon which to fall back but his own extensive combat skills. Yes, Sushi enjoyed working alone, but enjoyment didn't figure into tonight's equation.

The Cuban, known on the streets as Famous Amos, was a notorious pimp and drug dealer, specializing in the really hard stuff. He was a celebrity – hence his nickname – throughout Brooklyn, where he made his base of operations, and the only reason he hadn't been arrested was that his reputation for callousness and brutality frightened the police just as much as it did the civilian populace. Indeed, more than one cop had been murdered trying to apprehend him.

Thanks to his notoriety as one bad son of a bitch, Famous Amos felt entitled to keep a high profile, rather than cower in the back alleys like most criminals. The prostitutes – mostly white slaves, and young girls smuggled over by the boatload from China – and drug peddlers who worked for him were a common sight throughout Brooklyn's poorer, dirtier neighborhoods. As for Famous Amos himself, he spent much of his time touring his turf in his pink Cadillac convertible with the giant steer's horns mounted on the front grille, the fluorescent green fuzzy dice dangling from the thunderbolt-shaped rearview mirror, and the vanity license plates that read 'OH DADDY'.

Famous Amos had been Sushi's personal project over the course of the past week. He had managed to elude Sushi twice, the second time last night when the ninja had interrupted his pursuit of the criminal to save the elderly couple from the gang of Red Cobras. Sushi vowed that there would not be a third escape in the man's future.

Staying well back, but still keeping the garish Cadillac in sight, Sushi finally tailed Amos to a large storage warehouse, its fenced-off yard dotted with forklifts and big, empty crates casting eerie, monstrous shadows in the pale moonlight. Perched like a gargoyle atop a cornice stone across the street, Sushi watched with interest as Amos brought his convertible to a screeching halt in front of the warehouse – his two right tires parked improperly on the sidewalk – jumped out of the car without opening the door, strode up to the gate barring his entry to the property, and blew off the single padlock with a shot from his Browning 9mm, not caring who heard.

Joey Tusker opened his mouth in a gaping yawn, and rubbed his tired right eye with his free hand. His left hand grasped a clipboard upon which he had spent several of the past hours recording the inventory of the dusty, spacious warehouse. And what was that inventory? Mountains and mountains of huge wooden crates containing home appliances; refrigerators, freezers, washing machines, clothes dryers, dishwashers, ovens, televisions, microwaves, computers, and toasters. They were all stacked one atop the other, and stretched out like the rolling highs and lows of the Swiss Alps for what seemed like miles, lending the warehouse's interior an eerie, labyrinthine atmosphere that made one feel quite dwarfed, and instilled in one the paranoid and silly, yet somehow very believable fear that one might be beset upon at the next corner by a bloodthirsty Minotaur.

These appliances hadn't seen the light of day since they were first packed and shipped from their factories, and most of them would continue to depreciate here inside their crates for years to come. After all, they were just surplus; the end result of overly zealous, overly ambitious manufacturing. Perhaps they would all be carted away and destroyed sometime in the very distant future, if the company ever decided it needed the warehouse space for the storage of more valuable, higher priority merchandise. For the moment, however, Joey Tusker was stuck on the regular nightshift, wandering around the enormous warehouse like a child lost in a forest of towering sequoias, jotting down complete lists of this, that, and quite a bit of the other, and listening to his own lonely voice echo hollowly off the moldy, cobweb-covered walls. It wasn't what he had pictured himself doing on those Career Days back in elementary school when the policemen, firefighters, and doctors had all come to visit and share the magical mysteries of their crafts with the eager young minds of tomorrow, but then, there weren't that many jobs available for someone who had been released just recently from prison.

Joey yawned again, and was in the process of deciding whether or not he was due for another coffee break, when he heard a familiar voice ring out from somewhere near the warehouse's entrance.

"Joey! Joey, I know you're in here! There ain't no place for ya to run! I know you're in here, an' I'm gonna kill ya!"

Joey gasped with fear and dropped his clipboard to the concrete floor. The clatter it made carried, echoing throughout the confines of the rectangular building, and Joey was much distressed to hear angry footsteps stop, change course, and draw nearer to his position.

"I hope you're scared, Joey! I hope you're pissin' your pants like a little girl! I hope ya know what I'm gonna do to ya when I get my hands on ya!"

Joey *was* scared, and he *did* know what the unwelcome intruder would do once he got his hands on him, and, if ever there had been a time in Joey's life when he had wanted to piss his pants, now was that time.

"I'm comin' for ya, Joey! There ain't no place on this planet ya can hide from me! There ain't no hole deep enough for ya to crawl into!"

Despite his pursuer's comments on the futility of hiding, Joey fled deeper into the maze of crates, hoping that he could eventually reach a back entrance, fruitlessly trying the lids of random boxes along the way, hoping against hope that one would open to reveal an empty interior in which he could cower.

"I ain't playin' games with ya no more, Joey! I'll tear this whole fuckin' place apart if I have to!"

Joey jumped as he heard a box crash to the floor alarmingly nearby. His pursuer was getting closer. Perhaps he was even on the other side of this wall of crates, heading in the same direction, ready to intercept him at the next junction! Yes, that had to be it, because the footsteps were getting louder! Or was that the blood pounding in his ears? Joey didn't know. At this moment, he didn't know anything. He was operating solely on instinct, and his instinct told him that he was going to die unless he could do something to elude the predator that was stalking him so relentlessly.

Changing direction and running off to the left, Joey frantically looked around for something – *anything* – he could use as a weapon, but his desperately darting eyes found nothing but storage crates; miles and miles of storage crates, penning him in on all sides, rearing up in front of him at every turn, as if working consciously in alliance with his stalker.

The cold sweat of terror dripping from his panicked body, Joey continued running, opting for any direction that would take him further away from those pursuing footsteps, gritting his teeth with the effort of blocking out the threatening taunts of that hated voice. In his haste, he caught the toe of his right shoe in a pothole of uneven concrete, and, in what seemed to Joey to be slow motion, crashed to the floor, facedown. It took him three seconds to scramble to his knees, throw a glance over his shoulder, and realize that the race was over.

"You've gone an' made me real mad, Joey!" hissed Famous Amos, towering over him, looking almost absurd in his rainbow-striped jacket, high-heeled alligator boots, and tiger-skin hat complete with purple plume. "Why'd ya have to do it, huh? We used to be friends! Why'd ya have to go an' open your big, fat mouth?"

"Amos, I had to!" said Joey. "I told ya, I'm going straight! I don't want no more o' your kinda life! I was just rottin' in jail, thinkin' about all the mistakes I made, and then they promised me early release if I told 'em what they wanted to know!"

Amos growled, and seized Joey by the front of his shirt, hauling him to his feet, only to send him sprawling back to the floor with a fierce punch to the jaw.

"They busted a whole boatload of 'em, ya piece o' shit!" he screamed, furiously. "I don't get these sluts for free, y'know! I gotta pay through the fuckin' nose, an' I don't get no refunds just 'cause the cops pick 'em up!"

Amos growled some more as he kneed Joey in the groin, punched him in the stomach, then gave him another crack on the jaw, but this time he didn't let his victim fall. Instead he held onto him by his shirt and began administering a series of stinging, punishing slaps to his face.

"And thanks to your blabbin', Louis got picked up!" he continued counting Joey's sins. "Louis was one o' the best I had workin' the street! He always had the stuff his customers wanted, an' he always brought home a shitload o' cash! So that's more you've cost me! All in all, I'm barely breakin' even right now, and I'm up to my neck in heavies wantin' to know the reason why! All...because...of *you*!"

His eyes flashing with rage, Amos punched Joey one more time, hurled him to the floor, tore his Browning 9mm from its holster, and leveled it at Joey's crumpled, gasping form.

"You're just lucky I ain't got the time to do a razor job on you!" he snarled. "Say hello to Satan for me!"

Amos' finger had begun curling around the trigger when a strange, almost alien sort of scuffling sound drifted down from the shadowy rafters high above. In his state of heightened anxiety and frenzy, any unexpected noise was enough to distract Amos, and he felt the back of his neck crack a little bit as he jerked his head upwards to face the darkened ceiling.

"What the hell is that?" he asked no one.

"It...it...it could be...r-r-rats," stammered the terrified Joey. "B-b-bats, maybe."

"Rats! I hate fuckin' rats!" hollered Amos, pointing his gun at the ceiling and blindly firing off three loud, resonating shots, as if expecting to slug the unseen pests.

The gunshots, still echoing off the walls, were answered by more scuffling, followed by the metallic 'schlink' of a sword being drawn from its scabbard and the eloquent 'twongk' of a taut rope being cut, and the last thing Amos – still looking up – ever saw was an immense, wooden storage crate plummeting down from the inky blackness of the warehouse's upper reaches, allowing him just enough time to scream but not enough time to move out of the way.

The crate smashed down onto the floor with a deafening thunderclap, breaking away pieces of the concrete floor, and creating great, billowing clouds of dust. Much of the wooden crate itself fell away and clattered to the floor, revealing the remnants of a badly damaged dishwasher, crumpled like an accordion. Amos' right arm – the only piece of him still visible – was sticking limply out from underneath one of the collapsed pieces of crate, the Browning still clutched tightly in his hand.

Joey was too incredulous to move, speak, look around, or do anything but gape in awe at the sight. He had been just two seconds away from certain death, the vicious criminal's gun aimed and ready to send a hot bullet lancing through his racing heart. But then…well, then *this* had happened! But what had caused it to happen? Was it mere chance? Had the rope holding the crate aloft been weak, and, by some incredible stroke of good fortune for Joey, just happened to snap when Famous Amos – pimp and dope dealer extraordinaire, and untamable terror of the borough – had been standing directly beneath it? That seemed pretty far-fetched, but what other possible explanation could there be?

Joey received his answer when the figure in black appeared, swooping down to the floor and landing lithely on his feet, his back to the scene. Without a word to the ex-con whose life he had just saved, he began strolling coolly and confidently towards the warehouse's main entrance. Joey, realizing that this was the man to whom he owed his salvation, scrambled hurriedly to his feet, calling after him.

"Hey!" he cried out. "Hey! Hey, come back, dude! Ya saved my life, man! That was just…amazing! Is there anything I can do to repay you?"

Sushi stopped, and looked back over his shoulder to face the other man. "Keep treading the straight and narrow," he said, "or I just might have to come back and drop a box on *you*."

Joey gulped nervously, and took a few steps back, bumping into the fallen dishwasher. He looked down and saw the pale hand, still holding the gun, and called out once again to the stranger to whom he owed his continued existence.

"Um…er…well, what should I do with Amos here?" he asked.

"Inventory him," said Sushi.

Gary was sitting comfortably on the ledge of a three-story building, much like a child sits on the edge of a pier with its legs dangling over the water, enjoying the roast beef on rye and can of Dr. Pepper he had purchased from the 7-Eleven, when he heard the loud 'thud' resonating from a few blocks away, and he knew that the despicable public menace known as Famous Amos had ceased to walk the earth. Gary smiled to himself as his teeth tore off another bite of bread and meat. Sushi had been noticeably preoccupied with Amos' downfall over the past few days, and everyone who knew Sushi knew that once he set his mind to something, he could be downright obsessive about seeing it through to his ideal conclusion, often at the expense of other matters which he deemed less important. Gary was glad that this particular crusade was over. The ninja would be a lot easier to live with now.

At least until another mission gets a hold of his endorphins, thought Gary, as he swallowed his current mouthful, only partially chewed, and resumed his cell phone conversation.

"I swear, Mr. Parker, I really don't know nothin'," said the nasally voice on the other end of the line.

"Bullshit, Lenny," said Gary, in a rather more good-natured, amiable tone than a two-bit punk like Lenny deserved. "It's impossible for you to know nothing. Everybody on both sides of the business knows that you've always got your slimy little ear pressed to the ground."

"Will ya cut me a break already?" Lenny sounded as if his old nerve trouble was beginning to play up again. "People tell me to get a real job, but they should try bein' a snitch. Everybody's always after me for info, and I gotta keep it all straight. If it's not you breathin' down my neck, it's cops draggin' me down to the precinct every five minutes, or gangsters and other assholes dunkin' me upside-down in water. And then there's the hazards o' the job! More and more guys are assumin' I'm the one snitchin' 'em out these days, and they keep comin' by to express their displeasure in no uncertain terms. And you want me to talk to you about Kubritz? The fat man'd *murder* me!"

"Come on, Lenny, you owe me big time," said Gary, swallowing another mouthful of sandwich and washing it down with a swig of Dr. Pepper. "Remember when I went out of my way to keep you out of jail?"

"You beat the shit outta me!"

"Well, you were going to violate your parole and skip town," said Gary. "Obviously you needed some sense knocked into you. And what about the time I stopped you from having sex with that HIV-positive hooker?"

"Again, you beat the shit outta me!"

"But only for your own good, Lenny," said Gary, finishing off his soda and tossing the empty aluminum can onto the rooftop behind him. "And let's not forget the copy of *Rocky III* you still owe me after you broke the one I lent you."

"Again, you beat the shit outta me!"

"And it damn well served you right," said Gary. "That's the one where he fights Mr. T, y'know. Come on, Lenny. You don't have many friends, but I've got to be one of your best."

"For a best friend, you sure do beat the shit outta me a lot," said Lenny, sulkily.

"And I'll do it again unless you tell me what I want to know," said Gary, wolfing down the last of his sandwich and licking a drop of mayonnaise from his left thumb. "And be quick about it. This may not be a peak hour call, but it's still costing me."

"Okay, okay," Lenny relinquished, his voice heavy with defeat. "You said you wanted to know if Kubritz was working on any major operation at the moment, right?"

"He's always working on a major operation of some sort," said Gary. "I just need you to fill in the details."

"I don't know many details," said Lenny. "Honestly, I don't. All I know for sure is that he's connected to those kidnappings. Y'know, the broads who've disappeared over the past few days. And this is just a rumor, but I hear he's hookin' up with one o' them towelhead terrorists they jailed recently."

"An Arab terrorist?" Gary's interested peaked at this. "It wouldn't happen to be one of the douchebags responsible for bombing that office building in Queens last year, would it?"

"Right on the money," said Lenny, a touch of the old excitement coming back into his voice. "The leader. Calamari Salami, or whatever his name is."

"Qasim Al-Fulani," Gary groaned. "Shit."

Gary ran a pair of fingers over his suddenly aching left temple as his memory took him back to the horrifying news clips of last August. Just like every other New Yorker, he could still see, in his mind's eye, the cataclysmic fireball ravenously devouring the five-story building that had served as a place of employment for over one hundred people. He could see the building quaking and convulsing with spasms as it toppled completely to the ground, hurling the burnt remnants of human beings through its shattered windows like spitballs from a soda straw on its way down. He could see the surrounding buildings catching fire, and he could see the street erupting into chaos and panic, and he could see police officers and firefighters and paramedics and pedestrians all being injured or killed by falling pieces of masonry and basketball-sized chunks of flaming debris that shot through the air like meteorites, and, for what must have been the millionth time, he silently cursed Qasim Al-Fulani and his five colleagues who had been responsible for the carnage.

As their sworn duty demanded, the Vigilantes had taken charge of the situation, and had managed to track down and capture all six of the terrorists, including Qasim himself, before they could escape back to their native Pakistan. After they had been turned in to the police anonymously, they had been found guilty at trial and shipped off to separate maximum security prisons throughout the country. Qasim Al-Fulani was now stowed safely away in what was literally a hole in the ground, banished from civilization and cut off from the world of man for the remainder of his natural life.

"Kubritz and Qasim? I don't see how that's possible," said Gary. "As far as anyone's concerned, Qasim no longer exists. The closest he comes to human contact on any given day is the anonymous hand that slides his food tray through the slot in his cell door."

"Ain't no place Kubritz can't get to," replied Lenny. "And I swear that's all I know. Can I hang up now? *Night Court* is comin' on in five minutes."

"Yeah, Lenny. And thanks. I'll buy you an ice cream next time I see you."

Gary turned off his cell phone, pocketed it, and stared blankly out into space, his eyes fixed on the face of the brownstone apartment building across the street, its innocent residents totally oblivious to the storm Gary felt sure was coming.

A partnership between Kubritz and Qasim? Somehow I'm not completely sure that's what the world needs right now.

With his elbow on his knee and his chin in his hand, Gary allowed his mind to unwind and stretch out as he eyed the shadowy silhouette – framed behind a set of lacy, white curtains – of the slender young woman undressing in front of a third floor window directly parallel to his vision, divesting herself slowly of her blouse, bra, and skirt in such a sultry and deliberate manner that Gary couldn't help but feel she was putting on a special show, just for him. The show soon ended, though, and the silhouette, its hair now drawn up into a perky, flirty ponytail, melted away from view, doubtless preparing to spend the remainder of the night in bed.

Bed, Gary reflected. *I remember what that used to feel like.*

Gary heaved a weary, hollow sigh as he swung his legs back up over the ledge, and stood, his hands pressed flatly against his hips as he arched his back, tensed his thighs, and rotated his head twice. A few soft, inconsequential cracking noises that are the common result of stretching one's muscles after an extended period of sitting reminded Gary that he wasn't twenty-nine anymore.

Why did I ever allow myself to turn thirty? Shit, I'm halfway to sixty. And a third of the way to ninety. Well, maybe I'll get lucky and some psycho'll nail me with a bullet before I have to experience life as an old man.

Trying to put the morose thoughts of human mortality – particularly his own – out of his mind, Gary stretched his arms up over his head and yawned. He hadn't slept a wink in the past forty-eight hours, and since the neighborhood seemed reasonably peaceful, he would have liked to go home to the silent darkness of his bedroom, where he could strip down naked, hurl his clothes into a randomly selected corner, and crouch on the floor, resting on his heels and knuckles like a primitive missing link. Then he would cease to be Gary Parker, intelligent *Homo sapiens* with fears, worries, regrets, and problematic emotions, or Gary Parker, the clandestine crimefighter, who regularly risked his life to help people he didn't even know for reasons that he himself often failed to fathom. Instead he would be simply a beast that existed in solitude, forsaking all of man's troubles and obligations, requiring nothing more to sustain himself than oxygen with which to fill his lungs, as he re-energized the flesh-and-blood urn that imprisoned his spirit, emerging from the darkness only after the life force he had lost had been regenerated. It was a method of retreat that Gary employed often in order to retain his sanity, and it was a ritual as essential to his emotional well-being as was food and water to his physical health. After staring continuously into the face of unadulterated, irredeemable evil that took the form of creatures who looked just like him, he had no choice but to seek isolation in his own personal darkness, sealed safely away from everything that put him in mind of the world at large, with only his own demons for company, if he was to continue resembling anything even remotely approaching human.

And other people think their jobs drive them crazy.

But he couldn't go home; not yet. Exhausted though he was, there was still another matter that demanded his immediate, undivided attention. So, adopting a casual stance, with his hands thrust into his jeans pockets, he turned to face the far side of the rooftop, blanketed in shadow, and cleared his throat ceremoniously.

"You can come out now," he said.

An amused little laugh rippled across the rooftop, followed by the authoritative clicking of stiletto heels.

"You knew the whole time that I was there, didn't you?" said Janet, her long legs carrying her with great strides into the moonlight.

Gary nodded.

"We never could get the drop on each other," she said. "Our frequencies are way too intertwined."

"I thought you were in prison," said Gary.

"I was," said Janet, "but you know me. I like to move around."

"You do realize, of course, that I'm going to have to knock you silly and take you back."

"Oh, fighting is all we ever do," said Janet. "Why don't you ever take me to a nice restaurant?"

"Janet, if there was ever anything between us, it was a long, long time ago, and far away from here."

"Why are all men so terrified of commitment? We could be fantastic together, sweetie."

"I'm really quite tired, Janet," said Gary, rolling up his sleeves and assuming a fighter's stance. "I'm in no mood for the usual repartee. If we're going to have another duel to the death, let's belt up and get on with it already."

"Aw, you're no fun anymore," said Janet, with a mock pout. "But I suppose it was bound to happen in our relationship, just like it happens in everybody else's. We used to go at each other furiously from dusk till dawn, but now you just want it over nice and quick so you can fall asleep."

The blatant double meaning of Janet's phrasing was not lost on Gary, and it only served to annoy him further. Being addressed in such a familiar fashion by a woman whom he knew to be an insidious, unprincipled killer levied upon him a degree of personal offense that left a foul stink in his nostrils, and every encounter with this longtime enemy left him itching for a hot, cleansing shower. In many ways, Janet was the physical embodiment of Gary's inner turmoil. Seemingly undefeatable, and staunch in her refusal to disappear forever and leave him in peace, she represented all of the monsters that Gary couldn't vanquish and all of the challenges he couldn't overcome. Essentially, Janet was Gary's most overpowering demon.

"We're two sides of the same coin," she had said to him once.

Although the very thought of himself and Janet sharing some sort of fateful, spiritual link was enough to send chills coursing through his body, Gary often had to wonder to himself whether his lifelong foe wasn't right. If there were 'coins' in the universe that carried the burden of two souls forever connected by some grand, cosmic design, then it was easy to believe that he and Janet were 'heads' and 'tails', being flipped constantly into the air by a divine thumb and slapped down onto the back of a divine hand. Gary wasn't sure that he believed in the idea of soul mates, but if the world's relationships did turn on such a mystical system, then his and Janet's long acquaintanceship of rivalry and hatred was most likely ordained by some higher power.

The spiritual quickly manifested into the physical as Janet leapt at Gary like a panther, her every muscle cord tensed and ready to perform its function to the fullest as she danced and dodged around him, delivering several playful kicks to his sides with the pointed toes of her shoes. Each time he spun to face her, she had already moved further along the track of the circle, and whenever he tried to break away, she was always right there in front of him like a cat blocking the escape route of a cornered mouse.

Fuck knows how she does it in those heels, Gary marveled.

Gary was, by all accounts, among the most dangerous hand-to-hand combatants in the world. Having been trained by his native government to be essentially a killing machine for use on occasions when the deployment of such a dangerous, emotionally barren warrior was warranted, Gary was well-versed in three different martial arts, and knew thirty-seven different ways to kill a man with his bare hands. His hand-eye coordination and reflexes were so acute that the common muggers and street punks he encountered almost daily, who fought with nothing more than their adrenaline and their clumsy fists, might as well have been moving in slow motion. With his high threshold for pain – conditioned into his nervous system by endless hours of unimaginable torture administered by his own handlers – rounding out the package, he could have been considered a kinder, gentler John Rambo. In spite of all of this, however, Janet had always proven to be more than a match for him. Her speed, skill, and endurance consistently rivaled his own, and though he was loath to admit it, past encounters had him suspecting that she actually surpassed him in the brute strength department.

Tired of Janet's games, Gary executed a roundhouse kick that landed against her left set of ribs, and was pleased with the sharp yelp of pain that followed. Janet was quick to retaliate, however, leaping in close and smashing her bony knuckles into Gary's jaw, sending him sprawling backwards with a stream of blood running down onto his shirt.

If only I could get her interested in meeting new people...

Gary rolled out of the way just in time to avoid being stomped on by both pointed heels, then performed a backward somersault that carried both his feet up into Janet's chin, knocking her back while he regained his footing. Janet recovered quickly, however, and fell onto her hands, using her impressive upper body strength to propel herself feet first like a missile at Gary's torso. The impact sent Gary flying halfway across the rooftop, and the only thing that prevented him from tumbling three stories into the street was a kidney-jarring landing against the concrete ledge.

I remember when three consecutive life sentences in prison actually meant something, he reflected.

His entire midsection singing with pain, Gary lunged stubbornly forward, dodged a high kick to his head, and thrust his fist into Janet's abdomen. Solid though the hateful woman's stomach was, Gary was still rewarded with a windy 'huwuff' sound as she exhaled heavily and stumbled backwards.

"Didn't your mother ever tell you that it's not nice to hit girls?" she asked.

"Yes," said Gary, "but she also told me not to play with guns and to stay away from drink. For better or worse, I was never a very good listener."

Having quickly regained her breath, Janet flipped forwards, sprang off her hands, and caught Gary's head between her ankles, and, using her momentum to complete the handspring, drove his head into the rooftop and ended up standing tall over his upturned face. Thoroughly annoyed, but not the least bit stunned, Gary launched his right leg upwards to kick Janet in the backside, sending her forward onto her knees. Then, with the speed of a striking snake, he leapt to his feet, wrapped one arm around Janet's neck, and used his free hand to grasp her short hair and tug her head to the side.

"Say 'uncle' now or I'll *break* you!" he hissed through clenched teeth, spitting tiny globules of saliva and blood.

Instead of saying 'uncle', Janet tensed her back, shoulders, and legs, then somersaulted forward, carrying Gary with her and rolling him over like an armadillo. Caught off guard and thrown upside-down, Gary lost his compromising grip on Janet and found himself flat on his back, and before he could make another move, Janet's knees landed hard on his chest, driving the wind from his lungs and sending a tidal wave of pain up his spine. The last thing he saw before everything went black was the fist rocketing towards that vulnerable spot right between his eyes.

Janet's lips curled into a smile of satisfaction as she regarded her unconscious enemy, like a spider regarding a helpless fly it has just cocooned. Her eyes gleamed with almost childlike amusement as she tousled his hair, stroked his bruised cheek with her long, sharp fingernails, and licked a blood smear tenderly away from the left corner of his mouth. Then she asked the question she had been waiting to ask since the fight had begun.

"Was it good for you too?"

Carolyn was sitting at a small, two-person table in a secluded corner of the Dunkin' Donuts on Nassau Street, munching on a cinnamon raisin bagel laden with lite cream cheese and doodling blueprints on her napkin of the Fabarm FP6 shotgun she was modifying in her spare time. It occurred to Carolyn, as she took a cautious sip of her Hazelnut coffee and decided that it still hadn't cooled quite enough to drink, that her mind was occupied almost constantly with devising new and innovative ways to kill, maim, or otherwise disable dangerous criminals, and she wondered briefly if this one-track thinking was part of her problem when it came to attracting and keeping men. After all, common sense dictated that her bad track record in Cupid's garden couldn't be blamed entirely upon her big-boned stature. There were plenty of other big women out there, and they all seemed to manage just fine. Maybe her quartermastering job with the Vigilantes had cut off too much of her ultrafeminine side, and potential mates were taking her for a dyke. Ah, well. After the experiences Carolyn had had with the last few men to whom she had dared get close, she figured it might actually be a good thing that she remained so unattached. On the other hand, here she was, sitting alone at a table designed to seat two, and she paused in her scribbling long enough to think about how nice it might be to have someone sitting across from her for a change.

Almost as if God wished to prove once and for all that He did indeed have a sense of humor, a man carrying a chocolate coconut cake donut and a large cup of steaming French Vanilla coffee approached the table, set down his food, and drew out the empty chair. The grating noise that the bottoms of the chair legs made against the tile floor caught Carolyn's attention, and she looked up from her napkin to see a tall, skinny individual in a powder blue leisure suit and matching fedora, a broad, death's head grin spread out across the bottom of his ghoulish face.

"Is this seat taken, ma'am?" asked Henry Hugo.

If Carolyn was surprised, she didn't show it. Instead she simply fixed the dandily dressed newcomer with a glare of utter contempt, her eyes narrowed, her lips pursed, and her cheeks flushing.

"What the hell do you want?" she asked, coldly.

"Only a little bit of time to catch up with an old friend," said Hugo, lowering himself onto his chair and crossing his long legs with the elegance of a grand duchess sitting for high tea.

"A friend?" said Carolyn, contemptuously. "Is that what you call the woman whose fiancé you murdered?"

"My dear Carolyn, that was nearly three years ago," said Hugo. "Can't we let bygones be bygones? Come, now. Why not give ol' Henry a big, sloppy kiss?"

Hugo took Carolyn's hand in his and raised it to his thin lips, but Carolyn pulled away, angry and disgusted. But she would *not* get upset. No, she would *not* give this reptilian bastard the satisfaction of seeing her get upset.

"Mmmmm," said Hugo, closing his eyes and arching his brow in ecstasy as he masticated his donut. "Absolutely divine. It'll probably go straight to my thighs, but it is *soooo* worth it. You know, I really am a complete and total whore for chocolate. Heh. I guess you could say I'm a fudge-packer in more ways than one."

Carolyn glowered at Hugo, and clenched her fists in her lap as she remembered Bruce Little, her third fiancé. He had been a good man. Kind, intelligent, witty, and handsome, and after the two stinkers she had been through previously, Carolyn was ready to believe that Bruce was 'the one'. But he had also been a money launderer for a particularly nasty racketeer called Robinson "Crusoe" Jackson. Carolyn had first met Bruce when the Vigilantes had busted up one of Jackson's more prominent car theft rings, and despite being on opposite sides of the chess board, they had taken an instant liking to each other. They had begun eventually to see each other socially, and it wasn't long afterwards that Bruce had dropped to one knee and asked Carolyn to marry him. Carolyn had accepted his proposal, on the condition that he go straight right away.

Bruce had happily obliged, using his four years of college to obtain a well-paying job at a prestigious marketing and advertising firm, but divorcing himself from the illicit side of his life had proved to be more difficult than he had imagined. Robinson "Crusoe" Jackson had not taken kindly to the betrayal, nor had he relished the thought of a clever loose end like Bruce running around unchecked with too much information stored in his mind. So he had hired Henry Hugo to remove Bruce from the picture.

Hugo had taken his sweet time with the job, stalking Bruce, tormenting him at every turn, dogging his every step like a sadistic phantom, threatening him with the constant specter of imminent and untimely death, until a searing bullet between the eyes seemed kind by comparison. Carolyn had watched with growing horror as Bruce had transformed from a handsome, healthy, happy specimen of bold and confident manhood into a sickly and paranoid shell of his former self, characterized by dark circles under his eyes from lack of sleep and a nervous tic in his neck from the constant looks over his shoulder.

"I swear to you we'll keep him safe, Carolyn," Gary had promised her, solemnly. "He's the man you love, and that makes him family. We'll do everything we can to guard him, and the next time I see Hugo, I'll put a bullet in his brain."

The slippery Hugo had proved too cunning and elusive for even the Vigilantes, however, and one sunny morning, while Gary himself was escorting Carolyn's fiancé to the grocery store, a bullet had lanced cleanly through the center of Bruce's neck and shot out the front of his throat. A geyser of blood spraying from his ruptured pulse, Bruce had stumbled forward, made a clumsy, desperate grab at a nearby lamppost, then fallen facedown on the sidewalk, dead.

Carolyn fancied that Gary had taken the tragedy almost as badly as she had.

"And I have simply fabulous news," said Hugo, sucking a glob of chocolate suggestively from the tip of his middle finger. "We're going to be seeing each other regularly again, only this time it'll be on a purely professional basis. It just so happens that you're the one my current employer has hired me to target. Well, you and your crimefighting brothers and sisters, of course."

Carolyn heard a distinctive 'click' emanate from beneath the table, and noticed that Hugo's right hand was in his lap.

"Confoundingly enough, he wants you alive," said Hugo. "I don't usually work that way, but the price is right. So, if you'd kindly come with me, I'd be much obliged. But by all means, finish your coffee and bagel first. There's no hurry; no hurry at all. After all, the night is young, you're unstrung, and I'm well-hung!"

Carolyn had taken just about all she could at this point, what with her memories of Bruce choking her up, and the continued sight of Hugo just plain making her choke, so she pushed her coffee cup and half-eaten bagel to one side and leaned over the table until her face was mere inches from Hugo's. The icy glare she gave him proved enough to make even the cold-blooded assassin blink.

"Who do you think you're threatening, you murdering cockroach?" she hissed. "You can play yourself up all you like, but outside of your own twisted little fantasy world, you're nothing more than a little, little worm who just happens to be good with a loud toy that every ten-year-old boy likes to play with. Take away your gun and you're nothing but a worthless, pathetic bug waiting to be stepped on. And you'd better believe, you piece of crusty dogshit, that I'm going to do the stepping!"

Carolyn seized Hugo's slender left wrist and twisted hard, evoking a yelp of pain from the killer, then whisked the fedora from Hugo's scalp and poured his own scalding hot French Vanilla coffee over his head. While Hugo screamed, and fumbled blindly for the napkin holder, Carolyn, a look of grim satisfaction on her face, rose with grace, dignity, and composure from her chair, and was met by an off-duty policeman who had been dining upon a Boston Kreme five tables away.

"What's going on here, ma'am?" he asked.

"Everything's all right now, officer," said Carolyn, turning to leave the establishment. "It was simply a matter of his getting ideas above himself."

Gary Parker, Gary Parker
Dormez-vouz? Dormez-vous?
Sonnez les matines, sonnez les matines
Ding dang dong, ding dang dong.

Clawing his way through a thinning veil of darkness, closer and closer to what was shaping up to be one mad bastard of a headache, Gary wondered from whose larynx that song was lilting. He knew that *he* wasn't singing it, but he didn't recognize the voice that was. Was he even hearing it at all? Perhaps it was just in his mind, akin to the ringing in his ears and the sensually deep, husky female voice repeating, 'Was it good for you too? Was it good for you too?'. But the song was definitely from his childhood. He remembered sitting behind a desk in a drafty classroom, singing it along with the rest of the children as the overweight, over-perfumed music teacher taught them the correct pronunciation of the French lyrics. And he chuckled to himself as he remembered his own, naughty version of the song that cast aspersions upon the sexuality of the French. He couldn't quite recall the full verse he had composed in those carefree childhood days, but he was fairly sure that it concerned Brother John letting another Frenchman have it in the rear end with a 'sausage'.

It's quite extraordinary when one stops to consider it, Gary thought, steadily regaining lucidity. *We Brits, as a people, never cease to be amused by the comic nuances of the male genitalia. And farts. Farts are funny too. If you want to get a laugh anywhere in the UK, just blast one right out. And then there's transvestites. They're hysterically funny. Nothing pleases a true blue Britisher more than the sight of a man in a dress. It's really amazing the sort of thing we find humorous. But even given all that, we're still not as bad as the Americans. These Yanks'll laugh at anything. They even laugh at* Saturday Night Live.

Having finally rambled his way back to consciousness, Gary moaned, and fluttered his eyelids a few times, bracing himself against the sting of the bright light that poured into his pupils. He ran his dry tongue over his dry lips and immediately recalled his rooftop duel with Janet. He couldn't remember beating her, so that probably meant that she had beaten him. So, the thing to figure out now was what had happened after his lights had been put out, and where he was now. He tried to move, but found he couldn't, and for one terrible moment he thought he was paralyzed. Then he rolled his eyeballs downwards in hopes of examining his body, and he realized he was in restraints.

He was strapped to the front of a big, metal slab, not unlike the one that had served as the bed for the Frankenstein Monster. The slab was situated at a diagonal angle so that he was facing the wall at the far end of whatever the hell room this was. His neck, elbows, waist, knees, and ankles were all secured to the slab with strong, metal shackles, rendering him effectively immobile, and his hands had been inserted into a pair of globe-shaped gauntlets, from which protruded a number of colored wires, attached to either side of the slab. His shirt, socks, and shoes had all disappeared from his person.

"Ah, our guest is coming around," Gary recognized the voice, made coarse by expensive tobacco, immediately.

"Kubritz," he spat the name.

"Yes, and you are Mr. Gary Parker, precisely the man I've been wanting to see," said Kubritz, plunging his chubby hands casually into his jacket pockets and thrusting out his massive gut. "The next time I see her, I must compliment your friend Janet on her prompt delivery. She certainly knows how to earn a paycheck."

"Janet's working for you?" said Gary. "Wow. I knew she was a psychotic, amoral, dark-hearted bitch from hell, but I did credit her with just a little taste."

"How do you like the office?" asked Kubritz, ignoring the remark. "It's not the primary seat of power, but it's such a nuisance to lug all this heavy equipment from one room to the other, so second best will have to do. Permit me to introduce my trusted assistant, KnuckleDuster, so called because of his extraordinary steel hands that can rend iron and shatter concrete."

"How do you do?" KnuckleDuster greeted him with a nod.

"Give the toffee-nosed 'well-bred bad guy' routine a rest, Kubritz," said Gary. "What am I here for?"

Kubritz took a big draw on his cigar and exhaled a thick plume of smoke into the air, then smiled wickedly, his flabby jowls folding back to reveal his square, yellowing teeth.

"I know about your clandestine crimefighting operations, Mr. Parker," he said, his bushy, black eyebrows coming together to form a fur headband. "I know there are ten of you in all, and, for reasons of my own, I am in a bit of a hurry to exterminate the lot of you. The trouble is, I don't know where to find any of you. So you are going to tell me what I want to know. You are going to tell me the location of your base of operations, as well as the locations of the private dwellings of each of your friends."

"No, I'm not," said Gary, matter-of-factly.

"If you do not cooperate, you will be broken down by means of painful physical torture," said Kubritz. "Upon my signal, my friend KnuckleDuster will throw that switch over there, and those gauntlets on your hands will send enough electricity coursing through your body to light up *Dick Clark's New Year's Rockin' Eve.* Do I make myself quite clear?"

"Crystal," Gary answered.

"Very well, then," Kubritz puffed out a plump smoke ring and adopted a casual stance, leaning back against his desk. "Let's start with your headquarters. Where is it?"

"Piss off, marshmallow ass," Gary said, quite calmly.

Kubritz tipped a nod to KnuckleDuster, who threw the switch eagerly. A blast of burning energy jolted through Gary's body, and he screamed.

"I'll ask again," said Kubritz. "Where is your headquarters?"

"In your mother's pants," said Gary.

Kubritz nodded to KnuckleDuster again, and another wave of electricity tore through him. Again he screamed, but it seemed worse this time, and he was left writhing and gasping for several seconds after KnuckleDuster turned off the juice.

"Where is your headquarters?" Kubritz asked for the third time.

"He likes it hard, he likes it hard, Brother John, Brother John..." Gary began to sing, weakly.

Kubritz nodded again to his sadistic minion, and this latest attack was the worst yet, giving Gary new insight into the plight of the common lightning rod. By the time it was over, his breath was coming in ragged gasps and his body was drenched with sweat.

"Where is your headquarters?"

"Jabba the Hutt called," said Gary, breathing heavily. "He wants his chins back."

"Oh, honestly," Kubritz rolled his eyes. "This is a waste of my valuable time. This time give him something to really think about, m'boy."

KnuckleDuster nodded with a grin, and threw back the switch. This time the torture went on for nearly thirty seconds as the goddess of anguish made love to Gary's body in sixty-nine different positions, and he screamed until he thought his throat would go raw. It seemed like every living cell in his body was being torn apart by some incredible energy, and only death could relieve him. But death would not come. He had only more of this to look forward to, and his formal training in torture resistance was providing him little comfort. No matter how many times he mentally recited dirty limericks, or the lyrics to Billy Joel's 'We Didn't Start The Fire', it still hurt like bloody hell. Finally the power was cut, and Gary was free to sag as limply as his bonds would allow, wheezing and shuddering as the remnants of the electricity still hiccupped through him.

"Now, how did that feel?" asked Kubritz.

"Imagine getting…a full-body massage…from Freddy Krueger," Gary said hoarsely, between gasping breaths.

"And you crave still more of this punishment? Come now. Tell me what I want to know, and all of this will be over."

Gary simply glared at Kubritz in angry, impotent defiance.

"Answer me, damn you!" shouted Kubritz, losing patience.

"All right, all right," said Gary. "The fact of the matter is, I do have something to tell you."

"Now, that's more like it," said Kubritz, tapping a rain of cigar ash into his golden ashtray. "Let's hear it."

Gary closed his eyes, took a deep breath, then locked his gaze with Kubritz's. "You're so fat," he said, "that when you go swimming, fishermen fire harpoons at you!"

Kubritz's eyes snapped wide open, and his mouth popped into a bright red, surprised 'O' shape, causing his Montecristo to tumble from his lips and begin burning a hole in the expensive carpet.

"What…what did you say?" he asked.

"You're so fat," Gary continued, "that if you sat on a quarter, it would break into two dimes and a nickel!"

Kubritz opened and closed his mouth like a goldfish, at a loss for an appropriate reply. To think that any man alive would have the balls to speak to him this way! KnuckleDuster merely looked on, equally astonished.

"You're so fat, you'd have to be baptized at Sea World!" Gary drove another insult home.

"Why...why you insolent, insignificant little...worm!" Kubritz sputtered, his broad face turning a deep shade of crimson. "You've no right to speak to me that way! You're nothing compared to me! I'm ten times the man you are!"

"Yeah, especially from side to side," said Gary.

Kubritz's teeth gnashed together loudly enough to break the sound barrier, and the cigar smoke still lingering in the air around his head made it appear as if steam was shooting out of his ears.

"Fry the bastard!" he commanded KnuckleDuster, clenching his fists so tightly that his fingernails drew blood from his palms. "Fry him like a pig on a spit!"

Behind his shades, KnuckleDuster's eyes glinted with delight, and he threw the switch one more time, and it was then that everything ended for Gary Parker. The unrelenting electricity ravaged its way through his helpless body like a fire through a dry forest. Any capacity for coherent thought was robbed him as he shook and jolted wildly against his unyielding bonds. For Gary Parker, life no longer held meaning, and the universe was no longer real. All that was real was the monstrous fist of agony that was crushing him, dragging him down into the inky depths of hell where no one could hear him scream.

A slender, bespectacled man who had been picked on and persecuted by his peers nearly every day of his childhood and adolescence, Dave Sullivan had developed an inferiority complex as towering and ungainly as a certain ape's ascension of the Empire State Building, and in his adult life as an unremarkable office drone, he felt the constant, overwhelming need to compensate for all his nameless shortcomings. One of his most recent compensations had come in the form of the purchase of a giant, intimidating SUV; a 2001 Ford Escape. Colored a manly dark green, and standing tall above the conventional traffic astride its fifteen-inch tires, the SUV was outfitted with a 3.0L Duratec V6 engine with two hundred horsepower, which, when combined with the Class II Trailer Tow Package for which he had opted, allowed the vehicle to tow up to thirty-five hundred pounds, even though Dave Sullivan didn't have anything that required towing. The vehicle was furnished with all sorts of nifty features – everything from air conditioning to power windows to refrigerated cup holders – but Dave derived the most pleasure from the rear seats' ability to fold back completely, thereby creating a cavernous space of sixty-three cubic feet. Why, Dave reckoned there was room for a whole other car back there! He rarely used the space for storing cargo, however.

Lying on her back in the rear of the SUV, Dave's boss' secretary moaned with pleasure as her nylon-clad ankles were gradually pushed nearer and nearer to her ears by Dave's continuous thrusts against her pelvis. She was a leggy blond called Britney, with terrible shorthand but a spectacular pair of tits, and she also happened to be another of Dave's compensations. With Britney, Dave could exit his mundane skin temporarily and become an entirely different person. When he was with Britney, he wasn't a boring little computer programmer with astigmatism, a pocket protector, and a marginally effeminate facial structure. He was a stallion, a studmuffin, and an iron giant, gracefully bestowing orgasm after orgasm upon his adoring conquest. Only once did he have to squeeze those ripe breasts, plunge his lizard-like tongue into that hungry, rosebud mouth, and stare hypnotically into those wide, china blue eyes, and he felt like the biggest, strongest, most powerful man in the world. Only one thing at this point could reduce him once again to the worthless, cowering pantywaist he was the other twenty-three hours and fifteen minutes of the day, and that was the unwelcome ringing of his cellular phone.

His erection losing potency instantly, Dave pulled hastily out of Britney, reached for his phone, and answered it.

"Hello, dear," he said to his wife, trying hard to control his breathing and keep the tremor out of his voice. "Yes. No. Yes, I'm sorry I'm late, but something...came up."

"I'll say it did," Britney giggled, poking her pedicured toes playfully at his excited member.

"Shhh!" Dave hissed, covering the phone's receiver with one hand. "What, dear? Oh, that was just the radio. You know I like to have it on when I'm working."

"And you like to have it off all the rest of the time," Britney smirked.

"Quiet!" said Dave. "What? No, dear, I didn't mean you. That was... erm...that was just Rob. Yeah, he insists on talking to me, even though he knows they're playing my favorite song. That's right, 'Rocket Man'. You know, the one about the guy not being the man they think he is at home?"

"Nice touch," Britney purred.

"I have to go now, honey. Work is murder. I promise I'll be home as soon as I can, okay? Okay. See you soon. Bye."

Dave switched off his phone and breathed a sigh of relief, and Britney came up behind him and draped her arms over his shoulders, circling his nipples with her long, pink fingernails while she nibbled on his right earlobe.

"When are you going to tell her about us, lover?" she whispered in his ear, her breath like a warm summer breeze.

"Well...I haven't exactly worked it out yet," said Dave. "It's tricky, you see. Everything is in her name. I could lose it all if she...well...you know..."

"Yes, I think I do know," said Britney, icily, the warm summer breeze turning instantly to frost.

The girl didn't have time to make further comment on Dave's spinelessness before a fist came smashing though the tinted window just inches from her head.

"Well, look what I've found here," Janet grinned, broadly. "A love nest. Say, you wouldn't mind if I joined the action, would you?"

Dave and Britney stared at the intruder, their eyes and mouths wide open.

"No? Well, in that case, I'll have to insist on going solo."

Janet pulled open the back of the SUV, grabbed Dave and Britney by their respective ankles, yanked them out of the vehicle, and watched with amusement as they rolled and tumbled across the pavement, picking up grit and pieces of crushed gravel on their bare skin like human Velcro.

"Well, squeeze my titties and get chocolate milk!" Janet exclaimed. "It's true what they say about guys with big cars! You really are trying to compensate for a tiny dick!"

While Dave and Britney scrambled away in mortified shock, Janet jumped into the driver's seat and turned the key in the ignition. The engine purred to life, the air conditioning roared back into action, and the numerous stereo speakers resumed crooning out a perfect, static-free rendition of Don McLean's 'Crying'.

Sissy music, thought Janet, extracting the CD from the player and tossing it out the window. *Now, where did I put that...?*

Janet reached into the pocket of the leather jacket slung casually over her shoulders and produced a copy of Marilyn Manson's *Antichrist Superstar* album. She fed the CD into the hungry player, which slurped it up eagerly and began belting out the obscene chords of 'Irresponsible Hate Anthem'.

Now that's more like it, thought Janet. *Seeing as how I have money again, I might as well start driving like the financially secure.*

Janet threw her commandeered vehicle into reverse, loving the big, bulky feel of the machine as it swung around to face the parking lot's exit, then slammed her stiletto heel down hard on the accelerator. Layers of rubber peeled themselves from the tires as she careened across the lot and out onto the street, leaving twin trails of smoldering black goo and an offensive odor of burnt rubber in her wake.

At precisely the same moment that Janet was bringing Dave and Britney to a premature climax, Carla was preparing to return to night duty, having slept away the afternoon. Her routine upon waking was always the same. She spent twenty minutes working out, waking up her muscles and getting her blood pumping with a variety of calisthenics that she found most suitable for taxing her legs, arms, back, and abdomen. Then she washed down under a three minute shower of cold water, and toweled off while downing an untoasted Pop-Tart – frosted raspberry this time – for energy. Then she went to her closet and retrieved her suit.

The black leather bodysuit was a holdover from Carla's cat burglary days. Together with the boots and gloves, also made of leather, it fit her like a second skin from collarbone to toe, making it easy for her to perform her agile maneuvers, and making it just as easy for her to make any dark corner or shadowy niche her hiding place. In days of yore, she had worn a hood-like mask that attached to the collar of the suit and concealed all of her head, save for her eyes and nostrils, but she had rather gladly discarded that particular accessory once she'd declared her burglary days officially over. As a crimefighting Vigilante, she went barefaced.

The suit's accessories and equipment that had aided her in becoming an urban legend back in her native Madrid were just as useful in her war on the scum of New York. The compact launcher mounted on her right wrist fired a retractable grappling cord as strong and reliable as steel cable, with three sharp little hooks on the end that could bite into almost any surface, including metal and stone. A pair of highly sensitive hearing aids that Carla took almost everywhere enhanced her auditory senses many times, allowing her to hear footsteps or voices at the far end of a long corridor, or the clanking of tumblers inside a safe's combination lock. She carried a pair of night-vision goggles for seeing her way through pitch blackness with midday clarity, and a pair of thermal vision goggles for easy detection of human heat signatures and laser tripwires. Her belt buckle, at the press of a button, became a blinding flashlight, and the suit itself was littered with places to carry and conceal the numerous tools of the trade, including knives, lockpicks, computer disks, smoke pellets, and just about anything else required by a woman of Carla's unique talents.

Once zipped, snapped, buttoned, and buckled snugly into the suit, Carla made for her bedroom window and climbed out onto the fire escape, where she made sure to close the window securely behind her – this was New York, and you couldn't trust anyone – and, with the simple thumbing of a button, fired her grappling line straight up. It seized the ledge of the building's roof, and within seconds, Carla was on top of the neighborhood.

Nice night, Carla thought, a warm breeze blowing through her shoulder-length hair as she regarded the blue-black sky above, its scattered collection of twinkling stars visible even through the perpetual air pollution of one of Earth's largest cities. *It's nights like this that make me happy I can come up this high and really breathe a little.*

Carla was interrupted in her enjoyment of the agreeable weather by the horrifically irritating sound of squealing tires, shrieking out their fiery protests in all eight compass rose directions, the nerve-shredding sound waves bouncing off the walls of the nearby buildings like a ping-pong ball between paddles, the lingering echo drilling itself ruthlessly into Carla's ears and threatening to decalcify her spine. Simultaneously, a dark green SUV roared out of the parking lot down at Carla's right and skidded onto the street, missing by inches a collision with an oncoming Mazda 6, whose driver immediately thrust his head out the window and began shaking his fist and yelling curses at the retreating larger vehicle. Carla paused just long enough to ascertain the SUV's intended direction, then took off running across the rooftop.

Now, it could be that this is merely a case of an incredibly discourteous driver, thought Carla, *but prior experience fills me with doubt.*

Her advantageous position atop the roof allowing her to cut corners that even the maniac behind the SUV's wheel could only dream of, Carla arrived swiftly at an overlook point above the next street and waited for the runaway vehicle to carom around the corner. When it did, Carla estimated the vehicle's current speed in miles per hour, along with the length of street it had to traverse before drawing even with her, then counted silently to five, and dove majestically from the roof.

Her timing was as impeccable as always, and, just as she had planned, she landed in a neat somersault atop the SUV's broad roof with a loud 'thump' that shook the vehicle. The bullet that came blasting up through the metallic roof mere seconds later, missing Carla's left ear by no more than an inch, proved indisputably to Carla that the driver's intentions were hostile. Crawling over to the driver's side, uncomfortably aware that she was now placing her belly directly over the hole that the bullet had made in the roof, she dangled her head upside-down over the side and peered into the open window. A tall black woman with a gun in her left hand scowled back at her.

"All right, sister, let's see your license and registration," said Carla.

Janet responded by sticking the gun in Carla's face, but, before she could squeeze the trigger again, Carla grabbed Janet's wrist and twisted hard to the right. Janet shrieked in pain and dropped the weapon, which clattered away down the street and fired a shot harmlessly into the brick façade of an apartment building.

"All right, you've just earned yourself a breathalyzer test, and at least a medium-grade ass-kicking," said Carla. "Now pull over!"

Carla grabbed the steering wheel with one hand and yanked it to the left, causing the SUV to cut across to the other side of the street and ride up onto the sidewalk, but Janet wrestled it back under her control, never letting up on the accelerator, even as the vehicle sideswiped a newsstand, sending newspapers and magazines exploding into the air like confetti from a novelty volcano. Janet took advantage of the momentary confusion and landed a hard punch to Carla's face. Stunned, Carla fell from her precarious position, but before she even hit the pavement rolling, her grappling line had already shot out and snagged the trailer hitch protruding from the SUV's back bumper, and now she was being dragged through the street on her belly at fifty miles per hour, her body weaving in and out of traffic in a deadly game of crack-the-whip. The fact that her skin wasn't being shredded off by the layer reminded her why she put up with the heavy leather material of her suit, even during the hot, humid dog days of summer.

Gritting her teeth and breathing heavily, ignoring the burning pains in her legs and the wind-knocking bellyflops against the pavement assaulting her stomach and breasts, Carla pulled herself steadily up the length of her taut line, inch by inch and hand over hand, wind-induced tears blurring her vision, until she was within arm's reach of the bumper. A few more seconds and she would have been able to remount the vehicle. That, however, was when Janet happened to speed through the four-way intersection.

Ignoring the halting beacon that was the red light, Janet roared onwards without hesitation and just barely missed having her rear end knocked all the way to the scrapyard by a Chevy Cavalier coming from the left, which, although smaller than the SUV, was bearing down fast, encouraged by its own beckoning, permissive green light. Carla, however, did not manage such a fortuitous escape. Instead, her prone form was struck by the nose of the Chevy and flung clear across the intersection.

After a series of clumsy rolls, tumbles, and somersaults, she finally came to rest in the entrance of a dead end alley, her eyes closed, her limbs askew, her breathing shallow. A homeless wino who had been squatting in this particular alley for several weeks now and had come to consider it his personal property glared resentfully at the unmoving newcomer, and demanded in the firmest of tones that she find someplace else to spend the night. The wino was pigheaded and stubborn, and reluctant to relocate, but when he finally realized that his unwelcome guest was clearly not going to leave, he got begrudgingly to his feet, spat on the homewrecker and flipped her the bird, and moved on.

The first thing of which Gary became aware upon his groggy, sluggish return to consciousness was the unforgiving hardness of the concrete floor on which he was lying flat on his back, and his feelings about this sensation were nothing if not ambivalent. On the one hand, the floor's firmness felt good against his abused muscles. On the other hand, his head still felt like the Queen of Hearts had cut it off and used it as a croquet ball, and lying on the concrete like a giant paperweight, allowing a highly irritable degree of light to penetrate his burning eyes, wasn't helping matters. So he decided to rise to his feet, carefully and gingerly, weathering a sudden, brief dizzy spell as he did so. Once upright, he passed a hand over his throbbing skull, rubbed his stinging, watery eyes, and looked down at his body. He was still minus his shirt and shoes, and, as he observed the constellations of small, black burn marks dotting his exposed flesh, memories of his previous ordeal came flooding back to him. Then he wondered why he was still alive.

"Ah, you're awake," said a booming, disembodied voice that seemed to be coming at him from all sides.

Gary looked around, and deduced that he was in a large basement of some kind, with a concrete floor and walls, and a number of steel pillars holding up the ceiling. It looked like a big, empty parking garage, and the only exit he could see was a closed elevator with no visible call buttons. As for people, he saw none.

"I wagered that you would remain unconscious for approximately eight hours," said the amplified voice, its boastful, condescending tone bouncing off the stone walls. "Thanks to your kind cooperation, I am now ten million dollars richer."

"So, what happened, Norman?" Gary addressed the empty room, certain that Kubritz, wherever he was, could hear him. "Last thing I remember, I was being fried like an egg on a Mexican sidewalk."

"Yes, I was going to have you killed right then and there," said the voice of Kubritz, with a smooth, velvety quality that put Gary instantly in mind of Donald Pleasance stroking his Persian cat. "But then I devised a much more...entertaining idea."

Gary didn't have time to ask the question he was sure he'd regret before he heard a soft, humming noise behind him, and turned to see the elevator doors sliding open to reveal the largest human being Gary had ever seen; an enormous black man clad only in a pair of khaki drawstring trousers and sporting a heavy, golden bracelet around each meaty wrist. He stood not an inch below eight feet tall, his naked chest swelled to the size of a barrel – or maybe even a barrel and a half – and his arms and legs looked like tree trunks, rippling with thick cords of muscle.

"Mr. Parker, this is Mr. Bojangles," said Kubritz, pure relish dripping from his words. "We call him that because he likes to dance on people's heads. He'll take good care of you while I attend to more important matters of business. By the way, I've wagered a cool million on you not lasting more than five minutes, so don't let me down."

With that final word came the resounding 'thunk' that indicated the concealed loudspeaker going dead, and Gary knew he was now alone; alone in this very large, very empty, very doorless chamber with a man who made Charlie look almost normal-sized by comparison.

"Howdy," rumbled Mr. Bojangles, his voice deeper than the Pacific Ocean, and deploying enough vibration to make the hairs on the back of Gary's neck stand on end.

"Howdy," Gary replied, apprehensively. "How're you doing this morning?"

"Good," Mr. Bojangles grinned broadly from ear to ear, displaying two rows of ivory white teeth that looked strong enough to bite an iron rail in half. "You, on the other hand, ain't doin' so good."

"Tell me about it."

"I will."

With that, the immense man cracked his knuckles loudly enough to shatter glass and began stomping towards his prey, his bare feet seeming to shake the ground with every step. Gary watched every move that those huge, powerful legs made and wished that he could be somewhere else. Anywhere else.

First Janet re-enters my life and beats the ever-loving shit out of me, he thought, *then I get char-broiled to tender, juicy perfection, and now this. All in all, the past twelve hours have been pretty craptacular.*

Mr. Bojangles' ham-sized fist came flying at Gary's head, and Gary dropped quickly to the floor and rolled between the giant's legs, feeling the breeze caused by the swing even as he came up behind his enemy. He then brought his right leg up and kicked Mr. Bojangles solidly in the balls, but the behemoth merely turned and grinned at him before delivering a vicious backhand that sent Gary skidding halfway across the room like a skipped stone across the surface of a pond.

As he came to rest against a steel pillar, Gary's comprehension of the degree of trouble he was in reached a new level. A kick to the giant's crotch had proved ineffective. That had never happened before. No matter how strong or intimidating an enemy had been in the past, they had all crumpled as helplessly as everyone else after being dealt a whack in the sack. But not this time. Mr. Bojangles' genitals were just as strong as the rest of him.

Gary scrambled to one side just in time to dodge another punch from Mr. Bojangles – and was not in the least bit comforted by the sight of the small dent the giant's fist left in the pillar – but was not quick enough to escape being seized by the wrist by the larger man and yanked off his feet. Gary grunted in pain as he felt something in his shoulder shift in a way that the design of human anatomy did not appreciate, nor allow to go unpunished, and Mr. Bojangles roared with laughter as he spun around twice, swinging Gary by his captured limb like a toddler swings a teddy bear, then threw him over to the other side of the room.

I've been thrown out of better bars than this, was the absurd thought that ran through Gary's mind as he crashed against the wall.

Mr. Bojangles belted out a rich, loud belly laugh that actually seemed born of genuine joviality and amusement, and stalked towards Gary once again. Gary picked himself up, his headache worse than ever, and noticed immediately both the pain that was lancing through his right shoulder and the odd angle at which his arm was hanging. Employing a technique he had learned not from training, but from Mel Gibson in *Lethal Weapon 2*, Gary drove his dislocated shoulder against the wall in order to insert it back into place, crying out in pain as he did so.

Mad as hell, and all too aware that he was never going to beat this Sasquatch of a man if he didn't start taking the offensive, Gary lunged forward, past Mr. Bojangles' groping arms, and began slamming his fists into the giant's abdomen. Punch after punch found its mark on the man's hard, washboard stomach, but Mr. Bojangles didn't seem to be bothered in the least. On the contrary, it was Gary's knuckles that were feeling the results. It was like punching a brick wall.

At what appeared to be his own leisure, Mr. Bojangles raised one fist high into the air, then brought it down on Gary's head like a mallet. Gary made the sound of someone stunned by a moving vehicle, and collapsed to the floor. Mr. Bojangles, his grin as broad as ever, picked him up with both arms and wrapped him in an inescapable bear hug. Gary's feet dangled a full three feet above the floor as the giant held him aloft, tightening his grip around his midsection with every breath.

Gary writhed in the giant's double-armed grasp, using all the fading strength he had left to push against Mr. Bojangles' entwining arms, feeling like a cork trying to slip its way out of the neck of a champagne bottle, but the brute's grip seemed unbreakable, which was more than Gary could say for his own spinal column, which was complaining loudly as his vision began to go fuzzy.

The distortion of his vision infused Gary's mind with the strategy that would be his last chance at getting out of here alive. In order to survive, he had to concentrate his attack upon the only part of his enemy's body that wasn't abnormally strong or protected by layer upon layer of calloused muscle.

The distress calls from his ribs and lungs egging him on, Gary thrust both his thumbs into the giant's eyes and pressed hard. For the first time, Mr. Bojangles stopped grinning and actually cried out in pain, but didn't relax his grip. Infused with the satisfaction of having hurt the brute, Gary pressed harder. His thumbs dug into the eyes, pressing harder and harder still, evoking more screams of agony from the giant. Finally, the enormous arms relinquished their grip and the hands clapped themselves over the eyes. Gary dropped to the floor and started running immediately as Mr. Bojangles collapsed to his knees, covering his eyes and wailing.

Gary knew he had to get out fast. This wasn't as effective as what Odysseus had done to the Cyclops. Mr. Bojangles would be back on his feet and seeing through his stinging eyes again in seconds, and now that he had royally pissed off the giant, the fun and games would be over. Mr. Bojangles would tear through him like an 18-wheeler through a Volkswagen Beetle. So Gary grabbed the only object he could see in the entire room – an unassuming fire extinguisher hanging on the wall – and ran for the elevator.

Using the extinguisher as a battering ram, Gary smashed it against the elevator doors with every ounce of force his furiously pumping adrenaline could muster. They didn't open, so he backed up and slammed into the metal doors a second time, then a third, praying to high heaven that they would open and release him from this lions' den, but nothing gave. Indeed his efforts made nary a dent in the shiny, reflective surface of the doors, and it was just after he had slammed the extinguisher against the doors for the fifth time, refusing to surrender and go quietly into that good night, that his heart had occasion to sink at the sound of an angry, bellowing roar from the other side of the room, followed by a flurry of fast, thundering footfalls. Mr. Bojangles was stampeding towards him, burly arms pumping at his sides like pistons, a freight train in human form, apparently intent on running him crudely down.

More in the name of self-defense than anything else, Gary hurled the battered fire extinguisher down at Mr. Bojangles' legs. The charging brute tripped over it and his considerable momentum carried him headfirst into the doors, which finally gave way beneath his impact. Gary gaped, disbelievingly.

Not exactly what I had in mind, but okay, thought Gary, as he sprinted into the elevator and repeatedly jabbed the button displaying a '1' before Mr. Bojangles had the time to get his wits together.

"Ow! Jeez, Eva, take it easy!" Carla complained to Leeza as the Vigilantes' doctor prodded the tender bruise on the side of her head with her long, bony finger. "I was hit by a car, y'know."

"It serves you right," said Leeza, unsympathetically. "You're a rash and careless child, and its only by force of pure, dumb luck that your back wasn't broken."

"Thanks, Mom, you're the best," said Carla, sitting upright on one of the beds in the Rat Hole's infirmary.

"How do your ribs feel?" asked Leeza, never allowing any sarcastic comment to derail her concentration from her work.

"Better, since you taped them," answered Carla.

"It will take some time for your skin burns to heal up," said Leeza, recording every detail of the examination meticulously, as she always did for each of her fellow Vigilantes. "I have some ointment for that, and some painkillers for your superficial aches and pains. They'll go away soon. Any questions?"

"Can I have a lollipop?" Carla asked, affecting the voice of a little girl who expects a reward for behaving herself.

Leeza, notorious for her lack of a sense of humor, snorted, and turned to file away Carla's chart, saying no more. Carla smiled to herself, stretched her arms up over her head, then alighted from the bed and walked out into the Rat Hole's lounge where the majority of the Vigilantes were congregated. These early, post-sunrise hours usually constituted their 'down time'.

"You okay, Carla?" Charlie asked her, looking up from the previous day's *USA Today*.

"Just the usual sprains, bruises, and lacerations, big guy," said Carla. "No sweat. Say, does anyone know if William is coming by today? I need him to help me get my rebellious laptop to do my bidding."

"Something tells me we won't be seeing him all weekend," said Carolyn.

"Don't tell me he's been grounded again," sighed Carla. "He's really got to stop that. I mean, what if we need him in an emergency? If we need him to hack into the security mainframe of a building where a bunch of ruthless terrorists are holding and threatening to execute a group of hostages, saying, 'Sorry, but my mom isn't letting me go out today', just isn't going to cut it."

"He isn't grounded," said Charlie. "He's got a date."

"A hot date," added Zeke, wisps of cigarette smoke slithering out from the tight gaps in his teeth. "From what he tells me, she's a real peach."

"Really? Well, good for Will," said Carla, happy for her younger teammate. "I knew he'd find his social bearings eventually."

"There are no traffic cops on the road of life, so we all travel at different speeds," mused Buzz, typically philosophical. "Some go very fast in their fancy sports cars and accept the risk of becoming involved in a terrible accident; some ride buses and look at the scenery while they wait to arrive at their destination; still others ride bicycles in the side lane. I was a walker at William's age. The handicapped have become more integrated into society now, but forty years ago no one was overly interested in dating the blind kid."

"I'd have thought the ugly girls woulda been throwin' themselves at ya, Shades," said Zeke, demonstrating his usual complete lack of tact.

"I never had much of a teenage social life," said Carolyn, reflectively. "It's amazing how a broad girth can turn you into an absolute pariah."

"I remember my first date," said Peg, her chin resting gloomily in her hand. "I was thirteen, and it was a disaster. I was so nervous I got a migraine and threw up all over the guy. Adolescence was not an easy time for me."

"When I was a kid, I was busting windows and stealing color TV sets," said Charlie, joining in the sharing. "A dumb-ass punk through and through. Took me a long time to get off that path."

SUMMER OF THE VIGILANTES

"Shit, this is depressin'," said Zeke. "Next thing y'know, ol' Eva's gonna come in and tell us about hidin' under tables in Berlin. Ain't there anythin' happy we can talk about?"

"Well, June first is coming up," said Carla.

"What's June first?" asked Charlie.

"Morgan Freeman's birthday," answered Carla. "I thought it might be a good excuse to exchange gifts. After all, he's been in some good stuff, right?"

"*Driving Miss Daisy* is overrated," was Carolyn's reply.

"But *The Shawshank Redemption* and *Million Dollar Baby* are terrific," said Charlie. "Mind ya, I didn't care much for *The Sum Of All Fears*," said Zeke.

"It was a Ben Affleck movie," said Carla. "You weren't supposed to like it."

Before the Vigilantes had the opportunity to indulge this particular tangent further, the door that served as the Rat Hole's only entrance flew open, banging against the wall, and Gary appeared, stripped to the waist, breathing heavily, hunched slightly, and dotted with cuts, bruises, and burns.

"Gary, you look like hell," said Charlie.

"What on earth happened to you?" asked Carla, approaching him with concern as he lumbered into the center of the room. "Leeza, we need you out here!"

"No, no, I'm fine," said Gary, shrugging her hand gently from his shoulder. "It looks worse than it is. I just need a drink."

He caught the spark of surprise and nervousness in Carla's deep, soulful eyes, and hastened to clarify.

"Of water," he added, quickly. "I mean a drink of water."

Gary filled a paper cup at the water cooler, drank it down in two big gulps, then flopped down into the nearby La-Z-Boy recliner.

"And a Tylenol the size of a football," he added, rubbing his forehead with his fingertips. "I could use one of those as well." "So, what happened?" Peg repeated Carla's question.

"Kubritz," Gary answered. "He tried to feed me to Goliath's big brother. A huge son of a bitch. Even bigger than you, Charlie."

"Wow," said Charlie, smiling with amusement as he crossed his muscular arms over his barrel chest. "I think I'd like to meet this guy."

"Better you than me," said Gary. "The next time he sees me, he'll probably want to use my lungs and intestines to make balloon animals. You look a little battered yourself, Carla. What did you get into?"

"Carjacker," she replied.

"Anyone we know?" Gary asked.

"No, I'd have definitely remembered," said Carla. "Big black bitch with a killer left hook, wearing a leather outfit that made mine look almost normal by comparison."

Before Carla even finished describing the culprit, Gary's fist clenched tightly and abruptly around his paper cup, crushing it as if by automatic reflex.

"Janet," the name was a curse coming off of Gary's lips.

"Who?"

"An old...acquaintance of mine," Gary explained. "We go way back. We were kids together, in fact. I've known her for as long as I can remember, and we've always been at each other's throats. Sometimes I think our respective lives are just one big contest arranged by the gods to see who kills who first. If she's going to be running rampant around New York, you all need to be aware that she's a sociopathic killer with absolutely no conscience whatsoever. She's a strong, skilled fighter, and I can't think of a single thing she fears. Her very existence is an obscenity, and the mere fact that she's roaming free makes me want to buy a ton of spam and three hundred bottles of purified water, and hide in the basement."

"Well, that's good news," grumbled Carolyn, rolling her eyes.

"Oh, it gets even better," said Gary. "Janet, uncharacteristic though it may be, appears to be working for Kubritz. That's how I ended up in Fatty Arbuckle's clutches in the first place. But instead of simply killing me when he had the chance, Kubritz seemed more than a little interested in making me tell him where we all live and where the Rat Hole is. If I didn't know better, I'd say he was trying to collect us."

"Actually, you might be right," said Carolyn, rubbing her chin, looking at no one in particular. "I also received a visit from an old 'friend' last night; Henry Hugo, the assassin who killed Bruce three years ago. In between his usual incoherent ravings about how fabulous he is, he mentioned that he had been retained by a very rich man to help capture the ten of us and bring us in alive."

Gary's tired eyes darkened at the mention of Hugo's name, and he scowled. The score still required settling.

"So, in summary, Kubritz knows about us, and he's hired some top-notch talent to come after us like exterminators after cockroaches," said Carla. "I'd say the next few days ought to prove interesting, to say the least."

"Norman Kubritz, Henry Hugo, and Janet, all on the same bill," Gary muttered, mostly to himself, gazing at the wall. "What the fuck did I ever do to deserve that?"

Standing before Kubritz's desk with his head bowed and his big hands clasped sheepishly behind his back like a chastised schoolboy in the headmaster's office, Mr. Bojangles stared at the floor with eyes that were still red and aching while his perturbed employer evaluated, on no uncertain terms, his recent performance.

"Exactly how big of a fucking imbecile are you?" Kubritz bellowed, slapping his big hand angrily down onto his desk with enough force to send his Ming vase full of red and white roses toppling to the floor with a priceless crash. "I lock you in a basement with an unarmed man one-third your size, and you allow him to escape! All you had to do was kill him! It was perfectly simple! Sometimes I think the most muscled part of your anatomy is your head, you useless oaf!"

"Sorry, boss," said Mr. Bojangles, who could have taken Kubritz's head off with one punch.

"You'll be even sorrier when I dump you back in that prison where I found you!" Kubritz threatened, belching smoke like an enraged dragon.

"All body and no brains," said Henry Hugo, sprawling like a pampered housecat on the leather couch. "Just the way I like 'em."

"Dear Malik, I must beg your pardon for the bumblings of my incompetent staff," said Kubritz, turning to the Arab standing next to him.

"Quite all right, Norman," said Malik. "Though it may be a cliché, it really is difficult to find good help these days. I'm sure there will be opportunities aplenty to achieve our ends."

"Unfortunately, Parker proved remarkably resistant to torture," said Kubritz, chomping moodily on his cigar. "We were unable to make him divulge the locations of his accomplices."

"Is that what you want to know?" asked Janet, her statuesque, scantily-clad form draped over a leather armchair. "Hell, I know where they are. Even in prison I kept constant tabs on Gary. Consequently, I know all about his friends too."

"You know where they live?" Kubritz, surprised, spun to face her. "But why didn't you tell us this before?"

"You never asked," she said.

"Well, I've gotta admit, that's one chick flick I really enjoyed," said William to Rachel, as the pair of them walked out of the cool, dimly-lit cinema and into the dry heat of the sunbathed parking lot. "I'm really more of a sci-fi geek. Y'know, aliens busting out of people's chests, and the Austrian Oak telling everyone he'll be back. But this movie really did appeal to me."

William didn't think it prudent to add that the primary reason he had so enjoyed the film was because he had spent most of its running time stealing discreet, peripheral glances at Rachel's nipples reacting to the air conditioning, and getting high off the extremely agreeable scent she was wearing.

"I loved it," said Rachel. "It was so romantic. Didn't you love the part at the end when they found each other in the park?"

"To be completely honest, I would have liked it a lot more if the Predator had come along, beheaded them both, then strung them up by their ankles and skinned them," said William, as he unlocked and opened for Rachel the passenger side door of his father's car. "But just disregard that. Like I said, I'm a real sci-fi geek."

"I don't think you're a geek," said Rachel, climbing into the car, her hand shying instinctively away from her seat belt's metal buckle that had been baking in the sun for over two hours. "So you have different interests than all the jocks and popular kids. That doesn't make you a freak of nature."

"Thanks," said William, not knowing what else to say, though his heart was warmed. "Y'know, I've got the car for the rest of the day. You wanna get something to eat?"

"Yeah, that sounds good," said Rachel. "Y'know, this is the most fun I've had with a guy in a while. When I'm out with Jason, he always drags me wherever he wants to go, like I'm some kind of accessory who's supposed to just go with the flow. It's nice to be asked my opinion for a change."

"Guys like Jason have no class," said William, growing bolder by the moment, as he climbed into the driver's seat and inserted the key into the ignition. "They've got all those rugged good looks, and they waste them on trying to dominate everyone they see."

Rachel smiled sweetly, and looked at William for a moment. Then, taking the boy completely by surprise, she leaned over and kissed him full on the lips. The kiss lasted five seconds, and when she finally pulled away, William was left with a dreamy, dumbstruck expression on his face.

"Y'know, you don't have to be rugged in order to be sexy," said Rachel, winking playfully.

William was unable to reply. The unbelievable yet undeniable fact that he had just shared lip-to-lip contact with a young woman who was hot enough to cook a steak by sticking it between her legs was too much for his brain to process, and he remained frozen in time.

"So, what do you feel like?" Rachel asked. "If you like Chinese, I know a great little place not far from here."

Still in suspended animation, William continued to stare blankly into space, like a robot gone offline, with the same dumb expression on his face.

"Would you like me to drive?" Rachel asked.

"I think you'd better," said William.

Stocknorton Super-Maximum Security Prison, situated in a patch of rural Genesee County countryside, where it had towered like a dark, foreboding Frankenstein's castle for over one hundred years, was one of the strongest, most secure federal prisons in the United States, rivaled only by the ADMAX prison in Florence, Colorado. It was a well-guarded, impregnable fortress where the very worst of humanity's dark side was stowed away for safekeeping and forgotten by civilized society. Here in the underground catacombs of six-by-eight cells and narrow, poorly ventilated corridors were the rapists and murderers, the terrorists and cannibals, and the dangerously demented animals whom a jury had not been content with sending to a mere mental institution after the unspeakable acts they'd committed, but whom the Constitution still protected from being condemned to the electric chair.

Because of the nature of the men it housed, Stocknorton was hard as hell. The guards wore bulletproof body armor and visored helmets and carried a small arsenal of weapons at all times, including batons, pistols, tear gas grenades, stun blasters, pepper spray, Plexiglas shields, and 'nut guns', so called because of the acorn-sized rounds they fired like miniature cannons.

The cells were small, cramped, overheated 'boxcars', with solid steel doors rather than bars. The cells didn't contain much, but then, there wasn't room for much. Just a filthy little toilet, and a cot that was nothing more than a concrete slab with a two-inch-thick rubber mat on top. Prisoners remained inside these cells for twenty-three hours per day, usually being let out only for an hour's exercise in the corridor just outside their stuffy quarters. Prisoners never saw each other, as there was no congregate exercise, dining, or religious services, and no work opportunities. As for visitors, most inmates received none, and those who did were allowed no more than thirty minutes per week.

It could be said that Qasim Al-Fulani had done a better job of adapting to this lifestyle than most of his fellow inmates, whose pitiful cries and maniacal screams could be heard echoing almost constantly off the underground's walls of stone and steel. Perhaps he just had a stronger constitution for this sort of thing, or perhaps the knowledge that he had been put here in recompense for the horrific mass murder of American citizens provided him with an adequate measure of inner peace and contentment. Or perhaps he knew something no one else did.

Whatever the reason, Qasim Al-Fulani seemed blissfully at peace, lying on his back on his cot, his fingers laced on his chest, his eyes closed as if he were napping, when the electronic 'pleep' of a keycard being inserted into its slot sounded from the corridor outside, and the steel door of his cell slid open.

"You have a visitor, scumbag," said one of the two armed guards standing in the doorway.

Without saying a word or making eye contact with the guards, Qasim sat up on his cot, slowly, observing the policy of making no sudden movements. The guards then advanced on Qasim and, wasting no time, cuffed his wrists behind his back, chained his ankles together so that he could take steps of only six inches at a time, and clasped something like a dog collar around his neck. One of the guards attached a chain leash to the front of the collar and began leading Qasim out of the cell and down the corridor towards the visitation room, with the other guard bringing up the rear, keeping his stun blaster pressed threateningly into the small of Qasim's back all the while.

"Please empty your pockets and place all objects in the tray," the guard requested.

Malik suppressed a sigh of tedium, and rolled his eyes with impatient tolerance as he produced from his pockets a cellular phone, a leather wallet containing five credit cards and nearly two thousand dollars in cash, and a handful of change adding up to one dollar and eighty-three cents, and deposited it all in the plastic tray provided. He then turned out the lining of each of his pockets to prove that they were now indeed empty. The guard inspected each of the items carefully in turn, then handed them back to Malik, while another guard ran the metal detector wand up and down his frame.

"Would you please remove your turban, sir?" asked the guard who had inspected the items.

"Is that really necessary?" asked Malik.

"I'm afraid it is, sir."

Rolling his eyes again and sniffing huffily, Malik removed his turban, and even shook it up and down like a handkerchief a few times in order to demonstrate that it was truly nothing more and nothing less than a customary Islamic head covering.

"Thank you, sir," said the guard. "Now, please insert your right arm into the X-ray machine."

"What?"

"Your cast, sir."

"Oh, for the love of Allah…"

"I'm sorry, sir, but caution is our watchword here at Stocknorton," said the guard, as he watched the broken bones of Malik's hand appear on the X-ray screen. "A razor blade could easily slide into a cast next to the skin."

"A lot of good a little razor blade would do somebody in a place like this," said Malik. "So, that's it, is it?"

"Yup, you're cleared," said the guard. "Thank you for your cooperation. Officer Weston will take you to the visitation room."

The guard called Weston nodded, and gestured for Malik to follow him down the corridor. There were no cells here. This was the administrative level, home to several offices, including the warden's, the necessary laboratories and medical facilities, and an employees' lounge. All of the doors leading off the hallway into these areas were made of steel, however, and the entire section was patrolled by a generous number of armed guards. Despite the incredible odds against any prisoner getting out of his cell, let alone making his way up here where the surface dwellers toiled, the institution certainly wasn't taking any chances.

That's all right, thought Malik. *It will make the coup all the more satisfying.*

Malik and Weston finally reached the end of the long corridor to be greeted by a set of steel double-doors, which schussed open at the behest of Weston's keycard to reveal the visitation room; a small chamber partitioned into two halves by a thick layer of bulletproof glass. A table with a base-mounted microphone resting on top of it sandwiched the glass on each side, and the accompanying plastic chairs were the only other objects in the room. Qasim Al-Fulani was already sitting patiently on the other side of the glass, his wrists, ankles, and waist chained securely to his chair, which, in turn, was bolted to the floor.

"You've got half an hour," said Weston. "If you want out before then, just press that call button over there."

With that, Weston departed from the room, closing and locking the doors behind him. Malik smirked to himself, then turned, walked over to his chair, and sat down. He pressed the ON switch on his microphone's stem, then thumped the head a few times with his knuckles, causing a shrill whine to ring out from Qasim's connected microphone on the other side of the transparent barrier.

"Don't do that, you great big imbecile!" exclaimed Qasim, cringing. "It's a microphone, not a telegraph key!"

"It's glorious to see you again, Qasim," Malik said into the microphone, a smile spreading across his ruddy face. "You're looking well."

"As they say, you can't keep a bad man down," said Qasim, also smiling.

"How are you keeping?" asked Malik.

"Three meals a day and a roof over my head," said Qasim. "It's marvelous how these Americans take such pains to look after even their greatest enemies."

"Can we still talk here?" asked Malik.

"Nothing has changed since the last time you visited," said Qasim. "Those cameras up there watch us, but there are no listening devices. I suppose they feel there is no need for them. Phah. These Americans always think they are so safe, but they will never be able to take enough precautions. We will always get to them somehow."

"Well, they're about to learn yet another lesson in the folly of presumption," said Malik. "I came primarily to tell you that the operation for which we have been waiting these many months will finally be launched tomorrow night, approximately thirty-four hours from now. Even as we speak, Norman is putting the finishing touches on the necessary arrangements."

At the mention of Kubritz, a look of distaste spread across Qasim's face.

"I've said it before and I'll say it again, my old friend," he said. "You are unwise to ally yourself with Western infidels, especially one as corrupt and despicable as this Kubritz. They are unreliable and untrustworthy, and they think of nothing but their own pleasure. That is why they can never defeat us. Because, unlike our own noble warriors, they are unwilling to pay the ultimate price and embrace their own destruction for a cause. We do not need them, Malik."

"On the contrary, Qasim," said Malik. "Without Kubritz's money and limitless resources, this operation would be impossible. There are precious few other men on the planet who would be able to pull off something such as this. Besides, Kubritz isn't so bad. I've dealt with him for many years. I know him. And if you can't trust him, then trust me, and believe me when I tell you that he will deliver the goods."

"I do trust you, Malik," said Qasim, abandoning his negative tone. "You've always been a very good friend to me. If you say everything is set, then I believe you. Now tell me, have you been keeping an eye on my affairs as I requested? How stand my training camps in the northwestern mountains of Pakistan, my opium fields in Afghanistan, my oil wells in Iran, and my luxurious mansion, draped with curtains fashioned from the skins of a hundred Israeli whores?"

"They are all in fine keeping," said Malik. "I do have one bit of regrettable news about your enviable harem, however. Two months ago, one of your women was beaten and raped by a pair of bandits. Naturally, I was compelled to put the woman to death after she had allowed her person to be so violated."

"I see," said Qasim. "Which one?"

"Aishah," answered Malik.

At this, Qasim's face contorted with pain, as if he had just been kicked in the groin, and he groaned into the microphone.

"*Ebn el metanaka!*" he lamented. "Why Aishah? Of all of my women, why Aishah? She was so good! So warm! So...tight!"

"I know, my friend," Malik tried to console him. "I know. It is such a damnable waste, like a purebred Arabian stallion being slaughtered for dogfood. And it shadowed my heart with great sadness, even as I brought my sharpened blade down upon the back of her neck. But I knew you would be loath to keeping a woman who had been soiled."

"Quite right," Qasim admitted, shaking his head sorrowfully. "Yes, you did the right thing, Malik. A woman who has been raped cannot be allowed to go on living in disgrace to herself and her master. But, oh, how I shall miss fucking her. How I shall miss those moist, red lips wrapped around my rod, and that rough tongue licking my chest devotedly. She was an angel, Malik, an angel."

"Try not to dwell on it," said Malik. "Remember that there are over three billion other creatures just like her in this world, and once you are a free man again, you will have your pick of them."

"Ah, freedom," said Qasim. "My soul takes wings at the prospect. I grow weary of these damp, dreary surroundings. I long to shuck off the yoke of these imperialist overlords who would have it that their cause is just. I long for the warm kiss of the Arab sun on my face, and the friendly embrace of Arab sand between my toes. Oh, dearest Malik, how I yearn to be once more in the cradle of the mysterious, enchanted desert I have called home since born from my mother's womb."

"And you will, Qasim, you will," said Malik, rising from his seat. "But now I fear I must be off, as I have some last minute details to attend to. Mustn't let the infidels have all the fun planning this picnic, eh?"

"Certainly not," said Qasim. "You know, these Western dogs think they have it all figured out. Theirs is the most advanced of societies, blessed with frivilous technology, abundant resources, and obscenely relaxed laws. Practically a utopia when compared to our world of fascism, poverty, and squalor. Indeed I wouldn't be at all surprised if they looked down upon us as though we were mindless, futile insects; ants. But consider this, Malik; what would their picnic be...without our ants?"

Malik's face broke into a broad smile, and he chuckled with interspersed hisses through grinning teeth as he pressed the red call button that would summon the guard.

"Qasim, my dear fellow, you have always had such a delightful repertoire of metaphors," he said. "You truly are a treasure. I look forward to many more conversations like this one in the near future. But, until tomorrow night, may God bless you and keep you."

Keith was a chubby, unwashed little man in a tatty pair of jeans, a raggedy hooded sweatshirt, and a baseball cap reading 'Defend Freedom – Kill Your Congressman' clamped snugly over his mop of unruly red curls. He had a scraggly brown beard, a squint in his right eye, and a sloping, neolithic forehead you could ski down. His teeth were rotting, his hands were never clean, and his beer belly spilled out over his Chicago Bulls belt buckle as if it were host to a seven-month-old fetus. He was five feet and three inches of vulgar, odious fly bait, and Carolyn had learned early on in their relationship to dread these unpleasant but necessary business meetings.

"As you can see, we've got a lot of new stuff for the summer line," said Keith, as he thumped the trunk of his banged-up, long-suffering Mazda hatchback with his fist, opening his portable stall of merchandise for Carolyn's viewing pleasure. "Assault rifles, bazookas, rocket launchers, you name it and we've got it here at Keith's One-Stop Emporium. What can I do ya for?"

"I'll be needing five more Micro Uzis," said Carolyn, referring to her mental shopping list. "And the good stuff this time. None of your secondhand garbage that you can't push off onto the drug dealers. One of the damned things jammed on a partner of mine at a very inopportune moment, and the only reason you're still alive is because I convinced him that you're one of the best merchants around."

"I'm very distressed to hear that, Miss Carolyn," said Keith, sniffing loudly as he wiped a sleeve across his crusty nose. "As you well know, I take great pride in stocking a wide range of high quality items. May I compensate you for the inconvenience with a free tear gas bazooka? Just got them in yesterday. Absolutely the cutting edge when it comes to storming crack houses. It fires a grenade from as far away as seventy feet. You don't even have to get close to the action before every last one of 'em staggers out choking."

"Fine, order me one when you get the Uzis," said Carolyn. "And a new AK-47 wouldn't go unappreciated either. And I presume you have my regular purchases ready?"

"Assault rifles, flash bangs, sonic grenades, Tasers, flying buzz saws, high-caliber handguns, and bulletproof body armor, all at the warehouse, nestled in Styrofoam peanuts and ready to move to their new home," Keith replied, proudly.

"Good," said Carolyn. "The usual pick-up spot will be fine. Anything else of particular note?"

Keith grinned, flashing his yellowing gumlines, reached his arms deep into his trunk, past the sample display of handguns, rifles, explosives, and small cannons, and produced what looked like a metallic tennis ball.

"We're calling it the hedgehog for the moment," said Keith. "I've been saving it especially for you 'cause I knew you'd love it. This bad sonofabitch, on remote-controlled command, shoots out precisely one hundred and twenty-seven needle-sharp projectiles at force sufficient to rocket them right through a man's throat, or even his chest. Ideal for clearing out crowded rooms. At five thousand bucks apiece, I'm robbing myself. Interested?"

"Put me down for three to start with," said Carolyn, trying not to sound too eager. "And that'll be it for now."

"A pleasure as always, Miss Carolyn," said Keith, tipping the brim of his cap and slamming the trunk on his samples. "And take care. I wouldn't want my best customer getting her head blown off."

"And you stay out of trouble, Keith," said Carolyn. "You know the rule. If any of your weapons are directly involved in more than two murders per month, I won't be able to protect you from Gary. He barely tolerates you as it is."

"Why do you think I have my boys regularly combing crime scenes for my guns?" Keith winked, flopping down into his car's driver's seat.

"Now, if you'll excuse me, I've gotta get moving. I have a three o'clock in the Bronx. Some commie whacko who's interested in surface-to-air missiles. Those things can take down commercial jets, y'know."

Carolyn did her best to pretend she hadn't heard that as Keith gunned his engine and pulled clumsily out of the alley – knocking over a pair of garbage cans in the process – and began roaring down the street, gray fumes belching from his corroded exhaust pipe. He was definitely a slimeball, and unquestionably a menace to society, but he was a necessary evil with whom the Vigilantes had no choice but to co-exist. After all, one couldn't buy Keith's special brand of merchandise at any old Wal-Mart.

Carolyn walked the remaining three blocks to her apartment building, entered the lobby, and strode over to the elevator, where she pressed the '3' button. When she arrived at the floor that housed her residence, she walked down the nicely decorated corridor – with its Oriental carpeting, and floral paintings hanging on the wall – turned a corner, and stopped in front of her own door, marked '357'. She inserted her key into the lock and pushed the door open, planning to have a shower, a bite to eat, and a short nap before sealing herself away inside the apartment's second bedroom, which she had long ago converted into her home workshop. (She was particularly eager to resume work on that fire-spitting Cabbage Patch Doll.) But then a sharp dart struck her just above her collarbone, and she gasped in surprise.

"Too many people have mistaken my amiability for tolerance, Carolyn," said Henry Hugo, sitting cross-legged on the sofa, for once not grinning that inane grin of his, the gun that had fired the dart clenched in his fist. "You ruined my favorite suit last night. Coffee stains are a total bitch to get out."

"What the hell is this?" asked Carolyn, pulling the dart from her neck and throwing it to the floor, as if it were a repulsive insect that had bitten her.

"Trank dart," said Hugo. "Very quick. You'll be out in less than a minute. And you have only Kubritz to thank that it wasn't a bullet instead."

Carolyn snarled, slammed the door shut, and pulled a Remington 7400 from a dusty, battered golf bag hanging on the coat hook behind the door, then leveled it at the seated intruder, aimed through already blurring vision, and pulled the trigger.

Nothing but an impotent 'click'. Obviously Hugo had gotten to it first.

Carolyn uttered a four-letter word, then her eyes rolled back in her head, and an irresistible darkness forced her down onto the floor.

"Okay, you're good to go," said the guard at the entrance to LaGuardia International Airport's sprawling freight section, as he slammed down the back door of the UPS van and fired a thumbs-up to the driver. "Sorry 'bout the wait, but ya gotta watch these things, y'know."

"I understand completely," KnuckleDuster sat in the driver's seat, outfitted smartly in the courier service's trademark brown uniform and cap, but still sporting his dark sunglasses and black gloves. "Can't be too careful these days. Y'never know what those bastards'll get up to."

"Right," said the guard, hitching his thumbs in his belt and spitting to the side. "If there's one thing nine-eleven did, it made us all equal. If honest, hard-workin' joes like you an' me have to put up with a little inconvenience, then so do these rich pricks with their own jets. Talk about havin' too much of a good thing. Getting packages delivered to your plane? If y'ask me, the sonofabitch deserves a little hassle."

KnuckleDuster chuckled, threw the guard a working man's salute, then put the van back into gear and drove across to the hangars housing the private jets belonging to the rich and famous. When he came to the hangar marked '106-A', he alighted from the van and entered the six-digit access code on the hangar's electronic keypad, prompting the massive electronic double-doors to slide open with a loud, grinding whir and reveal the sleek, stylish jet hibernating within.

Malik's personal aircraft that carried him, along with seven other passengers and all the comforts of home, from his lavish estate in the desert just outside Las Vegas to anywhere in the world that it took his fancy to go, was a Bombardier Learjet 60 equipped with powerful Pratt & Whitney PW305A engines with forty-six hundred pounds of thrust behind them, and winglets and delta fins to reduce drag and enhance directional stability. The smoothest, fastest ride in its class, the jet could rocket Malik to fifty-one thousand feet, then cruise high above bad weather and other air travelers at Mach 0.81. With its high-speed performance, mid-size comfort, luxurious cabin space, stellar good looks, and 2,496 nautical-mile-range that allowed Malik to jump continents the way children jump mud puddles, the enviable jet was the Arab's pride and joy. He kept the inside immaculately clean and decadently furnished, and, if even so much as a scratch dared to show its face on the plane's shiny, silver sheen, he promptly commissioned the best buffers in the business to see to it.

Where some people fussed over their children, their pets, or their homemade crafts, Malik fussed over his jet.

KnuckleDuster drove the UPS van into the hangar, brought it to a halt near the rear of the plane, threw up the van's cargo door like a window shade, and turned down the ramp. He then disappeared inside the van for a few seconds, and re-emerged pushing a metal dolly bearing a large wooden crate five feet high, three feet wide, and pocked all over with small airholes. Painted in bold, black letters on the front of the container was 'FRAGILE', and 'THIS WAY UP' complimented by a thick, upward-pointing arrow.

KnuckleDuster produced what looked like a garage door opener, pointed it at the jet, and pressed one of the remote's two buttons. Fluidly, and without a single rusty squeak, the ramp leading into the plane's cargo section unfolded from the rear of the flying machine's trim belly. KnuckleDuster slid the remote back into his pocket, then began wheeling the burdened dolly up the ramp, whistling tunelessly as he went.

Inside the cargo section were four young women, completely naked, and bound to metal cots with leather restraints on their wrists, waists, knees, and ankles. Each had been sedated into unconsciousness, and KnuckleDuster thought they looked quite peaceful in their sleep.

Each was fiercely attractive in her own way. There were two voluptuous blonds with tanned *Playboy* centerfold bodies, blessed with flawless skin, large breasts, long legs, and perfectly rounded behinds. There was one fair-skinned brunette, petite but curvy, with pouty lips and arched eyebrows. And there was one shiny-brown Latina woman, plump in all the right places, 'with enough spice in her ass to sprinkle some hamburger and salsa in there and call it a taco,' KnuckleDuster had assured Malik.

The young women were being guarded vigilantly by two tall Arabs with flint eyes and big biceps, who never spoke a word and ignored KnuckleDuster altogether as he pried open the front of the crate with his steel hands and extracted the unconscious girl from inside, using his fingers to snap the restraints that had held her upright during transit, allowing her to collapse dopily onto the floor, facedown.

Here she is, gents," said KnuckleDuster to the impassive Arabs, their hands folded and at their waists. "Sweet number five in the flesh. A tight little Asian teen with pink, perky titties and big, innocent eyes, as ordered. Tell your boss to have her look up at him while she's seein' to him down there. That's how you get the full effect. Looking into those eyes, he'll drop his load twice as hard, I guarantee."

Maintaining their stubborn silence, the Arabs each seized one of the girl's arms, dragged her over to the only vacant cot remaining, and went about their work fastening down her limp form. They did not turn to face KnuckleDuster again.

Snobs, thought KnuckleDuster, as he turned to leave the plane. *We're all in the same business anyway. Just 'cause I work for a rich American and they work for a rich towelhead doesn't mean we can't be civil to each other.*

KnuckleDuster stepped off the ramp, then used the remote control to fold it back up, leaving the precious cargo sealed tightly away. Then he headed back to the UPS van, but before he had taken two steps, a delicious thought crossed his mind, and a wicked grin broke out on his face.

Turning back to the plane, KnuckleDuster removed the glove from his right hand and, snickering evilly, pressed the tip of his forefinger into the flying machine's polished metal, creating a fingerprint-sized indentation no more than three centimeters in depth.

It'll drive him nuts, thought KnuckleDuster, suprememly satisfied. *Absolutely fucking nuts. That idiot at the gate was right. A rich yahoo like him does deserve a little hassle.*

"For someone who says he's never kissed anyone before, you're pretty good at it," said Rachel from her current position beneath William in the backseat of the car that had brought them to this secluded corner of the Home Depot parking lot.

"I've been making a study of movie and TV characters doing it for the past sixteen years," said William. "I should hope I picked up something."

Rachel giggled, and William lowered his mouth back down onto hers, reintroducing his hungry young tongue to the girl's. She sighed softly, and William stroked his fingers through her hair, enjoying the vibes of affection and adoration coming his way. They – whoever 'they' were – always said that behind every great man there stood a great woman, and, at this point in time, William had absolutely no trouble finding the truth in that. Why, he couldn't remember the last time he had felt so strong; so confident; so infused with raw pride and machismo. Making out tenderly and passionately with this beautiful girl, knowing that she wanted him as much as he wanted her, was a self-esteem booster to be equaled by no other.

"Mmm," moaned Rachel, finally breaking the kiss, looking into

William's eyes. "William, you're a great guy. I wonder...would you do something for me?"

At this point, William would have cut off his right arm and beaten his best friend to death with the soggy end if Rachel had asked him to.

"Would you take off your glasses?" she asked, caressing the left side of his face. "I'd like to see you without them."

They were William's spare pair, to replace the glasses that Jason had stomped on the previous afternoon. They were adequate, but they were two prescriptions behind and were giving him a bit of a headache, so, if Rachel wanted him to take them off, then off they would come.

"That's better," said the girl. "I can see your eyes so much better now. You've got really nice eyes, y'know. Ever thought of getting contacts?"

"Truthfully, the idea of sticking little pieces of chemical-drenched plastic into my eyes has never really appealed to me," said William.

"Well, here's something that will appeal to you," said Rachel.

The girl closed her lips on the side of William's neck, just a hair to the left of his pulse point, and nibbled and sucked, very gently, at the spot she had selected while William reveled in the magical tingling sensation that ran the entire length and breadth of his titillated body. When she finally pulled away, a bright red spot had appeared on his flesh where her mouth had been.

"You can show that off to your friends," said Rachel, smiling like the tantalizing seductress-in-training she was.

For the past several minutes, William had been debating the merits of making a certain move that would more than likely elevate his interactions with Rachel high above kissing. On the one hand, Rachel seemed to be sending out all the signals, but, on the other hand, bodily trespasses of this sort could be awfully risky. These days you practically had to get the girl to sign a notarized statement of consent or you were liable to be locked up for rape, no questions asked. Would Rachel accept the advance he had in mind, or would she stand him up in front of a jury, who, in today's 'enlightened' society, would readily and righteously find him guilty, essentially because it would be a female's word against his?

After taking due time to weigh the pros and cons, William decided to damn the consequences.

Clapping his mouth over Rachel's in yet another steamy oral embrace, William ran both his hands over the girl's breasts, relishing the feeling of her hard nipples poking up into his palms and almost convulsing with the satisfaction of knowing that he had finally arrived at the party, a little late but with one hell of a guest on his arm. As William had hoped, Rachel reacted positively to this, and she arched her back a little, grinding her stomach against William's blood-engorged member.

"My shirt, Will," she gasped, in between lip smacks. "Put your hands up my shirt."

The giddy teenager was only too happy to comply, as Rachel bit at his lips and continued gyrating her pelvis against his crotch. From kissing to dry-humping in no time flat! This was fantastic!

A couple of hours later, as the sun began saying its good-nights to the Big Apple, William and Rachel said their good-nights to each other, parked at the curb outside Rachel's house. With one more warm, deep kiss that seemed to come straight from a wet dream, and a rub to her new boyfriend's inner thigh, Rachel got out of the car, flashed a supermodel smile through the passenger side window, and said she'd see him again tomorrow, the tone of her musical voice heavy with the promise of delights and pleasures to come.

William took a deep breath and sighed with utter happiness, enjoying the erection that had not relented once during the course of the entire day, as he watched Rachel's gorgeous butt wiggle up the driveway and disappear into the house. He didn't know how he was going to be able to fall asleep tonight.

As he began pulling away from the curb, he shot a glance into the rearview mirror, and was not altogether surprised to see the glowering figure of Jason not a block away. Even from this distance William could see the twisted scowl of jealousy and hatred darkening his enemy's face.

Well, that cinches it, thought William, as he drove off down the street towards home. *This is, bar none, the absolute best day of my life!*

The bus came to a brake-squealing halt at the designated stop just two blocks from Buzz's apartment building, and the blind psychologist – who had made a career of helping other people see things clearly – rose from his seat and stretched one arm out in front of himself at chest level as he walked up the aisle. Once he reached the front of the bus, he handed what he knew to be a one dollar bill to the portly driver, and was given three coins in return. He held the coins in his hand for a few seconds, then smirked at the driver.

"Give me the nickel, you old bastard," he said, good-naturedly.

"Whazzat?" said the driver.

"Nice try, Hank, but you'd be hard-pressed to find a blind person who can't easily tell the difference between a nickel and a penny, which is what you've tried to con me with here," said Buzz.

"Dang," said Hank, taking back the penny and replacing it as Buzz requested. "You're never gonna let me pull one over on ya, are ya? How'd ya know, anyhow?"

"A nickel is much heavier than a penny," said Buzz. "Broader and thicker too. Plus, the penny stinks of copper."

"Oh."

"Additionally, Lincoln's profile on the penny faces right, whereas all other coin profiles face left," said Buzz. "A man like me, who reads with his fingertips, can tell right away what he holds in his hand."

"Awright, awright, enough already," said Hank, utterly defeated. "Jeez, sorry I asked. But it ain't over till it's over. I'll think o' somethin'."

"Hank, Hank, Hank," tsked Buzz, shaking his head. "There are none so blind as those who refuse to see."

"Get off my bus and don't come back," said Hank, continuing the banter that had been a staple of Buzz's evening commute home for some time now.

"Oh, I'll be back all right," said Buzz. "And I'll bring friends. Deaf people, mute people, and people in wheelchairs. By the time I'm through with you, you'll think you've pulled transport duty for the Special Olympics."

Leaving Hank to wonder if Buzz actually intended to make good on this threat, the psychologist smiled to himself and descended the bus' two big steps, moving past the folded-open door and out onto the sidewalk. With a flick of the wrist his white cane extended to its full length, and he began tapping it rhythmically against the concrete thoroughfare stretched out before him as he strode briskly forward with the cool confidence of a man who could see beyond the veil of darkness to every obstructive fire hydrant, every yawning pothole, and every loping pedestrian clutching the ensnaring leashes of their yappy little dogs. He didn't stumble or misstep once in his skillful navigation of the sea of innumerable hazards, all of them zealously eager to trip up a victim who wasn't paying them due attention. Having been completely blind since the day he had first opened his eyes fifty-five years ago, Buzz was well used to literally feeling his way through life.

Entering the foyer of what he knew to be his building, Buzz executed a sharp right turn and approached the elevator. With a light touch, he ran his fingers over the buttons, counting them in his head until he found the one that would transport him to the fourth floor. He pressed it, then stepped into the elevator car when he heard the soft hum of the doors sliding open.

Mere seconds later the familiar 'ding' sounded, and Buzz stepped out and began walking down the right side of the hallway, his hand brushing against every metal doorknob he passed. He knew he was almost home once he had counted five doorknobs.

Upon reaching the sixth doorknob, Buzz stopped, fished his key out of his coat pocket, and, using his forefinger as a guiding figurehead, inserted the key into the lock and turned it to the right. He then pushed the door open and entered the dwelling he had called home for many years, yet had never seen.

Discarding his cane by the door – the assistance it lent him was entirely unnecessary for the navigation of the familiar layout of his own apartment – Buzz headed toward the kitchen, the thought of the leftover roast beef and mashed potatoes in his refrigerator already teasing his taste buds.

And that was when he heard the 'click'.

As was the case with many similarly afflicted people, a lifetime of blindness had compensated Buzz with a boost to his other four senses. His sense of taste was sharp enough to pick out ingredients that no one else could detect in various foods, his sense of smell was discerning enough to tell the difference between a wet dog and a wet cat, and his sense of touch, as demonstrated earlier to Hank the bus driver, was sensitive enough to serve almost as a pair of eyes. But reigning chief above all was his extraordinary sense of sound, and there were very few people on the planet who could hear as well as he. Indeed a person of average hearing would never have detected the soft 'click' of the light switch by the door being flipped, but Buzz picked it up easily, not only because of his superior hearing, but because the sound was so utterly alien to him. Never before had a 'click' like that emanated from the living room. In all the time that he had lived in this apartment, he had never flipped that switch once. After all, what use had he for light switches?

The approaching footsteps were cushioned by the soft shag carpet, but Buzz heard them anyway, and he surprised the intruder by moving quickly to the left and doubling back to the door to snatch up his cane, extending it once again and thrusting it like a fencing foil in the direction in which he had last detected the intruder. A yelp of pain was his reward as the tip of the cane connected with the mystery man's kidneys.

"Not so easy to sneak up on a blind man, is it?" sneered Buzz. "I'll teach you to pick on the handicapped. Just you get over here and take your medicine. I've got something better than a birch switch here for you."

"Shaddup, pops," said a second man, coming from the side and grabbing hold of the cane. "We all here have had a long day, see, and we ain't in no mood for any trouble from you."

"So, there's more than one of you in here, eh?" said Buzz. "Shame on you, tag-teaming a man with no eyes. Shame on you!"

The only response Buzz received from the intruders was a swift blow to the side of his head. Losing his footing, he fell and struck his left temple on the corner of the coffee table, his shades skewing as he sprawled out on his back on the floor and collapsed reluctantly into unconsciousness. It would be a misstatement, however, to say that everything went black for Buzz, because, in Buzz's world, everything was black all the time.

Does it wake you in the night, Peg? Do you spring from your bed, screaming and drenched with sweat as the vivid picture of your mother's clammy, bloated corpse slouching in the bloodstained bathtub rushes back to the forefront of your memory with the force of a bullet train? How long does it take you to stop hyperventilating after seeing that swollen, purple belly, those glazed, bulging eyes staring up at the ceiling, and that arm dangling limply over the side, blood running in rivers from the gash in the wrist, down over the yellow knuckles, and off the tips of the rigid fingers? No cause to be embarrassed about it, naturally. Fuck, it would certainly wake me *up! What a horrible thing for an eight-year-old child to see...*

"Shut up," said Peg, clenching her teeth and squeezing her eyes shut, doing her level best to maintain control.

Does it wake you in the night, Peg? Do you toss and turn and burn with shame as your intimate fluids soil your bedsheets at the bid of your masochistic memory, as you are taken forcibly back, time and time again, to that night when your cherry was finally broken off? To that dark high school parking lot, so duplicitous in its outward veil of tranquility? To that van in the far corner, well out of sight of the road, rocking back and forth like a boat on a choppy lake? You don't even remember their names, do you, Peg? And they almost certainly don't remember you. The air inside that hell wagon was choked with pot smoke. But you remember the sensations, don't you, Peg? The stinging in your eyes caused by the smoke. The blistering burns on your wrists caused by the thick rope used to tie your hands behind your back. And of course, the hot, fleshy stiffness of one boy thrusting himself up your ass while the other forced himself down your throat. Oh, I remember how you cried and cried the whole time, but you really should have given up struggling and just relaxed and let it happen. After all, a girl's first time should be special, right?

"Shut up!" Peg screamed, grabbing her head with both hands and shaking it, as if trying to dislodge it from her shoulders. "Get out of my head, you bastard! Go away and leave me alone!"

Don't be such a crybaby, you little bitch! I'm not going anywhere! I've always been with you, and right here's where I plan to stay! I don't care if you've managed to survive into your mid-thirties, despite the overwhelming odds against such longevity in your case! You'll always be a weak, frightened, pathetic little chit of a girl, no matter how old you get! It doesn't matter how many doctors you see or how many pills you pop! No matter how many times you try to get better, you'll always fail! And I hope you keep failing, and keep failing, and keep failing, until you have no choice but to give in and we both take that final swan dive off the top of the George Washington Bridge together!

"Shuuuuut uuuuup!" Peg shrieked, as she slammed her head hard against her bedroom wall, then fell back onto her rear end, slightly stunned.

"Holy shit, Peg, are you all right?" asked Chloe, the call girl with whom Peg had been sharing her bed for the evening.

"Fine," Peg muttered, sitting on the floor, rubbing her eyes like an injured child. "I'm just fine."

Chloe moved to help Peg up, placing her hands gently on her trembling shoulders, but Peg shrugged them violently off.

"Don't *touch* me!" she shouted. "Why is everyone always trying to *touch* me?"

"Okay, okay, I'm sorry," said Chloe, backing off. "But what's the matter? For a minute there, it looked like you were having some kind of fit."

"None of your fucking business!" snapped Peg, rising to her feet. "Why don't you just fuck off? I don't need you for anything else tonight!"

"Peg, I don't want to leave you like this..."

"Oh, right, the money!" said Peg, turning to retrieve her purse. "Heaven forbid you should ever leave without your money! How much is it this time?"

"Peg, that's not what I'm concerned about, and you know..."

"Let's see, you got here at eleven and we fucked twice...the usual two hundred should cover it," said Peg, throwing a handful of crumpled bills unceremoniously at Chloe. "Now, get your clothes and get out of my sight!"

Chloe locked eyes with Peg for a few seconds, frowning as only a woman can, then threw on the haltar top and mini-skirt she had come in, and, leaving her payment unclaimed on the floor, marched to the door and pulled it open.

"Y'know, you and I have known each other for a long time," she said, looking back at one of her most frequent clients. "I thought we were friends, but sometimes I just don't know. You've been there for me in the past, Peg, and you know damn well that I've been there for you, totally free of charge. But just keep it up, girl. Keep it up, and I won't be there for you anymore."

Then she was gone. Peg stomped across the room, slammed the door hard enough to knock a picture off the wall, and shouted at the top of her lungs.

"That's right, get out of here, you dirty whore! You dirty, stinking, filthy whore! And don't come back or I'll kill you! You hear me? If you ever come back here, I'll choke you so hard every sleazeball you've ever blown will suffocate!"

Shrieking unintelligibly, beating her clenched fists against the sides of her head, Peg threw herself facedown onto her bed and sobbed. She sobbed until her mouth went completely dry and the howls of misery gave way to coughs for air, all while her fingernails tore little holes in the sheets.

"I'm sorry, Chloe," Peg croaked to the empty room, waterfalls of tears cascading down her cheeks. "I'm sorry. I didn't mean any of those terrible things. I really didn't."

After she had finished venting the worst of her raw emotion, Peg got up slowly from the bed, donned her purple terrycloth bathrobe, and walked to the bathroom, where she filled a cup with cold water and drank it to moisten her hoarse throat. Then she filled it a second time and downed two tranquilizers. The dosage was twice what she was supposed to take, even under circumstances like these, but it was certainly better than swallowing the entire bottle with a liquor chaser and going straight to bed after leaving a brief, explanatory note, which is what she most definitely would have done in the not so distant past.

Peg knew that she was a trainwreck. She had been ever since she could remember, and it only got worse when the sadistic voices in her head forced her to recall the grim watersheds of her past, such as her mother's suicide, or her rape at the hands of two goons looking for a good time. When these visions crashed over her like waves of cold salt water on jagged rocks, not even her numerous prescription medications were enough to keep her completely in line.

Sitting back down on her bed, Peg opened the drawer in the top of her nightstand and pulled out a lighter and one of the many loose cigarettes rolling around inside. She flicked the lighter a couple of times, finally got the flame to appear, and lit the cigarette. Then she threw the lighter back into the drawer and sucked greedily at the poison she was introducing into her body. It usually helped calm her down.

These things are gonna kill me, she reflected, tendrils of smoke wheezing forth from her mouth like little demons exorcising themselves into the open air. *Not sure how I feel about that.*

Now, sitting in her bedroom, alone and shaking, with nothing but her own devils and the dancing wisps of smoke for company, Peg began to feel even more remorse over the awful way she had treated Chloe. After all, Chloe was a good friend, and had always been someone that Peg could go and talk to. Or do other things with. She wished that Chloe was here right now. She wished that Chloe could hold her and tell her that everything was going to be all right.

Peg's bisexuality had long been cause for personal embarrassment to her, and her sexual promiscuity, though a seemingly irremovable aspect of her nature, always made her feel dirty and low. That was why she kept that side of her personality to herself, and though her fellow Vigilantes were the closest friends she had in the world, only one of them knew about it. That one was Buzz, who had been counseling her for quite some time, helping her wade through the wretched, murky quagmire that was her tortured psyche. He had told her long ago that, while he couldn't absolutely apply this theory to Peg's compulsive need for intimate female companionship, her desire to be with so many different partners – many of them strangers – could be traced back to the trauma of the rape, as many victims of sexual abuse tend to act out their pent-up frustrations and aggressions sexually. According to Buzz, the reason that Peg spent many a night trolling the 'business districts' for action, a scarf wrapped around her head and a pair of dark sunglasses concealing her eyes, was so she could 'act out'. She never felt any better afterwards, though. She just felt empty, used up, and alone, like a dirty, crumpled, partnerless old sock at the bottom of the hamper.

Well, no use dwelling on it, I guess, Peg thought with a sigh, as she killed her cigarette in a glass ashtray sitting atop her night table. *Might as well try and fall asleep. Those tranks'll be kicking in soon. Maybe I'll feel better in the morning.*

With a yawn and another sigh, Peg fixed her bedsheets and was about to divest herself of her robe when she became keenly aware of the smell of smoke; not the cigarette smoke that still hung heavily in the air like a toxic memory, but the distinct, pungent odor of something on fire, emanating from the living room.

Certain that she hadn't left any electrical appliances running, Peg exited the bedroom and followed the smell to the living room, where she found the curtains adorning the window closest to the kitchen alive with dancing, orange flames.

What the hell...?

Peg looked hurridly around, trying to remember where she had put the fire extinguisher, but didn't have the chance to call up the requested information before the pointed steel toe of a leather boot struck her in the back of the head, just above her neck, and without so much as a whimper, Peg lost consciousness and crashed to the floor. Towering over her fallen form was Janet, her hands on her hips, a wicked, sadistic smile playing about her face.

"Wow, that was easy," she said to herself. "I guess that after a lifetime of fighting guys like Gary to a standstill, you tend to forget how pathetic the average, untrained person really is."

Ignoring the flames that continued to consume the curtains, Janet lifted Peg off the floor, threw her over one shoulder, and exited the apartment via the window that led out onto the fire escape.

"Boardwalk. Friggin' typical," Zeke grumbled. "And by the time I've made it 'round the board once, all the good properties have already been bought up."

"You just wait'll I get a hotel on there," said Charlie, sitting across from Zeke, on the other side of the Rat Hole's long conference table, the Monopoly game board between them. "It'll suck the marrow from your bones."

Zeke muttered to himself, and thrust a wad of colorful play money grudgingly into Charlie's open palm, while William snatched up the dice and took his turn at throwing them. The twin cubes bounced onto the center of the board and punched the cheerful visage of the mustachioed Rich Uncle Pennybags on the nose.

"Reading Railroad," said William, after moving his pewter hat five spaces. "Who's got the Reading Railroad?"

"I do," declared Sushi, the fourth player in the entrepreneurial quartet. "And, Zeke, keep your worthless Baltic Avenue card away from my pile."

"Cork it, Japzilla," said Zeke. "It's your fault I'm losin'. Ya shoulda let me be the car. I always win when I'm the car."

"Zeke, we all rolled for the car and you lost," said Charlie, rolling the dice while William paid Sushi. "Get over it."

The dice came up nine, directing Charlie's ship to the Electric Company.

"I'll buy that," he said to William, who was serving as the banker.

"Oh, great," grumbled Zeke, slouching down in his chair and crossing his arms moodily, like the poor sport he was.

"And, while it's still my turn, I'll build some houses on the greens," Charlie continued.

"Now there's a fuckin' surprise," said Zeke, sarcastically.

"Now, at last, it's my turn again," said Sushi, rubbing his hands together. "And as you can plainly see, dear friends, I control this entire side of the board. Reds, yellows, Water Works, and the B&O."

"Typical Jap," said Zeke. "In the country for just five minutes, and he wastes no time in buyin' up everythin' he sees."

"Careful, Zeke," said Sushi, "or I just might buy your hundred-year-old, good-old-boy American institution, and turn it into a sprawling Japanese corporation for manufacturing computer chips."

"Thanks for letting me join in the game, guys," said William, while Sushi moved his coveted car six spaces. "I just had to get out of the house for a while. My mom and dad wouldn't stop asking questions about how my day with Rachel went."

"That reminds me," said Charlie. "How'd your day with Rachel go?"

"You want a punch in the mouth?"

"No, seriously."

"Seriously, it went great," said William. "Fantastic, actually. Spectacular, even."

"What does she look like?" asked Charlie. "Is she cute?"

"Cute? Try hot," said William. "Believe me, she's a real duct tape ripper."

"What's a duct tape ripper?" asked Zeke.

"A term I've come to use to describe extremely sexy women," William explained. "You see, back in junior high, I knew this kid called Eric Varney. Now, Eric's pubescent hormones were almost always in a state of over-stimulation, and because of this, he often suffered public embarrassment due to ill-timed, indiscreet erections whenever a hot chick happened to walk by. So, one day, he got this brilliant idea of duct taping his dick to the inside of his thigh, thereby restraining it. You with me so far? Well, this new and innovative method actually worked for the first few hours of the school day, but then lunchtime arrived. I was standing right behind him in the lunch line, and he was standing right behind Sarah Thurgood, and Sarah Thurgood was a hottie, let me tell you. And on this particular day she was wearing a tight little babydoll top and a skimpy pair of cutoff shorts. Well, I don't think I need to tell you what happened next. Just take my word for it when I say that everyone in the lunch line could hear that duct tape ripping out of place."

"So, in summary, a duct tape ripper is a true force of nature," Sushi smiled. "Congratulations, William. You do us all proud."

"Sixteen-year-old sexpots," Charlie grinned, scratching his chest. "I wonder what our friend Leeza would have to say."

"I'll tell you what she'd have to say," said Zeke, thrusting his right arm upwards in a 'sig heil!' salute and sticking the forefinger of his left hand horizontally beneath his nose to simulate a Hitler mustache. "She'd say, 'Mien Fuhrer! Human feeling eez not practical and does not compute! Ve did not conquer ze Europe by jumping into ze bed wiz each ozer every five minutes!' "

Everybody burst out laughing at this, and Sushi spewed out the orange soda he had been drinking, drenching his play money and 'Get Out Of Jail Free' card. William, reveling in one of those all too rare and infrequent instances in his life that truly made him feel like 'one of the guys', went on to boast to his friends about the events that had taken place that afternoon in the backseat of his father's car. What William refrained from telling them, however, was that, in less than twenty-four hours from this jovial moment, he would be, inarguably and irrevocably, a man.

Despite their relative intimacy over the course of the day, William would not have dared broach the subject. Rachel herself had pitched the proposition that they get to know each other on that level, and though William had been stunned that any girl would want to go that far after just one real date, not one fiber of his being was able to present a convincing argument for declining the titillating invitation. He was sixteen, after all. It was high time he lost his virginity, and if he had the chance to lose it to an absolute goddess like Rachel, then it was indeed an opportunity to be seized with both hands.

William kept this from his fellow Vigilantes because he knew they would just try and talk him out of it by presenting the concept of sex to him in all sorts of negative, world weary ways, and they'd ask him repeatedly whether or not he was sure he wasn't making a huge mistake. That was the trouble with hanging out with guys two or three times his age. They could, at times, be irritatingly paternalistic. Besides, this was a very personal thing for William, and he decided he would rather keep it to himself for the time being.

"All right! Community Chest!" exclaimed Zeke, reaching for the card pile. "This is where ol' Zeke's luck changes. Maybe there'll be a bank error in my favor, or maybe my life insurance'll mature, or maybe...aw shit, go to jail!"

"Zeke, back in Japan, we have a saying for Monopoly players of your caliber," said Sushi.

"Oh yeah? And whazzat?"

"You suck."

"Brother, if you weren't a friend..." glared Zeke, shaking his fist threateningly at the ninja.

"All right, guys, all right," said Charlie, fulfilling his usual role as referee. "Let's save the oxygen for something worthwhile. Did Gary tell either of you anything more about that Stocknorton tip?"

"Stocknorton? The supermax prison?" asked William. "The veritable fortress that FDR earmarked for Hitler if the military ever managed to capture him and bring him back to the States? That Stocknorton?"

"The same," said Zeke. "Gary got a tip from a reliable snitch that somethin' big is gonna go down there real soon."

"It might even involve Qasim Al-Fulani, though we're not sure of that," Sushi added. "The snitch said he saw an Arab visiting the prison on a couple of occasions."

"Well, there can't be much trouble coming out of that place," said William. "I doubt Alexander the Great could have taken Stocknorton."

"Alexander the Great couldn't light Norman Kubritz's cigar," said Sushi. "And if Kubritz is involved somehow, as Gary seems to think, then it certainly gives one pause."

The game, up to this point so vibrant with life and good humor, suddenly fell deathly silent. The dismal notion of a partnership between one of the world's most powerful gangsters and one of the world's most feared terrorist leaders was turning everybody's stomach. Finally, after a full minute of mood-dampening silence, William was the first to speak up.

"It's my turn," he said, somberly. "Somebody hand me the dice."

Only one of Henry Hugo's personality traits could truly be said to contend with his sadism and sexual deviance, and that was his unabashed, unbridled narcissism. As vain as a peacock, and as arrogant as a pedigreed cat that hasn't once in its life known the taste of canned food, Hugo generally considered himself a traveler of a higher path than most mortal men, and perhaps that made it easier for him to destroy life callously, as if it meant nothing, as he saw most of his victims as little more than inconsequential insects, not even worthy of being swatted by a man so glorious as himself.

Hugo's extreme narcissism spilled over into his sex life. Never once, while engaging in sexual relations with another man, had he ever allowed himself to be sodomized; to be made another man's 'bitch'. Oh, no, that would be utterly unacceptable. He, Hugo, was the bitch-maker, never the submissive. He, Hugo, was always on top; always in charge; always dealing out, rather than receiving. He would sink to his knees for no man. To do such a thing would be to surrender his superiority.

Because of this narcissism, Hugo generally missed out on recreational activities with the brawny, muscular set that dwarfed his own skinny lankiness, so his love interests often ended up being scrawny, timid pipsqueaks who enjoyed being abused. Just as typical were his liaisons with young boys, for Henry Hugo, among his many other wicked classifications, was a shameless pedophile.

Hugo hadn't always been inclined towards young boys. The fetish had seized him about ten years ago on a paid assignment to terminate Bernardo Fernez, the ruthless Brazilian drugs kingpin. In the traditional cold-blooded style that had allowed him to survive so many years in the business, Hugo had infiltrated Fernez's mansion, dealt silently and effortlessly with two patrolling bodyguards, and snuck into the master bedroom where the big man himself lay helplessly asleep, blissfully unaware of the terrible fate that was about to befall him.

Hugo's soulless eyes glimmered in the darkness, and he licked his lips with anticipation as he placed the tip of Li'l Dick's barrel gently against Fernez's forehead. But as his long, bony forefinger curled around the trigger like a viper, he heard a soft, sleepy sigh that could not possibly have come from the man, and actually seemed to be emanating from behind.

Turning his head slowly, Hugo beheld Fernez's son – petite lad of just five years – standing in the open doorway, one hand rubbing a tired eye, and the other clutching a raggedy teddy bear by an arm whose stitches were pulling loose. The boy was groggy and seemed only half awake. Perhaps he had had a bad dream and was here to consult his father on the best course of action, or perhaps he just wanted a drink of water (kitchen water, not bathroom water). It was even possible that he was sleepwalking. Hugo really didn't know. All that mattered was that the boy was there, staring the globe-trotting assassin squarely in the face.

The little brown-skinned boy was the very picture of innocence, with his small button nose, his eyes so bright and sparkling even when clouded with the damp mist of sleep, and his shiny, black hair that fell adorably down into his face, and Hugo couldn't help but be enchanted by the specter. Somehow the sight of this boy stirred within him emotions that he was not at all used to feeling, and the infinitesimal sliver of humanity that lived a trapped and tortured existence inside Hugo's black heart was touched as if by some mystical power, and, for the first, last, and only time in all of his wicked career, Henry Hugo stayed his hand.

Reholstering his gun, Hugo turned away from the sleeping Fernez and walked past the unmoving child, tousling his hair indulgently as he departed silently from the bedroom.

Over the course of the ensuing days, Hugo became deeply ashamed of the weakness he had exhibited, and, after much wrestling with his self-image, decided to even out his karma by killing the man who had sent him to kill Fernez. This did nothing to expunge the infection from his brain, however, and he had spent his life since in a hellish game of tug-o-war between longing to forget the experience and trying desperately to recreate it.

The Giddy Grasshopper, one of Henry Hugo's favorite hot spots, was a gay nightclub in the center of Greenwich Village. Boasting a fully stocked bar, an expansive dance floor, and a huge stage on which brawny men in thongs pranced to the songs of Madonna and Cher, the lively club was frequented by the more raucous and adventurous element of the homosexual community. Men wearing dresses, men wearing skimpy shorts, and even men wearing nothing at all partied heartily within the gaudily decorated walls, 'neath the multicolored, seizure-inducing strobe lights.

Hugo loved the Grasshopper, and he made sure to stop in at least once whenever he happened to be in New York. By the same token, Hugo was one of the Grasshopper's favorite gals, and nearly all of the regular patrons knew and adored him. Indeed, whenever Hugo came bursting through the main entrance, striking a stylish pose and belting out one of his favorite one-liners from *Will & Grace*, the thundering dance music stopped short and everyone applauded and cheered wildly and rolled out the red carpet – sometimes literally – for him.

"Great to see you back in the big city, Henry," said the head 'waitress', a fairly convincing transvestite who came to greet Hugo at the door, take his hat and coat, and lead him to his usual table.

"It's great to be back, Taffy," said Hugo, planting an affectionate kiss on the transvestite's faux beauty mark before sitting down. "What's new?"

"Things are pretty much as you left them," said Taffy, handing Hugo a folded, laminated menu and striking a match to light the table's single candle. "Marty and Samson have broken it off for the fifth time this month, Lucky Ducky is still having unprotected sex with guys down at the AIDS clinic, and I'm still saving up for the operation. As for Lonnie and Lou, they moved up to Vermont and had the whole thing properly documented."

"Yes, I heard about that," said Hugo. "They invited me to the ceremony, but I was on business in Bei Jing at the time. I sent them a blender, though."

"Funny, isn't it?" said Taffy, snapping a pink bubble from the gum 'she' was chewing. "The people who get together. I mean, you remember how they were, Henry. Who would ever have thought that Lonnie and Lou, of all people, would end up ball-and-chaining?"

"It's a mad, mad, mad, mad world," said Hugo. "Or at least it had better be. And now that I think of him, how's old Georgie?"

Taffy pointed to the stage across the room, upon which a creature that seemed to have the general figure of a woman but the shrunken genitalia of a man was dancing like a slut in heat, discarding various pieces of underclothing and reveling in the hurricane of dollar bills being thrown by the hooting, cheering members of the audience.

"That's right!" the transgendered performer was exclaming. "Show Li'l Cupid you love her! Remember, the prettier I am, the more money I make, and the more money I make, the prettier I am!"

"That's Georgie?" said Hugo. "But he used to be a prestigious, successful bank manager. Money, cars, a huge house. What on earth turned him into *that*?"

"You really broke his heart the last time you were here, Henry," said Taffy. "He just sort of broke down; crashed completely."

"I am blameless," said Hugo, defensively. "He knew what we had. Now, tell me what tonight's special is."

"Grilled beef tenderloin, drizzled with the chef's own special sauce," said Taffy.

"And by special sauce, you mean..."

Taffy smiled and nodded, slyly.

"Absolutely not," said Hugo. "You know I can't eat that stuff. Makes me queasy. Perhaps I'd better just skip dinner and move on to dessert."

"All right," said Taffy, taking back Hugo's menu and handing him a key. "He's in room four. It's a good thing you called ahead, love, because it took some doing to find a kid of the precise description you gave. After some haggling, he agreed to the full work-over for two thousand dollars."

"Two thousand? I distinctly remember telling you that I didn't want to pay a penny over fifteen hundred."

"I'm afraid he charges extra for the fairy princess costume," Taffy shrugged. "He says it's his sister's and that she'll have his head if he tears it."

"Hmph," said Hugo, standing up from the table. "Kids these days are getting far too above themselves. Thinks he can give me orders, eh? I'll teach him a little respect for his elders. I'll fuck his tight little ass raw."

"Enjoy yourself," Taffy called after Hugo as the assassin eased his way politely through the sea of sweaty dancers, on his quest for the corridor at the back of the club that led into the private bedrooms.

I certainly will, thought Hugo, as he inserted the key into the lock of room four and turned the doorknob. *Fairy princess, eh? I hope the skirt is one of those short, poofy ones with a petticoat.*

Hugo entered the bedroom, furnished sparsely but comfortably with an overstuffed armchair, a big beanbag, a faux fireplace, and a queen-sized bed. He had expected to see a small boy in drag sitting patiently on the bed, his stocking feet dangling adorably over the floor, a tiara resting atop his crown of golden curls, and a gorgeous pair of gossamer butterfly wings growing from his back. What he found was a grown man dressed in jeans and a black jacket, pointing a gun directly at his (Hugo's) crotch. Hugo recognized the man immediately, and he greeted him in his usual salutatory manner, as if this was not in fact a disappointing and inconvenient development.

"Why, if it isn't Mr. Gary Parker," Hugo said with a smile. "Don't tell me you've come over to our side."

"No, although you do have a marvelous floor show," said Gary. "I thought it was time we had a little chat."

"Oh, by all means," said Hugo. "But first, I trust you won't mind if I inquire as to what you've done with my date for the evening?"

"I boxed his ears, gave him a Snickers bar, and sent him home to his mother," said Gary. "You're a sick bastard, Hugo."

"A man must be allowed his own convictions," Hugo replied. "Now, what shall we talk about? My, my, it's been a while since we last touched base, hasn't it? I think the last time was when I saved Carolyn from a terrible fate as a homemaker. I've been worried about you since then, Gary. I've been meaning to ask you, are you okay?"

Gary's eyes narrowed and his jaw clenched as Hugo dredged up the Vigilantes' past failure to protect Bruce, but he kept his temper.

"You're working for Norman Kubritz, and you're coming after us," he said. "That much I know. Now I need you to fill in a few blanks for me.

Like how Kubritz knows about us, and why he's so interested in gathering us all up alive. And think carefully before you answer these questions, Hugo, because the first time I sense you're lying to me, I'll shoot off your left nut."

Hugo chuckled and shook his head. "Norman was right," he said. "You have absolutely no idea what's going on. I must say, Gary, I had more respect for your intelligence than that."

The hitman reached a hand into his pocket.

"Hold it!" Gary barked.

"Relax, love, I'm just going for a cigarette," said Hugo, his hand reappearing holding his lighter and cigarette case.

"Enjoy it, Hugo," said Gary. "Because I promise I'll kill you before the cancer can."

"Forgive me if I refrain from trembling with fear," said Hugo, placing the cigarette between his thin lips and raising the lighter. "I try not to stress out over little things like old enemies with grudges. It's very bad for the complexion."

Hugo flicked the lighter then, and a blinding flash of white light filled the room, prompting Gary to cry out in surprise and clamp his eyes shut.

Crafty bastard! thought Gary, knowing that it would be at least two minutes before he'd be able to see clearly again.

"Silly boy!" scoffed Hugo, landing a solid punch on Gary's jaw, sending the Vigilante tumbling backwards. "Did you really think I'd allow myself to be caught off guard so easily? Do you have any idea how many times I've been in this situation?"

Hugo didn't give Gary a chance to answer before administering a swift kick to his head. Gary groaned and rolled over onto his side, rubbing his eyes furiously.

"It's not safe for a working girl like me," Hugo continued to rant, kicking Gary sharply in the ribs. "Big, strong men like you are always trying to take advantage of little ol' me. In my line of work, a mastery of sneaky tricks is a must. Just count yourself lucky I left my coat at the door. The flower in my buttonhole spits acid like a fucking puff adder." *That's right, loudmouth, keep talking,* thought Gary, rolling to the side in time to avoid another painful kick. *Keep talking with that ridiculous, nails-on-a-chalkboard voice of yours so I can pinpoint you.*

"I don't know what Kubritz has in mind for you," said Hugo, "but whatever it is, you surely deserve it just for being such a brainless, bumbling moron. Did you honestly think you could take me? You, a common street thug, and I, one of the world's most sought after professional killers? You are nothing compared to me, and I ought to kill you right here just for the insult!"

Avoiding still another contemptuous kick, Gary rolled back onto his shoulder blades, braced them against the floor, and sprang up onto his feet. Before the surprised Hugo could react, Gary drove a powerful punch directly into the center of the assassin's face, sending him flying backwards into the wall.

"Aaaaaahhhhh, shaddup!" said Gary, doing a fair impression of an exasperated Warner Bros. cartoon character.

Sitting in a crumpled heap against the wall, Hugo groaned, blinked a few times, then screamed in pain as he sniffed and a huge glob of blood oozed from his right nostril.

"By nose!" he hollered. "You've broken by nose! You undinking fool, you've disfigured be!"

"And that's not all I'm about to do," threatened Gary, his vision finally starting to clear, though bright sparks of pink and silver continued to dance like rollicking pixies before his eyes.

His vanity compelling him to hide his bent and bleeding nose behind one hand, Hugo scrambled to his feet and bolted from the room. Gary took the pursuit, and the chase led the two combatants out onto the vibrant dance floor packed with leather-clad revelers.

"Sobody help be!" Hugo shouted, trying to make his voice heard over the loud dance music. "He's tryik to kill be!"

Evading the clutches of two large, hairy bikers coming up from behind, Gary leapt up onto the long bar and slid down the length of it on his knees like a mechanical rabbit at a greyhound racetrack, sending bottles, glasses, ashtrays, and bowls of nuts flying in all directions, and landed facedown on the stage with a heavy 'thud', frightening away a pair of transvestites who had been giving their all in a spirited performance of 'Sisters'.

Ow, thought Gary, getting to his knees. *Memo to me: Just because Jackie Chan does it, it's not necessarily a good idea. Kiddies, don't try this at home.*

Before Gary could pull himself to his feet, he was torpedoed soundly in the midsection by a running football tackle and knocked flat on his back.

"So, you like it rough, do you?" snarled Hugo, the tackler, now sitting astride his torso. "Then let Mummy give you what you want!"

With that, Hugo plunged into Gary's side the knife he had snatched from a table, and gave it a brutal twist. Gary screamed in pain, and brought his knee up hard to jab Hugo at the base of his spine, and the assassin arched his back in tingling agony and fell off to one side.

Jumping to his feet, Gary grabbed the knife by its wooden handle, and, with one solid yank that precipitated another scream, pulled it from his body, prompting a thin but insistent spout of blood to begin pouring from the wound.

Brandishing the knife in one hand and covering his injury with the other, Gary advanced on Hugo with the intention of cutting off the hitman's testicles and force feeding them to him, but he was struck down mid-stride by one of the bouncers, finally springing into action, who hammered him hard across the back with a chair in the manner of a professional wrestler.

Okay, now I'm pissed, thought Gary, dropping to all fours and taking another blow from the chair, while the crowd cheered wildly.

As the bouncer prepared to club him a third time, Gary rolled over onto his side and thrust his leg up to catch the chair, kicking it into the big man's face. Before the bouncer had a chance to recover, Gary leapt up and executed a devastating tornado kick that sent the big man flying backwards into a tripod-mounted spotlight, which collapsed beneath him with a loud 'crunch' and a shower of sparks.

Shouldn't seriously hurt the guy, but at least it puts him down for the count, thought Gary. *Now to deal with the Wicked Queen. Wait a minute, where'd he...?*

"So sorry to just cut and run like this," Hugo called out from the nightclub's entrance, still making the best attempt to conceal his damaged nose while he hurridly threw on his hat and coat, "but I have a bost urgent abbointment with by plastic surgeon!"

Producing another cigarette, Hugo lit it – with his real lighter – and threw it over to the stage, where it landed at Gary's feet. Two seconds later the cigarette exploded like a firecracker, with a loud bang and a buffeting but otherwise harmless blast that knocked Gary on his backside.

"An oldie, but a goody!" Hugo laughed, kicking the door open and sprinting out into the night. "Bye, now!"

Gary gave his head a quick shake from side to side, then clambered to his feet, leapt from the stage, and ran across the club, carving a path through the throng of confused, drunken patrons on his way to the door, but when he finally made it out of the building, he saw no trace of Henry Hugo in any direction. The cunning killer had melted seamlessly into nocturnal New York. He'd never find him now. But that still wasn't the worst of Gary's problems.

"Who the hell is gonna pay for all this?" a gruff voice thundered from inside The Giddy Grasshopper.

Gary headed back to the Rat Hole in a hurry.

Except for lunch and dinner, breakfast was Norman Kubritz's favorite meal of the day, and this morning, as was his daily custom, he took it in the casino's restaurant. Spread out before him on his usual table, distanced from the rabble who apparently had nothing better to do at nine o'clock in the morning then come to Fives & Lives, were eggs fried and scrambled, innumerable strips of greasy bacon, legions of crispy, juicy sausages, mountains of hash browns, thick pieces of french toast slathered with cream cheese and butter, a twenty-four inch stack of buttermilk pancakes – some with blueberries, some with chocolate chips – soaked with maple syrup, and two pots of steaming hot coffee.

"You're a pig, Norman," said Malik, sitting on the far side of the food-laden table, making do with a hard-boiled egg, and cucumber, tomato, and cheese on toast.

"A hearty breakfast is the foundation of a successful and triumphant day, Malik," said Kubritz, shoveling an entire fried egg – sunny side up – into his gluttonous mouth. "And today will most certainly be a success and a triumph. Tonight's the night, dear friend. Tonight's the night."

"I take you at your word that everything will run smoothly," said Malik. "Have all last-minute preparations been seen to?"

"Impeccably," said Kubritz, spearing a pair of pancakes with his oversized fork and biting into them as if they were a soppy popsicle. "Seven months of work and planning will at last bear their fruit tonight. You have nothing to worry about, Malik. Just be here at two in the morning and you will see our agreement honored."

"Not quite," said Malik. "You still haven't managed to capture all of these so-called Vigilantes, have you?"

"I have every intention of seeing it through," said Kubritz, devouring a ladle-sized spoonful of hash browns, then washing it down with coffee guzzled directly from the pot's spout. "They are a formidable enemy, but I've already taken three of them."

"Yes, two women and a blind man," said Malik. "When are you going to tackle the true threats?"

"Patience is a virtue, Malik."

"But sloth is a sin."

Kubritz's eyes darkened as he bit into a sausage. "For the sake of our friendship, I shall pretend you didn't say that," he said, wiping a chunk of scrambled egg out of his beard. "I told you I'd honor the agreement, and you should know me well enough by now to know that my word is my bond."

"I do know that, Norman," said Malik. "Please forgive me if I've offended you. It's just that I have a great deal of personal interest vested in this venture."

"Apology accepted," said Kubritz. "I know you're feeling a degree of stress that only heightens as we grow ever closer to our goal, but worry not. Uncle Norman will take care of everything."

Kubritz seized a slice of french toast in his sticky hand, sopped up a puddle of syrup with it, and stuffed the whole thing into his mouth before he had even finished swallowing the sausage, and he was just about to tackle another level of the pancake tower when the sniveling Phillips appeared, bowing at the waist repeatedly, his wrinkled coattails dragging along on the floor behind him.

"A thousand pardons for interrupting your *petit dejeuner*," he cackled, "but there is a gentleman downstairs with whom I think you will desire words."

"Hit me," said Gary.

"Are you sure, sir?" asked the dealer in the white shirt and black pants. "You've got seventeen showing already."

"What's the point in living if you can't do it dangerously? Go on, hit me."

The dealer shrugged his shoulders, and tossed Gary a card, face up. It was an eight of diamonds, putting Gary well over twenty-one.

"Ah well, first rule of gambling," said Gary. "The odds are always against you."

"Enjoying ourselves, are we?" said KnuckleDuster, approaching the table.

"Well, well, if it isn't my friend with his finger on the switch," said Gary. "Fancy a game?"

"Beat it," KnuckleDuster said to the dealer. "I'll take it from here."

The dealer, sufficiently intimidated, retreated as ordered, and KnuckleDuster took his place opposite Gary.

"You are one stupid son of a bitch," said the shaven-headed man, the numbers and symbols on the upturned cards reflecting in the lenses of his sunglasses. "You make a clean getaway, but are you satisfied with that? Like hell. No, you come back begging for more."

"A psychologist friend of mine thinks I'm somewhat self-destructive," said Gary.

"Do you have any idea who you're up against?" asked KnuckleDuster, dealing Gary, then himself, two cards. "Kubritz is a titan on this planet. There's no way you'll ever be able to beat him, and when that sad fact finally worms its way inside your thick skull, there's no place you'll ever be able to hide from him. If you only knew what he had in store for you…"

"I'd be shaking in my pants?"

"You'd be doing *something* in your pants."

Gary snickered, and flipped over his two cards, revealing their faces. They were a ten of hearts and a queen of clubs; an even twenty. He looked over at KnuckleDuster's cards and saw a ten of spades and a king of diamonds; also an even twenty.

"A draw," KnuckleDuster observed. "The house wins by default, and that illustrates my point perfectly. No matter how good you are, Big K always has the advantage."

"Not so fast," said Gary, holding up his hand and smirking a wicked smirk. "Hit me."

"You really are fucked up in the head, man," said KnuckleDuster. "You have twenty. You can't go any higher than that."

"Hit me," Gary insisted.

KnuckleDuster rolled his eyes and threw Gary a third card. Gary turned it over, and smiled when it revealed itself to be the ace of clubs.

"In blackjack, an ace can be counted as either an eleven or a one," Gary said. "With this ace and my two tens, I have twenty-one exactly. That means I win and you lose."

"How the hell did you know that was gonna come up next?" KnuckleDuster, almost incredulous, asked.

"I didn't," said Gary. "But, in many ways, the way I gamble reflects the way I live. I can take it easy most of the time, but when I'm going up against some dirtbag son of a bitch that I really want to beat, I'll take any chance offered me. And that's when guys like your boss lose the advantage."

KnuckleDuster scowled, and crumpled his cards in his metal fist.

"So, you think you're a real Mr. Smartypants, do ya?" he sneered. "Well, take a look behind you, dipshit."

Gary turned around on his stool and was not altogether surprised to find himself facing a hard washboard torso rippling with muscle. Craning his neck upwards gradually brought him into eye contact with the immense Mr. Bojangles, casting an oak tree-sized shadow over the blackjack table.

"The boss'd like a word," the giant rumbled.

"As would I," said Gary. "Perhaps the direct approach is best at this point. All right, let's go."

Gary rose from the stool, and Mr. Bojangles clasped his huge hands firmly around the Vigilante's arms while KnuckleDuster frisked him quickly and found not a single concealed weapon.

"Ya didn't bring nothin' at all?" Mr. Bojangles asked, confused. "Ya just walked in here unarmed?"

"Yup," said Gary. "I thought we could all sit down and talk this out like adults."

"You are one stupid son of a bitch," KnuckleDuster repeated his earlier sentiment.

Five minutes later, Gary found himself manacled by his wrists and ankles to a sturdy metal chair in Kubritz's main office, with Mr. Bojangles towering behind him, grinning inanely, and KnuckleDuster standing off to one side, clearly primed to defend his master should anything go unexpectedly wrong. Malik sat comfortably on the leather couch with an air of utter detachment and boredom, and the big man himself sat in his big chair behind his big desk, his big teeth chomping on one of his big cigars.

"You're a very interesting fellow, Mr. Parker," said Kubritz, twiddling the cigar between his index and middle fingers. "Twice I have tried to kill you, and back you come, like some stupid dog to an abusive owner. Tell me, are you some sort of masochist? Do you honestly think you'll be lucky enough to escape a second time? Why do you persist in this insane business?"

"Well, my friends kept telling me I should get a hobby," said Gary.

"Jest all you like," said Kubritz, "but your prattling witticisms will not save you now."

Gary knew that was perfectly true, and his mind fell instinctively back on his training.

Rule No. 371, Gary recited in his head. *If prattling witticisms can't save you, start bluffing.*

"So, you've got me at your mercy," Gary said aloud. "As long as I'm going to be dead in an hour or so, you might as well fill in the few little tidbits of your bollocking mad scheme that I don't already know, 'cause you'd better believe me, Norman, when I say that I've got you pegged.

I know you're behind the disappearances of those five women, and I know that you've got some kind of a beef with me and my friends, and I know that you've struck up a dark, perverse partnership with Qasim Al-Fulani."

"A partnership?" Kubritz snorted and chuckled at the same time. "Mr. Parker, I'm a respectable businessman. A captain of industry. One of the most highly respected men in America. I was *TIME* magazine's Man of the Year. Twice. What would I be doing in a partnership with a brutal, despicable, fundamentalist terrorist like Qasim Al-Fulani?"

"Go ahead and tell him the whole story, Norman," said Malik. "It might be amusing to see the look on his face when he hears the truth."

"If you want to hear the whole story, then I'll tell you the whole story, the basis of which is incredibly humble," Kubritz, leaning forwards on his desk and puffing out a huge cloud of smoke, said to Gary "You see, it all started with a bet – a wager, if you will – between my dear friend Malik and myself about seven months ago, the nature of which is immaterial. All you need to know is that I lost this particular bet, and, being both a good sport and a man of my word, was bound to abide by the conditions set down by Malik to which I had agreed previously. The first of these conditions was that I gather up five women, their personalities and physical traits adhering to the criteria Malik specified."

"I'm really quite into American women these days," Malik spoke up from the couch. "After a lifetime of fucking Arab women, I find them to be dull and unexciting. There's no joy in whipping a woman when she just lies there and takes it, sobbing pathetically. I want a real challenge. I want some headstrong, independent-minded shrews to tame. I want some bitches to break. I want to beat, rape, and abuse an emancipated, college-educated female until she's reduced to a whimpering heap of quivering flesh. Norman's generous gift of five American girls will make a fine addition to my harem. Why, I might even place them above the other girls and allow them to rule over my Afghan whores. After all, that's what you all want, isn't it? To dominate us?"

"Okay, that's one sick bastard, and counting," said Gary. "Are you a grade-A nutball as well, Edward Scissorhands, or are you just misunderstood?"

KnuckleDuster growled, and smacked his right fist into his left palm with a loud 'clank'.

"Ah, but that's just the first part," Kubritz continued, sprinkling a shower of cigar ash into the ever present golden ashtray. "If you liked that, you're going to love this next bit. I presume you know where Qasim Al-Fulani is being held?"

"At the bottom of one of the most secure dungeons this country has to offer," said Gary.

"Yes, Stocknorton is quite an imposing obstacle upon first glance, but no place is inaccessible to a man of my limitless reach. Tonight, approximately sixteen hours from now, Qasim Al-Fulani will be liberated."

"Now, that would be a neat trick," said Gary.

"How it is to be accomplished is no business of yours," said Kubritz. "All you need to know is that this was the second of Malik's conditions which I was obligated to meet after losing our bet. I promised to devote my full power chest of resources towards freeing Qasim Al-Fulani from prison."

"Qasim and I are very good, very old friends," said Malik. "It pained me to think of him locked up like an animal, his solid character and ingenious brain going to wicked waste. Such a man needs to be free, else how will he ever change the world for the better?"

"It was all arranged at Malik's behest," said Kubritz, waving a cloud of smoke away from his pudgy face. "For all I care, that uppity little sand nigger could rot in prison for the rest of his miserable life. I find terrorist attacks against great cities like ours just as distasteful as you do, Mr. Parker. They're bad for business. They frighten away the tourists."

"That reminds me," said Gary. "How'd you manage to open this casino anyway? If I'm not mistaken, you have to be an Indian in order to operate a gambling casino in this state."

"I'm one-sixteenth Cherokee," Kubritz flashed a large grin. "That bit of blood, along with the breaking of an influential pair of legs or the dropping from a roof of a carefully selected child, proved more than enough to convince the proper authorities that I had a perfect right to open and operate this establishment. But let us not get hung up on business matters. Let's press ahead to the juicy part of the deal. The part of the deal that concerns you the most. Malik's third and final condition. Why don't you take the honors, old friend?"

"Delighted," said Malik. "You see, Parker, my friend Qasim is generally a cool-headed man, but if he can be said to have one flaw, it is undoubtedly his vengeful nature. Being free from prison wouldn't be enough for him. No, in order to be truly content, he'd have to exact a complete and terrible revenge upon the people who put him there in the first place. And let's face it, Union Jack. That's you; you and your nine colleagues. That's why poor Norman has been devoting so much energy towards tracking you all down and picking you all up, even employing the most appalling people, like that faggot gunman and the Negress, to help get the job done. As of this moment in time, we have three of your merry band. The blind doctor, the woman scientist, and the woman quartermaster who curses like a man."

Gary's eyes narrowed, his face darkened, and his teeth gnashed together, and all thought of responding to Malik's self-important monologue with a sarcastic barb vanished from his mind.

"I swear, you shit-eating son of a bitch, if you harm them in any way..."

"Spare me your threats," said Malik, holding up a hand. "You're in no position to make them, as we now have you to add to the collection. And soon the rest will follow. The big nigger, the old woman doctor, the boy, the Spanish bitch. Yes, we have done our homework on you, Parker, just as I am sure you have done yours on us. And when we have chained the last of you to the wall, utterly impotent to do anything but accept the painful torture and messy death that await you, then Qasim shall have his fun."

A deep, rich chuckle from Mr. Bojangles and the quiet grinding of KnuckleDuster flexing his metallic fingers punctuated the silence as Gary worked to absorb all that he had just heard, unable to keep himself from feeling as if he had slipped into an alternate reality where absolutely nothing made sense.

"So, that's what this is all about?" he said, at last. "You're going to destroy the lives of five young women, and free one of the world's most notoriously vicious terrorists, all for the sake of a petty wager?"

"I'm a gambling man, Mr. Parker," said Kubritz, exhaling a smoke ring. "It's what I do."

"Stick him in the basement with the others, Norman," Malik suggested.

Kubritz nodded, and pressed a button on his desk, snapping open the shackles binding Gary's wrists and ankles. Mr. Bojangles gripped him tightly by both arms, pinning them to his sides.

"Any parting words, Parker?" Kubritz asked.

"I think you've got...egg in your beard," said Gary, raising one eyebrow, studiously.

Kubritz scowled, and wiped a chubby hand hastily across his bewhiskered triple chin.

"Still you persist," the crime boss glowered. "Haven't you realized by now that you can't get the better of me? Your cause is hopeless. Your impudent, pissant antics can't put even the slightest chink in my armor. You're a hapless worm, writhing along the ground, wallowing in your own slime, and that's all you've ever been. I am a god and you are an insect. You've no right to consider yourself my worthy rival."

"Yeah, yeah, if I had a nickel for every time some juiced-up supervillain gave me the 'how dare you challenge me' speech, I'd be able to empty the gumball machine down at the 7-Eleven," said Gary.

"Take him away," said Kubritz.

Still grinning, keeping Gary's arms pinned, Mr. Bojangles lifted him off the floor and carried him out of the room.

"Irritating little jackanapes," Kubritz grumbled, hissing out a stream of smoke.

"An insufferable fellow indeed," said Malik. "But I've a feeling he'll change his tune once Qasim gets hold of him. My incarcerated friend has been telling me, with no small amount of enthusiasm, about a new series of torture methods he's been studying involving hot coals and blunt knives. Should be a hell of a party."

"He's got a private jet at LaGuardia! Ya might find somethin' there! That's all I know! I swear that's all I know!"

That was what the punk had said when Carla had dangled him upside-down from the top of a ten-story building and threatened to make him the mozzarella cheese on an asphalt pizza, and it was her experience that most petty crooks with humble ambitions tended to crack and tell the truth when their lives were placed in serious jeopardy.

Now Carla scurried through the airport's isolated lot of hangars reserved for the aeronautic indulgences of the rich and famous like a rat through a maze, moving from one shadow cast by the early afternoon sun to another, avoiding the piercing, cyclopean eye of the occasional panning surveillance camera with ease.

It could be any of these, thought Carla, flattening her body against the wall of a hangar, and moving on only after the camera across the way had shifted its focus, having satisfied itself that all was right with its little piece of the world. *And even if I did manage to figure out which one I want, how would I possibly get inside?*

Carla didn't have to wait long for the answer to both her puzzlements to present itself in the form of a pair of large metal doors grinding noisily open about two hundred yards away. Crouching into a ball, making herself as small as possible, she watched as the doors folded open completely and two tall, muscular Arabs dressed in cotton pants and deafeningly loud Hawaiian shirts emerged from the hangar. They were talking to each other as they stepped out into the sun, and with her ultra sensitive hearing aids as finely tuned as ever, Carla had no trouble making out their words.

"So, where would you like to go first?"

"You know, I've never been to the Empire State Building."

"Good choice. Hey, have you heard the penny story?"

"The penny story?"

"They say that somebody dropped a penny from the top of the building, and it fell with such velocity that it cut clean through a man standing on the sidewalk below, killing him instantly."

"That is such bullshit."

"No, it's true!"

"Taimur, the Empire State Building is only about twelve hundred feet tall, so a penny dropped from the top would hit the ground at no more than two hundred and eighty feet per second. Now, taking into account a penny's flat, circular shape, chances are it probably wouldn't even break your skin. It would be no worse than an ordinary hailstone."

"Well, if you're so smart, why do people sell and buy penny helmets around the bottom of the building?"

"Because the corruption of America's system of capitalism and free enterprise knows no bounds. Now, talk no more of this."

Taimur grumbled to himself and punched in the code to bring the doors folding back over the hangar's entrance like the magical stone curtain sealing off the cavernous hideaway of Ali Baba's forty thieves. Then, as the doors began grinding and the two Arabs began walking, Carla began sprinting.

Last I checked, my personal best for the two hundred yards was twenty-one seconds, she thought, her legs a leather blur as she raced for the hangar. *Unfortunately, I doubt I have longer than twelve here.*

When she blew past one hundred and twenty yards, her breath whistling steadily through her clenched teeth, she tore a six-inch, pencil-thin baton from the side of her utility belt, pulled it on both sides to extend it to two feet, then, without missing a step, hurled it long-ways at the doors. The move was planned, timed, and executed flawlessly, and the baton wedged itself in between the two encroaching walls of aluminum, trembling but not giving way as it kept jammed open a space of twenty-four inches.

Reaching the hangar's entrance just four seconds after the baton, Carla turned sideways and slid in between the thwarted doors, which were groaning in constipated frustration, unable to comprehend what had halted them so effectively in their customary function.

Pausing to catch her breath and brush a lock of unruly black hair from her eyes, Carla studied the dormant plane she had come to see, and reflected upon the odious nature of its owner. From the research she had been conducting ever since Gary had mentioned Qasim Al-Fulani's visits with another Arab, Carla had been able to deduce that the man in question was a wealthy Afghan terrorist and arms dealer who went by the name of Malik. A further follow-up had established him to be an acquaintance of Norman Kubritz. Now the trail had led her here, to a private jet, with the ramp leading into the cargo section lowered invitingly.

That must be where Tweedle-Dum and Tweedle-Dumber came from, she reasoned. *Well, whatever's in there must be interesting, and it's my civic duty, on behalf of airport security, to poke my nose in.*

Carla didn't have time to scamper up the ramp, however, before she felt something leathery and strap-like hit her in the back, and suddenly found her arms bound tightly against her sides. She looked down just in time to see the two globular weights of the bola rope completing the bonding pirouette that entrapped her upper body. An instant later, something hit her hard in her side, and she crashed to the floor, her cracked ribs screaming their disapproval and insisting her entire body empathize with them.

"Hi there, playmate," said Janet, standing triumphantly over her, her stance casual, with one well-rounded hip thrust out provocatively.

Janet's latest dominatrix ensemble included a leather tube top equipped with a zipper between her large breasts, the same tight pair of leather pants, a spiked dog collar, a spiked belt, and a huge pair of leather stomping boots. The accessory which drew the bulk of Carla's attention, however, was the chainsaw Janet gripped in her right hand.

"Back for more, I see," she said, a wicked smile playing about her face. "Being beaten to a pulp and ground into the dirt really gets you off, huh? You're a lot like Gary in that respect. So, you want to spend a little quality time with Auntie Janet? Let me escort you to the honeymoon suite."

Janet effectively incapacitated Carla with another smash to her damaged ribs, then seized her by the back of her neck and dragged her cringing body up the ramp and into the bowels of the plane.

"So, I know that you and Gary are pretty chummy," she said. "Tell me, do the two of you ever get a good, sweaty, hardcore fuck going?"

Carla didn't have the breath for any sort of reply.

"Don't tell me you leave that perfectly good piece of dickmeat just lying around without ever hitting it," Janet continued. "He's experienced, well-built, knows how to use the tools of the trade. I'll bet he fucks you like a bitch in heat. I'll bet he throws your scrawny ass over a chair and makes you love it. And a petite little tart like you, he could jam you right down on his prick and spin you like a top."

Having reached the cargo section, Janet lifted Carla off the floor and threw her down onto a cot. Still struggling to suppress the agony in her midsection, Carla turned her head to the side, and, through teary eyes, saw five other women, naked and unconscious, strapped to similar cots.

"Who...?" she began to ask.

"Beats me," said Janet, unzipping her top and allowing her big breasts to pour freely out in an avalanche of soft flesh. "A bunch of girls that the ragheads were guarding. They wanted to do some sightseeing, so their boss dropped me an extra hundred grand for holding down the fort in the meantime. Looks like it was a good idea. It gives us a chance to really get to know each other. You know, I never liked playing henchwench to anyone's evil genius, but this Kubritz guy is definitely my kind of people. This business venture just keeps getting sweeter. Kubritz isn't a stingy bastard. He knows how to treat his help. Right now I've got enough money to swim in, like that Disney duck does. Plus, Gary's going to be horrifically tortured and maimed, and I get a sweet little Spanish pun'kin to play with."

"What about Gary?" asked Carla, able to speak again.

"Don't you worry your pretty little head about him," said Janet, pinching Carla's cheek. "Kubritz is entertaining him, along with all the rest of your friends, in his own way. But Mr. K generously agreed to let me have you, should you and I ever cross paths again. And here you are. Why, it's almost as if fate brought us together. It's karma, cupcake. We were meant to find each other."

Having divested herself of everything but the dog collar and boots, Janet hefted the chainsaw again, and, with a sadistic gleam in her eye, yanked the starter cord once, bringing the gas-powered cutting machine roaring to life with a terrifyingly loud bellow that indicated an insatiable appetite for destruction.

"I'm an adventurous girl," Janet shouted to make herself heard over the din of the saw. "I don't like to have sex the same way twice. I'm always experimenting. Just recently I thought about how wild it would be to fuck a person with no arms and no legs. It would certainly save the struggling. Of course, you have all your arms and legs, so we're gonna have to do a little amateur surgery first. By the way, you're not overdue for a tetanus shot, are you?"

Deploying all the strength her shoulders could muster, Carla heaved her body hard to the right and rolled off the cot just as her sadistic captor brought the buzzing blade arcing down onto the thin mattress, sending chewed-up little bits of foam rubber exploding into the air.

"No use playing hard-to-get!" Janet declared, kicking the cot aside and advancing on her prey. "Once I get 'em, they're got!"

The chainsaw made a truly terrifying noise as Janet squeezed the throttle control trigger repeatedly, and swung the weapon down at Carla, who somersaulted to her feet just in time to avoid being divided in two.

Gary was right, thought Carla. *This woman really is a psycho. I mean,* The Texas Chainsaw Massacre *was gory, but not even Leatherface wanted to hump his victims after he cut them up.*

With her arms still bound to her sides by the bola, Carla's combat options were limited. It seemed that, until she could come up with a really good plan, she would have to play a straight defense. So, as Janet moved in on her like a cat backing a mouse into a corner, the saw held out in front of her with both hands, Carla feinted to the right, then darted quickly left, dodging a lunge from the saw that would have bored a hole clean through her belly like a voracious termite through a soft, rotting tree stump.

"Come on, don't be so skittish," said Janet, her eyes aglow with bloodlust. "You know you'll love it. Why, just think about how much lighter you'll be!"

Janet leapt forwards from a crouching position, the dreaded saw held out at arm's length like a buzzing bayonet, going for Carla's kneecaps. Carla anticipated the move as soon as she saw Janet coil back like a spring, and she leapfrogged spryly over the other woman, hitching her heels up extra high. Janet corrected herself quickly, stopped on a dime, and spun around in a complete circle, whipping the savage saw through a rotation that claimed a fringe of Carla's ebony hair.

Can't keep this up all day, thought Carla. *Have to get control of the situation.*

Carla knew she couldn't keep dodging forever, and that she would win this fight only with the renewed use of her arms, and her resourceful mind could devise but one way to obliterate the ropes that bound them. It was mind-bogglingly dangerous, and a saner person probably wouldn't even have thought of it, but, as she fought for her life against this mad woman, she saw no other recourse.

Jumping back and to the right, Carla made a quick study of the method by which Janet thrust the saw in her direction, then compared it hurriedly with the mental snapshots she had been collecting of Janet's previous attacks. After running them through her mind in slow motion like action replays, she decided that Janet was pulling off mostly a combination lunge-swoop move with the saw. More than three quarters of the time, it was a vertical swoop that arced downwards from her collarbone to her belly, and she definitely shifted her weight to her right foot when she lunged. She always extended her long arms to their full reach at the widest point of the arc, and Carla's evasive maneuvers usually took her somewhere between fifteen and twenty inches out of harm's way.

With all of this in mind, Carla waited for Janet to strike again, and when she did, she actually took a step in the naked woman's direction, and quickly turned ninety degrees to the right so that she was standing sideways relative to Janet, and her right arm was directly in the rampaging saw's path.

If Carla had not calculated this maneuver with the precision timing and perfect placement that she had, she would have been horribly mutilated. The saw would have blasted through her upper arm and down into her side, and Janet would have had her for sure. But Carla's figuring was so spot-on that, instead of eating into her soft flesh, the arcing saw cut away her leather bonds as if they were tissue paper, only just grazing the skin of her arm as it did so.

Before the shredded remnants of the bola rope even had the chance to drift to the floor, Carla had already fallen onto her hands and kicked her legs straight backwards like a temperamental mule, sending the chainsaw flying away towards the back of the plane. She then sprang back to her feet, and before Janet could recover from the shock, punched the evil woman on the jaw.

I'm not making the same mistake you did, thought Carla. *No witty banter or jocular puns tying up the action. I'm putting you down now.*

Janet reeled from the blow, and threw a clumsy punch of her own which didn't come close to connecting. Then Carla smashed her leather-gloved knuckles into the space between Janet's eyes with enough force to kill a weaker person, and the wicked woman flew backwards, crashed onto her back on the metal floor, and lay still, blood running freely from her nose, her long arms and legs splayed awkwardly.

Honestly, the people I have to deal with, thought Carla, as she took a few deep breaths, ran a hand over her perspiring face, and checked her right arm to make sure the bleeding wasn't too bad. *No time to dwell on the glamorous part of the job, though. An anonymous phone call to the police is all the attention these girls really require from me. The boys in blue will take it from here. And after I've made that call, I'd better boogie back to the Hole and fill the others in on recent developments.*

Ignoring the discarded chainsaw still putt-putting uselessly away in the corner, Carla ran down the ramp, already detaching her cell phone from her utility belt in preparation to make the nine-one-one call.

The last glowing remnants of the westbound evening sun were filling the pale blue sky with streaks of pink, orange, and gold, and casting their long shadows over the rooftops, backyards, and sidewalks of the suburbs by the time William pulled up to the front of Rachel's house in his father's car, the backseat of which would always hold fond memories for him.

It was in this very car that I began my ascension towards bigger and better things, he thought, relishing his new status. *No more being pushed around, no more groveling in the mud, and no more jerking off to Internet porn. From now on, it's the finer things for me.*

With pride and confidence he strode up the short walk, climbed the two steps to the porch, and rang the doorbell. No more than five seconds later, Rachel opened the door and William practically swooned when he saw the little black dress that accentuated her breasts, hugged her every curve, and gave prominent display to her long, smooth legs.

"Hey there, stud," she said, sexily. "Don't just stand there. Come in."

William was only too happy to do so, and as he crossed the threshold into the kitchen, he felt a distinct oncoming of some spiritual force, almost as if God Himself was descending from the heavens in order to deliver to him a congratulatory pat on the back.

Excellent work, M'boy, William was sure He would say. *You've suffered long and you've waited patiently for your reward, but here you finally stand, as living testimony to the whole world that I do indeed create all men equally.*

Yes, this would definitely be a good night.

"Are you hungry? Would you like anything to eat?" Rachel asked, entwining her supple arms around William's neck and smiling into his bespectacled eyes.

"No thanks, I'm fine," said William.

Actually his mouth was so dry that he doubted his ability to swallow anything solid, but that was all right. After all, it was customary to raid the fridge afterwards anyway.

"How about a drink?" suggested Rachel, leading William into the living room and slinking over to the liquor cabinet in the corner.

"Er...well, okay. Why not?" said William.

William was not a drinker, and he doubted he would be even when he was of legal age. He had once sampled a sip of champagne on his parents' wedding anniversary, but had spat it out immediately and gulped down two glasses of Coke to kill the taste. His reaction had been similar when his father had given him a small sampling of beer. Additionally he didn't relish the prospect of using veritable poison to kill off his very valuable brain cells and erode his vital organs, and he had witnessed firsthand in Gary what ravages the curse of alcoholism could bring down upon a person's soul.

But he really didn't want to look like a wimp in front of Rachel. Besides, drinking booze was an established and accepted part of the sexual act, and he wanted this first experience of his to be as complete as possible.

Rachel bent down to retrieve the tiny silver key from its hiding place behind the cabinet – a fabric-stretching move that drove the breath from William's chest – then inserted it into the lock, turned it to the right, and opened the wood-framed glass door.

"My parents won't be back until tomorrow night," said Rachel, selecting a large bottle of vodka and going for a couple of glasses, "which means that if you'd like to skip school tomorrow, we could spend the whole day staring at my bedroom ceiling together."

William could think of no better way to spend a Monday, nor could he think of any reason to decline the invitation. His academic performance at present was average, but not in danger, and one more absence in the second-to-last month of the school year wouldn't hurt him. As for his parents, they certainly wouldn't be any the wiser. They believed he had gone to stay the night at longtime friend Paul's house, where the two boys would study a little, then kick each other's asses in the video game world and watch *Pulp Fiction* for the millionth time. (They wouldn't give his visit to Paul's a second thought, as Paul was the alibi he most often gave his parents whenever he was required to step out with the Vigilantes in the evenings.) He had already told them he would take the bus to school from Paul's house in the morning and see them that afternoon.

"Sounds great," said William, accepting his drink from Rachel and giving it a quick sniff, suppressing admirably the wave of revulsion that came over him.

Rachel beamed, put one hand behind William's head, and kissed him on the mouth, and William was astonished at his own gentlemanly restraint in not throwing his glass to the floor, tearing that teasing little dress from Rachel's gorgeous body, and doing her right there up against the wall.

"So, what'll we drink to?" the girl asked.

"Uh…"

"Well, it's not important anyway," she said. "Drink up."

Rachel clinked her glass against William's, then downed her drink in two gulps. William depleted his glass' contents in two gulps as well, his eyes, nose, and throat all feeling as if they were on fire as he struggled to maintain an indifferent façade. Rachel took both glasses, set them aside on a table, and drew William close to her again, curling one shapely leg around his left calf.

"You go on upstairs," she whispered seductively into William's ear while licking the lobe with the tip of her tongue. "My room is the first door on the left. I'll be right up after I take my pill. You get your studly self all ready for me."

Rachel kissed him one more time, thrusting her tongue past his lips, then turned, and, with an adorable wink, wiggled off into the kitchen. William stood rooted to the spot for a moment, exhaled heavily, then pumped his fist triumphantly into the air and bounded briskly up the carpeted stairs.

"Yes!" he exclaimed, under his breath. "Yes! I'm in! I'm in, I'm in, I'm in!"

Whistling a few bars from Beethoven's 'Ode to Joy', William found and opened a door decorated with a poster of a bare-chested Eminem, and dared to enter what he knew would become his ultimate pleasure dome.

William had never been inside a girl's bedroom before, but he figured the Shangri-la that now stretched out before him lived fairly up to his expectations. The décor, including the painted walls and thick pile carpet, was largely pastel and cheerful. There was a TV hooked up to a hybrid DVD player, a couple of cushioned chairs, a work desk on which rested a closed laptop computer and the most recent issue of *Cosmopolitan*, a closet probably jammed full of clothes, and a quilted bed – by far the most compelling piece of furniture in William's eyes – that played host to a small assortment of stuffed animals. There was also a dresser, atop which rested a large mirror, innumerable cosmetic and vanity items, and a framed photograph of Jason.

I don't think we'll be needing that, thought William, turning the photo facedown.

His inhibitions vanishing with each passing moment he spent in the perfumed room, William unzipped his pants and flung them over the back of a chair before he had the chance to talk himself out of it. His shirt, shoes, socks, and briefs followed, leaving him completely nude.

Glasses on or off? he asked himself. *Jeez, I hadn't thought of that. She liked me without them in the car yesterday, but I'll be able to see much better with them. I'll ask her what she thinks.*

William reached into the right hip pocket of his discarded pants and produced a small, square packet. He had purchased it at the drugstore that very afternoon, and now he tore it carefully open and was surprised to find the comprehensive network of diagrams that decorated the wrapper's interior.

I wanted a condom, not a model airplane, thought William, reviewing the diagrams studiously, making sure he wouldn't miss a trick and end up with a blooming family prematurely.

It was then that he heard soft footsteps on the stairs, and he quickly pulled back the bedsheets and jumped in, shoving aside a SpongeBob SquarePants and two Care Bears as he did so. He pulled the sheet up over the lower half of his body, fluffed the pink pillow resting behind him with a few elbow jabs, and, at the last second, decided to remove his glasses and place them on the bedside table, next to the clock radio.

If TV and movies are any example, this seems to be the conventional way to situate oneself, he decided.

"I'm coming, Will," Rachel called from the hallway. "Get ready for a life-altering experience."

Being the movie buff that he was, William should have been exceptionally mindful of a particular universal truth. Specifically, the time when things start going unbelievably well for a teenage social outcast or misfit is the time for that teenage social outcast or misfit to exercise suspicion and caution. Of course, a movie allows the viewer an omniscient glimpse at the workings and machinations of every central character, whereas real life, regrettably, only affords a person the sole perspective that is taken in through one's own eyes, however willfully blinded to the inevitable those eyes might be. Such as it was, William received the shock of his life when the door flew open and three familiar boys burst into the room.

"Surprise, Willy!" crowed Jason. "Getting comfortable?"

"Look at him!" chortled Randy. "He's totally bare-ass naked!"

"This is too fuckin' funny!" laughed Kyle. "He looks even paler and punier than ever!"

Horrified, William looked to Rachel standing in the doorway and saw that she was laughing too, a hand placed demurely over her lipsticked mouth as she guffawed it up along with her surprise guests. Then the awful revelation finally sank in as he realized that everything – the romantic interest, the flirting, the kindness, the backseat escapades, and the sexual proposition – had been lies. The incidents that had bolstered his self-respect and soothed his cynical adolescent heart had been nothing more than a cruel web of deceit designed to crush and humiliate him. The first girl ever to give him the time of day was a manipulative, cold-hearted serpent, and his first kiss had been nothing more than tantalizing bait inside an inhumane trap.

From paradise to hell in five seconds. That had to be a new record, even for William.

"Now, that's how it's done, boys!" Rachel crowed, triumphantly. "Any questions?"

"I gotta hand it to you, babe," said Jason, wiping a tear of laughter from his eye. "Honestly, I had my doubts that you could pull this off at all, let alone in just two days! Shit, I thought it would take at least a couple weeks!"

"He was so desperate to believe that someone actually liked him!" Kyle roared with laughter. "I can't believe he actually thought a hottie like you would ever wanna do a little twerp like him!"

Everyone continued laughing their silly heads off while William sat catatonically in the bed, utterly mortified, as red as a steamed lobster, and he didn't move until Jason grabbed the sheet that covered him and yanked it away.

"Holy shit, will ya look at that shriveled up little Tootsie Roll!" he crowed. "My dick only looks like that after I've been in the water! No wonder the dork never gets any!"

One hand covering his genitals, William leapt off the bed and scrambled for his clothes, but Jason and his two cronies snapped them up and held them above their heads, out of the shorter boy's reach. Desperate to regain a shred of his castrated dignity, William lunged at Randy, hitting him ineffectively in the chest in an attempt to recapture his pants.

"Dude, he's trying to get your shirt off!" laughed Kyle. "He's naked and he's all over you! Maybe he is a little fag after all!"

"I think he's gonna cry!" Rachel giggled.

"His ass is bright red! He's blushing all over!" exclaimed Jason.

As the relentless laughter and insults bombarded him from all sides, William's vision began to blur, and a thousand different negative thoughts and feelings poured into his mind. His ears began to buzz, and his nerves began to tingle, and he felt very, very hot, as if his body temperature had skyrocketed a hundred degrees above normal. His breath began to come fast and heavy, and his hands started trembling, and he could feel the part of his brain that gave him the ability to reason being overcome by thick, black patches of shadow.

Then he balled his hand into a fist and punched Randy in the crotch with every ounce of force he could muster.

"Stop...laughing...at me," William growled in a ferocious, guttural voice that was barely his own.

The larger boy shrieked in pain and doubled over, and William delivered a hard, double-fisted smash to his head, sending him reeling to the floor.

"I'm sick of being laughed at!" he hissed.

Jason made a run for him, his look of sadistic levity now changed to one of anger, but William snatched the laptop computer from Rachel's desk and swung it forcefully into Jason's face. The bully cried out in agony and staggered backwards, holding his nose. Then William raised the computer high above his head and brought it crashing down against his hated enemy's jaw. Now Jason turned and tried to move away, but William pursued him with the makeshift club, delivering several more blows to his back. Finally, as Jason was making his way out the door, William hurled the laptop like a stone and struck his retreating tormentor in the back of the head. Jason pitched forwards, landed facedown on the hallway floor, and lay still.

"You're not...going to laugh at me...anymore!" William snarled, turning his attention to Kyle, the last bully still standing.

Kyle threw a punch at William, but it didn't come anywhere near him as the smaller boy had already opted for the low road and torpedoed his entire body into Kyle's stomach. Kyle crashed against the wall, gasping and wheezing for breath, and William finished him off quickly with a drubbing from a chair.

"No one will!" he roared, turning to Rachel.

The girl screamed in terror and attempted to run from the room, but William caught her by her long, blond hair, and yanked her back towards him. He kneed her hard in the behind, casting her headfirst into the wall. She slumped to the floor, crying, and remained there, cowering with her arms over her face, while William went about exacting his revenge on the inanimate furnishings of the room. His adrenaline pumping deafeningly in his ears, he tore the bedsheets, decapitated the stuffed animals, overturned the dresser, desk, and night table, broke the mirror, tore down posters and pictures, scattered the clothes, and threw against the wall everything that it was in his power to lift.

Finally, after the entire room had been destroyed, William stood shakily in the center of the chaos, still breathing hard, still trembling, torrents of sweat running down his naked form, feeling rather the same as Dr. Jekyll must have felt after transforming back from Mr. Hyde. Then, after the ringing in his ears had finally ceased, and the worst of the pins-and-needles sensation had left him, he hastily donned his briefs, socks, shoes, pants, shirt, and glasses, and stomped downstairs.

Passing through the living room, William kicked in the glass door of the liquor cabinet and seized the large bottle of vodka. He looked around the room for a few moments, spied a couch that looked expensive and new, and proceeded to dump the vodka calmly and coolly all over it, making sure to disperse the alcohol evenly from end to end. Then he marched over to the fireplace, snatched up the book of matches that lay on the mantlepiece above, struck one, and tossed the tiny torch onto the drenched couch, which burst instantly into flames.

"Drink to *that*, you spiteful bitch!" he bellowed, storming out of the house.

Overweight, underpaid, and out of options, the real Mitch Dilton had hated his life. He was a lazy, middle-aged man with a limited education and an incredibly dull and unfulfilling job as a security guard at Stocknorton Super-Maximum Security Prison. He lived in a shabby, one-bedroom house that he couldn't afford to repair, and drove a bad-tempered clunker of a 1983 Dodge Diplomat that he couldn't afford to replace. His high cholesterol and risk of heart problems had deprived him of his favorite foods, damning him to a diet of oatmeal, rice cakes, and steamed vegetables. His wife had divorced him a year ago, her lawyer had taken him to the cleaners, and he hadn't seen his son – or half his paycheck – since. He had the onset of premature arthritis in his fingers, a hunk of Desert Storm shrapnel in his ass, and two cavities that he resolved would remain rotting in his mouth until he could find a dentist that would fix them for free. All of this tagged merrily along behind the most recent cymbal-clashing monkey on his back, which took the malevolent form of excruciating cravings for nicotine as he struggled to kick the cigarette habit. Sweat beads on his forehead and invisible insects crawling across his skin had become sensations of regularity that made his long, monotonous, graveyard shift hours – he usually clocked in from ten at night to six in the morning – infinitely worse. But the real Mitch Dilton no longer had cause to worry about any of these miseries, because the real Mitch Dilton had been killed, disposed of, and replaced two weeks ago.

Just as he had done every night for the past two weeks, the faux Mitch Dilton used his keycard to enter Stocknorton's big security center and was greeted only by the massive banks of computers wired to every alarm, surveillance camera, laser trip beam, automated machine gun, and electronic door in the prison. The only voice he heard in his ears was the humming of the costly equipment gobbling up its fair share of the taxpayers' money with every passing second, and the only eyes staring back into his were the numerous glowing monitors that showed him any corner of the complex he desired to see.

"I'm in," he said aloud.

"Good," crackled the voice of KnuckleDuster, coming in clearly through a tiny radio transmitter planted in the faux Mitch's ear. "Now you're going to fix the cameras. Go to the console at the front-center of the room – the one with the big monitor above it – and press the green, triangular button. You'll be asked to enter a password. Today's password is 'herbiethelovebug'. All lowercased, no spaces."

"You're kidding, right?"

"Get on with it."

The faux Mitch shrugged his shoulders and entered the unlikely password, after which he was treated to a bare-bones menu screen.

"The cameras in this prison each film on their own individual hard drives, rather than tapes or discs," explained KnuckleDuster. "From that console, you control every camera in the complex. Now, insert a blank loop into the program. Once you've done that, the cameras will maintain an unchanging front of an empty room or corridor. We'll be able to walk right past them without having our images recorded, and no one reviewing the false footage in the future will be the wiser."

Looks pretty straightforward, thought the faux Mitch, who had dabbled in this sort of thing before. *Ah, there we go.*

"Is it done?" asked KnuckleDuster.

"Piece of cake."

"All right, on to phase two," the voice crackled in his ear. "We're driving a marked prison van, so we're mostly above suspicion. I've already been granted access to the yard. We will now approach the building's main entrance. Come around and let us in. If you meet any other guards on the way, remember to act natural. You belong here. Say you're going to the lounge for a soda or something."

The faux Mitch nodded again, exited the security center through the only door, and began moving down the metallic corridor, making sure to adopt the real Mitch's lazy, ambling shuffle, slouching his back slightly, plunging his hands deep into his pockets.

"Hey, Mitch. Whatcha know?" a ruggedly handsome, sandy-haired guard appeared from nowhere and greeted him with a smile.

From his consistent studies of the real Mitch's life, the faux Mitch knew this to be the outgoing, overly friendly Pete Allen, and he knew how to reply.

"Hey yourself, Pete," he said. "How's your wife and kidneys?"

Pete laughed – with genuine humor, the faux Mitch feared – at the piece of ancient corn, and gave him a friendly punch on the shoulder.

"Actually, it's the girls' second birthday tomorrow," he said, proudly. "Or today, dependin' on how ya look at it. It is after midnight, isn't it? I'm tellin' ya, twins' birthday parties can be really rough. Still, I'd rather be there than here. I don't care for these night shifts, Mitch. I mean, this place is so secure that it'd be impossible for any o' these creeps to bust outta their cells, but it still gives ya the jitters just thinkin' about it. Am I right?"

"I try not to think about it," said the faux Mitch.

"I've heard stories," Pete continued. "They say this place is haunted with the ghosts o' the inhuman monsters who've died here over the decades. Ya remember Tad Milton?"

"Yeah, he was given early retirement last year," said the faux Mitch, recalling the information from his vast mental database of Stocknorton knowledge. "He was having heart troubles."

"Heart troubles, my ass," said Pete. "Tad was disgustingly healthy. Never used any of his sick days or anything. Then one day, during a lockdown, he got himself sealed inside the electroshock room down on the third level where all the real loonies live, and when they finally let him out…Mitch, his hair was completely white; as a *sheet*. And he couldn't stop shakin'. He never told anyone what happened down there, but it's pretty friggin' obvious that somethin' scared him shitless. And he was no good for anythin' after that. They had no choice but to let the poor geezer go."

"That's certainly a good Halloween story," said the faux Mitch, with just the right amount of skepticism.

"It wasn't Halloween, it was the middle o' summer," said Pete. "The spirits come out whenever they feel like it. You'll probably think I'm crackin' up too, but I could swear I've heard footsteps where there were no people, and heard laughter comin' outta empty cells. I don't know if the ghosts can actually hurt us, Mitch, but they're definitely among us, and they're extremely pissed off."

"Hmm," said the faux Mitch, wishing that Pete would shut up and go away.

"But y'know who I fear the most?" said Pete, grabbing the other man's shoulder suddenly, as if for spiritual support. "The Reaper, that's who. When he was free, he dressed in a black cloak that concealed his entire body, and he carried a long scythe that he used to hack people to death with. And there was no pattern to his killings; no method to his madness. He murdered indiscriminately, killin' every living person he laid eyes on. Just walkin' into his field of vision was what got ya killed. Ya could've been an old man or a child or a pregnant woman, it didn't matter to him. He just killed ya. They say that he was the very incarnation o' death itself; the real Grim Reaper made flesh. It's reported that his body count was close to a thousand by the time they finally caught him. And they say that when they removed his hood, he was so horrible to look at that they made him wear the cloak all through his trial, and he was still wearin' it when they sent him here. That was way back in the twenties. He lived to be a hundred and thirteen, and only died a couple o' years ago down there in his cell. He spent nearly *ninety years* in this prison, and he hated every single minute of it. I wouldn't be surprised if he stayed behind just long enough to slaughter every last one of us. And who knows? Maybe he's the one who got to Tad."

"Yeah, fascinating," said the faux Mitch. "Look, I was on my way to the bathroom..."

"Man, it gives me the shivers just thinkin' about it," said Pete. "Anyway, I'm meeting some of the other guys in the lounge. Denny brought *Who Framed Roger Rabbit* on DVD. That'll take our minds off this scary Reaper shit. Ya wanna join us?"

"Thanks, but someone's gotta man the security center," said the faux Mitch. "I really only came out to take a leak."

"Okay, then," said Pete. "You've probably seen it a hundred times already anyway. So have I, but I can never get enough o' that fuckin' rabbit. And I get Stonehenge in my pants every time his wife comes onscreen. She has tits to Tuesday all right. And that cigar-smokin' baby always cracks me up. See ya later, Mitch."

"Right, see ya," said the faux Mitch, already continuing down the corridor.

What an idiot! he thought to himself, after rounding the next corner. *Loudmouthed windbag. If you're gonna relentlessly talk someone's ear off, at least talk about something interesting. Fucking retard just keeps prattling on and on about ghosts and his kids' birthday and cartoon chicks with big jugs. Just yak-yak-yakkity-fucking-yak!*

The faux Mitch was still recovering from the mind-numbing experience when he reached the wide open, almost cathedral-like foyer that greeted both visitors and personnel using the prison's only standard entrance. The foyer was home to an X-ray machine, a metal detector through which all comers and goers were required to pass, and usually at least two heavily armed guards.

"Evenin', Mitch," said one of them, a well-built man called Rick, his visored helmet obscuring his eyes. "Your shift ain't over already, is it?"

"Naw, I'm here to oversee a prisoner exchange," said the faux Mitch, pressing the palm of his right hand flat against the electronic panel mounted on the wall inches from the three foot thick steel door leading out into the regularly patrolled yard. "We're sending one of our better-behaved boys to Rikers in exchange for one of their bigger nuisances. The island couldn't handle him. He's a real bastard. He put several guards and inmates in the infirmary on multiple occasions."

"How'd he do that?" asked Rick.

"He's a biter," said the faux Mitch, as the panel scanned the prints on his splayed fingertips – identical to those of the real Mitch – identified him as authorized personnel, and electronically commanded the huge door to slide open. "An animal. Would you believe that he actually managed to escape from the island on three separate occasions?"

"You're shittin' me."

"No, honest," said the faux Mitch. "He almost made it to shore once. The guards had to damn near run him down with a motorboat to recapture him."

"Well, he'll find that the game is played a little differently around here," Rick said, with a smirk. "Right, Nate?"

"That's for fuckin' sure," said the guard called Nate, hefting his 'nut gun' proudly. "He gets outta line once and I'll blast him up the ass with this. Rikers is gonna look like a summer camp to him in no time."

The door finally yawned all the way open to reveal KnuckleDuster dressed in a Rikers Island guard's uniform, and, slouching dejectedly in front of him, an Arab man in an orange prison jumpsuit. His ankles were clapped in leg irons, his hands were cuffed behind his back, and a leather muzzle kept his mouth shut.

"Is that to keep him from biting?" asked Rick.

"Yeah," said KnuckleDuster, pushing the Arab along in front of him. "You can leave it on him if you want, but I'd recommend having his teeth filed down too."

"You won't mind if we do a quick search," said Nate, in a tone that made it clear he was not seeking permission. "I don't doubt you Rikers boys are thorough, but we're called maximum security for a reason. I'm sure you understand."

"Of course," said KnuckleDuster. "By all means."

In quick but exemplary fashion, Rick and Nate patted their hands up and down the Arab's body, from his shoulders to his hobbled ankles.

"Clean?" asked KnuckleDuster.

"So it would seem, but give us a moment," said Nate.

With that, Nate yanked the Arab's pants unceremoniously down and thrust two gloved fingers up inside the man's anus, while Rick delivered a couple of light swats to the prisoner's genitals in order to expose anything he might have hidden in the area, during all of which the prisoner made no sound.

"Nothing there," said Rick. "Check his mouth."

"If you bite me, dipshit, I'll beat you to death right here," threatened Nate, unzipping the front of the muzzle, prying open the prisoner's mouth, and poking around inside with the same two fingers he had used to probe his backside. "Naw, he's clean."

Nate replaced the prisoner's muzzle while Rick pulled his pants back up, then they shoved him stumbling through the metal detector, which went off only because of his restraints.

"Here's all the paperwork," said KnuckleDuster, showing the two guards a clipboard laden with photocopied forms. "These are our copies. Your warden has already received his own."

"Everything seems to be in order," said Rick. "Go on through."

KnuckleDuster nodded, handed Rick his sidearm, then walked through the metal detector, which sounded off, loudly.

"Got something else you need to declare?" asked Nate.

"I'm afraid so, gentlemen," said KnuckleDuster, stepping back from the detector. "Promise you won't stare for too long."

KnuckleDuster pulled off both his black gloves, unbuttoned his cuffs, and rolled up his blue sleeves, allowing the room's fluorescent lighting to reflect off his steel prostheses with all the glimmering brilliance of a sunbeam off the hood of a brand new silver car.

"Holy shit!" exclaimed Nate. "What the hell happened to you?"

"Like you heard," said KnuckleDuster, a wry smile tugging at the corner of his mouth, "he's a biter."

Leaving Rick and Nate with their mouths hanging open, the faux Mitch led KnuckleDuster and the Arab prisoner out of the foyer and down the corridor.

"Did you have any trouble getting in?" KnuckleDuster asked his subordinate, once they were out of earshot.

"Not a bit," answered the faux Mitch. "Thanks to my change in identity, I can open any door and walk past any camera or security device in this place. Getting into one of the most secure prisons in the world was as simple as walking through the front door."

Reaching the elevator, the faux Mitch punched in the five-digit access code on the wall-mounted keypad, and the steel double-doors slid open to reveal an interior that was large enough to accommodate a dozen people comfortably. The trio stepped inside, and the faux Mitch jabbed the '2' button.

"He's down on level two, seven doors down from where we get off," he said. "On the right."

The speedy elevator had already descended to its destination and opened its doors by the time the faux Mitch had completed his sentence, and he led his two accomplices out of the car and down the new corridor, past rows of thick steel doors on either side. When the party reached the seventh door on the right, the faux Mitch reached into his left breast pocket, produced his keycard, and swiped it through the wall-mounted reader, and, with a clank and a hum, the door slid open, allowing access into – and out of – the little cell.

"Time to go, Qasim," said KnuckleDuster to the Arab terrorist lying quietly on his cot. "Your liberation is at hand."

"You must be the one they call KnuckleDuster, correct?" said Qasim, sitting up. "Malik told me to expect you."

"Exactly how much of this operation have you been briefed on?" asked KnuckleDuster.

"Not so much that I would mind hearing more," answered Qasim.

"Fine," said KnuckleDuster. "I'll give you the *Reader's Digest* version, since we don't exactly have all night. Now, this guard here actually works for us. His name is Carl Preston, but, thanks to a shitload of plastic surgery, voice work, and mannerism training, he looks, sounds, and behaves exactly like a former guard here called Mitch Dilton, right down to fingerprints, skin pigment, and number of fillings in his teeth, along with knowing even the tiniest details about Stocknorton, its personnel and inmates, and its inner workings that the real Dilton would know. No expense has been spared to transform him into a completely identical copy of Dilton, all for the purpose of granting us access into the prison. He will remain here for the next six months, doing Dilton's job and leading Dilton's life, so as not to arouse any suspicion. Then he will resign and disappear with a very generous pay package from Mr. Kubritz. And all this ties directly into the second aspect of the plan. Feast your eyes on this."

KnuckleDuster turned to the shackled Arab he had brought in, and, after undoing the various zippers and snaps on the leather muzzle, removed it from his face, leaving his features exposed for all to see, and Qasim let out an incredulous gasp when he got his first clear look.

"Why, he looks exactly like me!" he exclaimed.

"A volunteer was picked from among your most trusted and loyal followers to undergo the same procedures as Preston," KnuckleDuster explained. "He will take your place in here as a decoy and serve out the remainder of your life sentence for you."

"It's like looking into a mirror!" Qasim marveled. "My own mother wouldn't be able to tell us apart! Tell me, who is it?"

"It is I, my noble leader," the shackled prisoner spoke in Qasim's voice, bowing his head respectfully as he did so. "Rashid."

"Rashid! In the name of everything holy that's left in this world, I don't believe it! My old friend and faithful lieutenant? Can it really be you?"

"It is indeed, my noble leader," said Rashid. "When I learned of the operation to deliver you from the chains of the oppressors, I volunteered eagerly for this role."

"But you will be giving up your whole life," said Qasim. "You will have no choice but to remain here until the day you die."

"I have resigned myself to it, my noble leader," said Rashid. "I...I have accepted that the stature and meaning of my life is small when compared to yours. I have known you and worked with you for many years, and I have always seen you for the truly great man you are. But how can you be great when chained up in here like an animal in a cage? No, my noble leader, our cause needs your guidance and leadership, whereas my little role in the grand scheme can be easily refilled. I would consider it an honor and a privilege to surrender my insignificant life in the furtherance of your glory."

Qasim smiled warmly, his eyes moistened, and he placed one hand over his heart as he struggled to find words. It was clear that the man was deeply moved. Finally, he spoke.

"Rashid, you have made me glad," he said. "My breast swells with pride in our friendship. It is said that there is no greater love than that which compels a man to lay down his life for his friend. I am honored to be counted among your friends, Rashid. And while you are woefully mistaken in your assumption that I will ever be able to replace you, you ultimately do right by trading your existence for your master's. After all, what would this world be...without me?"

"The guards think we're making a prisoner exchange," said KnuckleDuster, removing the handcuffs and leg irons from Rashid's person and advancing on Qasim. "We'll put these on you and walk you right past the stupid jerks, out into the van I drove here, and be off without anyone being the wiser."

KnuckleDuster finished fastening the restraints to Qasim's wrists and ankles, then marched him out of the cell, and Rashid, with no visible show of regret, sat down on the cot where he would be spending the rest of his natural life as Preston swiped his keycard through the reader to close the door on him.

"Preston, you'll be staying here to finish out the rest of your shift after you've escorted us to the door," said KnuckleDuster. "Set the cameras back to normal and deactivate the loop. Make sure that no evidence exists that anything out of the ordinary has happened here tonight."

"Aye-aye, sir," said Preston, throwing KnuckleDuster a salute before the three of them began walking back down the corridor towards the elevator.

His mind overwhelmed with black thoughts of hatred and bloody retribution, William stormed into the Rat Hole and saw that the lights were off. No one was there. That was unusual, but agreeable. The last thing he needed was any witnesses to what he was about to do.

They'd just try to talk me out of it, like they were my parents or something, he thought, as he stomped across the lounge, making a beeline for the unassuming wooden door on the far side of the room, next to the water cooler. *Well, I don't need any parenting! For once in my life I'm going to be a man and stand on my own two feet! And if this is the only way to show the world that I'm not a weakling and a coward, then so be it!*

Arriving at the door, William snatched the key hanging from the nearby hook, thrust it into the lock, turned it to the right, and flung the door open, revealing a closet stocked with a daunting variety of weapons; blades, explosives, scads of Carolyn's pet gadgets, and lots and lots of guns.

This ought to do the trick, thought William, selecting a Magnum 44 handgun and holding it up to examine it appreciatively. *The same gun Clint Eastwood used in the Dirty Harry movies. It'll make a beautiful mess.*

William had just finished loading the gun with ammunition and was about to take his leave when he heard the bathroom door at the other end of the room creak open, and whirled around to see Leeza emerge.

"Where the hell did you come from?" he asked, startled.

"I've been in that bathroom for a solid hour," Leeza answered.

"At my age, one's body can be somewhat unpredictable. Speaking of unpredictable, what do you think you're doing with that gun?"

"I thought I'd give Rachel and Jason an early Christmas present," said William. "Right between the eyes. They won't feel a thing."

"So, I gather your coming-of-age rite didn't go exactly as planned," guessed Leeza, walking towards him.

"It was nothing!" William shouted, his voice shaky. "Nothing! It was all a cruel trick from the very start! Just a well-laid plan to humiliate and degrade me!"

"I see," said Leeza, able to work things out for herself without hearing the gruesome details.

"A guy can only take so much!" William shouted, becoming excited again, waving the Magnum carelessly around, fresh tears spilling from his eyes, projectiles of spittle shooting out from his gnashing teeth. "I have my breaking point too, y'know! And they're about to find that out!"

"Committing a double homicide isn't going to make anything better," said Leeza, approaching the wrathful teenager calmly and cautiously.

"On the contrary, I think it stands to improve my mood greatly," said William.

"Why don't you give me the gun, William?" Leeza suggested, gently, extending her hand.

"Back off!" the boy roared, snapping the Magnum up to aim the long train tunnel of a barrel at Leeza's chest. "Back the fuck off and don't come any closer, or I'll blow you away too! Don't think I won't! Just try me! Test me!"

"William, look at yourself," said Leeza. "You're not behaving rationally. You need to calm down."

"Don't tell me when to calm down! I'll tell *you* when to calm down!" William ranted, his gun hand trembling.

"William, please put down that gun before something goes wrong," said Leeza. "Don't make me fight you for it."

"Fight me for it?" a shrill, ironic laugh intermingled with his sobs of rage. "Did I hear you right, Grandma Moses? Old lady, you wouldn't be able to wrestle this gun away from me if I was unconscious!"

William barely had time to conclude this declaration before Leeza took a sudden, giant step forward, catching the boy off his guard, and struck him on the right side of his chest with the flat edge of her hand. William gasped in pain and collapsed to his knees, coughing and wheezing, while Leeza snatched up the gun.

"What...the hell...was that?" William groaned, pressing his hand against flesh that was already turning black-and-blue.

"Never tangle with an alumnus of the Hitler Youth," Leeza replied, opening the Magnum's cylinder and emptying the six bullets into her palm.

"Great," William winced, rising slowly to his feet once again, only to flop down into a nearby chair, his arms and legs stretched out in abject defeat. "I just got my ass kicked by a seventy-five-year-old woman. And up until a moment ago, I didn't think I could feel any worse. I guess I just don't understand anything. I give up. That's the only thing left to do. I give up."

"Don't give up," said Leeza. "Conquer. That's what I did. Too many people are slaves to their emotions, and it leads only to confusion and remorse. Conquer your emotions, young William. Let your head rule your heart. That's what I've always done."

"That's all very well to say, but what about the emotions you can't control? Like love, for example?"

"There's no such thing as love," Leeza stated, bluntly. "Not in the sense in which most people take it, anyway."

"What do you mean?"

"All this business about love being some sort of divine, universal force that fills people's hearts with magic and throws predestined soul mates together is a lot of stuff and nonsense," Leeza elaborated. " 'Love' is nothing more than a word we've assigned to a peculiar and as yet unexplained chemical reaction in our brains that clouds our judgment and handicaps our common sense. Moreover, it is my professional medical opinion that there are a number of people in this world who lack the capacity to fall in love, due to some sort of chemical deficiency in the brain. Hmph. The lucky ones, say I."

"Jeez, that's kind of a cold way of looking at it," said William.

"The truth is sometimes harsh," said Leeza, "but I'm afraid that so-called 'love' is just another intangible obstruction to the more important things in life."

"Like what?"

"Like ambition, success, and fully realizing one's own potential, rather than sacrificing all that one is worth and giving oneself up entirely to another mortal being," said Leeza. "How long does love last? These days it dies in the blink of an eye. But one's achievements – the things one has done to elevate oneself above commonality – live forever. Strive for that, William. Strive for greatness, and do not allow yourself to be weighed down by giddy simpletons who attempt to superimpose their problems and neuroses onto you. Emotions are like viruses, my young friend. They handicap you and your ability to succeed."

"I...suppose you make a couple of good points," William conceded, "but I can't believe that there isn't more to it than that. I just can't."

"Of course you can't," said Leeza. "In the thick of your despair, you turn to wishful thinking and unfounded hope, as do we all. But you'll learn the truth one day, even if you do not do yourself a huge favor and heed my counsel now."

As William sat sullenly, absorbing all of the poison-dipped words Leeza had just used to describe the emotion hailed widely as humanity's most positive and precious, he found himself suddenly regretting every joke that he and the other Vigilantes had ever enjoyed at the old woman's expense concerning her antisocial surliness. She wasn't merely the stereotypical 'cranky, cantankerous old bear with a heart of gold' for which most of her friends took her. Clearly here was a sad, bitter, lonely old harpy who had never been lovingly embraced by another human being, and had effectively pushed away anyone who had ever tried to get close to her. Born in a country that, at the time, had forged its young people from the fires of fear, hatred, and intolerance, Leeza's heart had shriveled like a raisin, and her once striking good looks had wizened under the ravages of time without ever being put to the practical uses for which they had been designed.

Weighing the keynotes of Leeza's little lecture, William could almost bring himself to be thoroughly and utterly convinced that she was a soulless, unfeeling shell, bereft of any and all affection or human spirit; as detached and cold-blooded as a reptile. But then he thought of her staring boldly down the barrel of one of the world's most powerful handguns, all in aid of preventing him from executing a mad plan that, while bearing no consequence for her personally, would have destroyed his young life and ended at least two others, and he knew that, on some level, she must care, and she must regard him as a friend. The feeling was there, buried however deeply, but it wasn't a characteristic that she cared to show to other people. It seemed to William that, in her own way, she had made herself just as vulnerable tonight as he had, and he felt a keen responsibility to reciprocate. Despite the sprawling difference in age, they were essentially the same; two confused, dejected individuals walking around lonely. As misery tended to appreciate company, William saw no reason why tonight should be any different.

"Enough philosophy," the boy said, wiping the back of his hand across his sore, red eyes before replacing his glasses and getting to his feet. "My stomach's growling. The drive-thru at Wendy's stays open till two. Wanna grab a bite?"

"I don't eat fast food," said Leeza, reverting immediately to type, her characteristic need to distance people rearing its head once more. "You Americans and your incessant gluttony for junk. It's disgusting. I shudder to think what you all must look like on the inside."

"Leeza, I'm trying to be nice here," said William. "Stop being such a bitchy old tight-ass. Take your nose out of the air, get down off your high horse, and come have a fucking cheeseburger. I'm buying."

Leeza's eyebrows raised almost undetectably for two seconds, then she seemed to lose an inch in height as her shoulders relaxed and her perpetual frown softened.

"I'll have a salad," she conceded, "but that's all."

Qasim Al-Fulani, now smartly clad in a navy blue business suit that eloquently set off his tall, muscular frame – accessorized with a pale blue turban, a pair of shiny black shoes, and a pair of glistening gold cufflinks in the shape of tigers' heads – stood proudly and triumphantly in the middle of the casino's basement, taking his time in lighting a cigarette, relishing his first luxurious puff since his incarceration nine months ago.

"You underestimate us, Parker," he said, his stance casual, the cigarette protruding from the corner of his mouth, his hands stuck into his hip pockets. "You really do. You and your whole misguided race of weak-willed, sanctimonious, gadget-crazy nincompoops."

Gary didn't reply.

"I suppose you think us to be cavemen," said Qasim. "Outmoded savages from an outmoded civilization. I suppose you think us to be dinosaurs, made all but extinct. But consider, Parker, that the most dangerous of dinosaurs never became extinct at all. The snakes, crocodiles, alligators, and sharks have all been going strong since the Mesozoic Era. They survived and adapted where their less intelligent and able brethren fell by the wayside, and after two hundred and forty million years of evolution, they are still feared, and they still rule with an iron fist over their own little piece of this mammals' world."

Gary didn't reply.

"It is the same with us," Qasim continued. "You Westerners may think yourselves to be far superior to us in the arenas of society, economy, and technology, but the very things that put you so far ahead will ultimately be your undoing. You grow soft, while we, possessing so much less than you do, are willing to give up so much more, up to and including our very lives. We are the dangerous dinosaurs, Parker, who pretend to be extinct while we lie in wait for the kill. We are not afflicted with the warm blood and doubting mind with which God cursed the mammal, and we're a far more effective enemy for it."

Gary didn't reply.

"Why, just look at the contemporary fears of your society," said Qasim. "You're all going out of your minds worrying about our getting hold of an atom bomb, which you know we would not hesitate to use in the furtherance of your destruction, yet you have silos full of the things – thousands of them – wasting away for want of a single purpose, and you do not fire a solitary shot! Why, if we were in your position we'd waste no time in exterminating you like an infestation of carpenter ants in a log cabin! It's your misguided conscience and rose-colored belief in the sanctity of life that makes you weak, and that is why you will never be rid of us!"

Gary didn't reply. He was in no condition. His naked body was suspended horizontally from the basement's ceiling, hanging limply in a tangled web of iron chains, his limbs spread-eagled so as to make his tortured lungs fight for every shuddering breath, ten-pound weights secured to his forearms and calves. His face was battered and bloody, his body was a roadmap of bruises from the severe beating Qasim had given him before hoisting him off the floor, and his jaw was slack as he gasped for air, hanging in exhausted acceptance of his fate, like a fly in a spider's trap.

"I do wish you'd contribute something to this discussion, friend Parker," said Qasim, looking up at his captive. "I had quite enough talking to myself when I was in that cell; the cell in which you put me. Well, the shoe's on the other foot now, isn't it, you great, steaming hypocrite?"

Qasim punched a large, red button mounted on the face of the nearest steel pillar, and the awful chains, like so many clutching fingers, released Gary's pain-wracked body all at once with a loud 'clank' that echoed off the concrete walls, and the helpless Vigilante fell fifteen feet, landed hard on the floor, and uttered a pitiful cry of agony, his limbs feeling as heavy and lifeless as leaden weights.

"We're missing something here," Qasim, standing triumphantly over his enemy's fallen form, scratched his chin and tapped his foot. "The experience isn't quite...complete. Certainly I'm having the time of my life here, but there's this peculiar void. I feel an additional element is called for."

Gary groaned. Qasim kicked him in the side.

"Quiet while I'm thinking," he scolded. "Now, what in the...ah yes, of course! How could I have been so negligent?"

Turning his back casually on his broken enemy, Qasim raised his hands into the air and clapped them twice. Mere seconds later, the door at the far end of the room opened, and the cockroach Phillips appeared, pushing a wheelchair carrying the person of Peg, still in her bathrobe, her wrists and ankles manacled securely.

"We need an audience," Qasim said.

"Gary!" Peg cried out with horror and concern as she beheld the state of her friend.

"Oh, Gary! Gary!" Phillips parroted in a shrill, mocking voice, waggling his fingers about and cackling like a forest imp.

"That's more like it," said Qasim. "Now that we've corrected that little problem, on with the festivities."

Still lying defenseless on his belly, like a run-down, discarded mechanical soldier, Gary watched Qasim march cheerfully out of his field of vision for a moment, then return promptly, carrying a wooden mallet in one hand, and four sharp, wooden stakes the size of railroad spikes in the other.

Oh, fuck, thought Gary.

"What are those for? What are you going to do?" asked Peg, frantically.

"Just you watch," said Qasim, "and know that your turn will come soon enough."

If I could just...stand up, thought Gary, tightening every muscle in his face as he endeavored to will his punished body to move, and actually succeeded in lifting his upper torso a few inches off the floor.

"Down, boy," said Qasim, stepping on Gary's back, pressing him down again beneath his heel. "We're just getting started."

Kneeling by his incapacitated enemy, Qasim pinched the length of Gary's right calf with his thumb and forefinger until he found the meatiest zone.

"Yes, that will do," he said, hefting the mallet in his right hand and one of the stakes in his left. "That will do quite nicely."

Then came the incredible pain, and Gary screamed as loudly as he could remember ever having screamed before as he felt the stake being driven through the back of his leg like a tent peg into soft soil, tearing through muscle beneath the force of each hammer blow, until he felt the spine-vibrating anguish of the stake's tip striking against the back of his tibia bone, barring its exit through the front of his shin.

"You monster! You bastard!" Peg shrieked, crying as she wrestled furiously against her bonds. "You monster! Stop it! You'll kill him!"

"He's not that lucky," said Qasim. "He has a long road ahead of him yet before his lights wink out for the final time. Now, let's move on to an arm."

Gary's body shuddered with agony, and his bottom lip bled from the force with which he had bitten down on it as Qasim moved away from the pulped flesh and geyser of blood that Gary's right leg had become and knelt beside his left arm.

"Enjoying yourself, Parker?" Qasim sneered. "You should have known better than to cross me. I swore I'd have my revenge, didn't I? Believe me, I'm just warming up. When it comes to matters of blood-soaked retribution, my imagination goes beyond all established limits. Even now, your blind colleague hangs by his thumbs in the other room, turning over and over in his mind the knowledge that I shall return soon to pluck out his useless eyes...and eat them!"

"I'm going...to kill you...you bastard," Gary hissed through clenched teeth, the stake still standing upright in his leg. "This time...I'm going...to kill you!"

"Order in the court!" Qasim demanded, bringing the mallet down on Gary's head. "Any further disrespect and you'll be fined!"

Gary groaned as Qasim clasped his left wrist, stretched his limp arm out to its full extention, positioned a stake over the center width of Gary's forearm, and smashed down with the mallet. Again Gary screamed, and off to the side, Peg could be heard retching into her lap, choking on phlegm and bile as she sobbed and wheezed uncontrollably. She tried to close her eyes, but Phillips pried and held them open with his fingers, forcing her to continue viewing the grisly scene.

"Oh, if I had a hammer," Qasim began to sing as he readied himself for yet another blow, "I'd hammer in the mooooorning. I'd hammer in the evening. All over this laaaaand!"

The hated mallet struck again, completing the stake's impalement of the arm, driving it between the radius and ulna bones and out the underside of the limb to strike against solid concrete. Unwilling to give the terrorist any satisfaction whatsoever, Gary endeavored to suffer in silence, but he could not stop several cries from escaping his raw throat.

"There, there, only two more to go," said Qasim, moving over to the right arm. "Then we'll do something with that tongue. A meat skewer, perhaps?"

Gary clenched his teeth together so hard that he thought they would break as he struggled to remain as stoic as possible under the inhuman circumstances, sweat pouring down into his squeezed-shut eyes and what seemed like gallons of blood spewing from his wounds. Qasim, enjoying himself immensely, was preparing to drive his third stake when the door opened and Malik appeared, a grave expression clouding his face which did not change even as he beheld, with callous indifference, the gruesome menagerie of gore and cruelty spread out before him.

"Qasim, I would require a word in your shell-like ear," he said.

"Could it possibly wait?" asked Qasim. "I'm really rather occupied."

"I'm afraid it's urgent," Malik insisted.

Qasim sighed – as if he were an astronomer being pulled away from a telescope's view of a rarely recurring comet – dropped the mallet and stakes, and joined Malik at the door. Blood pounding in his ears, Gary could make out only a few scraps of the conversation, but it didn't take the combined powers of Albert Einstein and Sherlock Holmes to deduce that the Arabs, particularly Qasim, were displeased about something.

"No!" Qasim was rasping. "No, no, no! I've waited too long and planned too well for this!"

"Use your head, you stubborn mule!" said Malik. "They outnumber us, and we can't risk you being sent back to prison! After the expense of this operation, Norman will never agree to another! The only prudent course open to us is retreat!"

"It's not fair! It can't end like this!"

"For the time being, it has to! Come! The tunnel comes out approximately four miles north of here. If we go now, we can make it."

Qasim glared, unblinking, at Malik, who matched the steely stare. Then he looked back over his shoulder at Gary, still helpless and at his mercy, and growled with frustration.

"Curse the gods!" he lamented. "All right, fine! I will accompany you, Malik, but this is far from over! I'll be back to finish what I've started!"

Gary watched the pair of them disappear, and wondered what on earth could have precipitated their hurried exit. Then he heard a squeal of surprise, a squishy sound, and a choked gurgle of surrender, and, with some effort, turned his head to see Phillips slump to the floor, a dagger driven directly through his scrawny neck.

"Sorry we took so long," said Sushi, the wielder of the dagger, as he struck the manacle binding Peg's right wrist with the blade of his *katana*, popping it open. "We had no idea."

"Holy shit, Gary," Zeke whistled, scratching his forehead. "Can I get you a Band-Aid?"

Gary mumbled something semi-coherently.

"Sorry, boss, I didn't quite catch that," said Zeke, holding his hat in his hands and lowering his ear closer to Gary's bleeding mouth.

"I said...get these fucking stakes...out of my body...dumbass."

Nothing like winding and squirming your way through an air vent to put your hips in perspective, thought Carla, popping open the grate at the end of the narrow tunnel and poking her head out into the darker, more confined section of the basement that housed the sprawling banks of machinery used for generating the thousands of volts of electricity necessary to power the energy-guzzling casino. *I might as well face it. As I get older, my metabolism is going to slow down and I'm going to have to cram in some extra gym time.*

Somersaulting out of the vent and landing on her feet, Carla was immediately aware of the electric presence in the dimly-lit cavern. Signs warning of high voltage were plastered all over the walls surrounding the humming, vibrating machinery, and as she turned to face the crackling monstrosities, her hair actually began to stand on end, responding to the static dancing through the air, making Carla feel as if she would burst into flames if she so much as rubbed her hands together.

Time to pull the plug on this popsicle stand, thought Carla, who had broken away from the rest of the group in order to do just that. *Looks complicated, though. If I pull the wrong switch...*

Carla didn't have time to finish working out her plan of attack before something cold and metallic seized her by the back of her neck and hoisted her off her feet as if she weighed nothing, and her hands leapt reflexively to her throat and clawed at the strong, tightening fingers as she kicked her legs impotently in the air.

"I daresay curiosity is about to kill another cat," growled a sinister voice from behind.

Carla said 'Urk!' as her assailant shook her up and down like a ketchup bottle, then flung her into the wall. As her face hit the wall and she slumped dizzily to the floor, she wondered briefly if what were supposed to be her super sensitive hearing aids were due for a tune-up.

I swear, if one more fucking idiot sneaks up on me today...

"Three points, and the crowd roars!" exclaimed KnuckleDuster, tearing off his leather jacket and gloves and tossing them aside, leaving himself stripped to the waist. "Not bad, eh? I lose my arms, but get these total gunboats in return! Just goes to show you that one man's crippling handicap is another man's claim to power!"

I used to fight normal people, thought Carla, pulling herself to her feet. *I know I did because I remember it. Joe Blow crooks with crowbars and guns. Those were the good old days. When did it become all about these psychotic, deformed refugees from Ripley's Believe It or Not!?*

"You shouldn't be down here, girly," said KnuckleDuster. "Mr. K doesn't like people going past the velvet ropes. I'm afraid I'm gonna have to give you a spanking, you naughty, naughty girl."

"I won't make it that easy for you," said Carla, launching herself feet first at the bare-chested, metal-armed man. "With me, you'll find you've got a fight on your hands!"

His reflexes surprisingly quick, KnuckleDuster seized Carla's right ankle before it could connect with his chest, spun around swinging her by the leg, then released his grip, letting her fly against one of the larger generators. The hapless Vigilante crashed into the towering machine and slumped to the floor, stunned.

"Haven't you heard a word I've said, you stupid bitch?" said KnuckleDuster, advancing on her. "I don't *have* any hands!"

"Turning tail and running at the first sign of trouble? I must confess to being very disappointed in you, Malik," Kubritz, flanked by a pair of armed bodyguards, spoke into his cell phone as he marched briskly down the corridor's river of red carpet.

"I hesitate to play the blame game, Norman," Malik's voice replied, "but if you had been more proficient in your pursuit of these undesirables, then it would not be necessary for Qasim and me to take this regrettable course of action. Such as it is, we must abide by a saying that is one of our people's oldest, and has particular relevance here."

"And that is?"

"When all your plans go tits-up, run like bloody hell," said Malik. "We are returning to the East. I'll see you in a couple of years when the heat's off. In the meantime, consider all debts settled."

With that final, curt sign-off, the phone went dead. Kubritz cursed under his breath, turned off the phone, and stuffed it into his coat pocket.

Lazy ingrate, he thought. *And he wonders why he isn't ruling the world yet. I shall have to deal with this myself.*

Emerging dramatically from the heavy, wooden double-doors leading from the 'Employees Only' area into the casino, Kubritz waddled across the vast room, pushing his way with polite urgency past frolicking gamblers, tray-bearing waiters, and scantily-clad cigarette girls until he reached the large stage, upon which a jazz orchestra was playing with soul, and being, for the most part, unabashedly ignored by the throng of chatty, dice-throwing, card-flipping pleasure-seekers.

"Excuse me!" Kubritz called out, taking hold of the microphone in one hand, while his stinking cigar continued to smolder between the index and middle fingers of the other. "Excuse me, everyone! Quiet down, please! If I could have your attention for just a moment, please!"

The crowd was excited, but it didn't take more than a few seconds for the commanding presence of one of the world's wealthiest men to calm them.

"Thank you," Kubritz said into the microphone, once all eyes were upon him. "Now, I know you're all having a good time..."

The crowd roared its approval, belting out cheers and applause for their generous, avuncular host, but even as they hoisted their glasses to him, Kubritz waved his pudgy hand for silence.

"...but I'm afraid we here at Fives & Lives have found ourselves suddenly in the middle of an emergency, and the casino, I am very sorry to say, is going to have to close down for the remainder of the evening."

Sighs and groans of dismay and disappointment filled the room like a thick, almost visible fog, but before Kubritz could attempt an acceptable explanation and insist that everyone file calmly and quietly through the exits, a patch of wall not twenty feet from where the crime king was standing seemed to explode outwards in a storm of swirling wood, metal, and concrete, and a large, human-shaped form rocketed through the air and came to a crash landing against one of the craps tables. Though he was covered in bruises and plaster dust as he hoisted himself to his feet and shook his head woozily, it was clearly Charlie, his tanktop ripped from his torso, his eyeballs still spinning from that last blow.

"Tag!" laughed Mr. Bojangles, storming into the casino through the hole, sporting a grin that would have made the Cheshire Cat jealous. "You're it!"

"Sir, this situation is getting out of control," said one of Kubritz's bodyguards. "I really think we should move you to a more secure location."

"Run? From them? Never!" said Kubritz. "They are of no more consequence than anyone else! Now that Malik is gone, my concern with them is minimal. I will not justify their petty actions with special treatment! On the contrary, I shall adjourn to my office."

"But, sir..."

Kubritz whirled around and slapped his open palm across the guard's jaw, sending the minion reeling backwards.

"I am Norman Kubritz, damn it! No one dictates to me, no one intimidates me, and no one ever gets away with this degree of impudence! In time I will retaliate against these savages, not because I fear them, but because they have inconvenienced me! When I am ready, they will taste the full extent of my wrath, and you, yourself, would do well to remember that nobody is greater than Kubritz! Nobody!"

With that, Kubritz dropped his furiously smoking cigar to the floor, stomped down hard on it with his thousand dollar shoe, then strode toward the elevator, moving effortlessly through the vibrant sea of panicking civilians rushing to get out of the way of the two giants dueling in their midst.

Jim Croce had been the one to warn the world against tugging on Superman's cape, and throughout Charlie's entire life, from his early adolescence all the way up to a mere ten minutes ago, he had always been Superman. He had always been the biggest, strongest man around, able to heft any common street thug off his feet and heave him into a brick wall with one careless flick of his wrist. He had always been the one wearing the cape on which no one dared tug. Such as it was, being blasted halfway across a room by the muscle power of another man's fist was a radically new experience for him. Mr. Bojangles had hit him hard; harder than Charlie had ever been hit before. It had actually hurt. Clambering to his feet, Charlie realized that, for once in his life, he was facing a hand-to-hand combatant on an even playing field, and worse, that he, himself, might actually be the disadvantaged party.

And I thought I was one big mother, thought the large Charlie, as the even larger Mr. Bojangles slammed his anvil-sized fist down onto the craps table, smashing through its surface.

"You've had it now, punk!" Mr. Bojangles chuckled with those rich, vibrating pipes of his as Charlie ducked a swing and swooped in to wrap his arms around the bigger man's torso. "Ya mighta been the strongest guy in your nursery school, but you ain't nothin' here!"

"Punk? Look who's talking," Charlie growled with exertion as he shoved Mr. Bojangles back up against the wall. "Which one of us here is the underpaid, unquestioningly loyal enforcer for the fat white man anyway?"

Mr. Bojangles snickered, and threw two punches into Charlie's face.

"Growin' up in the Bronx, ya learn it's a good idea to be on the winnin' team," he said, twisting Charlie's brawny arm behind his back, spinning him around, and casting him head-over-heels into a row of slot machines, which burst open and discharged hordes of quarters that cascaded down over his shoulders and back in rivers of silver.

"Oh, yeah, you're a winner all right," said Charlie, jumping to his feet before seizing a felled slot machine by its long stem and brandishing it like a sledgehammer at his enemy. "I see 'winners' like you in the old neighborhood all the time. Pop quiz, Leroy Brown. What's five times five?"

"Uh…"

"Exactly," said Charlie, smashing the one-armed bandit into the larger man's face.

Mr. Bojangles said, 'Oof!', and fell backwards, his bottom lip split and bleeding.

"Shouldn't have hurt too much," said Charlie, discarding the battered machine. "I only hit your head."

"You callin' me stupid?"

"No, 'stupid' would be a gross understatement," said Charlie. "You're one of the dumbest punk niggers I've ever met. Hell, boy, I haven't been this embarrassed since the O.J. verdict."

Mr. Bojangles, his grin shrinking, leapt off his backside and lunged at Charlie, knocking him down and taking hold of his throat.

"And what makes you so smart?" he snarled.

"You think I don't know where you come from?" sneered Charlie, groping at his enemy's sausage-thick fingers with one hand and punching at his enemy's face with the other. "You think I wasn't poor ghetto trash most of my life? You think I didn't break my fair share of kneecaps or boost my fair share of appliances? The only difference between you and me, boy, is that when I finally realized what an asshole I'd been, I didn't continue to wallow in it!"

Capping his words with a Herculean roar, Charlie threw Mr. Bojangles off to the side and leapt to his feet just in time to sidestep a bull-style charge from the larger man. Mr. Bojangles crashed into the wall headfirst, but spun quickly around again, completely unfazed.

"Why don't you get a real job?" asked Charlie, seizing a blackjack table and throwing it at his sparring partner, who caught it like a medicine ball and smashed it over one bulky knee. "You could make a fortune as a quarterback or a pro wrestler."

"Workin' for Kubritz is the tops," replied Mr. Bojangles, pitching a splintered piece of the table at Charlie's face with a force that would have carried a smaller man's head all the way to Cleveland. "He may be a pain in the ass sometimes, but he's got the whole world on his dinner plate."

"And when was the last time he offered you so much as a table scrap?" asked Charlie. "Can't you face facts, you brain-dead moron? You're nothing but a tool; completely expendable, and utterly useless for anything but the simplest and most indelicate of tasks. You're nothing to Kubritz. Guys like him just use guys like us."

"Whadda ya mean 'us'?"

"What, you think I'm just shooting off my mouth without knowing from where I speak? I used to *be* you," said Charlie. "Not all that long ago, I was a mob flunky just like you. I could take orders and break legs with the best of 'em. Being the idiot I was back then, I actually thought it was the only career open to me, after I'd squandered all the other opportunities life should have thrown in the path of a more deserving guy. It ultimately took an ass-whoopin' from a crazy white fool from England to make me finally realize that I could have just as much fun and get a helluva lot more satisfaction from putting the hurt on the bad guys instead."

"Wait a minute, wait a minute," Mr. Bojangles raised his open hands and laughed like Geoffrey Holder. "Lemme get this straight here. Are you preachin' to me? Are you tryin' to reach out to me? Ya think you're Sidney Poitier or somethin'? Doc Cosby? Brother, from where I stand, I've got two options. I could pay attention to what you're sayin', walk outta here, and maybe get an honest job baggin' groceries, or...nah, I'm gonna go with option two. That is, kick your ass and get a fat bonus for doin' it."

Mr. Bojangles seized the nearby roulette wheel with both hands, and, with one mighty yank, tore it from its base and proceeded to hurl it at Charlie like a great, red-and-black Frisbee. The wheel struck Charlie in the midsection, drove the breath from his body, and sent him hurtling through the air and out the casino's grand front entrance amidst a loud shattering of glass and crunching of metal.

All right, that does it! thought Charlie, as he crashed onto the sidewalk, the wheel still on top of him. *I'm done holding back! If he was anyone else, I'd pull my punches to keep from breaking his spine, but if he wants the full work-over, he can have it!*

Mr. Bojangles strode out into the street with the boastful, chest-swelled confidence of an undefeated prizefighter emerging from his locker room, and laughed with delight to see a handful of nearby pedestrians yelp and shrink away from him. Charlie kicked the roulette wheel at him, but Mr. Bojangles swatted it aside like a wad of crumpled paper, sending it careening into a fire hydrant, which erupted into a high-pressure geyser beneath the impact, blasting water in three directions. Mr. Bojangles lowered his head and charged at Charlie, who moved out of the way just in time to see his foe crash into the Plymouth Voyager parked directly behind him instead. The Voyager flipped upside-down and twitched its wheels helplessly in the air, as if it were a living thing trying to right itself, and Mr. Bojangles tore the driver's side door from the body with the same ease with which any other man would tear a drumstick from a Thanksgiving turkey. Before he had the opportunity to deploy the makeshift weapon, however, a whirling manhole cover came slicing through the air at a killer speed and struck him squarely between his broad shoulder blades. The giant said 'Uff!', and dropped to his knees, and that was when Charlie fell upon him, taking advantage of his enemy's temporarily disoriented state to rain down blow after double-fisted blow.

Truly ponderous as Charlie's brute strength was, the extraordinary levels of testosterone and adrenaline that coursed through every cell of Mr. Bojangles' structurally superior body allowed the brutish enforcer to shrug off the attacks delivered by perhaps the one man on Earth who could truly be considered his worthy rival in a round of fisticuffs, and, bracing his hands and knees against the pavement, he threw his assailant like a bad-tempered bronco would throw an inexperienced rider. Charlie flew five yards into a lamppost, which cracked in two and crashed to the ground with a loud 'snapkt' of light and a flurry of electrical sparks.

"Ya just don't get it, do ya?" Mr. Bojangles growled, still retaining a measure of his dumb grin, even as he wiped a war paint smear of blood across his face with the back of his hand. "I'm bigger and stronger than you! You can't beat me!"

Mr. Bojangles ran three yards, leapt the last two, and landed on Charlie, driving his shoulder into the Vigilante's chest. Charlie yelled in pain as the breath went out of him again, and Mr. Bojangles wasted no time in wrapping his hand around his enemy's face and slamming his head repeatedly down into the sidewalk.

"Ya like this, boy?" Mr. Bojangles laughed, as he cracked the pavement with Charlie's skull. "Ya like this? Does it feel good? Are ya havin' fun yet? Well, are ya?"

"Actually...it's not so bad," said Charlie, pausing between head-banging intervals.

"Because...while you're busy...expending your energy...all at once... I'm sitting back...and taking it easy...and storing up my reserves...so that when I'm ready...I can open up a can on you...so bad that your kids are gonna be born limping!"

Then it was Charlie's turn to grin as he brought both of his fists suddenly up and clashed them like cymbals against either side of Mr. Bojangles' head. The larger man shouted 'Gaa!' at the resulting pain in his ears, and that was when Charlie hit him with the triple head butt, forcing Mr. Bojangles further upwards and backwards each time until he slumped off of him.

While Mr. Bojangles remained on his knees, Charlie jumped to his feet and smashed the other man's face with a continuous, unrelenting series of full force punches – administered alternately by his right and left fists – that drew blood, bruised flesh, and loosened teeth. Then, in a spin in which Charlie managed to integrate a punishing kick to the face from his combat booted-foot, the Vigilante whisked up the Voyager's discarded door and slammed the window portion down over Mr. Bojangles' head, which broke through like the hard mass of bone that it was, resulting in a comic resemblance to a quintessential cartoon character whose noggin has been bashed in by a framed painting.

His eyes spinning in his head, his mouth gaping stupidly, Mr. Bojangles didn't have time to see the final battering ram-like punch that torpedoed into his face and knocked him flat on his back, where he lay sprawled out on the pavement, senseless and motionless, like the ogre that had plummeted from atop the beanstalk.

Breathing heavily, Charlie turned away from his defeated adversary and slumped into a sitting position on the curb, wiping one hand across his bloodied face and the other through his sweaty crewcut.

Well, I suppose that wasn't too difficult, thought Charlie, though he knew full well that the duel had been one of the most grueling tests to which he had ever put his remarkable strength. *Maybe I can keep my self-bestowed title of Strongest Man in the World after all. This must be how Popeye feels when he pounds down a can of spinach after getting his ass handed to him by Bluto.*

Hunching his shoulders and bowing his head, Charlie watched a thick glob of blood ooze from his right nostril and splatter down onto the pavement between his big feet. The reminder of his sustained injuries made him chuckle, and he smiled as he indulged himself in a private joke.

For those of us who are different, it's always nice to know there's someone out there who's a bigger freak than you are, he thought.

His face radiant with a smile that was the result of finding a perfect revelry between business and pleasure – sometimes he almost felt as if he were robbing Kubritz, as he would gladly maim and kill for free – KnuckleDuster punched his steel fist into a giant fan, and, showing no discomfort whatsoever as the whirling blades screeched, sparked, and shattered to a grinding halt against his extraordinary appendage, tore one of the blades free and stood over Carla like a mighty hunter preparing to behead a felled boar. She was still sitting with her back against the huge generator, her cracked ribs giving her hell as she tried to catch her breath.

"Come on in, take off your skin, and rattle around in your bones," KnuckleDuster recited with a smirk, placing the edge of the fan blade delicately against Carla's cheek like a giant razor.

"You really get off on this, don't you?" said Carla. "I mean, this is actually getting you excited, isn't it? You enjoy seeing women in disadvantaged, preferably battered conditions."

"Weeeeeellll...yes," said KnuckleDuster, totally unashamed.

"Does it give you a feeling of power?" asked Carla. "Does it make you feel big and strong? Hell, I'll bet it's the only way you can get off!"

"Play the psychoanalyst all you want," said KnuckleDuster, moving the fan blade down to trace the nape of Carla's neck, "but don't expect to get me riled up. I know I'm dysfunctional. Y'see, ever since Alyusha Davidov yanked me out of his daughter and turned my elbows into woodchips...well, when you find it impossible to disassociate an extremely painful experience like that from the sex that provoked it, then the only way you can ever truly enjoy sex again is by embracing pain as a natural part of it. And I had some great plans for you too, if I ever managed to catch you at my leisure. I was gonna put you on a spit and stick an apple in your mouth...but we don't have time for all of that. So give us a kiss, and we'll finish this nice and quick."

KnuckleDuster lowered the fan blade, bent at the waist, and gripped Carla's chin firmly in his hard, cold fingers as he moved his face towards hers. Before his thin, dry lips could suck onto Carla's mouth, however, the Vigilante moved her own face suddenly forwards and bit the prosthetic-armed thug hard on the nose. KnuckleDuster screamed as Carla's teeth ground in mercilessly, wringing blood from his proboscis like water from a sponge. He tried as delicately as he could to pull away, but to no avail, and it was only after taking firm hold of Carla's arms and applying his strength to squeeze insistently that she relinquished.

"Argh! You bitch! You fucking bitch!" he howled, stumbling backwards, his hands clapped over the remnants of his latest piece of anatomy to become grotesquely mutilated.

Not taking the time to form a sufficient quip, Carla leapt forwards from her sitting position, lunged in between KnuckleDuster's widely spread legs, and, now crouching behind him, kicked both her legs up like a mule, striking him hard in the small of his back, sending him falling forwards against the generator.

As all human beings are prone to do when they find themselves falling forwards, KnuckleDuster stretched an arm reflexively out in front of himself. The metal arm, driven by the momentum of its kicked wielder, smashed through the face of the generator as if it were cardboard, and the resulting voltage that blasted through KnuckleDuster's body proved sufficient to barbecue the man in seconds. He didn't even have time to scream as the electricity seized upon the excellent conductor that was his arm, using it to feed into every cell of his being on its way to the ground. When the electricity finally released him, and the power fizzled out all over the casino, the charred, blackened corpse rocketed backwards across the room, hit the wall, and crumbled into a smoking, smoldering heap of dismembered body parts, two slightly fused metal arms among the mess.

"Stop here, Taimur."

Taimur applied his foot to the brake, and the black limousine halted at the entrance to the hangar housing Malik's private jet. A nearly full moon hung silently and impassively as ever in the infinite blackness as Malik and Qasim emerged from either side of the back of the car.

"Oh, deplorable fate!" Qasim lamented, shaking his fist at the starry heavens. "Oh, reprehensible injustice!"

"Quiet!" said Malik. "Do you want the whole world to hear?"

"Do I want the whole world to hear how despicably I have been cheated? Absolutely!" Qasim replied.

"Like it or not, we must leave," said Malik, punching in the hangar's access code and stepping back from the doors. "There will be plenty of opportunities for vengeance in the future. Stop your moaning."

"Retreat is the thin end of the wedge, Malik! The lives of men like you and me are constant with overwhelming resistance and are defined by how that resistance is met!"

Qasim turned away from Malik to face the far horizon, decorated with thousands of blinking city lights, and spread his arms wide in an embrace of the damp night air, as if he were standing on the edge of a great precipice, overlooking the entire world.

"Look at them, Malik!" he said. "Can't you see them out there, with their anthems, and their emblems, and their armies stocked by mindless slaves, unlimited in their numbers and unquestioning in their destinies? A monstrous amassing of regulated forces, harnessed to unwieldy causes, headed by unworthy men, groping for unattainable empire! Even now, as they sit on high in their palaces of hypocrisy and disdain, they are ripe for destruction! Oh, how they loathe and fear me, Malik, because I am the avenger of God, annointed to chastise them for their sin! Repent, you powers of evil; you poisonous overlords of duplicity! Repent, and perish in the fires of your own hell! Your wickedness shall be punished for all time by Qasim! Oh, don't you see them, Malik? The satanic majority that must be washed away by the cleansing waters of retribution! Tell me you can see them, Malik! Don't leave me here alone in my knowing torment! Tell me you can see them!"

Malik remained silent throughout Qasim's impassioned monologue, primarily because he could think of nothing to say. He had to confess to being surprised by his old friend's recent behavior, particularly this raving, Hitleresque outburst. True, it had seemed to Malik on his scheduled visits to Stocknorton that Qasim had been growing ever more eccentric inside prison walls, but now he appeared positively manic. There was a strange quality of distance in the man's eyes, as if part of his soul had been transported to another place entirely.

"The only thing I'm telling you right now is to get your ass on that plane," said Malik, marching into the hangar, towards the sleeping jet. "The arid winds of the East beckon. You'll feel better once you're home."

The hangar's lights flashed abruptly on then, startling the two Arabs and halting them in their tracks on their way to the jet, and the clicking of what sounded like a thousand handguns and rifles followed immediately, the noisy echo snapping off the concrete walls and steel girders like the world's loudest bag of microwave popcorn. Positioned strategically all about the hangar, covering every possible angle from an effective line of fire, was a tremendous force of uniformed police officers and SWAT cops.

"Stop right there, the both of you!" bellowed a cop's voice, amplified through a megaphone. "You're under arrest! Get down on your knees and clasp your hands behind your heads, fingers laced!" In the instant it took to evaluate the situation, Malik realized he had no chance of escape. There were too many of them, and they had him too well covered. It was definitely a time for surrender. He'd oblige the police for now, and go quietly like a good boy, all the while trusting his money, power, and influence to extricate him later from this undesirable but unavoidable circumstance.

Qasim, however, was not quite so level-headed. He had always been brasher and more impulsive than Malik; a hot-headed maverick, even among fundamentalist terrorists. And, as Malik had observed earlier, Qasim's time in prison had diseased his mind, heightening his delusions of grandeur and perverting his sense of logic. Yes, the stagnant, stifling life within Stocknorton's walls had ultimately proven too much for a man of destiny like himself, and he was bound and determined not to be taken back.

He thrust his hand inside his jacket.

"Gun!" a cop shouted.

In no more than three seconds, Qasim fell to the ground with over four dozen bullets lodged in his body, and, an instant later, Malik crashed down on top of him, also cut to ribbons by the leaden hailstorm. Lying on his back on top of Qasim's corpse, already feeling the rhythmic beating of his own heart slow to a dead crawl, Malik rolled his eyes upwards and looked through red, blurry vision at his jet; his pride and joy; his wonderful toy with which he would never play again, and his ticket to safety and security, so close and yet so very, very far away.

Then his unrelenting eye for detail spotted the fingerprint-sized indentation in the plane's otherwise flawless body.

Where the hell did that come from? he wondered.

Then his vision went completely, and with one more ragged, blood-spewing cough, he died.

For the first time since the lavish casino's grand opening years ago, a day had arrived that saw Fives & Lives closed to the public as the minions of Norman Kubritz scrambled like a colony of worker ants to repair the damage of the previous evening's violence. Not only did the resort suffer now from an almost complete lack of electrical power, thanks to the destruction of the downstairs generators, but the battle between Mr. Bojangles and the large-muscled Vigilante had resulted in the trashing of much of the ground floor and its attractions. The casino itself, littered with broken slot machines, splintered card tables, shattered sculptures, and chunks of three walls, was a depressing sight and would take some time to repair completely. The attached rec center, through which Charlie and Mr. Bojangles had rampaged previously, was not much healthier by comparison. The snack bar and pool tables had been smashed, nine of the bowling alley's twelve lanes were no longer fit for use, and there were bumper cars and go-karts at the bottom of the swimming pool.

And above it all, like a dragon roosting atop a ravaged castle, dwelled the big man himself, puffing smoke as furiously as said mythical beast, seething behind his desk of power, his teeth and fists clenched tightly, his face purple with anger and indignation. He did not speak and he did not move. He simply sat in his chair, his huge, self-aggrandizing portrait hanging behind him, and glared into empty, silent space, fuming about how much media and legal attention was being focused upon him now, about how many of his projects and business ventures had been set back or damaged irreparably, and about how anyone – *anyone* – could have so much as dared this degree of impudence. His cigar smoke stinging his narrowed, yellow eyes and seeping into the pores of his saggy, jaundiced skin, he sat with the stillness of a craggy, dilapidated monolith, an incredible build-up of rage boiling just beneath his barely composed surface. He made a truly imposing picture, like that of a terrible, stern-faced guardian of purgatory, handing down damnations from on high. Nothing could rattle this man of power now as he blueprinted, coldly and single-mindedly, his plans for a swift and reverberating vengeance. Not even something so unexpected yet so predictable as the object of that planned vengeance kicking down his door and stomping into his office was enough to derail the cavalier fury from his bearing.

"Hi, Norman," scowled Gary, sporting bandages around his right leg and left arm. "Guess what? A funny thing happened on the way to the forum. Someone nailed my body to the ground."

"How did you get up here?" asked Kubritz, not one detectable note of surprise in his voice, as he moved his hand, slowly and easily, beneath the lip of his desk.

"I have a friend who's quite adept at pulling the doors off elevators," Gary answered, taking a few steps forwards, limping a bit. "The power was off, but it was easy enough to climb up the shaft. And I did it all for you, Norman. It's time for you to pay your debt to the piper."

Kubritz's chubby forefinger jabbed the little red button for which it had been searching, and the front of his enormous desk slid away to reveal the cyclopean business end of a large machine gun barrel. Gary hit the floor and rolled to the side an instant before a hail of bullets blasted out of the stationary turret, chewing into the far wall, filling the air with floating mites of disintegrated cedar wood paneling.

"It won't be enough to save you now, Norman," said Gary, standing up beside the potted palm tree in the office's right hand corner. "Judgment, swift and decisive, is coming your way."

A single bead of sweat materializing just above his left eyebrow, Kubritz pressed a second hidden button. A telltale 'pleep' sounded from within the palm tree's foundation of moist soil, alerting Gary to throw himself back into the center of the room a mere second before the mine concealed inside the pot exploded, incinerating the tropical flora and setting fire to the surrounding area.

"Strike two, Norman," said Gary, getting up and stalking purposefully towards his seated enemy.

His concern growing, Kubritz stood up from his chair and stabbed his third and final button. A loud 'clank' resonated throughout the large office, and the entire desk shot towards Gary on concealed rails, its velocity and weight enough to crush a man, but Gary simply leapfrogged over the mahogany missile, letting it crash through the wall behind him.

"What are you planning to do, Parker?" asked Kubritz, backing warily away. "Haven't you realized by now that I am utterly invincible? My power is limitless and my influence unending! I've been here for thirty years and I'll be here for another thirty! There's nothing you can do! There's nothing anyone can do! You can't lay so much as one finger on me!"

Gary stopped as he drew within five feet of Kubritz, then shook his head and let out a little snort of melancholy amusement.

"You still don't get it, do you, fats?" he said. "I'm a vigilante, unsanctioned by and unknown to all of those powers you keep wrapped so smugly around your little finger. All of the cops, district attorneys, and government agencies in the world can't touch me either, and I'm no more inhibited by the bounds of the law than you are. I've always said that it takes a lawless rogue to beat a lawless rogue, so let's cut the bullshit and tell it like it is. After forsaking all of the usual compunctions that would come with a more rigid adherence to society's perennial code, we're just a couple of assholes who don't follow the rules. So, what do you say? Feel like finishing this?"

"Come now, Parker," said Kubritz, almost appeasingly, as his beady eyes darted over to the sledgehammer standing silently in the corner – its iron head still stained red with H.J. Haberdash's blood – and he realized there was no way he'd be able to reach it quickly enough. "We're both sensible men. You must know that I've nothing personal against you. This whole unfortunate episode was just business. Regrettable, I know, but such is the way of things in our industry. Considering the superior intelligence we both possess, I'm sure we can arrive at some sort of... agreement that will permit us to continue on in peaceful co-existence."

A snarl darkened Gary's features, and he seized Kubritz by the knot of his wide necktie and punched him squarely in the center of his pudgy, piggish face. Kubritz cried out and staggered against the wall, blood dripping from his nose and mouth. Then Gary thrust his hand inside his jacket and produced a six-shot revolver, and any remaining trace of arrogance and superiority vanished from Kubritz's widening eyes as his face turned pale and his jaw dropped open.

"I understand you're a bit of a gambling man, Kubritz," said Gary, "so I'm going to do you the favor of letting this final confrontation of ours turn on chance. I assume you're familiar with a game called Russian roulette?"

Kubritz gulped, and the sweat came faster as Gary pushed the revolver into his trembling hands.

"There's one bullet somewhere in that gun," said Gary. "Spin the cylinder, put the barrel to your head, and pull the trigger. If you die, it'll damn well serve you right. If you live, I'll let you go."

Looking into Gary's emotionless eyes, Kubritz knew this was his best, if only chance. Turning the gun on his enemy was out of the question, as he had no idea where in the cylinder the single round resided, and outright escape from such an athletically superior foe was a supremely ludicrous notion.

"Roll the dice, Norman," Gary urged. "Take your chance."

His face a Niagara Falls of perspiration, Kubritz uttered a silent prayer to the Lady of Luck that had guided him throughout his life, blessing his hand in almost all ventures to which he'd applied it, then spun the cylinder once, raised the gun barrel shakily to his head, pressed the muzzle flat against his right temple, squeezed his eyes shut, and pulled the trigger. An explosive roar followed as a bullet blasted clean through Kubritz's skull, shot out of his left temple – leaving two gaping holes and a spout of blood in its wake – and embedded itself in the wall. Kubritz's eyes snapped open like window shades, and he crashed to the floor with a five hundred and ten pound 'thud' that must have shaken the entire building, blood squirting freely from both sides of his head.

Gary, his expression one of complete and utter passiveness, stepped over to the corpse, knelt down, and pried the revolver free from the fat fingers of the right hand. Then he stood up and flipped the gun's cylinder open, and five more bullets tumbled out into his open palm.

"First rule of gambling, Norman," he said, pocketing the rounds. "The odds are always against you."

Reclining comfortably in the spacious suite reserved especially for him in the posh first class section of the Boeing 747 passenger jet that was, at this moment in time, rocketing high above the restless, crashing crests of the Atlantic on its way to the teeming, sweltering city of Madrid,

Henry Hugo, his broken nose bandaged demurely, stifled a dainty burp and held up his empty wine glass.

"I think I'll try the *Chateau Lafleur* this time, love," he said.

"Certainly, sir," said a young, sandy-haired steward with a fine, muscular tone and two of the brownest eyes Hugo had ever seen. "Did you enjoy your stay in New York, sir?"

"Oh, not really, no," Hugo gave a weary sigh as the steward charged his glass. "Mostly business, really, and the whole deal fell through."

"I'm sorry to hear that, sir."

"So I've decided I'm due for a little vacation," said Hugo, taking a sip of the wine and smacking his lips, appraisingly. "Mmm. Quite agreeable. Soft, flavorful, and medium-bodied."

"I'm glad you approve, sir," said the steward. "It's one of our most popular French wines."

"Oh, I wasn't talking about the wine, darling," said Hugo, twirling his glass dismissively. "I was talking about you. You're much too tasty a specimen to be stuck in this dead-end job. How would you like to accompany me to a five-star hotel once we've landed?"

The steward was taken aback by this blunt proposition, but did his best to take it in stride, forcing a nervous laugh and maintaining his compulsory, hospitable grin.

"I'm afraid I don't lean that way, sir," he said.

"Not even for a million dollars?" said Hugo, producing a few thick wads of greenbacks from nowhere and plunking them unceremoniously down onto his dinner tray.

The steward's chocolate brown eyes nearly popped out of their sockets when they saw all that money, and Hugo knew he had him. Having approached unambiguously heterosexual men in this manner before, the wily assassin could see easily the furious battle of emotions raging across the sweating, speechless steward's face. A million dollars was a lot of money; more money than most people would earn in a lifetime of hard work, let alone an hour or two in the arms of a randy fag. Bitterly repulsive as the idea was to any straight man – and this steward was doubtless no exception – it was hard to conclude that a lifetime of prosperity and comfort wasn't worth a single evening of disgusting perversity which any mature, right-thinking man should be able to put easily behind him.

He won't be able to forget it, though, thought Hugo, grinning like the sadistic jester he was. *They never do. I can see he's made up his mind already. He's allowed his greed to win the day, though he hates himself for it. He'll take the money, and he'll moan and groan as I make him mine. And he'll be a rich man afterwards, but he'll find he's lost his soul. He'll spend the rest of his life doubting himself, despising himself. Every day until his death will be filled with resentment, depression, and self-loathing. All for a million dollars, which is just a fraction of what I receive regularly for relieving one of his kind of their useless life. Ah, what fools these mortals be.*

Hugo took another sip of wine and winked at the steward, who bowed his head somberly and pocketed the cash, his heart, mind, and spirit already burning with shame.

"Will there be anything else, sir?" the steward asked, quietly, his eyes lowered.

"Yes," said Hugo. "Fetch me the latest issue of *Cosmopolitan*. I understand there's an excellent article in there about '26 secrets that'll make him roar like a lion'. I've no doubt you could benefit from it. After all, I'm paying top dollar for you, and I expect to get my money's worth."

The steward nodded, sniffed back tears, and went off to fulfill the request.

Life, Henry Hugo decided, could be simply fabulous.

Sitting at the Rat Hole's conference table, directly across from Sushi, Zeke fixed the ninja with an Eastwoodish squint of defiance and curled his lips into a snarl.

"This is fer the championship o' the world," he uttered. "It all comes down to this. Draw."

Sushi, an equally combative expression on his face, extended his hand slowly and drew a card from the pile. It was yellow. He moved his blue gingerbread man to the nearest corresponding space, rounding the sweet, sticky marshes of the Molasses Swamp, drawing ever nearer to the utopian Candy Castle.

"Well played, Shinto Sambo," said Zeke, maintaining his steely eye contact, "but here's where it all ends for ya. You may wear the Monopoly crown, and you were definitely lucky at Parcheesi, but no one – *no one* – has ever beat me at Candy Land."

"There must be a first time for all things," Sushi replied. "Draw."

Jutting his chin out as far as he possibly could, Zeke regarded the situation. He wished he felt as confident as he sounded. True, his own red gingerbread man was only a few spaces behind Sushi's pawn, but it would take just one red card to bog him hopelessly down in the sugary quicksands of the Molasses Swamp, giving his wily opponent all the opportunity he needed to dig for that coveted purple card that would carry him triumphantly to the palace of King Kandy. Zeke knew that if he was to win, he would need a couple of really good cards in a row. If he could just get past that sticky spot, he figured his odds for victory to be at least even with Sushi's. So, he drew. And that was when the corners of his mouth drooped dramatically, and all color drained from his face, for stamped on the card was the cheery, smiling visage of a friendly, green gnome whom all Candy Land veterans respect and fear as their most dangerous enemy.

"Nooo!" Zeke wailed, crumpling the card in his fist as if it were a death sentence issued him by a fortune teller. "Nooo! Not Plumpy! Not fucking Plumpy!"

"Aha!" Sushi crowed. "Back to the Gingerbread Plum Trees with you!"

Zeke looked sorrowfully at the orchard in question, situated all the way down at the bottom of the board, just a few colored spaces from the game's starting point. Then his forlorn expression twisted and contorted into one of rage, and he flung the board and its accessories halfway across the room.

"You damn Jap, you're a cheater!" he bellowed, leaning across the table to get into Sushi's face.

"What did you call me?" the ninja asked, a very menacing tone entering his voice.

"You were the one who shuffled the cards! You were the one who insisted on going first!"

"The rules of the game state clearly that the youngest player goes first!" Sushi countered. "And you have a good thirty years on me, you loudmouthed, trailer trash redneck!"

"And I suppose it was just a coincidence that you got the Gramma Nutt card on your third turn and moved all the way up to the Peanut Brittle House while I stayed stuck in the Peppermint Forest!" Zeke continued to rave. "You're a cheater!"

The dagger appeared in Sushi's hand at lightning speed, its deadly point just centimeters from Zeke's jugular.

"You'll take that back!" the ninja demanded.

"My ass! You're a Candy Land cheater and I'll tell anyone who'll listen!"

"You'll take that back, or I shall have my satisfaction from a pint of your blood!"

"It's just like having children, isn't it?" Carolyn remarked to Charlie. "Gives us a glimpse of what we're missing, I suppose."

"This is the stupidest thing I've ever seen," said Charlie, looking up from the *TV Guide* crossword puzzle. "Two grown men arguing over a game that boasts among its merits an advancement system based on colors instead of counting. Leeza, why don't you give both of these nitwits a heavy sedative?"

"Zeke, would you like to tell me if things have improved for you concerning that matter we discussed the other day?" asked Buzz, hoping to segue into a quieter, more peaceful discussion.

Zeke snubbed Sushi with a dirty look and shuffled out of the conference room, moving towards the couch upon which Buzz sat, poring over another braille newspaper and nursing a large, tender bump on his left temple.

"Well, I gotta hand it to ya, Shades," he said. "You were right. Me an' Molly had a long talk two nights ago, an' we both got some feelings out into the open. Really cleared the air. An' we cleared out one or two… heh…other things, if I ain't bein' too subtle for ya. An' tonight I'm takin' her to Tavern-on-the-Green. She deserves it, and I can certainly afford it now, what with all we brought in from Kubritz."

"That's right, let's get that straight right now," said Gary, sitting comfortably in a recliner, the arm of which Carla was perched upon. "What's our profit for this little venture, Will?"

"Enough to keep us all very comfortable for quite some time," said William, whose prodigious mathematical skills permitted him the distinction of being the Vigilantes' official treasurer, "even after all the government agencies and crime syndicates that swooped in to take their pounds of flesh after Kubritz's 'suicide'. Among other things, we can refurnish the lab, which is something we've wanted to do since forever."

"So, all in all, we didn't come out of this too badly, I guess," said Peg, gently rubbing the sore spot on the back of her head.

"Naw, just the usual bruises, contusions, and impalements," said Charlie. "Business as usual, more or less. Hey, does anyone know who 'Dave of *Full House*' was? Seven letters with a 'u' in the middle."

"Coulier," William answered.

"Gary, are you sure you're doing okay?" Carla whispered so that the others couldn't hear.

"Don't I always do okay?" he replied.

"You pretend you do," said Carla, running her fingers affectionately across his bruised forehead, "but I know you. I can tell when you're rattled."

"I'm not rattled," said Gary.

"It's nothing to be ashamed of," Carla pressed. "After what you were put through…"

"Carla, I am not rattled!" Gary insisted, rather more harshly than he meant, causing his concerned friend to turn away, her hands folded in her lap, a downcast expression on her face.

"I really wish you wouldn't shut me out like this," she said, her beautiful brown eyes looking down at the floor. "It's not always easy, you know. Seeing someone you care about...when I saw the state you were in last night, I..."

Carla sniffed, and pretended to brush a strand of hair away from her eyes. Sorry for snapping at her, Gary slipped his arms around her waist and pulled her gently down into his lap, where she sat with her legs curled up and her head resting on his chest.

"It's all right, hon," he said, stroking her hair tenderly with his hand. "You're okay and I'm okay. We're both okay."

"I love you," she whispered.

"I know," he replied.

That was the only response Gary was able to give, and the only response Carla had expected from him. For the next few minutes they sat in silence, partaking in each other's emotions and drawing strength from each other's mutual, unacknowledged feelings while the rest of the room buzzed around them, just peripheral noise in a vacuum that didn't seem to have anything to do with either one of them. Then he gave her a little kiss on the cheek, and she looked him in the eye and smiled.

"I know something that'll cheer us up," Gary said, at last.

They exchanged mischievous glances, and smiled slyly to each other, an almost imperceptible nod passing between them.

"Leeza, I think my arm needs rewrapping," Gary called to the Vigilantes' resident physician. "Could you get me another bandage?"

As sore-headed as Leeza perpetually was, the one thing she never complained about was her duty to the medical needs of her colleagues, so, without a solitary sign of reluctance, Leeza rose from her seat and marched into the infirmary.

"Everybody watch this," Gary told the others.

An anticipative silence fell over the Vigilantes as they listened to the no-nonsense clicking of Leeza's heels on the infirmary's tile floor and the 'clunk' of the giant medicine closet being unlocked. Then a bloodcurdling scream ripped through the air on the wings of startled terror, and seconds later Leeza stomped furiously back out into the lounge, holding up the steel hand that had greeted her inside her cabinet, its fingers gnarled and outstretched in artificial rigor mortis.

"Which of you...*delinquents*...is responsible for this?!" she fumed.

Gary and Carla raised their hands sheepishly, snickering like a pair of naughty children, and they were joined promptly in their laughter by the rest of the group.

"That's it!" Leeza growled, throwing the hand to the floor with a loud 'clang'. "That is absolutely the last straw! I've had it with the lot of you! I'm resigning! I'm out! You ingrates can find someone else to bandage your aching backs!"

"That'll be the third time this month," muttered Carolyn.

"Come on, old girl, it was just a joke," said Gary.

"What is the matter with you, anyway?" Leeza asked. "Why do you do these things?"

"Because you're basically a terrible person," Gary replied.

Leeza emitted an exasperated growl and stomped back into her sanctuary, slamming the door amidst the continued chuckles of her colleagues, who acknowledged, silently, one by one, that their time of repose was coming to an end, and began to move anew towards their daily goals and objectives. Carolyn adjourned to her workshop, Peg adjourned to the laboratory, Sushi adjourned to the gym, and William, his free period almost over, adjourned altogether. Zeke, a Marlboro dangling from his lips, read through the day's edition of *The New York Minute*, memorizing effortlessly the gory details of every article involving a violent criminal offender who required the Vigilantes' special brand of 'seeing to', and Buzz perused the obituaries of the braille version for murder victims who required avenging, while Carla and Charlie prepped themselves to return to the surface to hunt down the city's ever present infestation of thieves, rapists, and killers, determined to put as large and crippling a dent in their number as possible. After all, the war was everlasting. Norman Kubritz was gone, but the devil lived on, and each of the Vigilantes knew that, by the end of this very day, the immense victory they had achieved would seem small, far away, and perhaps even inconsequential. The tirelessness of the forces of evil could be demoralizing at times, but that was what you got when you did this job. No medals or commendations or tickertape parades. Just a kick in the balls and a cruel reality check.

As for Gary, he elevated his right leg – still giving him hell – on a footstool, and used the remote to turn on the widescreen TV, already tuned in to the local news station, its anchor reporting on the latest exploits of the as yet unidentified serial killer who had, over the course of the past two weeks, been stabbing pregnant women and carving out and collecting their unborn fetuses.

"You're next, you gruesome son of a bitch," Gary said aloud. "You're next."

THE DEVIL TAKES MANHATTAN

Standing at just over six feet in height, Shang Fear was uncommonly tall for a Chinese. An imposing and enigmatic specter if ever one stalked the streets of nocturnal New York, he typically wore a ruffled white shirt, a black vest, tight black trousers, and a pair of black leather high-heeled boots, wrapping it all up inside a black, calf-length trenchcoat which enshrouded his sinewy frame, and billowed and flapped in his wake like a cape. His long, black hair was slicked back and tied up in a ponytail that hung to his shoulder blades, and he masked his emotionless, cold-as-flint eyes behind a pair of wire-framed sunglasses. A silver hoop earring dangled from his left earlobe, and he wore an emerald ring on the third finger of his bony left hand.

It was thusly attired that Shang Fear sat on a stool at the end of the counter in The Happy Trails Diner on the Upper West Side, availing himself of a very early breakfast – it was two o'clock in the morning – of scrambled eggs, toast, and bacon, and scanning his visored eyes over the previous day's edition of *The New York Minute*, his macabre curiosity taken particularly with the obituaries.

Because I could not stop for Death, he kindly stopped for me, Fear referred to one of his favorite Emily Dickinson poems. *The carriage held but just ourselves, and Immortality.*

An almost imperceptible smirk tugged at the corner of Fear's narrow mouth as he took in another modest forkful of egg – he had to admit to his fondness for Western cuisine done well, even if he did eschew any excessive degree of assimilation into America's cultural landscape – then rapped the countertop three times with the tip of his forefinger, signaling for service.

"Refill this if you please, waitress," he said, indicating his empty, milk-filmed glass.

"Certainly, sir," she said. "Anything else I can do?"

"No, I shan't be here much longer," said Fear, not looking up from his paper. "The inner man requires sustenance, but the night is ever waning, and there is much work yet to be done."

Scraping the rest of his plate clean and taking a thirst-quenching swallow from his refilled glass, Fear thrust his spidery hand inside the voluminous folds of his coat and produced a silver cigarette case and lighter.

"Oh, I'm sorry, sir, but there's no smoking in here," said the waitress.

Fear went on to extract a cigarette, place it between his thin lips, and light it as if the girl hadn't spoken.

"Sir, did you hear me?" she asked, somewhat timidly. "I'm afraid you can't smoke in here."

"Go attend to your other customers," Fear muttered, still refusing to dignify her presence with a glance.

Emboldened by the man's rude defiance, the waitress leaned assertively across the counter and reached for the cigarette, intending to snatch it away as a parent snatches an alien object from the mouth of a child, but Fear's own arm moved with the speed of a striking snake to seize the girl's wrist and twist it violently out of place. The waitress shrieked in pain, drawing the attention of the four other people patronizing the eatery at this wee hour, and Fear held her that way while his other hand lowered his sunglasses, allowing his dark, almost reptilian eyes to hold her captive as he stood and moved his face close to hers.

"It was Aristotle who said that we cannot learn without pain," he hissed, the dispassionate monotone of his voice wavering for the first time. "Perhaps *you* could make use of such an education. Are you listening, my girl?"

"You're hurting me!" she squealed.

"Be thankful that that is *all* I am doing," said Fear, "for if I were not in such an agreeable mood, your neck could easily have taken the place of your wrist. It happens that I am in the course of my regular meditations upon the events of the coming hours, and I am not likely to be aided in any way by the incessant chatterings of an inconsequential busybody such as yourself.

Now, do I make myself quite clear?"

"Y-yes!" the girl stammered, tears running down her pale cheeks.

"We are in complete and utter understanding?"

"Yes!" she sobbed.

"Then away with you!" Fear snarled, relinquishing his grip and sending the waitress stumbling backwards. "And do not expect a tip. You have earned a lesson instead, which I assure you will be of much superior value."

While the weeping waitress fled into the kitchen, Fear replaced his sunglasses, folded his newspaper and tucked it neatly away behind the napkin holder, and was preparing to leave before he found himself accosted by yet another undesirable, this one being the dumpy, ginger-whiskered, ruddy-faced man in his late forties who, it had not escaped Fear's keen notice, had been observing him studiously from the small table in the corner for the past twenty minutes.

"It really *is* you, ain't it?" the man said, his chapped lips forming a knowing smile. "I mean, it really is *you*, ain't it?"

"No," said Fear.

"Aw, ya may be able to fool some folks, but not ol' Gussy," grinned the man, tapping his stubby forefinger against the side of his potato-shaped nose. "Ol' Gussy's got a memory for faces, not to mention you're a pretty distinctive gent. Ya stick out in the mind. A gent like you, I'd know ya anywhere."

"How delightful for you," said Fear, still aiming to get away.

"Everyone thought you was dead," gushed Gussy. "Killed in that trouble a couple weeks back. But me, I knew better. I said to 'em all, 'God'd have to strangle that one with His bare hands. The illustrious gent's still out there, and anyone who says otherwise is a damn liar.' I knew you'd be back sooner or later, and here y'are. Say, could I bum a smoke offa ya? I seem t'ave run out."

"No," said Fear.

"Oh, this is a great moment for me," Gussy continued. "I've always wanted to meet ya face to face. You're my idol, y'know that? I think you're a great man, an' please pardon me if I'm jabberin' too much, 'cept I ain't never met a real celebrity before, but the very moment I saw ya walk in that door, I said to myself, 'That's him awright, and no mistake.' "

"Who *are* you?" Fear finally asked the odious little man.

"Oh, I'm sorry, ain't I made that clear?"

"No, you haven't."

"Please forgive me, but I get awful excited," said Gussy, sheepishly. "Here, take a gander at this."

Gussy thrust a hand inside his raincoat, pulled out what looked to be a rolled up bundle of papers, and handed it to Fear, who slid off the rubber band and found it to be a homespun newsletter entitled *Maniacs, Madmen, and Monsters Monthly.*

"Ya've heard of hero worship, right?" said Gussy. "Well, this is *villain* worship. Started out as just a hobby, really, but now my subscribers number in the thousands. Quit my dayjob and everythin'. Basically it's a publication for bad guy enthusiasts. Y'know, fans o' Charles Manson, or the folks who were secretly rootin' for the one-armed man on *The Fugitive.*"

"How very novel," said Fear, emotionlessly.

"We keep up to date on all the major crime figures," Gussy continued, "and as for you...well, what can I say, my man? The readers just love you! You've been Murderer of the Month three times! And now I run into you *here* of all places! Talk about a stroke o' luck! I'd give anything for an interview with ya!"

This unworthy wastrel thinks he can appeal to my vanity, thought Fear, exhaling twin plumes of smoke from his nostrils.

"So, how 'bout it?" asked Gussy. "Can we delve into your childhood?"

"My childhood?"

"Sure! Everyone knows that the most fascinatin' part of a psycho's life is his childhood! The head-shrinkers all say that a rotten, stinkin' childhood is what *makes* ya! An' a real whackjob like yourself must've had a doozy! My readers'll come in their pants when they read whatever you've got to say!"

"The eloquence of your proposition has persuaded me," said Fear. "Sit."

Fairly bursting at the seams with glee, the star-struck Gussy sat down on a stool, and Fear took the seat next to him.

"In Bei Jing," he began, holding his cigarette between his long, pianist's fingers, "my family came about as close to aristocracy as was permissible in a country ruled by a communist regime, and we owed our privileged lifestyle in its entirety to my father, Shang Tzu. He worked as a book-cooker and all-purpose accountant for a powerful crime boss called Kang Jin-Khu.

"Now, most gangsters the world over know the wisdom of keeping happy staff, and Kang was no exception. In exchange for my father's services rendered, Kang kept the house of Shang quite securely seated in luxury's lavish lap. We wore the finest clothes, enjoyed the finest foods, and dwelled in the finest houses. And of course, I was able to take advantage of a most superior education centered around philosophy and literature, as well as a strict and continuous tutelage in *wushu,* the Chinese martial arts. Although the mass populace of China was strictly regulated by the government, there was nothing but the best for us.

"Everything changed, however, with the approach of my thirteenth birthday. Though we had nothing to complain about when it came to the standard of living, my father had always been troubled by excessive greed; a handicap which clouds one's judgment and makes one careless. When Kang finally found the time to take a good look at the numbers and discovered that my father had been stealing from him for years..."

"The shit hit the fan," Gussy interrupted.

"I would not have employed that particular vulgar expression, but you've got the idea," said Fear. "Exercising the most sadistic and vengeful of wraths, Kang boiled my father alive in hot oil, then proceeded to round up the rest of my hapless family members and condemn them to the underground slave trade. My mother and two sisters, each quite attractive, were whisked from the block extraordinarily quickly. As for me...well, the great and powerful Kang opted to keep me for himself.

"He was very cruel to me at first, stripping me of my clothes, whipping and beating me until I bled, and clapping me in chains in a dark, damp, cold cellar, with only the rats for company and only discarded table scraps for nourishment, as if my father's sins had been so great that they necessitated my inheritance of punishment. Though I remained fiery in my resistance for quite some time, I inevitably grew weak and skinny and ill.

"Once it had become clear that my spirit was well and truly broken, Kang took me out of the cellar and placed me in a comfortable bedroom, where I was allowed to eat heartily and rest recuperatively, interrupted only by occasional visits from Kang's own personal physician. Finally, when I had regained my full strength, Kang dandied me up in a Little Lord Fauntleroy outfit, locked an electronic tracking bracelet around my right ankle, and versed me, in the softest and most patient of tones, in the details of my new life.

"He told me that he owned me, and that I was to do whatever he said, and I shall never forget the metaphor he used to illustrate my lowly position. He said, 'You are to me as is a dog to its master, and like all dogs, you have a degree of choice, albeit limited, in the matter of your destiny. If you are a good, noble, obedient dog, then you will be treated with the appropriate level of dignity and compassion. You will be fed well, you will be allowed to live in the house, and you will not be beaten. But if you are a mischievous, ill-tempered, disobedient dog, then you can expect to be punished regularly and severely, and to be treated with the disdain owed such an animal. And if you ultimately prove to be more trouble than you are worth, then I just might take you out into the yard and shoot you. Now, speak up, boy. What's it to be?'

"Surrendering to the hopelessness of my situation, I opted to go the way of compliance, and as is the case with many a rather-less-than-human domestic serf forced to survive and thrive under such circumstances, I eventually learned to fulfill my lot with a sense of satisfaction, and even pride. As valet and houseboy, I ran errands, fixed drinks, washed clothes, shined shoes, ran baths, looked after guests, did odd jobs, and cleaned and maintained the property both indoors and out, all with a growing devotion and loyalty to my master, and in return, as Kang had promised, I was allowed a soft bed and ample nourishment.

"But you mustn't think too harshly of him. He was kinder and more generous to me than was ever necessary. He gave me presents of books to read in my spare time so that I could continue my education, and he allowed me to continue my *wushu* training under one of the most skilled and qualified masters in the country. Though I remained as much a slave as ever, I daresay Kang often thought of me as a sort of ward."

Throughout the retrospective, the stars in Gussy's eyes had grown progressively brighter, and the grin on his beaming face had grown progressively wider. His cheeks were flushed and his breath was coming in excited bursts.

"That...was...incredible!" he exclaimed, as if he and Fear had just engaged in an extraordinarily gratifying act of sexual release. "I mean, that's just fucking *perfect!*"

"Is it?"

"I'll say! Better than I ever dreamed! No wonder you're such a twisted sonofabitch! With an exclusive like this, I can't wait to put out the next edition!"

Fear's leg kicked out sharply to the side, the hard, steel heel of his boot splintering two of the legs of Gussy's stool, and the amateur journalist fell straight downward, smashing his chin into the countertop and driving his front teeth directly through his bottom lip. Before the man even had time to scream, Fear seized him by the handful of short hairs atop his scalp, yanked him upwards, and slashed him deeply across the full breadth of his throat with a six-inch dagger produced magically from thin air.

"The superior man is modest in his speech, but exceeds in his actions," said Fear, dropping his choking, dying victim to the floor. "Not only do I value my privacy, but at my present maturity of thirty-two years, I prefer to leave the past behind."

While the writhing Gussy gurgled and gagged on his own blood, Fear took a napkin from the nearest holder and ran it once up and down the blade of his dagger, expunging the mess from the polished metal. Then, after returning it to the leather sling hanging from his shoulder inside his cavernous coat, the killer dropped his cigarette to the floor, stepped on it, and took his leave of the establishment.

I give it four out of five stars, he thought. *The eggs were just a bit too salty.*

It occurred to Alvin Bryce, even as he took an indifferent sip from his glass of ten-year-old *Dom Perignon* and stared morosely into the red, relentlessly flapping mouth of Mrs. Margot-Alice Meriwether, that the game of politics never ended, and once one had cast his hat into the ring, one was never allowed to take it back, tug the brim down over one's eyes, and depart with the haste of a man who has realized the terrible mistake he has made in putting under perpetual public scrutiny every opinion he might express and every action he might undertake unto the end of his tormented life. Even now, just seven months after winning the race for one of New York's senate seats and successfully ousting the incumbent old windbag in a coup that most political analysts called 'a welcome end to the reign of tired, out-of-touch, anemic, old Bernhardt, but a totally unexpected development when achieved by a relatively unknown young upstart with Mr. Smith-like ideals', Bryce was already regretting the blind ambition that had dropped him into the middle of this hurly-burly that sent him rocketing back and forth daily from Manhattan to Washington, D.C., in and out of the phony embraces of pompous, harrumphing geriatrics who saw themselves as the indispensable, authoritative backbone of the world's greatest democracy.

It occurred to him, in fact, that he'd rather be sailing.

"And then I said to her, 'What's love got to do with it, my dear? The man is rich!' But then, she's never been satisfied with all of the good things with which life has blessed her. I think it must be some sort of illness," Mrs. Margot-Alice Meriwether was harping on. "I mean, really! The man spends a single night with his secretary and she's ready to throw it all away. Foolish girl. I told her, 'Sadie, you don't go courting scandal just because of a little hurt pride. The man has money and standing, and I won't see you break up a perfectly good marriage just because some little floozy batted her eyes at him and led him astray. After all, it takes two people to create a problem.' Young people these days are far too self-indulgent. They'll do anything at the bid of emotion, and they never think of the long term. Wouldn't you agree, Senator?"

"What? Oh...erm...yes," said Bryce, trying to focus. "Yes, Mrs. Meriwether, this younger generation does seem rather mixed up."

"But *you're* a nice young man, aren't you, Senator?" the aged woman smiled – alluringly, she no doubt thought – and touched Bryce on the elbow.

Bryce pulled reflexively away, spilling a bit of champagne on the thick pile carpet.

"Yes...well, I try to be," he said, his voice cracking nervously. "It's been lovely chatting with you, Mrs. Meriwether, but I really must attend to my other guests."

Bryce turned and hurried off towards the far side of the lavish living room, tugging at his stiff collar and beginning to perspire as he navigated through the throng of high society elitists crowding up his Fifth Avenue penthouse apartment, beelining for the open french windows leading out onto the balcony where he hoped to suck in great breaths of the cool night air and subdue the illness he felt washing over him. These gatherings always made him anxious and tense, as did the people whom he perpetually invited – that awful hag Mrs. Meriwether always made Bryce feel like Dustin Hoffman's character in *The Graduate* – but the rules of society dictated he host them regularly so that he could be re-elected six years on, even if his reasons for his wanting to be re-elected currently escaped him.

"Ah, there you are, m'boy!" said J. Arthur Mitchell, a former senator and Bryce's self-appointed mentor who still called Bryce 'm'boy', even after his recent thirty-fifth birthday. "Haven't seen you in ages! How the hell are you?"

Mitchell threw his arm around Bryce's shoulders, pulled him in, and slapped him heartily on the back. More champagne spilled onto the carpet.

"Well, I'm doing just fine, sir," said the hapless senator, the butterflies in his stomach growing into bats.

"Aw, what's all this 'sir' crap? I've told you a thousand times, call me Jack."

"Yes, sir... I mean, Jack."

"So, how's it feel to be a member of the illustrious legislative branch at last, eh?" asked Mitchell, nearly knocking Bryce over with a friendly punch on the shoulder. "We're the best, y'know. Forget all that 'balance of power' crud. We run this great country almost single-handed. We make all the laws, we approve treaties with other nations, and we confirm Presidential nominations. And if we don't even *like* the President, we keep him hogtied by shooting down anything he tries to push through. And the President can't declare war. *We* declare war. And the judiciary can only stand by and watch, its only duty being to reinforce what we make up. Yes, sir, m'boy, you've certainly chosen well in your political vocation. S'no one more powerful on the face of this earth than a United States senator."

Yes, sir. I mean, Jack," said Bryce, chomping unconsciously away at his bottom lip, the perspiration flowing more and more freely, the glass slipping in his sweaty grip. "If you'll excuse me...erm...nature, you know..."

Unable to form anymore cohesive syllables, Bryce set his glass hastily down on the corner of a small table and lumbered towards the bathroom, almost hyperventilating as he pushed the door open. Closing and locking it behind him to shut out the hated buzz and chatter of the assembled hypocrites and sycophants, Bryce stumbled to the sink, ran it with cold water, and splashed some onto his pale face with his trembling hands. Then he looked in the mirror and saw a grotesque, almost demonic snarl cutting across his usually meek features. His teeth were bared, his lips were twisted, and his eyes were narrowed and icy.

I hate them, he thought, his fists clenched and shaking. *I hate them all!*

Then kill them! his reflection seemed to talk back to him. *Nothing could be simpler! You know you long for the release!*

No, I...

A sudden dizzy spell besieged him, and he slumped back into a wooden chair that he had placed next to the sink after suffering similar lapses of the senses. The snarl still on his face, he growled with what seemed like a great, embedded fury, and placed one quivering hand over his nauseous stomach.

Come on, Alvin, he urged himself. *Calm down. Get a grip.*

Breathing slowly and deeply through his nose, Bryce took his monogrammed handkerchief from his pocket and dabbed at his moist forehead while he waited for the tingly, prickly sensation inside his skull to subside.

"Senator," a voice on the other side of the door called to him, accompanied by a knocking that was almost enough to make Bryce swoon into a migraine. "Senator, I know you're in there. Open this door."

"I'm all right, Father," said Bryce, shakily. "I just had another one of my spells, that's all."

"Open the door and let me in," said the voice.

"I'd really rather not..."

"Do you defy your God?"

"No, it's just that I..."

"You *will* obey!" the voice commanded. "Upon pain of eternal damnation, you *will* do as you are told!"

Bryce sighed, and, with some effort, leaned forward to unlock the door, which swung open to reveal the stern countenance of Father Campion Earkhert, a tall, husky priest in his early forties. Darkening the doorway like a terrible minister of judgment, he sported a black cassock, a pair of bifocal glasses, and a short, conservative haircut. A rosary strung with pearls (and sterling silver beads for the Our Fathers), ready for use at a moment's notice, dangled from his royal purple waist sash.

"You know why you have these fits, don't you?" hissed Earkhert, pushing the door shut behind him. "It's because you're a low, vile, contemptible sinner! An infidel of the most offensive order! I am ashamed to have one such as you infecting my parish!"

"Please, Father," Bryce groaned, placing a hand over his watery eyes.

"Oh, don't beg anything of *me*! Get on your knees and beg forgiveness from God for all your despicable faults! I will take your confession *now*!"

"Father, do you really think this is the time..."

"*All* time is God's time! Confess!"

Bryce sighed, closed his eyes and bowed his head for a few moments, then ran his dry tongue over his upper lip and began to whisper.

"Father, it's been two weeks since my last confession," he muttered, looking down at the floor. "In that time I told lies, I passed a poor man on the street without giving him anything, I took the Lord's name in vain I-don't-know-how-many times, and I viewed a pornographic movie and I...I gratified myself while I watched. Also, I was rude to my ex-wife yesterday. I said something very nasty to her when she accused me of being wishy-washy."

"You *are* wishy-washy, Bryce, and that is why God hates you," said Earkhert. "You're a weak, pathetic excuse for a man, and you haven't the stuff it takes to make a soldier of Christ."

"I try to do good, Father," Bryce whimpered, a tear of remorse leaking from his eye. "I really do try."

"Then we shall start anew, and you may try again," said Earkhert, extending his hand.

"Kneel, and be forgiven."

Sobbing softly, Bryce slumped to one knee and took hold of Earkhert's sleeve, kissing the fabric devotedly.

"You're so good to me, Father," Bryce wept with gratitude. "So good."

"God is good, my son," said Earkhert, his tone much gentler now. "Through me, He purges you of evil. The Lord God is a sun and shield. The Lord will give grace and glory. No good thing will He withhold from them that walk upright. Do you walk upright, my son, forsaking the devil and all his empty promises?"

"I do, Father," said Bryce.

"Doth thou meditate on His law both day and night?"

"I do, Father!"

"Then may all workers of iniquity depart from thee, for the Lord hath heard the melancholy song of thine weeping," said Earkhert, drawing a cross on Bryce's forehead with his thumb. "Now the God of peace, that brought again from the dead our Lord Jesus, that great shepherd of the sheep, through the blood of the everlasting covenant, make you perfect in every good work to do His will, working in you that which is wellpleasing in His sight, through Jesus Christ, to Whom be glory forever and ever. Amen."

His head still bowed, Bryce rose slowly and shakily to his feet, tears of vindication staining his cheeks. Earkhert took up the senator's handkerchief and wiped them away, then gave Bryce a tender pat on the side of his head.

"Now say five Hail Mary's and strike your sinner's forehead harshly against the wall three times, and you shall find forgiveness," said Earkhert.

"Thank you, Father," said Bryce, truly grateful.

"Tribute to whom tribute is due, my son," said Earkhert. "It is the Lord Who watcheth over you all the days of your life, using my humble self as His instrument. Give your entire heart over to God, o lamb of tribulation, and just as surely as the meek shall inherit the earth, so shall you be gifted with all that you desire. Now, get on with your prayers."

"I...I'm afraid I haven't got my rosary with me this very moment, Father," said Bryce.

At this, Earkhert's eyes flashed with anger and his face flushed instantly purple.

"Wicked heathen!" he roared, slapping Bryce's face hard enough to send the young senator reeling backwards. "Am I to continue repeating myself unto the very end of the world? I've told you time and time and time again! *Always* carry your rosary! Take it everywhere! Keep it with you at all times!"

"I'm sorry, Father! I'm sorry!"

"Repentance without reform is meaningless!" Earkhert spat globules of saliva through clenched teeth as he tore his own rosary from his sash and began whipping his parishioner with it. "The next time I see you without your rosary, I'll have you excommunicated!"

Then Earkhert's violently heaving chest was seized by a coughing spell, and he finally relented his attack, hacking loudly and dryly as he backed towards the sink.

"Get out of here!" he sputtered in between coughs. "Get out of my sight, you inglorious infidel!"

Never prepared to wage an argument with God's intervener, the chastised Bryce scrambled to his feet and ran from the bathroom, hoping that providence would forgive him for upsetting the Father so.

Immediately after the door closed, Earkhert slumped wearily down into the chair by the sink and began a course of deep, steady breaths.

My Lord, throughout the course of my entire life, I have never once strayed from the path You have set for me, he prayed, silently, passing a trembling hand over his forehead. *I have stayed true to Your teachings, administered Your message, and made many a personal sacrifice for the sake of Your glorious name. And yet it sometimes seems You seek to test me further still, by throwing such hopeless sinners at my feet.*

Deep into that darkness peering, long I stood there wondering, fearing, doubting, dreaming dreams no mortal ever dared to dream before.

Towering in the doorway of the pitch black bedroom like some nightmarish fiend escaped from a child's closet, the only light reflecting off the dark sheen of his sunglasses being that cast by the thin shafts of pale moonlight permeating the Venetian blinds stretched across the bulletproof windows, Shang Fear was reminded of Edgar Allan Poe, one of his personal favorites because the man had so obviously been a mad genius with a macabre, tormented purgatory for a soul.

Allowing his eyes more than adequate time to adjust to the inky blackness, Fear slid his hand inside his coat and curled his long fingers around the hilt of the six-inch dagger, and moved, so lightly and noiselessly that he seemed to float, over to the king-sized bed where Ustin Pavla, head of the Russian mob since the death of Alyusha Davidov five years ago, lay on his back in peaceful slumber beneath the silken sheets, blissfully unaware of the imminent threat.

"While I nodded, nearly napping, suddenly there came a tapping, as of someone gently rapping, rapping at my chamber door," Fear whispered, delighting in his poetic revelry. " 'Tis some visitor', I muttered, 'tapping at my chamber door – Only this, and nothing more.' "

Gripping the dagger's hilt with both hands, Fear raised the weapon high above his head and plunged it down into the sleeping Pavla's belly. Pavla jolted awake with a heart-stopping scream and catapulted reflexively up into a sitting position, spitting blood all the way to the foot of the bed as he did so, but his assailant forced him back down with a firm hand on his throat and wasted no time in jabbing the dagger into strategic points about his chest.

" 'Be that word our sign of parting, bird or fiend!' I shrieked upstarting – 'Get thee back into the tempest and the Night's Plutonian shore!' " Fear shouted, with what could most be said to resemble glee in his ghoulish character.

"Aaaaagh!" Pavla screamed as his reddening eyes watched a geyser of blood explode from the left side of his chest.

" 'Leave no black plume as a token of that lie thy soul hath spoken! Leave my loneliness unbroken – quit the bust above my door!' "

"Bluaaackk!"

" 'Take thy beak from out my heart, and take thy form from off my door!' Quoth the raven, 'Nevermore!' "

"Urrrggh..."

With one last twist of the dagger, Pavla's heart stopped beating and his breath stopped coming, and all that remained of the erstwhile gangster was a mutilated, blood-soaked cadaver, its teeth clenched, its eyes bulging, its fingers still clutching the sheets at its sides. Fear pulled the dagger from Pavla's chest, like Arthur pulling the sword from the stone, and proceeded to use the blade to saw off the dead man's head.

"Alas, poor Ustin! I *killed* him, Horatio!" Fear paraphrased, as he held up at arm's length, like a trophy, the severed head by its hair.

Then the door slammed shut, completely extinguishing the already sparse illumination from the hallway, and a blast of fiery lead rocketed past Fear's head and embedded itself in the oak-paneled wall, missing its lethal goal by a margin of mere inches.

"I know you're in here, motherfucker!" screamed the voice of Yerik Pavla, Ustin's twenty-year-old son, brandishing a Remington 597 automatic rifle. "I've got you trapped!"

Without pausing for breath, Yerik fired off four more shots, each differing in altitude and spaced no more than three feet apart. Then there came the squishy, sickening thud of Ustin Pavla's severed head hitting the floor, followed immediately by the 'whish, swish, swoosh' of the lithe, agile Fear leaping into the air, hand-springing off the gore-soaked bed, and somersaulting through the darkness with all the unseeing confidence and grace of a bat, his majestic coattails whirling inexplicably about his superhuman form like a billowing parachute, even in the complete absence of moving air currents. Before Yerik could get off a sixth blind shot, Fear materialized behind him and drove the dagger, still stained with the elder Pavla's blood, into the small of his back.

"Action is eloquence," Fear hissed into the gasping lad's ear, gripping him firmly by the hair with one hand and twisting the blade ever deeper with the other. "Before setting out to achieve a goal, you must be cool and collected. You must be emotionless, dispassionate. Have a clearly-defined plan. Rehearse it. Deviate only when necessary. Let logic and reason be your gods."

Yerik screamed and convulsed as Fear yanked the dagger upwards, slicing it up the length of his spine as if cutting open a cardboard box.

"Did you honestly think you could so much as set a single one of my hairs out of place by storming in here like a mad dog and jerking off your itchy trigger finger? You rash and stupid punk!"

"You...you can't...do this!" Yerik choked on the words, blood spilling from his mouth. "We are...in good standing...with Norman...Kubritz!"

Fear raked the blade up through the back of Yerik's head, and the young Russian pitched forwards to land facedown on the ruined carpet, spongy morsels of brain tissue seeping out with the rivers of blood.

"Norman Kubritz is dead," said Fear, throwing the dagger into the floor next to the torn-open corpse. "Long live the *Dong Ji*."

"Here's another one you won't like," said the big Apache Indian in the deerskin vest and denim jeans. "What do you get when you stab a teenage girl in the chest?"

"I'm sure I don't know," the older, corpulent Chinese man sighed with boredom. "What *do* you get when you stab a teenage girl in the chest?"

"Well, I don't know about you, but *I* get an erection," said the Indian.

"Most distasteful," said the Chinese, sucking the stem of his tobacco-stuffed pipe.

"Oh, don't be such a snob," said the Indian. "You're trying not to chuckle. I can see the corner of your mouth twitching."

Waving his pipe dismissively, the Chinese leaned back in the chair he had borrowed from one of the downstairs cubicles and gazed out the large, rectangular window that overlooked the docks in this particularly cluttered shipping harbor on the East River, presided over by all manner of cranes and forklifts and piled high with innumerable wooden, plastic, and metal boxes of all sizes.

"I see our ship docking now," he said. "Shan't be much longer."

"Our usual front company, right?" said the Indian. "ChiWan Exports, Inc?"

"Precisely," said the Chinese, taking another puff on his pipe.

The comfortably reclining Asian was a man with no name, known simply as the Racketeer to even his closest associates, and though he was now in his autumn years with a fat belly and a case of emphysema that would make Big Tobacco blush, he retained the invigorating memories of a youth spent in proud service of his country, spying for communist China. He had been fast, strong, and intelligent. Whatever his environment, he'd adapted to it like a chameleon. One of the best of his era, he had been singularly responsible for bringing literally hundreds of duplicitous Westerners, primarily Americans, to stand before his government's public firing squads. Of course, that had all been before the ill-timed explosion that had destroyed the right side of his face. From that tragic day forward, the man called the Racketeer had wandered the earth a disfigured monster. The right half of his visage was burnt and boiled, his lips were twisted and black, and his right eye, useless and unseeing, bulged ever so slightly out of its socket, preventing the eyelid from closing completely over it. He was half deaf in his deformed right ear, his right nostril was caved in and inactive, and as he could no longer grow hair on the right side of his head, he kept his entire scalp shaved.

The Racketeer's Apache companion was Warren Winterhawk, a muscular Indian in his early forties, standing at about six-and-one-half feet tall, and perpetually clad in beads and animal skins, with his long black hair tied into multiple braids. Having grown up on the San Carlos Apache Reservation in Arizona – to this day one of the most impoverished living areas in the United States – Winterhawk was a grim-faced, battle-scarred thug with a limited education, and he made his way in the world exclusively from the utility of his body builder's physique.

"What merits the both of us coming down here tonight, anyway?" asked Winterhawk. "This is subordinate work. The usual supervisors would've done just fine."

"You mean you don't know about our honored guest?" said the Racketeer. "That ship out there, in addition to the usual guns and opium, carries extra special cargo in the form of an old associate of mine; the infamous ex-KGB man, Kolach Zarubezhnik."

"Really? I knew of our acquisition of a certain illustrious Russian, but I had no idea it would be him," remarked Winterhawk, cocking an eyebrow. "I'm quite impressed."

"The *Dong Ji* takes nothing but the best," said the Racketeer, a cirrus cloud of smoke escaping from the twisted, down-turned corner of his mouth. "He is the reason for our hands-on involvement in this otherwise procedural enterprise. I am here to make certain that all comes off without a hitch, and you, my able-bodied friend, are here to guard against any potential attacks by our many meddlesome antagonists. What with the warring mobs jockeying for position, the police stepping up their efforts against organized crime, and all these rumors of unsanctioned crimefighters hovering about the metropolis like territorial jungle beasts, this city is becoming less and less secure for the civilized businessman."

"Don't be afraid," said Winterhawk, attempting an alleviation of the Racketeer's apparent anxiety.

"Be mindful of whom it is you speak to," said the Racketeer, his ruined features forming a frown. "I fear no one. I simply believe, quite vehemently, in exercising all due caution."

Winterhawk was debating the merits of bringing up the persistent nightmares the Racketeer had suffered for a full year after two weeks in the cruel clutches of the Russian mafia when the dull, heavy 'ka-foomp' of a distant explosion rumbled across the harbor, and both gangsters cast their eyes out the window to see the destroyed bow of their ChiWan Exports, Inc. freighter alight with a roaring mass of flame.

"What the devil?" hissed the Racketeer, jumping too suddenly to his feet and grabbing his air-swelled chest with one hand.

"You take it easy," said Winterhawk. "I'll check this shit out."

The big Indian cracked his neck, straightened his raggedy headband, then charged towards the window and crashed through it, shielding his eyes with his muscular forearms as he flew out into the damp night air and plummeted thirty feet to the ground, making a noisy landing in a pile of empty, plastic crates. Hardly breaking his stride, Winterhawk flung the crates aside and stampeded towards the burning ship.

"What the hell was that?" Kolach Zarubezhnik asked no one in particular, having been nearly thrown off his feet by the sudden explosion that had rocked the mighty steel ship like a paper boat in a rambunctious child's bathtub.

"Well, it wasn't the engine backfiring," said a female voice from behind.

Zarubezhnik whirled around to face, at eye level, a black-clad woman dangling upside-down from the ceiling, suspended aloft by the grappling line hitched to her belt.

"Welcome to America, Gorby," said Carla. "If you came for the Egg McMuffin, you're in for a bitter disappointment."

Before the startled killer could react, Carla's gloved fist lashed out and struck him on the jaw, sending the heavyset man sprawling a full fifteen feet.

Patiently inhabiting the vast cargo hold below decks that had served as his dark, musty home for the past several days and nights, the potbellied Russian in his mid-sixties was a broad, burly man with a ruddy, bulldog face characterized by beady little eyes, a snub nose, and flabby, hanging cheeks. The forefront of his egg-shaped head was bald, but a thinning mane of curly, dark hair still grew from the back of his scalp and fell untidily down to the base of his thick neck. In his prime he had been one of the KGB's most vicious, cold-bloodedly efficient assassins, and even so ravaged by age and leisure as he now was, he was still an extremely dangerous man with whom to cross swords. For now, however, he wiped the blood coyly from his lips with the back of his rough, calloused hand, and crawled hurriedly on his knees towards the back of the hold while his two gun-toting bodyguards opened fire. After all, was discretion not the better part of valor?

"Kill the intruder!" one of the bodyguards shouted, as he and his partner began firing their machine guns in Carla's general direction.

"Anyone ever tell you you're antisocial?" quipped Carla, zipping back up into the shadows on the wings of her wire.

"It's an ambush!" declared the gunman who had given the initial order to attack. "How the hell did they get in here?"

"You left the key under the mat," said Gary Parker, materializing behind the man and dropping him to the floor with a hard knee to the kidneys.

With a snarl, the remaining gunman whipped his barrel in Gary's direction and prepared to ventilate the surprise trespasser, but before he could so much as wrap his finger around the trigger, he was rendered instantly unconscious by the skull-battering impact of a five pound sack of opium dropped on his head from above.

"And that's just one way that drugs can cause severe brain damage," said Carla, crouching atop a tall stack of crates. "Just say no, kiddies."

"Thanks, babe, I owe you one," said Gary, shooting his fellow adventurer a thumbs-up. "Seems to me there was a third one, though."

Gary's suspicions were confirmed by a sudden sharp pain shooting through the back of his head, delivered by the flat edge of Zarubezhnik's hard-boned hand, and the wise-cracking Vigilante fell to his knees with a grunt. An instant later his head was yanked abruptly back by his hair and the cold lips of a gun barrel were pressed against his right temple.

A Navy Arms New Model Russian Revolver, I think, Gary referenced his mental catalogue of firearms, even as the 'click' of the lethal weapon resonated in his ear. *44 caliber. Six shots, six-and-a-half inch barrel, forty ounces in weight, with a smooth walnut grip. Nice gun, but that's not to say I'd consider myself privileged to receive a cranial enema from one.*

"Who are you?" Zarubezhnik was snarling. "Speak, damn you! If those bloody Chinks have double-crossed me..."

"I don't know any Chinks," Gary said, quite calmly. "I know a Jap, but he insists they're two entirely different things. Not quite sure I believe him, though. By the way, Carla, feel free to jump in anytime. No rush or anything, y'understand."

In quick response, a dart fired from Carla's wrist launcher whistled through the stale air and embedded itself in Zarubezhnik's broad, shiny forehead. The fast-acting tranquilizer took immediate effect, and the Russian lay passed out on the floor a mere five seconds later.

"What were you waiting for, an engraved invitation?" Gary asked, irritably, rubbing the back of his head as he rose to his feet.

"It's fairly common knowledge that men resent being saved by women," said Carla, returning to floor level with an agile forward flip. "I didn't want to emasculate you."

Gary didn't have a chance to respond to the facetious jibe before a big hand seized him by the back of his collar and yanked him off his feet.

"You again!" exclaimed Warren Winterhawk.

"Well, if it isn't my old buddy Tonto," said Gary. "How's the Lone Ranger doing? Jeez,

I'd forgotten how tall you are. Shouldn't you be standing in front of a cigar store somewhere?"

"You're a real funny boy, ain't ya?" the Indian snarled, tossing Gary forwards to land hard on the cold, metal floor.

"Not according to the judges on *Star Search*," said Gary, somersaulting into a fighter's stance. "How else d'you think I got stuck in this lousy, dead-end job?"

Winterhawk lunged at Gary, but his smaller opponent ducked to the left and thrust his fist into the Indian's hard washboard stomach.

"Is that all ya got?" Winterhawk chuckled. "Our last fight shoulda taught ya that not even your strongest blow can hurt me!"

"I didn't want to hit you, Kimosabe," said Gary. "I wanted to give you something."

Winterhawk lowered his head to look down the length of his powerful torso, and finally located a strange object, about the size and shape of a quarter, attached to his hawk-shaped belt buckle.

"What the...?" he began to say.

Then the object exploded, and Winterhawk blasted off his feet like a giant firecracker and rocketed ten yards into an unstable mountain of crates, which collapsed all around him, burying him beneath an avalanche of heavy wood.

"Brother, if he was annoyed *before*..." Gary whistled, shaking his head mirthfully.

"What *was* that, Gary?" Carla asked.

"Carolyn's latest," he answered. "Intended primarily for when you want to destroy a small obstacle without causing any peripheral damage, but it works on big, sore-headed goons like him, too. Now, I suggest we leave the mopping up to the harbor cops and make a quick exit before Sitting Bull can get his shit together."

Of all of Manhattan's all-night watering holes of ill repute, from the raunchy Burning Bush strip club with its underage performers, all-girl orgies, and under-the-counter prostitution, to the flagrantly freakish fantasyland of The Giddy Grasshopper's homosexual nirvana, to the more mainstream den of iniquity that was The White Stallion, there was none so seedy, sordid, and abhorrent as Mick's Tavern, a wretched, run-down, ramshackle little pub down by the docks on the East River. It was a decrepit, dilapidated bar, with cracked, grimy windows, holes in the sagging roof, and bullets lodged in the walls. On the inside, the warped hardwood floor was stained with equal parts beer, blood, and urine, obscene graffiti decorated the walls, and the tables and chairs were rickety and unstable, having been deployed as makeshift weapons in many a spontaneous brouhaha. The low-wattage lightbulbs cast a dim, brown glow that strained even the most adaptable of eyes, the tiny billiards room in the back had long since fallen into hopeless disrepair and become a convenient place to take a shit – for those patrons who didn't feel like walking all the way across the street to the Texaco station – and the incredible odor of unwashed drunkards, coupled with the oppressive storm clouds of cigarette smoke, choked nearly all breathable oxygen from the air.

This was Mick's Tavern, an exclusive sanctuary for New York's criminal scum; a private social scene where the city's thieves, killers, sex offenders, street punks, and wanted felons could kick back for a few hours, have a drink, and forget about the wife they had strangled, the vengeful drug dealers they had messed with, or the money-grubbing lawyers who were fucking their ill-gotten savings straight to hell. Here in this repugnant, unkempt haven for society's dysfunctional cast-offs and reprobates, ugly hookers touted for business, amateur hitmen closed contracts, dirty cops in plainclothes took their weekly bribes, and big thugs and toughs cracked their knuckles and boasted about the legs they had broken.

One of the tavern's better-to-do regulars – who stopped by not because he couldn't find anything better to do, but because he enjoyed showing off for the useless, unskilled degenerates to be perpetually found there – was Gillard G. Gatsby, long a high-up enforcer for the Irish mob. A dandified eccentric, he spoke with a brogue as thick as Hudson River water, and adopted his persona from the mythical leprechauns of his native Emerald Isle, making a habit of dressing quite ridiculously in a green jacket, green vest, white silk shirt, green trousers, green shoes with shiny, gold buckles, and a green derby hat with a fresh four-leaf clover – plucked daily from his own greenhouse – stuck in the band. His hair was orange and curly, as was the pointed goatee on his chin, and as he leaned back in his chair with his feet up on the table, he twirled his diamond-topped cane lazily with his left hand and puffed smoke rings from a long-stemmed clay pipe cradled in his right, and regaled his gathered admirers with tales of his adventurous experiences in his chosen profession.

"An' would you believe it, m'lads, that after all that'd 'appened in the course o' that evenin', that I then found meself cornered in the very sanctum o' the fat boy 'imself, bein' accused o' cheatin' no less!" he dramatized, with all the talent of a professional storyteller. "Well, I wasn't after takin' too kindly to this accusation, as you may well imagine."

"*Were* you cheating?" asked Sally, a gaudily dressed hooker who tried to hide her advanced age, rather unsuccessfully, behind thick layers of make-up.

"O' course," said Gatsby. "He 'ad me dead to rights, caught on some 'idden camera, slidin' an ace o' diamonds down me sleeve, but buggered if I was content to 'ave the label affixed, bein' known about town as a man o' class an' refinement. Now, I'd 'eard tell o' the method by which ol' Mr. Kubritz enjoyed dispensin' with cheaters an' such, an' sittin' in that office, I could tell that the atmosphere wasn't quite right, 'specially when he reached for this whackin' great sledgehammer, 'efting it like it was a blackjack and sayin', 'Now, Mr. Gatsby, would you like to do this the painful way, or the *extremely* painful way?' in that pompous, blusterin' voice o' his."

"I know exactly whatcha mean," said a sinewy punk, sitting ass-backwards on a wobbly chair, a cigarette dribbling from his lips. "I used to work for Kubritz, and brother, he could put the fear of God into you with a single breath. Just one threatenin' word from him and your mind spun outta control."

"Not the case with I, m'laddo," Gatsby grinned, tapping the stem of his pipe against his right temple. "Keepin' perfect and unflinchin' command o' the ol' brainbox, I made good me escape from one o' the most feared criminal dens in the New York underworld. When he swung that 'ammer at me, I deflected it with me stick, then kicked him 'ard in the knee, and he dropped like a marble statue what's had its feet cut off. Then his blokey made a go for me —y'know, the one with the metal 'ands – but I jabbed him in the chest with me stick and switched on the ol' stun blaster and that saw him off good an' proper. An' that, dear friends, is how I, the Great Gatsby, single-handedly defeated one o' the greatest criminal minds o' our time."

"Wow," Sally gushed. "That's some story. You must be a really brave man."

"Real David and Goliath stuff," said Mick, the proprietor, himself an Irishman of seamy character. "You're a credit to the underdog, Gil."

"An' *I* say yer fulla shit, paddy," a gravelly voice rasped from the back.

"Who said that?" asked Gatsby, shooting up from his chair. "I demand to know who said that!"

The scraping of a chair being pushed out from a table sounded off on Gatsby's left, and an elderly albino man, his scalp bald, his eyes red, and his physique slight and withered, dragged himself into the light.

"You dare call me a liar?" Gatsby fumed.

"Yes! Liar!" the albino wheezed, pausing just long enough to spit out a ragged, phlegmy cough. "It's criminal slander you speak! Norman Kubritz was a giant of a man, quick of thought and unerring in direction, and if you had done even the slightest thing to provoke him, he would have brushed you right out of existence as he would have done a speck of lint on his cuff! One snap of that man's fingers and every killer in the city, including your own boss, would've been vying for your head!"

"Shit, Kubritz wasn't so tough," said Jackie T, a streetwise black man who made his living selling hard drugs to soft kids. "Offed himself in the end, didn't he?"

"Don't you dare believe it!" hissed the albino. "Maybe it was meant to look that way, but I know better! It was the Vigilantes! It had to be them! No one else could have done it!"

"You're senile, pops," said the serial killer called the Unicorn, so named because of the enormous wart in the center of his forehead. "There ain't no such thing as any Vigilantes. That's just a story the D.A. cooked up to keep us all runnin' scared."

"It *had* to be them!" the albino insisted. "As loath as I am to admit it, they had the capability to defeat Kubritz. A capability which you lack, Gatsby!"

"I'm warnin' ya, old man..." Gatsby growled through clenched teeth.

"What right have you to bandy the name of one of the greatest men this city has ever seen?" the albino continued his impassioned scolding. "You're nothing but a worm; a bottom-feeder! You tell stories to make yourself feel big, but you're *small*! You're a little, little man who cheats at cards, dishonors the dead, and tells tales in bars, and that's all you'll *ever* be, you lying, scavenging, whiskey-swilling, shit-eating shamus!"

The bullet from Gatsby's Glock 22 drove itself through the exact center of the albino's pasty forehead, and the old man flew off his feet and crashed onto his back, as if he had slipped on a patch of ice. Gatsby, his gun barrel still smoking, leapt up onto his table, shaking his fist and stomping his foot like the indignant imp he was.

"Does anyone else dare call me a liar?" he roared. "Who else doubts me word? Who else wants to taste the wrath o' the fightin' Irish? C'mon, I know you're all spoilin' for a fight! Honor yourselves with the privilege o' perishin' at the hands o' the Great Gatsby, just like that fucker over there! Stand up, lest ye all be cowards! Let all who challenge stand up!"

Then came an abrupt crash from the tavern's only entrance, and all of the patrons, including Gatsby, looked over to see the door broken off its rusted hinges and collapsed on the floor, yielding access to a tall, severe phantom of a man.

"*I* challenge," declared Shang Fear, his voice poisonous with menace, his right fist stickerbushed with splinters from its impact with the door, the cool, damp wind whipping at his coattails as it wafted in off the nearby, mist-blanketed water.

"Faith and begorra! Who the 'ell is this brazen, Chinkish interloper?"

"I am the banker of life and death, Gatsby," said Fear, "and I've come to inform you that you've been living on borrowed time for far too long!"

Before any of the tavern's rattled patrons could make a move to accost the strange newcomer, an object the size of a tennis ball flew from Fear's hand and exploded upon impact with the floor, filling the bar with a thick, black smoke whose wispy tendrils groped into every corner of the room, blinding the eyes and choking the throat. In the thick of the unnatural darkness that followed, there came the 'schlink' of a razor sharp sword being drawn, succeeded almost immediately by the squishy 'thud' of a head hitting the floor, and Mick, peeking out from his hiding place behind his counter, was just able to make out the grisly sight of the Great Gatsby's carrot-topped noggin rolling like a bowling ball across the uneven boards.

Other noises ensued. Flattening himself to the floor with both his hands clasped over his precious, balding scalp, the terrified Mick heard Jackie T scream as his stomach was impaled by something long and sharp. He heard the body of the Unicorn crash to the floor, a jagged chair leg protruding from his forehead that did much more to make him the namesake of the mythical one-horned beast. He heard Sally pinned up against the wall and shrieking in agony as Fear thrust his dagger up inside of her and scooped her out like a Halloween pumpkin. In horrific stereo sound he heard bodies thudding, blood splattering, guts squishing, bones breaking, victims howling, glass shattering, and furniture splintering, all melding together in a truly unholy din that could only herald the coming of the devil himself.

Then, just as suddenly as the chaos had begun, it ceased, and the smoke began to thin out. Mick, petrified with terror, remained on the floor behind the counter, praying frantically to any and every patron saint who would listen, while strange, scratching noises persisted from the far side of the tavern, alerting the hapless bartender that the harbinger of gruesome death still tarried on the premises.

Finally, when the dreaded, dangerous thumping of the butcher's boots seemed to indicate a cavalier departure, Mick reached up to the counter with one hairy arm, gripped the edge with trembling fingers, and pulled himself slowly and shakily to his feet. The atrocious menagerie of carnage and massacre that assaulted his teary eyes was enough to make him fall forwards onto the bar, retching. The place was a mess with severed limbs, decapitated bodies, spilled bowels, and poolings of blood. Not one patron had been left alive.

So hasty was Mick's panicked departure that the bartender didn't even notice the Shakespearean quotation Fear had left behind, painted across the wall with the fresh blood of his victims. It read, 'By the pricking of my thumbs, something wicked this way comes.'

Dr. Desmond Death, prestigious surgeon to the criminal elite and savvy wheeler-dealer within the black market of illicitly harvested body parts, was a tall, thin man with short, blond hair and pince-nez glasses, and though he possessed neither a practicioner's license nor a membership with the American Medical Association, the quality of his work and his commitment to his patients could not be denied, and this was why his exclusive little 'clinic' saw so many of the injured gangsters, mobsters, and other assorted murderers who were reluctant to take their urgent business to a legitimate hospital.

"Take note, Smedley," said Dr. Death, clad in his pale green scrubs and matching sanitary mask, as he and the similarly dressed intern regarded the unconscious form lying facedown on the operating table in front of them. "Being the pampered, halfwit son of an Italian Don doesn't necessarily mean never having to say you're sorry."

"Yes, Doctor," said the young Smedley, ever eager to learn from his mentor.

Dr. Death smirked behind his mask as he extracted the last of three bullets from his patient's right shoulder and dropped it in a tray with a ceremonious 'ka-tink' of finality.

"There, now, that wasn't so bad, was it?" said Dr. Death. "And to think the big baby wanted to be put under for that."

"It seems to me that a local would have been sufficient, Doctor," Smedley concurred.

"Indeed," said Dr. Death, "but this boy always takes things too far. That's what gets him into trouble all the time. If I were his father...still, I shouldn't complain. After all, the more people he pisses off, the more money I make."

Smedley didn't have the chance to nod in grinning agreement before the tiny operating room's only door creaked open, and a gorgeous blond creature – long of leg, plump of rear, pouty of lip, and ample of bosom – appeared, clad in an immaculately white nurse's uniform of the variety seldom seen outside of themed porno films, complete with ludicrously high heels, sheer white stockings, daringly short skirt, wide open blouse, and conscientious cap perched just so atop her golden tresses.

"Excuse me, Doctor," she said, in a melodious, breathy voice, "but you're needed out front."

"It would be unethical for me to leave my patient at this time," said Dr. Death, curtly.

"But it's kinda important," said the nurse, scuffing her toe shyly against the floor, her manicured hands clasped behind her back. "It's about that heart you wanted."

"Eh? What about it?"

"Well, the thing is, it's here."

"Ah, I see," said Dr. Death, removing his mask. "Well, that's another matter entirely. Smedley, be a help and finish stitching this up for me. And after you've done that, call Mr. Hannah and tell him that we've finally got that heart he's been needing and that he should get himself down here as soon as humanly possible."

Smedley nodded, and prepared to finish treating the young Italian's wound, while Dr. Death removed his smock, threw his bloody plastic gloves into the wastebasket, and marched briskly from the room, with the nurse at his heels.

"We've been waiting for this one for quite a while, haven't we, Doctor?" panted the nurse, skipping along at a quick trot – handicapped as her stride was by her tall shoes – her unrestrained breasts jiggling with every step.

"Indeed we have, my pet," said Dr. Death, reaching the end of the bare corridor and pushing through the door that stood between him and the waiting ambulance parked at the curb. "I don't mind saying there was a point there when I feared a suitable match would not be found in time, but there is something to be said for faith."

"You're such a wise man, Doctor," sighed the nurse, wearing her admiration for her employer on her sleeve.

"There will be ample time for praise later, my dear," said Dr. Death, indulgently. "And perhaps some fellatio to relax the tension."

Approaching the ambulance with the eagerness of a child approaching a gift-laden Christmas tree, Dr. Death threw open the double-doors at the back of the emergency vehicle to reveal the hoped-for sight of a small, styrofoam cooler sitting on the floor, and when he lifted the lid to peek inside, his pulse raced at the discovery of a human heart, dormant and unassuming, nestled securely in a bed of crushed ice; the biological pump that seemed so small and fragile now, yet had the power to keep a man's circulatory system running on full steam for a hundred years or more. Oh, what a complex and fantastic machine was the body human!

Dr. Death's pontifications were interrupted by the whip that seized his right forearm with an authoritarian 'crack' and pulled him forcibly back onto the sidewalk. Its wielder was a diminutive Chinese woman called Penelope Yin, all of five-and-one-half feet tall, dressed provocatively in a dark red tube top, an equally crimson pair of tight, low-cut capri pants, and demure red slippers. Now in her early forties, she was but an afterthought of the beautiful young flower she had used to be, and though she wasn't exactly decrepit, her face and body had both become hard and jagged, her skin was tough and leathery, and the occasional wrinkle or varicose vein couldn't resist making its presence known.

As a younger, more attractive woman, Penelope Yin had been trapped in a life of degradation and debauchery in one of Bei Jing's more upscale brothels, where she'd specialized in leather-clad sadomasochism and bondage play for the predominantly rich and famous clientele, spanking them with riding crops, clamping clothespins onto their nipples and testicles, and grinding many a foreign object into their backsides. She had done all of this because her state of economic desolation had left her little alternative, and even then the paycheck was never very dazzling; the brothel's owner and operator – her employer – had seemed convinced that a good banging was often welcome in lieu of some cold, hard cash. No, this life of chains and ball gags and putting crybaby wimps in diapers, all the while being bound in chains of her own by the communist oppressors, had not been not for her, and so it should hardly come as a surprise that, when the ripest of any likely opportunity to escape the brothel – along with China altogether – had come strolling into her backroom and asked for the works, Penelope had seized it with both hands.

Au-Yong Hai, the brother of the Chinese premier, had not been an infrequent visitor to the brothel. Penelope had caught sight of him there on at least twelve previous occasions, wallowing in infamy under his powerful sibling's protection and pissing away the family money on sexual frivolities. On those occasions he had always gravitated towards the abuse-the-girl-of-your-choice offers or the mother-daughter combos. He had never before expressed an interest in being dominated by a badass bitch in a spiked thong. Penelope had supposed he'd wanted to try something new, and that had suited her just as apples suit little green worms.

Having been given time beforehand to read over Au-Yong Hai's kinky requests, she had been fully prepped and ready for him when he'd entered her chamber. Truly enjoying herself for the first time in years, Penelope had let all of her titillating expertise work for her as she'd stripped Hai down, padlocked him inside of a snug, leather bodysuit that covered every inch of his body save for his nose, cuffed his hands behind his back, hobbled his ankles with shackles, and finally attached herself to her unsuspecting victim with an additional pair of manacles connected by a length of chain that led from his neck to her wrist like an unbreakable leash. Then, without hesitation, she had dragged him out into the center of the brothel, tore open her robe to reveal the plastique with which she had wired herself, and had announced coolly but meaningfully that if the premier didn't agree to put her on an airplane bound for Mexico that very night, he'd have to pick up his brother's remains with a pair of chopsticks.

After the plane's landing in a rural area several miles north of Mexico City, Penelope had informed the pilot that he was now free to fly himself and the still-restrained Hai back to the Far East, then strode confidently away into the wilderness, utterly proud of the way she had handled the situation. From there it had been the simplest of tasks to infiltrate the United States through its porous southern border, and a prosperous career in urban crime – which soon revealed itself to be one of her natural aptitudes – followed, and had been extremely kind to her ever since.

"Just what do you think you're doing?" Dr. Death huffed, glaring at his assailant as he freed his arm from the whip. "I wasn't made aware you'd be coming."

"I've been dispatched as an emissary of the *Dong Ji*," Penelope said, "to inform you that this heart will be the last delivered to you at the old price. A higher rate will have to be negotiated for all future transactions."

"What? Why?"

"Change in environment," Penelope answered. "With the death of Norman Kubritz, the underworld has become unstable and the assorted mobs are jockeying aggressively for position. Criminal activity has not so much increased as it has become exponentially more erratic and unregulated. It will be more dangerous, more difficult, and certainly more expensive for us to procure for you the usual...materials."

"I could always change my supplier," Dr. Death thought he sounded threatening.

"I think not," Penelope replied. "You'll do much better to remain with us. You see, we recently cracked open a few old blueprints of this 'clinic' of yours, and..."

"And what?"

"And, taking into consideration its age, its safety equipment, its location in this neighborhood, and its general state of decrepitude...well, we estimate it to be quite the little firetrap, if I'm not being too subtle for you."

Dr. Death's features shifted from indignity to confusion to rage as Penelope's meaning dawned upon him.

"Why, you petty, ruthless bitch!" he cursed her. "You people are villains! Monstrous, medieval villains!"

"Oh, come now," said Penelope. "We're not entirely bad. We know how to look after our long-term dependents. Just to show there's nothing but good will to be found here, we've brought you an additional little present completely free of charge or obligation. Boys, show the good doctor our olive branch."

Lau and Jin, the Chinese men who had been sitting silently in the ambulance's cab all this time, exited the vehicle and walked around to the back, where they reached in past the cooler, and, with visible effort, managed to haul out and drop onto the pavement an immense black man, clearly dazed, his meaty wrists cuffed behind his back in a pair of electric shackles designed to send painful, discouraging shocks coursing through the body of any captive who applied even a small degree of pressure or resistance against them.

"This is for you," said Penelope.

"I say!" Dr. Death exclaimed, all anger and resentment forgotten. "What a marvelous specimen! Such a body! Such musculature! Such potential for raw power! To think of the hardy, healthful, robust organs I could salvage from such a wonderful beast!"

"Help yourself," Penelope invited. "In fact, you'll even be doing the *Dong Ji* a service by killing him. He has proven himself an enemy. He attacked us on the way here, and it was quite the bother to subdue him."

"Oh, goody, goody, goody!" Dr. Death rubbed his hands together and fairly danced with joy as he turned to his sexy nurse waiting patiently on the sidewalk. "Nurse, fetch three strong orderlies and an extra sturdy gurney! We must begin examination as soon as possible!"

Lying docilely on the ground, Charlie groaned quietly, blinked his eyes to clear them of the blur, and cursed himself for being so careless. He didn't usually allow his own physical dominance to trick him into underestimating his opponent, but he did have to admit to an unhealthy overconfidence in this present situation. After all, it had only been three little Chinese, one of whom looked to be a prostitute. What real danger could they have posed? Plenty, Charlie had found out, as they had proven themselves to be skilled, organized fighters. While the two men had held him at bay, dodging his big arms agilely and leaping repeatedly in and out to take annoying jabs at him with their own hands and feet, the woman had blasted him from behind with a stun gun, the full discharge of which Charlie was convinced had been intended for elephants. After he had collapsed helplessly to the ground, his triumphant foes had wasted no time in restraining him with those damned shackles, and, with some difficulty – it had taken all three of them – heaving his heavy body into the back of the ambulance before continuing on their way. But now his vision was clearing, his body was feeling stronger, and the buzzing in his ears was finally subsiding to a point where he could make out most of his captors' chatter, and none of it gave him the impression that they were discussing something for which he'd like to stick around.

"Madam Yin, I must apologize for my prior harsh speech," said Dr. Death, appeasingly, as his nurse and orderlies returned, wheeling a very large gurney outfitted with leather straps and iron shackles. "As temperamental as our unique economy has become, there lingers in my mind no doubt whatsoever that our two parties will be able to arrive at a satisfactory and amicable new contract."

"Excellent," said Penelope. "I shall convey your good wishes to my colleagues upon my imminent return to their bosom."

"Must you rush?" asked Dr. Death, as he motioned for his nurse and orderlies to get started with the heavy lifting. "Are you sure I couldn't tempt you and your friends with a cup of tea, or some other such refreshment?"

"Quite sure, thank you," Penelope declined. "I mean no offense by what I'm about to say, but, in my experience, Americans know very little when it comes to the proper preparation, presentation, and consumption of truly fine tea."

For the past several minutes, while Dr. Death and Penelope had been exchanging varied pieces of dialogue in varied temperaments and tones of voice, Charlie had been playing possum, lying seemingly helpless in the midst of his enemies, gradually recouping his strength for the painful ordeal which he knew would be the breaking of his bonds, and as one of the orderlies drew near, Charlie made his move and bit the man hard on the leg with all the unrelenting meanness of a junkyard dog. It was an unexpected move that caught the assembled criminals completely off their guard for the few precious seconds required, and Charlie didn't waste them. Even as the wounded orderly hopped away on one bleeding leg, howling in pain, Charlie regained his own feet and channeled all of his diminished but still significant strength into the effort of shattering the shackles, which retaliated by channeling eager waves of electricity through his aching body with every ounce of force he applied in the name of freedom. It hurt a lot. He felt like he was on fire, burning up from the inside, but his straining muscles ultimately won out, and the torture stopped abruptly as the shackles broke apart just in time for Charlie to scream once and collapse to the pavement. Although only four seconds had elapsed since he had begun his agonizing struggle, to Charlie it had seemed much longer, coping with the malicious current coursing through every fiber of his rebellious body. As resilient as his faculties were, however, he was nonetheless obliged to remain a crumpled heap on the asphalt, trembling and breathing heavily as the menagerie of villains fell upon him, his muscles having been reduced temporarily to linguini.

Gonna have to roll with the punches and take the beating for a few moments, thought Charlie. *Play dead while I regain some energy.*

"Subdue him! Quickly!" Dr. Death bellowed. "Don't let him get back up!"

The three orderlies, bulky ex-cons all, took the initiative, hurling themselves onto Charlie and attempting to pin him, while Lau and Jin rushed into the periphery of the punch-up, crouched like coiled springs, ready to leap in at the crucial juncture with a punishing chop to their big foe's solar plexus.

"Keep strugglin', Sambo, 'cause this is sweet to me!" growled one of the orderlies, punching Charlie repeatedly in the face. "In prison I got fucked in the ass by niggers regular, and, as far as I'm concerned, this is payback for all o' ya!"

"I don't got nothin' personal against niggers," said the orderly kneeling on Charlie's stomach, "but you just guaranteed me stitches in my leg, and damned if I'm lettin' you get away with that!"

"Doc, we got him!" shouted the third orderly, holding Charlie in a headlock. "Get a trank into him already!"

"Be still, you magnificent creature!" Dr. Death, having hurriedly prepared a potent sedative in a hypodermic, scrambled towards the center of the mayhem, ready to plunge the needle deep beneath the skin of his reluctant organ doner. "You serve a greater purpose! You will help me give life to countless unfortunates! Give me your organs for transplants, your blood for transfusions, and your skin for grafts! Just think of the dozens of fully functioning bodies you'll complete! There are so many sores to heal! So many breaks to mend! So many wounds to bind!"

Then the three orderlies cried out in alarm as they were sent flying in different directions, and Dr. Death found his wrist locked in the crushing grip of a very big hand.

"Thanks," said Charlie, a wicked grin spreading across his black-and-blue face, "but I gave at the office."

A jarring punch, and the doctor tumbled over and struck the back of his head against the curb, rendering him senseless, while the nurse shrieked in fright and ran back inside the clinic with all the speed her impractical shoes could afford her.

Lau and Jin sprang into action, dancing around Charlie, hoping to again dazzle him with their fancy footwork, but the big Vigilante would not succumb to the same offensive twice, and the two Chinese were swatted aside by a pair of bone-shaking backhands. Then the trio of orderlies rushed him again.

Amazing how a little lie down can make you feel so much stronger, thought Charlie, side-stepping the most eager challenger, then seizing him by the back of his shirt and heaving him headfirst into a steel lamppost.

"Is that all ya've got?" asked Charlie, picking up the second orderly by the neck and hurling him into the side of the ambulance.

"C'mon, you black son of a bitch!" snarled the orderly who had expressed dissatisfaction with his love life inside prison walls, wielding a blade the size of a butcher's cleaver. "I'm gonna cut you up bad, you shit-eating nigger!"

An amateurish swipe with the blade was dodged easily by Charlie, and the orderly was pulled in close to his large enemy by a set of thick fingers that latched on to the front of his shirt.

"Have I ever told you how much I hate that word?" said Charlie, hunching a bit and hoisting the orderly up onto his tiptoes so that a gap of mere inches remained between the orderly's face and his own. "It's a foul, dirty slur. I hate that it's used constantly by practically all of our cultural figureheads, I hate that an entire generation of black youngsters is growing up hollerin' it to each other, and I hate Richard Pryor for giving it positive connotations in the first place."

Then came the crackingly loud headbutt that sent the orderly crashing to the ground, blood gushing from his broken nose, and Charlie looked around for someone else to hit. But there was no one. The doctor and his flunkies were all down for the count, and the three Chinese strangers had vanished.

Probably run into 'em again sooner or later, thought Charlie, prodding a loosened tooth with the tip of his tongue. *The bad guys never stay outta the picture for long.*

Whistling 'I'm An Old Cowhand' to himself, the occasional drop of blood passing his lips with the tuneful expulsions of air, Charlie trudged casually over to the abandoned ambulance, retrieved the cooler with the heart inside, tucked it under one massive arm, and strolled for one and a half blocks, breathing in the luxuriously cool night air and allowing the gentle humidity to massage his aching muscles, until he arrived at yet another ambulance, this one piloted by a youthful paramedic.

"One human heart, used," said Charlie, handing the paramedic the cooler through the open window. "See? I told you that if you followed the action, you'd get it. Just took a little longer than I anticipated to sort 'em all out. Now rush that to Roosevelt Hospital. I know of a few people there who'll be very glad of it. I'll mop up here."

"You're the salt of the earth, Charlie boy," said the paramedic. "A prince among men."

"Save the eulogy for when one of 'em finally does me in," said Charlie.

On one side of the stained wooden table in the attorney-client conference room of Police Precinct 5 sat Thomas Jefferson Zang, a skilled Chinese martial artist and gunman who had long ago adopted the name of one of the most renowned and accomplished statesmen in American history in order to better 'blend in'. On the other side sat Conroy O'Shea, an Irishman in his late twenties, lightweight and wiry but tough, sporting a military crewcut, a pair of blue jeans, and a t-shirt reading 'God Kill The Queen'. Formerly of the terrorist revolutionary group known as the Irish Republican Army, O'Shea was perpetually surly, and, had the chip on his shoulder been an actual chip, he'd have had no choice but to walk around lopsided.

"My organization's patience with you grows short, Mr. O'Shea," said Thomas Jefferson Zang, glowering at the handcuffed, disheveled Irishman. "The *Dong Ji* selected you because of your tenacity, your guts, and your 'problem-solving' skills, as it were, which are all qualities for which I admire your people. How unfortunate it is, then, that the Irish tendencies to drink to excess, act with utter impropriety, and casually disregard all consequences of one's actions appear to rule over all other, more desirable characteristics in your case."

"Get off my ass, ya bleedin' yella Chink," said O'Shea, who had been arrested three hours earlier for his part in a violent barroom brawl. "I awready done more 'an what I hadda do to show you poncey-arse gooks that I 'ave what it takes, an' I ain't doin' no more. Ya wanna fire me, then knock yourselves the fuck out, but I ain't gonna grovel."

"We want to stick with you," said Zang, masquerading as O'Shea's attorney in order to ensure a private conversation. "You impress us consistently, for all your faults. But we can't have all this loose cannon nonsense. You're no good to us behind bars. If you wish to be part of the future – our future – then you must fall into line. Guidelines must be followed and rules must be observed. Clean, conscientious organization; that's the name of the machine. Am I quite clear?"

"Ya hired me to do a job, an' I'm gonna do it," said O'Shea, "but it's gonna be my way. I been doin' this shit forever, an' I know how ta get things done, an' I ain't takin' lip from any gookish taskmasters. Now, am *I* quite clear?"

Zang maintained his stern, stoic façade, but on the inside he rolled his eyes and heaved a sigh of fatigue. He sometimes wondered if *all* Caucasians were so crude; so careless; so undisciplined and disorganized.

A race of sensationalist cut-ups, he thought. *Why, they're almost as bad as...*

Zang's thoughts were interrupted by a bloodcurdling scream, two gunshots, and a crazed interjection of what sounded like Shakespearian verse. Then a cop flew from the other end of the hallway and crashed against the wall, blood spewing from a nasty wound in the left side of his chest. Two more mangled officers were quick to follow, hurled through the air as if weightless.

Oh, no, Zang lamented. *Not him. Even he's not mad enough to attempt a stunt like this...*

" 'The superior man, when resting in safety, does not forget that danger may come'!" cried Shang Fear, confirming Zang's worst fears. "Confucius!"

As he had done during his earlier siege upon Mick's Tavern, Fear moved with all the speed and agility of a superhuman acrobat, bouncing off desks and ricocheting off walls as he disarmed or dismembered each of his oncoming enemies on his quest for the holding cells through the door in the back, knocking out lights and throwing down explosives and smoke grenades as he went. The police, surprised and disoriented, were at a loss to stop this single extraordinary man.

"You are Alonzo Esteban?" Fear, having reached the cells, asked a Latino detainee sitting on a wooden bench behind bars. "Unchallenged regent of drug, prostitution, and car theft rings all throughout Brooklyn?"

"Uh...yeah," said the man in the cell.

Esteban barely had the time to get the word of affirmation past his lips before something like a harpoon shot from the sleeve of Fear's coat and impaled the Latino's forehead, nailing his skull to the wall behind him. Then, just as a platoon of armed cops was surging into the room, Fear was departing through the high window, shattering it into a thousand crystal shards that rained down upon and around him like hailstones as he landed gracefully on his feet outside the station.

Supremely satisfied with the work he had just completed, Fear sheathed his blade, and was making a great show of brushing himself off when a green convertible, its top down, screeched to a halt in the middle of the street, forcing other cars coming from both directions to zig-zag evasively around it and careen up onto the sidewalks where they sideswiped and crashed into fire hydrants, lampposts, and storefronts and sent panicked pedestrians scattering for cover. Occupying the convertible were the adolescent persons of three Red Cobras, clad in their trademark red-and-black bandannas and denim jackets.

"Hey, fish-face!" the Cobra behind the wheel shouted at Fear, making himself heard over the din of honking horns, squealing brakes, angry cursing, and wailing car alarms. "Ya like noodles? Ya like to eat your noodles? Eat your noodles, ya slant-eyed fucker! Eat 'em!"

Then came the star-shaped muzzle flash of a discharging AK-47 assault rifle wielded by the Cobra sitting alone at the back, and Fear dove for cover behind a parked police cruiser as a hail of bullets cut through the air towards him, each of their snub little noses diabolically intent on his life. For a full thirty seconds, Fear crouched behind the cruiser while the bullets chewed into the vehicle, shattered the windows, and exploded the red and blue lights atop the roof, and the young Cobras howled and hooted with maniacal glee.

"You done got that math wiz now, Franky!" Devon, the Cobra at the wheel, chortled like a hyena as he threw the car back into gear and stomped down hard on the accelerator, peeling a half inch of rubber off the squealing, smoking tires before resuming his rampage down the street. "He ain't gonna be makin' no more Happy Meal toys, that's for fuckin' sure!"

'Youth is a wonderful thing,' thought Fear, standing upright as the car full of Cobras roared away. *'What a crime to waste it on children.'* *George Bernard Shaw.*

"All right, Danny, who's next on the list?" Devon asked his compatriot in the passenger seat.

"Well, we already offed a cop, a Jew, and a Chink," said Danny, consulting the checklist, "so all we need is a pregnant woman and a seeing-eye dog and this little scavenger hunt is over!"

"Let's do it fast!" said Devon, sending the vehicle careening sharply around a ninety degree turn. "I ain't lettin' Jag beat me this time! Are you sure that was a Chink back there?"

"Sure it was," said Franky.

"I dunno, man," said Devon. "They all look alike. Remember last time? We killed a Jap instead and got disqualified! There's no way Jag is gonna beat me that way again!"

Before the discussion could continue, the speeding convertible was bounced suddenly by the heavy 'thud' of something landing on the trunk, and Franky barely had enough time to turn and look behind him before a polished steel blade cut cleanly through his neck with one swift stroke, and his head toppled from his shoulders, rolled across the backseat, and came to rest upside-down in the cup holder.

"It is a youthful failing to be unable to control one's impulses!" said Fear, standing tall and impossibly steady atop the back of the careening car, his coat flapping in the wind like a bat's wings, the police motorcycle he had commandeered now falling behind, riderless, having served its purpose. "But I give no more pardon or indulgence to my callow, immature enemies than I do to my foes of greater wisdom!"

Danny fumbled for his gun, but his skull was split like a block of wood beneath Fear's guillotine-sharp blade before he even had the chance to heft it, and, in the subsequent instant, the same blade cut a slicing arc through Devon's wrists, separating them from the screaming boy's arms, though the hands continued clinging to the steering wheel at the nine-and-three position, as if elemental of some ghastly, gruesome farce. It was then the execution of a simple backflip that deposited Fear back upon the pavement, where he stood comfortably and watched the convertible speed on unguided for an additional six seconds, then hit the curb, buck sideways, flip over a fire hydrant like a gymnast over a pommel horse, and come to a terrible, upside-down crash landing through the center of a florist's picturesque front window.

Brats, thought Fear, pulling up his high collar and retiring discreetly from the chaotic scene as throngs of curious and horrified gawkers materialized around the twisted, mangled wreck.

Hell of a way to kick off a Sunday morning, thought Carla – dressed comfortably for a change in a white cotton blouse, knee length skirt, and lightweight raincoat to protect against the rain that had presided over the Greater New York Area for six gray, dreary, miserable days in a row now – as she stood passively under the blue-and-yellow striped awning of Peebles' Printing and Stationery, sipping from a styrofoam cup of cold coffee and watching the coroner's people pull the zipper closed on the black bodybag and lug it out through the front door of The Happy Trails Diner across the street. *So much for my week off.*

Carla shrugged, dropped the bad coffee into the garbage can at her side, pulled her jacket's hood up so as to save the percentage of her hair that hadn't already frizzed in the damp air, and resumed her stroll down the sidewalk – crowded as usual, even in weather like this – towards the subway station she visited nearly every day.

As she traversed the final city block stretched out between her and the entrance to the underground, she thought about the grim parade of atrocities with which she had had to contend the previous night – that business at the harbor, a bomb in a Jewish temple, a roving child molester, a wife-beater, and three separate muggings – and was forced to the conclusion that, on average, Saturday nights were simply the worst nights for crime. As perpetually dangerous and hostile as New York's five boroughs were, no other night could touch Saturday, and last night had been typically horrendous, even in spite of its being the week's only notable reprieve from the tiresome rain, uncharacteristically relentless for these latter days of June. The oppressive weather, Carla conceded, had to shoulder some of the blame for her present bad mood, but other contributing factors included the recent increase in her apartment's rent, the battle scar on her pretty cheek that was beginning to seem as if it would never vanish completely, and the odious direction in which civilization in general and New York City in particular was racing with ever mounting speed.

Sometimes I wonder if this mudball island is even worth *saving,* she thought, sullenly.

Carla was jolted rudely from her gloomy self-indulgence when a heavyset man in jeans and a gray hooded sweatshirt was shoved violently against her and they both stumbled out into the street, narrowly avoiding being flattened by a Toyota Camry. Seconds later the assailant stalked forward, revealing himself to be a tall, brutish-looking thug in torn pants and a leather jacket.

"What the hell...?" Carla ejaculated.

"Hidin' behind a broad, Bingo?" sneered the brute. "Ain't that jus' typical!"

"I'm not afraid of you, you stupid punk!" retorted Bingo, shoving Carla aside and balling his fists. "If you've got something to bring, Artie, then just try and bring it over here! I dare you!"

"Mr. Castle warned you 'bout what would happen if he didn't get his money this week," Artie growled, reaching for an ice pick hanging from his belt.

"Castle's a punk!" Bingo spat back.

"I'm gonna tell him you said that," said Artie.

"Oh yeah?"

"Yeah!"

"Oh yeah?"

"Yeah!"

"If Castle wants his money, he's gonna have to come himself and pull every last dollar out of my fat, pasty ass!" declared Bingo.

"Boy, I'm gonna rip your balls off and stuff 'em up your nose!" threatened Artie.

"Enough!" shouted Carla, seizing each of the disputants by their respective collars and yanking them apart with a strength that belied her petite frame, holding them both at arm's length like naughty schoolchildren. "I am so fucking sick of all of this! What the fuck will it take for all of you dickheads to treat each other decently for a change? To hell with all of you!"

With a snort of unrestrained disgust, Carla dispensed with both of the astonished barbarians, shoving them disdainfully back into the trash-strewn alley from whence they had come, and resumed her journey down the avenue, her fists now clenched at her sides and her legs taking longer, quicker, angrier strides.

Buffoons, she seethed, stomping down the stone steps that would take her beneath the wet, dirty street and into the labyrinth of tunnels that crisscrossed the Big Apple's underground like a subterranean beehive. *Feckless, pointless, parasitic morons. Day and night I'm out there in the trenches, chafing my ass in that stupid leather suit, risking my life, and for what?*

Finally arriving at the discolored patch of stone wall that marked the entrance to the Vigilantes' clandestine base of operations, Carla pushed open the camouflaged door, pressed her right thumbprint against the electronic panel set into the wall in order to briefly deactivate the security measures in the entry corridor, then threw open the second door and emerged in the Rat Hole's lounge, occupied by what looked to be the majority of the team, with Gary and Leeza being the only apparent absentees.

"Does anyone else ever get the feeling that the only reason Jesus Christ wants you to accept Him into your heart is so He can take you down from the inside?" she asked the room.

"Sounds like someone's getting a visit from her 'friend'," said Zeke, his disgusting, ever present cigarette puffing away like a chimney.

"That's right, Zeke, give me an excuse to pulverize you," Carla snarled. "I'm just in the mood."

"It's the weather," said Buzz, ever the calming voice of reason. "We're all feeling it."

"It's getting worse, y'know," said Carla.

"Yeah, the prediction for Monday and Tuesday is constant thunderstorms," said Carolyn, thumbing through the newest issue of *Scientific American.*

"I'm talking about the crime," said Carla. "I mean, what are we doing this for? The crime rate in this city is growing, despite our best efforts. My body's aching and my biological clock is ticking and it all seems so... futile! Reminds me of Moses. He gives up a cushy life in the Pharaoh's palace and breaks his back working to free the Israelites, and what does he get for his trouble? His people grovel in the dirt before a do-it-yourself golden calf and God stamps 'Admission Denied' on his ticket into the Promised Land. Sure, he gets a nice write-up in the Bible, but was he ever really happy?"

"Really hammering away with the religious descriptors this morning, aren't we," remarked William, his bespectacled eyes peeking out from behind his big computer monitor.

"I was raised Catholic," said Carla, extracting a can of Fresca from the refrigerator and popping it open with a carbonated 'snick'. "It's in my vernacular."

"She's right, though," said Sushi, standing rigidly to attention in front of the widescreen TV, his back to the others while he observed the grotesque images, deemed 'possibly disturbing to some viewers', being sent out over the airwaves of the local twenty-four-hour news channel. "Of late, the wind has been carrying something distinctly different; something bitter; something distasteful; something...ominous. I've sensed its coming for weeks. I've sensed the build-up of negative energy. With every step I've taken, it's dogged me. And now it grips the city, though I am at a loss to mark it."

"Okay, you can drop the whole 'mystic Jap' routine now, 'cause no one's buyin' it," said Zeke, coughing out a trio of snaking smoke wisps.

"Must you smoke those filthy things in here?" asked Carolyn. "Some of us are trying to breathe."

"Aw, a little second-hand smoke never hurt anybody," said Zeke.

"Actually, it kills," said Carolyn.

"Yeah, and a penny saved is a penny earned," retorted Zeke. "What's your point?"

"What are your thoughts, Peg?" asked Charlie, massaging a big, purple bruise just above his right temple.

"Oh, I'm a carton-a-day girl myself," said Peg, "but I do have the courtesy not to impose it upon people who place a greater value on their general health."

"No, I mean about the crime situation," said Charlie. "Would you say there's been a sharp increase lately?"

"Rape, murder, drugs, people behaving like animals," Peg sighed. "Why should it all come to a grinding halt now?"

"If the FBI's official website can be believed, crime in the city of New York has risen dramatically over the course of the past month alone," said William, consulting the online statistics. "But what's the catalyst?"

Then the Rat Hole's only entrance swung open once again and Gary appeared, a purple-and-yellow silk kimono wrapped flamboyantly around his frame, a bright orange, papier-mâché dragon's head concealing his face, and a large, white take-out box of fragrant leftovers clutched in his left hand.

"I don't want to make any unfair generalizations," he said, his voice muffled slightly by the dragon's head, "but, for a predominantly hard-working race, those Chinese sure do know how to throw a party."

"Hey, Gary, I haven't seen you around for the past couple of days," said Charlie. "Where've ya been?"

"Chinatown summer festival," Gary answered, pulling off the dragon's head to reveal his own flushed visage. "It was a riot, even in the rain. Parades, dancing, fireworks, open markets. I even got to be the apparatus for a pair of female Chinese gymnasts!"

"The what?" asked William.

"The apparatus," said Gary. "Y'know, like the pommel horse or the parallel bars. There I was, kneeling on my hands and knees in the middle of the street, stripped to my briefs and covered in chalk dust, with two beautiful young girls dancing spritely around on my back! It was fantastic! Oh, and of course they had tons of great food there as well. Anyone want an egg roll? Fried wonton? I brought plenty."

"I'm sure we're all thrilled, Gary, that you had such a wonderful time while some of us were getting our butts whipped doing actual work," said Carla, glaring disapprovingly and crossing her arms in refusal to partake of the Oriental delicacies being passed around the room, "but we were just talking about something rather serious."

"You mean the huge and horrifying spike in criminal activity as of late?" said Gary, his intuition as sharp as ever. "What do you think I was doing in Chinatown in the first place? Investigating, my dear Watson. After all, it all stems from there."

"From Chinatown?" asked Buzz.

"More specifically, the Chinese mob," Gary elaborated. "But it was only a matter of time, I suppose. Look, we took out Norman Kubritz just over a month ago, right? Well, that leaves a great big vacancy at the top tier of New York's criminal hierarchy – a vacancy that hasn't been there for decades – and you can bet that the competition for that spot will be fierce. From what I've observed over the past several days, the Chinese sector is currently doing the most ruthless and efficient job in making their way to power's peak, using uncharacteristically bold guerilla tactics to win this little gangland war they've initiated, aggressively wiping out as much of their competition as possible."

"Wait a minute," said Charlie, swallowing the bulk of an egg roll in a single gulp. "I ran afoul of a group of Chinese last night. They didn't appear to be up to anything too unusual, though they did give me some trouble."

"I think that if we scratch the surface, we'll find that a lot of the crimes we've encountered lately have carried the influence of the Chinese mob," said Gary.

"I have no love for the Chinese," Sushi stated. "They're unscrupulous, underhanded, and untrustworthy. And their eyes are too close together."

There was no time for any of the less xenophobic Vigilantes to respond to Sushi's declaration before the door flew open once again, this time slamming angrily against the wall with enough force to break a tiny crack in the wallpaper, heralding the arrival of Leeza, the tenth and final member of the team to materialize. This morning she looked even meaner and surlier than usual, perpetually sour though she was. Her eyes were black, her jaw was set, her fists were clenched, and her shoulders were trembling as she glared at her nine colleagues, seeming to lock eyes with each and every one of them simultaneously.

"You all enjoy a great many jokes at my expense," she began, her voice dangerous with quiet rage, "and for the most part, I let them pass, as I consider your boorish, juvenile humor beneath my notice. I take your snide remarks about my country and my national heritage in stride, as I acknowledge the black, monstrous stigma that will hang over my homeland for generations to come. You call me 'Eva Braun' and I shrug it off, as I know you think you're merely being flip, and do not realize the hurt and shame you're repeatedly dredging up. But I will not forgive you this latest and most atrocious infraction against my person, and I have come down here one last time to inform you all that I am taking my leave of your graceless company and quitting this ridiculous occupation."

"Quitting? Leeza, what are you talking about?" asked Gary, who didn't relish the prospect of scouting a new physician. "What's happened? I don't think I've ever seen you so upset."

"When Carla came in all riled, I figured she might be on the rag," Zeke chuckled. "I'd suggest the same here, but this old girl's drier than a month-old dog turd."

Zeke barely had time to affect his usual shit-eating grin before Leeza wiped it from his face with a blow from the hard plastic handle of the telescoping umbrella she clutched at her side.

"You've had this coming since the day I first met you!" she snarled, bringing the umbrella handle back down to punish the other side of Zeke's face in turn. "You're a lewd, uncivilized pig! Filthy, obscene, slovenly degenerate! You're probably the one who did it! You think painting a swastika on my door is a cute little joke, you vile, perverted, tasteless scum? You think the Third Reich is funny? You think any right-minded

German looks back upon that disgraceful chapter in our history with pride or amusement? I should beat you until you bleed!"

"Ow! Ow! Stop it! Get off me, you crazy old bitch! I have no idea what you're talking about!" Zeke hollered, raising his forearms to his face in an only semi-successful attempt to defend against Leeza's continuous batterings.

"That's enough!" Gary barked, seizing his septuagenarian teammate by the elbows and forcing her down into a chair. "Leeza, what the hell is the matter with you?"

"I am *not* a Nazi!" the old woman bellowed. "I have never *been* a Nazi! And I have had more than my fill of innuendo from the lot of you! Whichever one of you is responsible for painting that ugly black swastika on the outside of my door last night is going to answer for it, right here and now! Let the culprit speak up, damn you, and let me see the true color of your nature!"

Each of Leeza's nine colleagues glanced around the room at each other, exchanging looks of confusion and bewilderment.

"Leeza, I have a very hard time believing that anybody here would do something like that," Gary said, at last.

"Well, who else?" the elderly doctor demanded. "You all seem to find no small amount of pleasure in my discomfort!"

"A little teasing is one thing," said Charlie, "but a swastika? That's different. That's not right."

"Well, *someone* has to be responsible," said Leeza, beginning to calm down at last.

"Don't neo-Nazis sometimes paint swastikas on the doors of Jewish households?" suggested William.

"That isn't really pertinent to the matter at hand, Will, but thanks for participating anyway," said Gary.

"So, you're not really leaving us, right, Leeza?" asked Peg.

"No, I suppose not," the older woman sighed, "since you all swear ignorance. But surely you must realize how distressing this is for me."

"Of course we do," said Buzz. "Your reaction is perfectly understandable."

"I'll tell you what," said Gary. "We'll see if we can't track down whichever vandal is responsible. And later today, Zeke'll go over to your place with his can of white paint and cover it up for you."

"The hell I will!" Zeke protested, the dark bruises already forming on his face. "After she damn near beat my brains out? Forget it!"

"If you don't do it, then you won't get your salary from the Beck take-down," said Gary, simply.

"This ain't fair!" cried Zeke. "I'm bein' singled out 'cause o' my blue-collar status! What, no one else here can paint a door? Hell, even Shades over there could paint a door, and he's so blind that if I plugged his nose, handed him a piece o' shit, and told him it was a Twinkie, he'd eat it!"

"And it's that interminable condition of diarrhea-of-the-mouth that landed you this assignment in the first place," said Gary. "If you have anything more to say, *my* place could always use a little touching up."

Zeke said, 'Hrmph!', folded his arms, and remained silent, though the indignation came off him in waves.

Campion Earkhert – handpicked by God, as were all ministers of the Catholic faith – had received the calling at the age of fourteen, and, after graduating high school, had gone on to attend New York City's prominent St. John's University, where he'd earned a Bachelor of Science degree while dabbling extensively in the liberal arts. After his four years there, the next procedural step was enrollment at St. Vladimir's Orthodox Theological Seminary in Crestwood, New York, where he began his three-year quest for his Master of Divinity degree. Of course, he would never have been allowed to progress so far in life if anyone had seen him, at the tender age of seven, pushing that little girl in front of the city bus; nor if anyone had been able to prove that he had been the one, in his first year of junior high, to stab one of his classmates to death with a screwdriver; nor if he had been implicated in the savage beating of a homeless man a year later; nor if he had been seen slipping arsenic into the punchbowl at his senior prom.

The change in his environment upon his admission into college seemed to suppress and even pacify Earkhert's natural psychosis, however, and his dark side remained buried for years, even for the better part of his junior year at St. Vladimir's, with its eleven acres of lush, green surroundings, beautiful buildings, and lively, wholesome, community-oriented campus lifestyle. For his first seven months at the seminary, Earkhert was the very embodiment of what a priest-in-training should be, attending devotedly to his studies and participating enthusiastically in chapel and choir activities. Then, on an unusually hot and humid night in late April, he and a fellow student became involved in a bitter, protracted argument, and the following morning a body was found in the basement of the campus' chapel.

There was no holding Earkhert's bloodlust after that. The beast lying dormant inside of him had tasted its first kill in half a decade and it craved more. St. Vladimir's quickly became home to a masked fiend whom the media dubbed 'The Praying Mantis', and before the academic year was out, nine more seminarians had succumbed to his wicked reign of unholy terror, including the girl who had been drowned in the private lake on the campus' northwest property line, the young child of a married couple who had been hanged by his neck from one of the swingsets, the two victims of hideous disembowelment, the four students who had inhaled anthrax from the venerable pages of the chapel Bible, and the professor who had been found crucified upon the trunk of a giant oak. Naturally, this sort of behavior brought about an immense conflict within the aspiring priest, so, out of the necessity to adapt came Earkhert's twisted realization of his holy mission to serve the Lord through the consistent extermination of 'sinners'; a label which he affixed to every living person but himself.

The seminary itself saw little of the same violence during Earkhert's second year, when his field assignment as a prison minister at the Men's House of Detention on Rikers Island took him out into a broader world and introduced him to all sorts of interesting new people, most of whom were just the sort of loathsome, despicable sinners he had been looking for. The institution was packed to overflowing with blasphemers and heathens, and his clerical status placed him high above suspicion, so, with his rosary in one hand and an inmate's toothbrush sharpened to a deadly point in the other, Earkhert set about discreetly pruning the prison population.

Senior year was the time for aspiring priests to be assigned to a New York City parish, where they would get a taste for the real thing under the auspices of that parish's usual minister. Earkhert was sent to the Church of Holy Martyrs in Brooklyn where he assisted Father Patrick Donnelly. He was a kindly, popular, and highly respected old gentleman whose generosity and compassion seemed to know no mortal bounds, and the entire community grieved for months after his brutal death by stabbing in the far corner of the unlit parking lot behind the church.

Earkhert graduated *summa cum laude*, received his Master of Divinity degree, was ordained into the priesthood at the age of twenty-six, and had since remained within the urban boundaries of the Big Apple, as it had proven itself over the years to be an ideal venue for killing sinners. Presently – as for the past twelve years – he presided over a decent-sized flock at Our Lady of the Blessed Sacrament on the western side of Chelsea, and he always made certain that the Sunday morning Mass, for which the most people turned up, had his parishoners glued to their pews.

"And so we must ask ourselves," Earkhert enthused loudly from his place of respect and power, standing tall behind his wooden pulpit at the front of the church, "will the Lord cast off forever? Will He be favorable no more? Is His mercy clean gone, and hath He forgotten to be gracious, and hath He in anger shut up His tender mercies?

"Remember the paralyzing horror with which St. Francis beheld the gates of hell, leading to that most terrible of places where there is neither rest, nor consolation, nor hope! The prisoners of hell are given great strength by their fury and despair, and they do repeatedly dash themselves against the gates in a desperate bid to break free, but they do this in vain, for in hell there is nothing stronger than its massive, unyielding gates! Do you hear that terrible, growling thunder rolling over hell? That is the gates grinding open, and they open for *you!*"

By this point the flock was rapt with attention and fear, and one or two small children had begun to cry.

"And when St. Francis saw the size of hell was infinite, his blood was frozen with terror, for not in height, nor depth, nor length, nor breadth could he see any end to it!" Earkhert continued, the airy sleeves of his cassock flapping about as he made his usual, flamboyant gestures. "The air was choked with a fog of fire, and there were sweeping whirlwinds of fire, and fiery hailstones raining down from above, and fiery rivers of burning pitch and brimstone flowing in all directions, and floods of fire rolling throughout hell like waves of the sea!

"And into this sea of fire, the souls of the wicked are pulled down and drowned! The fire of hell burns the souls of the wicked, as it was prepared for them! Imagine such fire! You may have seen a house afire, but you have never seen a house *made* of fire! Hell *is* a house made of fire! Take a spark out of the kitchen fire and throw it into the sea, and it will go out. But take the tiniest spark from hell and throw it into the sea, and it will not go out. But, in one moment, it will dry up all the waters of the ocean and set the whole world ablaze! The fire of earth is a pale reflection of the fire of hell. Fire on earth gives light, but fire in hell is dark. Hell is one long, everlasting night of impermeable darkness, and the damned cannot even see as they are choked by sulfurous smoke, and they cry rivers of tears, and shriek and howl and wail as if they are dying!"

Now more children were crying, and a handful of grown women had joined them, pressing tissues to their eyes and noses and stifling their sobs. To Earkhert, this was better than a standing ovation.

"And St. Francis saw condemned souls, brushed away by the calloused left hand of God, falling into hell, and written in fire upon their foreheads were their unforgiven sins! And the devils seized them and brought them before the monstrous Satan, so large that he occupies all of hell, and so fearsome that St. Francis vowed he would rather burn for a *million years* then look upon his indescribable face for a single second!"

A child in the second row began wailing, and its mother did her best to quickly hush it as Earkhert fixed her with a look that could have withered a fig tree.

"And the souls were sentenced by that unspeakable beast who rules hell even as he is its prisoner, and rushed to the nightmarish cells that were to be their homes for evermore!" Earkhert went on, pounding his pulpit with both fists. "And St. Francis wept as he saw the unfortunate souls beaten and tortured and taunted relentlessly by their devilish jailers, and though they did cry out, they knew they did so in vain, for the Lord had ordered them, 'Depart from Me forever!', and their torment would endure for all eternity!"

Half the congregation was weeping now, and everyone was crossing themselves frantically.

"The man on earth, when hungry, looks for bread, and at last finds it. The man on earth, when in pain, looks for his pain to lessen, and at last it does. The man in hell looks for the burning to cease – but it doesn't. And he is left with nothing to think about but the everlasting anguish and how it will *never* cease. He is given no relief, no one comes to comfort him, and he has not even death to look forward to!"

Now children were hiding under the pews, tears were staining good Sunday clothes, prayers were being uttered in English, Latin, and Spanish, the clicking of rosary beads was nearly deafening, and anyone who wasn't crying was holding their head in their hands, trying desperately to escape their priest's accusatory leer. It was time for the dramatic finish.

"A lost soul cried out from the depths of hell, begging the Lord for mercy and forgiveness and salvation, and the Lord replied, 'Unhappy soul! I do pity you, for I did not create you for sadness, but for happiness! I wished you to be in heaven, not in hell! How could I wish you to be in hell? Consider what I did to *save* you from such a tragic fate! Do you remember how I put your happiness above My own, leaving My heaven and descending to earth where I was persecuted and scourged and pierced with giant thorns? Do you remember how I was nailed to the wood of the cross and made to die in shame and cruel agony? And what was all that for? So that you could continue to break My laws over and over and over again, knowing full well that hell would be your everlasting punishment? Yes, my child, I do pity you, but I cannot help you now, though I thought of nothing else during all the days of your earthly life, during which you repeatedly spurned My undying love and actually seemed to grow weary of My concern for you. You did not want salvation when it was Mine to give, so how can I give it to you now? Depart from Me now forever, unfortunate soul, for I know thee not!'

"Here ends the lesson."

Earkhert closed his Bible with a loud, decisive slap, and stepped down from his pulpit to prepare Holy Communion for his parishoners, still weeping and trembling as they got to their feet, while the organist – herself visibly shaken – began playing 'The Bread That Gives Life'.

"The body and blood of Christ," Earkhert muttered, dipping a paper-thin wafer into a golden chalice filled with wine and placing it upon the first parishoner's offered tongue.

"Excuse me, Father," whispered an altar boy sidling up to Earkhert's right side.

"Away from me, Satan!" Earkhert commanded, dealing the boy a disciplinary blow to the ear. "Do not interrupt while the consecrated host is being administered!"

"But there's a lady to see you in the vestry, Father!" said the boy. "She says it's urgent!"

"By the annunciation of Mary!" Earkhert cursed. "I'm struggling to save souls here, and you bring me feather-brained females! Oh, very well. But the receiving of the Holy Eucharist must not be interrupted. Get the other boys to help you in the continuance of this most holy sacrament, and I will hasten to ascertain the nature of our visitor's business."

Handing the chalice to the altar boy, Earkhert climbed back up past his pulpit, motioned to the organist to continue playing, and strode into the small, private room far behind the tabernacle, pushing the black, velvet curtain and several spare cassocks aside as he entered.

"Who dares trespass against the sanctity of this house of God?" he asked what appeared to be an empty room.

"No need to get yourself worked into a frenzy, Father," said a smooth, sultry female voice emanating from the corner behind the vestment case. "It's only little ol' me."

Earkhert's eyes lit up like twin tongues of fire on Pentecost as he took in the divine vision of a tall, toned, statuesque woman in her late thirties, strikingly attractive with long, supple limbs, a severe bob of blond hair, and a pair of red, bee-stung lips that probably could have been used as a flotation device in the event of an airplane disaster. She wore nothing more than a pair of costume devil horns on her head and a red thong which allowed for the affectation of the matching pointed tail. The 'bitch' tattoo just below her pierced navel was visible, and she held a large, shiny red apple in her right hand.

"Ah, Millicent, my sweet child," Earkhert grinned, lecherously. "You look as ravishing as ever. Let me guess. You're a horny little devil?"

"Millicent? I go by many names," purred the scantily clad woman, wiggling her skinny hips as she advanced on the wicked priest. "You can call me Satan, Lucifer, Beelzebub, Diablo, Queen of Darkness, Morticia Addams..."

"You try to tempt me," said Earkhert, taking a step back. "Blessed is the man that walketh not in the counsel of the ungodly, nor standeth in the way of sinners, nor sitteth in the seat of the scornful!"

"Bite the apple, man of God!" Millicent hissed, thrusting the fruit into the priest's face.

"I most certainly will not!" Earkhert refused.

"Take a bite," Millicent persisted, "and your eyes shall be opened, and you shall know unparalleled joy and great personal satisfaction!"

The long, manicured fingers of Millicent's free hand plunged into Earkhert's groin, and the priest, needing no further encouragement, opened his mouth, lunged his head forward, and bit the apple nearly in half in his eagerness.

"Slave of Satan, now you must uphold your end of the bargain!" said Earkhert, chomping the apple fiercely, spitting out chunks as he wrapped an arm around Millicent's neck and pulled her in for a long, hard kiss on those lovely, swollen lips. "Get thee down on thy knees and deliver what was promised! And tell me the things I want to hear!"

Looking up into Earkhert's face all the while, Millicent lowered herself to her knees, licked her tongue over her delicious lips, hoisted the priest's cassock high enough for her to crawl underneath, then let her long, sharp fingernails graze the sensitive skin of Earkhert's scrotum, reciting the lyrics to the Rolling Stones' 'Sympathy For The Devil' sexily as she worked.

"I've been around for long, long years," she said, huskily. "Stolen many a man's soul and faith. I was around when Jesus Christ had His moment of doubt and pain. Made damn sure that Pilate washed his hands and sealed His fate!"

Earkhert moaned loudly as he felt Millicent wrap her pouting lips around his rigid member, and she continued to speak with her mouth full.

"I watched with glee as your kings and queens fought for ten decades for the gods they made," she mumbled, saliva and the first comings of sperm dribbling down her chin. "And I shouted out, 'Who killed the Kennedys?', when after all, it was you and me."

"Suck it, you fucking little sinner!" Earkhert shouted, not knowing or caring if the people in the chapel could hear him. "You blasphemous heathen! Love the serpent! Make love to the serpent that deceived you in the Garden of Eden!"

"Just as every cop's a criminal, and all the sinners saints," Millicent continued, having a harder time forming the words now that her tongue was fully depressed and working hard at Earkhert's tip, "as heads is tails, just call me Lucifer, 'cause I'm in need of some restraint."

Earkhert let out a loud, high-pitched scream, as he always did when brought to orgasm, and discharged what must have been a gallon of come into Millicent's mouth. She swallowed what she could, but there was no preventing the bulk of it from spouting out of her nose and bubbling over her lips.

"Aaaaahhh," Earkhert sighed, shoving the messy woman out from under his cassock and flopping down into a convenient chair. "The pleasures of release! Thank you, my dear. I'd be lost without you."

"Same time next week?" asked Millicent, picking herself up off the floor and wiping her hands and face on a spare cassock. "I know you like it on Sundays."

"That will be most agreeable," said Earkhert.

"Oh, and it'd be great if you could stop by my place some time over the next couple of days," she added. "My niece requires her next...Bible lesson."

"Ah yes, your niece," said Earkhert, nodding thoughtfully. "She's a difficult girl to reach, but I suppose that's what this job is all about, isn't it? Reaching the unreachable. That's what our Lord Jesus Christ did, after all, bringing prostitutes and tax collectors into His fold. Very well, I shall see her tomorrow morning. But if you could see to it this time that she is unable to bite me, I would be much obliged."

The largest Asian community in North America, the bustling Chinatown is a thirty-five block area nestled in Lower Manhattan, due north of the Financial District, and is packed densely with herbal medicine shops, barbershops, acupuncturists, food markets stocked with amazing varieties of glassy-eyed fish and exotic fruits and vegetables, secondhand shops hawking everything from precious stones to socket wrenches, hundreds of restaurants, and, on the southernmost end of Mulberry Street, across from Columbus Park, a small assortment of funeral parlors, the most lavish and financially prohibitive of which was Mourning Dove, owned and operated as a legitimate front for the doings of New York's Chinese mob. Known as the *Dong Ji*, or 'The Motive', this particular faction of Chinese criminals had been operating out of Chinatown in one form or another for the better part of a century, and had successfully weathered and outlasted decades-long turf wars with formidable rival gangs, including the infamous Hip Sings and On Leongs.

The *Dong Ji's* longtime president was a very old man called Kun-Cho Fang whose withered legs and spine confined him to a wheelchair, while his weak lungs compelled him to cart his breath of life around in a tank. His speech was slurred with the ravages of past strokes, and these days he found himself moving about as little as possible so as to avoid incurring his severe arthritis pain. Fang had been on the scene for as long as any man alive could remember, and some said that he had even been around in the time of the legendary Mock Duck. This would have required Fang to be of an age in excess of one hundred and twenty years, but no one who looked upon the wizened old invalid could find that especially difficult to believe. Though he was feeble in body, however, he was a terror in mind and spirit, and those enemies of his whom had satirically nicknamed him 'the fairy godfather' found that they had done so to their own detriment.

Directly under Kun-Cho Fang was a perennial council of five of the *Dong Ji's* most exceptional members, each of whom had proven their value through many a trial by fire, and, as a group, assisted the president in running the organization, answering only to him. They called themselves the Faustian 5, describing their willingness to get the job done by any wicked and devilish means necessary, and the longest-standing member of this 5, the horribly disfigured Racketeer, stood before his crippled employer in the large, lavishly furnished room designated the 'Director's Office', holding his unlit pipe in one hand and his chest in the other, while he recounted the events of the previous evening.

"Winterhawk informs me that it was the same people with whom we've had trouble in the past," he rasped. "We were able to rescue Mr. Zarubezhnik before the police arrived, but I'm afraid the cargo was a total write-off."

"A Pyrrhic victory," Kun-Cho Fang croaked, his wrinkled, prune-like head lolling to one side. "That shipment was worth billions. I am very displeased with the way you conducted yourselves last night."

"That's bullshit," said Warren Winterhawk, one of the *Dong Ji's* few non-Chinese members, and the only non-Chinese ever to join the ranks of the Faustian 5. "Everything went according to plan until the explosion, and it was too late to do anything after that."

"With all due respect, Fang, I think you've been cooped up in this congenial little funeral parlor for too long," said the Racketeer, making no attempt at disguising his tone. "You've forgotten what it's like outside these safe, comfortable walls."

Ignoring the resulting, inevitable pain that seemed to jump onto his back like a chimp and spread throughout his entire midsection, Fang lashed his arm out with improbable speed and seized the unsuspecting Racketeer's wrist in a surprisingly vice-like grip. The nerve he pinched made the Racketeer cry out and drop to one knee.

"You would be wise to remember that, in spite of my physical impairment, I am still one of the most feared men in this city," Fang snarled, holding his wincing subordinate fast. "You would also be wise to remember where you were before you joined our illustrious company. As I recall, you were sharing space with fleas and cockroaches in a dockside flophouse, your grotesque appearance disenfranchising you from even the most basic circles of society. You've done quite well for yourself here, oh ostracized one, but with a snap of these ancient fingers I could order your death. Perhaps our lovely Miss Penelope would oblige?"

"Certainly would," said Penelope Yin – herself a member of the Faustian 5 – sitting cross-legged on the sofa. "Sorry, Elephant Man. I like you, but you're more than my job's worth."

"And you dare suggest that *I* am losing something?" Fang gurgled out something that sounded like a hoarse, menacing chuckle. "Just you remember who is in charge around here. Know your place, comport yourself with a little more humility, and don't give me reason to terminate your employment!"

After one more hard squeeze, Fang released his grip on the Racketeer's wrist and shoved him to the floor, and the Racketeer cried out again as he landed on his bad hip and fumbled through his coat pockets for his inhaler.

"You don't have to be so rough with him," grumbled Winterhawk, helping the Racketeer to his feet as the deformed gangster sucked greedily at his inhaler's nozzle. "He ain't exactly a spring chicken, y'know."

"He is decades my junior," said Fang. "If he is feeling his age, then perhaps *he* would like to spend some time inside these 'safe, comfortable walls'. Pheh. Take him over there and sit him down. And make him face the wall. I tire of the sight of him."

One of these days, old man, thought Winterhawk, letting the Racketeer lean on him as he walked him over to the overstuffed armchair in the corner. *One of these days, you're gonna learn you can't treat people this way.*

"I understand, Penelope, that you also experienced some trouble last night," Fang continued his debriefing.

"Quite unexpectedly, on a routine organ delivery," she confirmed. "This is the most interference we've had to weather for quite some time. It's as if something is drawing special attention to us."

The loud, furious blast of exploding gunpowder retorted from the foyer, followed immediately by the shouted command, 'Out of my way, lackey!', and Thomas Jefferson Zang, the fourth member of the council, stormed into the office, one of his twin Beretta U22 Neos handguns smoldering in his hand.

"Zang, I've told you repeatedly not to shoot the staff," said Fang. "Some of them are legitimate."

"Well, he was vacuuming where I was walking," said Zang, reholstering his gun. "And, after spending the past eight hours in a police station lockdown, I am in a very foul mood."

"What were you doing at a police station?" asked the Racketeer, having regained his breath at last.

"Oh, that idiot O'Shea got himself arrested and I had to bail him out," said Zang. "Then all hell breaks loose and I end up being held in detention for the rest of the night, all because of that deranged, puerile, unbalanced, crackbrained sociopath!"

"I do believe Zang speaks of our good friend and colleague Shang Fear," said Fang.

"He's a maverick!" Zang elaborated. "A careless, dissident, self-indulgent douchebag!"

"Hello, fans," said Shang Fear, the fifth and final Faustian, standing suddenly in the doorway, his slender frame filling it commandingly.

"You!" Zang snarled, whirling to face Fear, closing the gap between them with two angry steps. "You crazed asshole! What the fuck do you think you're doing? You're jeopardizing everything we've worked so long and hard to achieve!"

"If I were running things, we needn't have worked so long and so hard," Fear replied.

"Oh, you two are always fighting about something," said Penelope. "You're like a pair of little boys."

"No, Zang is right," said Fang. "You alluded earlier to some undue degree of attention being drawn to our activities, my dear. I regret that one of our own – one who ought to know better – is to blame for this."

"Surely you can't mean me," said Fear, arching his thin eyebrows and putting a hand to his chest in mock dismay.

"You have always been a bit of a rogue, Fear," said Fang, grunting with discomfort as he shifted his weight from one side of his chair to the other. "Always a bit too frivolous; a bit too unrestrained. I have tolerated it thus far because of your tremendous ability, but in our current circumstances...you are causing problems. Don't think that being 'cooped up' in here, as our friend the Racketeer put it, prevents me from knowing where you are and what you are doing at all times. I am very displeased with your immoderate behavior of late. Need I remind you of the sensitivity of these present times? Norman Kubritz is dead, and for the first time in more than thirty years, the *Dong Ji* has a chance to regain and build upon its past glory. The Delegates have been gathered, and our labors have nearly reached fruition, and this organization can no longer indulge your assorted peccadilloes."

"But I'm the very model of restraint," said Fear.

"Restraint is not murdering a man in a well-lit diner in front of four witnesses!" Fang snapped. "Restraint is not brawling with a gang of common street punks! Restraint is not staging a one-man assault on a tavern filled with personalities familiar to the police!"

"The place is a notorious watering hole for the criminally inclined," said Fear. "I was merely trimming some fat; cutting away some dead flesh; eliminating some competition."

"I sent you out last night to assassinate the head of the Russian mafia!" said Fang.

"And I did exactly that," said Fear, placing a cigarette between his lips and lighting it up.

"You killed everyone in the house, then burned the house down!" Fang was wearing his fury on the outside now. "Not only did you make an immense spectacle of the entire operation, but you committed a grievous atrocity against those whom we would hope to have as our allies! And put that cigarette out at once!"

"No," said Fear, coolly taking a drag.

"How dare you defy your master in that fashion!" growled Thomas Jefferson Zang, outraged.

"Master?" Fear smirked. "Just as the moon is master over the day?"

While Zang sputtered at the insubordination, Penelope Yin attempted an appeal of logic.

"Fear, you know that Fang's oxygen tank is highly flammable," she said.

"Really?" said Fear. "That's so frightening."

A cruel, crooked smile pinched the left side of Fear's mouth, and, in what appeared to all present to be slow motion, he flicked the lit cigarette in Fang's direction, and it surely would have struck the old man's oxygen tank if Warren Winterhawk hadn't lunged forward, caught the cigarette in his big fist, and smothered it promptly.

"You daft maniac!" Zang bellowed, crossing the last threshold of rage and reaching for his handguns. "I'll kill you for your antics!"

Zang moved fast, but Fear moved faster, yanking from its decorated hardwood scabbard a magnificent Chinese broadsword, its hilt adorned with hand-braided brown leather and red silk sashes, and its twenty-six inch steel blade now pressed threateningly against Zang's jumping Adam's apple.

"Anytime you think you're ready, lapdog," said Fear, reveling in the indignant, defeated look in the eyes of the perpetually envious Zang.

"Enough!" Fang barked, coughing as he leaned forward. "Stop acting like children! We must not let internal squabbles distract us from our unfinished task! Michelangelo Marzari, head of the Italian mafia, is still alive. Fear, I will give you this chance to redeem yourself. Tonight, kill him! And I want it done properly and discreetly! Is that understood?"

"Of course it's understood, you dried-up old currant," said Fear, his coattails whirling behind him as he turned to leave. "You need tell me only once."

"The rest of you know what you're doing," Fang addressed his four remaining lieutenants. "Go about your business. Except for you, Zang. You stay behind for a moment. I would require a word."

"My ears are yours, leader," said Zang, after his colleagues had departed and closed the door behind them. "About what must we speak?"

"You've never liked our Shang Fear," Fang observed, getting straight to the point.

"He's an unhinged, irrational, extravagant lunatic," said Zang. "A dangerously loose cannon if ever there was one."

"How would you say you compare to him?" Fang asked. "In the arena of combat?"

"I am his equal, my leader."

"Equal? I hardly think so, my boy. Your skills are formidable, but Fear's are still more impressive."

"But, Fang, that's not fair..."

"It is certainly fair," said Fang. "He has done more good work for this organization than any other man, and we all just now saw how easily he could have cut your throat at the bid of your challenge. He is the most accomplished martial artist and weapons master I have seen in all my long years, and you are no more equal to him than nine is equal to ten."

Zang opened his mouth to say something, then closed it again, bowed his head, and lowered his eyes.

"I am sorry I am such a disappointment to you, my leader," he said, on the verge of tears.

"But that is not to say you could not one day *become* his equal," Fang continued. "That is, if you felt up to replacing him."

Zang's head snapped back up, and he regarded his employer with wide, inquisitive eyes.

"My leader, what do you mean?" he asked.

"His many talents aside, Fear has become a worrisome liability," said Fang. "I do doubt his sanity, as well as his loyalty, his company altruism, and his ability to continue to be any sort of asset in the future. His termination is an avenue I have been considering for some time now, and this morning's display has only served to help me arrive at what seems to have been the inevitable conclusion. And I want you to handle the affair."

"My leader, are you ordering me to carry out his execution?"

"You are the only member of the *Dong Ji* for whom success in such a venture is conceivable," said Fang. "Not even those among your fellow Faustians could challenge Fear and live. Though you are not his equal, my boy, I have every confidence that your own talent and resourcefulness will allow you victory over the erratic, self-absorbed creature Fear has become. I have already provided the time and place. He will be in Little Italy tonight, stalking Marzari. Do it then."

"I thank you deeply for giving me this opportunity, my leader," said Zang, bowing low. "I will not let you down. Fear will be dead this night, and then you will see which of us is truly the greater combatant."

"Relent, boy!" Father Campion Earkhert commanded, pursuing a cherubic young altar boy vigorously through the maze of pews in the empty church, a solid brass candlestick clutched in his right hand. "You cannot escape your retribution! I played football for St. John's!"

"But, Father, it was an accident!" the terrified altar boy pleaded desperately, while scrambling to stay ahead of his priest's wrath.

"Dropping the consecrated host – the body of our Lord – upon this filthy floor is no accident, but a travesty!" Earkhert roared, nostrils flaring. "You'll pay dearly for that sacrilegious indignity!"

Coming finally within striking distance of the fleeing altar boy, Earkhert lashed out furiously with the candlestick, dealing a harsh blow to the back of the unfortunate youth's head.

"And another one for the Son, and a third for the Holy Ghost!" Earkhert spat.

Before the priest could rain any additional blows down upon the stunned and prostrate form of the fallen altar boy, however, he felt a big hand seize him by the back of his stiff, white collar, and the next thing he knew, his head was fully immersed in the wall-mounted font of holy water by the church's main entrance.

"Hate to interrupt you while you're doing the Lord's work, Father," said Charlie, his unbreakable grip snapping Earkhert's head back up after a full five seconds of submersion, "but guess where I just came from?"

"My disinterest in your unholy antics cannot be measured in finite terms!" Earkhert sputtered, barely able to see through the dripping wet lenses of his glasses.

"I've just been dealing with one of your parishioners," said Charlie. "He barged into a movie theater showing an R-rated film and started shooting the place up. Before I knocked him out, he told me *you* told him to do it. Been belching out pillars of fire and brimstone again, Father?"

"If my words move people, and give them the strength to eradicate evil wherever they may find it, then I feel nothing but pride!" Earkhert declared.

"No Christian in their right mind would believe a word of what comes out of your poisonous mouth, Earkhert," said Charlie, shoving the priest down onto the nearest pew. "However, there does seem to be a number of poor, gullible fools out there who are blind enough to take you for a messenger of God."

"To these people, I *am* God!"

"A lot of people before you have made that same declaration, only to be jostled harshly from their comfortable delusions. I always knew I'd have to do something about you eventually. I won't kill you now because this is still a house of God, even with you *in* it, but you'd better watch yourself, 'cause I officially have it in for you now."

"Contemptible heathen! You dare threaten God's chosen intermediary?"

"Certainly do," said Charlie, his big combat boots clomping across the hardwood floor as he moved over to the dazed altar boy, still sprawled facedown before the tabernacle, as if genuflecting. "But in the meantime, I'm taking this boy to a hospital, because he's more important than you are."

"I'll see you in hell for this!" declared Earkhert, leaping to his feet. "The Lord is my light and my salvation; whom shall I fear? The Lord is the strength of my life; of whom shall I be afraid? When the wicked, even mine enemies and my foes, came upon me to eat up my flesh, they stumbled and fell!"

"Stuff it," said Charlie, turning his broad back on Earkhert and marching out of the church, the concussed altar boy cradled in his arms.

Head of the rogue crime syndicate known as the Harlem Hellfighters – mostly blacks, with a handful of Cubans and Puerto Ricans thrown in for seasoning – Tyrone Smits was a pot-bellied, bald-headed black man in his mid-forties, with markedly pointed ears and three gold teeth in his upper set. Having risen from rags, he enjoyed wearing smart business suits to perpetuate a touch of class and sophistication, but the small arsenal of weapons he kept concealed about his person – pistols, Tasers, switchblades, brass knuckles – spoke to his true, thuggish nature.

On Sundays, Tyrone Smits liked to take in a movie at a run-down, ill-attended, five-screen cinema in one of the dirtier, more dangerous parts of Harlem that had yet to be touched by the neighborhood's recent renaissance. Owned and operated by two septuagenarian brothers from Los Angeles, the Dreamland Cinema was a drafty, dirty, vandalized shell of its former self, but the promised attractions – hit movies from yesterday's imagination – never missed their curtain calls, though many of the seats were broken, and the screens were torn and smeared with filth. This week's marquee included *Planet of the Apes*, *Rosemary's Baby*, *The Birds*, *Willy Wonka and the Chocolate Factory*, and *Rocky II*, and it was the fifth of these that Smits was presently viewing from the third row of the trash-strewn theater, munching on gooey clumps of Raisinets – his favorite movie-going confectionery – and firmly elbowing the Racketeer seated next to him..

"Know what I like about Rocky?" he asked the elderly Chinese.

"Well, I suppose there's the story about a scrappy underdog who strives against impossible odds and triumphs in the end," wheezed the Racketeer, puffing on his pipe. "It's generally known that you Americans find that sort of thing agreeable."

"Watch the way he fights," said Smits, pointing up to the screen as Rocky clobbered Apollo Creed to the mat. "See his hands? He's not keepin' his left up. Rocky never does. Six movies an' he never wastes time with defense. He doesn't cower or cringe. He lunges at his opponent with both fists flailing, an' lets his body and head take any and all blows like a shock absorber. He's not weak or hesitant or afraid. He just charges in an' keeps poundin' an' poundin' till it's over. That's the same technique I like to employ."

"That might explain why the *Dong Ji* is acquiring your Harlem Hellfighters, rather than the other way around," the Racketeer rasped.

"I'm not complainin'," said Smits, popping another Raisinet into his mouth. "The way I see it, it's a win-win situation. Your group's backing will make the Hellfighters even stronger, an' I get to stay in charge."

"Subordinate to the *Dong Ji*. Do not forget that."

"Yeah, yeah."

"Hey, will you two morons shut up down there?" a white man in the very back row – the theater's only other guest – shouted angrily.

"Hey, shut the fuck up!" Smits shot back, turning in his seat. "Just shut the fuck up! Y'hear me? Shut the fuck up!"

"I came here to watch the movie, asshole!" the other man hollered. "Why don't you two fags get a room?"

Even in the theater's insufficient lighting, Smits could see well enough to fire six bullets through the heckler's torso, shredding the man's seat and splattering his blood all over the back row.

"I told you to shut the fuck up, dickbreath!" Smits screamed at his unresponsive victim.

"I think I've grasped the meaning of what you were talking about just now," coughed the Racketeer. "Was that really the most prudent course of action?"

"White man in Harlem," Smits muttered. "Serves 'im right."

"I think there's gum on my shoe," said the Racketeer.

"Yeah, there's all kinds of shit on this floor," said Smits.

"The *Dong Ji* would like to formally express their gratitude and convey their appreciation for your cooperation in this matter," said the Racketeer, producing a fat envelope from within his jacket and handing it to Smits. "You're one less gentleman we had to replace."

"Hey, I just wanna be on the winnin' team," said Smits, tucking the envelope inside the folds of his own jacket. "When I heard about this coup you Chinks were plannin', I knew where I should be standin'. I've worked long and hard to get where I am today. Didn't wanna lose it all. Didn't wanna end up like those other mob leaders. If you can't beat 'em, join 'em, that's what I say."

"You're a very sensible man for a Negro," said the Racketeer, rising to his feet and shuffling out into the aisle, reaching for his inhaler as he did so. "We will see you again later."

Smits nodded and turned his attention back to the screen just in time to see Rocky deliver the killing blow to Creed, while the stooping

Racketeer lumbered up the aisle towards daylight, gasping repeatedly into his inhaler as he went.

The pink and orange rays of evening sunlight – glimmering all too briefly through the sky's blanket of pregnant rain clouds – were kissing the city good night by the time Kolach Zarubezhnik found himself on Chinatown's elbow-shaped Doyers Street, nicknamed 'the Bloody Angle' because of the ongoing insistence that more people have died there than at any other intersection in the United States. Not at all worried about loitering here past sunset, Zarubezhnik pushed open the entrance to The Laughing Rabbit Tea Parlor – ringing a pleasant little bell as he did so – and entered a cool, quiet, comfortably lit sanctuary decorated with exquisite calligraphy hanging upon the walls, and fine ceramic teapots and golden Buddha statues sitting upon shelves and windowsills all about the circular establishment. A Chinese opera skit was being acted out upon the small stage at the front of the main restaurant, and an enclosed room off to the left sold exotic-looking lamps and brushes.

When in Rome, do as the Romanians do, Zarubezhnik chuckled to himself and ordered a cup of Junshan Silver Needle tea.

Easing himself down into an overstuffed armchair next to a crystallized window through which a dying sunbeam shone with purely Eastern splendor, Zarubezhnik let out a relaxed sigh – this was the first time he'd been off his feet all day – and allowed a chirpy little finch in a suspended cage and the lilting melody of an unnamed Chinese piano concerto to soothe him as he held his flowered teacup with both large hands and waited for the beverage to cool.

The Russian's meditations were interrupted by the arrival outside of a very long, white stretch limousine with tinted windows, a glittering, rotating disco ball for a hood ornament, and a loud dance tune blaring from its stereo speakers. While Zarubezhnik took a tiny sip of his steaming tea and watched with curiosity from the distorted view his window provided, a tall, lanky chauffeur with a handlebar mustache half the size of his bean-shaped head disembarked, smoothed out any rogue wrinkles in his jacket and pants, dropped two shiny quarters into the parking meter, then took the long walk all the way to the back of the limo, where he pulled open the door for his boss.

The man who got out of the limo was a fat, bronze-skinned, Mediterranean type in his mid-forties, with greasy, black hair combed tightly back, a pair of orange-hued sunglasses obscuring his eyes, a loud Hawaiian shirt completely open to display his hairy chest and trio of gold medallions hanging from his neck, a pair of khaki shorts, and a pair of beach sandals on his big, brown feet. His arms and legs were veritable forests of black, matted hair, and his left hand was wrapped around a soppy meatball-and-mozzarella sub.

Surely that can't be him, thought Zarubezhnik.

"Well, if this isn't one of the deadest joints I've ever seen," said the strange-looking newcomer as he entered The Laughing Rabbit. "What are Happy Hours like? Does everyone re-cross their legs or something?"

"Are you Ambrosi Pancrazio?" Zarubezhnik asked, hesitantly.

"At your service," said the newcomer, taking an oversized chomp out of his sandwich and dribbling meat sauce onto the floor as he extended his right hand to Zarubezhnik. "And you must be the bolshie with the long name I forgot."

"Kolach Zarubezhnik," the Russian introduced himself, shaking Pancrazio's hand, then wiping his own hand discreetly on the front of his jacket. "Do sit down."

"So, you're one of this so-called 'Delegation'," said Pancrazio, plopping himself down into the chair opposite Zarubezhnik.

"And you're another," Zarubezhnik observed, taking another sip of tea. "Tell me, how did they come by you?"

"Well, I've been big in the Italian mafia in Los Angeles for quite a few years now," said Pancrazio. "Y'see, I'm old-school, born and bred in Sicily. Out there, they like a boy with roots. I was doin' all right – nothin' to complain about, y'know – but the offer these gooks made is way more appealing."

"Yes," said Zarubezhnik. "I came all the way from Russia to take advantage of a similar offer. It just goes to show that one must keep an open mind about new career opportunities."

"Right," nodded Pancrazio, talking with his mouth full. "I had to kill a few old friends to make 'em all see it my way, but I finally got my affairs straightened out. They don't like it when you get the itch to move on to greener pastures, y'know."

"That's very true an' all," said a younger, wiry man approaching the newly acquainted colleagues, a cup of fragrant Oolong tea in his right hand. "They hate it when you wanna leave the company, an' no mistake. I'm ex-IRA meself, an' it was bleedin' hard to get outta there. They all start puttin' in their monocles an' sayin', 'No one escapes from Stalag 13!' an' such. Fuck me, but this tea is good. I usually prefer a pinter, but this really is bloody delish, isn't it?"

"And who, if I may ask, are you supposed to be?" Zarubezhnik queried.

"Conroy O'Shea, from the Irish end," said the newcomer. "Mind if I join you gents?"

"No, please, you're just in time," said Zarubezhnik, consulting his gold wristwatch. "Actually, it's ten minutes past the hour. Our hostess is late."

The greeting the gathered threesome had been awaiting came abruptly in the form of a razor-edged Chinese fan thrown with deadly precision into the wall behind them, followed immediately by the surprise spectacle of one of the opera skit's female performers suddenly executing a high backflip from the stage, handspringing off a table, and culminating with an impressive triple lutz that sent her colorful robes, sashes, and mask flying away to reveal the diminutive but commanding person of Penelope Yin standing authoritatively in the trio's midst.

"I apologize for my tardiness, gentlemen," she said, letting her hair down, and adjusting her lipstick and eye shadow with the aid of a compact mirror, "but, for reasons of caution, I had to observe each of you as you arrived. I'm sure you understand."

"Sure," said O'Shea, his Irishman's heart typically more tolerant with the trespasses of the fairer sex. "Very nasty bit o' business, this."

"I'd have thought you'd know each of us well enough by now to place with us a degree of trust," said Zarubezhnik, with all the surliness of an airline passenger whose bag has been searched one too many times.

"You're back-stabbers and sell-outs, the lot of you," said Penelope, snapping the compact closed and giving her hair a final disdainful toss over her shoulder. "Why should I trust any of you?"

"Now, you just hold those hackles, little lady," said Pancrazio, thumping his hairy chest and emitting a juicy belch as the last of the gooey sandwich disappeared down his gullet. "Now, we all came over here to do some business, and, last I checked, there were gonna be huge benefits all around. Mutual prosperity an' such. I agreed to do it your way, but I didn't agree to be looked down upon like some bug. From what I've heard so far, we're all very important to your plans."

"Indeed you are," said Penelope. "Thanks to your ambition and drive, gentlemen, we all stand ready to attain quite a lot of power. Your imminent positions as kings of New York have been vacated of their prior honorees and prepared for you. You have been gathered here this evening in order to be officially welcomed into the fold of the *Dong Ji*. Under our supreme guidance, your new enterprises will flourish. You will reward us, we will reward you, and a system will be laid down that will keep the New York underworld firmly under the control of the Chinese throughout the entirety of the next century."

Bloody arrogant gooks, thought O'Shea.

"There is but one minor obstacle remaining," Penelope continued, "and it will be eliminated tonight. All systems should be set into full operation by tomorrow morning. I cannot divulge any further details here in this public setting, but we may all speak freely once the three of you have accompanied me back to Mourning Dove – in your own time, of course – where you will be given the full remainder of your necessary information."

It was at the tender age of fourteen, after nearly two full years of loyal, obedient service to his master, Kang Jin-Khu, that the young Shang Fear was first seduced by the middle-aged gangster. It was an inevitable deflowering, given Kang's power over Fear, who by this time had come to idolize the man and was zealously eager to please the only patriarch and role model he knew. The boy's rite of passage into adulthood had not been conducted with any degree of cruelty or brutality, as would a callous rape. Far to the contrary, Kang had taken the nervous, impressionable youth in hand, tutoring him gently in the ways that a man pleasures himself, showing him how to kneel between his master's open thighs, and instructing him in the most effective way to utilize his hands and fingers, and, as the hot, humid evening wore on, his lips and tongue.

After that evening of sweat-soaked passion and discovery, during which man took boy to his naked body and imparted the knowledge that passes exclusively between such a pair, the young Fear spent at least four nights a week between the silk sheets of his master's big bed – doe-eyed, adoring, and utterly undressed – and no one was more surprised than Fear himself when he grew up to be something other than completely queer.

Fear was not homosexual. He had shared his bed with no man since leaving Kang's service. To say that he was enamored of women, however, would be an overstatement. Yes, he slept with a certain sort of woman when the mood took him, but he didn't make a regular diet of them. The frequent urges just weren't there, be it Kang's fault or not, and in his present life he found himself satisfied with a state of near celibacy. And when those rare cravings of the flesh did begin tickling the soft, warm skin of his loins, and he was drawn into the embrace of an attentive female who would kiss him and fuck him and give him fellatio and tell him how good he was, he treated the whole degraded exercise as merely an obligatory release of his tensions; a necessary diversion for an hour or so as he flushed it all out of his system. Fear had sex for the same reason that other people visited the dentist or worked out to aerobics tapes; it wasn't always something that he particularly enjoyed, but his ongoing good health necessitated it.

Of course, there were some sexual encounters Fear relished above others, chiefly those with women of character and scruple similar to his own; a dark, sinister, entirely amoral Medusa was his ideal mate, and, as type attracts type, he had found such a creature with whom to share his bed in his fine two-story house on Eighth Avenue on Manhattan's moneyed Upper West Side – far away from the less dignified Chinatown – near Central Park, where he liked to walk and smoke on his less hectic days.

"Take it, bitch!" Janet hissed, her long fingernails digging into Fear's skinny ribs as she thrust the eight inch, plastic dildo deep into Fear's anus, her firm pelvis colliding with his tough behind. "Take it all, you bitch! Say it! Tell me you're my bitch!"

"Yes! Yes, I am!" Fear groaned, his own fingernails tearing holes in his bedsheets, his sinewy body bucking back and forth as the tall black woman kneeling behind him took him doggy style. "I'm your bitch! Fuck me!"

"That's right!" said Janet, giving the strap-on phallus an exquisite twist that made Fear rear up like a horse. "That's what I want to hear! I've got you where I want you now!"

Then a 'schlorp', and an almost tear-jerking feeling of emptiness for Fear as Janet suddenly pulled completely out.

"Now, beg me to put it back in," she snarled, wickedly.

"No!" Fear howled, his backside already missing the divine fullness.. "That's not fair! Finish the job!"

"Beg me to finish the job, bitch!" Janet demanded, her hands placed stubbornly on her hips, the dildo extending absurdly from the belt around her waist. "Beg me to finish fucking you! Beg me to treat you like a bitch and fuck your insides right up your throat!"

"No, Janet, please don't make me beg," Fear shook his head, looking forlornly down at his mattress, every one of his muscles and tendons tensed and sticking out like a porcupine's quills as he shuddered with shame. "Please don't make me say it!"

"Say it, candy-ass!"

"All right, all right, I'm begging you!" he relented. "I'm begging you, finish me! Stick it back in and fuck me rotten! Fuck me, you heartless whore!"

Fear screamed with both pain and pleasure as Janet drove the dildo back past his anus' puckered lips, and he humped and gyrated for an additional two minutes and seven seconds before turning abruptly and punching Janet in the face.

"You dare to make me beg?" he seethed, breathing heavily as he clambered from the bed and seized a readily available flute staff, eighteen inches long and sturdy enough to shatter any given bone in the human body. "You need a lesson in who your lord and master is!"

Somersaulting backwards just in time to avoid a deadly swing from the small staff, Janet divested herself of her imitation penis with a flick of the wrist, then sprang off the wall behind her and torpedoed headfirst into Fear's midsection, wrapping her long arms around him, tackling him to the floor, biting him ravenously on the side of his neck, and grinding her genitalia against his.

"Feed me, darling, I need it!" she gasped through her sucking.

His teeth gritted furiously, Fear growled maliciously as he lifted his staff as high as he could, then drove the end of it down into the base of Janet's neck, squarely between her shoulder blades. Janet let out a loud grunt and went limp, and Fear, with the strength of a bodybuilder three times his size, rose to his feet with her body sprawled across his heaving shoulders, then roared like a champion wrestler and dashed her to the floor. An instant later, the shiny blade of Fear's broadsword was resting upon the dazed woman's throat, and she opened her eyes and allowed a sultry smile to spread slowly across her bruised, sweaty face.

"Thanks, hotcakes," she said. "That was real good."

"My life is richer for knowing you, dear Janet," said Fear, tossing the broadsword aside with a careless 'clang'.

"You should be careful, though," said Janet, rolling onto her side and propping her head up on one arm like a posing nude. "Be less of a pain in the ass to your boss. I wouldn't want to lose such a good fuck to 'judicious pruning'."

"Is that a note of concern I detect in your voice?" asked Fear, moving to put his pants on.

"Concern? Fuck you, Confucius. I'm here strictly for the exercise. You mean about as much to me as any of the other billion egg rolls out there. But, like it or not, you're one of the few men on the planet who can do what it takes to satisfy me, and I'd hate to see that go to waste."

"Oh, those fools talk a hard game," said Fear, donning his white shirt and buttoning the collar, "but they're paper tigers, the lot of them; snakes with no venom. Without me, their second-rate syndicate would never get anything accomplished. Certainly not with that useless old man in charge, with his feeble notions and outdated ideas. Hmph. Their dependence upon me would be laughable if it weren't so pathetic."

"No one's irreplaceable," said Janet.

"I am," said Fear, tying his black silk tie around his collar and slipping an arm through his vest. "I'm off to work now, in fact. Have to kill someone. It's not even a difficult mark, but they still need me. The tired old invalid practically begged me to do the job."

"Well, my mother warned me against shacking up with a career man," sighed Janet, rising gracefully to her feet and stretching. "Oh, well. Before you dash off, would you do one little thing for me?"

"Forget it," said Fear, disappearing into his coat. "I'm not taking all this shit off again."

"You don't have to," said Janet. "I just want you to hang me."

"Hang you?"

"Hang me."

"Normally I'd love to, but I'm not sure I have the time right now."

"Aw, sure you do," said Janet, clasping her hands in front of herself like a little girl. "Please hang me. Please, please, pretty please with sugar on top?"

"Well...all right, I suppose," said Fear. "Get over there."

Smiling, Janet skipped over to a noose hanging down from the high ceiling, put her head through it, then tightened it around her neck. Fear made a quick but flawless job of tying her wrists behind her back and binding her ankles together, then strode over to a wall-mounted lever which operated a brief system of pulleys and winches rigged about the room. Pulling the lever down, he watched with satisfaction and excitement as Janet was hoisted gradually off the floor, and he chuckled as he listened to her choking and gagging, and his penis sprang to attention inside his pants as he watched her large breasts heave with the effort of breathing and her bound feet wriggle in their reflexive effort to regain terra firma.

"All right," Janet croaked, at last, her face turning purple, her eyes fairly bulging from their sockets. "All right. You can let me down now."

Fear didn't pull the lever back up, however. Instead he folded his arms across his chest, and, with a most devilish smirk playing about his face, strolled slowly over to his suspended companion, placed a hand on her quivering stomach, and softly kissed her navel, which was now at his eye level.

"Beg me," he said.

Tall, slender, and sturdy, Leeza was remarkably fit for her age, but even in spite of the rigid diet and exercise to which she had adhered her entire adult life, she found herself leaning now against her apartment's defaced door, breathing heavily and clutching her tightening heart with one trembling hand. On her way down the quiet, empty hallway she had been certain she'd heard the dogging squeak of stiff Gestapo shoes behind her, and she had fairly run most of the way from the foyer to her apartment, clambering frantically up four flights of stairs rather than wait for the elevator, refusing to cast a glance behind for fear of seeing a stocky man with a black trenchcoat and fedora, pince-nez glasses, and ivory-handled walking stick in limping but steady pursuit. She'd been like this all day. It was silly, she knew, and there weren't many things that could frighten a woman of Leeza's emotional constitution, but the swastika – and its implications – had her spooked.

Stupid old woman! Leeza chastised herself. *Stupid, senile old woman! What would the others think if they could see you now? They'd all have a lovely laugh, wouldn't they? Pull yourself together, you useless old fool!*

Willing her nervous heartbeat to slow, Leeza snorted determinedly, drew herself up to her full height, and shoved her door open, pushing past the despised swastika and into her apartment. And *he* was there. Yes, *he* was there, standing rigidly to attention in the center of her living room, in front of her rarely watched TV, every bit as horrible as he'd appeared in life, with his ridiculous mustache, soup bowl haircut, and tan military uniform, complete with red armband, clunky gunbelt, and black, shiny jackboots.

"No!" Leeza shouted aloud. "I won't have this! I *hate* you! I've *always* hated you! This is my home, and you are not welcome! Leave me!"

Leeza gritted her teeth, balled her fists, and squeezed her eyes shut, and when she opened them again three seconds later, the intruder was gone. Of course, he had never really been there in the first place.

Just a hallucination brought on by stress, she told herself. *I've had a nervous day, and I'm tired, and my stomach is empty. There's nothing wrong with me that a little rest can't put right.*

Setting her handbag down on the coffee table, Leeza shrugged her shoulders a few times to relax the tension, performed a few lazy head circles, then exhaled slowly and heavily and strode confidently into the kitchen where she planned to fix herself a cup of hot tea and something good to eat.

She washed her hands, started the water boiling, then opened the refrigerator door, and the bomb rigged to the appliance exploded just as its operator had intended, destroying most of the kitchen instantly and flinging Leeza through the air like just another chunk of debris, back out into the living room where she crashed against the far wall and crumpled to the floor, her right arm bent at an odd angle, blood seeping from a number of cuts and lacerations all over her motionless body.

As Shang Fear wafted like a phantom into what remained of the receding neighborhood of Little Italy via Mulberry Street, he recalled the first time he had been deployed to kill someone. Like many of the experiences that had made him the man he was today, he had been introduced to the finer points by his master, Kang Jin-Khu. Once the most feared and revered crime boss in Bei Jing, Kang was blunting his edge in his old age, and the region's other major gangsters were losing respect for him and eyeing his position with hungry glares, as is common among the jackals that sit back on their haunches and salivate, waiting patiently for the strongest member of the pack to hit the ground. Kang was not so soft in the head as the council presumed, however, knowing full well that they conspired to terminate him and usurp his territory, and he used his advantage of surprise to full effect, not sending an army of assassins to eradicate his treacherous foes, but sending the young Shang Fear – now seventeen years old and a master of numerous different styles of martial arts – instead. Kang trusted in the loyalty, efficiency, and cold-bloodedness he had drilled into Fear's mind over the years, and the bid paid off with interest. While the dozen or so enemy mobsters were conducting a final meeting around a long, rectangular table in a safe boardroom, Fear dropped from an air conditioning duct in the ceiling, an elastic rope secured about his ankles like a bungee cord, and a machine gun gripped in his hands. Wasting not a single bullet, Fear cut the entire council to ribbons in less than thirty seconds, splattering the walls, floor, and furniture with blood and shredded flesh.

After Fear's roaring success that ensured Kang's retention of the lion's share of the Bei Jing underworld, the proud crime boss removed the electronic tracking bracelet from the boy's ankle and appointed him to be his personal bodyguard and part-time assassin, in which capacity Fear went on to kill a lot more people, discovering along the way that he quite enjoyed it.

It's always fortunate when a young man is able to conceive of his true vocation early in life, thought Fear, a grim smile tugging at the corner of his mouth.

The middle-class restaurant called Gambini's was well known as the front for the New York section of the Italian mafia, and though it appeared closed for the night, Fear knew the big man himself, Michelangelo Marzari, would be inside with his cronies, reviewing any conceivable number of shady business deals into the wee hours. So he broke the lock on the front door with the point of his dagger and let himself in.

The place was dark, quiet, and empty, with the wooden chairs turned upside-down neatly atop the bare, round tables, and, from the look of things, no lights on in the kitchen. Fear wondered briefly if he could have been mistaken about Marzari's location, but then he spied a single table towards the back, decked out with a red-and-white checkered tablecloth, three or four different pasta dishes, an uncorked bottle of red wine, and a stocky, balding man sitting very still, his back to him. It was Marzari all right.

" 'The sentence – the dread sentence of death – was the last of distinct accentuation which reached my ears'," Fear whispered to himself, taking another leaf from Poe's book. " 'What sweet rest there must be in the grave.' "

Fear traveled lithely across the dining room, drawing his broadsword from its scabbard as he went, but when he touched Marzari on the back of the neck, the gangster fell over, slumping face-first into a plate of lasagna.

Already suspecting the truth, Fear pulled Marzari upright, turned him around, and looked down into the tomato sauce-covered face to see that someone had beaten him to the punch. The man was as dead – as Dickens would have said – as a coffin nail.

Fear didn't have time to search out the rat he smelled before a pair of barbed probes shot into his back, blasting an unnecessarily brutal amount of voltage through his body, and he screamed in anguish as he crashed helplessly to the floor, his muscle tissue contracting violently.

"Now we see who the better man truly is," said Thomas Jefferson Zang, standing over his fallen rival, an X26 Taser in his hand. "I don't need all your dazzling moves and fancy turn-a-phrase. I just wish Fang had been here to see me take you down in one simple move."

Zang snapped his fingers and the enforcers Lau and Jin appeared beside him.

"Cook him," he ordered. "I'm stepping outside for some air."

While Zang turned his back on the crumpled, twitching Fear and made for the door, Lau and Jin hefted the prone assassin by his underarms and dragged him into the kitchen, where they shoved him inside one of the large ovens, secured the locking mechanism, and turned the dial well past five hundred degrees. Then they folded their arms across their chests, stood on either side of the oven, and waited.

So much for the immortal Shang Fear, Zang scoffed, standing outside in the warm, luminous glow of a streetlamp. *Hmph. I'll bet that's not even his real name. He probably changed it just to scare people. Well, you didn't scare me, you overconfident fool! You weren't a challenge at all! No, you were pathetically hapless! I'm almost disappointed by the ease with which I conquered you! I was hoping I'd get to knock you around a bit to pay you back for many a past indignity! Ah, well. At least now I am finally rid of your reckless antics and tiresome boasting, and I shall at last be given my due from Fang!*

Then a tremendous explosion sounded forth from the back of Gambini's, sending a pillar of flame shooting skyward through the restaurant's roof, engulfing the dining room, shattering every window in the place, awakening the alarms of three cars parked nearby, and propelling Zang clear across the street.

Hitting the sidewalk hard with his face and jarring loose two of his teeth, Zang clambered quickly to his knees and whirled around to face the blazing restaurant, and he was astonished to see Shang Fear – his hair and clothes slightly singed, with little flames dancing upon his coattails – emerging from the inferno like Shadrach from Nebuchadnezzar's furnace. Briefly, Zang wondered how Fear could ever have escaped such a trap, but then he noted, with growing amazement, the cigarette lighter clenched tightly in the man's fist, and remembered that Gambini's ovens were gas, not electric.

I don't believe it! Zang marveled. *The barking mad fucker blasted his way out!*

"Did you leave the gas on, dear friend Zang?" asked Fear, advancing on his former colleague. "Because I think I smell something burning!"

"Stay back!" Zang screamed, suddenly terrified as he scrambled clumsily to his feet and fumbled for his gun. "Get away! Don't come any closer!"

As always, Fear was faster than his jealous rival. When the frantic Zang finally managed to pull out his pistol and point it at Fear, the better man kicked the gun straight up into the air, chopped the side of Zang's neck hard with the flat edge of one burned hand, whirled around once and kicked him to the ground, then caught the falling gun in his other hand, and, directing it straight downwards, pumped three bullets into Zang's prostrate form.

"It's going to be a busier night than I thought," Fear muttered to himself, as he slipped the pistol into the folds of his coat and began walking back down Mulberry Street towards Mourning Dove.

Housed inside an old, inconspicuous brick building on Amsterdam

Avenue, dawdling far behind any semblance of the modern fire code, was The Burning Bush, one of New York's raunchiest, most debauched strip joints, where one could get off any number of deviant ways and most state and federal laws were checked at the door. Indeed, hard drugs were as prevalent as any item on the menu, many of the girls who stripped and danced and auctioned their bodies were underage, and identification was sought rarely. More like an actual brothel than any other Manhattan establishment, The Burning Bush was a favorite nighttime destination for sexaholics and nymphomaniacs, and this was why it enjoyed Peg's frequent patronage.

"Come on, I'm waiting! Give it to me for real already! Fuck me! Fuck my brains out!" she shouted, lying on her back on the bar, her little black dress hiked up above her hips, as a middle-aged businessman knelt between her widely spread legs, driving himself repeatedly forward like a piston.

With the assembled spectators chanting 'Fuck her sideways!' and 'Nail her good!', and Peg taunting him viciously, the sweaty-faced businessman redoubled his efforts, grabbing her pelvis on both sides and accelerating his thrusts, but it still wasn't enough.

"Give me a break!" Peg continued deriding the man who had been the quickest to accept her club-wide invitation to give her what she needed. "Are you going to fuck me, or just poke around inside me like my gynecologist? If it helps turn you on, pretend I'm a little boy! Fuck me, you limp noodle!"

The crowd laughed, and the grunting businessman kept going, but after another thirty seconds Peg lost all patience and pulled herself backwards, off of the half flaccid penis.

"Forget it, shorty," she said, pulling her dress back down and fixing her hair. "You had your chance and you blew it. As for the rest of you boys, you'll just have to wait till next time. I've lost the taste."

With that, Peg slung her leather purse over her bare shoulder and walked briskly to the other side of the bar, where she ordered a vodka gimlet, lit up a Virginia Slim, and noted that her loss did not seem to be felt sorely by the pack of randy men, as the next male-female team had already mounted the counter.

Well, it's Ladies' Night, Peg reminded herself. *That always means there's plenty to go around.*

"How you tonight, Peg?" asked the bartender, a Hungarian bodybuilder named Ervin, whose talent for mixing a killer martini vindicated his poor grasp of the English language.

"So-so, I guess," said Peg, polishing off half the gimlet with one sip.

"I'm kind of disappointed that my stick-up turned out to be more of a hold-up, if you know what I mean."

Ervin gave her a confused look.

"Never mind," she said.

"Well, I always enjoy to be watching you, Peg," said Ervin. "You are a...um...what is word for..."

"Slut?"

"Yes. Slut. Is that good?"

"Depends on who you ask, I suppose."

Crossing her long legs and allowing her dress to ride up provocatively, Peg swiveled around on her stool, her drink in one hand and her cigarette in the other, treating her eyes to the antics of the man and woman on the bar, the stripper on stage rubbing her silicone breasts up and down the brass pole, the pair of drug dealers on the purple couch receiving attention from a set of blond triplets, and finally fixing her gaze on the sight of a pair of tattooed skinheads cooperating in lifting a young girl up onto a pool table. The girl was very beautiful, clad in a dress similar to Peg's that showed off her creamy white skin, shapely legs, round behind, and squeezable bosom. Her eyes were green with long, dark lashes, her nose was small and pretty, her blushing cheeks were festooned with cute constellations of freckles, her pouty, swollen lips looked like they would be right at home wrapped around a cucumber, and her long, curly mane of fiery red hair cascaded down past her naked shoulder blades. She certainly looked like sex on two legs, but Peg noted that the girl appeared reluctant to engage the skinheads in the recreation they had in mind.

"Hey, Ervin," said Peg, turning back to the bartender. "Who's that girl over there?"

"Who?" asked Ervin, craning his neck while wiping out a glass. "Oh, that Vicki."

"Vicki? I haven't seen her in here before."

"She come sometimes. She young. Only seventeen."

"Don't tell me you're letting children in here now."

Ervin shrugged. "For you, she look like child?"

"I have to admit, no. But shouldn't somebody do something? She obviously doesn't want anything to do with those creeps. What's happening over there is practically rape."

"If she not want it, she not come dressed like that," said Ervin, dismissively.

"Okay, then *I'll* do something," said Peg, downing the last of her drink, stubbing out her cigarette, stepping down from her stool, and striding purposefully over to the pool table serving as the altar upon which the girl, Vicki, was to be 'sacrificed'.

She slut, but she crazy, Ervin shook his head as he moved to fill another drink order.

"Excuse me, gentlemen," Peg addressed the skinheads, arriving just as the one splaying Vicki's legs had unzipped his pants, "but what exactly is it that you think you're doing?"

"What does it look like, ya nosy bitch?" asked the skinhead pinning Vicki's wrists. "We're about to give this little ho a bit of the ol' ooh-ah ooh-ah."

"Well, we've got to talk about that," said Peg.

"Fuck off, bitch."

"Look, I know this little tramp is as juicy as a summertime peach picked right off the tree," said Peg, "but she's not for you. She belongs to Mr. Crest."

"Who the fuck's Mr. Crest?"

"You don't know Mr. Crest?" asked Peg. "You're lucky. He's a mean, wicked, ruthless old sonofabitch, and he doesn't like anyone fucking his girls besides him. See that down there?" Peg indicated the dainty red rose tattooed on Vicki's right ankle. "That's his brand. That means that those titties are his, that ass is his, and that little pink flower between her legs is most definitely his, and that means trouble for all of us if you don't zip up and back off. Because not only will he track you down and kill you, but the last time I allowed one of Mr. Crest's girls to get fucked by the likes of you, I was shitting blood for a week. Seriously, you should see my asshole. It looks like a train tunnel. So, how about it? Just save us all a world of misery and go bother someone else."

The skinheads stared hard at Peg, then turned back to their prospective victim, a look of uncertainty in their eyes.

They're buying it, Peg thought.

Then the skinhead with his pants open snickered, and seized the fabric of Vicki's short dress, ready to hoist it up.

"I ain't scared o' nobody, and I ain't scared o' your dipshit boss," he sneered. "This bitch is gettin' a reaming from yours truly, right now."

"All right, all right, you have me over a barrel," Peg sighed, opening her purse and producing a tantalizing amount of one hundred dollar bills bound together with rubber bands. "If you punks won't listen to reason, maybe you'll listen to this. Now, let's hear it. How much will it take for you two bozos to get lost? A thousand? Two? Three? I can go as high as five. What'll it be?"

The skinhead with the dangling dick still seemed unconvinced, but his buddy at the other end of the pool table had dollar signs in his eyes. Peg knew she had them now, and, not for the first time, she thanked the stars that her position with the Vigilantes kept her financially solvent.

"We'll take the five and go," the astounded skinhead said at last.

"Hey, wait a minute..." his buddy began to protest.

"Dude, no bitch is worth that much. Come on, we'll find another one. Let's take the cash and get outta here before that Crest guy shows up."

"A very wise decision," said Peg, handing over the bundled greenbacks.

"Fuck you," said the disappointed skinhead, as he and his buddy pocketed their payoff and took their leave of the establishment.

"All right, girl, they're gone," Peg said to the girl still lying prone upon the green felt of the pool table. "You can get up now."

Carefully the girl sat up, smoothed a few wrinkles out of her dress, tossed her magma-colored hair back over her shoulder in a move that nearly buckled Peg's knees, then turned to face her knight in shining armor.

"Thanks a lot," she said. "I really appreciate it. I *so* didn't want to get screwed by those jerks. How did you come up with that story?"

"The ability to think on your feet is important to a person like me. I'm Peg."

"Really nice to meet you," said the girl, stepping carefully down from the pool table. "I'm Veronica, but I like to be called Vicki."

"Good," said Peg. "So, now that the introductions are out of the way, perhaps we could discuss how you might like to repay me."

Letting this suggestion hang in the air, Peg laid a hand boldly on Vicki's firm right breast and slowly circled the pointed nipple with the tip of her thumb. Vicki, far from being scandalized, smiled mischievously, took hold of Peg's slender wrist with her own manicured fingers, and raised Peg's hand to her luscious mouth.

"Well, I'm sure I can think of something, seeing as how I do owe you in a big, big way," she said, kissing each of Peg's knuckles softly in turn while gazing directly into her eyes. "You don't have a problem with my age, then? How old are you?"

"You mind your manners," said Peg, penetrating Vicki's mouth with her forefinger and letting her suck on it. "I don't care that you're a teenager. As far as I'm concerned, anyone who looks like you should be put to good use, and damned often. And am I correct in presuming that you're not a virgin?"

Vicki nodded her head, Peg's finger still in her mouth.

"Good," said Peg. "I don't like virgins. They never have any idea how to do things properly."

"I know how to do a lot of things," said Vicki, extracting the finger and winking playfully. "You wanna do it in the backroom, or out here in front of everybody?"

"We won't be doing it here at all," said Peg, draping an arm over the young girl's exquisite shoulders and leading her to the club's exit. "I've got fresh batteries and a full bottle of K-Y Jelly back at my place. Come on."

Shang Fear had been betrayed before, most notably at the age of nineteen, by his master, Kang Jin-Khu. He still seethed to remember how badly he had been misused by his mentor and father figure on that last, fateful day of their relationship, after an entire adolescence spent guarding him, killing for him, waiting on him, and pleasuring him in bed. He still seethed to remember how Kang had cast him upon the rocks, discarded him as casually as an old glove, and disregarded all they had meant to each other with one cold, callous turn of his cheek. He still seethed to remember the night he had killed Kang Jin-Khu.

Fast approaching was the seventh anniversary of the day Kang had taken Fear under his wing, and the lad was as happy as ever in his master's service. He took great personal pride in the way he kept house, the assassinations Kang assigned him were pure recreation, and he was as pliant and eager to please as a lovesick schoolgirl when taken to the paternal gangster's bed. Yes, that particular part of his duties was most enjoyable, no matter how many kinky new ideas – bondage, cutting, defecation, asphyxiation – Kang had thrown into the mix over the years, and it hardly came as a surprise to him when his master had requested he braid his hair into twin pigtails and don the alluring plaid skirt, white blouse, knee socks, and black patent leather shoes of a Catholic schoolgirl. He was only too happy to oblige Kang in any way he could, and if his master desired a tight, virginal little tart that would squeal like a stuck pig on her hands and knees, then that was what Fear would give him.

When the anticipated moment of seduction finally drew nigh, Fear, having made himself as convincing as possible, sat demurely upon the edge of his master's king-sized bed, his legs crossed, his hands folded daintily in his lap, awaiting the entrance of his domineering lover. But it wasn't Kang who pushed open the bedroom door and stared with lustful eyes at the cross-dressed youth. Rather it was a notoriously homosexual gangster by the name of Tso Yeoh; a powerful man with whom Fear knew Kang wished to curry favor. And just like that, Fear saw things as they really were; just like that, his vision became clear; just like that, he realized that Kang Jin-Khu – his master, his lover, his *father* – had whored him out.

The next few minutes of Fear's life were engulfed in blind, blackened rage. He didn't even remember killing Tso Yeoh, though the shattered picture window and the bloody stain on the sidewalk far below Kang's penthouse apartment were testament to the deed. Likewise he had only the fuzziest of memories of bursting out of the bedroom, knocking the surprised Kang to the floor, leaping onto his chest, and wrapping both hands around his neck.

"How *dare* you!" he had hissed through clenched teeth, making every effort to choke the life from Kang's body. "After all that I've done for you! After...*all*...that I've...*done*...for you!"

A full twenty minutes expired before Fear returned to coherence; a full twenty minutes before his breathing normalized, his face lost its beet red hue, and he was finally able to remove his fingers from the dead man's neck, now marked with a set of ten deep, purple indentations. After that, there was nothing left to do; nothing left but to have a good cry, change his clothes, pack up what few personal effects he desired, make a quick withdrawal from Kang's vault, then take his leave of the now hateful, tainted place that had been his home throughout his formative years.

It was Kang's face Fear pictured when he returned to Mourning Dove, kicked open the Director's Office door, pulled the late Thomas Jefferson Zang's handgun from within his coat, and leveled it at the openly astonished Kun-Cho Fang.

"As a general rule, I detest Oscar Wilde," he said, "but he did say one thing which seems particularly apt here. Specifically, 'A man cannot be too careful in the choice of his enemies.' You, old man, have made a very grave mistake."

"Yes, I imagine I have," croaked Fang, sitting like a shriveled, lumpy toad in his wheelchair. "That is, in supposing that that young idiot Zang could do a single thing right." Then his aged, squinting eyes came into focus, and the reality of his situation became apparent to him. "Wait a minute. Fear, what are you doing?"

"You always knew I killed people, Fang," said Fear. "Whatever made you think *you* were exempt?"

Fear squeezed the trigger, and Fang's oxygen tank exploded, engulfing the wretched man in a ball of flame, and as he screamed and flailed his arms helplessly, Fear closed the door on him and stepped back out into the hallway, where the noise had brought the three remaining members of the Faustian 5 running.

"What in hell is going on in here?" demanded the Racketeer.

"This is a funeral parlor, is it not?" said Fear. "Well, then, I am simply overseeing a cremation."

"Fear, what have you done?" asked Penelope Yin, her eyes widening.

"I've killed the old fucker, my dear," said Fear. "Something I should have done ages ago. Things around here will be run much more efficiently now that *I* am in command of this organization."

"But this is outrageous!" the Racketeer exclaimed. "You can't just usurp authority..."

"As if any of you could stop me!" retorted Fear. "Fang was a crippled old invalid, but now you will have to get used to a leader who rules with the strength of a hundred men! Accept this change in the status quo, and we shall all prosper like never before! Or defy me, and I'll massacre the whole damned lot of you!"

Each of the three criminal elite, though stunned by the events of the past few minutes, retained the capacity to evaluate their circumstances. The Racketeer had disliked and mistrusted Kun-Cho Fang for some time now, and was not the least bit saddened by the smell of burning flesh emanating from the closed office. Additionally, he knew that his chances of survival outside the sovereignty of the *Dong Ji* were unfavorable, and he doubted his life would be worth a plug nickel without the affiliation. He was too old and too sick to leave.

Penelope Yin, who had long regarded Fear with quiet curiosity and amusement, found herself infuriated at what he had done. As far as she was concerned, Fear had stepped way over the line in killing the *Dong Ji*'s longtime president and strategist, and if the choice had been hers, the punishment for his treason – for 'twas no less than that – would have been a messy, prolonged disembowelment. But, like the Racketeer, she didn't want to leave. So she resolved to weather the issue for the time being, rein herself in, and at least pretend to be in concurrence.

Warren Winterhawk had never liked Fear, knowing full well the nature of his diseased, psychotic mind, and he bristled at the thought of being his subordinate, but he saw little he could do to rectify this unpalatable turn of events. True, he was a strong, resilient fighter, but he was as nothing when measured against Fear's prodigious talents, and as his primary role within the *Dong Ji* had always been that of an enforcer, he was in no position to challenge anyone who declared himself to be the company's leader.

"I shall take it by your silence that we are in agreement, then," said Fear. "Excellent. Believe me when I say that the *Dong Ji*, in times to come, will undergo a renaissance unlike any seen before in organized crime. Our plans to bring the city to its knees shall continue. Our new Delegation shall unite us with other armies of darkness all across New York. We shall strike down our enemies with the terrible, swift sword of a god, and scatter any and all resistance to the four winds! Very shortly our power will be the *only* power! We are building a legacy here, dear friends, and it belongs to all of us!"

Ten minutes had elapsed since Peg and Vicki had shared a combined fourteen orgasms, and now Peg lay on her side amid the rumpled bedsheets, staring at the wall and chewing away at her bottom lip, while Vicki spooned against her, her soft arms embracing the Vigilante's curved midsection, her perfect lips kissing the lobe of her ear.

"That was unbelievable," the young girl murmured in between kisses, nuzzling Peg's neck lovingly. "Seriously, that's, like, the best sex I've ever had. You're amazing, Peg. I'm so glad we met."

Peg was completely unresponsive to all this attention. Her back turned to the girl with whom she had just shared such a deep and magical intimacy, she remained silent, and even went rigid as Vicki's hand began venturing down past her quivering navel. The fact of the matter was that Peg wasn't crazy about being touched after sexual release had been achieved, much less having to actually cuddle with whatever convenient, accommodating creature had been handy to provide the service. She needed her space, and this gooey-hearted girl was all over her like an octopus. It wasn't acceptable to Peg's equilibrium, and she put her foot firmly down when Vicki attempted to remount her.

"Cut it out!" she insisted, shoving the surprised girl forcefully to the floor. "I'm not into that, all right? Look, we had a good time, but now we're done, okay? It's not like this was gonna be a relationship or anything. Jeez, don't you know what a one-night stand is? I picked you up, I brought you home, we fucked each other's brains out, and now we can get on with our separate lives. Okay? We're done. I have no more use for you. You can hit the road whenever you feel like it. Get the picture?"

Throughout Peg's dismissive little diatribe, Vicki had remained seated on the floor, the corners of her mouth turned down, her eyes moist but not leaking a single tear. She was clearly disappointed, but far too seasoned to fall to pieces over something like this, and after Peg had finished telling her what was what, she rose to her feet with as much dignity as she could salvage and reached for her dress hanging over the side of the dresser mirror.

"I'm sorry," she said at last, quietly, her eyes downcast. "I guess I misunderstood. I'm used to casual flings. I don't know what on earth made me think this was different. I guess I just felt...well, it's not important. I'll leave you alone now. But...could I sleep on your couch till morning? Then I'll be gone, and I won't bother you anymore."

"Yes, yes, here," said Peg, throwing a pillow at Vicki. "Do whatever you want. Just don't come back in here again."

Hugging the pillow to her chest, Vicki nodded silently and walked out of the bedroom, leaving Peg free to stretch out and fall asleep.

But Peg didn't fall asleep. She *couldn't* fall asleep. For nearly forty minutes she tried, but the glowing red numbers on her digital clock radio finally drove her to madness, and she threw off her single cotton sheet, got out of bed, and opened her door, her destination in mind being the living room.

Shit, she cursed herself, turning the hallway corner and catching sight of Vicki, her body configured on the three-cushion couch in the most comfortable position possible, her dress covering her like a blanket. "Vicki, are you awake?"

"Yes," the girl sighed, softly.

"Listen," Peg began, taking a seat on the edge of the couch, next to Vicki's crossed ankles. "I'm sorry. I mean, I'm sorry for what I said. It was mean and cruel and it wasn't at all fair to you, because you don't know the whole story. The plain, simple truth is I'm not...well, I'm not exactly what you'd call a normal person."

"I don't think I am either," said Vicki.

"No, but you're not listening," Peg continued. "I mean, I'm really fucked up. I've had a hard, traumatic life, and it's left me the worse for wear. Emotionally I'm a wreck, dependent on mood stabilizers, and liable to fly off the handle over the smallest thing. You should see my medicine cabinet. It looks like a candy kitchen for the Rolling Stones."

Vicki giggled.

"And I'm suicidal too," Peg added. "Let's not omit that from the package. I've tried to kill myself so many times, I've got Dr. Kevorkian on my speed dial."

"Oh, so that's what this is," said Vicki, tracing a finger gently along a faded scar that spanned the width of Peg's left wrist. "I wondered about that."

"And don't even get me started on my sexuality," Peg went on, crossing her arms over her chest. "You see, I had...a very bad experience when I was about your age, and these days I'm a bisexual nymph. I can't get enough, and I don't care where it comes from. Add everything up and I'm a complete freak."

As Peg lowered her head and looked at the floor, Vicki propped herself up on one elbow and caressed the older woman's shoulder gently with her other hand.

"I don't think you're a freak," she said. "I think you're great. You're a kind person. You're a tender, passionate lover. And now here you are talking to me about your problems. You're awesome, Peg."

"And I think you're great too, Vicki," said Peg. "And that's the problem. It wasn't supposed to be like this, y'see. When we met, I didn't regard you as anything more than another lay. You were to be a fix for my addiction, that's all. But when we were having sex I felt something… different. Y'know, something I've never felt with anyone else. Something good. And it really kinda threw me for a loop."

"And that's why you wigged out on me in there," said Vicki, sympathetically. "Because you were disoriented, and maybe just a little bit frightened."

"Yes," said Peg. "You're absolutely right. I'm not used to feeling those kinds of feelings with my partners. Usually they mean nothing to me, but you…you meant something."

"Then we're agreed," said Vicki. "Because you meant something to me too."

"Marvelous, isn't it?" Peg sighed, still looking at the floor. "The first person in a long, horny parade of discarded partners who actually makes me feel good beyond the physical, and the only way I can express myself is to yell at her and throw her out of my bed. Pretty sick, huh?"

Vicki smiled, sat up next to Peg, and put her arm around her.

"You know," she said, "I once had a boyfriend who used to say something that always put things into perspective for me. He said, 'God wants us all to be different, so He fucks up each of us in a different way.' "

Peg laughed. "I like that one," she said. "So, would you like to come back to bed and give the cuddling another try?"

"The cuddling can wait," said Vicki. "Right now I want you sitting on my face."

"I hate Monday mornings, and I hate algebra," William complained to no one in particular as he pored over his math textbook and three worksheets spread out across a table in the least cluttered corner of the Rat Hole's lounge, a mere twenty-five minutes before he was due to be at school. "There's no way I'm gonna be able to finish this in time for second period. Man, I'll be glad when summer vacation finally starts."

"Coffee order!" Carolyn announced, returning to the Hole carrying a cardboard tray laden with cups of steaming Dunkin' Donuts coffee. "Who had the Cinnamon Spice?"

"I did," said Peg, taking the cup and blowing gently over the coffee's surface.

"You certainly look like you could use it, girl," said Carolyn. "Those bags under your eyes are heavy enough to get checked by airport security."

"I was up all night working on a new project," Peg replied, figuring that qualified as at least a half-truth.

"I had a Dunkin' Decaf," said Buzz.

"One completely pointless blend of hot, brown water for our resident mind-bender," said Carolyn, handing Buzz his selection. "And let's see, the Hazelnut's mine, and here's your French Vanilla, Sushi."

"Did you get my Café Blend?" asked Charlie.

"It's right here, breaking my arm," said Carolyn, handing the big Vigilante a cup half the size of a movie theater popcorn tub. "Hasn't anyone ever told you that too much coffee is bad for you?"

"But I only drink two cups a day," said Charlie, defensively. "Besides, I don't exactly get a lot of sleep, y'know. Want a sip before you go, Will?"

"No thanks," said the boy. "I can't run the risk of stunting my growth."

"Here's your beer, Zeke, you grubby, drunken misfit," Carolyn continued, handing over the Miller six-pack she had been holding in her other hand. "And where's Gary? I got him an Original Blend and a Boston Kreme."

"Haven't seen him since yesterday morning," said Charlie, swallowing a huge gulp of coffee and wiping his mouth with his wrist. "He's seemed very preoccupied lately; very busy with something."

"Ya never know what that crazy horse thief'll get up to," said Zeke, already halfway through his first bottle. "We oughta run a feature. Y'know, 'Where In The World Is Gary Parker?' or somethin'. Ya can jus' picture that, can't ya?" He affected a deep, narrative tone. "Today, Gary's on the run from the authorities with the death mask of Pretty Boy Floyd, hiding out in the Reptile Gardens of Rapid City, South Dakota, wondering why all the exhibits are trying to eat him."

Carolyn didn't usually appreciate Zeke's sense of humor, but she had to admit to being tickled by this particular interjection of satire, as it sounded very much like Gary indeed. The group was quick to learn, however, that Zeke's jest had actually somewhat understated the incredible truth, as Gary came bursting energetically through the door just seconds later, sporting one of the most outlandish, vaudevillian ensembles his immoderate mind had yet conceived. Nearly unrecognizable to his colleagues at first, his face was blackened with shoe polish, his lips were exaggerated with white paint, an enormous, woolly afro wig wobbled like a mountain of jelly atop his head, he was dressed in a tatty suit of old clothes that would have looked more at home on a scarecrow, and he held a jingling tambourine in his right hand.

"Mornin', y'all!" he greeted his nonplussed friends, warmly.

"Gary, I know your fetish for disguises," Carolyn spoke up at last, "but a blackface minstrel? I swear, your behavior grows more and more bizarre with each passing day."

"I'm sure I don't know what you mean," he replied. "Hey, anyone wanna see me do 'Jimmy Crack Corn'?"

"I suppose I should be indignant," said Charlie, "but really, I'm just astonished that you've managed to go this long without being diagnosed with galloping schizophrenia."

"All right, seriously, I was up in Harlem and I thought this would help me blend in," said Gary, discarding the fright wig and tambourine and wiping the shoe polish from his face with his raggedy sleeve. "Instead, as it turned out, a group of four or five guys began chasing me and throwing bricks. I guess it is a bit cheeky, isn't it? Anyway, the important thing is that I had a nice, long chat with a reliable snitch that I keep up there, and I've finally got the lowdown on the Chinese mob's big plans."

"Well, don't keep us in suspense, boss," said Zeke, polishing off one bottle, tossing it aside, and reaching immediately for another. "What's the unglad word?"

"You guys are gonna love this," said Gary. "Remember yesterday morning when we were talking about the *Dong Ji* killing off a lot of their major rivals and competitors and fighting their way to the top of the food chain? Well, last night they finally achieved their grand ambition. They've devised and put into action a winner of a plan to give themselves control over most of the organized crime in New York City."

"Care to elaborate?" Charlie requested.

"Of course," said Gary. "You guys are definitely gonna want to hear this. Unbelievable as it may seem, the *Dong Ji* has actually managed to kill off the big bosses of the Russian, Italian, and Irish mobs."

"Big deal," said William. "So the mobs will select new leaders."

"Ah, but there's the rub," Gary continued. "The mobs don't get to select their new leaders. The *Dong Ji* has already done that for them."

"Come again?" said Carolyn.

"They – the *Dong Ji*, I mean – have actually conquered these other mobs and taken control, kind of like when a large corporation buys up several smaller companies. Yes. Yes, that's exactly what they've done. They've executed a hostile merger."

"So, blue-collar criminals are turning into white-collar criminals," Peg observed. "Or is it the other way around?"

"They all bleed the same color," said Sushi, fingering the hilt of his *katana*.

"You haven't heard the most ingenious part yet," Gary went on. "Honestly, it really is frightfully clever, and they conducted the whole affair right out in the open, under our very noses. Do you know what they've done? They've gathered together a group of operatives to serve as diplomatic middlemen between themselves and their new acquisitions. As you can well imagine, these mobs – dragons with their heads cut off – aren't particularly happy about being effectively owned by a lot of Chinese, so the *Dong Ji* has filled the leadership positions with men of the same nationalities. Take, for example, that Russian gangster Carla and I ran into the night before last. I've since learned that he's the new leader of the Russian syndicate."

"But you said the *Dong Ji* is running these mobs now," said William.

"They are," Gary affirmed. "These new leaders are mere puppets through which the *Dong Ji* channels its orders. They've been installed for the sake of harmony and smooth relations. Pride and identity are very important to crime syndicates, and this way the separate mobs each appear to have one of their own running the show and can maintain at least the appearance of independence, while it's really the Chinese who dictate and regulate their every move. Everybody wins."

"So, as of last night, three of the biggest criminal forces in New York are under Chinese control?" said Sushi.

"They've got the Harlem Hellfighters too," Gary added. "They didn't have to kill that bastard Smits, though. He caved in to them. He sold his soul to save his ass."

"Sounds like a whole new ballgame," said Carolyn. "We're not dealing with just a mob anymore. Now we're dealing with a conglomerate."

"Will, could you bring up the *Dong Ji* file, please?" Gary requested.

"Like I've really got the time for this," William muttered, tapping a few computer keys to bring up the desired information on the large computer monitor at the front of the room.

"Here are the *Dong Ji*'s six high-ups," said Gary, pointing to the grid of six photographs filling the screen. "We know all of these guys. They're all very nasty customers, but the good news is that Kun-Cho Fang and Thomas Jefferson Zang were both killed just last night. That knocks them down to four, making our job that much easier."

"Hey, that's the woman I ran into the other night," said Charlie, recognizing Penelope Yin. "If I had known who she was, I would have made breaking her neck my first priority."

"And that's Warren Winterhawk, the Indian," Sushi pointed to the picture of the square-jawed Apache.

"Right," said Gary. "He's the muscle of this upper echelon. He's nowhere near Charlie's class, but he does have an unusual advantage in most fights, thanks to a particular operation he had a while back. It probably took about twenty years off his life, but the man feels no pain. His central nervous system is completely numb, making him more resilient than any normal person."

"He ain't tangled toe-to-toe with me yet," said Charlie, cracking his knuckles loudly. "He may be painless, but nothing short of a jackhammer between the eyes can make me cry out either."

"And then there's our old friend the Racketeer," Gary continued.

"You're not serious, are you?" asked Carolyn. "Ol' Yin-Yang Face is still kicking around? He's been one good, strong cough away from a hole in the ground for years now."

"Men like him always live forever," said Sushi, his arms folded.

"And speaking of immortality, I'm sure we all recognize this fellow," said Gary, pointing to the final photograph.

Peg let out a little gasp and put her hand to her mouth. "Oh, no," she said. "Not him."

"Is it who I think it is?" Buzz asked. "But I was under the impression he'd been killed in that police shoot-out a few weeks ago."

"Shang Fear? Killed? Careful, Shades, that borders on crazy talk," said Zeke. "Chink's like a fuckin' cockroach."

"He's their leader now," said Gary. "The *Dong Ji*'s leader. He took control after Fang died. He might even be the one who killed Fang in the first place, if my source is to be believed."

"So, Shang Fear is now the most powerful criminal in New York?" said Carolyn. "What a jolly thought. Thanks for that, Gary. I might wet the bed for the rest of my life."

"Well, it's been a scream, guys, but my time's up," said William, gathering up his school supplies and stuffing them into his backpack, which he slung over his right shoulder. "English Literature waits for no man. Shit, I'm so screwed. I'm still only on page five of *Pride and Prejudice*."

William was in such a rush that he almost collided head-on with Carla, hurrying in as he was going out.

"Hey, Carla, where've you been?" Gary asked. "You missed a whole briefing."

"I just came from New York Presbyterian," she said, quietly, her face betraying distress and bewilderment. "Leeza's there. She was taken there last night by paramedics after a bomb went off in her apartment."

"*What?*" said Peg, giving voice to each of the stunned Vigilantes' concerns. "My goodness, is she all right?"

"She has a mild concussion, lots of second-degree burns, and her right arm is broken," said Carla. "The doctors say she was lucky. When I saw her just now, she was sitting up in bed and eating breakfast. She'll be all right, but..."

The room went quiet for a few moments.

"Oh, I just don't get it!" Carla blurted out. "I mean, it would be different if it was someone like me, or you, Gary, or you, Charlie, but Leeza...she's the *doctor*, for heaven's sake! An old woman with a stethoscope and a bottle of painkillers! If someone had a hit list with our names on it, she'd hardly be number one with a bullet!"

"Calm down, Carla, it's okay," said Gary, slipping a reassuring arm around her shoulders.

"We've got to take this steadily. The most important thing is that she's not too badly hurt and that she's recovering well. A lot worse could have happened."

"Yeah," said Zeke. "For one thing, they could've missed her altogether."

"That's way out of line, Zeke!" snapped Buzz, surprising his colleagues with his departure from his usual even tone. "The poor woman might have been killed!"

"Zeke, what did I tell you before about that mouth of yours?" Gary chastised him. "If all you're going to do is upset everybody, then keep your trap shut."

"We should make it a priority to find the party responsible," said Buzz. "Whoever it is might try to finish Leeza off, or they may come after any one of us next."

"Duly noted," nodded Gary. "So, you all know the agenda for the next few days. Catch the mad bomber, and put the kibosh on the Chinese. Any other business before we go out there and make the world safe for democracy?"

"Well, there might be something," said Charlie, scratching his chin, thoughtfully. "I hate to bring it up now, seeing as how we've got all these other baddies to deal with, and especially because I don't see him becoming a huge threat, but there's something you all should know about a certain priest…"

Not twenty minutes ago, Father Campion Earkhert had concluded his Monday morning

Mass, shooed away the thirty or so parishioners who had attended, and, with the church now empty and peaceful, had taken a seat at the table behind his pulpit, eager to resume work on his personal project upon which he had labored meticulously nearly every day for the past two years; a bold, incisive new catechism embodying all the true and earnest properties and elements of the Catholic faith as they were meant to be – Earkhert's pen reinforcing God's everlasting law with iron and steel – its purpose being to supplant and replace all present, erroneous perceptions of the faith, to return the worldwide flock to its roots, and to snatch Christ's one, true Church back from the heathen jaws of laxity, liberalism, decadence, and Vatican II. Once he was certain it was perfect, flawless, and without want for a single improvement – once he was certain it was finished – he would send it to the Pope for approval.

And let no Catholic intermingle with a non-Catholic, Earkhert wrote, continuing the chapter he had begun the previous evening, *and let no Catholic take to their wedding bed a non-Catholic, for in giving their God-granted lives over to the heathen, they shall be ignored by the hand of God, and exiled to hell forever and ever. The unbelievers – the infidels who have turned their backs on the Church – are ugly in the Lord's sight. Let them alone, for they be blind leaders of the blind, and if the blind lead the blind, both shall fall into the ditch. Be ever faithful to the Lord, and be ever mindful that the wages of sin is death, but the gift of God is eternal life through Jesus Christ.*

"Excellent," Earkhert commended himself. "How can His Holiness in Rome deny that this be the way and the truth and the life? Oh, Father, I strive and succeed to return You to the people."

Before Earkhert could again touch pen to paper, however, he was disturbed by the creaking of the heavy oak doors at the front of the church swinging open, and, looking up from his composition, saw a tall, thin man dressed all in black, framed against the outer sunlight like an angel barring the entrance to paradise, the tails of his long coat flapping dramatically in the breeze.

" 'And thus I clothe my naked villainy with old odd ends, stol'n forth of holy writ; And seem a saint, when most I play the devil.' " said Shang Fear, advancing into the church. "Shakespeare."

"You!" Earkhert leapt from his chair, snatched a heavy, brass crucifix from the wall, and held it out at arm's length in front of himself. "Perfidious apostate! Iniquitous antichrist! It is written that the devil cannot see inside the house of God! For in the time of trouble, He shall hide me in His pavilion! In the secret of His tabernacle shall He hide me! He shall set me up upon a rock!"

"Oh, do hush up," said Fear. "I am not a religious man, Earkhert, as you well know, but even I can see what an abomination you are, standing upright in that cassock, clutching the graven image of another man's God in your bloody, sinner's hand."

"What business have you here, hateful idolater?" asked Earkhert.

"Business indeed," said Fear, approaching the pulpit. "I come to you with a proposition."

"As did Lucifer when he did try to tempt Christ in the wilderness!" Earkhert replied.

"I have been blessed recently with a most sudden advancement in my career," said Fear, "and I now find myself at the head of one of the most sprawling criminal organizations this city has ever known. I have my long-term plans, of course, but I entertain a particular ambition with which I suspect you can assist me. Without revealing all the details just now, I require a spectacle. A momentous event that will shake not only this metropolis, but this entire nation to its very core. I have no interest in ruling from the shadows. I wish to inform the people of this city, with as much violence and carnage as possible, that I have arrived; that I am the new sheriff in town, so to speak."

"And what has this to do with me?" asked Earkhert, fingering his rosary at his side lest his soul be cursed by Fear's mere presence.

"A temporary partnership would be conducive to both our ends," Fear explained. "My design is twofold. Not only will it establish firmly my new authority, but, if you join me, you will be assured the opportunity to destroy many of the people you call 'sinners'."

Earkhert's eyes widened at this, and his heartbeat accelerated instantly. The prospect of washing away sinners was always a stimulating one. Just as Tom Cruise had had Renee Zellweger at 'hello', New York's newest crime lord had Earkhert hooked irrevocably now, but still, the priest didn't want to sound too eager.

"What need have you for me?" he asked, warily.

"Your parishioners," said Fear. "Are they obedient in your sight? Do they heed your words?"

"My sheep listen to my voice," said Earkhert. "I know them and they follow me. My countenance mesmerizes them. They hang upon my every syllable, for they know I deliver to them the gift of Christ. If I commanded it, each and every last one of them would lay down their lives in my name."

"Earkhert, my new partner," Fear permitted a rare grin to part his lips, revealing two rows of ravenous, off-white teeth, "that's precisely what I wanted to hear."

"And then the cop says, 'Ma'am, that's not a tree. That's your air freshener.' "

Upon his completion of the humerous anecdote, Zeke slapped his knee and guffawed loudly enough to draw a leer of disapproval from an orderly out in the hallway. Leeza, reclining in bed with her right arm in a cast and a bandage wrapped around her cranium, was markedly less amused.

"That doesn't make any sense," she said. "Why would the blond woman have thought that her air freshener was a tree?"

"Because it was shaped like a tree," said Zeke.

"But if she purchased the freshener herself, and made the conscious decision to hang it from her rearview mirror, how could she have possibly become so confused?"

"Quit bustin' my balls, Eva Braun!" said Zeke, exasperated. "It's just a joke! I was tryin' to cheer ya up!"

Answer me this, Zeke," said Leeza, notorious for her lack of a sense of humor. "When, in all the time that we've known each other, have you ever known me to be cheery?"

Zeke had to concede that point. Never so much as cracking a single smile during her long acquaintanceship with Zeke and the other Vigilantes, Leeza seemed to be in a perpetual state of irritation, like Rudyard Kipling's rhinoceros with the itchy cake crumbs festering beneath its skin.

"All right, out you go," said a stout, elderly nurse, entering the room abruptly and clapping her wrinkled hands a few times, as if shooing a dog. "Visits for this morning are over. You can come back this evening if you like, but for now I'll have to ask you to leave."

"Jeez, Eva Braun and Nurse Ratched both at once," Zeke passed a hand over his forehead and stood up from his chair. "That's too much for me. Don't worry, lady, I'm goin'." He hesitated just long enough to steal one of the strawberry-flavored hard candies from the dish on Leeza's bedside table. "See ya later, ol' gal. Gary said he'd come see ya tonight, if he didn't get killed first. Ah, the glamour, the glamour."

"Imbecile," Leeza muttered, as Zeke's graceless footsteps grew fainter and fainter until the big, empty hallway swallowed the sound completely. "Well, nurse, don't keep it a secret. How many more days and nights am I to be incarcerated in this home for invalids?"

"Oh, you're leaving immediately, ma'am," said the nurse, producing a hypodermic needle, holding it up to the light, and giving it a quick squirt before closing in on her helpless patient.

"What?" said Leeza. "Hey, just a minute now. What's that? What are you doing?"

"You may experience some momentary discomfort," said the nurse, clinically, before plunging the needle directly into a vein in Leeza's left wrist.

"You look here, you blasted bedpan jockey!" Leeza ranted. "You're not fooling anyone! I'm a doctor! What have you done to me? I'll have your job! I'll...I'll..."

Then Leeza's eyelids dropped, her muscles went limp, and her head hit the pillow like a lump of lead.

That's it, dearie, thought the nurse, unlocking the brake on the castor-equipped bed and preparing to wheel it out of the room and down the hallway. *Get some sleep. And dream a little dream of me.*

The TV weathermen had been wrong; the predicted rain had never arrived. After seven days of gloom, the heavy, black clouds shadowing the metropolis had retired at last on a westbound wind, and the sun was beaming brilliantly over the entirety of America's greatest city, the tall, silver skyscrapers reflecting the rays of light like immense mirrors. The only obscure corner of the city seemingly untouched by the new illumination was the docks area down on the East River, where shadow and shade claimed eminent domain over all, and it was here, atop the flat roof of a two-story warehouse, that Shang Fear stood proud and tall over the territory he knew was now his.

I've finally done it, he thought. *I've finally accomplished that of which I dreamed years ago. Ruler of all I survey.*

Wearing his coat drawn down over one shoulder, like Lady Liberty in her majestic toga, Fear closed his eyes contentedly and breathed in the cool, dry breeze wafting in off the water. In the parking lot below, two squawking seagulls fought over a stale french fry. Several blocks to the south, a gunshot took a life.

I like this area, thought Fear. *Yes, I could be at home here. Here I shall establish my auxiliary headquarters.*

"Well, well, look who thinks he's king of the world," said a woman's voice from behind.

"Hello, Janet," said Fear, not turning around. "So, you've heard about my recent rise to power?"

"News travels fast through the underbelly," said Janet, her stiletto heels clicking loudly on the rooftop's concrete surface as she slithered over to Fear. "But I'd hardly use the word 'power' to describe what you have. You're a thug, Confucius, same as you ever were; a psychotic, hot-tempered thug with a serious impulse control problem."

"High praise indeed, coming from one such as you," said Fear.

"And that's exactly my point," Janet continued. "You're no better than the rest of us. You can force all the petty crooks and knee-breakers in the world to work for you, but it'll take just one bloody tantrum from you to show 'em that you're no mastermind and that the only constructive use for your brain is as an exhibit in a glass jar in a college criminology class. 'Cause you're not a big man, Fear. You're just a delusional weirdo with a Napoleon complex, and no matter how hard you try to be the Green Hornet, you'll always just be Kato. Might as well accept it."

Fear's jaw tightened imperceptibly.

"So, I have a half hour window scheduled before my next senseless act of violence," said Janet, slipping a long, sinewy arm over Fear's reedy shoulders. "Wanna find a room somewhere and fuck?"

Fear answered by seizing Janet's wrist in his own vice-like grip, bending down into a squat, and flipping the leather-clad woman over his back and off the edge of the roof, watching with supreme satisfaction as she fell twenty-five feet into a pile of empty wooden crates.

"What a splendid head, yet no brain," he said, leaping into a forward somersault that carried his own person safely to the ground.

"Lover, you have no idea what you've just done to yourself!" hissed Janet, her body covered with splinters, the familiar, excited bloodlust in her eyes as she stood and advanced. "I think it's time you and I reevaluated our relationship!"

Her head lowered and her muscles tensed, Janet lunged at Fear, not fifteen feet away, but the *Dong Ji*'s new leader sidestepped, wrapped a leg around the woman's neck, and held her like that while he unsheathed his broadsword and slashed a half inch deep cut across the full breadth of her back. Then he spun and released her, flinging her face-first into a wooden post at the edge of the nearest pier.

" 'To be great is to be misunderstood', dear Janet," said Fear. "Ralph Waldo Emerson."

An animalistic growl escaping her bleeding mouth, Janet leapt to her feet, feinted to the right, then weaved left and threw a kick at Fear's face, but the man moved his head out of the way with remarkable speed, delivered a disabling chop to Janet's offered ankle, then grabbed her by the back of her neck and cast her sprawling forwards, facedown in the dirt. When she tried to stand up again, her ankle gave out on her, and she screamed as she collapsed again.

Fear fell upon her like a jungle cat upon its prey, hammering her face with punch after relentless punch, as if trying to break through her skull and finger her soft, squishy brain. This was pure indulgence for the sadistic Fear, and he relished every blow he landed. By the time Janet's nose had cracked, her eyes had swollen, and her black-and-blue face had become drenched in her own blood, Fear was laughing giddily.

"Neitzsche said, 'What does not destroy me makes me stronger.' Do *you* feel any stronger, Janet?" Fear giggled like the lunatic he was, hoisting Janet effortlessly over his head and preparing to hurl her into the side of a nearby forklift. "I know that *I* feel like a brand new man!"

Janet hit the forklift with a bone-jarring, whiplash-inducing impact that threw her neck out of joint, and even though she was barely conscious by this point, Fear was far from through. Wrapping his long fingers around her throat, he lifted her off the ground and held her dangling in the air – though he was far less muscular than she – and proceeded to drive his broadsword directly through her left thigh, skewering it like a piece of meat. He then hacked deep into her left side, chopping out flesh like a whittler cuts a notch into a piece of wood, loosing a squirting stream of blood before throwing her like a piece of refuse over to the edge of the nearest pier.

Janet's animal instinct, which had always dominated her human side, told her that she was dying, and that her only chance for survival, albeit a remote one, was to stand up; stand up and fight. She was bloody and broken and twisted – more thoroughly counted out than ever before – but she had to stand up. So she reached up for one of the pier's wooden posts with her trembling right hand and used it to pull herself slowly, shakily to her feet, just in time for her reddening vision to see Fear's tendinous claw emerge from the folds of that infinite coat, clutching the handle of a pistol.

"Stalin said, 'A single death is a tragedy. A million deaths is a statistic,' " said Fear, taking his time in aiming the gun. "But your death, dear Janet, shall be neither."

The bullet rocketed through the left side of her chest in a haze of blood, and her body stiffened and arched before falling backwards off the pier and into the water with a splash of finality.

"Now *that's* entertainment," Fear chuckled, reholstering the weapon, turning his back on the scene, and setting off in the direction of Chinatown. "I wonder who else needs killing today? There must be somebody. After all, the whole town's abuzz."

While Fear departed cheerfully, the limp and lifeless Janet floated on her back in the red, murky water beneath the pier, and she would have gone under within minutes if a hand hadn't grabbed her by her short hair and pulled her back onto land.

Setting her gently down on the ground, Gary turned her over onto her belly and thumped her between her shoulder blades with a few solid punches to make her cough up the water she'd swallowed. Blood came with it. Then he conducted a quick examination of her injuries, determined that she was near death, and briefly considered choking out of her what little life remained.

No, he thought. *No, that would be too easy. After all this time, it was never meant to end like that.*

Gary divested himself of his jacket and shirt, used the combat knife strapped to his calf to cut them into long strips, then used the strips to bandage Janet's bleeding wounds.

I don't know who's going to kill you, Janet, he thought, lifting her into his arms and carrying her off. *By all rights it should be me. Bu, one thing's for sure. Whoever finally does succeed where so many others have failed, it's not going to be that evil, soulless prick.*

Vicki had been putting off going home ever since she'd left Peg's apartment hours ago, but it couldn't be avoided forever, and the girl now found herself standing hesitantly – chewing her lip with the same unnamable dread and trepidation of a deer wandering past the quiet danger of a hunter's base camp – in the paved driveway of the attractive Victorian home in Astoria, Queens, not at all relishing the idea of going inside.

Offering up a heavy sigh to the inevitable, Vicki weighed her chances of weathering the coming storm. It was well past eleven o'clock now, but today was Aunt Millicent's day off, and she usually slept late. Perhaps, if she was quiet, she'd be able to escape her wrath. Nervously she took off her noisy heels, padded to the front door, took the house key from the flowerpot on the second concrete step, and very cautiously pushed open the door and entered the well-furnished living room. The place was silent as a crypt; a house at peace, for a change.

I think it's all right, she told herself, daring to hope. *I think I've gotten away with it.*

Then she squealed in surprise and pain as she was yanked abruptly backwards by her hair and something like a steel dog collar attached to a chain was clasped and locked around her neck, and she realized that she hadn't gotten away with anything.

"And just where have you been, you little bitch?" asked Aunt Millicent, giving the metal leash a hard tug. "You've been out, haven't you? All night! When I ordered you to clean this fucking carpet!"

"But I did clean it, Aunt Milli!" Vicki defended herself, timidly. "I worked real hard on it, with the soap and everything! It's really, really clean!"

Millicent scowled, then lashed out to her right with her long, angular arm, and knocked a vase to the floor. Flowers, water, and broken glass hit the carpet.

"Now it's dirty!" Millicent barked. "Clean it again!"

Vicki gulped, and chewed her bottom lip some more.

"Honestly, I don't know what to do with you sometimes!" Millicent shouted, still holding her niece by the chain. "I take you in, I give you a nice place to live and three nutritious meals a day, and all I ask in return is that you do what you're told! But do you? No! Missy, the carpets upstairs look even worse than this one! That fence out there still needs a second coat of paint! And you completely botched the windows!"

"But...but I cleaned the windows, Aunt Milli! All of them! Inside and out!"

Millicent raised her eyebrows, pursed her lips, and slapped Vicki hard across the face.

"They're streaky!" she bellowed. "Not to mention you're behind on the laundry! Do you know, you little bitch, that I woke up this morning and I didn't have a bra to put on!"

"But it takes too long to wash it all by hand, Aunt Milli!" Vicki cried, her eyes beginning to well up. "Maybe...m-maybe if we got a machine..."

This suggestion earned the girl another stinging slap.

"Lazy, lazy, lazy!" Millicent scolded. "And just what are you going to do when the bomb drops and all the machines go dead? Hm? What are you going to do then, you stupid child?"

Another slap.

"And what's this sinful rag you're wearing?" Millicent continued her persecution. "It's plain to me what you've been doing, you dirty little slut! Is that how your parents raised you? Did my brother and his wife raise a slut? Is this what I get for showing a little compassion and letting you out of your chains? Well, I'm certainly all the wiser now! From now on you'll be chained all the time! And don't bother complaining about how hard it is to get upstairs, because I won't want to hear it! Now, lean over the couch arm!"

"Oh, Aunt Milli, please, no!" Vicki's eyes widened with terror as the color drained instantly from her face. "Please, not that!"

"Do as I tell you and get over there, or it'll be all the worse!" Millicent threatened.

Shaking and whimpering, Vicki moved over to the couch and bent herself forwards over it so that her face was pressed against the cushion and her backside was up in the air, while Millicent stomped to the other side of the room and took an expertly crafted wooden cane down from its place of prominence upon the wall. Millicent had purchased it at an Amish fair in Pennsylvania two years ago, and, to add insult to injury, had asked the craftsman to inscribe upon it the name 'Veronica' in large, extravagant lettering.

"Aunt Milli, please..." Vicki begged one last time for clemency.

"Girl, this is already gonna hurt you a lot more than it's gonna hurt me!" the cruel woman rebuffed. "Do you really want to stretch it out?"

Vicki didn't even have time to take in another full breath and grit her teeth against the coming assault before the cane struck her squarely in the rear end, and she screamed.

"That's it, child! Scream! Scream away your sins!" shouted Millicent, swinging the cane with two hands, like a baseball bat.

Vicki screamed again as the cane struck her a second time, and her tears began flowing freely now.

"You think I want you here, bitch?" Millicent growled, as a third crack from the cane made Vicki wail in anguish. "You think I need this shit from you? The only reason I have anything to do with you is because I loved my dear brother so, God rest his soul! You'd better watch yourself, girl, or I'll sell you to the first pimp who asks! We'll see how much you like being a slut when someone else is reaping the benefits!"

A fourth blow, then a fifth, then Millicent returned the cane to its rack upon the wall, where it loomed over Vicki's head as a constant threat, and Vicki slid weakly off the couch arm and collapsed to the floor, sobbing uncontrollably and trembling with the pain.

"Stop that sniveling and get up!" Millicent demanded. "Make yourself presentable. We have company arriving in just a few minutes. The good

Father Campion Earkhert is coming to help save your wicked, ungrateful soul."

Between the sobs and shudders, Vicki managed to find breath enough for a response.

"Aunt Milli, no!" she cried. "You know what he does to me! You know what he makes me do!"

"Quiet!" Millicent shouted.

Then the doorbell rang, and Vicki knew she was doomed.

"That'll be him now," said Millicent, marching to the door. "Don't you dare embarrass me!"

"Millicent, my darling child!" Earkhert boomed, arms outstretched, as his hostess ushered him into the living room. "So nice to see you again, and looking as pretty as ever. I must say, though, I do miss the devil's horns."

"Not in front of the girl, Father," Millicent whispered hastily to the priest. "And who's this you've brought with you?"

"Eh? Oh, why this is our venerable Senator Alvin Bryce," said Earkhert, introducing the meek, mild man who had ventured in behind him. "New York's hope for the new millenium. I hope his presence here is acceptable. I'm currently helping him through something of a spiritual crisis, and I thought it would be good for him to sit in on this."

"Oh, well, hello there, Senator," said Millicent, extending a hand, which Bryce shook, limply. "It's a privilege to meet you. I think I voted for you, in fact. Of course we'd be happy to have you join us. Can I get you something to drink?"

"He's fine," Earkhert answered for him. "Now for the girl."

"She's right here," said Millicent, indicating the wounded, frightened creature on the couch, doing her best to sit comfortably on her raw behind.

"I can see you've been administering some of the Lord's justice yourself, my dear," said Earkhert, drawing close to Vicki and setting down the tote bag he had brought with him. "That's admirable, but just be sure you don't put me out of a job."

Millicent giggled, and invited Bryce to sit down in an armchair, while Earkhert plopped himself down next to Vicki, who refrained from shrinking away only because she feared the return of the disciplinary cane.

"Now then, my child," Earkhert addressed Vicki. "Have you been behaving yourself since our last visit?"

"She certainly has not," said Millicent, folding her arms across her chest. "She's been nothing but trouble."

"I see," said Earkhert. "Vicki, my child, have you been studying your text?"

"I...I try to, Father," said Vicki, her voice wavering. "That is, as much as I can."

"Did you read what St. Matthew says about the Last Judgment?"

"Yes, Father, I...I think I got that far."

"Would you read it for me now, please?" Earkhert requested, producing a Bible from the tote bag and handing it to Vicki. "Chapter twenty-five, verse thirty-one."

Her hands shaking, Vicki took the Bible and opened it to the first book of the New Testament, being very careful not to tear any of the thin, fragile pages (Earkhert had punched her in the face last time she had done that). Then, her breath still coming somewhat unsteadily, she began to read aloud, though her agitated state caused her to stumble over more words than she would have normally.

"When the Son of Man shall come in His glory, and all the holy angels with Him, then shall He sit upon the throne of His glory. And before Him shall be gathered all nations, and He shall separate them one from another, as a shepherd divideth his sheep from the goats. And He shall set the sheep on His right hand, but the goats on the left. Then shall the King say unto them on His right hand, 'Come, ye blessed of My Father, inherit the kingdom prepared for you from the foundation of the world.' "

"Stop there," said Earkhert, holding up a hand. "Do you understand what that means, child?"

"I think so, Father. The sheep on His right hand are saved and are going to heaven, but the goats on His left hand are doomed to burn in hell."

"That's absolutely right," Earkhert nodded. "And when the time of the Last Judgment does arrive, wouldn't you rather be a sheep?"

"Yes, Father."

"Of course you would. Now, read us the fifty-first Psalm."

Vicki nodded, anxious to cooperate, and turned to the specified page.

"Have mercy upon me, O God, according to Thy loving kindness; according unto the multitude of Thy tender mercies, blot out my transgressions. Wash me thoroughly from mine iniquity, and cleanse me from my sin. Create in me a clean heart, O God, and renew a right spirit within me. Cast me not away from Thy presence, and take not Thy holy spirit from me. Restore unto me the joy of Thy salvation, and uphold me with Thy free spirit."

"Very nice," said Earkhert. "And that is God's benevolence, my child. Ask for forgiveness, and you shall receive it. With one prayer, a goat may be turned into a sheep."

"Yes, Father."

"And as I'm sure you know, Vicki, I'm here to turn you from a goat into a sheep."

"Yes, Father."

"My favorite part of the job," he smirked. "Hold her, Millicent. And pay attention, Bryce.

I want you to absorb this."

Before Vicki could even think about making a futile attempt at escape, Millicent grabbed both her arms by the wrists and pulled them behind her back, pinning them firmly. Vicki squirmed and struggled in vain, then gasped as Earkhert produced from his tote bag a cigarette lighter and, to Bryce's shock and horror, flicked it to life and held the orange flame against the girl's bare shoulder.

Vicki screamed.

"This is nothing as compared to the fires of hell, child!" Earkhert shouted to make himself heard over Vicki's unending cries. "In hell the damned burn forever and ever, all over their bodies! Imagine that! To burn in an inferno for all eternity! This is what happens to the goats, girl!"

"For mercy's sake, Father, what are you doing?" asked Bryce, frantically. "You're hurting her!"

"What she is feeling now is nothing compared to her everlasting punishment in hell!" said Earkhert, still having to shout. "Now shut up and watch! Maybe you'll learn something! I'm about to give her emergency communion!"

"What...what's an...emergency communion?" Bryce asked.

"For lost causes like this one, mere wine won't do the trick," said Earkhert, taking the cigarette lighter away at last and rummaging once again through his bag. "Her kind has committed too great an offense against God to receive communion sweetly and in fellowship with other Catholics. They must receive salvation bitterly, as will those left behind after the Rapture! Fluid made holy by the body of God's chosen intermediary!"

Bryce didn't have time to inquire about what on earth that meant before Earkhert came up with a funnel, and a clear plastic bottle filled with a yellowish liquid.

"Oh, my goodness," Bryce uttered, disbelievingly. "That's not..."

"It certainly is," Earkhert grinned, failing at last to hide his sadism. "Tip her head back, Millicent, and hold her nose."

Continuing to restrain both of Vicki's arms with one hand, Millicent pinched her niece's nose closed until the girl was forced to open her mouth to breathe, and that was when Earkhert stuck the stem of the funnel between her lips, unscrewed the bottle, and dumped its contents down the funnel. Vicki began spluttering immediately, trying to spit the vile stuff out once the funnel had been removed, but Earkhert kept her jaw clamped shut with both hands until she swallowed the mouthful of what the bad priest had once referred to as 'Christ's blood lite'.

Bryce, feeling as though he was going to be sick, held his stomach with one hand and turned away.

"Keep watching!" Earkhert commanded. "We're not finished yet!"

Before Vicki even had time to gag on the taste of the salty, bitter drink, she found herself bent over the couch arm once again, her dress hiked up above her waist, and Earkhert forcing himself roughly inside of her.

"This is what happens to goats, you wicked child!" the priest screamed. "This is what will happen to you in hell! The devil has precious little to distract him from his torment, and he will take you as his concubine! He will fuck you night and day! And remember that in hell there will be no sinful condoms to protect you from his fiery outpouring! You'll be burned alive! Burned alive!"

Right on cue, Earkhert ejaculated inside of Vicki, then pulled out and readjusted his cassock, leaving the savaged girl where she lay, for she had not the strength nor the will to move.

"And the same goes for you, Bryce, you contemptible heathen!" Earkhert pointed an accusatory finger at the terrified senator. "Behold this ruined harlot, and know that a similar fate in the bowels of hell awaits you!"

"No!" Bryce cried, leaping out of the chair and falling to his knees in front of the priest. "No! Please, Father, no! Don't let it happen to me! Save me, I beg you! I'll give you anything!

I'll do anything you say! But please, save me from such a horror!"

"Stay at my side, and you will always be safe," said Earkhert, helping Bryce to his feet. "Well, Millicent, it's been quite a productive session, but I doubt there's anymore I can do here for the time being."

"Thank you so much for coming, Father," said Millicent. "You know, so many priests don't make proper house calls anymore."

"It was my pleasure," said Earkhert, taking his tote bag with one arm and Bryce with the other. "Truly."

A ninja in plainclothes was still a ninja. Two punks from the Lower East Side, who had come to Chinatown looking for trouble, had learned this the hard way when Sushi – clad not in his ninja garb, but in a plain white t-shirt and a pair of cotton cargo pants – had flattened them both in under twelve seconds and stowed their unconscious bodies in a convenient dumpster.

"Oh, my!" gasped the Chinese woman whom the punks had been in the process of mugging. "Well, I don't know where you came from, but I owe you my life! How can I thank you?"

"I can think of no better way than for you to go about your business," suggested Sushi, turning away.

"Oh, but there must be some way I can express my gratitude," said the woman, grabbing him by the shoulder. "Will you take a monetary reward?"

"Ma'am," said Sushi, brushing the hand away as if it were an insect, "I'm happy I was able to help, but..."

"But what?"

"But I don't really like you, all right?" he said, at last. "It's nothing personal, but neither this neighborhood nor your people are – if you'll pardon the expression – my cup of tea."

Sushi turned on his heel and resumed his walk down Chinatown's central avenue of Mott Street, not needing to look back to know that he had upset the woman, and his conscience might have bothered him if he were not so hardened against such emotional weakness.

I saved her purse and her jugular, he told himself. *What more does she want? A hug?*

Five blessedly uneventful minutes later, he arrived at a sturdy brick building designated Winds From The East, a fashionable Chinese restaurant which the Vigilantes – and not many others – knew to be a front for *Dong Ji* business.

Gary could have given this scouting assignment to any of the others, thought Sushi, entering the air-conditioned dining room at the peak of the lunch hour, the odor of Chinese cuisine forcing its way up inside his nose. *And yet he gave it to me. I think he did it just to annoy me. Well, there doesn't seem to be anything too unusual here. I expect all the criminals have gone out to lunch as well.*

"Excuse me, waiter," said the portly man sitting in the booth to Sushi's right. "Could I have a second order of moo shi pork, please?"

Sushi regarded the portly man with the appropriate degree of disdain. "I'm not on the staff here, sir."

"Oh, sorry, my bad," laughed the portly man. "You'll have to forgive me. I just saw you – a Chinese guy in a white shirt, standing around – and figured you for the waiter."

It took Sushi precisely two seconds to seize the portly man by the front of his green sweater and yank him right out of his seat.

"Listen very carefully, you ignorant jackass!" he hissed into the portly man's face. "I'm...not...Chinese!"

"Okay, okay! Innocent mistake! I'm sorry!" the portly man tried urgently to make amends. "Um...Korean?"

Sushi released the portly man with a guttural sigh and resumed his survey of the establishment, but there was nothing unusual to be seen; just a lot of New Yorkers enjoying their midday meal. To the left was a family of five, dining on tangerine beef, chicken fingers, egg rolls, and rose shrimp. A bit further on was a lovey-dovey couple feeding morsels of beef to each other with chopsticks, and giggling. In the booth behind them, a seafood treasure of lobster, crab, shrimp, and scallops was being excavated. And in the back, at an isolated table for one...yes, yes it was. Shang Fear in all his gruesomeness, lunching on tender spring lamb, stir fried with broccoli, cauliflower, and mushrooms in Hunan sauce.

"I know you, don't I?" said Fear, looking up as Sushi approached his table. "It's on the tip of my tongue...ah, yes, you're one of Parker's lot. Well, reports of your demise have been greatly exaggerated. I thought I'd heard the Jap had died."

Sushi's response was to snatch up Fear's two chopsticks and plunge them into the rice bowl so that they were standing straight up; a grave insult to any well-bred Chinese.

"Something on your mind?" asked Fear.

"You," Sushi answered.

"Perhaps we should adjourn to the backroom," Fear suggested, finishing his cup of Wuyi Rock Tea in three gulps, dabbing at his mouth with a napkin, and rising from his chair. "Come."

Sweeping his coat theatrically around himself, Fear led Sushi twenty feet to a door marked 'Employees Only', turned the knob, and pushed it open to reveal a cozy lounge area with plush couches and chairs, an unlit fireplace, decorative lanterns and pottery, and a restored antique table as the room's centerpiece.

"After you," invited Fear.

"Oh, no, please, I insist," said Sushi.

"Very well," said Fear, ushering Sushi in and closing and locking the door behind them. "Now, before you cultivate any incorrect ideas about this situation, let me assure you that I am prepared to tell you absolutely anything and everything you desire to know."

Sushi glared at Fear, his arms crossed.

"I mean it," said Fear. "I am an open book. If you are curious about anything at all, you have but to ask."

"You're kidding, right?"

"Not at all," said Fear. "My dear fellow, I've waited my entire life to be atop the heap, so to speak. I've waited my entire life to play the game from this position, observing my rules. And the game just wouldn't work without the very noblest contribution from you, the opposition. How could the criminal experience of a lifetime be complete without a hero doing his level best to thwart me? The game is simply no fun if one is playing it all by oneself."

"You're insane."

"Possibly," Fear conceded, "but no great genius is without an admixture of madness. Now, come and sit down. We are going to play *Jiuling*, the Chinese drinking game."

Sushi, still not quite certain what was to take place here, sat at one end of the antique table. Fear sat across from him, and clapped his hands three times, apparently signaling some unseen party.

"The rules to this *Jiuling* are simple," he said. "This is a *Jiuling* of riddles. Since you are my guest, you may go first. You will pose to me a riddle, and I shall have no more than thirty seconds to solve it. If I fail to solve it within that time, then I must take a drink, and you may ask me any question, which I must answer truthfully. If I succeed in solving the riddle – or, if you are confounded by one of *my* riddles – then I get to ask *you* a question, which you must answer truthfully."

"I warn you, I have a high tolerance for alcohol," said Sushi. "It doesn't inebriate me."

"Oh, we won't be drinking alcohol," said Fear. "I rarely touch the stuff. No, our taste today will be leaning towards the more...exotic."

Now a door that Sushi hadn't noticed at the other end of the room opened, and a Chinese waiter carrying a digital kitchen timer and a tray laden with little plastic cups – each holding about three teaspoons of red liquid – appeared.

"Thank you, boy," said Fear, taking the timer and setting it to thirty seconds. "That should do nicely. Now, away with you."

While the waiter bowed and hurried off, Sushi regarded the numerous cups inquisitively. What was this stuff, anyway? When Fear had described the chosen beverage as exotic, Sushi had hardly thought he'd meant tropical punch. It possessed a peculiar smell, however; an odor that Sushi couldn't quite identify, yet found disquietingly familiar. And upon dipping his forefinger into one of the cups, he found the mystery fluid had a surprising thickness to it. Not as thick as, say, chocolate sauce, but certainly thicker than water. Finally he licked the fluid from his finger with the tip of his tongue, and the horrible realization came to him.

"Blood!" he cried, astonished. "You mad lunatic, this is *blood*!"

"Donated by a man no longer employed by the company," said Fear. "Don't worry. I assure you it's completely clean."

"You expect me to *drink* this, you animal?" Sushi growled, pounding the table with his fist, sending ripples through the cups.

"If you don't want to play, you're welcome to leave," said Fear. "But this is the only way you may learn anything."

Sushi stared hatefully at Fear, his teeth and fists clenched. He didn't relish the thought of participating in this depraved, perverted exercise, but, at the same time, he was glad that he was the one whom Gary had sent, for he doubted that any of the other Vigilantes – including the indomitable Gary – would have had the constitution for this. Sushi – though it would be an experience that would haunt him until the day he died – would be able to handle it, and if degrading oneself like this was truly the only way to shed light on the plans of one of New York's most dangerous criminals, then it was all the better that it had been the ninja who had come.

"And, begin," said Fear, pressing the START button on the timer.

"All right, have it your way," said Sushi. "A woman has seven children. Half of them are boys. How is this possible?"

"The odd child is a hermaphrodite," said Fear, almost immediately, as if he weren't even taking this seriously.

"Wrong," said Sushi. "*All* of the children are boys, so both halves of the group are male."

"Excellent!" Fear applauded. "I can see you're getting into the proper spirit of the thing. Well, bottoms up!"

Fear snatched one of the tiny cups from the tray, tipped his head back, and drained it into his mouth while Sushi, utterly disgusted, watched.

"Now it is my prerogative to ask a question, correct?" asked the ninja.

"You've earned the privilege," said Fear. "Fire away."

"What have you – that is, you and your organization – been doing over the past several days?" he asked.

"Preparing for greatness, of course," said Fear. "Making sure that the *Dong Ji* is number one on every list. Speaking for myself, I've been growing accustomed to the trappings of power, exterminating a few pests, and preparing a special surprise for the city."

"And what would that surprise be?" asked Sushi.

"Uh-uh, naughty boy," Fear smirked, waggling a finger. "Have you forgotten the rules so quickly? One question per riddle. The milk is cheap, but it isn't free."

"Fine," said Sushi. "A man makes a bet that he can remain completely under water for ten minutes without using any special equipment or breathing apparatus. He wins his bet. How?"

Fear scratched his chin thoughtfully for a few seconds. He was tempted at first to say that the man had been inside a submarine...but no, the ninja had said that the man hadn't used any special equipment. Then, like a flash, the answer came to him.

"He filled a glass with water and held it above his head for ten minutes," said Fear.

"Right," Sushi sighed.

"Now it's my turn to pose a question," said Fear. "My dear fellow, I would like to know why you and your colleagues do what you do. Why do you put so much time and energy into the fighting of crime?"

"Because this city is fast becoming an urban wasteland, and the legitimate authorities are far from capable of handling it all on their own," Sushi answered. "Just look at people like yourself. You and your organization require our particular brand of...special attention. If we – with our extraordinary resources and talents and 'take no prisoners' attitude – didn't take a stand against evil like yours, then you would have taken over long ago."

"And what precisely is it that compels you as individuals to take part in such escapades?" Fear asked, fascinated.

"Uh-uh," said Sushi. "One question per riddle."

"Of course," said Fear. "A man was born in 1955, but is only thirty-three years old today. How is this possible?"

Sushi turned this over in his mind until he had only a few seconds left, because he really didn't want to have to drink the blood. Finally he had to come out with the only answer he could think of.

"The man was cryogenically frozen at age thirty-three," he said, just as the timer went off.

"Incorrect," said Fear. "1955 was the number of the hospital room in which he was born. Now, please, help yourself to a drink."

Sushi grimaced as he picked up one of the little cups and held it at eye level.

Cannibalism, he cursed Fear and all his Chinese kind. *That's what this is. Just when you begin to think that there's still something that separates us from the animals, you meet a man like* him.

"Are you going to drink that blood, or just cuddle it all day?" asked Fear. "Go on, down the hatch."

Steeling himself for the ordeal, Sushi parted his lips and poured the three teaspoons of blood into his mouth. Fuck, it was awful! Syrupy as it drizzled down his tongue and into his throat, warm and gooey, leaving a coppery taste and fatty texture in his mouth. He wanted to be sick immediately, but he kept himself under control.

"Now, that wasn't so bad, was it?" Fear smiled. "You've already heard my next question. I wish to know what makes the individual members of your merry band so devoted to this cause for justice. What drives you? What obsesses you so?"

"Many of us could be considered outcasts, undesirable to society," said Sushi. "Tragic losses, criminal backgrounds, handicaps, or other stigmas. We're all trying very hard to put those things far behind us. Maybe our collective outrage at injustice compels us to action, or maybe we just do this as a distraction from insanity. Either way, I think we've done the world some good."

"Interesting," said Fear. "See if you can untie *this* one. If a man tells you, 'Everything I say to you is a lie,' is he telling you the truth, or is he lying?"

As the timer ticked off the seconds, Sushi focused on the riddle, determined not to be confused by the scrambled concept. He stretched it out and spun it around and turned it inside-out, and at last, just as the timer was about to beep, he came out with his answer.

"He's lying," Sushi said. "He has to be, because if everything he tells me is a lie, then it would be impossible for him to tell me the truth. And even though he's lying when he says *everything* he tells me is a lie, at least *some* of the things he tells me can be lies, as is this."

"Very well done," said Fear. "Your question?"

"What's the big surprise you mentioned you had in store for the city?" asked the ninja.

"Ah, now we're getting to the meat of the matter," said Fear. "Well, here's the rundown. You know there's a subway station in Times Square, correct?"

"Of course."

"Oops! Not anymore!"

"What?"

"Well, that statement is a bit premature, actually," said Fear, idly fingering the emerald in his ring. "The station won't be blasted to smithereens until the top of tomorrow morning's rush hour. I'm sending in a suicide bomber, armed with ten pounds of C-4 plastique. That seems to be the fashionable way to do it these days."

"But that's the busiest subway station in New York!"

"Well, of course it is. That's why I'm going to blow it up."

"But why? What will it profit you?"

"You mean aside from giving me that warm, fuzzy feeling all over? It will announce to the world my arrival, and establish my prominence in the hearts and minds of millions. It will be the glorious start of a long, blood-soaked process of taking this city apart, skinning it to its bare bones. This generation will see me in its collective nightmares for years to come!"

Sushi jumped to his feet and went for his *katana*, intent on dealing Fear a quick beheading, but his fingers closed around empty space, and he remembered that he hadn't brought any of his weapons with him.

"Don't get so worked up, dear fellow," said Fear. "Calm yourself. After all, wouldn't you like to know my suicide bomber's identity? That information might come in handy."

Sushi remained standing for a few seconds, then snarled, and sat reluctantly back down. The cunning Chinese was right. He couldn't afford to quit now. Too much was at stake. But he didn't know anymore riddles. How could he learn the identity of Fear's kamikaze accomplice when he had no more riddles? There had to be some sort of puzzler he could throw at Fear.   Finally, after two minutes of probing his brain, he remembered something Zeke had told him a long time ago. It was stupid and juvenile, but it was the only card he had to play.

"All right, you son of a bitch, answer me this one," the ninja challenged. "What is the difference between a light on and a hard on?"

Fear furrowed his brow and squinted into space, stroking his chin with his long, spidery fingers while the wheels in his mind spun furiously. At last his thirty seconds expired, and the timer beeped.

"All right, what's the answer?" he asked, reaching for his next cup.

"The difference is, you can fall asleep with a light on," Sushi answered.

Fear gulped down the blood like a shot of liquor, and, in spite of himself, smiled.

"Very clever," he said. "Most amusing."

"Well, out with it, then" Sushi demanded. "Who is your bomber?"

"Why, it's none other than popular Senator Alvin Bryce himself, the distinguished gentleman from New York," said Fear. "That's the beauty of the whole plan, really. For New Yorkers, the blow will be twofold.

Not only will they get to deal with a horrendous terrorist attack, but they'll also be left completely dismayed by the actions of their idol of the moment."

Sushi was feeling a little dismayed himself.

"But how could you have possibly gotten Bryce to do this?" he asked.

"The answer to that question will cost you another riddle," said Fear.

Growling something incoherently, Sushi shot up from his chair and slapped the tray of cups hard with his hand, sending blood splattering across the wall.

"I'm through playing games, you fuck!" he roared. "Tell me the rest of what I want to know or I'll break your spine over my knee!"

Then Sushi heard a dull 'thud' that seemed to come from a long, long way away, followed quickly by an overpowering numbness, then everything went black. Unconscious on his feet, he fell forwards, hit his head on the table, and collapsed to the floor.

"Whadda ya want me to do with him now?" asked Warren Winterhawk, towering over Sushi's fallen form, rubbing one fist with the other.

"Throw him out in the street," said Fear, dismissively. "I suppose it's just as well that you were forced to incapacitate him. After all, there's no fun in making the game *too* easy for the opposition, now, is there?"

Sitting in the center of the fourth row in another empty theater in the Dreamland Cinema, Tyrone Smits popped greedy handfuls of Raisinets into his mouth and kept his other hand resting easily on the butt of the 12-gauge pump-action shotgun sitting in his lap like a cat. He was watching *Planet of the Apes* – one of his all-time favorites – and grinned with a movie lover's pleasure as he watched Charlton Heston swept up in the net in the middle of the town square, and heard him growl, "Take your stinking paws off me, you damned dirty ape!"

That's right, Omega Man, you tell those fuckers to go stick it, he thought.

Smits had heard about the massive, sudden shake-up within the *Dong Ji's* upper ranks, and he had heard about what had happened, just this morning, to the other members of the erstwhile Delegation. It should have worried him. It should have made him nervous that that scramble-brained fruitcake Fear had obviously no use for him. But he kept his cool. After all, he hadn't clawed his way up the ladder from lowly street punk to the top of the Harlem mob by lacking cunning, fortitude, and pure bloody guts. If Fear was looking for a rumble – and Smits was sure he was – then a rumble was what he would get.

The primed grenade landed with a 'thunk' in the crevice of the semi-folded seat to Smits' left. His eyes darted to the explosive for half a second, then, with an agility that belied his age and build, he leapt over the rows in front of him to safety, diving for cover, the shotgun clutched tightly in his hands, as the entire row of seats in which Smits had been sitting was blown to shrapnel.

I knew he'd send his flunkies, thought Smits, ignoring the indignant outcries of the muscles he had pulled.

Bullets whizzed over his head, and another grenade went off in the fifth row. A splintered armrest bounced off Smits' back. Gritting his teeth, he waited for a brief lull in the firing, then sprang up quickly and let off a round from the shotgun. One of three Chinese hitmen screamed in anguish as his right arm disappeared in a mist of red.

"You fuckin' Chinks can suck my big black dick!" shouted Smits, yanking back on the shotgun's pump handle to simultaneously dispense with the spent shell and load a fresh one into the chamber.

"It's a madhouse! A madhouse!" Charlton Heston screamed onscreen, as Smits fired again, obliterating the wounded assassin's midriff, then hit the floor and crawled on his elbows and knees under the seats as the dead man's two remaining colleagues, machine guns blazing, took up the task of avenging their fellow.

Bullets chewing into the seats above his head, Smits ignored the bits of popcorn and pieces of sticky Sour Patch Kids attaching themselves to his suit like barnacles to the bottom of a ship, and stretched out with his left arm to grab a discarded Pepsi can rolling his way. Hoisting himself into a crouched position, remaining out of sight, Smits readied his shotgun and threw the Pepsi can up and to the far left. As he had hoped, the sudden movement caught the nearest hitman's attention, and he fired at it automatically. That little distraction was all Smits needed. Before the bullet-riddled can clattered to the floor, Smits popped up from his hiding place like a Marine up from the underbrush and blasted the hitman's head from existence.

Three little, two little, one little Chinkish boy, Smits counted, pulling the gun's pump handle again and returning to his crawlspace beneath the rows of dilapidated seating.

Finally exhausting his ammunition, the third and final Chinese threw his firearm aside, pulled a serrated machete from his belt, and began plunging it vigorously through the bottoms of randomly selected seats, hoping to run the unyielding blade through Smits' skull.

"Where are you, you darky spearchucker?" the Chinese asked aloud, carving an entire seat away from its kin.

"I'm right here, sucka!"

Appearing from nowhere, Smits swung the fire extinguisher by its nozzle like a mace, smashing it into the hitman's right temple. The hitman spun off his feet like a pirouetting ballerina and crashed to the filthy floor, a lake of blood forming around his head.

Now that's what I call a Chinese yo-yo, thought Smits, shouldering his shotgun and turning towards the illuminated EXIT sign. *Sorry, Hes. Have to finish the movie another time. Right now I got wontons to fry.*

"Who does that arrogant fuckface think he is, anyway?" asked Warren Winterhawk, lifting a heavy wooden crate up onto a metal table down in Mourning Dove's embalming facility, and breaking it open with one frustrated blow from his fist.

"Calm yourself, my musclebound friend," said the Racketeer, also at the table, fat plumes of smoke rising from his pipe.

"I'm gonna kill him," the Indian grumbled, reaching into the crate and producing a brick of C-4 plastic explosive, its weight just in excess of one pound. "I mean it, I'm really gonna kill the bastard. Look what he has us doing! Flunky work! Like we're nobody! Any idiot could do this! I'm telling you, it really burns my ass!"

"You speak with conviction," said the Racketeer, watching his disgruntled colleague produce additional bricks and begin to arrange them in a pyramid.

"I didn't sign up to work for that drooling psycho," said Winterhawk. "I'm not the Muttley to his Dick Dastardly!"

"I beg your pardon?"

"The Smee to his Captain Hook!" Winterhawk made it clearer. "I'm a Faustian! I earned it! And he sticks me down here and tells me to unpack this shit for his own tiny agenda! I hate comin' down here anyway. Gives me the creeps."

"Do try not to sound so much like a stereotypical, superstitious Indian," said the Racketeer. "Your people put far too much stock in spirits, and look where it's gotten you."

"If he keeps disrespecting me like this, he's gonna find out he's not so indestructible," muttered Winterhawk.

"Are you committed to what you're saying?" the Racketeer asked, chewing thoughtfully on the stem of his pipe. "You're not just blowing steam?"

"Hell yes, I'm serious," said Winterhawk, unloading the tenth and final brick and placing it atop the pyramid. "If the time is ever right..."

"That time may come sooner than you think," said the Racketeer. "I've been giving the subject careful thought, and I've concluded that if a tactless madman like Fear can seize control of everything so easily, then why not someone of equal, if not greater talent? Why not me? Why not the *both* of us?"

"Whadda ya mean? You and me, in charge of the whole *Dong Ji?*"

"Why not? With my brains and your brawn, we could own this town. The only obstacle in our path is Fear; a careless and undisciplined rogue with no favor curried him. He will be vanquished easily. I've already spoken with the priest involved, and he's agreed to modify his end of the deal to suit our needs, in exchange for a very generous donation to be made to his church. I had planned, originally, to go into this alone, but I would value the partnership of one such as yourself. After all, though I am sharp in mind, I am feeble in body, and you would make up for that most amply."

"What about Yin?" asked Winterhawk. "Is she in on this?"

"Fuck her," said the Racketeer, waving his pipe dismissively. "Three's a crowd."

Winterhawk rubbed his square chin with his big hand for a few moments, giving the proposal due thought. True, challenging Shang Fear in any arena was dangerous, almost to the point of being suicidal, but if this plan of the Racketeer's succeeded, of which the disfigured Chinese seemed certain, then he, Winterhawk, would be in a position of high power, heading up what had grown to be New York's most potent criminal organization, working alongside the Racketeer, for whom he had respect at least.

"Tell me the plan," he said, at last.

Shang Fear was lying peacefully in an open, stainless steel casket with a lustrous black pearl finish in Mourning Dove's decadent showroom, a bouquet of five bright yellow daffodils clutched against his chest, when Penelope Yin made her brusque entrance, her eyes flashing with rage, a Medusa 47 revolver clenched tightly in her trembling right hand.

"I've just learned what happened this morning!" she hissed, spittle flying from between her clenched teeth. "A bomb exploded at The

Laughing Rabbit, killing Zarubezhnik, Pancrazio, and O'Shea! Three of the four Delegates, gone up in smoke!"

"Yes," said Fear, rising like Dracula. "It is regrettable only that Mr. Smits was not among their number, but I have already dispatched a team of operatives to take care of him separately."

"Why are you doing this?!" asked Penelope, her voice shaking as she leveled the revolver at Fear. "You're ruining everything! *Everything*! When I think of all the time and effort we took to bring those people together under us, so that we could rule..."

"I do not require the assistance of inferior outsiders!" proclaimed Fear, looking both absurdly and majestically like a ship's steadfast, questing figurehead as he sat upright in the casket, still clutching the daffodils. "I am above men such as they! From this day forth, I oversee all mob activity myself!"

"That's impossible!" said Penelope. "The organization is sprawling!"

"It is only an impossibility when conceived in the futile minds of mere mortals such as yourself!" Fear replied. "The single aim of any man's life is self-development! Self-realization! Self-actualization! That is how the few extraordinary people in this world rise above the masses of mediocrity! You, dear Ms. Yin, exist for the sole purpose of carrying my greatness upon your shoulders! Through self-actualization, I have made myself a god! I am *your* god, and you shall worship me!"

"You rabid lunatic!" Penelope screeched, curling her finger around the revolver's trigger. "I saw this coming! I should have done this last night!"

Fear turned to face her directly, and extended his bouquet of five daffodils towards her with one hand, and the sudden realization of what was wrong with this whole scene hit her like a ton of bricks.

"Daffodils!" she shrieked, her eyes widening with horror. "There *aren't* any daffodils this time of year!"

From each blossom shot a steel wire, and affixed to the end of each steel wire was a razor sharp prong the size of an arrowhead. All five of these flew into Penelope's chest, burrowed through her midsection, and burst out of her back before embedding themselves in the wall behind her. Writhing like a worm impaled on several hooks, she gasped and gulped, remaining on her feet until Fear threw down the faux flowers; then she crashed to the floor, the wires stretching through her eviscerated body and across the room looking like so much gore-covered dental floss.

These people all seem awfully keen to get themselves killed, thought Fear, climbing out of the casket and taking his leave of the showroom, walking down the hallway towards the funeral parlor's front entrance.

Ah, well. No time to dwell on it just this minute. There's work to be done, and I'm obviously the only person I can trust to do it right.

"Hello, you beautiful day!" he exclaimed aloud as he threw open the building's glass double-doors and stepped out into the parking lot, opening his arms to embrace the warm, glaring sunlight that seemed to be shining specially for him.

The day replied by throwing at him a long, black hearse from Mourning Dove's own fleet, behind the wheel of which sat Tyrone Smits, screaming obscenities and loaded for bear, missing Fear by mere feet as the wily Chinese scrambled quickly around the corner of the building.

"You ain't escapin', ya yellow motherfucker!" he bellowed, scraping against the building, taking off both paint and the driver's side mirror as he floored the accelerator in his ambition to run Fear down. "I'm gonna fuck you up bad!"

Why doesn't anybody like me? Fear wondered, drawing his broadsword and turning to run back towards the oncoming car.

"Eat this, shithead!" Smits roared, firing an Uzi out the window as he sped on.

Dodging the bullets as easily as if they were moving in slow motion, Fear leapt up onto the hood of the car, stabbed his sword through the windshield and into Smits' right shoulder, then withdrew the sword, and ran the length of the hearse's long body to jump off behind it. Smits grunted in pain and covered the wound with his left hand, but did not lose control of the car. On the contrary, he executed a tight U-turn that peeled at least an inch of rubber off the tires, and, with hardly any slowing down, rocketed back towards Fear.

"Till you've messed with a mad nigger from Harlem, you don't know what messin' is!" Smits screamed, missing Fear – somersaulting out of the way just in time – by no more than three inches. "You're all mine now! Kiss my black ass and die!"

Driving around in a wide circle, Smits pulled the pin from a grenade with his teeth and hurled the explosive out the window in Fear's direction, but Fear, standing rooted to the spot, struck the grenade with the wide edge of his sword, batting it back through the window and into the car, where it landed snugly between Smits' thighs.

Oh, shit... thought Smits.

A thunderous blast, a dazzling fireball, and the hearse was propelled up into the air, where it flipped three times before crashing back to earth, cartwheeling over the asphalt, and sliding upside-down into the side of the building, exploding a second time, and disappearing completely into the cocoon of fire and smoke. Fear sheathed his sword, straightened his coattails, brushed the debris from his ponytail, and dusted off his hands.

As busy as I am, I'm beginning to think I should seriously consider moonlighting for the police department, he smirked, walking away from the twisted, burning wreck. *After all, I've done more to clean up this town over the course of the past few days than the cops have done all year.*

"Anytime you're ready, Peg," said Carolyn, lowering her protective goggles over her eyes.

Peg nodded, and turned the dial on the electric beaker, sending the boiling brew of chemicals through the connecting plastic tube and into the rectangular metal casing.

"So far, so good," Carolyn noted, once the entire mixture had drained.

Then the casing exploded with enough force to drive both women back from the table, scattering its components to the lab's four corners and emitting a foul stench that set off the sprinklers.

"Oh, come *on!*" Carolyn growled, striking the tabletop with her gloved fist in frustration. "This stuff costs money!"

"I still think we're using too much nitro," suggested Peg, crinkling her nose and waving the black smoke away from her face.

"No, no," Carolyn shook her head. "If anything, we should be using more."

"Did you used to be a mass murderer in a former life?" asked Peg. "Because you sure talk like one."

"Peg, making a bomb is just like making a batch of cookies," Carolyn explained. "The first time you do it, you follow the recipe to the letter. Then, once you've sampled the result, you think about how the recipe could be improved to better suit you personally. You take a little bit less of this, and a little bit more of that, and what have you, and ultimately it becomes your own design. No, I know how to make a bomb, and I'm doing everything right. It could be the way *you're* mixing the chemicals."

"Now, just a minute..."

Fortunately, the ringing of Peg's cell phone interrupted the argument, and she flipped it open and answered it on the second tone, still ignoring the torrents of water raining down from the ceiling, soaking her to the skin.

"Hello? Oh, hi...um...Bob. Just a moment." She covered the mouthpiece with one hand, and turned to the Vigilantes' quartermaster. "Um...Carolyn, could you...?"

"Personal call, right?" Carolyn smiled. "Understood. I think my last one was in 1947. I'll go see if I can get these blasted sprinklers turned off."

"Okay, speak," Peg said into the phone, after Carolyn had departed.

"Who's Bob?" asked Vicki's voice.

"You," said Peg. "You're Bob. When we're not alone, anyway. Y'see, my friends don't actually know that I have a taste for both snails and oysters, to paraphrase that line from *Spartacus*. What's up?"

"Well, I'm...I'm just calling to tell you I have to miss our rendezvous tonight," said the girl. "I...came down with something late this morning, and I feel really crappy."

"Yeah, you do sound kinda beat-up."

"You have no idea."

"I'll bet you picked something up at The Burning Bush. There's no telling what you could catch at that place. I always stick a rubber glove down the front of my panties when I go there, just in case."

"I think it's more like a head cold," said Vicki. "Anyway, I'm really sorry. I was totally looking forward to seeing you again."

"Yeah, me too," said Peg. "It would've been nice to bang someone I actually liked for a change. But you just worry about getting better. I'll be able to tide myself over until you're back in the saddle."

The pause on Vicki's end of the line told Peg that she had probably said too much.

"So...you'll be seeing someone else tonight?" the girl asked.

Now it was Peg's turn to pause. "Vicki, I laid it all out for you last night," she said, at last, striking her forehead with the heel of her palm, punishing herself for letting her evening plans slip. "I like you a lot, but I...I just don't know if I can be monogamous."

"Oh. I see."

"Vicki..."

"No, it's all right," said the girl, a sort of sad emptiness suddenly deflating her voice's vivacity. "Really, it is. I probably won't be able to get out of the house for a while anyway, and there's no reason why you shouldn't enjoy yourself. Gotta go now. My head is killing me."

"But, Vicki..."

The phone clicked, and the line went dead, and Peg was left alone in the Rat Hole's big, empty lab, the sprinklers still drenching her, the color running out of her blouse, her wet hair slopping down into her face.

Shit, she thought.

Back in the Victorian house in Astoria, Vicki barely had time to place the receiver back upon its cradle and move her hand out of the way before Millicent came raging into the room and brought the sturdy Amish cane down hard upon the phone, smashing the girl's only line of communication with the outside world.

"Who were you just talking to?" Millicent demanded, thrusting the end of the cane into her niece's face. "If you called the police again, so help me, I'll cut off all your little toes!"

"No, Aunt Milli, I didn't!" Vicki cried, stumbling backwards, tripping over the iron ball chained to her right ankle. "It was just a friend! Honest!"

"You don't have any friends, girl!" hissed Millicent. "Your whole life is inside these walls, and don't you forget it! Step out of line once more – just once more – and I'll order that bullwhip I saw online the other day!"

"No, Aunt Milli, please!"

"Then get upstairs and clean that bathroom!" Millicent ordered. "And if it isn't sparkling from top to bottom by the time you're done, I'll make you do it all over again with your *tongue!*"

Knowing full well that this was not an idle threat, Vicki started moving, but the ball-and-chain manacled to her ankle made it difficult, and the shackles on her wrists weren't helping her balance. Millicent scowled and struck the small of Vicki's back with the cane. Vicki yelped.

"I said, get moving!"

Vicki got moving.

Chelsea's last operating cattle slaughterhouse – a holdover from the glory days of the Hudson River Railroad – was a huge, rectangular building sequestered discreetly behind a cluster of brownstones and tenements, as regularly busy as any such facility in the Midwest, but removed judiciously from the controversy of the public eye. Whereas its brethren had steadily died out over the course of a century that had seen the neighborhood modernized and molded into a residential district, this slaughterhouse still surged with activity Tuesday through Saturday, and the inhabitants of the nearby apartment buildings could hear loudly and clearly the pounding of heavy machinery, the clanking and popping of tools, and the mass mooing of hundreds of doomed, clueless cows being herded single file to their fate.

Leeza was screaming, not because she had finally come to her senses inside the heart of this bastion of death, tied up on the cold tile floor, while the thick, acrid stench of raw meat choked her nostrils, but because she was being drenched continuously by a waterfall of leftover animal blood, gushing from an open pipe in the ceiling high above her. Helpless to move, and crying hysterically – the first tears she had shed in years – she writhed and vomited as the blood dyed her entire body red.

"Well, you certainly don't look as if you're enjoying yourself," said the croaking, gravelly voice of her captor, speaking for the first time. "I don't think that one can fully appreciate a bloodbath until one has truly experienced it."

The captor pulled a lever mounted on the wall, and, with a 'schlakt' that echoed all throughout the big, empty room, the torrential blood flow came to a halt. Though her wrists were tied behind her back, Leeza did her best to shake the blood from her hair, face, and eyes, and she got her first really good look at her surroundings, taking in bloodstains on the walls, automated production lines laden with grisly tools of the trade, steel catwalks high above, and row upon grotesque row of dead, dripping cows hanging upside-down from enormous hooks. She also got her first look at her captor.

The heretofore unidentified menace was an elderly woman of about Leeza's age, though the similarities ended there. Whereas Leeza was strong, healthy, and perhaps even relatively attractive for her time of life, this other woman was a gargoyle. She was a hunched, square-shaped ghoul with yellow, peeling skin, bulging varicose veins, gray hair thinning to the point of baldness, withered muscles beneath sagging, jaundiced flesh, and a wrinkled, pock-marked face with chapped lips, crooked teeth, and sunken, bloodshot eyes.

"Rather disconcerting, isn't it?" she said, kneeling on one stubby knee to face Leeza eye to eye. "To be surrounded by all this death, even if it is only cows. Being cradled in death's cold embrace is something from which one never quite recovers."

"Who...are you?" Leeza gasped, just able to breathe again.

"Don't recognize me, eh? Well, I can't say I'm surprised. It's been about sixty-five years since we last saw each other, after all. Let me give you a little hint."

As Leeza sat nonplussed, the ugly old woman rolled up her right sleeve and showed her captive the pale, liver-spotted underside of her forearm, tattooed with a six-digit number in faded blue ink.

"Oh, no..." Leeza gulped.

"Oh, yes," her captor croaked.

"Avigail?" Leeza whispered, hoarsely. "It can't be. Is it…I mean…is it really you?"

"After a fashion."

"But I…I thought for sure you were…"

"Dead? Sorry, better luck next time."

"Avigail, I swear, it was never my intention…"

"Don't you lie to me, you black-hearted traitor! You knew exactly what you were doing! You knew what you were doing to me, even after all our years of friendship! Yes, Leeza, I do still recall those happier, carefree days we enjoyed as children together. They are my life's only happy memories. I am sorry to have learned that they meant less than nothing to you!"

"Avigail, that's not true!" Leeza protested. "You were my best friend!"

"Well, you certainly had a peculiar way of showing it!" said Avigail, clenching her wizened fists, her rage boiling just beneath the surface.

Leeza bowed her head somberly, and looked at the bloodstained floor.

"1933," said Avigail, reflectively. "That was the year the Nazis took power. We were just little children, you and I. All our memories of Hitler standing behind that podium, screaming his head off and waving his arms extravagantly, come from the black-and-white newsreels we saw after the fact. The change in Germany's political climate went completely unnoticed by us. Little did we know that we would both soon become utterly swept up in it all, just the same as any other German citizen. You see, it was so easy for Hitler to take control because nearly the entire country saw him as their savior; as their ticket out from under economic depression and the Treaty of Versailles. But can you guess who *didn't* see him that way?"

Leeza nodded, her eyes downcast.

"It started off badly enough," Avigail continued, "with the signs in shop windows reading 'No Dogs or Jews', and the Star of David we were forced by law to sew onto all of our clothing. Then came the propaganda against us, accusing us of being inherent carriers of disease; accusing us of being the source of all earthly evils; accusing us of being parasites that contaminated the German blood! Our fellow Germans lashed out at us, dragging us out into the streets and beating us while policemen just looked on. The government took away our rights and told us that we couldn't educate our children or hold religious services. They took away our property and forced us to live miserably in the ghettos. And you know what the next step after that was, don't you?"

Again Leeza nodded, her eyes moistening anew.

"They began rounding us up," said Avigail. "We disappeared steadily from society, and no one did anything about it, or even stopped to wonder why! My family hid from them for a year, and we were just beginning to think we might escape the Third Reich's unjust persecution, when they came for us. And do you know *why* they came for us? Do you know *how* they knew where to find us?"

Another miserable nod from Leeza.

"Say it, bitch!" Avigail hissed. "I want to hear you *say* it!"

"Because I told them where you were," she admitted, quietly.

"Yes," said Avigail. "Yes, you did. In spite of our close friendship, you betrayed me and my family to the Nazis. What a malicious, cold-blooded thing to do!"

"But I didn't know!" Leeza cried. "I...I can't excuse myself, but I didn't *know*! None of us did! Hitler's influence and charisma and silver-lined promises were enough to make an entire nation turn away from its conscience and ignore the truth! I was just a little girl! I thought that by telling the authorities about you, I was doing my patriotic duty! I thought I was doing my country a service! I didn't know what would happen! I...I was just a stupid, eager little kid who thought she was doing her bit!"

"Well, your 'bit' got me, my mother, my father, and my little brother all sent to a Polish death camp!" Avigail snarled. "And don't you dare try to tell me that you know what that hell was like, because one who hasn't experienced it can't even begin to imagine! In a way, it was quite like a larger version of this very slaughterhouse. It was a place designed specifically to maximize the efficient extermination of innocent lives!"

"Avigail, I've never begged anything of anyone in my entire life," said Leeza, tearfully, "but now I'm begging you not to go on."

"Shut up!" screeched Avigail. "You need to hear this! You need to know what you did to me!"

"Avigail, I..."

"The conditions were inhuman! Do you know how long the winter is in Poland? To this day I still shiver in temperatures below eighty degrees! Many people died of exposure and disease before they could be executed, and still others died of starvation. You know, I remember a few people who actually turned to cannibalism in order to survive, eating the flesh raw off the bones of corpses. Not that it did them any good, as we all shared the same, ultimate fate; summary execution by our sadistic captors! As you can plainly see, I managed to survive until the camps were liberated by the Allies, but for what? I lived to see my mother and father lined up, along with dozens of others, in front of a huge ditch that they themselves were forced to dig, and then mowed down by a firing squad! I lived to see my little brother and all the other younger children herded into gas chambers and showered with poison! I lived to endure hard, senseless slave labor, and I lived to see the horrific medical experiments performed upon my people by the maniacal doctors, and I lived to see the skins of slaughtered Jews fashioned into vests and lampshades! And here's a little-known fact that rarely makes it into the history books; as bad as the wartime food shortages were in Allied nations like Great Britain, they were never quite as bad in Germany, and do you know why? Because the Third Reich didn't let six million Jewish bodies go to waste!"

"You...you can't mean..."

"I mean exactly that!" Avigail shrieked. "Somewhere in Germany, in a slaughterhouse very much like this one, the bloody carcasses of my mother, father, and brother were hanging on hooks!"

Leeza moaned with sorrow and disgust, and the stink of the blood with which she was covered finally made her throw up in her lap as she collapsed fully into tears.

"But don't weep for me, old friend," said Avigail. "Weep for yourself. Because the people who work here won't return until tomorrow afternoon. There's no one coming to save you, just as there was no one coming to save me. Think on that as the night wears on. I'll be back tomorrow morning to send you to join your fascist regime in hell."

Tha-thump. Tha-thump. Tha-thump.

"Her heartbeat is steady now. She'll pull through. All she needs now is rest."

Tha-thump. Tha-thump. Tha-thump.

"Thanks, doc, I owe you one. But I think you'd better go now. This bitch is mental, and I don't know what she's gonna do when she wakes up."

Tha-thump. Tha-thump. Tha-thump.

"All right, then. I'll send you my bill. And tell Leeza I hope she feels better soon."

"Will do."

Tha-thump. Tha-thump. Tha-thump.

Janet opened one swollen, purple eyelid, and, out of the corner of her blurred vision, watched the middle-aged man with the white coat and medical bag depart through an open door and close it softly behind him.

"I thought he'd never leave," she rasped, lisping a bit.

"Ah, the sweet, harmonious chords of that voice, forever calling me to thy side," said Gary, appearing at her left elbow.

"Where the fuck am I?" she asked, finding it difficult to move her neck and look around.

"In my bed," Gary answered.

"You're not one to let an opportunity slip by, are you?" said Janet. "Say I'm sentimental, but I don't want to die looking at your ugly, shit-eating face."

"You're in my bed because you need to heal up," said Gary. "You'd be dead by now if I hadn't brought you here and retained a doctor. He was just a stand-in, I'm afraid. Our usual doc got blown up last night. Still, I've come to trust this fellow's discretion, and he's proven himself a handy pinch-hitter in the past."

"Well, what was the diagnosis?"

"Fear beat the ever-loving shit out of you," said Gary, "but really, your biggest problem was the loss of blood. Once we capped that, everything else was fairly superficial; some broken bones and lots of cuts. That's a brace on your neck, your nose is broken, and your ribcage is half the man it used to be. That's why you might be having trouble breathing, by the way."

"I seem to have a vivid recollection of being shot in the chest," she groaned. "How did I cheat *that* one?"

"Fear may be an unsurpassed master of martial arts," said Gary, "but he doesn't use a gun often enough for his aim to be as perfect as he thinks it is. One of your ribs deflected the bullet just enough for it to miss your heart."

"What heart?"

"I can hear the old Janet coming back already," said Gary, placing his hand on the doorknob. "I just know I'm gonna regret this, but I'm extending to you an invitation to recuperate here for as long as you like. I'd take advantage if I were you, as you'll find it very difficult to get around with those injuries. Next time the police spot you, you won't be able to outrun them."

"Fuck you."

"The remote and *TV Guide* are on the night table. Why don't you watch something with cute little bunnies in it?"

"Fuck you!"

Gary snickered to himself and shook his head as he stepped out of the bedroom and into the living room, closing and locking the door on his nemesis.

"I still think you're crazy," said Carla, standing by the couch, her arms folded.

"So do I," said Gary. "Can I get you something to drink?"

"I'll have a Diet Sprite, if you can spare one," she said. "You should have let that monstrous woman die the death she deserved."

"Yeah, yeah, I know that me saving Janet is kinda like Robin Hood saving the Sheriff of Nottingham," said Gary, reaching into his refrigerator to extract a can of Diet Sprite for Carla and a Dr. Pepper for himself, "but after spending the whole of our lives trying to kill each other, I just couldn't let it end like this. It would be so...wrong; wrong, and anticlimactic. When Janet is finally killed – when her body lies utterly destroyed, and that dark, demonic excuse for a soul is exorcised once and for all – it'll be me who does it. I *deserve* that privilege. To allow someone like Shang Fear to do it would've been like...well, like letting the French topple the Soviet Union. He just didn't have the right."

"But that's not the whole story, is it?" said Carla, knowingly, as she and Gary clinked their soda cans together and lowered themselves onto the couch.

Gary took a long drink, then wiped his mouth on his sleeve and heaved a heavy sigh. "No, I suppose it isn't," he said. "As much as it frightens me, and as much as I hate myself for it, I think there must be a deep, dark place in my heart for Janet. If not, why on earth didn't I kill her years ago? And since *I'm* still breathing unassisted as well, I can only assume that the unacknowledged feeling is mutual. Ours is...a complicated relationship."

"You're telling me," said Carla.

The two of them were silent for a few minutes while they drank their sodas and stared into space, and Carla ran her fingers through Gary's hair. Then Gary chuckled to himself.

"What?" asked Carla.

"It's nothing."

"Oh, come on, tell me!"

Gary curled his lips into a wicked, ironic smile, and looked Carla dead in the face.

"Y'know, I lost my virginity to that woman," he cackled, gleefully.

"What? You lost your...oh, you have *got* to be shitting me."

"No, it's true!" Gary pledged. "When we were fifteen. Really, I...I hadn't thought about it for the longest time."

"Well, you can't just blurt out something like that, then let it rest!" said Carla. "You have to give me details. Now."

"Oh, there wasn't much to it, really," said Gary, a thoughtful, almost nostalgic tone coming into his voice. "It was just a few days after my mother died, see. Huh. I never thought of it this way before, but maybe that's why I tend to block it out. Anyway, my father had died years earlier, so I was waiting to be moved in with an aunt in Liverpool who had agreed, fairly cordially, to see me through the remainder of my adolescence. In the meantime, however, I was rattling around an empty flat all by myself, amidst mountains of cardboard boxes and plastic bags packed with the trappings of my short life. And then, on one typically gray, rainy London afternoon, Janet showed up at my door. I still don't know why we clicked like that, after an entire childhood of being at each other's throats, but... Carla, I hardly recognized the girl. She was actually *nice* to me. She had actually come to cheer me up. She brought booze, and a fine selection of naughty movies from her uncle's stash, and she even brought me *Dirty Harry*, because she knew it was one of my favorites."

"Well, I certainly don't find *that* surprising," said Carla. "That scene in the empty football stadium – where Harry is torturing Scorpio for his victim's location, and Scorpio is screaming in vain for a lawyer – is very you, Gary."

"Yeah, that Dirty Harry sure is a class act, isn't he?" Gary smiled with the memory. "Anyway, we hung out around the flat together for three days and nights, like real friends, and I have to confess I was truly grateful for the company."

"Uh-huh. And when exactly did you get to your dirty sex?"

"Oh, it was either the first or second night she stayed with me, I don't recall precisely which. We were both a little drunk, and Janet asked me if I wanted to touch her tits, and even back then they were about the size of friggin' basketballs, so I couldn't possibly say no. Everything after that was a teenage boy's wet dream come true. Looking back, I believe it was her gift to me. I think she was trying to express something to me which... just couldn't be fulfilled."

"Wow," said Carla, finishing her drink and crushing the can on her forehead. "And I thought my mom's relationship with her hamster was confusing."

"Something else is bothering me as well," said Gary, leaning forward like Rodin's *The Thinker*, pulling thoughtfully with his fingers at the beginnings of a goatee on his chin. "Janet is one of the most formidable hand-to-hand combatants I've ever faced, even though she's never received any formal training. She's strong, quick, agile, and resilient. Most of our grudge matches end in draws. I've never been able to score a decisive victory over her, for all my training that made me one of the British Secret Service's most dangerous operatives. But today, in under fifteen minutes, and with seemingly little effort, Shang Fear annihilated her completely. It really helps put into perspective how truly dangerous this maniac is. This isn't going to be easy."

"Meanwhile, you've got the Spider Woman living in your bedroom," said Carla.

"Even Janet has to acknowledge her limits," said Gary. "She's banged up very badly. I doubt she'll be much trouble for a while."

A heavy 'thud' resonated from the bedroom then, followed by a scraping sound and a smashing of glass. Gary stood up quickly from the couch and jogged over to the bedroom door, which he unlocked and threw open to find his houseguest gone, out a broken window.

"You were saying?" said Carla.

"Shit," said Gary.

District Attorney Theobold Hatcher – at last regaining consciousness after a long, vexing night of distressing dreams and unsettling apparitions – couldn't remember dying. He could sense no change in his constitution, nor did he feel like he had transcended the physical or the earthly; he felt the same now as he always did upon waking in the morning. Yet here he was, lying in state in a beautiful mahogany casket in Mourning Dove's showroom, surrounded by bouquets of fragrant flowers and cherished mementos from his mortal life. The room was dark and closed up, but enough of the pale morning sunlight was shining through the slats of the windows' Venetian blinds to illuminate his surroundings.

Draped upon the wall directly ahead was a huge banner bearing Hatcher's image – a warm, charismatic smile leering at him mockingly – with 'We'll miss you, Theo!' splashed grandiosely above it, and his birth date and the present date hyphenated beneath. On the wall to the right, a black-and-white film of a procession of his friends, colleagues, and loved ones walking past his casket and bidding him their last farewells was being projected by an old, wheezy machine that hiccuped and lost the thread every now and again.

He looked down to examine his own physical form, feeling that there must be some mistake, and he was astounded to find himself wearing the navy blue suit in which he had always planned to be buried. Even more alarming were the five bloody holes peppering the front of his white shirt.

I've been shot! his mind cried out. *Some murdering scum got back out onto the streets and shot me!*

A 'sproing' noise to the left seized Hatcher's attention, and he turned to see the decaying, skinless remains of a cadaverous corpse sitting straight up in the open casket next to his, its bulging eyes and gaping, toothless mouth staring horribly into space. Hatcher screamed, and joining him in his screams were a dozen other rotting corpses, all springing up from their caskets like grotesque jack-in-the-boxes, all with bits of rotten flesh hanging off their limp and lifeless bones, all seeming to be inviting themselves into the game with their own unbearable shrieks and wails. Hatcher squeezed his eyes shut, clapped his hands over his ears, and screamed some more. He screamed until he was out of breath. He screamed until the left side of his chest felt tight. He screamed until he collapsed back into his casket, as dead now as he had been led to believe previously.

"Now, I'm sorry, but that was priceless!" Shang Fear chortled, turning the lights on and appearing at the late D.A.'s side. "You should have seen the look on your face! Oh, I never get tired of this gag, no matter how many times!"

Still chuckling, Fear slammed the casket's lid closed on Hatcher, turned off the clicking film projector, and pressed the concealed button that would return the mechanical corpses to their dormant rest inside their boxes.

What a bracing start to the new day! thought Fear. *How glorious it is to be in charge! A man feels as though he has a reason to get up in the morning.*

"Stay back! Let me through, I say! I must see the one called Shang Fear!" cried a voice from the hallway.

What in the hell...?

"You tread in the way of a power far greater than yourselves!" declared the voice, likely addressing the guards in the corridor. "Show me to Shang Fear, or I will wreak your destruction!"

Anticipating the worst, Fear drew his sword and assumed the proper stance, but Senator Alvin Bryce – adorned proudly with a belt laden with five pounds of C-4, and clutching a push-button detonator in his right hand – was the last person he expected to see barging through the door.

"Treachery!" Fear lamented. "My plans, they go awry!"

"I've been sent by the Holy Father to give you rebirth, Shang Fear!" said Bryce.

"You sniveling twerp, don't you dare press that button!" Fear commanded, brandishing his sword at the senator.

"It's all right, Shang Fear!" Bryce insisted. "I was afraid also, but there is no need! The Lord of hosts is with us! Cry out now unto Him, and He will hear you, and deliver you from Satan! When your mother and father forsake you, He will take you up! Through God, we shall do valiantly, for righteous is He, and upright are His judgments! It is better to trust in the Lord than to put confidence in man! I see that now! So magnify the Lord with me, Shang Fear, and let us exalt His name together, and we shall not die, but live, and reap the bountiful harvest of paradise!"

"Bryce, I'm warning you!"

"Through works of faith and labors of love, let us make a joyful noise unto the Lord of our salvation! For the Lord is Alpha and Omega, the beginning and the ending! Be not afraid, Shang Fear, for we will go to Him together, and He will absolve us!"

"Earkhert, there's nowhere in this world or the next that you'll ever be safe from me!" Fear cursed the absent traitor.

Then Bryce's thumb came down hard on the button, and the Lord's fiery judgment washed everything clean.

Coughing loudly, and attracting flies, Gary was lying down on a wooden bench in a quieter corner of the Times Square subway station at 42nd Street and Broadway. When Sushi had finally come to his senses – in a heap of garbage in one of Chinatown's more dangerous dead end alleys, a mangy, fish-breathed cat standing atop his chest, licking his face – and had returned to the Rat Hole to inform his colleagues of the latest developments, Gary, as always, had been able to advise coolly on the most prudent course of action. With the confidence and grace of a general donning his chain mail for battle, he had slipped into a dirty, battered, worn-out hat and coat borrowed from Zeke's wardrobe, adorned his face with an obviously fake beard of gray, gin-soaked whiskers, plunked a bottle of ginger ale into a brown paper sack, and made a bed for himself in the station directly beneath a 'No Loitering' sign, where he had waited watchfully for the morning commute to kick into high gear. It was now nearly eight-thirty, however, with still no sign of Alvin Bryce or any known member of the *Dong Ji*.

"All right, sir, move along," said a uniformed member of the station's security personnel, dealing a few gentle but insistent prods with his baton to Gary's right shoulder.

"Let me alone, ya young pup," Gary grumbled, affecting the voice of a man twice his age. "Ain't it bad enough, what with the world an' the state it's in an' all, without one so wet behind the ears as yourself disturbin' an old man's peace?"

"I'm sorry, sir, but you can't stay here," said the security guard.

"So ya say, my little fireside soldier," Gary grunted, scratching his backside and spitting as he got to his feet, "but would ya say such if I were the President o' these United States, or p'raps one o' you kids' popular music entertainers or such? Would I be allowed to stay here then? Surely I would, says I. But, on the contrary, bein' a gentleman who requires a little bit o' shelter more urgently than any o' those distinguished personalities, I must be turned out with all due haste, left to wander like a Hebrew in the wilderness, so's that better men than I may not take offense at my smell. It's criminal the way we're bein' treated. I'll have you know I lost an arm for MacArthur."

"Sir, it's perfectly clear to me that you have both your arms intact."

"That's 'cause I stuck around long enough to pick it up again afterwards. I could show ya my Purple Heart if I hadn't already pawned it for a few paltry dollars, along with my daddy's ring and antique watch fob. Hrmph. Ya prob'ly don't even know what a fob is, do ya, boy? Ya prob'ly think Desert Storm is a bath salt, don't ya?"

The security guard rolled his eyes and shuffled away to another part of the crowded station. He didn't need his ear jawed off by the inane ramblings of a drunken nincompoop. He had dislodged the vagrant beggar from the bench, and as far as he was concerned, his work was finished.

And to think the Midtown Players spurned me for not projecting from my diaphragm, Gary chuckled to himself.

A string of blue language was the next sound to arrest his attention, and he turned to the left to find the Racketeer, as ugly as he'd ever been, leaning against a nearby pillar, fiddling with his pipe and cigarette lighter.

" 'Scuse me, sir," Gary rasped, sidling up to the old Chinese, "but ya seem to be enjoyin' no end o' trouble with that most unsympathetic o' simple devices."

"The fluid's gone," the Racketeer replied, stifling a cough against his sleeve.

"Then please allow me to help your gentle self," said Gary, plunging his hand into his coat pocket and pulling out a book of matches, which he handed to the Racketeer. "That's better than a lighter any day o' the week and twice on Sundays anyways. Helps the flavor an' such."

"Thank you very much," said the Racketeer, flipping open the book and plucking a match.

" 'Tis nothing, noble squire, but a small courtesy to help move you along in the day's right direction. After all, we vets must look after our own, for no one else will, though they do try to bring us crashin' down at every opportunity that presents itself in golden, glitterin' splendor. What did happen to you anyway, oh brother? Fall on a landmine?"

The Racketeer frowned, but didn't say anything as he struck the match and held it to the barrel of his pipe. Three seconds later, the nitroglycerin packed inside the match's head exploded with the heat, and the left, unravaged side of the Racketeer's face caught fire as he fell backwards, screaming in pain, while many nearby commuters had already begun scattering in panic.

"Really, Carolyn is almost my ideal of a woman, y'know that?" said Gary, discarding the hat, coat, and beard and standing tall over the injured gangster, fists clenched, ready to engage his foe in mortal combat. "I think she must get most of her ideas for weapons from Bugs Bunny cartoons."

While the Racketeer was busy slapping at the flames dancing across the ruined flesh of his face, he retained the presence of mind to kick out and jab Gary in the shin with the blade protruding from the toe of his right shoe. It wasn't poison-tipped, as had once been Chinese government issue, but the sting was enough to make Gary drop to one knee.

"You!" the Racketeer screamed with fury. "You'll pay for this! You're fucking dead!"

Gary and the Racketeer both leapt to their feet and pulled their pistols at the same moment, and, in the midst of the chaos they had caused, they stood still and quiet, face to face and gun to gun, their right arms intersecting with each other at the elbows, their hands thrusting their weapons into each other's faces.

"Y'know, you'd think a guy who makes as much money as you do could afford a proper plastic surgeon," he said. "And that eye! That fucking eye! For the sake of all the little children, wear a patch over it!"

The Racketeer growled something that wasn't really a word, actual froth dribbling from his twisted snarl, but before he could apply the appropriate pressure to his gun's trigger, a thin cord of some strong material lassoed itself around his neck from behind, yanked him off his feet, and cast him to the ground where he lay gasping and searching urgently for his inhaler.

"Well, so much for subtlety, huh?" said Carla, the wielder of the cord.

"Believe me, Carla, I went into this thing with every intention of playing it quiet," said Gary. "But then I saw an irresistible opportunity to field test Carolyn's new matches."

"Hands behind your head, lady!" a security guard shouted, training his gun on Carla. "Hands behind your head with your fingers laced, and kneel down on the ground, or I shoot!"

"No!" roared Warren Winterhawk, stampeding in from nowhere, swatting the guard casually aside, and wrapping both arms around Carla's midsection. "She's mine!"

"And Tonto joins the hunt!" Gary exclaimed. "Listen, Kimosabe, I still don't have that five wampum I owe you, but I know I can get it together if you'll give me just another day or two."

"Shut up!" Winterhawk bellowed, throwing Carla at Gary, knocking both Vigilantes down in a heap.

"Jeez," Gary whistled. "Good thing I didn't wear my *Bonanza* t-shirt, eh?"

"Kill them, Winterhawk!" the Racketeer commanded, sucking at his inhaler. "Break their necks before they can interfere further!"

His teeth grinding like an axe against a stone, Winterhawk smacked his right fist into his left palm and advanced on the stumbling pair, but his steps were halted by a huge hand that seized him by the top of his head and, amazingly, whisked the big Apache off his feet and swung him around twice like a hammer before relinquishing its grip and sending him flying through the air, all the way to the other side of the station, where he finally crashed against the side of a dwelling N train bound for Queensboro Plaza, his impact denting the metal, shattering a window, and rocking the car on the tracks.

"Now that, boys and girls, is how you scalp an Indian," Charlie grinned as he opened his hand and let flutter to the ground the vast bulk of hair he had yanked free from Winterhawk's cranium.

"Couldn't you just kiss the big, lovable lug?" smiled Gary.

The almost simultaneous cocking of two handguns drew attention to a pair of security guards on the left, the butts of their weapons clenched with both hands, their concentration steely and not in the remotest danger of being derailed by the screams and cries of panicked civilians charging past them.

"Drop your weapons and get your hands in the air, all of you!" demanded one of the guards. "This is your last fucking warning! Drop your weapons and get on your knees!"

The Vigilantes' decision about whether or not to comply was made for them when the Racketeer, still lying on the ground behind the guards, brought his Mini Uzi to bear and spewed several rounds of ammunition into their backs, dropping them like rabbits, wisps of smoke rising from the numerous bullet holes.

I could have handled that, Gary thought. *I could have dealt with them non-lethally. You're going to pay for that, Racketeer. You're going to pay for smearing their blood all over my hands.*

His inhaler having given him his second wind, the Racketeer rolled upright, leapt to his feet, and began running and strafing, now clutching a Mini Uzi in each hand, firing off a stream of bullets which Gary and Carla hit the floor to avoid, while Winterhawk roared his return to the fray, running up behind Charlie and leaping onto his back. The big Vigilante shook around in every direction, like a gorilla attempting to dislodge a smaller mammal, but Winterhawk retained his position, his own muscular arms wrapped tightly around Charlie's neck, like a stubborn cowboy refusing to be thrown by a bull.

"Gonna take more 'an that, you black son of a bitch!" the Indian hissed into Charlie's ear. "I don't feel a thing!"

Snarling at Winterhawk's vain attempt to choke him, Charlie was finally successful in ridding himself of the piggy-backer when he thundered backwards and smashed the Apache against a stone pillar that shook with the impact, though the Indian was on his feet again before Charlie could even turn around.

Unhindered by any sense of pain that, by this point, would surely have crippled a normal man, Winterhawk lunged forwards at Charlie, throwing punch after exuberant punch into the big Vigilante's face and torso, running on the limitless adrenaline and raw power afforded a man who feels no ailment, and though Charlie was larger and stronger than his *Dong Ji* enemy, he nonetheless found himself being driven steadily backwards across the platform overlooking the train tracks.

"Gonna own this town, shithead!" Winterhawk bellowed, forcing Charlie to the edge of the platform. "Gonna kill you, then I'm gonna own this town!"

"We already bought Manhattan from you people, fair and square," Charlie rumbled, catching Winterhawk's fist in his hand and holding it tight. "You can't have it back."

Still holding Winterhawk by the fist, Charlie hauled back with his other arm and punched the Indian squarely in the gut with a sledgehammer uppercut, lifting him up high into the air, then releasing his grip on his fist. Winterhawk crashed into the far wall, then landed facedown on the third rail, which embraced him with dancing, blue arcs of electricity that burned the life out of him in just three seconds. Charlie spat a globule of saliva down onto the charred body, and it sizzled.

"Say hello to the Great Bear Spirit for me," he muttered.

With the majority of civilians now stuck in a swelling, crushing glut at the station's entrance, pushing and shoving against each other in their desperation to vacate the underground, Gary and Carla had a blessedly open field in which to engage the Racketeer, who was crouching inside the Metrocard booth, using it as a pillbox while he fired intermittently at the two Vigilantes. A bullet lanced through Carla's right leg, and she cried out and dropped to the floor.

"You okay, sugar puffs?" asked Gary, leaning out from behind a pillar and firing a few covering shots from his Beretta 96.

"A minor setback, cinnamon bear," Carla answered. "Toss me a match, will you?"

Still firing on the Racketeer's position, Gary plunged his other hand into his pocket, withdrew the book of matches, dropped it to the ground, and kicked it over to Carla, who selected one of the camouflaged grenades and struck it alight.

"Who'd ever imagine that fighting fire with fire could be so much fun?" she smirked, before throwing the match in the direction of the booth.

The booth exploded in a blaze of flame and shrapnel from which Gary and Carla shielded their eyes, and the Racketeer was thrown several yards, all the way to the turnstile, his clothes smoking, his flesh badly burnt.

"You...fuck!" he hissed, groping for the Mini Uzi that had landed next to him. "Even if you kill me...you'll still lose!"

The Racketeer was surprisingly quick in getting to his feet and bringing his gun to bear, but Gary was quicker still, firing four bullets directly into the gangster's chest. Streams of blood squirted out from beneath the Racketeer's torn, tarnished shirt, and he stumbled backwards against the turnstile, which, for the lack of a token having been dropped in its slot, refused to yield against the man's weight.

"Can't...breathe!" he gasped, coughing up blood, and even now fumbling for his inhaler. "Quickly! Somebody...get me...a glass of... water!"

Then he slumped to the floor, dead, and an eerie quiet fell over the station, now devoid of the throng of commuters who had run to save their skins.

"So, is that a wrap or what?" asked Charlie, rejoining his colleagues.

"Not quite," said Gary, helping Carla to her feet, letting her lean on his shoulder. "The baddies are dead, but why were they here to begin with? They'd hardly want to be down here if Bryce was going to cave the place in. And where *is* Bryce, anyway? No, something doesn't smell right, and I'm not talking about the guy you barbecued on the tracks."

As if by instinct, all three pairs of eyes gravitated in unison towards the same dimly-lit, ill-attended corner, where, tucked cozily behind a bench, there sat an innocent-looking attaché briefcase.

"Oh, shit," said Carla.

Shifting Carla over to Charlie, Gary raced over to the briefcase, smashed the combination lock with the butt of his gun, threw it open, and groaned loudly.

"It's a time bomb," he said. "A big one. There must be at least five pounds of C-4 here."

"So, either Fear changed his plans, or the Racketeer had his own design in store," said Carla, as she and Charlie came over for a closer look.

"I defused a bomb once when I was in the Army," said Charlie, "but it didn't look anything like this. How much time's left?"

"Just over a minute," said Gary. "There are two wires here. Red and green. If I cut the wire leading to the timer, the bomb'll fizzle. Problem is, I don't know which wire it is."

"And if you cut the wrong wire, we all get to see what our insides look like," said Carla.

"Well, it's always the red one in the movies," Gary ventured.

"But what if they were counting on us thinking that?" said Charlie.

"Yeah, the green wire is a little less obvious," said Carla. "Then again, maybe color coordination never even occurred to them."

"Well, time is marching on, and we've got a fifty-fifty chance of getting it right," said Gary. "Hand me your cutters, Carla."

With thirty-four seconds left, Carla took her miniature wire cutters from her utility belt and gave them to Gary, who resumed staring at the ticking briefcase bomb.

"If anyone has any last-minute gut instincts, now would be the time to speak up," he said.

"Go with red," said Charlie, decisively.

"Red?" asked Carla. "Are you sure?"

"No."

"Then why did you say it?"

"Because I think it's prettier than the green wire."

"You *what*?"

"Well, I don't have the user's manual for this thing, y'know! Maybe you have a better idea?"

"I'm getting a really strong vibe from green," Carla said.

"No, I really don't think so," Charlie shook his head. "It's gotta be red."

"Well, I say green," said Carla.

"Well, you'd better make a decision, and damned quickly," said Gary, as the timer reached fifteen seconds.

"You cast the deciding vote, Gary," said Carla. "Red or green?"

"I think I'm gonna have to go with red," he said.

"Well, congratulations, Gary, you've just killed us all," grumbled Carla.

"Down to the moment of truth," Gary muttered, opening the cutters and preparing to shear the red wire. "If the Man upstairs owes you a favor, now's the time to call Him on it."

Carla and Charlie both shut their eyes, and, as the timer ticked down to three seconds, Gary snipped the selected wire in twain. The timer blipped to a stop at one second, and the low, gentle hum the device had been emitting ceased.

"Well, that was a bloody near thing," Gary exhaled, wiping a hand across his perspiring brow.

"Never in my entire life have I been so happy to be wrong," Carla sighed. "But how did you know, Gary? How did you know to cut the red one?"

"Elementary," he said. "Look here. It says 'TIMER' on it."

"Oh, you *asshole*!" Carla shrieked, slapping him in the head.

"But Sushi said Fear was planning to use *ten* pounds of C-4," said Charlie.

"Right," said Gary. "So what happened to the other five?"

Shang Fear had emerged from the stainless steel casket – turned on its side amidst the wreckage and rubble of what had once been the most expensive funeral parlor in Manhattan – like a hermit crab emerging from its shell. It had been the humble metal box that had saved his life, cocooning him against the cataclysmic blast that had reduced Mourning Dove and all its secrets to an ashen, smoldering heap at the southernmost edge of Chinatown. And though his castle now lay in ruins, only one thought occupied his mind.

Earkhert!

The bad priest, already caught up in the excitement of what he could accomplish with the money given to him by the Racketeer in exchange for sending the bomb-strapped Bryce to Mourning Dove instead of Times Square, hadn't known what had hit him, and when he regained consciousness hours later, he found himself stripped naked and tied with rope to nothing less than a wooden cross standing upright in a patch of solid concrete down by the East River docks.

"Welcome, Father," said Fear, stepping in front of Earkhert, the cool river breeze whipping at his coattails at the same time that it lashed itself painfully across Earkhert's exposed flesh, "to your redemption."

"What devil's work is this?" asked Earkhert, his teeth chattering. "What blasphemy? Darest thou lay a hand upon God's child?"

"Judas Iscariot was God's child," said Fear, placing a cigarette between his lips and flicking open his lighter, "but he did betray his Lord for thirty pieces of silver, then killed himself in remorse. You betrayed *me* for money, Earkhert, and unless I'm very sorely mistaken, your faith tells of a special place in hell for traitors. Let's call this your...baptism of fire."

It was then that the trussed-up Earkhert was at last able to identify the noxious odor that had tickled his nose hairs upon his waking. Kerosene. He and the cross were both soaked in it.

"In God I have put my trust!" he screamed, writhing against his mock crucifixion. "I will not fear what flesh can do unto me! I will not fear, though the earth be removed, and the mountains carried into the midst of the sea! The Lord is my refuge and my fortress! Yea, though I walk through the valley of the shadow of death, I will fear no evil, for He is with me! He prepares a table for me in the presence of mine enemies! Surely goodness and mercy shall follow me all the days of my life, and I will dwell in the house of the Lord forever! O Lord, deliver me from my enemies and them that persecute me! Lift up Your countenance upon me, Lord, and give me peace!"

"You always wanted to be like God, Earkhert," said Fear. "Well, now you can *die* like God!"

With that final condemnation, Fear took the cigarette from his mouth, and, pinching the safe end between his thumb and forefinger, touched the lit tip to Earkhert's chest, and the priest and the cross burst into flames, to much screaming and wailing on Earkhert's part.

"You'd best get used to that burning sensation," said Fear, flicking the cigarette into the water. "From what I hear, it's rather a bother down there."

"Nazi executions were brutal, but, for the most part, they were quick," said Avigail, freeing Leeza from her chains and hauling her to her feet with one hand, while brandishing a pistol in the other. "So I shall extend to you the same courtesy. I've seen enough torment and suffering to last me ten lifetimes. I've no desire to keep you hanging. A single bullet to the head, and it will be finished."

"Before you kill me..."

"Don't try to beg your way out of this!" spat Avigail, thrusting the gun into Leeza's face. "This is going to happen! You can't squeeze blood from a stone, and you can't squeeze mercy from a heart that's made of the stuff!"

"I'm not going to plead for my life," said Leeza, quietly. "You've made me feel as if I don't deserve it anyway. No, the only thing I'll beg is your forgiveness."

"My forgiveness? You must be joking!"

"Avigail, you're right to blame me for what happened to you. It's true that I didn't know any better, but ignorance is no excuse for anything. With or without the knowledge, my conscious and deliberate actions contributed directly to the ruination of your life. If I were you, I'd want me dead too. I know that my sins are huge, old friend, but perhaps one fine day, many years from now, when you're lying upon your deathbed, you'll find it in your heart to forgive this stupid old fool – and even better, that innocent, unsuspecting child with whom you used to play in pre-War Berlin."

Avigail listened quietly to Leeza's short speech in its entirety, but, by the end, her features hadn't softened.

"I could almost believe you mean it," she said.

"Of course I mean it," Leeza insisted. "You're not looking at this thing from both sides. After the War finished, and the truth about Hitler's death camps came out, I was overcome with guilt and remorse! When I learned of the fate to which I had doomed my best friend, I wanted to kill myself! I could only assume that you were dead, and that I might as well have been your executioner! Avigail, did you really think that I could ever have forgotten about you? Your memory has haunted me every day for the past six decades, and while you claim that I've been your personal demon throughout that span of time, it's just as true that you've been mine."

Leeza's remorse was heartfelt and sincere, but Avigail's ears were deaf to it. Pursing her chapped lips, furrowing her weathered brow into a frown over her dark, sunken eyes, the woman was decidedly unmoved, and that came as no surprise to Leeza. This poor, wretched survivor of tribulation was no longer alive; not really. Avigail – the true Avigail, with a heart that pumped blood, and a soul nourished by hope – had died ages ago, along with her family, in that camp. The Avigail who now stood before her was merely a shell, kept alive only by nature's cruel design, and no fire could provide the light or warmth necessary to pierce the eternal darkness.

"All right, you've had your say," said Avigail. "You can't say I didn't let you account for yourself. But that's enough talk now. I didn't bring you here to talk. I brought you here to die."

It hadn't occurred to Avigail that Leeza might actually make an effort to escape her fate, so the Vigilantes' physician had the element of complete surprise on her side when she lunged aggressively forward, just as her captor's crooked, calloused forefinger was curling around the trigger, and struck the side of Avigail's gnomish head with the cast on her right arm. Avigail grunted and stumbled backwards while Leeza ran as fast as she could for a door which she perceived to be an exit.

"You lying, treacherous bitch!" Avigail screeched, holding her head with one hand and aiming the gun amateurishly with the other. "You're not escaping! I've waited too long for this!"

Leeza heard the loud, angry retort of a gunshot, and screamed, but the bullet missed her by inches. A second bullet, closer this time, was quick to follow, and Leeza changed direction, scrambling off to the left and hiding behind a row of slaughtered cows. The animals were hanging above the floor like a meaty curtain, and the third bullet Avigail fired was stopped by the thick hide of one of the beasts.

Avigail howled unintelligibly, threw down the gun in frustration, and snatched up a buzz saw – its serrated, circular blade used specially for the cutting of bone – and Leeza went on the run once again as its jagged teeth tore into the carcasses behind which she'd been hiding, shredding them zealously, spewing strands of red meat like party streamers.

A mere thirty feet ahead of Avigail and the roar of that terrible saw, Leeza reached the elevator that would carry her to the metal catwalks high above, pulled the sole lever with her good arm, and breathed a sigh of relief as the mechanism coughed to life and chugged its way up, noisily.

"That won't help you!" Avigail hollered, running towards the stairs that would take her to the same level. "I'm still coming!"

Before Avigail could reach the stairs, however, she slipped in a slick of blood, flew off her feet, and crashed down onto her back, screaming in agony as her ancient bones broke like glass, and the saw, which had landed against her chest, began chewing its way in.

Not hesitating for an instant, Leeza ran for the stairs as quickly as her aged legs would allow, hoping to reach Avigail in time to save her.

"I'm coming! Avigail, I'm coming!" she shouted. "Hang on!"

Avigail's screaming ceased a full fifteen seconds before Leeza was able to reach her side, and when she finally did arrive, it was clear to Leeza that her former friend was dead. If the internal maiming that the fall had dealt her hadn't killed her, then the saw buried deep in her chest certainly had.

For several minutes Leeza knelt beside the body, staring forlornly at what had become of this human being with whom she had once been so intimately connected. Carefully she extracted the buzz saw – still grinding away – from the chest, turned it off, and dropped it with a 'clunk' to one side, then passed her hand over the staring, jaundiced eyes, closing them for the final time. Crying openly now, Leeza took Avigail's hand in hers and caressed the lifeless fingers, pressed her tear-streaked face against what was left of Avigail's breast, and bawled.

"So, I guess this means I killed you *twice!*" she moaned. "Oh, Avigail! Oh, Avigail, I'm so sorry!"

With the destruction of Mourning Dove, the *Dong Ji* had moved itself completely out of Chinatown with the haste and efficiency of an army breaking camp, and it had taken the best part of the day for the Vigilantes to ferret out the very imminent threat of Shang Fear. There had been a lot of leg work, and low-tier criminals all over Manhattan were separated from valued body parts during interrogations conducted by Gary's crimefighting coalition, but the mystery of the mad killer's whereabouts had finally dissolved along with the last fiery streaks of the summer sunset, and now Gary broke the surface of the East River a full ten minutes after his initial submergence and realized he had a dead striper down the back of his shirt.

I really wish the city would clean this mess up, he thought, extracting the slimy fish and discarding it along with his SCUBA apparatus. *The water down there is practically chewable. I could probably clean my toilet with the stuff a bit deeper down.*

Treading water, he craned his neck to look up the starboard side of the big ChiWan Exports, Inc. freighter, and knocked the water out of his ears to hear the screams and cries of hapless Chinese thugs being dispatched left and right on dry land.

Sounds like Sushi has things well in hand over there, he thought, as he listened to the din of the ninja taking Fear's forces apart piece by piece, and thus providing Gary with the distraction he required. *You can always rely on him in a melee.*

Spitting out the last remnants of river scum still lingering on his tongue, Gary pulled a pistol-shaped grappling gun from his waistband, pointed it up towards the clear night sky, and squeezed the trigger, firing a line of thin, steel cable that arced up towards the stars with a 'twizz' sound and snagged the metal safety rail high up on the ship's deck. A second squeeze of the trigger and Gary, both his hands wrapped tightly around the butt of the gun, was whisked quickly heavenward, out of the murky water and up to the deck, where he stood soaking wet and shivering a little in the breeze. Then he heard an amused, utterly unsympathetic laugh – like that of a spider regarding a new fly in its web – and felt a jolt of searing pain rip through him as the blade of a Chinese dagger embedded itself in his right shoulder with a wet, squishy 'thuck'. Cursing through clenched teeth, he gripped the dagger's hilt and pulled it out, then turned to see the fantastic figure of Shang Fear – two inches taller than Gary, and bearing the countenance of the arrogant elitist he always pretended to be – standing royally atop the ship's high, chimney-like ventilation shaft, his coattails dancing in the wind, seeming to move as independently as Medusa's snakes.

" 'And I feel that the period will sooner or later arrive when I must abandon life and reason together, in some struggle with the grim phantasm, Fear,' to quote aptly my beloved Poe!" he howled, drawing his broadsword and twirling it madly above his head. "Welcome back, Mr. Parker! So nice to have you with us once again!"

"I wish the feeling could be mutual, douchebag, but I crossed you off my Christmas card list ages ago!" he replied.

Fear laughed haughtily, and leapt forward, body flat and arms outstretched like a skydiver, and, just as it was beginning to look like a jump even he couldn't survive, he executed an Olympic triple somersault that culminated in a typically perfect landing just five feet from his foe. Before Gary could react, the edge of the broadsword had already cut across the front of his torso, slicing away his sopping shirt and marking a start to the bloodletting.

"I still carry the calling card you left me during our last encounter," said Fear, pulling back the lapels of his coat and ripping open his vest to reveal the scarred words 'Gary Wuz Here' cut into his chest with a knife, just above his left nipple.

"Yes, I remember that," said Gary. "I was in a bit of a mood that day. Felt like humiliating you."

"You succeeded beyond your wildest ambitions," said Fear. "You could have killed me with that same knife, but instead you mocked me, as if I were not worth the trouble. Tonight, here and now, I will show you how that feels."

Moving too quickly even for Gary's extraordinary reflexes to match, Fear cut another shallow gash across the Vigilante's torso, this time a bit lower down, bleeding the belly.

"You'll be fortunate if I decide to cut off your head before I allow you to bleed to death, Parker," he said, spinning to avoid a counterthrust from Gary's dagger, and chopping his sword into Gary's side.

Brushing a lock of wet hair out of his eyes, Gary blinked a few times and tried to get his mind in order.

Pull yourself together, Parker, he told himself. *You're better than this. You were top of your class in knife fighting, remember? Don't let this asshole throw you off with cavalier vanity. Toughen up.*

Breathing through his nose, Gary assumed a proper stance, and beckoned to Fear with a waggling finger.

"You wanna get hot, Fear?" he asked. "You wanna get nuts? Then let's stop talking and do it! You think your inner demons are so frightening? Wait'll I show you mine!"

Smirking like a goblin who has just swallowed a brand new soul, Fear spun on his high heel, swung his sword up in an arc, and brought it crashing down against Gary's dagger, which he held defensively while Fear tried to force his own blade further.

"I'm glad you brought up the subject of demons, Parker," he said, his face just inches from Gary's. "I've always found your behavior fascinating, and, before I kill you, I'd like you to tell me why it is you do what you do. For what do you daily risk your life and limb? Not for the betterment of the world, surely, for as Confucius said, 'I have not seen a person who loved virtue, or one who hated what was not virtuous. He who loved virtue would esteem nothing above it.' So, what drives you, Parker? Vengeance? Absolution? Thrills?"

"Well, I really shouldn't be telling you this, it being a trade secret and all," said Gary, kicking Fear in the gut and slashing the dagger across his knuckles, "but our dental is excellent."

"I've done some amateur analysis of your character, Parker," said Fear, cutting a red river up the full length of Gary's right arm, "and I know there must be some madness in there somewhere."

"You don't have to be crazy to do this job," said Gary, twisting away from a sword swing and taking another swipe at Fear's hand, "but it sure helps."

"I think your true, most basic motives are far more sinister than even you may realize," said Fear, swinging his sword like a baseball bat and connecting directly with Gary's left thigh. "I don't think you're a hero at all. I think you're a murderer."

"Now if *that* isn't a case of the wok calling the kettle black," said Gary, darting to the right and jabbing Fear in the shoulder.

"You kill people," said Fear, dealing Gary a serious cut to his left wrist and watching with delight as the blood pulsed out of the opened artery and splashed onto the steel deck. "You rationalize it in your own quaint, mortal way by calling them 'evil', but who are you to decide who deserves to die for their sins? Who are you to deprive any man of that most precious gift which is life? Are you, in your own way, any more perfect than those very criminals against whom you crusade? Does not this culture of yours maintain its faith in a loving, merciful God Who will forgive any misdeed? What do you imagine He would think of your dark, controversial pastime? I kill people because I like doing it. What's your excuse?"

This blitz of questioning caught Gary completely by surprise, and his concentration was derailed just long enough for Fear to deliver a vicious series of cuts that crisscrossed his torso like lines on a roadmap, and now the blood ran off him in rivers.

"Aristotle said, 'We are what we repeatedly do.' And what is it that you do, Parker?"

"I kill animals like you!" Gary lunged angrily, carelessly forward, and Fear ran the edge of his sword along his back as the Vigilante stumbled to his knees.

"No, Parker, you don't kill animals. You kill people. Just like your victims do. Just like I do. What sets you so high above the rest of us? Your sense of morality? Is it your highly developed conscience that gives you the right to pass sentence on your fellow beings? Come to terms with it, Parker. Dancing restlessly beneath your skin is a serial killer, the same as all the rest of your kind in that you pursue a specific archetype of victim; in your case, criminals. You're a mass murderer, my friend, and you can't escape that. Remember Nietzsche's words; 'He who fights with monsters might take care, lest thereby he become a monster. If you gaze for long into an abyss, the abyss gazes also into you.' After all the gazing you've done, that abyss has found a kinship with you, Parker."

Gary snarled like a wild man and tried to stab his hated enemy in the belly, but Fear kicked him in the groin, then cut a swath across the top of his collarbone, spraying blood off to the right and casting the Vigilante back on his haunches.

"Emerson said, 'We do what we must, and call it by the best names,' " Fear continued, dealing out another broad swipe with his sword that cut Gary across the chest and knocked him on his back. "You, Parker, must kill. Instead of preying upon the hapless and innocent, you slake your bloodthirst with the dregs of society and call yourself a crimefighter, but you've no fewer notches on the barrel of your gun than any other outlaw. Do my words not ring true?"

Gary wasn't given the chance to answer, as Fear's sword hacked hungrily into his right thigh and ran all the way down to his ankle, slicing open the skin, but even in the midst of all the pain and blood, his trembling fingers were able to quest out like feelers and grasp a short length of metal chain lying inconspicuously off to the side, disregarded as carelessly as a squashed snake on a highway.

"And what makes you a killer, Parker?" asked Fear, driving the point of his sword directly through Gary's left shoulder. "What makes you so angry? Some tragic loss in your past, perhaps? That's usually how it works, isn't it? Have you sentenced yourself to this fate as a means of atonement for failure to protect someone dear? Is this so-called life of yours actually a self-imposed punishment? 'What other dungeon is so dark as one's own heart? What jailer so inexorable as one's self?' to quote Nathaniel Hawthorne."

Concealing the chain behind his back, Gary – fastly becoming anemic – climbed back up to his knees even as Fear's sword nipped off a bit of his left earlobe.

"Or perhaps there's another reason," Fear suggested, cutting Gary's forehead and watching the blood run down into his eyes. "Do you believe, as did Voltaire, that every man is guilty of all the good he didn't do? Hmph. As for myself, I shall once more cite Emerson, who observed that every hero becomes a bore at last."

"So, you like quotations, do you, you fucking son of a bitch?" Gary panted with his increasing loss of vitality, his color gone, blood drooling from his mouth. "Well, here's one that I think suits you particularly well! It's Rudyard Kipling's, and, if I remember my school reader correctly, it goes something like, 'He wrapped himself in quotations, as a beggar would enfold himself in the purple of emperors!' "

Leaping off his feet with a speed and strength that Fear could never have expected, Gary lunged at the madman and whipped the chain hard into his face, and Fear stumbled backwards, dropped his sword, and screamed as pieces of his cheeks, lips, and nose flew away.

"Quoting great thinkers doesn't make you human!" Gary growled, whipping the chain again, this time at Fear's chest. "And stealing their ideas doesn't make you sound impressive! Far from being sophisticated, you're nothing but a savage!"

Feeling dizzy, but determined to press his advantage, Gary threw the chain into Fear's maimed face, then snatched up the dropped sword, and, with an exertion that almost made him swoon, swung the weapon hard enough to sever Fear's left arm at the elbow. The limb hit the deck with a 'thud', and blood spewed freely from both the useless lump of meat and the mutilated stump still attached to the villain's body.

"You really want to know why I do this, you shithead?" Gary asked the screaming Fear. "Ask any cop why he sticks to *his* job. It's all about that one case. That one nightmare that needs to be exorcised. That one victory that becomes the personal highlight of an entire career. Whether it's catching a pedophile who's fucking his five-year-old son to death, or nailing an arsonist who gets his jollies by burning down nursing homes, it's that one real-life monster that comes along very occasionally that establishes a crimefighter's self-worth. Why do I kill your kind, Fear? Why do I embrace my inner monster? Because it takes a monster to beat a monster, and someone's gotta do it!"

Feeling weaker and sicker with each exhalation of air, Gary lunged forward once more and thrust the sword straight into Fear's belly, jamming it in as hard as he could until it came out through the hateful man's back, impaling him completely. Then he dropped down onto his side, lying in what had become a veritable lake of his own blood, gasping for breath, attempting to keep his vision clear just long enough to see his enemy die.

Remarkably, Fear was still standing, as tall and straight-backed as ever, though shaking like a leaf as he gripped the sword's hilt with his remaining hand, and, with a cold, deathly shudder, extracted the blade slowly and carefully from his midriff.

"Did you think...I'd let you have...the last word?" Fear stammered, using the modicum of strength left to him to raise the gore-dripping weapon once more into the air, squarely above Gary's head. "If I am to die...then I'm taking you with me."

Already feeling the life force slipping away from him, Gary knew this had to be it. He had no way of stopping that final, killing blow from splitting his skull when he couldn't even roll over to save himself from drowning in his own blood. Yes, this had to be it. Good-bye, world; hello, great beyond. I hope I did right, because I sure as shit don't want to spend all of eternity in a bonfire with this crazy jackass. I just wish I had told Carla...

But the killing blow didn't come. Instead Gary heard a quick, low whistle lance through the air, ended abruptly by a strange 'thunk', and he looked inquisitively upwards to see Fear standing as still and as silent as a mannequin, his eyes and mouth open, the sword still gripped in his hand, and a crossbow bolt stuck cleanly through his neck, his Adam's apple speared on the end like a kabob.

As Shang Fear's dead body crashed to the deck, Gary grunted and groaned and forced himself to his knees so that he could look out over the rail and learn the identity of the talented archer who had saved his life. Though his vision was blurred, it didn't take him but a few seconds to make out a tall, shadowy figure – wielding a crossbow in its right hand – perched majestically atop the outstretched arm of a crane just one eighth of a mile away.

He recognized Janet instantly. There was no mistaking that silhouette.

What a terrific friend she is, Gary thought, just before he lost all consciousness.

"So, you looking for action, or what?" asked the thirty-something hooker leaning against the storefront of Cashbox Clyde's Buy, Sell & Trade, a cigarette in her mouth, her hands plunged into the pockets of her cutoff shorts.

"Are you addressing me?" asked Peg.

"Sure," said the hooker. "Girl, this is the fourth time you've been back to this end of the street. You lookin' for a little lez play?"

"How would you know what my sexual preferences are?" asked Peg.

"Hon, all the rent boys are over by that fag joint in the Village," said the hooker, cocking her head southward. "If you wanted pork, you'd be there. Such as it is, I think you've got a hankering for some tuna instead. I'm not wrong, am I?"

"And you're into that?"

"You kidding? For an extra hundred, I'll do your dog."

"I don't have a dog," said Peg, approaching the hooker and pushing two fifty dollar bills into her hand. "You'll have to make do with just me. What do I call you?"

"It's your money, sweetheart," said the hooker. "Call me whatever you like."

"Vicki," Peg said, almost immediately, a wistful look coming into her eyes. "I want to call you Vicki."

"Cute. Let's go."

Before Peg could depart with her new companion, however, her attention was arrested by the shrill, indignant holler of a very familiar voice, and she threw a glance over her shoulder to see Leeza – clad in only her hospital gown – wresting herself away from the clutches of a uniformed police officer. She looked exceedingly haggard and frazzled, and, alarmingly, she was covered in something that looked a lot like blood.

"Get your hands off me, you filth!" Leeza was screaming at the cop. "Don't touch me!"

"Lady, I'm just trying to help you," the cop protested.

"I don't need your help! I didn't need your help when the tanks rolled into Berlin and blew up the street where I lived, and I don't need it now!"

"Leeza!" Peg cried out as she ran to join the fray, having already told her hooker that she could keep the hundred bucks and maybe they'd meet again at a more convenient time. "Leeza, what on earth's happened to you?"

"Oh, Peg, thank goodness for a familiar face!" said Leeza. "This oaf thinks I'm a war criminal! I keep telling him it was all a mistake! I keep telling him that I didn't mean for any of it to happen! But will he listen? No, he'd rather brutalize a defenseless woman! Damn this war, Peg! Damn this war for what it's turned all of us into!"

Peg stared at Leeza, wondering what in the world the elder Vigilante could be rambling about.

"Do you know this woman, ma'am?" asked the cop.

"Yes, officer, I do," Peg nodded. "Has she done anything?"

"Just disturbing the peace, yelling and screaming about I dunno what."

"Would it be all right if I took charge of her, then?" asked Peg.

"I wish you would," said the cop. "I'll bid you good evening, then."

"Yes, you clear off!" Leeza bellowed at the cop's retreating back. "Go find some other poor German girl to ravish! I didn't start this war, you know! I don't deserve such treatment!"

"Leeza, hush up!" Peg hissed, keenly aware of the crowd they were drawing. "What's gotten into you?" Then, more gently, "Leeza, do you know what year this is?"

"What? Of course I do, you stupid girl! Do you think I'm senile? My mind's as sharp as a tack, and it always will be! Growing older doesn't necessarily go hand-in-hand with losing your mind, you know! And what are all you people staring at?"

"Come on, Leeza, I'll take you home," Peg put an arm over her colleague's shoulders and began leading her down the street, away from the curious eyes of strangers.

"Would you...would you stay with me?" Leeza asked, quieter now. "I know that I don't often ask, but...I just don't think I want to be alone tonight."

"Of course I will," said Peg. "You don't even have to ask. After all, we're friends, right? We're there for each other. We can order something good for dinner and watch TV. Nothing like a little idiot box to take your mind off...whatever this is that's bothering you." Then she added, completely without thinking, "Hey, y'know what they're running on HBO tonight? *Schindler's List*. I've never seen it before. Have you?"

Leeza started crying again.

"I feel like I've been violated by Edward Scissorhands," said Gary, the next morning, sitting opposite Carla in a booth in the dining room of Winds From The East, two chopsticks and a small heap of chicken bones discarded on the plate in front of him.

"Yeah, you look like some kind of Band-Aid mummy," said Carla, finishing off her egg drop soup.

"And still, I let you drag me back here," Gary rolled his eyes.

"The owner's a friend of mine," said Carla. "Lives downstairs from me. With the *Dong Ji* gone, he can go back to running the place himself, and I want to support him."

"I'm overdue for a tetanus shot, y'know," said Gary. "My jaw could be frozen shut in a matter of hours."

"I think I might like you with your jaw frozen shut."

"Smartass."

"Carla!" a Chinese man in a smart, black suit approached the table with a jovial greeting. "I'm so happy to see you. And you too, Mr. Parker."

"Hello, Mr. Ting," Carla smiled. "How does it feel to be reaping your own profits for the first time in ages?"

"Oh, it feels very good indeed, Carla, thank you," Mr. Ting was all teeth and gums as he grinned and chuckled, almost clapping his hands with glee. "And I see that you are ready now for your fortune cookies."

Mr. Ting snapped his fingers and a waiter appeared, carrying a silver tray bearing two of the trademark Chinese confection, and Gary and Carla took them.

"Am I going to find the check inside mine?" Gary asked.

"Oh, no, Mr. Parker, your meal is on the house," said Mr. Ting. "It's the very least I can do."

"Thanks very much," said Carla.

"May your fortunes be as sweet as mine," said Mr. Ting, bowing before leaving the pair alone again.

"Well, let's see what fate has in store for yours truly," said Gary, crushing the cookie in his hand and extracting the tiny slip of paper.

"Aren't you going to eat yours?" asked Carla.

"You're not supposed to. No one really likes the taste."

"I do."

"Small wonder," said Gary. "Look at what you Spanish use for pastry. A thin little pizza crust with some powdered sugar sprinkled on it. This isn't a cookie. A cookie is something made with eggs and butter and chocolate chips, or something that you can twist apart and dunk in a glass of milk. Leave Santa this sorry excuse for a cookie on Christmas Eve, and he'll come to your room and wake you up just to slap you silly."

"When did you say your jaw was going to freeze shut?" asked Carla, running her eyes over her fortune. "Oh, looky here. Apparently I have a beautiful soul, and my lucky number is six. What does yours say?"

"The enemy of my enemy is my friend. Ain't that the truth," said Gary, thinking of Janet and her crossbow. "Take me home, Carla. I don't want to start off my two vacation days by missing the start of the *MacGyver* marathon."

Carla smiled warmly, and linked her elbow with Gary's as the two Vigilantes stood up and strolled over to the exit. As people are prone to do, she folded her fortune neatly and slipped it into her pocket, but Gary didn't keep his. Instead he crumpled it up and threw it into a trash can. He didn't want Carla to see that it actually read 'You think you've won your golden crown, but I'll be back for another round.'

He didn't know how the cryptic message had gotten inside his fortune cookie, and he didn't want to know. It honestly didn't intrigue him in the slightest, nor did it fill him with any bothersome feelings of dismay or foreboding. Shang Fear was dead, and he wasn't about to entertain any absurd notion to the contrary. After all, there were some things just too ludicrous even for Gary to believe.

THE QUALITY OF LIFE

A stretch of largely desert terrain, underlined by the long, winding flow of the Rio Grande, the United States-Mexico border goes on for nearly two thousand miles and is the world's most frequently crossed international border, guarded by an understaffed, under-financed patrol of federal police. With forces concentrated on the larger border cities, much of the boundary line is left unattended, including the patch of sandy beach on the cusp of the relatively small Mexican town of Piedras Negras. Here, alone on the vacant beach, was a ramshackle wooden hut that served as home to an American expatriate called Skip; a shiftless bum and onetime bank robber, half white and half Mayan.

Nearly every morning, sometime around eleven o'clock, Skip would rise from his unkempt cot, scratch the lice out of his hair, stomp any new rats, throw on his old, dirty overalls and shirt, and stumble out into the blinding sun, where he would pick up the wad of cash and the two duffel bags left there for him the night before. He'd pocket the cash, then carry the duffel bags down to the Rio Grande – just a few quick strides from his front door – where he kept a motorized go-fast boat tethered to a wooden post. Stealthy, seaworthy, virtually undetectable by radar, and capable of speeds of up to fifty knots, the boat was built from solid, darkly colored fiberglass, with a thirty foot, v-shaped offshore racing hull.

Clearing his throat of the nighttime phlegm with a series of loud, unbecoming hacks, Skip would throw the two duffel bags into the boat, then pilot the stylish craft to the other side of the river, crossing illegally into his hometown's American counterpart of Eagle Pass, Texas. Upon reaching the opposite bank, he would heft the bags again and walk half a mile to a diner called Tito's Eggs N' Things, where he would take a seat in a booth by a window, order two fried eggs with bacon and hash browns and a cup of black coffee, and wait for his friend Jyro to arrive. Although he and Jyro had been working together for some time now, Skip could never bring himself to trust anyone completely, and he found it difficult sometimes to suppress the nagging fear at the back of his mind of Jyro one day missing the rendezvous, having been replaced by a team of armed SWAT cops. Skip worried needlessly, however, as Jyro – taller, handsomer, and always better groomed than Skip – showed up just as fashionably late this morning as on every other, strolling casually through the door, just as the cruder man was finishing his first egg.

"Why can't you get here on time for once?" Skip hissed, as Jyro took the opposite seat. "I'm gonna have a freakin' heart attack one o' these days!"

"Keep eating like that, and I'd state it to a medical certainty," said

Jyro, politely refusing the menu offered him by the waitress. "Yes, I'll just have a black coffee and a cranberry muffin, thank you, dear," he told the girl, sending her off with a slap to her behind.

"Man, I'm really getting sick of this work," said Skip, talking with his mouth full. "I'm tellin' you, my nerves can't take it. Y'know I keep the go-fast fueled an' stocked at all times, right? First sign o' trouble an' I'll be headin' for the Gulf so fast it'll make your dick spin."

"Relax," said Jyro, reaching for a packet of butter and a plastic knife as his order was placed before him. "You're a part of the General's organization. That means something, y'know."

"Yeah, it means we could end up serving twenty years in a federal pen," said Skip, wetting his mouth with a nervous sip of coffee.

"On the contrary, it means we'll *never* end up serving twenty years in a federal pen," said Jyro, breaking his muffin in half and slathering butter onto one of the pieces. "The General knows what he's doing. He knows strategy."

"How can you say that?" Skip asked. "He just got done with a three year sentence up north!"

"His arrest wasn't his own fault," said Jyro. "I've told you this before. The whole unfortunate incident was precipitated by the bumblings of certain incompetent staff who are no longer with the company. Besides, can you think of anyone else capable of running this whole thing from a jail cell all that time?"

"From what I heard, it was his second-in-command doin' most o' the overseein'," said Skip.

"All the same, you've nothing to fear so long as the General protects you," said Jyro, dabbing at his lips with a napkin. "Oh, and I'm to tell you that from now on there'll be *three* bags."

"Three? Aw, man, you gotta be shitting me!" Skip moaned.

"With a proportionate raise in salary, of course," said Jyro.

"Great," Skip rolled his eyes. "Maybe I can use it to hire Johnnie Cochran."

"Cochran's dead."

"Well, I feel myself empathizing already."

"Calm down, and lower your voice," said Jyro, rising from his seat and dropping a ten dollar bill onto his empty plate. "People are staring. Finish your food, go home, and try not to make a public spectacle of yourself. Some of us have real work to do."

Skip chewed nervously on a strip of bacon while Jyro bent at the knees to pick up the two duffel bags, clutching one in each fist.

"See you tomorrow," he said, before walking out the door.

Hot August night, thought Sushi, his mask clinging uncomfortably to his perspiring face, as he flipped agilely through the upper scaffolding of the Queensboro Bridge and cast an eastward glance toward Long Island City.

These were the final days of the final month of summer in New York, and few living souls could recall a more intense heat wave than that which had set the grand metropolis ablaze for nearly two weeks now, with little in the way of relief. On a daily basis humidity was at one hundred percent, and the mercury bubbled up into the triple digits. Sushi hated these long, hot, hazy periods because the natives tended to grow restless and cause trouble. This sort of oppressive weather brought out the very worst in the city's criminal element. Sushi wasn't after the smalltime crooks, rioters, and carjackers tonight, however.

The ninja had just swung around the bridge's final pillar, arriving effectively in Queens, when a burst of static exploded in his right ear, and he nearly lost his balance.

"Stop doing that!" he barked into the tiny microphone attached to his hidden earpiece. "I could have been killed just now! What the hell do you want?"

"Hey, don't shoot the messenger," crackled the voice of William. "Gary just wants me to tell you to get a move on."

"Tell him to go hang himself."

"*You* tell him to go hang himself. He's in one of his moods."

"I noticed."

"Can you see Bronson from there?" William asked.

"Of course I can," said Sushi. "It's only a block away. Tell our intrepid leader to start eating my dust, because I'll be there in no time."

Descending to rooftop level, Sushi sprinted, leapt, and somersaulted across the tops of the smaller buildings that made up this dreary, industrial section of New York's largest borough, traversing the area with an ease that would put him at least ten minutes ahead of his colleagues, and finally arriving at the tall electric fence cordoning off the premises of the Bronson Chemicals plant, bathed in the bright, white light of the full moon.

Towers of steam rising off the asphalt all around him, Sushi threw a single *shuriken* throwing star into the eye of the security camera mounted atop his section of the fence, then drew from his utility belt an object that looked like a simple key ring flashlight. Pressing the ON switch, however, revealed it to be one of Carolyn's many handy tools; a concentrated laser beam with which Sushi cut away enough of the fence's high voltage wires to grant himself entry.

Not even the pall of moonlight could betray the black-garbed ninja as he flowed through the darkness and shadows like the very breeze, his mastery in the ways of stealth and invisibility indisputable, and, when he finally reached the main building, scaling the sheer wall with the aid of his spiked gloves and boots was simplicity itself.

Running to the center of the roof, Sushi used the small laser to cut open the single air vent he found, then slipped lithely inside and followed the claustrophobic shaft for a good forty seconds before finding another vent, this one set in the ceiling of a carpeted, door-lined corridor of what must have been the plant's administrative level. A uniformed security guard, his face turned away from Sushi's position, stood stubbornly between the ninja and the door he wished to access. Sushi used the laser to cut two of the grate's fasteners, causing it to swing silently open, then dropped down into the hallway to land on his toes, as light on his feet as a cat. The guard only moved – and then for just a moment – when Sushi grabbed him around the neck from behind and shoved the chloroform-soaked rag in his face.

After dragging the unconscious guard to a shadowy corner behind a tall, potted plant, Sushi wasted no more time on subtlety, and kicked open the door of which he knew to be the security station. Inside, another lone guard leapt to his feet in surprise and went for his gun.

"Hold it!" Sushi commanded. "I didn't come here to hurt you, but make another move and I'll crush your windpipe before you can get that thing halfway out of its holster!"

The guard hesitated long enough for Sushi to hurl a fast-acting tranquilizer dart into his right shoulder, and even as the guard collapsed senselessly back into his chair, the ninja was already at the main computer bank that controlled alarms, cameras, and emergency doors throughout the facility. The system was vast, but simple, and within minutes all security measures were down.

"All right, things should be relatively clear now," Sushi spoke into his microphone. "Two civilians down, by the way."

"It's about bloody time," the voice of Gary Parker growled in the ninja's ear. "Next time, why don't you take all night about it?"

"Next time, why don't you do it yourself?" Sushi snapped back.

"Can we just shut up and do this already?" asked William. "Some of us don't have forever and ever, y'know. If my parents find out I snuck out again, my life won't be worth a three dollar bill."

Six minutes later found Gary and William – both equipped with face masks over their noses and mouths – inside the largest room of the building's lowest level. Giant steel vats of hazardous material bubbled noisily below a web of metal catwalks, each suspended walkway leading to a different computer terminal, at one of which William now sat, his bespectacled eyes fixated on the glowing monitor, his fingers flying across the keyboard with practiced dexterity.

"And...done!" he said at last, closing down the program and ejecting a compact disc from the computer's drive. "I've downloaded all of the most incriminating stuff. There should be way more than enough evidence there to prove to the authorities that Bronson Chemicals is processing opium into heroin for local drug lords."

"Good," said Gary, slipping the disc into his jacket pocket. "Tell Sushi to meet us outside. We're done here."

"Y'know, you've been acting kind of strangely over the past couple of days, Gary," said William, falling behind Gary's quick strides towards the nearest exit. "Let's just say you haven't been your usual, jocular self. Are you all right?"

"Hardly ever," Gary muttered, surlily. "What difference does it make to you?"

William answered with an 'Urk!', and Gary whirled around to see the diminutive but menacing figure of Edwin Bronson, his left arm wrapped around William's neck, his right hand pressing the barrel of a pistol to the boy's temple.

"I'll be asking for that disc, if you can bear to part with it," he said. "Just take it out, place it on the floor, and kick it over here, or the boy dies!"

"I'll give you this last chance, Bronson," said Gary, quietly and dangerously. "Let him go and I'll take you in alive."

"No, this is *your* last chance!" threatened Bronson, pressing the gun more firmly against William's head. "The disc! Now!"

Growling, Gary thrust his hand into his pocket, but Bronson didn't have time to order him to do it slowly and with two fingers before a throwing star flew in from nowhere and bit into the industrialist's gun hand. Bronson screamed in surprise and pain, and dropped his weapon. William scrambled clear, and Gary hit Bronson like a missile, grabbing his lapels and heaving him up off his feet and over the catwalk's safety rail to dangle him high above a fifty-five gallon vat of boiling opium gum.

"So, putting a gun to a sixteen-year-old kid's head makes you feel safe, does it?" Gary snarled, shaking Bronson in midair. "You don't feel so safe now, do you, fuckface? Got anymore aggression to work out of your system? Why don't you take a poke at me?"

"Gary, this isn't necessary," said Sushi, standing twenty yards down the catwalk. "We've got the evidence. Let's take him to the police."

"They'd only let him go again," Gary hissed.

"Please! Please don't drop me!" Bronson pleaded, kicking his legs in impotent distress. "I give up! I give up! I'll go peacefully! Just please don't drop me!"

"What's the matter, Bronson?" asked Gary. "Don't you want to experience your all-time high?"

Bronson screamed again as Gary let go and watched him plummet directly into the steaming vat with a tremendous splash and a satisfying sizzle.

"That's the only way to deal with these people," Gary muttered, mostly to himself. "That's the only language any of them understand." Then, turning to Sushi, "What the hell did you think you were playing at? If your aim had been off, he could've blown Will's brains out!"

"My aim is never off," said Sushi, indignantly. "Besides, I was thinking of saving young William's life. What were *you* thinking of?"

"I had the situation well under control!" Gary snapped. "Your grandstanding only broke my concentration and forced me to improvise! Do that again and you're fired!" Then, to William, "And if you can't look after yourself during the most basic of field missions, then *your* ass will be history too! If you want to remain a part of this team, then you'd better not put any of us in such a compromising position ever again!"

"How long did you say he's been like this?" asked Sushi, as Gary stormed out of the room.

"Almost two weeks," said William. "It's like he's not himself lately. He's always angry, flying off the handle like you saw just now. And I hate to say it, but I'm sure I've smelled booze on him once or twice. We've all tried to talk to him, but you know how he is."

"Yes, I do," said Sushi. "That's why I'm worried."

Any normal evening, The White Stallion would have been jumping with drunken clubbers, sexed-up dancers, and twenty-four-hour party people. Tonight, however, the popular nightclub was swarming with grim-faced police officers, homicide detectives, and forensics experts taking statements and photographs, quelling the glut of civilian and media interest, and collecting tiny pieces of evidence with tweezers and rubber gloves. Carolyn was there as well, and as she craned her neck to glance past the yellow police tape and into the private bedroom that housed the crime scene, even she – with her worldly experience – had to admit that it was a truly grisly sight.

The victim of what could only have been a crime of pure passion, the mutilated prostitute was sprawled untidily over the queen-sized bed, much of her blood-soaked body reduced to chopped hamburger. Her face had been hacked with a knife, and the eyes, nose, ears, and lips were all gone. Whole clumps of blond hair had been torn viciously from her scalp, her throat had been slashed from end to end, her breasts were lumps of bloody meat, and her belly had been cut clean open, the organs inside stabbed repeatedly. Indicating a certain sexual nature to the murder, the woman's vagina had also been slashed, and some foreign object – absent from the crime scene – had been forced deep inside.

"Sure is a mess, ain't it?" said a gruff-voiced detective coming up on Carolyn's right, his McDonald's coffee going cold in his left hand. "You from homicide?"

"Detective Andrea Beckworth," Carolyn lied, flashing a false badge. "Any ideas?"

"Not too hard to figure, considering the state of the victim," said the detective. "Plus, we got a fair description of the killer from the John the girl was...servicing. Unharmed, miraculously, but then, men don't seem to be this dirtbag's MO. The poor slob's over there right now, having a nervous breakdown."

"What did he say?"

"Exactly what we expected him to say," said the detective. "The intruder was dressed all in black – black coat, black pants, black gloves and boots, black felt hat turned down in the middle – with a black bandanna covering his face, and a big knife in his hand. That was already enough for us, but then we found this."

The detective handed Carolyn a clear, plastic baggie containing a handwritten note, reading:

She screams good. She loves to scream. I say, 'Baby, talk soft', but she just screams and screams. Little sluts ain't worth it, though. Think I got a rash. Itches.

From Hell.

"Jack the Ripper," said Carolyn.

"Yeah, the same sick sonofabitch who's been killing hookers all over town for the past month," said the detective. "He's a slippery one, I'll give him that. His pattern's become fairly predictable, but he's always in and out, under the radar, before we can close the noose."

Carolyn nodded her head, sympathetically. The latest street-stalking media darling – taking his inspiration from one of history's most infamous serial killers – had been at large for the past thirty-two days, coming out at night to attack and butcher prostitutes, and even the Vigilantes had to admit failure thus far in the tracking down and apprehending of the mysterious culprit. By police count, this unfortunate girl was the Ripper's twenty-first victim, and his identity remained secret.

Having seen all she needed to see, Carolyn plunged her hands into her coat pockets and turned away from the gruesome scene, already forcing the hideous images from her mind so that she could get a good night's sleep before returning to the Rat Hole in the morning and resuming the hunt.

Enjoy yourself while you can, Jack, she thought. *Because, with the Vigilantes on your trail, your days are numbered.*

Cashbox Clyde's Buy, Sell & Trade was a secondhand store nestled in the Garment District. Long a commercial staple of Thirty-Fifth Street, it was a dirty, unkempt little shop packed to overflowing with used sporting goods, old exercise equipment, burned out electronics, and ponderous heaps of discarded books and video tapes, all ripe for the picking should a customer be courageous enough to commence haggling with Clyde himself; an overweight, middle-aged man who perpetually sported a scruffy, graying beard, a red flannel shirt, and a Yankees baseball cap, and who could almost always be found lounging disinterestedly behind his counter, his feet up, his nose stuck in the sports section of the daily paper.

It was quarter of eleven now – Clyde knew this because he had actually taken the trouble to fix up one of his old grandmother clocks, once his ancient wristwatch had finally given up the ghost – and, after putting away half a bottle of bourbon and gratifying himself with help from an old, tattered copy of *Juggs*, he was left with nothing to do but prepare for a night's retirement in the backroom, where he slept on a rusty, banged-up old cot that none of his customers would ever want to buy anyway, and the last thing for which he was in the mood was the loud, intrusive banging now sounding at his door.

"We're closed!" he barked. "Come back tomorrow!"

The door broke completely off its hinges and crashed to the floor, and Clyde whirled in alarm to see a large black man in Army fatigues filling the doorway. This was Ron Grimace, a Vietnam veteran with a flash temper, and a psychotic streak facilitated by the effects of post-traumatic stress disorder and Agent Orange poisoning, under the yoke of which he still suffered night terrors and voices in his head. An AK-47 assault rifle was slung over his right shoulder and a huge combat knife hung from his leather belt.

"Now you're open," said Grimace, stepping inside the shop and standing to one side of the doorframe.

Now there was room for the next intruder to enter, and, though he was short in stature, his was an even more unsettling countenance than Grimace's. He was dressed from head to toe like the Invisible Man, sporting a tan trenchcoat over a raggedy sweatshirt and jeans, a pair of sunglasses over his eyes, and strips of amateurishly applied bandages over most of his exposed skin, though plenty of his ugly, rotting face still showed through. This was Jimmy Jay, a cruel and sadistic hitman, vicious and calculating in his methods, and ever ruthlessly efficient despite the horrific AIDS virus that had all but consumed him.

Looking like a zombie escaped from a George A. Romero movie, the wretched Jimmy Jay was a sickly, walking corpse, almost leper-like in his ongoing physical deterioration; the very embodiment of the modern plague itself. Ever too nasty to succumb, he shambled along with all the poise and posture of a sleepwalking Quasimodo, his head bowed low, his arms dangling limply at his sides, and his feet merely scraping along the ground. He suffered from chronic nausea, diarrhea, and swollen glands, his ashen skin was pocked with red lesions, and his esophagus was so inflamed that he had trouble taking nourishment. Fevers, sweats, and chills besieged him relentlessly, and he had to squint to see through his blinding eye infection.

Diagnosed with the killer virus shortly after sharing a single dope needle with a crowd of dozens, Jay had been given eight months by his doctor to get his affairs in order, but there had proven to be no cause for haste. His infection was now in its third year.

"Hi, Clyde," Jay rasped, with a voice that Death himself would use. "It's come time to pay your taxes."

Jay took his place on the other side of the doorframe, and from between he and Grimace emerged a third man. This was Max Shepherd, a tall, distinguished gentleman in his early fifties, with a full head of salt-and-pepper hair, and craggy, Eastwoodish features. He wore a navy blue business suit that had cost more than most people's houses, and he leaned on an ebony walking stick topped with a golden eagle's head – a bullet had shattered his right kneecap ages ago, and he still walked with a pronounced limp. Clyde was right to be intimidated by this man – though he tried hard not to show it – as he was an experienced gangster, his past exploits including racketeering, human trafficking, extortion, arms dealing, gambling, black marketeering, various types of fraud, and a brief but violent tenure with the Ku Klux Klan.

"What the hell do you want, ya creep?" Clyde channeled his anxiety into anger. "And you owe me a new door!"

"I've come to you once again on behalf of the General," said Shepherd, ignoring the man's cries of indignation. "As you have been informed, he wishes to acquire your little piece of this city's narcotics trade, and he is prepared to make you one of two very generous offers. If you wish to keep your fingers in the pie, so to speak, then you are welcome to come aboard the General's organization and work for commission. If you would rather wash your hands of the whole, dirty business, then the General will be more than happy to buy you out for far more than you're worth. I have presented these options to you before, and you expressed indecision. The General was willing to give you time to think it over, but I'm afraid your time is up now. The General needs your decision, and he needs it now."

Clyde narrowed his eyes, and scowled at Shepherd.

"Jus' who do you think you are, you rich, high-talkin' faggot? This is *my* store, and I been dealin' here for years, and there ain't nobody that's gonna take away what's rightfully mine!"

"You do realize, of course, that the General has taken control of virtually every other steady drug supply in the city," said Shepherd, as unconcerned with as he was unsurprised at Clyde's reaction. "You're one of the very last dealers in New York who does not work for him."

"An' it's gonna stay that way!" Clyde vowed. "Down with big business! Down with conglomerates! Up with the small businessman! And you can tell your precious General, direct from me, to go and fuck himself!"

"I see," said Shepherd, producing a monogrammed handkerchief and using it to polish the head of his cane.

Then Clyde could hear the slam of a car door emanating from outside, followed by a series of brisk, steady footsteps that resonated like those of a horse's iron hooves, and he retreated behind his counter in terror at the sight of the next man to appear.

A tall, muscular man in his mid-fifties, General Salvador Ramos was a near perfect physical specimen of humanity. Possessing a firm, rippling, Adonis-like physique – the sort of statuesque build revered by gay Renaissance artists – his chest was broad and proud, his skin beautifully bronzed, and his arms and legs characterized by thick, sinewy cords of muscle. A graying crewcut topped his flecked scalp, and his chiseled features were accentuated by two sharp, black eyes, a hawkish nose, and an exceedingly square jaw. He would have been impressive enough standing naked, but, such as it was, he was immaculate in a beautiful blue dress uniform, with four shiny silver stars and Mexico's golden coat of arms – a righteous eagle strangling a seditious snake in its talons – decorating the epaulets. The front of the coat was heavy with medals and decorations that jingled with the slightest movement, and they jingled now as Ramos approached the counter.

"Hello, Clyde," he said, his voice smooth as velvet.

"Shit!" Clyde yelped. "I...I didn't know you were out of jail!"

"Yes, it's good to be free and catch up with some old friends," said Ramos. "I must say, though, I'm very sorry to hear about your decision. Is that final, then?"

"Well...er...I..."

"All right," Ramos heaved a faux sigh, then turned to face his waiting lieutenants. "If you insist. Gun, Grimace."

Grimace took the AK-47 down from his shoulder and handed it to Ramos, who hefted it like a pro and pointed it at Clyde. Clyde didn't even have time to scream before the General pulled the trigger and sprayed a hail of bullets into his torso, propelling the shopkeeper-drug dealer back against the wall, where he lingered for just a few seconds before slumping as a bloody pulp to the floor.

"If I may say so, sir," said Grimace, "you're a real surgeon with that weapon."

"All in aid of the bigger picture, Grimace," said Ramos, handing the rifle back to his subordinate. "Alas, behold that to which I have been reduced."

Ramos' contempt for his present circumstances would come as no great surprise to one privy to the man's background. In his native Mexico, he had been revered and worshiped as a military hero. Hailed as a fighting General – and before that, a fighting Colonel – who wasn't averse to rolling up his sleeves and getting his hands dirty, he had been used for years as the face of the people's army, his image appearing frequently on promotional posters as a rough-and-tumble Rambo type, a blazing machine gun gripped in his hands, a smoldering cigar clenched between his teeth. Praise was undying for the bold, two-fisted tactics he had employed against radical revolutionary groups and guerilla terrorist organizations, the infamous Mexican Proletarian Party and the Twenty-Third of September Communist League among them. Still more popular was his overseeing of the army's turn back towards pressing domestic issues – natural disasters, organized crime, and the illegal drug trade – with which the civilian police force was unable to cope unassisted. There was no question in anyone's mind that Ramos was a hero, and a fine role model worthy of any Mexican youth's admiration. That is, until a monumental mistake on Ramos' part revealed him for what he truly was; a powerful drugs baron, using his station, and the resources of the army – an institution already shrouded in mystery and corruption – to both facilitate and disguise the means by which his clandestine companies produced and distributed narcotics all throughout the Western hemisphere.

Ramos was dishonorably discharged, and left with not a penny to his name after the government's seizure of all his assets and holdings. The Associated Press, ever eager for the fall of a giant, was quick to nickname him 'the Mexican Mobster' and 'the South-of-the-Border Overlorder', and, after a handful of attempts on his life by the authorities, Ramos fled in disgrace to New York, where he ultimately settled into a niche in the city's criminal underbelly and began blueprinting his ascension from the ashes.

For a time it had seemed that Ramos' star was once again on the rise as he set about building a new cartel, utilizing the people and opportunities he'd found running rampant within one of the world's largest, most corruptible cities, and he had just begun to remember the taste of power and success when an outlaw group of vigilantes had brought him tumbling down. The ultimate result of that conflict had been his three-year incarceration at Hudson Correctional Facility, but now those three long years had finally passed, and here he was, hungry again; hungry for strength and glory lost; hungry for revenge.

The city is almost mine, he thought, relishing the near fruition of his plans. *And if I can't rule it, then I'll destroy it instead.*

Not forty minutes ago, over on the Bronx River Parkway, a brief but horrific gun battle had broken out between rival gangs the Red Cobras and the Deer Hunters. All participants had been under the age of twenty, and armed with automatic weapons. Twelve gang members and civilians had been declared by the police to be dead on arrival, an additional fifteen had been shuttled off to hospitals, and the rest of the punks had made good their escape, free to terrorize the local populace another day. However, as the authorities bagged bodies and hosed the rivers of blood off the pavement, the mood in the humble house in Morrisania in the South Bronx was decidedly more upbeat.

Charlie was sitting on the couch in the dimly lit, modestly furnished living room, at ease in his olive green tanktop and Hagar the Horrible boxer shorts. Sitting in his big lap was Krystal Harris – an attractive black woman in her late thirties, and owner of the house – clad in her white cotton bra and panties. With her arms entwined around his thick neck, and his huge hand moving up and down her curled-up legs, they held each other in the rosy afterglow of love-making, surrounded by the remaining scraps of pizza crust, Italian sausage, mushrooms, breadsticks, and chicken bones, while Bruce Willis shot his way through *Die Hard* on the twelve inch TV.

"Baby, that was real good," Krystal smiled, her head resting against Charlie's powerful chest, his steady heartbeat thundering in her ear. "Y'know, there's a chance I just might get to like you."

"Here's to that," said Charlie, taking his second bottle of Miller Lite from the six-pack on the couch arm and popping the cap off with one flick of his big thumb.

"There's just one thing I want to ask you about," said Krystal.

"Ask away," said Charlie.

Krystal asked with her fingernails, pushing them deeply, firmly into a spot between Charlie's chest and stomach. Charlie winced and grunted in discomfort.

"I knew it!" said Krystal, triumphantly. "When you didn't want to take off your shirt, I *knew* it! What are you hiding?"

Charlie sighed, but didn't resist as Krystal pulled up his tanktop to reveal a very large, very ugly, very fresh scar carved in a jagged, diagonal path from his big, black nipple down to just above his cavernous navel.

"Oh, my gosh!" she gasped.

"Really, sweetheart, it's nothing," said Charlie. "It's not as bad as it looks."

"It couldn't be," said Krystal. "If it were, you'd be dead."

"Some stupid punk with a knife just got lucky, that's all," said Charlie.

"If he'd gotten any luckier, you'd be a canoe," muttered Krystal, climbing off of Charlie's lap and bending down to pick up her jeans. "Honestly, Charlie, I don't want to be one of those women who's always nagging her man about his job, but sometimes I really wish you'd just quit this whole thing."

"Now, Krystal, I thought we talked about this," said Charlie, leaning forward to set his beer down on the coffee table.

"You made it sound like you were some kind of cop," said Krystal, zipping up her jeans and reaching for her blouse. "From the way you described it, I expected you to have normal hours, a disability pension, and a bulletproof vest."

"We have vests," said Charlie, standing up to don his own jeans, "but you certainly can't blame Carolyn for not being able to find one that'll fit me. Baby, I can't quit doing what I do. You knew that when we started this relationship."

"I know, I know," Krystal grumbled. "And so far, I've been able to deal. But can't I worry about you, Charlie? Aren't I allowed to worry? I mean, you spend a large part of your days and nights out on the streets, provoking dangerous criminals into fights! In this city, provoking just an average Joe Blow into a fight is practically suicide, never mind a mad dog killer with a mile long rap sheet and half a pound of coke up his nose! Baby, this isn't normal behavior!"

"I know," Charlie bowed his head. "Believe me, honey, I know it can be rough, but I've gotta do it. I've just...gotta. It's what I'm here to do. After so many years of my life wasted, knowing that my actions make the world a better place is what fulfills me. Nothing has ever made me feel that good, baby."

"Nothing?" asked Krystal. "Not even...us?"

Charlie didn't know what to say. "Do you want me to leave?" he asked, at last.

"No," Krystal shook her head, somberly. "No, of course I don't want you to leave. I really care for you, Charlie, and I want you in my life, and if I have to coexist with this bizarre lifestyle choice of yours in order to hang onto you, then so be it. I just wish I could truly understand all of this."

"But you do understand," said Charlie. "I know you. Every time you think of Michael, you understand."

Michael was Krystal's eight-year-old son who had been indirectly responsible for bringing his mother and the Vigilante together two months ago. Being a single mother, Krystal had to work fulltime, while praying daily that Michael would be able to make his way safely home from school on his own, traversing the dirty streets and alleyways of one of New York's seediest, most dangerous neighborhoods. The boy usually reached home without incident, but his turn to plumb the Bronx's underbelly inevitably arrived – shortly after the school year had given way to summer vacation – in the cozy, familiar setting of Jimbo's convenience store, not two blocks from home.

Michael was perusing the candy display at the check-out counter, agonizing over what to buy with the seventy-five cents burning a hole in his pocket, when the hand came to rest gently upon his right shoulder.

It was a skinny, limp-wristed hand belonging to a pale, cadaverous man with a bushy beard, bad acne, and a stubby ponytail protruding from the back of his head like a topknot.

"Hi there, boy," said the man, in a laryngitic whisper of a voice. "Candy lookin' good, huh?"

"Yeah," said Michael. "I can't decide what to get."

"Well, what do you like?"

"All of it."

"Good for you, boy," the man smiled, revealing two front rows of crooked teeth. "Tell ya what. I'll buy you any three you want."

"Wow! Really?"

"Really! Go ahead and pick 'em out!"

"Have I seen you in here before, mister?" asked the young woman behind the counter. "Because my friend Michael knows he's not supposed to talk to strangers, right, Michael?"

"Uh-huh," said Michael, who was busy picking out a Milky Way, a Nestle Crunch bar, and a packet of Peanut M&M's. "I think I'll take these, mister."

"Excellent choices, boy," said the man. "And tell me, boy. Do you like comic books?"

"Yeah!" Michael exclaimed, feeling like it was his birthday.

"Do you like Batman?"

"Spider-Man's my favorite."

"Mine too!" enthused the man, taking the latest issue of *The Amazing Spider-Man* from the rotating magazine rack. "So, whadda ya think? Will that do it for you?"

"Yeah! Thanks a lot, mister!"

"Well, we seem to have a satisfied customer here," said the man, producing a ten dollar bill from a mangy billfold and pushing it across the counter to the disapproving cashier. "Just ring those up, please, and we'll be on our way."

"Sir, I don't mean to be rude, but I don't think you should be buying those things for that boy," said the cashier. "It's plain to me that you aren't acquainted with him at all."

"The customer is always right, miss," said the man.

"Sir, I don't want to have to call the police."

The man's eyes darkened. "Now, see here, miss..."

"Lookin' for a good time, mister?" asked the deep, bass voice of Charlie, approaching from behind, carrying an armful of potato chips, pretzels, and soda.

"What's it to you?" the man asked, indignantly. "What kind of world is this where a guy can't do a little something nice for a child without having suspicion cast upon his motives?"

"And I suppose you were gonna give him a ride home in your car as well, right?" said Charlie.

"If he wanted," said the man.

"Uh-huh," Charlie rumbled. "Mister, why do I get the feeling that I could find your name, address, and photo under a certain category in a certain Internet database?"

The man gulped nervously as Charlie leaned down to whisper in his ear.

"Now, I'm not gonna hit you in front of the kid," he said, "but you better get outta here now, or you'll be in a whole new world of pain that astronomers can't even see with a telescope. And if I see you around here again, I'll bury you."

The man departed with all due haste, and Charlie sprang for the promised gifts himself, then escorted Michael home, where he and an eternally grateful Krystal first made each other's acquaintance.

"Of course I love what you did for Michael," said Krystal, "and, even if I live to be a hundred, I don't think I'll ever be able to fully repay you. And I don't really want you to stop doing your good work. It's just that... oh, baby, I do worry about you."

"I know, hon," said Charlie, opening his big arms. "Come here."

Krystal went to him, and they embraced, hoping their shared feelings for each other were powerful enough to ward off any worry or doubt nagging at either one of them.

"You can count on me, hon," said Charlie, running his large fingers through her hair as she nuzzled his chest. "I'm always gonna be here. There's no criminal strong enough to take me away from you."

"Just keep telling me that," she said.

"But I don't want to think about criminals right now," said Charlie. "You know what I *do* want to do?"

"What?"

"I want to suck the marinara from your fingers."

Krystal laughed as Charlie swept her up and dropped her back down onto the couch, where the two lovers resumed their canoodling for another minute and a half. Then the back door leading into the kitchen banged open, and, a moment later, a fifteen-year-old boy appeared in the living room. This was Leon, Krystal's other son. His t-shirt bore an image of an angry Malcolm X, with the words 'The chickens are comin' home to roost!' emblazoned beneath it, his ratty blue jeans hung down around his ass, and he carried a scratched-up skateboard over one cold shoulder.

"It's past eleven o'clock, young man," said Krystal, sitting up and becoming all business. "Where have you been?"

"Out," said Leon, surlily.

"Hi there, Leon," said Charlie, trying to be friendly.

"Aw, gee, hi, Charlie," Leon sneered, sarcastically. "It's real nice to see you here. By the way, my dad paid a lotta money for that couch, so I hope it's comfortable for you while you're humpin' my mom."

Charlie found the rudeness distasteful, but he didn't feel it was his place to discipline Krystal's child. Besides, he was used to it. Whereas Michael had taken to Charlie like a duck to water, Leon had hated the Vigilante from day one.

"Leon, I can't believe the things that come out of your mouth!" Krystal scolded. "Apologize, now!"

"Fuck that shit," Leon muttered, turning towards the stairs.

"What did you say?" asked Krystal, moving after him. "What was that you said?"

"Nothing," said Leon.

"Oh, you are grounded, mister!" Krystal shouted up the stairs after him. "Do you hear me? You're grounded for a week!"

"Yeah? Then where are you and the third wheel gonna snatch your precious moments?" Leon called back down to her.

"Go to your room!"

"Y'know, sometimes I wonder if it wasn't Dad who left *you!*"

"How dare you! Your father was a drunk and a bum, and I'm working all the time so I can give you a good home with everything you need!"

"Yeah, a good home, with my mom playin' the slut for a total stranger, right out in the middle of the living room! No good home would be complete without one!"

"Why are you behaving this way?" asked Krystal, welling up with tears. "Honestly, I don't know what's the matter with you! You're out of the house all the time, you never tell me where you're going or what you're doing, and then you come home and treat me like this! What am I supposed to do with you, Leon? Really, I don't have a clue!"

"And I doubt you ever will," said Leon, disappearing into his bedroom.

Krystal watched the door close on her eldest son, then put her face in her hands and started crying, softly. Charlie put his arm around her.

"You okay, hon?" he asked.

"Oh, Charlie, I'm so sorry about all that!" she sobbed. "I'm so embarrassed! I just don't know what his trouble is, and I'm lucky if he says five words to me in a day!"

"He's a teenager," said Charlie. "They're all a bunch of little punks. I was kinda like him when I was his age. I think I might be part of the problem, actually. I think he resents me for trying to take his father's place."

"Oh, it's not just that," said Krystal, blowing her nose with a tissue from the box on the table. "His problems really started last year. He was misbehaving in school, cutting classes and getting in fights, and his grades were dropping. He got suspended three times. I tried talking to him. I tried threatening him. I tried punishing him. Nothing worked. Then he started staying out late at night and seeing a whole new crowd of people that he won't introduce me to, and more than once he's come home smelling of cigarette smoke."

"Yup, that all sounds pretty familiar," said Charlie, scratching the back of his head. "I could try to talk to him if you'd like, although I don't think he'd listen. In case you haven't noticed, he doesn't like me very much."

"But maybe that would help," said Krystal, tilting her face to look up into Charlie's. "He's been missing a father figure. Maybe if he had a man-to-man talk with someone who was once in a similar situation – someone who grew up in a bad neighborhood like this one – maybe he'd understand why certain things are so bad."

"Possible, I suppose."

"Maybe he'd even grow to like you a little."

"Well, I wouldn't set my hopes *too* high."

"And if you get through to him, you could tell me what I could do to help," said Krystal, becoming more and more enamored with the idea. "You could tell me what it is exactly that I'm doing wrong, and what I need to do to better accommodate him."

"Now, don't go hanging this all on yourself," said Charlie. "It's not your fault."

"But he's my son," said Krystal. "I have to take responsibility for how he turns out. I...I just want to be a good mother to him."

"You're a fantastic mother," said Charlie. "Don't doubt that for a second. Kids like Leon just get mixed up sometimes, that's all. He's a textbook angry young man. There are tons of 'em running around all over the place. But as long as he has you, he's not alone."

More tears from Krystal as Charlie folded his arms around her and tried his best to be comforting. That was what she needed now; comforting, optimism, and positive energy. He saw no reason, in the thick of this tender moment, to tell Krystal that the odor he had detected clinging to Leon had not been that of a cigarette, nor did he think any good would come of pointing out that the boy's red-and-black denim jacket was unmistakably in the style of the Red Cobras.

Cry, and the world cries with you. Laugh, and you laugh alone.

"No! You've got it wrong! It's the other way around!" protested Gary, tumbling through a multitude of psychadelic distortions of what he had always taken to be reality. "Let me out of here! Somebody let me out of this rabbit hole!"

Mother always said, 'Life is like a box of chocolates. You never know which one contains the razor blade.'

"No! No! How am I here, and wherefrom? Who made me, and what?"

I can stand the sight of worms, and look at microscopic germs, but Technicolor pachyderms are really too much for me!

"No! Leave me alone! I'm not insane!"

Insanity is a perfectly rational adjustment to an insane world.

"Help! Heeeellllllp!"

I am not the type to faint when things are odd or things are quaint, but seeing things you know that ain't can certainly give you an awful fright!

"No! You're nothing but a pack of cards! Who cares for you?"

Of the two natures that contended in the field of my consciousness, even if I could rightly be said to be either, it was only because I was radically both.

"No! I am one! One, I say!"

All work and no play makes Gary a dull boy.

"Allison! Allison, where are you?"

A victim of the modern age! Poor, poor girl!

"Allison, say something so I can find you! Is that the baby crying? Or is it *me* crying? Oh, help me, Lord, if You exist! Show me the way out of this hell!"

Villains! Dissemble no more! I admit the deed! Tear up the planks! Here, here! It is the beating of his hideous heart!

"No! Get away from her, you bastards! Die, die, die, die!"

To be...or not...to be? That...is...the...quest...

"Aaaaaaahhhhh!"

Clawing at his bare chest with his fingernails, as if trying to rid himself of some evil embedded within, Gary screamed up at the full moon hanging high above Central Park like a cold, omniscient eye and bled down his torso before falling off his widely splayed legs and hitting the ground with a 'thud' that brought him back to semi-consciousness right in the center of the teardrop-shaped Strawberry Fields memorial garden dedicated to the memory of John Lennon, slain just a short distance from the designated 'quiet zone' bounded by shrubs and trees and woodland slopes.

You lied to me, Johnny, thought Gary, morosely, lying flat on his belly in the damp grass. *You lied to all of us. Because there* aren't *any strawberry fields, are there?*

Shirtless and shoeless – clad only in a pair of old, worn-out cargo pants – Gary climbed to his knees and pulled his Beretta 96 from his waistband. His aching, angry eyes studied the beautiful weapon, sleek and silver, with its checkered black plastic grip, squared trigger guard, grooved front and backstraps, tritium night sight, inertia firing pin, ambidextrous safety mechanism, and ten-shot magazine. It was a good gun – especially since Carolyn had rendered it so much more than the sum of its parts, making the model capable of feats for which it had never been intended by its original manufacturer – and it had served him well in his war against crime. But how could a war effort be sustained when the soldier himself was so weary? The never-ending conflict had drained him completely. It was time to retire. People like him, however, didn't retire from anything.

Growling like an animal, gritting his teeth furiously, Gary turned the gun around and pressed the muzzle against the center of his forehead, his thumb in place, ready to push back on the trigger that would fire the round that would take his tortured soul from this world.

"You want a piece of me?" Gary roared, his face turning purple with rage. "You want a fucking piece of me? Then take it, you son of a bitch! Take it!"

"Gary?" said a familiar voice, coming in from one side. "Gary, I hope you won't think I'm trying to stick my nose where it doesn't belong, but you really, really don't look too good right now."

Gary heaved a weary sigh, lowered the gun, and turned his head to the right to face Carla, clad in the leather bodysuit that typified her nightwear.

"How did you find me?" he asked, emotionlessly.

"You always come here when you're sulking," Carla answered.

"It helps me remember what I'm fighting for," Gary muttered. "At least it used to. These days it seems my greatest enemy is myself."

"Will told me about what happened at the Bronson plant," said Carla, moving in closer and touching him gently on the shoulder. "Would you like to talk about it?"

"No," said Gary, decisively.

"I'm really worried about you, Gary," she continued. "You've been like this for too long. I mean, you've had your fair share of dark patches in the past, but you've always been able to find your way back. This time you seem lost."

"Not lost," muttered Gary. "Just resigned."

"Come on, Gary, you're stronger than this," said Carla. "Don't go down this way."

"If you've gotta go, go without a smile," he replied.

"I really wish you'd agree to talk to Buzz," said Carla. "That's part of his job, y'know.

To help straighten out any of us who happen to fall off the edge of the world. It's a hard life we're living, Gary. We all come down with the sickness from time to time. It's easy to give in to anger and despair and self-pity, but you can't do it. Not if you want to live."

"Who says I want to live?"

"Don't talk like that, love."

"And don't call me that!" Gary snapped. "I'm not your 'love'! When have I ever loved you? Have I ever shown you any encouragement? Any indication that I'm at all interested in being loved by you?"

"No," said Carla, softly. "It just comes to me involuntarily, I guess."

"Well, stick a sock in it, then," he said, sullenly. "And stay away from me. You'll live a richer life."

He turned away to face the memorial's focal point – the word 'Imagine' spelled out amidst a circle of inlaid Italian marble – and Carla could see the metal flask stuck in his back pocket.

"When did you start drinking again?" she asked, unable to disguise her alarm.

"When I got thirsty," said Gary, unscrewing the cap and taking a swig.

"Just like that? Even after all the work you put into drying yourself out?"

"Especially after all that. Cheers."

"You're disgusting," said Carla, her eyes darkening as a new, contemptuous tone came into her voice. "Look at you! A true champion of justice! How low and pathetic you seem now! If I hadn't been raised Catholic, I'd tell you what I really think of you!"

"Here's to that," said Gary, raising his flask into the air.

"Give me that!" Carla demanded, snatching the flask from his hand.

"I never took you for the type to give up easily, Gary, but can't you see what a pitiful wreck you've become? Just a naked, drunken, suicidal bum, ranting incoherently to himself in the park in the middle of the night! You used to eat scum like that for breakfast! How does it feel, knowing that you've changed into that which you most despise? We've all watched you sink lower and lower over the past several days, but I'm not going to watch any longer! This has gone on long enough, and it's time for you to get your shit together!"

"I wouldn't do that!" Gary snarled, the gun suddenly back in his hand and pointing directly at Carla. "If Buzz were here right now, he'd tell you that I'm very fucking far from being in my right mind! And I'm very thirsty!"

"You want to shoot me? Go ahead! It'll almost be worth it, just to see you slurp this cat piss up out of the dirt!" She dashed the precious flask to the ground, sending its contents spilling out across the well worn pathway. "So go ahead, you ugly drunk! Lick it up! I know you need it!"

Even in his delirium Gary moved with a speed and finesse unmatched by most human beings, and his fist struck Carla's face like a brick, sending her spinning off her feet to crash face first onto the ground. More surprised than hurt, she attempted a quick recovery of her footing, but though she too was a formidable hand-to-hand combatant, there was no denying that Gary's talents eclipsed hers any day of the week, and she found herself helpless to resist as her incensed friend seized her by the back of her neck, yanked her upright with one hand, then punched her in the gut with the other.

"You've had this coming for a long time!" he growled, dealing Carla an elbow jab that knocked her back to the ground. "You've been an insufferable nag from the moment I met you! I think it's about time I reminded you who calls the shots around here!"

Carla could do nothing but gasp painfully and breathlessly as Gary gripped her by her slim shoulders, hoisted her once more to her feet, and propelled her into a thick tree trunk, but before he could continue with the impromptu lesson, his attention was arrested by the lilting echo of a strange, drunken laugh dwindling down from atop the magnificent, twin-towered San Remo apartment complex nearby. Turning to gaze up towards the top of the seventeen-story main structure, he could make out two shadowy figures – grown men both – dashing and stumbling erratically back and forth, pushing each other playfully, and seeming altogether unsteady on their feet.

Good, he thought. *Something to distract me for five minutes.*

Retrieving his gun and sticking it back in his waistband, he ran his hands up over his sweaty face and through his unkempt hair, then began striding purposefully out of the park.

"Well, are you coming or not?" he asked Carla, throwing a brief, unconcerned glance over his shoulder at the leather-clad Vigilante, just now climbing to her feet, one hand dabbing at her bleeding bottom lip.

"If for no other reason than to keep an eye on you," she muttered, following his lead.

"One! Two! Three!"

At the final count, Dickie and Chester – two brothers who had decided they were due for a night off from their usual work at the neighborhood chop shop – charged towards each other from opposite sides of the San Remo's broad roof, their heads lowered like a couple of rams. At the center of the roof their skulls collided with a thunderous 'crack', and both men fell backwards onto their rear ends.

"Wow!" exclaimed Chester. "This shit is really good! I didn't feel a thing!"

"It's fuckin' incredible is what it is!" said Dickie, finally taking the time and effort to remove his leather belt from his left arm, where it had been serving as a tourniquet. "Lemme tell ya, this stuff is as pure as you can get! Made real good! Not a lotta contaminants in it!"

"Where'd ya get it?"

"Some posh faggot in the Village. I've been saving it for a whole week!"

"You don't have the money for Village dope, man. 'Specially not from a faggot. Fuck, man, a fag dealer is worse than a Jew banker."

"Not as it stands now, bro!" Dickie chortled. "Ain't ya noticed? Drugs are on the rebound, baby! And it's a buyer's market! Tons of dealers all over the city, all selling for cheap! I dunno or care why, but over the last several months we been goin' back to the eighties, man, with everyone – black or white, rich or poor, young or old – getting stoned outta their minds every day of the week!"

"I liked the eighties," said Chester, reflectively. "A guy could get a fix without worryin' about undercover cops."

"And that's the way it's gonna be again, little bro, if the big brains behind this resurgence have anything to say about it! Now, get up there and walk that rail!"

"What?"

"You heard me," said Dickie, pointing to the safety fence bordering the edge of the roof. "I wanna see you walk that rail like a balance beam."

"Are you out of your fuckin' mind? I'll fall!"

"Yeah, I should've known you wouldn't have the balls," said Dickie. "Your dick must be the size of a pencil, y'know that? And I don't mean a regular pencil. I mean one of those mini golf pencils. One that's been used a few times already."

"My dick's bigger than yours!" said Chester, defensively. "I'm the one who takes after Dad, remember!"

"No, you're the one who takes after Uncle Greg!" said Dickie. "I bet you have to use a magnifying glass and a pair of tweezers to take a piss!"

"That's it! We're gonna settle this right now! Drop your pants and start stroking!"

"Gladly!" Dickie accepted the challenge, pulling out his penis and gripping the shaft with his right hand. "All I gotta do is think of Jenna Jameson and mine'll be stretchin' all the way to Jersey in no time!"

"Hey! Don't you dare think of Jenna Jameson! *I* think of Jenna Jameson!"

"Well, why can't we *both* think of Jenna Jameson?"

"Because there's no way I'm gonna be able to get it hard if I'm thinkin' about you strokin' and thinkin' about Jenna Jameson while *I'm* strokin' and thinkin' about Jenna Jameson!"

"Fine, fine! Have it your way!" Dickie relented. "I'll think of Briana Banks instead."

"No, you can't think of her either!"

"Why the fuck not?"

"Because I like to pair her up with Jenna Jameson, and how do you s'pose I'm gonna be able to reach my maximum hardness if you cram yourself right into the middle of my lesbian sandwich?"

"You are such a dipshit, y'know that? Okay, then *you* tell me! Who can I think of?"

"I don't know! Just leave my girls alone! You like big tits, don't ya? Why don't you think of Pamela Anderson?"

"I can't think of Pamela Anderson! That skank has hepatitis! I stick my dick in her and it'll fall off! Besides, I've never seen her naked."

"Well, what about Halle Berry?"

"She's all right for a black chick, but I prefer white meat."

"Oh, for fuck's sake! We're gonna be freezing our dicks off in the wintertime before you come up with somebody to think of!"

"It's your own fuckin' fault! You and your sexual insecurity! Honestly, if you had a chance to fuck Jenna Jameson and Briana Banks, would it really even matter if I was there as well?"

"I hate to be cruel, boys," said Carla, appearing suddenly on the left, "but if it'll help settle this rather noisy argument, I'd say that neither one of you is particularly impressive." Her eyes lingered on Chester. "Huh. Uncircumcised. Y'know, I've never actually seen one of those before. It's kinda cute."

"Not you again!" lamented Chester, as he and his brother tucked themselves hastily away and zipped up their flies. "Look, we don't know nothin', okay?"

"Your bloodshot eyes and trembling fingers tell me otherwise," Gary, coming in from the other side, rasped menacingly. "I always said you were a pair of real jerk-offs, but I never meant it literally. Now, if you losers aren't too doped out of your minds, you can tell me where, when, and how you got that junk, and who gave it to you."

"Man, whadda ya wanna be botherin' us for?" asked Dickie. "It's just a little smack. We're not hurtin' nobody. There must be tons o' muggers and murderers in this city that you could be harassin' right now. Why pick on us?"

Gary grabbed Dickie by the front of his shirt and yanked him towards him. "Because, like you said, this city is becoming a drug toilet again," he hissed, "and I don't like it. We've been working very hard over the past couple of months to combat the industry's exponential climb. Maybe you'd like to know what I did earlier tonight. I executed the man most likely responsible for manufacturing that garbage you just shot into your veins. Wanna know how? I boiled him! Cooked him with his own opium! Now, are you gonna tell me what I want to know, or not?"

"Honestly, man, I don't know nothin'!" said Dickie.

"I don't believe you," said Gary.

"Really, I'm totally in the dark!" Dickie insisted. "I've always been straight with you, ain't I? I picked this up in a fag bar in Greenwich! A guy named Timmy Rasputin operates outta there! I got the stuff from him!"

"You're lying to me, Dickie."

"No, it's the truth! Scout's honor!"

"Rasputin's dead, Dickie."

"What? How do you…"

"Because I killed him three weeks ago, Dickie."

"Oh, shit."

"I have an idea," said Gary, murder glimmering in his eyes. "Let's get *really* high!"

Dickie said 'Urk!' as Gary yanked him off his feet, swept him over the safety fence, and held him out in thin air, nearly four hundred feet above the ground.

"Tell me who's orchestrating this drugs spike!" Gary demanded. "I know you know!"

"I dunno! I dunno! Don't drop me! Please! I dunno!"

"What the hell are you doing?" Chester demanded, rushing forward. "Let him go!"

"No, don't let me go! Don't let me go!" implored Dickie.

While Carla reeled in Chester with her grappling line and rendered him unconscious with one swift kick to the head, Gary shook Dickie like a tambourine, as if trying to make the facts fall out of his pockets.

"Tell me who's behind it all, Dickie! Tell me, or I drop you!"

"I can't! He's a fucking killer! They all are! You know how brutal these drug lords are! They really get off on it!"

"Who's dangling you off the side of a building right now? Me or them?"

"Please!"

"You're starting to feel heavy, Dickie."

"I can't!"

"My arms are getting tired."

"I'll do anything! Just please don't make me..."

Gary let go with one of his hands, and Dickie screamed.

"All right, all right!" he relented, nearly hysterical. "You wanna know who's at the top of the game? It's the General, okay? It's the General! The fucking General!"

"Don't lie to me, you junkie piece of shit!" Gary snarled. "The General's in jail! I put him there!"

"He got out a few weeks ago!" Dickie insisted. "His boys handled most of the heavy lifting in his absence, and now he's come back to take up the reins again! It's the General! I swear it's him!"

Gary furrowed his brow, then turned to Carla. "Has it been three years already?" he asked.

"Yeah, I guess it has," she said. "Boy, time sure does fly, huh?"

Gary turned back to face the terrified Dickie. "Thanks," he said, before relinquishing his grip completely and watching with unnatural relish as the man plummeted seventeen stories and landed in the courtyard below.

"Time may fly," he said, dusting off his hands, "but *he* sure doesn't."

Wide-eyed and open-mouthed, Carla stared in astonishment and horror at Gary, then lunged forward, lashed out with her right arm, and wrapped her hand around his throat.

"What the fuck did you do that for?" she demanded, furiously. "He told us what we wanted to know! You can't kill a snitch after he cooperates! We rely too heavily on stool pigeons to let this sort of thing happen! If this gets around, no one in all of the five boroughs will want to talk to us!"

His lip curling into a snarl, Gary grabbed Carla's wrist, yanked the hand away from his throat, and pinched the nerve that made his fellow Vigilante cry out in pain and collapse helplessly to her knees.

"Listen to me very carefully," he growled into his suffering friend's ear. "If you *ever* raise a hand in defiance of me again, I will take that grappling rope of yours, and I will use it to hang you by the neck from the first lamppost I can find! Are we clear?"

"Y-yes!" Carla cried.

Gary gave her an extra hard pinch for emphasis, then released her, and disappeared from the rooftop before she even had time to brush the tears of pain, anger, and bewilderment from her eyes.

> *At the far end of town, where the Grickle-grass grows,*
> *And the wind smells slow-and-sour when it blows,*
> *And no birds ever sing, excepting old crows...*

Theodor "Dr. Seuss" Geisel had composed that verse in order to illustrate the Street of the Lifted Lorax, but he could just as easily have been describing the Bowery; the dismal, neglected thoroughfare blighting Manhattan's Lower East Side. One of the city's most notorious streets, and longtime 'skid row', the impoverished, crime-shadowed area warned most decent people away, but 'decent' wasn't the breed surging through the district in droves of late, drawn, as if by instinct, to one oasis in particular.

Mr. Happy's Bar & Grill – situated where the Bowery intersects with the tawdry, underpopulated Delancey Street – enjoyed a state of relative good repair compared with the broken bleakness of its surroundings. Its doors and windows actually locked, the restrooms were usually passably clean, and a bright pink neon sign hung out front, flashing the message 'Topless Tuesdays! Over 21 Only!'

On its exterior, Mr. Happy's Bar & Grill resembled any other dive where a working class grunt could hang his hat for half an hour, shoot a game of pool, and enjoy a steak and a beer for under ten bucks, so long as he was willing to disregard the occasional hair on his plate and didn't take exception to stomping his own cockroaches. Indeed it was primarily the blue collar crowd who stopped by the eatery, but once inside the front doors, a visitor would discern right away that this was no mere burger joint.

The large dining room boasted only a few conventional tables and chairs, being far more generously furnished with couches, waterbeds, beanbags, and overstuffed armchairs. The lights were turned deliberately down low so that the assorted customers had to strain to see each other clearly, and the overall atmosphere – while defined by a certain pulsing, unnamable energy that crackled as tangibly as raw electricity in the air – was far too subdued, too sedate to be confused with that of any public restaurant in the world. No, there was no abundance of convivial conversation or nonchalant banter here. No friendly, bright-eyed wait staff or glossy, laminated menus. And, although available to those who asked, not that many beers or steaks. Instead of fillet mignons and french fries, long lines of powdered cocaine decked the counters and tables, and instead of sopping up blood from a side of beef done especially rare with a flaky buttermilk biscuit, patrons paid for the privilege of indulging in a marijuana cigarette or shooting up with a longed-for heroin fix before reclining in a comfy seat and letting nature take its course. Yes, Mr. Happy's Bar & Grill was a drug club in disguise; a secret sanctuary where an entire subculture of narcotics zombies could purchase the slow-killing poison of their choice at a bargain rate, then kick back and enjoy it without being bothered by anybody.

The proprietor of Mr. Happy's – just as colorful and as full of sin as the establishment's valued patrons – was a middle-aged man called Dirty Otis. This was the stage name with which he had christened himself some twenty-five years ago upon the start of his career in pornographic film. Like many of the industry's male performers, he had ultimately moved on to directing his own features, and his perfectionism, attention to detail, devotion to his fans, and pride in his work had made him one of the more popular auteurs in the business. (With the advent of DVD technology, Dirty Otis had seen to it personally that all of his archived works were restored and re-released on the new format, and he'd made certain to carve out the time necessary to add audio commentary and other bonus features to each one.)

Dirty Otis still directed regularly – churning out original works, as well as installment after installment of some of his best-selling series, which included but were by no means limited to the *Father Knows Breast* series, the *JurASSic Park* series, the *Dennis the Ass-Raping Menace* series, and the award-winning line of *One, Two, Freddy's Cumming For You* horror spoofs – but he no longer played an actor's role. Some said this was because he had let his body go in his forties, while others insisted it was because he had become stricken with hepatitis. The prevalent Internet rumor was that all the cocaine and heroin he had used as a younger man had finally rendered him impotent, though this was pure conjecture and had never been confirmed.

The big, blond brute standing by the door was Tove, a muscular Scandinavian born with severe mental retardation, whom Otis, out of the goodness of his heart, had long employed as a bouncer. The man was brawny and intimidating, with dull eyes, a permanent scowl, and a low IQ of thirty-seven. He spoke only in monosyllabic grunts – and thus, never asked for a raise – and displayed no knowledge of the difference between right and wrong. He could not function independently in any semblance of a 'real world' environment, so Otis let him live in a small room in the back.

Unlike the ill-fated Cashbox Clyde, Otis had taken the path of least resistance when General Ramos had begun collecting drug dealers like butterflies, and had allowed himself to be absorbed by the General's organization. As a result, Mr. Happy's had become not only a spoke of the company, but also a regular stomping ground for Ramos' cohorts, and Otis had found the opportunity to strike up a friendly rapport with most of them, including the coolly aloof Max Shepherd.

With welcome assistance from his ever present walking stick, Shepherd entered the establishment through the front door, ignored Tove's grunt of recognition, and began making his way through the throng of junkies, stoners, and crackheads littering the floor and furniture like so many discarded articles of unwashed laundry. Shepherd could see that, as usual, business was good. Squatting and slouching in the dark, fitting themselves into any available corner and cranny, were people sticking themselves with needles, people sucking on bongs, people popping pills, and people smoking just about anything that could be smoked. People from all over the city had come in tonight for a cheap fix, and most of them were calm and sedate, zoning out on their own private, personal highs, although a midget off to the right did choose this particular moment to jump up onto a table, point his chubby forefinger towards the ceiling, and cry out, 'De plane, boss, de plane!', much to the amusement of his friends.

"Out of the way, degenerate," Shepherd snarled, using his good leg to kick the head of a prone patron lying only semiconscious on the floor in front of the bar.

"Hey, go easy, Max," Dirty Otis implored from behind the bar. "The customer is always right, remember?"

"Junkie scum," muttered Shepherd, who never used drugs himself, and held those who did in the lowest possible esteem.

"Well, it's a living," said Otis, checking his titanium wristwatch, then turning towards a microphone situated next to the napkin holder. " 'Scuse me a moment, but it's getting to be that time again."

Shepherd scowled disapprovingly, and adopted an at-ease stance next to a tall stool while Otis flipped the microphone's ON switch and cleared his throat loudly.

"It's midnight, ladies and germs!" he boomed to the assembled revelers. "Does everyone know what it's time for?"

"Whitewash!" the crowd, coming suddenly alive, shouted back at him in unison.

"What?" said Otis. "I don't think I quite caught that!"

"WHITEWASH!" the crowd shouted the word again, sounding like a *Wheel of Fortune* studio audience.

"Lemme hear ya *want* it! Lemme hear ya *need* it! Lemme hear ya *love* it!"

"Whitewash! Whitewash! Whitewash! Whitewash!" the crowd chanted, fairly bursting with anticipation.

"Then here comes the nor'easter!" declared Otis, at last satisfied with the reaction. "Let it snow, let it snow, let it snow!"

Otis' forefinger jabbed a button underneath the lip of the bar, and a huge neon sign reading 'WHITEWASH' sprang up from the floor on stilts to the accompaniment of numerous colored disco lights flashing on and the dense, deafening roar of Guns N' Roses' 'Welcome to the Jungle' belting ferociously through the crackly, but loud, stereo sound system. Then a huge section of ceiling over the center of the room opened up, and pounds and pounds of powdered cocaine poured out, like desert sand from a trap inside a cursed mummy's tomb, making sugared donuts out of the screaming, laughing junkies as they scrambled in rioting hordes, like children burrowing through a fresh snow bank.

"What a bloody, shameful waste," Shepherd grumbled, voicing not the first of many objections to this practice as he watched the lesser mortals wallow in their own futility.

"Aw, come on, Max," said Otis. "Y'know, this gimmick's been really good for business. Ever since word of mouth got around that we drop ten kilos of free coke on the crowd every night, I've actually had Tove turnin' people away at the door! Besides, the General is havin' us practically give the stuff away anyway. A lotta the other dealers have a problem with the low, low prices Ramos has been imposing on all of us, but not me! My bar's never been so full!"

"The General's methodology is far from sound, in my opinion," said Shepherd, his legs splayed two feet apart, both his hands resting atop his cane. "He gives himself undue credit for being Machiavellian, but he's an unbridled lunatic if ever I've seen one, and I wouldn't find it at all surprising if he ends up posing a very serious threat to this business I've been cultivating in his absence."

"Careful there, Max," Otis cautioned. "Even the walls have ears, y'know."

"It was *I* who built this, Otis, not him," Shepherd continued. "He languished in prison for three years, relying on me to make certain everything on the outside went smoothly. I orchestrated virtually this entire takeover! *My* efforts made this sprawling organization what it is today, and I say it's a damn cheek for him to think that he can just storm back in here after three years away and usurp all my control over this extremely lucrative industry which I'm on the verge of cornering! And it's an even greater insult when he shoots my superb business policies straight to hell by saturating the market with product so inexpensive that we're actually taking a loss!"

"Ramos said he wanted everyone in the city hooked," said Otis. "If that's what he wants, then I guess this is the best way to go about it."

"He ought to be struck down!" Shepherd snarled.

"Y'know, Max, it wouldn't kill ya to try to be less of a penny-pinching old Scrooge. I mean, you're doin' all right, ain't ya? How many thousands o' dollars did that nice suit you're wearin' cost ya?"

"It is not my own, personal income from this enterprise that concerns me," Shepherd sniffed. "My forays into various other fields have availed me of enough fortune to last me several lifetimes."

This was most certainly true. Not only had Shepherd amassed grotesque sums of money in banks all over the world, but these days, as a side to his criminal activities, Shepherd served as the Chief Financial Officer for Westley-Browne Foods; a Fortune 500 company with an annual revenue typically approximating twenty-five billion dollars, Westley-Browne was one of the world's largest processors and marketers of beef, pork, and chicken. The company commanded roughly one hundred and twelve thousand employees working at over three hundred facilities and offices in seventy-nine countries, with its corporate headquarters based conveniently in New York City. Enjoying the responsibility of overseeing the sprawling company's corporate finances, financial risks and planning, and record-keeping, Shepherd had been embezzling from Westley-Browne for years.

"My concern lies with the welfare of the business," Shepherd continued. "Yes, we are profitable, but competition is so fierce that we cannot afford any drains. If we show just one sign of weakness, our enemies will be at our throats and we'll lose everything before we know we've been robbed!"

"I've seen this a thousand times before, Max," said Otis. "I call it *Julius Caesar* Syndrome. Ever seen that play?"

"Of course I have," Shepherd sniffed, haughtily. "And how did an uncultured heathen such as yourself become familiar with it?"

"Now, Max, that's not fair," Otis frowned. "You know I don't like it when you stereotype me as lowbrow, just because I shoot porn instead of sweeping epics, and won my most prestigious award for *From Russia With Lust* instead of *Gone With the Wind*. You know damn well that I take great pride in my work, and it just so happens that I once directed a flick inspired by *Julius Caesar*. It was nominated for five awards by three separate academies, I'll have you know, and it came out so good because of the extensive research I did before going into the project."

"All right, Otis, I'm sorry," said Shepherd, somewhat sincerely. "You've been a good friend to me, and I didn't mean to offend you. What was this film of yours like?"

"It was called *Friends, Romans, Horny Men*, and I told the story from the female perspective," said Otis, always eager to talk about his work; that old, familiar twinkle of pride coming into his eye whenever he was asked to do so. "Instead of Caesar, I gave Rome a queen, and when all the senators finally stabbed her to death, they 'stabbed' her with their dicks instead of knives. I had ten dudes going down on one chick in that scene, and it almost won Best Orgy Scene of the Year!"

"Sounds quite stimulating," said Shepherd, emotionlessly. "Why didn't it? Win, I mean?"

"The trouble was that Best Lesbian Orgy Scene wasn't a separate category that year," Otis lamented. "They were all lumped together, and I got robbed by the sixteen co-eds all fuckin' each other in *Cyborg Sorority 7*."

"Ah," said Shepherd.

"Anyway," said Otis, "I was tellin' you about *Julius Caesar* Syndrome. Cassius wants Caesar dead, right? 'Cause he thinks he's better than Caesar. He thinks that if he could just get a shot at that power seat, he could do ten times as good as that chump Caesar. But what happens after Cassius and the rest actually kill Caesar? Everything goes straight to hell. There's corruption, a brief war, and by the end of the play, Cassius is just as dead as Caesar is. The moral of the story is, don't rock the boat and you won't drown."

"You know, Otis, there are times when you remind me, seemingly quite effortlessly, of how wise your experience has made you, and how insightful you can be," said Shepherd, fingering his cane handle. "Then there are other times, like this one, when you just sound like a complete idiot."

"Yeah, yeah, I don't know anything," said Otis, rolling his eyes as he produced a bottle and filled a glass to the rim with bourbon. "Here, have a drink and forget your troubles."

Shepherd said, 'Hrmph', picked up the glass, took two quiet, dignified swallows, then reassumed his scowl.

"How can I forget my troubles?" he lamented. "I'm up to my neck in them."

"Try not to sound so Jewish," replied Otis.

"The Harlem Hellfighters are the last bastion of resistance against us," said Shepherd, ignoring the jibe. "They haven't taken too kindly to our usurpation of their primary franchise – that is, the buying and selling of illegal narcotics – and have declared open war on us. For an organization of uneducated rogues, they don't lack strength and ability, and their reckless, continuous sabotage of our operations is becoming a worrisome nuisance."

"Y'know what else I hear about them?" Otis leaned over the bar to whisper. "I hear they've got, like, five tons o' the shit stored up in a warehouse up there somewhere. Barrels and barrels of pure, uncut, white gold!"

"I wouldn't doubt it," said Shepherd. "Harlem probably never foresaw an era that would see it jarred from its lead position in the urban drug trade. Little wonder they have such a ponderous inventory at the ready."

"Just imagine havin' five tons, all in one place!" Otis exclaimed. "I'll bet that's somethin' ol' Ramos would love to get his hands on."

"They need to be crushed," said Shepherd. "Decisively. If our intention truly is to corner the market, then the Hellfighters must be the next ones to go. There will be no cooperation, no peaceful coexistence with stubborn brutes such as they. They'll reoccur, like a painful rash, continuing to jeopardize and disrupt. If we are to flourish and prosper, then they must wither and die."

"And they're not the only ones," said Otis. "What about Gary?"

"Gary who?"

"You know who I'm talkin' about, Max."

"Forget him," said Shepherd. "He's a nobody; a negligible detail. He and his ragtag rabble of do-gooding outlaws are far too trivial to worry our heads about now."

"If you wanna get an idea of how many cocky bastards have said that before you," said Otis, "walk into the offices of any major metropolitan newspaper and ask to see the archived obituaries."

"You know how I feel about defeatism, Otis," said Shepherd, tapping his cane handle against Otis' left shoulder.

"You don't know him like I do," said Otis.

"I wasn't aware you knew him at all."

"We were casual friends at one time," said Otis. "Well, maybe 'acquaintances' would be a better word. We could take or leave each other in a snap, but it was better than talkin' to the wall, know what I mean? I shared room and board with him a few years ago, back when he was goin' through his bad patch."

"Bad patch?"

"Ain't you ever picked up a comic book? It's the same for all crimefighters. Something bad happens to 'em and they decide to take it out on the readily accessible street scum. I dunno what happened to him before he came here from England, but it fucked him up bad. Haven't even talked to him in years, but when I knew him he was crazy. He was always doin' real fucked-up shit like drinkin' window cleaner and wrestlin' with junkyard dogs. He got as close to the edge as anybody can without fallin' off, then one day he just up and disappeared. Now it sounds like he's gone back to his old ways, from what I hear on the street. Accordin' to witnesses, it isn't any black man who's been killin' our dealers and burnin' up our surplus. It's a white man with a Beretta, a British accent, and an attitude problem the size of Alaska. He was always a real psycho inside, and now he's got a raging mad-on for us, and no matter what you wanna say or believe, he's worse than any ten of the Hellfighters put together. With the Hellfighters, it's nothing personal. They wanna kill us because it's the right thing to do for their business. But Gary's a wild-eyed fanatic with a death wish, and he won't rest until every last one of us is in either a pine box or a six-by-eight cell."

"And I'm supposed to be shaking in my shoes, I suppose?" Shepherd scoffed. "Grow up, Otis. There are no monsters in your closet, the Boogeyman doesn't live under your bed, and Gary Parker is very little threat to a serious businessman such as I. Let him go on doing what he's doing, accosting muggers and carjackers and tying them to lampposts outside police stations. The future of New York belongs to our kind, Otis, not his."

"Take that up with him when you meet him face-to-face," said Otis. "Because he will get around to you eventually, and when he does, you'd better make sure your life insurance is paid up."

Shepherd didn't have time to further decry the efforts of vigilante crimefighters before the ear-splitting roar of a revving engine 'bbbrrrrraaaaappp'ed outside, and, an instant later, a man on a motorcycle came crashing through the big front window, yelling 'Waaaa-hoooo!', clad from head to toe in spiked leather, his face obscured by the tinted visor of his helmet. A Molotov cocktail left his gloved right hand and shattered against a long, red couch which burst immediately into flame, sending panicked junkies scrambling for cover, only to be cut down by a hail of lead blazing in through the broken front window courtesy of two big machine guns strapped to the forearms of a large, bare-chested black man.

"It's the Hellfighters!" Otis exclaimed, crouching down behind the bar. "Third time this week! Down, Max!"

Demonstrating impressive agility for a middle-aged man with a bum leg, Shepherd vaulted over the bar in one move and hit the floor at the same time Otis popped back up again with a MAC-10 machine pistol in each hand.

"I am sick to fuckin' death of getting that window replaced!" he snarled, squeezing the triggers, spraying bullets back at the big bruiser outside.

While Otis and the machine gunner exchanged fire, and countless stupid, dope-brained junkies bumbled into harm's way in their clumsy, misguided attempts at escape, the motorcycle guy continued his circulation of the establishment, rocketing like Evel Knievel from one tabletop to another, his spiked tires clinging to sheer surfaces and cutting the ankles out from under unlucky patrons, the heated blast from his engine stirring up the scattered cocaine into a blizzard. Tove chased after him, but wasn't clever enough to take advantage of the club's confined spaces and outmaneuver the invader. It was as the biker performed a neat trick, driving straight up the side of a wall and back-flipping down again to crush Tove beneath his wheels, that the third surprise came. A patch of roof over the bar exploded in a whirl of flame and splinters, and Harvey King, one of the Hellfighters' favorite sons, slid down on a rope, firing a Mini Uzi in any direction he happened to turn.

Somersaulting across the floor, Otis rolled out from behind the bar just in time to avoid being ventilated by King, and just in time to nail the machine gunner at the window with seven lethal shots to the torso. Knowing he was now in King's blind spot, Otis concentrated his aim on the biker, but the biker threw another Molotov his way, blocking him with a wall of fire.

"Barroom blitz! Barroom blitz!" the biker shouted gleefully, bouncing off yet another table and landing on his back wheel.

The biker didn't have time to take another fancy turn before a throaty, animalistic roar overpowered that of his engine, and the seven inch, carbon steel blade of a Ka-bar combat knife buried itself in his belly. Riderless, the motorcycle went flying off into a corner, and Ron Grimace, the muscle-bound wielder of the knife, screamed like a triumphant gorilla as he held the impaled, faceless biker writhing on the blade high above his head, the dying man's blood pouring down into the insane warrior's face.

"It's about time he fuckin' got here," Otis muttered to himself, searching for a position from which he could take a shot at the dangling King.

"What the fuck's all the noise out here?" Jimmy Jay demanded, finally emerging from the men's room where he had spent the past half hour shitting out the lower half of his digestive system. "My headaches are bad enough without all this!"

"Jimmy! Knife!" Otis cried out.

"Where is he?" Jay demanded, yanking a switchblade from his belt loop and flicking it open. "You know I don't see so good anymore!"

"Ten minutes past twelve, and six feet up!" Otis replied.

The knife flew from Jay's jaundiced, peeling hand in the direction specified by Otis, and cut cleanly through the rope to which King was clinging, dumping the jerry curled assassin to the floor.

"Seize him, Tove!" Shepherd commanded, regaining his feet now that the danger was past. "Grab that black fucker and bring him over here!"

Obediently, Tove picked up King by his shoulders, carried him over to the bar, and plunked him down onto a stool, and Otis found himself almost pitying the Harlem gangster. Max Shepherd was notorious for his vicious, hair-trigger temper – those who had witnessed his tantrums firsthand often referred to him as 'Mad Max', though never to his face – and Otis knew that anyone who angered him to this fiery degree was not about to have an easy time of the proceeding minutes.

His teeth set, his eyes fairly bulging from their sockets, Shepherd wiped a trail of spittle from his chin, took one giant step forward, and slapped King hard across the face. Three more slaps followed, administered with both the front and back of the hand, delivered so harshly that the man's dark face turned red.

"Try and bring *me* down, will you?" Shepherd snarled, his eyes crazed with hatred. "*I'm* going to win this war, not you! *I* deserve power and command, not you! I'll kill you, and any pompous, strutting, rank-pulling lunatic who gets in my way! You filthy, insolent, fucking little... *punk*!"

Shepherd dealt King's head a hard rap with his cane, then knelt down, picked up Jimmy Jay's switchblade, and handed it back to its owner.

"You know what to do," said Shepherd. "Grimace, hold his mouth open."

Grimace's strong, bear-like paws pried open King's jaws and tilted his head back while Jay stepped forward, rolled up his left sleeve to reveal his lesion-covered arm, and held it over King's face.

"Now, cut!" Shepherd commanded.

Bothered not at all by the pain – small in comparison to his daily ordeal – Jay grinned nightmarishly as he dug the switchblade into the underside of his forearm and cut a long, wide gash down its length, spilling his poisonous blood in thick globs all over King's frantic face and into his open mouth.

"That's the AIDS virus you're drinking!" Shepherd declared, watching with satisfaction as King choked and gurgled on the infected fluid. "Take a good look at this sick fucker here, because in a few weeks you'll look just like him! Now, Otis, get your trained monkey to throw this dumb nigger out of here!"

While Tove hefted the sputtering King once again and carried him towards the door, stepping over, around, and through the remains of patrons who hadn't made it to safety earlier, Jay closed his switchblade and tied a tourniquet around his arm, and Shepherd turned to Grimace.

"You're the muscle, you idiot!" he spat. "You're supposed to be here in case something like this happens!"

"Sorry, Mr. Shepherd," said Grimace, in a decidedly unapologetic tone. "It won't happen again."

"Where the hell were you, and what were you doing?" Shepherd demanded. "Look at yourself! You're covered in blood! That couldn't all have come from the jackass on the bike! What happened?"

"I killed some people I shouldn't have," Grimace answered, his deep, steady voice unwavering.

"Blast it, not again!" Shepherd groaned, slapping himself in the forehead. "Who the hell was it this time? Someone nobody will miss, I hope!"

"Bunch o' Deer Hunters," said Grimace.

"Deer Hunters? You brainless fuck-up! We *need* the Deer Hunters! They're one of the largest street gangs in New York, and we need them for distribution purposes!"

"Thought they were Viet Cong."

"There *is* no Viet Cong! It's all in your stupid, fat head! Look, are you sure all of them were dead?"

"Hacked 'em to ribbons."

"And there were no witnesses?"

Grimace shook his head.

"All right, good," said Shepherd, beginning to breathe a little easier. "With any luck, they'll blame the Cobras. With all our other enemies breathing down our necks, the last thing we need is a reprisal from those delinquent savages! But just you see how much farther you can try my patience, you oaf, because I grow tired of cleaning up your messes for you!"

"Calm down, Max," Otis implored. "Remember what the doc said about your blood pressure. I've got your pills right here if you need one."

"Just shut up! All of you! Shut up and leave me alone! I need to think!"

"Jeez, what a sorehead," Otis muttered, after Shepherd had thundered off. "He thinks *he's* got problems. Just look at the state of this place! This is gonna cost a fortune, I can tell already!"

"Get away from me, you stupid cat!" Gary growled, kicking at the stray feline that had found its way up to the rooftop of the Salvation Army store on Orchard Street on the Lower East Side. "I don't need your pity! I don't need *anyone's* pity!"

Walking the precarious ledge overlooking the avenue that had served the neighborhood as a major shopping strip for nearly two centuries, Gary directed another kick at the stubborn cat and almost lost his balance.

"And wipe that smug look off your face!" he ranted at the unresponsive animal. "Even at my worst, I'm better than you!"

The cat arched its back and hissed, but didn't retreat. Gary took a swig of whiskey from his flask, then spat it onto the cat's head. The cat yowled indignantly, and scrambled to the center of the roof.

"What makes you so smart, anyway?" Gary snarled. "You furry little bastards are always raving about how you're so much smarter than dogs.

Where the hell do you get off, anyway? Look at your cultural figureheads! Sylvester gets his ass handed to him by a canary, Tom can't even catch Jerry's diapered nephew, and Garfield's the poster boy for dangerous obesity! And who do the dogs have? The noble Toto, the faithful Pluto, the charismatic Goofy, that really smart one from *Inspector Gadget*, and Lassie, who's probably got even more brains than Flipper! You should be ashamed of yourself!"

The cat licked its paw and began to wash behind its right ear. Furious at the animal's conceit, Gary threw his flask at it, succeeding at last in driving it off.

"I *hate* this!" Gary screamed into the night, his face tilted up towards the mocking stars, his fingers clawing at them as if trying to bring them crashing down around him. "What do you *want* from me?"

Gary stomped to the center of the roof, retrieved his flask, licked the taste of whiskey from the rim, then turned slowly around in a full circle and recoiled at the sight of all the immense buildings surrounding him. His city dweller's heart had used to thrill at the tall monoliths of glass and steel reaching up from the ground to touch the sky, but they were no longer magnificent or awe-inspiring now that Gary could see them for what they were; mere piles of sculpted concrete and twisted metal, erected as a boast for those rich enough to find use for such decadent facilities. And now they seemed to close in on him like a grove of bowing trees or a ring of resting prairie schooners, making him feel trapped, stifled, and claustrophobic in the midst of what had been known for decades as the capital of the world. They were the fingers of an unseen giant, forming a cage for his body and spirit. They were the walls of the Forbidden City; inside their possessive embrace, one was as an emperor, but beyond the boundaries of this great and powerful island, one was as nothing. It was an exacting toll – one's soul for one's survival – but could it really be that way? Could it really be that Manhattan was the last stronghold of humanity, and that all outside that golden metropolis had perished ages ago? It sounded just crazy enough to be true, and Gary was in such a state of mind as to believe anything that sounded crazy.

"Y'know, I could get locked up for talking to myself!" Gary hollered at thin air. "Doesn't anyone else have something to say? Isn't there another contribution to be put forward here? Another voice to be heard?"

Right on cue, a shriek of terror – punctuated by the sickening smack of a clenched fist colliding with a soft, fleshy face – answered him from the dark, constrictive canyon of a dead end alley three buildings over, in between a sidewalk café and a Jewish paraphernalia store called Menorahs, Etc.

Danger, Will Robinson! thought Gary, his strong, athletic legs propelling him with ease over a narrow gap between his rooftop and the next. *It's always something, isn't it? Why can't they all just leave me alone?*

Gary reached the two-story high rooftop of Menorahs, Etc. in seconds, then crouched like an ape on the ledge overlooking the alley and stared down into the inky shadows helping to conceal what was surely an act of villainy, his eyes adjusting almost instantly to the thicker blanket of barely illuminated darkness. His probing gaze was met by the sight of two young toughs in gang colors – both black, one sporting a waterfall of dreadlocks down the back of his neck, the other opting for a smooth, shaved scalp – wrestling with a panicking, disheveled young woman. One of the punks pinned her arms behind her back and forced her down onto her knees while the second punk used his knife to cut away the front of her short dress.

A rape, huh? Gary rolled his eyes, his chin resting on his hand. *Well, that makes for a nice change of pace. I mean, I only stop about a hundred of these a day, right?*

The screeching of tires, followed immediately by an amplified, authoritative voice bellowing, 'All right, scumbags, hold your dicks!', pierced the nocturnal quiet, and Gary, the two punks, and the imperiled girl all looked over to the alley's only entrance to see a police cruiser freshly arrived at the curb, blocking the only escape route. A uniformed cop clambered out of the driver's seat, his right hand hovering just a few inches from the butt of his side arm.

Huh. And who says there's never a cop around when you need one? thought Gary.

"You fuckin' idiot!" Baldy cursed, slapping his friend on the head. "I told you he'd find us!"

"Fuck off, Gargan!" Dreadlocks, retaining his grip on the girl's wrists, hollered at the approaching cop. "This is a private party!"

Gargan replied by tearing his baton from his belt and hurling it through the air. The larger end struck Baldy's left temple and he crashed to the pavement, his consciousness doused like the frail, fragile flame of a candle.

"So, what have you boys been up to this evening?" Gargan, drawing nearer, asked.

"In case you didn't notice, pig, we're tryin' to get somethin' goin' here!" said Dreadlocks. "Piss the hell off!"

"Would you like to know what *I've* been doing?" asked Gargan, as if Dreadlocks hadn't spoken. "I've been spending the last three hours getting the shit kicked outta me by a bunch of dealers who can't find a market for baking soda!"

At this, Gary's eyes narrowed, his teeth clenched, and the blood of impassioned anger flooded back into his cheeks.

One cop in the whole neighborhood, and he's bent, he thought.

Gargan threw the plastic baggie full of Arm & Hammer in Dreadlocks' face, covering the punk with the stuff, then lunged at him, grabbing the girl around the neck and holding her with his left arm, and punching Dreadlocks in the gut with his right fist. Dreadlocks groaned and doubled over, and Gargan socked him on the jaw, dropping him to his knees. A kick to the face, and the next thing Dreadlocks knew, he was lying flat on his back with Gargan's foot planted firmly on his chest and the cop's handgun pointing down at the space between his eyes.

"You cocky little shit!" Gargan spat, his finger curled around the trigger. "Thought you'd set me up, huh? Is that what you were trying to do? Nobody fucks me, you little jungle monkey! *Nobody!*"

"Get off, man, get off!" Dreadlocks cried, squeezing his eyes shut so he wouldn't have to look at the gun. "I'm sorry, all right!"

"Damn right you're sorry!" Gargan shouted. "Open your eyes and watch this!"

Taking the gun off Dreadlocks, Gargan turned to the left and fired three times, pumping three bullets into Baldy's sprawled body.

"Holy shit, man!" Dreadlocks exclaimed.

"Now, boy, if you don't want that to be you, then get off your black ass and hold this bitch for me!" Gargan commanded.

Dreadlocks, freed from Gargan's heel, scrambled obediently to his feet and clasped the sobbing girl's shoulders while Gargan unzipped his pants and tossed Dreadlocks a pair of handcuffs. Not having to be told what to do, the punk snapped them around the girl's wrists.

"If she bites, hit her with that," said Gargan, pointing to his baton still lying on the ground next to Baldy. "If she's good, maybe I'll let you have the sloppy seconds. You niggers like skinny white women, don't you?"

Dreadlocks didn't have time to reply before an unknown hand reached down from above, grabbed the misguided youth by his long braids, and, with one mighty yank, hoisted him up into the shadows. A short scream of surprise, then a loud, sickening 'crack', and Dreadlocks fell back to earth, his body unmoving, his head lolling at an odd angle.

"What the fuck...?" Gargan wondered.

"Y'know, I don't hate cops," Gary, appearing suddenly behind Gargan, growled in the man's right ear, pressing the muzzle of his Beretta against the base of his skull. "Quite the contrary, I admire them. That's why I try my best to help make their job just a little bit easier. No, I have no contempt for your uniform, sir; just the man inside of it."

"How dare you pull a gun on an officer of the law!" Gargan rasped, staring straight ahead, unmoving. "Who do you think you are, you faceless, cowardly thug?"

"Protect and serve, isn't that supposed to be your motto?" asked Gary, ignoring Gargan's interruption. "Yeah. Yeah, I can see how this whole pathetic scene could be construed as you protecting and serving, right? Free the girl. Now."

Slowly, Gargan's right hand let go of the girl's arm and lowered itself to his belt, where it lingered just a moment too long next to his gun. Gary corrected the crooked cop with a sharp blow to the back of his head.

"You're not dealing with rubbish here!" Gary emphasized. "I could break your neck with two fingers! Now do as I say!"

Wincing with the pain now shooting through his skull, Gargan produced the tiny, silver key, turned the girl roughly around, and removed the handcuffs. The girl, tearful and nearly hyperventilating, screamed one more time, and retreated hurriedly to the relative safety of a row of metal garbage cans.

"Now what, Mr. Hero?" asked Gargan.

"Now we weigh the courses of action," Gary answered. "Obviously I can't turn you over to your own people. That badge of yours is a veritable 'Get Out Of Jail Free' card, especially if you're turned in by a civilian with no particular evidence against you. So, as I see it, there are two options. I can let you go, or I can kill you right here. Care to guess which way I'm leaning?"

"If you're waiting for me to beg for mercy, I'm not gonna do it," said Gargan.

"Suits me," said Gary. "Saves time."

Gary pulled the trigger, Gargan's head burst open like a piñata, and the girl screamed again.

"Put a sock in it already, you stupid slut!" Gary shouted at her. "For fuck's sake, have some composure! Hell, it's mostly your fault that all this happened in the first place! Look at you! You walk around this neighborhood in the middle of the night, dressed like that, and then have the gall to be shocked when someone actually responds! That's just like a woman! You say you don't want to be objectified, but deep down inside you're all whores, and what's more, you get off on it! You tease and tantalize, deriving your pleasure from the knowledge that every man who lays eyes on you will want you! Well, these three creeps here most definitely wanted you! Are you satisfied?"

Gary reholstered his gun with a snort, then turned his back on the hysterical girl and made for the alley's entrance and the idling police cruiser, whose radio had begun spitting static mixed with inquiries and commands.

"Car 32! Car 32, come in!" a female voice crackled. "Are you still in the Orchard Street area? A man over there has just reported hearing gunshots in the street, and we'd like you to check it out."

"This is Car 32," Gary flopped down into the driver's seat, picked up the radio, and spoke into it. "I've just killed one of your boys in blue. If you want a piece of what he got, I'll be driving around for the next hour or so with the siren blaring. Always wanted to do that, y'know."

Switching off the radio, Gary slammed the door shut, turned the key in the ignition, and stomped down hard on the gas pedal, peeling rubber off the tires as he took off towards Delancey Street, the red and blue lights atop his stolen transport flashing wildly to reflect the madness and confusion running rampant over his tortured mind.

Keith, the fat, odious little man who operated a weapons stall out of his gray Mazda hatchback, was parked under a lamppost on Elizabeth Street, sitting in his car's driver's seat, munching on a messy meatball-and-mozzarella sandwich, when he heard the tapping at his vehicle's back window. He cast a glance into his rearview mirror, and his eyes widened and he swallowed hard as he beheld the newcomer. It was a girl. A stunningly cute blond, petite – she couldn't have been an inch over five-foot-three – with fair, supple skin, and her short, flaxen hair braided into twin pigtails. She wore a pair of Daisy Duke cutoffs, a tight t-shirt reading 'Too bad you can't touch 'em, huh?', a pair of pink-and-turquoise flip-flops on her demure feet, and a bulky leather purse slung over one shoulder.

"Well, well, now," said Keith, clambering out of his car, dribbling tomato sauce down the front of his shirt. "Whose little girl are you?"

"Are you Keith?" asked the girl.

"Absolutely," said Keith. "And it's not my birthday for another month, but I won't tell anyone if you won't."

"I need a gun," said the girl.

"Oh," said Keith, visibly disappointed. "Well, you came to the right place, 'cause guns is what I got."

Tossing the rest of his soggy sandwich down onto the driver's seat, Keith bent down to pull the lever that would pop open the trunk.

"Quite a selection, wouldn't ya say?" said Keith, proudly, inviting his pretty customer to browse the display of pistols, rifles, and machine guns freely. "What's your name, honey?"

"Just call me Tomboy," the girl said, her lovely green eyes perusing the weapons.

"Tomboy? That's a funny name. I had you pegged as more of a girly-girl."

"I am," the girl explained. "My brother used to tease me about it all the time by calling me 'Tomboy'."

"Well, Tomboy, is there something specific you're interested in?"

"I just need a gun. Nothing fancy, nothing complicated. Just something that shoots bullets. And not too expensive."

"I know jus' what you're lookin' for, li'l missy," said Keith, reaching in towards the back of his display and producing a small handgun. "This here is a Smith & Wesson 317 AirLite. Pretty, isn't it? Made for someone just like you. They've taken to callin' it the Ladysmith now, as a matter o' fact. Eight shots, aluminum alloy, smooth combat trigger, short spur hammer, weighs well under a pound. I can let ya have it for five hundred."

"I'll take it," said Tomboy, already practicing holding it at arm's length and aiming. "Cash, right?"

"If ya please."

Tomboy took down her purse, opened it, and handed Keith five bundles of five twenties each, then dropped the pistol in the bag and zipped it closed again.

"Well, you sure do know your own mind, missy," said Keith. "Can I interest you in anything to go with it? I know how you ladies love to accessorize. Maybe a nice, fashionable shoulder holster? Or I could fudge you a carrier's permit if ya like."

"No, thanks," said Tomboy, slinging her purse back over her shoulder and turning to leave. "I'm only going to use it once."

After ditching the stolen police cruiser on the front lawn of a known member of the Green Party, Gary returned to his apartment – neglected and unattended for several days – to find the lock broken and the door ajar.

Great, he thought, yanking out his Beretta, cocking it, and kicking the door open. *This is just what I need.*

He heard noises coming from the kitchen; pots banging, dishes clattering, and cupboard doors opening and closing. It sounded like someone was looting the place.

Whoever you are, you picked the wrong night, Gary snarled. *And you'd better not be touching my Mr. Coffee.*

Not standing on ceremony, he kicked open the swinging door to the kitchen, and, upon learning the intruder's identity, found himself wishing for just a plain, ordinary burglar.

"Hi, lover," said Janet, leaning against the counter, her long legs crossed. "I've been waiting for hours."

"What the hell do you want?"

"Now, is that any way to talk to a gal? And after I got all prettied up for you, too."

Gary lowered his gun and blinked his eyes a few times, and now he could see that Janet wasn't clad in her usual ensemble of dominatrix leather. Instead his longtime enemy was uncharacteristically formal in a black, strapless dress that clung tightly to her every curve and ended several inches above her knees, with her feet strapped into a pair of classy, open-toed heels. She had further adorned herself with a gold necklace, a pair of diamond earrings, and a certain pleasant scent that reminded Gary of...well, some sort of flower, even if he couldn't pin down precisely which.

"Do you think I look nice?" she asked.

Gary couldn't deny the stirring in the front of his briefs.

"What are you doing here?" he asked.

"Word on the street is you've lost your mind," Janet smiled. "When I heard, I thought maybe you'd finally let your real self out. I thought maybe there'd be a chance for us."

"I've no idea what you're talking about."

"Oh, do stop playing these games, Gary," Janet shook her head. "We know each other too well for that kind of messing about. You know just as well as I do that our relationship has always had that underlying tone; that special potential. And now that you've embraced your dark side – now that you've finally come to accept that which I always knew was inevitable – now we can at least give it a try. Now, sit down. I'm making us an early breakfast."

Gary, nonplussed, felt he had no choice but to sit down at the table while Janet turned back to face the stove, atop which a frying pan full of beaten egg, sliced cheddar cheese, and chopped green pepper simmered. On a second burner was a pan of sizzling bacon, and on a third was a pan of pancake batter, already browning.

"Y'know, you really don't look after yourself properly, hon," said Janet, using a spatula to turn over the omelet. "I had to go buy all this stuff myself. Betcha didn't know I could cook, did you? Well, I took the class, just like every other girl in school. After all, if my parents weren't going to feed me, then I had to do it myself."

"Your father went to prison when you were six months old and your mother was a whore," said Gary.

"That's what I mean," said Janet. "You like your bacon really crispy, right?"

"Janet, this is crazy."

"Is it? I wonder."

While Gary shook his head and rubbed his right temple, Janet turned off all the burners, and used the spatula to heap the omelet, bacon, and pancakes onto two plates, then set the plates down on the table and went to the refrigerator.

"I thought the occasion called for more than just orange juice," she said, producing a chilled bottle of *Chablis* '96 and two long-stemmed wine glasses. "They say you're supposed to drink it cool, not cold, so I only left it in there for a couple of hours. And the guy I stole it from said it was a really good year."

"You seem to be trying awfully hard," Gary commented.

"This is how normal couples do things," replied Janet, finally taking her seat next to Gary as she poured the wine. "I made breakfast, so you can buy us dinner someplace nice."

For the first time in days, Gary actually felt a smile tugging at the corner of his mouth.

"Janet, you are undoubtedly the most..."

"Eat your nice food before it gets cold," she said, spearing a piece of pancake with her fork. "I didn't slave over a hot stove so that you could go hungry. For goodness sake, get something nourishing inside you. You look like shit."

Gary shook his head again, this time in surrender to the whimsy of the bizarre situation, and scooped a forkful of the runny omelet into his mouth. After chewing it for just a second, he realized with surprise that it was probably the best he'd ever tasted.

"Do you like it?" she asked.

"I can't believe it," he replied.

"Y'know, it was always meant to be this way," she said, setting down her fork and putting a hand to Gary's left cheek. "Written in stone. Just you and me against the world."

"I think you might be right," said Gary.

"Tell me you love me, Gary," Janet whispered, as she nibbled on his earlobe. "I know you love me, but I need to *hear* it. Tell me you love me, Gary."

"I do love you," said Gary, huskily, gripping Janet by her bare shoulders and pulling her in close. "I love you more than I can say."

"No one's ever loved me before," said Janet, digging her long fingernails into Gary's back and scratching, as a cat will with its claws when it's being affectionate.

"I've *always* loved you," said Gary, closing his mouth over Janet's and kissing her deeply.

"I was your first," she panted, pushing her tongue against Gary's.

"My first, and my best," he replied.

The two fell out of their chairs in unison and became entangled on the floor. No longer desiring to restrain himself, wanting nothing more than to give in after thirty years of foreplay, Gary bit Janet's neck, and tore the flimsy dress from her beautiful black body. Janet gasped with pleasure and dispensed with Gary's pants with similar enthusiasm, and the raw, feral, unbridled sex that proceeded lasted for hours and hours on end.

> *At first cock-crow, the ghosts must go,*
> *Back to their quiet graves below.*

"He's really gone this time," said Charlie, joining his fellow Vigilantes in the Rat Hole's lounge early the next morning, the air conditioning at full blast to stave off the diabolical heat that pervaded even this level of the underground.

"I've tried to initiate discussion a few times now, but he won't confide in me," said Buzz, the only Vigilante present unable to see for himself the Theodosia Garrison verse written upon the wall in black, dried blood.

"It's Gary's type," said Peg, who had analyzed a sample of the blood taken from the second comma, "so, odds are he used his own."

"Well, we all knew this was bound to happen, didn't we?" said Carolyn, gazing into the soul of the macabre graffiti like an abstract oil painting. "I mean, Gary isn't exactly the most stable person in the world. All you have to do is look at how he fills his life; how he spends every waking hour of his time. His eccentricities, at times, can be downright spooky."

"Oh, stop trying to sugarcoat it, Carolyn," said Peg. "Gary's a great guy, and we all adore him, but we all know what he's really about. We all know that, on some level, he must be insane."

"Yeah, you're one to talk," muttered Zeke, a smoldering Marlboro protruding from either corner of his mouth. "By the way, are there any flowers left on your wallpaper at home or have you gone an' picked 'em all off?"

"Hey, I've got my medication, so shut up!" Peg snapped back.

"You guys are right, though," Carla sighed, her voice troubled. "I mean, he's had his problems in the past, but this time he's drowning."

"Drowning his liver is what it looks like," said Carolyn. "Surely you all must have detected a certain drunkenness in his countenance over the past several days."

"He fell off the wagon and landed hard on his stupid, self-indulgent backside," said Leeza, her arms folded disapprovingly across her chest.

"Last night I found him in the park, eating his gun and yelling at Lennon," Carla continued.

"The Marxist?" asked Leeza, raising a confused eyebrow.

"The Beatle," Carla clarified. "And just a few minutes later, he murdered a snitch. In cold blood."

"Which one?" asked Carolyn.

"Dickie O'Halloran."

"Aw, shit!" Zeke cursed. "Now I'll never get that fifty bucks back."

"He killed Edwin Bronson as well," Sushi spoke for the first time, "though he would have been more useful to us alive."

"Y'know what was *really* bad?" William chimed in. "That incident two nights ago when he beat up that woman who was carrying cocaine inside her baby's diaper. The 'real' Gary would never have done that."

"This *is* the 'real' Gary," said Sushi. "His cocoon has finally cracked. If you think this is something, you just wait until his new wings have dried."

"I don't think that's true at all," said Charlie. "Gary is one of the finest men I've ever met, and I admire him immensely. I can't believe it's the 'real' Gary, but what we're definitely seeing here, for some reason, is the 'old' Gary coming back to the forefront. Not all of you were here when this little garden club of ours was initiated, but this is how he was back then. He was mean, tormented, suicidal, erratic, and doled out executions to lesser offenders when a swift blow to the head would've more than sufficed."

"But that was six years ago, back when he was really pissed off," said William, who had been with the Vigilantes for only two years, but had heard stories. "I thought he was better."

"People like Gary can't always get better without help," said Buzz. "Help which he consistently refuses."

"Does anyone know what made him like this anyway?" William asked.

"He's always been quiet on that front," said Carla. "The most I've ever been able to deduce is that he lost a loved one to an act of violence. It's why he got into crimefighting in the first place."

"He really did get a lot better with time," said Charlie. "Leeza had him on some pretty heavy duty meds for a while, though. He was totally unpredictable. Sushi, tell 'em all about the thing with your sword."

"Oh, please, not that," Carolyn groaned, putting a hand to her forehead. "I get nauseous every time I think about it."

"What? What?" William demanded. "You guys are always talking about 'the thing with the sword'. I must be the only one here who hasn't heard this story."

"He came to me at his very lowest state," Sushi reflected. "I've never seen any man look so thoroughly dehumanized as did Gary that day. With a tongue that slurred every sad, desperate syllable, he bade me unsheath my *katana* and hold it out in front of me. When I did so, he threw himself upon it, and, my trembling hands still gripping the hilt, I watched in alarm as he slid down the length of the blade, his blood tarnishing the polished steel before dripping off and pooling at my feet."

"Holy shit," William gasped.

"It pains me to even think it," said Carla, "but if he's reverting, we can't have him in charge. He'll have to be made to step down, at least temporarily, for everybody's sake. Carolyn, you're our recognized second-in-command. Can you take the reins until this is sorted out?"

"Yes," Carolyn nodded, without hesitation.

"Well," a familiar, melancholy voice lilted from the direction of the Rat Hole's only entrance, "it seems as though I've been made superfluous."

Each of the Vigilantes turned their heads abruptly to see Gary leaning against the doorframe, his arms folded in casual disregard of the conversation he had no doubt overheard in its entirety, and they were surprised – but could not be truthfully said to be astonished – to see their temperamental leader sporting a suit of flimsy, imitation chain mail around his torso, metal gauntlets and boots upon his hands and feet, and a Phantom of the Opera mask over the left side of his grim face.

"Gary, why are you dressed like you're gearing up for an amateur production of *Spamalot*?" asked William.

"So, this is what all you fair weather friends talk about when I'm not around, eh?" said Gary, ignoring the question. "Stabbing me in the back? Taking everything *I've* worked for out from under me? Looking for an excuse to brush me off? Well, I've got news for you double-crossers.

This isn't a public company! The shareholders don't have the option of bouncing the founder from the leadership position!"

"Gary, it's not like that at all," said Carla, approaching him cautiously. "We just don't think you're feeling very well right now, and we want you to have a rest. And what's all this you're wearing?"

"I am Beowulf," Gary answered. "Anointed by fate as steadfast defender of the meek, slayer of the devil's children, and all-round personable fellow."

"Oh, for pity's sake," Leeza muttered, rolling her eyes.

"What's with the silly mask, then?" Carla continued to probe.

Gary smirked a macabre, ironic half-smirk, then put his left hand to his face and removed the mask, revealing a frightening mess of scratches, scars, and cuts beneath. His skin was red and raw, lesions were torn open, and even his gums on the left side of his mouth were bleeding. With his disfigured left side's stark contrast to his normal, attractive right, he did indeed look like the yin and the yang.

"Oh, my..." Carla drew back in alarm, her hand over her mouth. "Gary, what have you done to yourself?"

"It was inevitable," he replied. "For, you see, though I am Beowulf, I am also Grendel."

Possible dissociative identity disorder, thought Buzz.

"Gary, love, this is serious," said Carla, moving in close and taking him by the shoulders. "We need to get you some help."

"I told you not to call me that!" Gary shouted, transitioning from relative calm to fury in the blink of an eye, smashing his gauntlet into Carla's face, sending her reeling backwards.

"Gary, that's enough!" barked Charlie, delivering a subtle nod to Leeza, who disappeared quickly into the infirmary to retrieve a sedative.

"And you can go fuck yourself as well, John Henry!" Gary hollered at him.

"Oh, I *know* you didn't just call me that," Charlie frowned.

"I seem to recall a promise I made to you last night, Carla, concerning your ever rising up in defiance of me again!" Gary continued his tirade. "You talk a good mutiny, my girl, but I have the feeling that if I were to tear off that skirt and pull down that slutty little thong of yours, I'd find you don't have the balls to take me on!"

"Gary, please try to calm down!" implored Carolyn. "We're not against you! You have no enemies here!"

As if alerted by instinct, Gary thrust his right arm behind him and seized Leeza's wrist in his gauntlet's vice-like grip, making her cry out in pain as the hypodermic fell from her fingers.

"Uh-huh," he said. "And that's why you were all watching this conniving witch try to take me from behind, right? Y'know, it's true what she said last night! It really is just me and her against the world!"

Gary squeezed harder, and the bone in Leeza's arm – freshly healed from the incident two months ago that had led to its breaking – snapped loudly, dropping the elderly woman to her knees in agony. Gary kicked her out of his way with the pointed toe of his steel boot, then turned once again to face the others.

"Let that be a lesson to the rest of you!" he declared. "Your brute strength won't help you against me, you big ape, and the Jap's fancy ninja techniques are useless! And you, Carolyn! Not even in your wildest dreams are you capable of creating a weapon powerful enough to halt me in my tracks! I'm still the sheriff around here, and anyone who feels like disputing that fact can take it up with me personally! Now, if you'll all excuse me, I'm off to East Broadway for a brunch date. Shalom!"

"Jeez, what a fuckin' loony," Zeke whistled, after Gary's flamboyant departure.

"My arm," Leeza moaned through clenched teeth, cradling the crippled limb against her chest. "It's broken."

"Sushi, William, help Leeza see to that arm," Carolyn ordered, assuming her new rank without delay. "Honestly, I can't believe he did that. And, Zeke, get a sponge and a bucket of hot water and scrub the blood off that wall."

"Why should *I* have to scrub the blood off the wall?" Zeke protested. "Why can't someone else scrub the blood off the wall? Why am *I* always the grunt? Why am *I* always given the menial tasks to do around here?"

"Because it's what you're good for," Carolyn replied, curtly. "Get on with it."

"Everyone knows why Gary chose you for his backup," Charlie said quietly to Carolyn, approaching her for a discreet word, while Zeke stomped like a surly child over to the sink. "Your intelligence, leadership ability, and cool head do you credit. But I'm still very worried here. I mean, if Gary could break Leeza's arm just 'cause he was angry, then what's he been doing to complete strangers?"

"I haven't shared this thought with the others," said Carolyn, "but I feel I can tell you. Anticipating for several days that I might be asked to step up to the plate, I've been keeping my ear very close to the ground, and from what I've heard, Gary's become one of the most violent and unpredictable offenders out there at the moment, though we can thank our lucky stars he's still exercising his wrath exclusively against criminals. If he should ever turn on innocent people, however..."

"Like he just did with Leeza," said Charlie.

"Right," Carolyn continued. "Then we'd have no choice but to take him down ourselves. And, as he's quite right in pointing out that not a one of us – not even you or Carla or Sushi – is capable of overpowering him, I fear a crushing amount of lethal force might end up being our only option."

"Either that or putting him in a wheelchair for the rest of his life," said Charlie, "which, for someone like Gary, is a fate even worse than death."

"It's not easy to think about, I know," Carolyn sighed, rubbing her right temple. "Believe me, I've been thinking about it almost nonstop for the past week."

"I have faith in his better nature," said Charlie. "He's in a bad spot right now, but everything I know about him tells me he'll bounce back soon."

"Hey, what're you guys talking about?" asked Peg.

"Just the ongoing drug problem," said Carolyn, shooting Charlie a sideways glance. "Carla, you said you picked up a juicy piece of information last night, didn't you?"

"As a matter of fact, I think I know who's behind this recent flooding of the drug market," said Carla, massaging her sore jaw. "Dickie O'Halloran said it was the General."

"General Ramos?" said Charlie. "But he's in jail."

"Actually, he got out a few weeks ago," said Carla, her hands on her hips.

"I remember Ramos," said Carolyn. "Very ambitious, with lots of resources. I have no trouble believing that he could have been orchestrating this whole narcotics revival right from his jail cell. And it makes sense, too. Being in the entourage of one man would explain the increased organization and efficiency displayed of late by the city's dealers."

"So we'll run with that idea for now," said Carla. "After all, we've got to clean up this cruddy mess somehow. It's already getting so you can't walk down the street without some space cadet puking on you. Drugs'll always be a problem in a city like this, but taking the General out of the picture will at least put things back to abnormal."

"And in the meantime, what are we going to do about Gary?" Charlie inquired of Carolyn, following her through the laboratory and into her workshop as the meeting adjourned.

"Remember that old Reagan campaign ad?" she replied, making a beeline for her cluttered workbench. "The one with the bear?"

"Vividly," said Charlie, recalling the metaphorical propaganda. "Some say the bear is tame, while others say it's dangerous, and no one can really be sure who's right."

"So," said Carolyn, hefting a heavy grenade launcher and plunking it into Charlie's arms, "doesn't it make sense to be just as strong as the bear?"

One of the many towering edifices of glass and steel ruling over the north side of Wall Street, the seventy-story Westley-Browne Foods building scraped the sky as New York City's sixth tallest monolith, and, despite its tiered upper structuring, went a long way towards providing a canopy for the lush Financial District, blocking out the sun with effectiveness equal to that of a ceiling of vast, green vegetation spread out across the rafters of a rainforest.

Inside the manmade mountain, the entire fifty-eighth floor – a veritable beehive of activity buzzing around corner offices, overworked photocopiers and paper shredders, and mazes of cubicles – belonged to CFO Max Shepherd, and all of the men and women toiling on this level of the gargantuan corporate machine answered directly to him. This included Krystal Harris, Shepherd's personal secretary – capable of typing sixty words per minute and taking shorthand at the rate of spoken language – who had just activated her computer's screensaver and strolled down the corridor to the employees' lounge for her twenty minute coffee break, as she did every morning at precisely four minutes past eleven.

"Hi, Krystal," said Helen, a fellow secretary who worked for one of Shepherd's assistants, waving cheerily from the leather couch in the corner, next to the tall rubber plant in the brass pot. "What's the glad word this morning?"

"Not much at all, really," Krystal sighed, filling a Styrofoam cup at the coffee machine before joining Helen on the couch. "The boss is even crankier than usual today. I'm telling you, girl, it's no picnic being the sounding board standing between 'Mad' Max and the rest of this crazy world."

"I admit I don't envy you," said Helen, taking a sip from her cup and re-crossing her legs. "Mine may grab a handful of my ass every chance he gets, but at least he doesn't shout."

"Oh, I get my fair share of that, too," said Krystal. "Even when he's angry, he still finds time to prod me. Sometimes I go home with so many bruises, I feel like an overripe cantaloupe."

"Y'know what really bugs me?" said Helen. "When they pretend they're reaching for something and they brush their forearms across our breasts. I mean, like we're really supposed to not notice that, right?"

"It's the complimentary shoulder massage I dread," said Krystal. "You're just going along, doing your job and minding your own business, when you hear him say, 'You look awfully tense.' Next thing you know, he's towering behind you, grinding his hands into your shoulders and stealing glances down the front of your blouse."

"You could always file sexual harrassment," suggested Helen.

"That wouldn't stop him," Krystal lamented, taking her first drink of coffee, now suitably cooled. "The man's a force of nature. Y'know that old story about how Pecos Bill lassoed a cyclone, pulled it to earth, and rode it like a bucking bronco? Well, Shepherd's the cyclone all right, but in his version of the story he threw poor old Bill to the ground and stomped him to death."

"Speaking of forces of nature," Helen's eyes lit up, "how's that incredibly gorgeous boyfriend of yours? Has he gotten tired of you yet, and does he go for white women?"

"Charlie's just fine!" Krystal laughed for the first time that morning. "And don't get any ideas, girl, because that man is mine!"

"I remember when he came here to pick you up that one day," said Helen. "My word, the size of him! I swear I could see my reflection in his biceps!"

"Helen..."

"I'll bet he's really fantastic in bed, right?" Helen continued to press. "Seriously, he must be hung like a fire hose! He probably has to put it down one pant leg!"

"Helen!"

"Well, I'm only speaking to reason!" said Helen. "I mean, just look at him! The physics speak for themselves!"

"Sometimes I wonder why I tell you anything at all," said Krystal.

"Miss Harris!" a familiar voice bellowed from the corridor. "Miss Harris, where in blazes are you?"

"Your destiny's calling," said Helen.

"Miss Harris!" Max Shepherd shouted, his face flushed vermilion as he stormed into the lounge. "What the devil are you doing in here, sitting on your duff and gossiping when there's a stack of papers a mile high sitting on your desk? And that spreadsheet still isn't finished! What are you being paid for, woman? I ought to have you replaced with one of the cleaning ladies! At least they're not averse to rolling up their sleeves and doing a little good old-fashioned work!"

"But it's just my coffee break, Mr. Shepherd," said Krystal, doing her best to maintain an even tone.

"When I was starting out, we didn't have coffee breaks!" Shepherd spat, banging his cane on the couch arm, making both Krystal and Helen jump. "If I don't see you back in your chair in two minutes, you're fired!"

Shepherd spun on his heel and began limping back towards the open door again when he seemed to suddenly remember something and whirled back to face his long suffering secretary.

"Oh, and about the coffee mug on your desk," he said. "The one that says, 'I used up all my sick days, so I called in dead.' "

"Yes, sir," said Krystal. "I keep my extra pens in it."

"Not anymore," said Shepherd. "I dashed it to pieces at the bottom of your wastebasket."

"What? Why did you do that?" asked Krystal, rising to her feet.

"Because it reflects poorly upon this company in general and upon me in particular!" Shepherd shouted, hitting the couch arm again. "Westley-Browne Foods is a happy place to work, Miss Harris! A happy place! I'll not have any negative propaganda casting dark clouds over our friendly, comfortable work environment!"

"But, Mr. Shepherd..."

"And when I tell you to do something, I don't expect to be subjected to any of your tiresome female backtalk! I expect you to do what your ancestors did when mine gave them an order! Bow your head, shuffle your feet, and say 'Yessuh, boss'!"

"Wow," said Helen, after Shepherd had departed, Krystal watching him go with clenched fists and teeth. "He must have said at least a dozen things just now that you could use to get him fired."

"What's the use?" Krystal sighed, gloomily, taking one more drink from her cup before dropping it into the nearby wastebasket. "Force of nature, remember? I'll see you later."

'Teddy' Callahan – so called by those who knew him because of his uncanny resemblance, in both appearance and nature, to a cartoon bear – was an obese curiosity of a character who owned a Coney Island seafood eatery called Davy Jones' By The Sand along the Riegelmann Boardwalk on the sun-drenched beach, where it stood to do plenty of business by the mass throngs of people looking either to soak up some rays or to cool off in the salty sea on a day like this when the big, brass ball in the sky burned down with enough energy to set the very air ablaze.

Though his air-conditioned restaurant was packed, Teddy himself resided – as he did on most days – in the private room behind the bustling kitchen, where he rested his ponderous girth upon a giant beanbag and consumed sticky honey straight from the jar while tapping his foot and bobbing his head to the lively tempo of 'The Teddy Bears' Picnic'. Approaching him now were two beautiful young women clad in bear's ears, paws, and tail – an outfit akin to the quasi-bunny costumes worn by Hugh Hefner's girls – called Pooh and Paddington, carrying a shiny silver platter between them, upon which rested a bright red, steaming lobster.

"Ah, yes, every teddy bear who's been good is sure of a treat today!" Teddy chuckled, salivating as he rubbed his fat hands together. "There's lots of marvelous things to eat and wonderful games to play! Come now, my lovelies! Sing! You know the words!"

Joining in the melodious revelry as commanded, the girls set about preparing Teddy for his gourmet lunch. Pooh tied a plastic bib around the fat man's neck, while Paddington set the lobster platter – along with a fork, a nutcracker, and a fresh jar of honey – down on a TV tray in front of him.

"Keep singing, my little cubbies!" Teddy laughed, unscrewing the lid from the honey jar and dropping a big dollop of the sweet stuff onto the lobster, like a scoop of vanilla ice cream onto a slice of blueberry pie. "I can't hear you! Beneath the trees where nobody sees, they'll hide and seek as long as they please, 'cause that's the way the teddy bears have their picnic!"

Foregoing the fork and nutcracker entirely, Teddy used his big hands to rip the lobster's tail from its body with one cracking, crunching yank, sending bits of shell and meat flying all over the place as he sucked on the open end like a snow cone.

"Picnic time for teddy bears! The little teddy bears are having a lovely time today!" Teddy sang while he chewed, his mouth full of lobster and honey. "Watch them, catch them unawares, and see them picnic on their holiday!"

"Nice to see you relaxing for a change, Callahan," said Sushi, sarcastically, having materialized without sound and now blocking the only exit.

"Oh, for pity's sake, it's the idiot in the spandex again!" Teddy grumbled, clearly put out at this interruption of his lunch hour.

"Lose the girls, Callahan," Sushi commanded. "We need to talk."

"I have no wish to discuss anything whatsoever with you," said Teddy, snapping open the side of a claw with his fork, "least of all during my private luncheon!"

"I want to know the details of your most recent deal with Edwin Bronson," the ninja persisted.

"Bronson was killed last night," said Teddy, swallowing a mouthful, noisily. "Everyone knows that. Hell, it was probably you who did it."

"Everyone also knows that you and Bronson were frequent collaborators when it came to your mutual benefits," said Sushi.

"I'm a legitimate businessman now," said Teddy, sucking the honey from the remains of the tail. "I've done nothing illegal. Who says I've made any recent deals with Bronson?"

"That flunky of yours who lives up in Chelsea," said Sushi. "Oh, he didn't part with the information easily, but in the end he favored keeping his fingers above keeping your secrets, and while he was packing his thumb in ice and groping for a tourniquet, I believe I heard him stammer something about a rather large quantity of potassium cyanide; a quantity measurable by the ton, if I'm not mistaken."

Teddy glowered darkly at his unwelcome visitor, then wiped a sticky hand across his rubbery lips. "Take a powder, girls," he said, gutturally. "Man talk."

Pooh and Paddington departed as ordered, and Sushi moved out of the doorframe to stand before Teddy, his hands on his hips, his feet spaced broadly apart.

"So, what about it, Callahan?" he asked again. "Would you like to tell me about the cyanide, or shall I fix it so that that goop you love so much is the only food you'll ever be able to swallow again?"

"You can't threaten me, you son of a bitch," Teddy growled, banging down his fork. "I'm not afraid of you."

"Yes," Sushi insisted, leaning in close so that his masked face was mere inches from Teddy's, "you are."

"Look, Bronson didn't tell me why he wanted it, okay?" the cornered criminal offered. "The fact is, I needed the stuff taken off my hands as it was, and I didn't care how, so long as I made my money back. Besides, when you're shifting a load like that, it's customary not to ask too many questions."

Sushi stared hard into Teddy's wet, brown eyes for a few seconds, then his nimble fingers picked up the sticky fork and twirled it.

"I shall ask the same question once again," he said, "and if you don't provide me with something a damn sight more helpful, I shall give you an amateur tracheotomy with this. Now, think very carefully before you answer, and bear in mind that just because I fight crime, that doesn't automatically make me a nice person."

"I tell you, I don't know why he wanted it!" Teddy tried to sound more outraged than nervous. "He could have been handling the catering for Lucrezia Borgia for all I care!"

"The largest chemical manufacturer in the state gobbles up three tons of cyanide and you don't even bat an eye?" Sushi growled, seizing Teddy by the front of his shirt and actually lifting the heavy man a few inches out of his chair. "That's not good enough, fat man! I want the *real* answers!"

"I don't know anything!" Teddy insisted, perspiring openly now.

"Then let me put it another way," said Sushi. "If you have no information, then you are utterly expendable, and there is no reason in the world why I should let you live to see another sunrise!"

"All right, all right!" Teddy relented at last. "Look, I'll get on the horn with the boys who handled the transaction, and reconnoiter with my usual contacts at Bronson's place, and see what I can learn about where the blasted stuff ended up! Is that good enough for you, you brute?"

"For now, I suppose it will have to be," said Sushi, releasing his grip on Teddy and turning towards the door. "I'll see you again tonight, at which time I'll expect you to have made progress."

"You know, it won't be like this forever, you dirty Jap!" Teddy shouted at Sushi's back, hoisting himself to his feet, thrusting out a damning finger, and knocking his food tray over in the process. "The status quo will change! It always does! You'll get yours, and I'll be laughing myself silly when you do!"

"Don't get so bent out of shape, Teddy," Sushi said, in his trademark over-the-shoulder manner, just before departing. "It makes you dribble."

Swinging the aluminum baseball bat like a major leaguer, the Red Cobra called Tash smashed to pieces the parking meter outside Augustine's convenience store on Union Street in Flushing, Queens, sending quarters exploding in all directions along the pavement. An elderly woman walking past with a brown paper bag full of fruits and vegetables stopped in her tracks and gaped, her mouth open.

"What you lookin' at, bitch?" Tash snarled, turning on her.

The woman gasped, clutched her bag more tightly, and took off running down the street as quickly as she could. Tash snickered, then turned to an admiring Leon.

"Y'see that? That's respect. Ya join the Cobras an' everyone gonna be afraid o' you. That what you want, right?"

"More than anything," Leon answered, like a good soldier. "I want that respect! I wanna shake up this lousy neighborhood! Jus' 'cause they out here don't mean they safe from us!"

"You got it right, dawg," said Tash, bumping his fist against Leon's. "You gonna fit right in. Now, you been runnin' with us for a little while now, watchin' how we do things an' shit. Now it's your turn. O'er the next couple o' days is when you're goin' through your initiation, see. Ya gotta do some shit, and if ya do it, you're in. I'm the guy who's gonna be tellin' ya what shit to do, an' makin' sure ya do it. Got it?"

"Jus' tell me what to do, and my ass is *on* it," Leon replied.

"I like your attitude, dawg," Tash chuckled. "That shit makes a nigga proud. Okay, check out that trash can over there."

Leon moved back into the alley, over to the metal trash can indicated by Tash, and lifted the lid. Waiting patiently inside were a sawed-off shotgun, a can of gasoline, and a humble cigarette lighter.

"You take that shit and you fuck up that store there," said Tash, pointing directly towards the open entrance to Augustine's, the store's overtaxed air conditioning system gasping its effluence out into the street. "Don't matter how long you take, but we ain't leavin' till it ain't there no more."

Leon weighed the shotgun in his hands, any nervousness he might have felt completely overwhelmed by the feelings of excitement and raw power now coursing through his veins like a drug. The very sight and feel – fuck, it even *smelled* good – of the powerful firearm intoxicated him with a new, unfettered freedom never tasted by the sad, pathetic peons of the system; those hapless, unimportant ants scurrying for their own survival, neither feared nor respected by anyone. Whether it was the white man in his ivory tower, driving himself to an early grave just to stay ahead, or the black man in his lowly ditch, resigned to doing society's dirty work, neither one of them could be said, from this moment on, to be more powerful, more significant than Leon.

Leon had never used such a weapon before, but he had had ample opportunity to observe the other Cobras making good use of them, and he was confident in his ability to wield it with equal finesse. So, with the gun in his right hand, the gas can in his left, and the lighter in his back pocket, the purposed young man charged into the tiny establishment like a stormtrooper, kicking over the potato chip rack and blowing a hole in the ceiling with the firearm.

"Awright, nobody move!" he bellowed. "Everyone just stay right the fuck where you are!"

'Everyone' was the Korean clerk behind the counter – who didn't speak much English, but was quick to throw up his hands in the universal gesture of surrender – and a middle-aged man by the ice cream treats who tried instinctively to make a run for the backroom. Leon fired the gun again, and the man's right knee exploded all over the frosted glass of the freezer case.

"I said *don't* move, motherfucker!" Leon, almost startled at his own assertiveness, scolded the howling, bleeding victim before whirling to face the terrified clerk.

"Heads up, Chinaman!" he hollered, before letting loose a third blast that disintegrated the cash register, sending its charred remains spiraling up into the air and clattering against the big front window.

A fourth blast destroyed the one visible security camera mounted upon the wall above and behind the clerk's position, then Leon banged the gas can down on the counter.

"Pour this all over the place or I'll blow your slant-eyed head off!" Leon commanded.

"*Chapi! Chapi!*" the clerk cried.

"Shut the fuck up and do what I tell you!" Leon barked, thrusting the shotgun barrel into the clerk's face. "Get pourin'!"

His hands trembling, the clerk picked up the can, stepped slowly out from behind the counter, and, shooting constant, nervous glances at Leon, began pouring the gasoline onto the floor.

"Get it all over the place!" ordered Leon. "Splash it on those shelves too! And hurry the fuck up! I ain't got all day!"

A fifth pull of the shotgun's trigger turned the slushie machine into a sticky, spouting fountain of red and blue, and the sixth and final discharge from the weapon brought one of the fluorescent lights crashing down in a shower of sparks.

"Ain't you done yet, ya fuckin' gook?" Leon roared at the clerk. "You better hope you can run faster 'an that!"

With a casual disregard that did his ambitions credit, Leon pulled the cigarette lighter from his pocket, flicked it to life, then tossed it underhand towards a puddle of gasoline that had pooled in a dip in the floor. It lit up instantly and set the whole store ablaze, and the clerk screamed in terror as he dropped the gas can with a 'clang' and bolted for the door.

"Wait! Please! Don't leave me! Help!" cried the wounded man lying on the floor.

After a second's hesitation, the clerk doubled back hurriedly, grabbed the man by one shaking, outstretched hand, and dragged him howling across the floor towards the exit, leaving a wide trail of blood behind. Leon, unconcerned, watched them flee.

They won't tell the cops nothin', he thought, proudly. *They'll be too scared.*

"Holla back!" he shouted triumphantly aloud to Tash, leaning casually against a lamppost half a block away. "Ya see that shit? *I* cooked that shit! Gimme some love up here for it, man!"

"Passin' with flyin' colors so far, dawg," Tash praised his recruit, slapping his open palm into Leon's. "Now, ditch that gun and let's go."

"Ditch the gun?" Leon queried. "But I ain't wearin' gloves, man. My prints are on it. Shouldn't I take it with me?"

"Bein' a Cobra means you a known offender, nigga," said Tash. "You gonna be walkin' around dressed like a punk, so everyone see you gonna know you bad anyways. In this game here, ya gotta have the balls to step up. You got the balls, nigga, or you just jivin'?"

"Oh, I got the balls all right," said Leon, throwing the shotgun into an alley without further hesitation. "I got the fuckin' balls, all right!"

"I knew ya did, dawg," Tash smiled approvingly, and punched his protégé on the shoulder. "C'mon. I hope ya know how to jack a car, 'cause we gotta get to Brooklyn. I got a special treat for ya."

The cocktail was a unique blend of three parts hard bourban and one part ordinary household bleach. Gary had invented it as a teenager, and, over the years, had introduced it only to his closest, most responsible friends, with the advice that they down it quickly – the taste really was as despicable as a hard knee to the groin – and in small doses, so as to avoid poisoning. He mixed one such cocktail for himself now, and handed another to Janet, for whom he had named the bitter drink all those years ago, and who was still sprawled comfortably on Gary's bed, her long limbs entangled in the disheveled sheets, her perfect body glistening with a mist of sweat after the hot afternoon's rigorous session of love-making.

Love-making? Was that what he and Janet had done? He supposed so.

"Wow!" Janet exclaimed, after knocking back the drink with nearly enough force to break her own neck. "This shit's terrific!"

"It took a lot of trial and error," said Gary, his eyes watering furiously after he'd consumed his own, "but I finally got the proportions right, so you get the kick of the bleach without committing suicide."

"Man's never-ending quest to escape his own inner torment really is an art form, isn't it?" Janet smirked, licking the rim of her glass. "I love your new look, by the way. The left side of your face makes me so wet."

"Kill me."

"Not yet."

"Why not?"

"Because it's what you want me to do."

Gary heaved a sigh as he sat on the edge of the bed, his back to Janet, his eyes fixed on the milky film on the bottom of his glass.

"You wouldn't have believed how readily they all turned on me," he said.

"Forget them," said Janet, wrapping one long leg around Gary's midsection and pulling him back down beside her. "I'm the only person in your life who matters now."

"Yes, I suppose you're right," Gary mused, thoughtfully, gazing up at the whirling blades of the ceiling fan.

"Y'know, we oughta blow out of here," Janet suggested, after a brief silence. "Pull up stakes and move someplace nice and private."

"Like a South American rainforest," Gary muttered, wistfully, "or a mountain in the Australian outback."

"Now you're getting the idea," said Janet, giving Gary's genitals an affectionate squeeze before alighting from the bed and heading for the bathroom. "You hold that thought, and make me another one of those drinks. I'll be right back."

Gary shrugged his shoulders in abject acceptance of the passing of his old life, then heaved himself onto his feet, glasses in hand, and made for the kitchen. As he passed the room's only window, however, a shrill cry of distress reached his ears, and he stopped and looked outside to see a young woman being manhandled by a couple of punks in the alley four stories down. The punks were grinning nastily, and the woman was crying and choking hysterically as her assailants slapped her face, pulled her hair, pinched her naked breasts, and played tug-o-war with her arms.

For what seemed an age, Gary stood rooted to the spot, gazing out the window, his eyes narrowed and his teeth grinding as he watched the attack unfold, a storm of indecisiveness raging in his mind. Finally he shook his head, then slammed the window shut and pulled down the blind.

None of my affair, he thought.

Letting her body weight rest upon the strength of her sturdy toes, her chin supported upon her right hand, Carla crouched near the edge of the flat roof of Avery Fisher Hall on the north side of the famed Lincoln Center for the Performing Arts and looked down with only casual interest upon the bustling crowds of normal people scurrying hither and thither across the wide marble plaza, watching them with the same unacknowledged envy with which a troubled child might observe a teeming anthill.

Lucky slobs don't know how good they have it, she thought. *I wish I could take the time to do some of the things they do. Why, they show three thousand performances here each year, and I've never even been to one.*

The fourteen acre complex did indeed seem to be overflowing with liquid streams of busy pedestrians swelling in from five streets and mingling in a collective pool of vibrantly colorful humanity, and everyone appeared to have someplace to go, whether they were waltzing elegantly to a theater or opera house to attend a show, rushing eagerly over to one of the many fantastic sights that just this tiny piece of Manhattan had to offer the spellbound, or merely passing through on their way to Columbus Circle, the Hotel des Artistes, or Central Park. One young couple wasn't going anywhere at all, but was just sitting on the rim of the large fountain, caressing each other's shoulders and kissing as the water sprayed behind them.

Oh, get a room, Carla thought, grumpily. *Yes, yes, we're all very happy you've found each other, but must you remind the rest of us of our inadequacy?*

With a sigh, Carla drew herself up to her full height and stretched her arms above her head before extending her right wrist, plotting a swift, aerodynamic course for the Museum of American Folk Art just across the way.

Hope Butch is in a friendly mood, she thought, just before firing her grappling line and stepping off the edge of the roof.

Butch McQueen was the large, masculine lesbian, as shapely as a block of cement and twice as hard, who managed the MegaHuman Gym on 66th Street, a mere stone's throw from the Museum. Now in her early forties, Butch had entered the wild and unpredictable world of women's boxing in 1986, and had spent her subsequent years in the ring going toe to toe with some of the sport's most awesome female talent. She'd clobbered her way up the ladder of opponents, vanquishing and humiliating them one by one, until she finally beat Greta the Grizzly in

1992 and claimed as her own the title of world Heavyweight champion, and she'd held onto it for ten prestigious years before ultimately suffering her own defeat at the hands of His Gal Doomsday.

The blood hadn't even been wiped completely clean from her bruised, battered face before she had decided to one day reclaim the belt, and she had been in rigorous training ever since, using the gym's facilities more often than any five of the regular members combined. Butch's obsessive dream of returning to greatness was what served as the basis for Carla's acquaintanceship with her, for in order to help finance what would be an expensive comeback, Butch had long ago attained a lucrative night job as a distributor for Salvador Ramos' organization.

As Carla threw open the big doors and entered the air-conditioned gym, Butch McQueen was right where the Vigilante had expected her to be; presiding over the middle of the boxing ring, shifting her weight from one big, booted foot to the other as she threw flurries of aggressive one-two punches at a pair of focus pads strapped to the hands of a much smaller woman, who flinched fearfully at every practice blow and even winced with discomfort as some of the stronger impacts vibrated up the lengths of her arms.

"Keep 'em up and hold 'em steady, ya little girly-girl!" Butch was barking at her sparring partner. "I can't hit 'em if they're flailin' all over the place!"

"Watch your footwork, Butch!" Carla, approaching the ring, advised. "Remember, you don't want your opponent luring you too far away from the center and into cramped quarters."

Startled by the new voice, Butch took a step too far, threw herself off balance, and clipped the smaller woman on the side of the head. The smaller woman yelped an 'Oof!', and collapsed into the corner, stunned, while Butch cursed loudly and turned to face Carla.

"Dammit, girly, I done told ya not to come aroun' here in them sexy leather pants," Butch scolded her visitor. "Breaks my concentration."

"Sorry," said Carla, hurdling agilely over the thick, elastic ropes and into the ring. "I know you're busy, but we need to talk."

"Aw, an' here I was hopin' this was a social call," said Butch, grasping a water bottle in her oversized mitt and squirting the revitalizing fluid down her parched throat and onto her red, sweaty face. "Don't tell me you're still with that goofy *Mission: Impossible* team, lovey. Awright, awright, what the hell is it this time?"

"I have a few questions about your moonlighting gig," said Carla. "You're in Ramos' network, right? I don't suppose you ever get to see any of the bigwigs."

"Nope," Butch shook her head, water droplets flying from her short, spiky hair. "I'm on my own out here. It's just like being a salesperson for any legit company. They send me the product, they tell me how much to charge for it, and when my stock is depleted they take their profits and I take my commission. Then they give me more to sell."

"Uh-huh," said Carla. "Well, there are lots more drugs on the streets lately, and they're a lot cheaper too. Even free, in some cases. The number of addicts in this city is multiplying by the day, and it's all stemming from Ramos' influence. Can you tell me anything about that?"

"Honey, if you're gonna monopolize my time like this, at least make it worth my while," said Butch.

"What did you have in mind?" asked Carla.

"You're a halfway decent fighter, right?" said Butch, kicking a ratty cardboard box full of abused equipment over to Carla.

"Well, I'm not formally trained in the boxing method," said Carla, "but I have seen all the Rocky movies, plus *Million Dollar Baby*."

"All I ever get aroun' here is fraidy li'l novices. Gimme a match so's I can gauge my current strength. If you win, I'll tell ya whatever ya wanna know. If I win, you eat me out in the shower afterwards."

"Okay, there's no way in hell that I'm doing that," said Carla.

"Then ya better not lose, sweetcheeks," said Butch, gesturing insistently towards the box.

My week just keeps getting better and better, Carla sighed to herself, bending down to reach into the box and extracting a pair of old, worn-out boxing gloves, duct taped in several spots. "All right, Butch, what'll it be?"

"Fight to a knockout," said Butch, as Carla laced up her gloves. "Queensberry Rules. No kicking, biting, or wrestling, and no blows below the waist." She smirked. "Not until afterwards in the shower, anyway."

"Uh...this isn't something you just happened to have lying around, is it?" Carla asked, holding a chewed-up, plastic mouth guard at arm's length between her thumb and forefinger, as if it were a tiny lizard she had caught by the tail.

"Oh, don't be so precious, girly," Butch rolled her eyes. "I don't have mono."

What a glamorous life I lead, thought Carla, sticking the guard in her mouth and assuming the conventional stance, her legs two feet apart with her right foot a half-step behind her left, her right fist held beside her chin while her left hovered six inches before her face. "All right, come on. Get it out of your system."

"Y'know, it's almost too bad," Butch smiled. "I sure do hate to mess up that pretty little face o' yours."

Without standing on further ceremony, Butch lunged forward and threw a jab at Carla's chin, but Carla stepped back and parried the punch, deflecting the larger woman's fist to one side. Butch threw another jab, then threw a cross punch for a one-two combo, but the Vigilante bobbed beneath both shots, weaved to the left, and came up inside her opponent's still-extended arm, and the burly woman didn't have time to react before Carla jabbed her in the collarbone, then followed up with a quick left hook to her liver in classic Spanish style.

"Nice moves, cupcake, I'm impressed," Butch lisped through her mouth guard, stepping back while keeping her left up. "I was gonna hold back on ya a bit, but now you're askin' for it."

Another lunge forward, quicker this time, and Carla felt her stomach catch fire as Butch's gloved fist found a home in the center of her belly. Then she let out a loud 'Owoof!' as Butch's other fist connected with the side of her head and dropped her to the mat.

"Ready to throw in the towel yet, princess?" Butch grinned down at her toppled opponent.

"The hell I am," said Carla, regaining her feet, glaring defiantly. "Tell ya what. If you can knock me down again, I'll be your towel girl until the day you get that damn belt back."

Butch feinted to the left, then threw a right, but Carla ducked it, bobbed to the outside, and jabbed the bigger woman on the chin. Butch shrugged it off with ease and hooked Carla in the side before the Vigilante could pull her defense back up. A one-two combo was quick to follow, but Carla slipped quickly left, then right, bobbing to the inside unscathed and delivering a sharp uppercut to Butch's jaw.

I had you all the time, big mama, thought Carla. *Not fun to be toyed with, is it?*

While Butch still reeled from the powerful uppercut, Carla thrust five consecutive punches into the boxer's thick, bulky torso, then dealt her a right hook that smashed clear across the upper half of her face. Butch screamed in anguish and crashed to her knees, one gloved hand covering her eyes.

"Ooooowww!" she howled, spitting her mouth guard out onto the mat. "Oooooowww! You little bitch, you knocked out my contact lens! It scratched the cornea, you little whore! Ooooowww!"

"I'm sorry," said Carla, with what could have passed for sincerity, as she took hold of Butch's meaty wrist and tried to pull her hand away. "But there's no way I was going to go down on you. Here, let me look at it."

"Don't you think you've done enough?" Butch snapped, pushing Carla away, revealing her blood-red left eye in the process. "Ow! Oh fuck, this hurts! Fuck!"

"Well, if you're gonna be a sore loser, the least you can do is hold up your end of the bargain," said Carla.

"You crazy bitch, I have to go to the hospital!" Butch clambered to her feet.

"You've got plenty of time," Carla insisted.

"Shit, I can't even see out of it!" Butch grumbled. "Look, I know just about as much as you do. Ramos is flooding the market with cheap drugs in order to get everyone hooked and put his competitors out of business. Why? Hell if I know. Sounds like good economic policy to me."

While Butch hastened to unlace her gloves and fumbled for a cold towel, Carla considered what she had just been told. Good economic policy? Could it really be that simple? A bid to control all drug activity in New York? No. No, that seemed just a bit too pedestrian for a grandiose lunatic like Ramos. Another scheme – a far more sinister scheme – had to be in play here.

Turning what seemed like a limitless number of ludicrous possibilities over and over in her mind, Carla unlaced her gloves and moved forward to toss them back into their box when she heard a 'crunch' emanate from beneath her right foot.

"Oops," she picked up her foot, then blushed, sheepishly. "Now, don't get mad, Butch, but I think I just found your contact."

"What a slob that Bronson was," grumbled Ramos, bent over a desk in the chemical plant's administrative office, throwing documents, charts, and computer print-outs in all directions. "No wonder he was killed last night. If a man fails to conduct his life in a neat and orderly fashion, then what sort of end can he expect? Plenty of the old spit-and-polish, Shepherd.

That's the key to healthy living."

"The popular consensus among our people is that Parker's outlaws are responsible," said Max Shepherd, guising admirably his annoyance at being pulled away from his important duties at Westley-Browne Foods.

"Undoubtedly," said Ramos. "And they'll be dealt with as well, in time. Meanwhile, Bronson's death, though untimely, is virtually inconsequential. These files confirm, as I already understood to be true, that he had already fulfilled his obligations to me. His part in my plan is complete."

"And may one inquire, General, as to the nature of said plan?" asked Shepherd.

"Shepherd, we've been over this," said Ramos, sternly, eyes locking with his subordinate's. "For the time being I do not wish anyone but myself to be privy to all the details. I have availed you of what you need to know, and that is certainly enough."

"With respect, General," Shepherd said through his teeth, "I am your second-in-command..."

"Still a very long way down from the top rung, and don't you forget it," Ramos cautioned him, thrusting out a forefinger. "Don't think I'm unfamiliar with the rumors, Shepherd. When it comes to gossip, prison walls are very thin indeed. While on the inside, I heard several unsettling stories about you getting ideas above your station; stories about you taking for granted rather more authority than I ever licensed you."

"Filthy, ugly lies," said Shepherd, his fist tightening around the handle of his cane. "I was merely anticipating your whim. That is, doing what I thought you, yourself, would do."

"Were you? I wonder. Do watch yourself, my friend."

Shepherd's outward visage remained one of calm obedience, but inside he was seething. Ramos' continued impudence was fast becoming too much to swallow. It was bad enough being subordinate to such an inferior man, but to be chastised and disregarded like some dog was an almost overwhelming affront to his sensibilities.

"Get Grimace in here and have him gather up these papers," ordered Ramos. "All of this needs to be destroyed before the authorities can get their hands on it. We'll take the whole lot back to Otis' pub. We have no further use for this place."

And I have no further use for you, thought Shepherd, turning his back on the General and hobbling sourly to the door.

Bubba Bigfoot's, easy to find on Harlem's main thoroughfare of 125th Street – christened informally by the locals as Martin Luther King, Jr. Boulevard – was a popular soul food restaurant with cuisine magnificent enough to draw in not only half the neighborhood daily for lunch and dinner, but also regular, non-black business from the surrounding area. Among the patronage of all colors dining within the four walls of the clean, kempt eatery was Jimmy Jay, hunching miserably next to a garbage bin, reaching inside with his bandaged fingers to fumble for anything that hadn't been polished off completely.

Someone likes it with a little too much hot sauce, Jay thought, tears stinging his yellow eyes as he tried to force a tidbit of rescued drumstick down his screaming, convulsing esophagus. *Yuck.*

"Hey, you!" an apron-clad waiter shouted from behind. "Yeah, you, man! Get outta here, ya bum! You're makin' the customers sick!"

Jay, his hideous visage enough to shock the sensibilities of any clean-living man, turned to face the waiter, who recoiled, taking several reflexive steps back.

"Shit!" he exclaimed.

"Yeah, that's the word I'd use too," Jay replied.

"I didn't know it was you, man!" said the waiter. "Just stay away from me, man! Stay the hell away!"

How tiresome, Jay thought, as the waiter turned and made a dash for the kitchen. *Perhaps it would save time if I just got myself a silver bell to ring, and a sign saying 'Unclean'.*

Wiping the back of his hand across his mouth – peeling a layer of skin away from his lips with the action – Jay moved to follow the waiter into the kitchen, alarming the busy chefs as he shambled into the clattering, steaming center of culinary activity.

"I'm here to see the Emerald," Jay rasped, trying to make himself heard over the clanging of pans and the hissing of boiling water.

"Get outta here, you sick fuckin' honkey!" shouted the chef who appeared to be in charge.

"Not until I see the Emerald," Jay insisted.

"Brother, you ain't seein' the Emerald anymore 'an we are, 'an we never do!" declared the head chef, defiantly.

Though his worsening condition had made him considerably slower on his feet, the virus hadn't touched Jay's inherent talent for resolving a situation quickly and with as little fuss as possible, and the head chef didn't have time to move before the long, razor sharp carving knife whistled through the air and impaled the center of his right hand.

"Let me see the Emerald," Jay demanded of the screaming chef, "or I'll come over there and rub that open wound all over myself!"

Crying and moaning, the chef tried as gingerly as he could to remove the knife, and tipped his head in the direction of a huge, upright freezer built into the wall at the kitchen's far end. Receiving and understanding the message, Jay proceeded uninterrupted to the freezer and heaved it open to reveal the interior of an elevator.

Nice to know I've still got it, thought Jay, pulling the door closed and pressing his thumb against the button marked with a downward-pointing arrow. *At least I'll be able to die with my boots on.*

After a journey of seconds, the elevator halted, and the door opened on a long, white, undecorated corridor illuminated with fluorescent lights set into the low ceiling. It took Jay over three minutes to reach the far door that was his destination, and when he at last arrived and opened it, he found what appeared to be a hospital room; featureless, colorless, and almost completely sterile. On either side of the door he had just entered was a man with an automatic rifle, and the pair of them now swung around to point their weapons at Jay's head. On the other side of the room, directly across from Jay, stood two more men, similarly armed, flanking the very thing Jay had come to see.

Between the two gunmen towered a monstrous, mechanical apparatus containing a beautiful black woman in her late twenties. Held upright in a perfect crucifix position, the girl's modesty was preserved by a purple latex bodysuit, while her hands and feet were encased inside electrical units of unknown purpose, and a spider-shaped device remained attached at all times to her upper torso, facilitating the continued beating of her heart. An IV tube providing all necessary nourishment fed into her right arm. Devoid as Jimmy Jay was of most human feeling, he couldn't deny a twinge of empathy for this stranger trapped inside the humming machine, totally reliant upon the life support it provided; this stranger who was doomed to forever watch the world go by from the opposite side of a protective shield of Plexiglas; this stranger who, like him, clung to every breath with the weakest of grasps. And he went on to wonder how in the world this girl – this fragile, helpless, immobile victim of a cruel, debilitating handicap – had ever managed to become the leader of the Harlem Hellfighters.

"Well, well," said the lilting voice of the Emerald, looking down at Jay from her higher position. "An intruder in my inner sanctum. And a member of General Ramos' merry band, no less. What could this possibly be about?"

"I come under the white flag of truce, my lady," said Jay, bowing his head respectfully, "in hopes of receiving fair monetary reward in return for some information I think your people will find quite valuable."

"The Hellfighters do not require nor desire any form of assistance from outsiders," said the Emerald. "Tell me why I shouldn't order these men to shoot you."

"Because if your men ventilate me with those rifles, then my blood is going to be all over this room," Jay replied. "My blood is lethal to the very touch, my lady. Think of me as Chernobyl. If I blow, then all of you will wither and die."

"You make your point," said the Emerald. "Very well, then. By all means, divulge this information."

"Our two syndicates are currently fighting a drug war," said Jay. "However, I am well aware that drugs are far from being the only thing with which your organization is concerned. There is also prostitution, for example. Quite a large ring, as I understand it. But you've been losing girls lately, haven't you?"

"I'll not deny it," said the Emerald. "And I'm sure you know why."

"The serial killer known to the public at large as Jack the Ripper," Jay nodded. "With his undying zest for turning hookers into dogmeat, your business must be suffering."

"And what can you do about it?"

"I can give you the Ripper's identity," Jay answered. "His true face is known to me, and, for an equitable fee – medication and painkillers aren't cheap, you know – I will impart this knowledge to you."

"I see," said the Emerald, a slight smile crossing her face. "Well, Mr. Jay, I'm sure we can work something out."

On the far side of the construction site that dominated the Brooklyn avenue of Court Street, where an ancient brownstone had been condemned and demolished to make way for the neighborhood's new strip mall, Leon groaned in pain and crawled on his hands and knees towards his switchblade, lying open and discarded near a frame of semi-hardened cement. Festooned with a roadmap of fresh bruises and cuts, the boy reached for the knife with his right hand, but was stopped short of his goal when a heavy boot stomped down hard on his wrist, pinning him to the ground.

"Ain't tryin' to leave the party, are ya?" snarled the big, surly, waterfront type standing on his hand. "We ain't through with you yet."

Snickering, the brute reached down, grabbed Leon's nose between his two middle fingers, and squeezed hard enough to make the boy holler. He arched his back in agony, and another punk – skinnier and shorter, but just as mean – rapped him soundly across the shoulder blades with an iron crowbar, forcing him back down onto his belly.

"Tash!" Leon gasped through clenched teeth. "Help! Please!"

"Hell, nigga, don't look at me," said Tash, leaning against a bulldozer a few yards away, his arms folded in complete, cold-hearted refusal to help. "Ya wanna run with the Red Cobras, then you gonna be up in the face of every major fightin' force in New York. That means cops, rival gangs, crime syndicates, and every vigilante group that gets it in their minds to make the streets safe from us. Ya wanna be a Cobra, ya'll gonna be doin' a shitload o' fightin', so I gotta satisfy myself you up to the challenge."

"This one ain't no Cobra," said the big thug, kicking Leon in the face with the toe of his other boot. "Just a worm."

Leon didn't appreciate that bit of criticism. His sense of self-worth was at a dangerous low as it was, and the last thing for which he was in the mood was a diatribe of abuse from a pea-brained bruiser whose teeth looked in need of a good scrubbing with a pad of steel wool. He wanted respect, damn it, and wasn't that why he had ventured to join the Cobras in the first place? He could do this. While it was true he knew nothing of expert combat, he was just as good at brawling as any other kid from the ghetto. He could do this!

The light of his newly discovered capacity for violence flickering into his eyes, Leon lunged for the switchblade with his left hand, snatched it up, and slashed a deep swath across the ankle of the big thug, who cried out in pain and crashed down onto his backside, howling. Able to move freely again, Leon jumped to his knees and kicked backwards like a mule, catching the other thug completely by surprise and smashing his right knee out of joint, sending him falling similarly backwards. Before the shrieking thug even had time to fully assume the customary horizontal position, Leon had already moved to exact a lasting, malicious vengeance against him, taking a final whack at his right hand with his switchblade, severing the unfortunate punk's forefinger.

Now the bigger thug, pressing on in spite of the severed cords in his ankle, lumbered towards Leon on the support of one foot, his dark eyes a raging storm of murder. Leon, temperance and fairness all nonsense to him now as adrenaline and lust for power soaked into his every pore, snatched up a nearby jackhammer, turned it on, and drove the jabbing bit through his foe's left knee, pulverizing flesh, muscle, and bone, and putting the brute down a second time, this time for good.

"Come see me when ya get outta the hospital," Leon said to the screaming, vanquished brute, "and I'll be glad to sign your cast for ya, bitch!"

"Nigga, that was hardcore!" Tash praised his younger cohort, giving him a congratulatory punch on the shoulder. "That was some sick, fucked-up shit, man! I didn't know you had all that! I'm givin' you bonus points for cripplin' his ass!"

"You'll do more 'an that!" said Leon, growing bolder. "Quit runnin' trials on me like some motherfuckin' lab rat! I want in *now!*"

"You almost there, dawg, you almost there," said Tash, tolerantly. "Ya jus' got one more thing to do to prove that you're really, really ready. And tonight, since you as good as in anyway, we all gonna show you the finer points o' one of our more lucrative business practices. I think you gonna like it."

The last several hours of the dwindling day had seen Gary on a citywide crawl from one disreputable saloon to another, and by the time the fiery orange sun had finally set – though the ever present heat seemed no less oppressive – he had hunkered down in a dark corner of Seymour's House of Ale on Lafayette Street. He had consumed four large glasses of Irish whiskey at this one establishment alone, to say nothing of the rich, diverse variety of spirits that had disappeared inside of him earlier in the evening, and he had more or less achieved that happy state of not yet being thoroughly numb from head to toe, yet not being quite able to make out his own hand in front of his face either. It was a holding pattern of consciousness that left him alert and aware, yet uncaring.

"To New York, the city that never sleeps," Gary mumbled to himself, raising his fifth glass to toast his adopted home. "It can't sleep, because it's a whore and it has to work nights."

The glass went to his trembling lips, and the amber liquid drained down his throat, and Gary could feel his gore and bile stewing in rebellious outrage. He figured the lining of his stomach must have been coming away by the layer now.

"How green was my valley," he mumbled, no longer knowing truly what he was talking about, "and how yellow was the ribbon I tied 'round the old oak tree."

Ignoring the odd, uncomfortable looks he was drawing from the people at the surrounding tables, Gary bellied up to the bar, empty glass in hand, and slapped his palm noisily down onto the counter.

"Barkeep!" he called. "Time for a little visit from my old friend, Mr. Jack Daniel's, right? Gotta wash this Irish piss outta my mouth."

"I think you've had enough, fella," said the bartender.

"Not nearly," Gary replied, pushing his glass forward. "Fill 'er up."

"No can do, pal," the bartender shook his head. "This ain't that kinda place. You wanna get completely shit-faced, you'll have to do it somewhere else. Here you're cut off."

Now any pretense of amiability or social grace vanished from Gary's countenance like a puff of evaporated steam, and his left hand reached over the bar to grab the bartender by the front of his shirt and pull him forwards.

"My money's just as green as anyone else's," he growled, dangerously. "This is the last time I'm going to ask you nicely. If you continue to fuck with me, the bad man is going to come out." He used his right hand to pull open his jacket, giving the bartender a glimpse of his holstered Beretta. "Get the picture?"

By this time, patrons had begun shrinking away from what appeared sure to become the center of something very unpleasant, and two civic-minded individuals were approaching Gary cautiously from behind, intent on keeping the situation from escalating out of control.

"Come on, buddy, let's not have any trouble," said one of the men, closing in on Gary's left side, while the other took his right. "Why don't you sit down with us, and we'll call you a cab."

The men weren't small – they both stood about six feet tall and probably weighed over two hundred pounds – but it was a matter of little effort for Gary to seize them with either hand, hoist them off their feet, and throw them bodily across the room. One of the men smashed into an empty table by the restrooms, and the other crashed into the jukebox, which responded by bursting into a chorus of 'School's Out'.

"Anyone else?" Gary asked the room, his eyes, though hazy with the fog of poison, illuminated by an eerie, distant fire that burned with altogether inhuman zealotry.

No one moved to challenge him, so Gary cleared his throat, adjusted his genitals, and headed for the door, thinking it prudent to depart before the bartender got on the horn with the police.

I know when I'm not wanted, he thought, strolling casually out into the night. *I don't need a ton of bricks to fall on me.*

"Hey, there you are!" exclaimed Janet, swinging like an orangutan down from the roof of the neighboring shop. "You ran out on me, buster! But I knew I'd find you eventually, so long as I kept following the trail of puke stains and property destruction."

"Can't you leave me alone for just five minutes?" Gary groused. "A man needs time to himself. He can't spend every hour of every day being smothered by the attentions of some clingy, hen-pecking female."

"Well, I like that," Janet glared at him, her hands on her hips. "Here I am doing my damnedest to accommodate you and make you feel comfortable, giving you all my love and attention, holding your head above water when everyone else in this big, shitty world would just as soon watch you drown, and all you can do is stand there, sloshed as you are, and call me a nag!"

Gary was about to respond with something quite clever and cutting when a loud 'clang' off to his right turned his head towards the apartment building across the way, and he saw a teenage boy in blue jeans and a hooded sweatshirt clambering out of a fifth story window and onto the fire escape. Slung over his shoulder was a burlap sack filled with four or five small appliances, and he was chuckling to himself.

As if by automatic reflex, Gary flew with the swiftness of the winged Mercury to the fire escape, and reached the fifth story with three vaulting, vertical leaps that any circus performer would have envied, his drunkenness no handicap in the face of his extraordinary physical talent. Swinging up through the bars of the iron scaffolding, the Vigilante somersaulted to a perfect ten-point landing directly in front of the kid and kicked him hard in the chest, knocking him back against the safety rail behind him.

"Just what the fuck do you think you're doing?" he snarled at the adolescent thief sitting startled and winded against the safety rail. "What the fuck is going on here?"

While the kid struggled to catch his breath, Gary snatched up the sack, turned it over, and dumped its contents out onto the metal walkway. There was a toaster, two DVD players, a laptop computer, and a small TV.

"Oh, yes, that's very clever!" Gary growled, seizing the kid by the front of his sweatshirt and hoisting him to his feet. "Very clever indeed! A commendable night's work! Should fetch you about two hundred bucks at any decent pawn shop! You little shit, what the hell is your problem?"

"Hey, man, what's up?" the kid asked, nervously. "I'm just tryin' to score a little swag! I ain't botherin' you!"

"You're damned right you're bothering me!" Gary snarled, giving the kid a hard shove into the safety rail. "You're bothering me more than anyone I've met today! Y'know, I meet people like you all the time! And do you know what I do to these people when I meet them? I *kill* them!"

"That's right, kill the little wanker!" Janet, having finally caught up, smiled as she bounded up to join the fray, her eyes alight as her addiction to senseless violence resurfaced. "Dash him to the ground!"

Gary lunged forward to grab the kid by the chin, and the kid screamed as the Vigilante bent him backwards over the rail.

"One little push from me is all it would take to end your worthless life!" Gary continued. "Why shouldn't I do it? Why shouldn't I give you that final shove and laugh at you as you fall?"

"So get on with it already!" Janet pressed.

"No! Please! Don't kill me, man!" the kid begged, his arms flailing helplessly.

"Why not?" Gary asked. "You've obviously already made the decision to chuck your life into the gutter! What makes you so deserving of a second chance? What's so special about you? What separates you from the rest of us?"

"Please! I'm only seventeen!"

"So you're young! Does that make you any less despicable?"

"*I'll* push him if you like," Janet volunteered.

"Please! Please!" the kid was crying now, tears streaming down his pimply face.

"Your youth isn't a free pass to do whatever the hell you want, y'know!" Gary raged, his red face just centimeters from the kid's. "You can't do things like this! Don't you see that you can't do things like this? You don't have the *right*! You don't have the right to just storm into another person's life and turn it upside-down, robbing them of their security; of their happiness; of their prerogative to go about living their lives without becoming prey for disgusting vermin like you!"

"I'm sorry!" the kid wailed, utterly broken. "I'm sorry, okay! I'll put it all back! Just don't kill me, man! Please, please don't kill me! Please!"

Exhaling a series of guttural growls, Gary glared at the terrified kid for a few seconds more, then – much to Janet's dismay – pulled him back from his precarious position and dropped him to his knees on the walkway.

"Get it through your head, kid!" Gary leered at him, his own clenched fists trembling with anxiety. "You're going to die if you keep this course! D'you understand? You're going to *die*!"

"I understand! I understand!" the kid sobbed, groveling at Gary's feet.

"You *must* understand!" Gary insisted, almost pleading. "I'm telling you this because I want to *help* you! All I've *ever* wanted to do is help people! I *never* wanted to turn into what I am now!"

Before the kid even dared look up again, Gary had already gone, his tormented spirit vanished into the darker recesses of the immense beast that was one of the world's largest cities, beating a hasty and haunted path for the Upper West Side.

Oh, no, you don't, thought Janet, giving quick pursuit. *You're not getting away from me that easily.*

"No, no, no! Cut, cut, cut!" Otis bellowed, jumping out of his director's chair and waving his arms impatiently at the nude actors on the set of his *Pirates of the Caribbean: The Curse of the Black Dick.* "This is a fucking fiasco! Where did I dig you people up, anyway? I saw more convincing pirates in *Muppet Treasure Island*!"

"Otis, this is the fifth time you've stopped this scene!" one blond woman, clad in only an eyepatch and red-and-white bandanna, complained.

"I'm glad you spoke up, Mandy, because you're the one who keeps blowing lines!" Otis snapped. "Did you even read the script? Can you even read at all? The line is 'Yo ho ho, and a bottle of cum!', and it's not my job to tell you that, you dumb, blond bubblehead!"

"Hey, ease up!" protested one of the male performers. "For pete's sake, it's just a porno! It doesn't have to be gold!"

"What's your name?" Otis asked.

"Ross," said the actor.

"You're fired, Ross," said Otis, jerking a thumb in the direction of the door. "Put on your pants and get off my set."

"But..."

"But nothing!" Otis ranted. "See what it says on the back of my chair over there? Do you see what it says?"

"It says 'Director'," Ross mumbled.

"Fuckin' right! That means *I* call the shots! *I* give the orders! You wanna argue with somebody, go to your parents' house and tell 'em what you really do for a living! But you don't argue with *me*, pal! Get outta here! You're off the picture!"

"But we can't finish this scene without the Long Johnson Silver character!" Mandy protested, as the defeated Ross gathered up his clothes and skulked away.

"I'll give Eric a call first thing in the morning," said Otis. "His dick is a half inch shorter, but he's less expensive and much more cooperative than that prima donna! And let that be a lesson to the rest of you! Think about what you're doing, people! Every time you come to work you're putting yourselves on film that will endure, in one form or another, until the end of time itself! Countless people will critique your performances over and over again, long after your age and faded looks have forced you to retire from the profession! Y'know what happened to me just last week? A young man spotted me at the drugstore and asked me for my autograph! He said he knew me from *Chitty Chitty Gang Bang*! I did that film *twenty years* ago, people, and it's part of the adult movie subculture to this day! Think about your legacy! If you're going to devote your life to making movies, wouldn't you like them to be good ones? Well, wouldn't you?"

After a few seconds' pause, the cast members nodded their heads slowly and mumbled in the affirmative.

"Right," said Otis. "Remember, just because it's porn, that doesn't mean it has to be slapdash and lazy! We're entertainers here, and we're providing people with a valued service. Have a little pride in yourselves! Now, clear away this mess, and we'll move on to the scene with the virgin sacrifice!"

While the cast and crew members began changing costume and moving the props around, getting rid of the ship's hull, potted palm trees, and treasure chest full of Spanish doubloons (actually spray-painted bottle caps) that were part of the Cunnilingus Island set, Otis collapsed back into his chair with a heavy exhale and wiped the back of his hand across his receding hairline. Here, in the backroom of Mr. Happy's Bar & Grill, he was provided an almost ideal studio in which to film the bulk of his movies. The room was big, and empty of furniture, and, with the right props and scene settings, could be made up to look like just about anything. No, location was never a problem for Otis. It was the actors – those spoiled, temperamental cattle – who routinely gave him headaches.

"Y'know, a lot of people say this is what it was like to work for John Ford," said Peg, who had been sitting quietly on the sidelines since the commencement of the evening's shooting.

"The things I endure for my craft," Otis sighed.

Peg, whose interests were perpetually ruled by the blatantly sexual, had been a friend of Otis' for some while. Sometimes, if neither of them had anything more constructive to do, the two of them would go out for a drink and while away the evening exchanging views on their favorite positions or discussing the finer points of the female orgasm, and, providing the agreement to refrain from talking shop was upheld, Otis would occasionally permit Peg the pleasure of sitting in on the filming of one of his pictures.

"I like the way this one is shaping up, though," she said. "I really do. It's about time someone made an adult flick with a bit of swashbuckling in it. There aren't enough directors out there with the vision to recognize that some of us like a little art mixed in with our smut."

"My feelings exactly!" said Otis. "After all, just because the viewer is probably jerking off throughout the entire film, why should that negate the viability of a good story or compelling characters? Wouldn't a feeling of genuine sympathy for the girls onscreen just make a lesbian orgy that much more enjoyable? Call me a snob, but I like to think that I cater to the smarter, more discerning pervert."

By this time the set in front of Otis and Peg had been transformed, turned into a native village made up of straw huts. Sand was strewn upon the floor, thick vegetation – both live and artificial – bordered the 'clearing', and in the center of it all stood a pyre of kindling.

"That's where the natives'll burn the virgin, sacrificing her to their pagan god," Otis explained to Peg.

"You're going to use real fire?" Peg raised her eyebrows. "Isn't that a bit dangerous?"

"Not at all," said Otis. "See that fellow over there? The guy in the chief's headdress? He's an expert in pyrotechnics. He tells me he handled some of the special effects for *Backdraft*, in fact."

"Well, I still can't imagine who you could have found who would be willing to brave the inferno for a porn startlet's standard paycheck," said Peg.

"That's the beauty part," Otis grinned, slyly. "She's not a professional. She's just some girl I picked up on the street. Homeless, y'know, and looking for a way to earn money. She asked if I wanted a blowjob, and I offered her a brief role in my film instead. I decided to be generous and give her a hundred bucks. This way, everyone wins. I get a spectacular snuff scene on the cheap, and she gets something solid in her stomach for the next couple of days."

"You're all heart, Otis," Peg rolled her eyes. "So, where is she?"

"That's her now," Otis pointed across the room. "Not bad, eh?"

From the anecdote Otis had just related, Peg had expected to see a plain, perhaps even homely little skank with fat hips, blotchy skin, and scratches on her face, but the gorgeous creature lashed with rope to a wooden pole and being carried towards the pyre by two of the other actors was anything but. To the extreme contrary, she was a beautiful, nubile young girl with creamy white skin, long, shapely legs, a perfectly rounded behind, exquisite breasts, a face sculpted artfully from marzipan, and a thick mane of hair so red that it might have been on fire. Far from being an undesirable, she was a sexual goddess. Not just a girl tied to a pole, but an Aphrodite standing naked in a clam shell. A girl whom Peg would have taken to bed in the blink of an eye. A girl…

Wait a minute!

"I know her!" she exclaimed, bolting up out of her chair and rushing over to the pyre upon which the girl now lay. "I know this girl!"

"Huh. Small world," Otis muttered.

As Peg drew even with the pyre, the curves and contours of the girl's near perfect body became more and more familiar. The red rose tattooed on her right ankle, the Little Dipper-shaped constellation of freckles just above her left buttock, and the single, adorable beauty mark nestled to the right of her trimmed triangle of scarlet pubic hair all stood out prominently in Peg's mind, and when she finally got a good look at the girl's face, her suspicions were confirmed.

It was Vicki all right.

"I don't understand," Peg gasped, her eyes wide. "Where did you say you found her?"

"Downtown Brooklyn," said Otis. "Just wandering around, dirty and hungry, waiting for me to come along and exploit her. I know what you're thinking. Who knew that part of town held such a wealth of untapped talent, right? I mean, this is like finding gold and oil in Alaska!"

Dumbfounded as to how in the world the lively, vivacious girl with whom Peg had shared a brief but meaningful affair just two months ago could ever have found herself reduced to this, the concerned Vigilante tried to speak to her.

"Vicki," she whispered in the girl's shell-like ear. "Vicki, it's me. Peg. Do you remember me? What's happened to you?"

Receiving no response, Peg took Vicki's chin in her hand and tilted her beautiful face so that she could see her head-on, and, after brushing away a lock of silky red hair, she was startled to find the girl's eyes blank and expressionless, the whites clouded and milky, the pupils dilated.

"Has this girl been drugged?" she turned angrily to Otis.

"Just a little dope to make it more authentic," Otis shrugged, casually. "Human sacrifices are often drugged before a ceremony, y'know. It's nothing she didn't agree to earlier."

"I'm sorry, Otis, but you're going to have to find someone else," said Peg, loosening the ropes that bound the vapid girl's wrists and ankles to the pole. "This young lady is coming home with me right now."

"Now, wait just a minute here!" barked Otis, jumping back out of his chair and stomping onto the set. "Just who do you think you are? I'm congenial enough to allow you a behind-the-scenes look at stuff the rest of the world will only be able to see on the DVD's outtake reel, and you repay me by disrupting my whole production? Lady, I'm already way behind schedule! You're not taking that little tramp anywhere!"

Peg's face darkened then, and her eyes seemed to shoot daggers as she glared directly into Otis' poor excuse for a soul. The pornographer actually took a couple of steps back as the Vigilante – tall for her gender, and certainly taller than Otis – leered threateningly at him, hands on hips and teeth set, menacingly.

"I'm not one of your little whores, Otis," she said, slowly and quietly so he'd understand. "You can't tell me jackshit about what I can and can't do."

While Otis stood by with his mouth open, and more than one of the actors present smiled a discreet smile of satisfaction, Peg untied the final knot, rubbed Vicki's wrists and ankles briskly to ensure the circulation of the blood, then wrapped a handy blanket around the naked girl, gathered her up in her arms, and strode towards the exit.

"Oh, and by the way," Peg couldn't resist tossing one more remark over her shoulder before departing, "I hated *Alien VS Sexual Predator 3*. It really ruined the whole trilogy for me."

"Grrrrrrrrr!" Otis growled, gnashing his teeth and banging his fist down upon the vacant pyre.

New York City's 'forgotten' fifth borough is a hilly, suburban, almost alien realm called Staten Island, fourteen miles long by seven miles wide, populated predominantly by the white, politically conservative middle class. The Verrazano-Narrows Bridge being the only solid conduit connecting the island to the rest of New York, Staten Island has often been a favored retreat for wealthy city-dwellers, and, for generations, most notable business tycoons, crime bosses, and Mafia kingpins associated with the metropolis have maintained weekend or summer homes there.

One such mansion, long a fixture of a particularly green section of the Hamilton Park neighborhood, currently served as the permanent residence of one transplanted cosmopolitan who did most of his commuting to and fro via the Staten Island Ferry. He didn't stand out from the crowd during the daytime, but at night, his curious, all-black outfit, which included the black bandanna obscuring his face, made him a noteworthy apparition, and certainly a most unlikely inhabitant of such a fine and stately home.

"Getting to knooooowww you, getting to know all abooooouut you," Jack the Ripper sang in his grisly, guttural voice, as he used his big knife to strip the skin leisurely, layer by layer, from his latest victim's body, suspended upside-down from the ceiling by a length of rope binding her ankles, dripping blood and other juices onto the hardwood floor. "Getting to liiiike you, getting to know you like meeeee."

Will you stop that? grumbled the other man inside the Ripper's twisted mind. *It's grating on my last nerve. If I handed you a bucket, you still wouldn't be able to carry a tune.*

"Aw, shut up, you old grouch," said the Ripper, dismissively. "Let me have my fun."

I suppose you'll want to fuck her next, disgusting necrophile that you are, the other man grunted, contemptuously.

"Depends on what time I have," the Ripper replied.

Well, I think it's damned inconsiderate of you, said the other man. *I have to use the body too, after all. Think about how I must feel, knowing my penis has been inside a corpse!*

"I don't necessarily like everything *you* do either," said the Ripper, eviscerating the dangling cadaver's belly and getting his first good look at the small intestine. "But like it or not, we're stuck with each other. So you be you and I'll be me, okay?"

Perverted degenerate, the other man muttered.

The Ripper's argument with himself was interrupted by a loud, unmuffled 'vrrooooom!', accompanied by a chorus of yelps, yowls, and war cries out on the expansive front lawn, and the masked killer rushed to the window to see a group of nine black men storming towards the house, firing machine guns into the air, tearing up the grass from their seats astride an assortment of motorcycles, four-wheelers, and ATVs.

"It's the Hellfighters!" the Ripper exclaimed.

Impossible! said the other man. *They never come out this far!*

"Use our eyes, you fool! It's them! The full force of the Burning Cross Corps!"

This is your fault! said the other man. *This whore was obviously the straw that broke the camel's back! I told you they wouldn't suffer you for much longer!*

"Don't be an idiot!" the Ripper fired back. "It's you they're after! Why else would they come here, of all places?"

Obviously they've discovered who you really are!

"Who *I* really am? Let's get one thing straight, dickhead! *I'm* the real persona here!"

You? Preposterous! I'm the genuine article, you indelicate lout!

"Oh, really? Well, if that were true, could I do this?"

The Ripper raised his six-inch knife, still dripping with the girl's blood, and plunged it into his right thigh.

Ow! You mindless maniac! That hurt! You're just as crazy as they say you are!

"And don't you forget it! Remember, I brought you into this world, and I can take you out! I'm just nutty enough to do it! Now, to dispense with these intruders!"

No! You can't do it! I know what you're thinking, and you can't do it! It's a disastrous idea!

"It's a fantastic idea!"

I won't let you!

"Brother, you haven't got a choice!"

Throwing his black coat over his shoulder like a cape, the Ripper ran from the room and charged across the mezzanine overlooking the foyer and down the adjacent hall, just as the house's big front door exploded inward in a hail of splinters and sparks and the Hellfighters came roaring inside, racing around the circular room until each of them had found a place to stand.

"So where is he?" queried one of the larger Hellfighters, alighting from his bike and giving his shotgun an affectionate pump.

Before anyone could hazard a guess, all the lights went out, blanketing the room in darkness, and the next sound anyone heard was a thick, wet gurgle, followed promptly by a heavy 'thud'. At once, the smell of death began to choke the air.

"What the fuck...?"

The Hellfighter didn't have time to say anything more besides 'Hurk!' as a long, sharp knife lanced through the back of his neck, and two men standing near him felt something warm and wet spray their faces.

"He's got the drop on us!" one Hellfighter screamed. "Everybody watch out!"

The Ripper was already gone, however, having hacked his way to the destroyed doorway and made good his escape, already a safe distance from the house, sheltered by a line of trees bordering the property.

This is your last chance! declared the adversarial voice inside the Ripper's head. *Reconsider, and I'll give you the evenings to go along with the nights!*

"Too late, buddy boy!" the Ripper cackled, gleefully. "*I'm* in control now!"

The Ripper jabbed his thumb down onto a button on the device sitting in the palm of his hand, and the three-story mansion imploded instantaneously, collapsing in on itself as it crashed to the ground with a thunderous din, burying everything inside – the Hellfighters included – beneath tons of immoveable rubble and debris.

No! Damn your eyes, you unthinking fool! You've destroyed everything!

"Hey, we put that bomb there for a reason, remember? You knew this was bound to happen someday. Besides, we still have the penthouse."

I liked the mansion!

"And speaking of the penthouse, perhaps it's time we adjourned to Manhattan for the night. In light of recent developments, I think there's somebody with whom we should have words. After all, the enemy of our enemy is our friend, correct?"

No! Not him*! You know how I feel about* him*! I won't allow you to embroil us with* him*!*

"Calm yourself, old man, before you give us both a heart attack. You know I'm not crazy about him either, but I see no other option. Without his intervention, the Hellfighters will surely overwhelm us, be it sooner or later. No, my symbiotic soul mate. If we are to remain healthy, we have little choice but to call upon the General."

Buzz was jarred from a sound sleep by a loud rapping at his door, continuous and unrelenting in its determination to bounce him out of bed. Groaning, he rubbed his sightless eyes with one hand and fumbled for the talking clock on his bedside table with the other.

"It is three-oh-seven AM," said the clock's electronic voice, once Buzz had managed to finally locate and press the device's largest button.

Muttering incoherently to himself, Buzz clambered to his feet, threw on his burgundy bathrobe, and shuffled steadily out of the bedroom, down the hall, and through the living room, the assistance lent him by his cane unnecessary for the navigation of his apartment's familiar layout.

"Who is it?" he asked, testily, opening the door with the chain still on.

"It's me," said Gary. "Can I come in?"

"Do you have any idea what time it is?"

"I know, and I'm sorry, but...I'm ready, Buzz. I'm ready to talk. I *need* to talk. I almost killed a kid earlier tonight because he lifted someone's toaster. I need to hash this out, and I need your help. Please."

Buzz heaved a heavy sigh, then unlatched the chain and opened the door wide enough to permit Gary entrance.

"All right, come in and sit down," he said.

"You're not going in there without me," said Janet, pushing her way in.

"Buzz, this is Janet," said Gary, wearily. "My significant other since the day I was born."

"If you want her to sit in, she can," said Buzz.

"It's not a question of what I want," said Gary. "Fate lashes us together, no matter what happens."

While Gary and Janet sat down side by side on the couch, Buzz walked over to a desk in the corner and retrieved his dark glasses and a small tape recorder.

"Where would you like to start?" he asked, taking a seat in an armchair.

"I don't know," said Gary. "I mean, you're the expert. Where would *you* like me to start?"

"You don't mind if I record our discussion, do you?" asked Buzz.

"No, go ahead," Gary consented.

Buzz loaded a tape into the recorder, pressed the PLAY and RECORD buttons simultaneously, then set the recorder down on the coffee table in front of him.

"How about we start with your behavior of late?" Buzz, settling back, suggested. "You must be aware of how manic and eccentric you've become over the past couple of weeks. Can you tell me anything about that?"

"I don't understand it myself," said Gary, holding his aching head in his hands. "My mind is all over the place. One minute I'm climbing the walls, the next I'm flat on my ass. One minute I'm sick as a dog, the next I'm strong enough to wrestle twenty men into submission. I'm up, down, sideways, backwards, and inside-out, with different emotions pulling me in all directions, and most of the time I just feel like I'm going crazy. Sometimes I lose control of myself, or forget who I am. Sometimes I'm floating above my body, watching myself doing things. Sometimes my five senses are blitzed by some fantastic energy that overwhelms me like a flood smashing through a dam. It's like I'm a twisted, contorted reflection in a funhouse mirror that's been shattered into a thousand pieces, and I can't pull myself together. It's like I'm not myself at all anymore, Buzz. It's like I don't even have any essence of being to keep myself cohesive."

"Keep talking, lover," Janet purred, tucking her legs up onto the couch and slipping an arm over Gary's shoulders. "My nipples are getting hard."

"Hmm," Buzz nodded, as if he had understood precisely what his friend had just said. "I've long feared you could eventually become the victim of such a syndrome."

"What syndrome?"

"You've lost yourself, Gary," the psychologist explained, "and should it really come as any great surprise? You don't balance yourself well. Your lifestyle is so off-kilter you could be a Jackson Pollock painting. Not only do you devote your entire life to combating crime, but you permit yourself no retreat from it. Day and night you're out there, confronting murderers, rapists, child molesters, drug dealers, and heaven only knows what else, with absolutely no respite; no withdrawal; no time for reflection, distraction, or the pursuit of pleasure. Is it any wonder that you feel as if you're burning up from the inside out? Human beings were never meant to endure that which you consistently bring down upon yourself, Gary."

"You make it sound as if I have a choice," said Gary. "I know no other way to live – to survive. I must lose myself in action, lest I wither in despair. Alfred Lord Tennyson said that, y'know."

"Oh, great, I'm fucking a philosopher," Janet rolled her eyes. "Your brain was never the most attractive part of you, Gary."

"And of what would you despair, Gary?" asked Buzz, ignoring Janet's interruption.

"My humanity. If I don't keep pushing myself, keep driving myself...I never wanted to be like this, y'know. I wanted to help people. I wanted to be a defender. I wanted to be a hero."

"I believe you," said Buzz. "Is that why you enlisted with the British Secret Service?"

Gary groaned wearily, rubbed his eyes, then pulled his flask from his pocket.

"I know you don't like to talk about your past, Gary," said Buzz, sympathetically, "but if you truly wish for me to help you, I'm afraid I see no way of avoiding it."

Gary took a long drink from the flask, wiped his mouth, and stared at the floor.

"So, you want to know the whole story, huh? All right, I'll tell you the whole story. Where should I start?"

"At the beginning."

"Fine. From the beginning, then. I signed up with MI5 when I was nineteen. See, the Cold War had ended just recently, and we were all excited because all of that moldy old spy stuff was finally kaput, and we were going to have the chance to get to grips with the villains of the twenty-first century. Guerilla terrorists in the streets, suicide bombers in the subway, and bank robbers with jetpacks strapped to their backs. It was gonna be one hell of a time, and my desirable physical condition was a guarantee that I wouldn't be left back at the office to file papers. No, sir, I'd be right out there where it was happening. I figured it'd be a blast, and a great way to fight crime in style, so I signed my name on the dotted line and answered my country's call. Then I went into training and spent a long time getting into tiptop shape. They drummed it into me real good, until I was capable of the kinds of feats I pull off on these mean streets every day. Top of my class, Buzz, and I don't mind bragging about it. The final verdict, in fact, was that I was too good for MI5's conventional agenda, so they sent me over to Custodial Division."

"Something tells me you're not referring to the cleaning corps," said Buzz.

"Only after a fashion," said Gary. "It was called Custodial Division because we were in charge of 'cleaning and maintenance' concerning certain volatile domestic issues that no other arm of the government was allowed to touch. It was a small subdivision of MI5 with only about half a dozen active agents at any one time, and knowledge of its existence was given out very sparingly. Only those who absolutely needed to know were let in on the dirty little secret. Other folks, including the Prime Minister, most of Parliament, and the royal family, were kept deliberately in the dark."

"Very hush-hush indeed," said Buzz.

"There was a good reason for that," said Gary. "Y'see, Custodial Division wasn't even legal. It was more like a Gestapo than anything else."

"I'm sure you're exaggerating," said Buzz.

"Am I?" Gary smirked mirthlessly and took another swig from his flask. "Y'know, I was really excited when I started working for them. In some ways I never grew up, and I'd always fancied myself as an action hero, kicking down the door of an enemy base with a blazing gun in each hand, killing the evil mastermind, scooping up the damsel in distress, and blowing out of there just seconds before the whole place went up in a mushroom cloud." He took another drink before continuing. "I had such aspirations. In just my first week I was going to crush the IRA, demolish the fascist and communist parties, weed out the Arab terrorists, jail every gangster in London, and get 'Rule Britannia' declared the new national anthem. I was a starry-eyed patriot of the first order, but you'd be surprised to hear where that attitude got me."

"Are you allowed to talk about this?" asked Buzz.

"No, but I don't give a fuck," said Gary, sullenly. "It's about time at least one of you knew the truth about me. I was no hero, Buzz. Just a blunt instrument to be wielded by despotic thugs who were never held accountable for their decisions. You want an example of my typical workday? I'll give you a real honey of an example." He took another long drink, then burped. "I think it was my second year. Britain and France were embroiled in yet another petty dispute over something that really didn't mean anything at all to the average citizen of either country. Britain was determined to come out of the argument on top, so they sent Sir Thomas Mumford across the Channel. He was a congenial old bloke, and one of our smartest diplomats, and he was very popular with the Queen's loyal subjects. But I guess some of the powers that be decided that any contribution he'd make as a diplomat was small in comparison to the contribution he'd make as a martyr."

"You mean..."

"Yup. While Mumford was enjoying a cup of coffee and a croissant at a sidewalk café on the Champs-Elysees, I snuck into an empty office building right across the street and did my Oswald impression with a sniper rifle. Naturally the British were furious, and the French had egg all over their faces. After that fiasco, they had no choice but to concede to Britain's demands."

"Ooh, I love it," Janet moaned, rubbing her thighs together.

"Well, Gary, I...I can certainly see how something like that might weigh heavily upon a man's conscience," said Buzz, unable to disguise his reaction completely. "But surely that sort of thing wasn't typical of your work."

"Oh, you don't think so, eh? Well if you liked that, this next one'll kill you. It concerned this average, everyday slob who happened to be a photographer for one of those sleazy tabloid rags, see. Now, don't ask me how, but the guy had managed to get some prize-winning pics of the PM dressed in drag and jerking off to one of those kinky 'chicks with dicks' videos. Naturally when the high-ups became aware of the photos, they decided to qualify them as a threat to national security. And, as usual, that's where Custodial Division came in to clean up the mess. They ordered me to capture the pics and terminate the photographer, and gave me carte blanche to do it. Don't care how you do it, they said. Just keep it quiet."

"So...what did you do?"

"Oh, you would've been proud of me, Buzz, ol' boy," said Gary, his tone heavy with irony. "You would've seen me for the true champion of justice I was. You want to know what I did? I abducted the guy's twelve-year-old daughter from her school, took her to one of our safe houses, slapped her around a bit, snapped some shots of her bruised, tear-streaked little face, and sent them off to her dad with a note informing him that if he ever wanted to see her alive and intact again, he was required to come alone, with all the photos, to the address I provided. Of course, the poor bozo came. I kept things quick and to the point after that. I shot him once in the head, right in front of the girl, then recovered the pics from the body, called up the woman I had just widowed to tell her where she could come and pick up her daughter, then took a quick bathroom break before heading back to the city. And that, my friend, is the true story of Gary fucking Parker, defender of justice and champion of the weak and oppressed."

"Ooh," Janet was still moaning, her eyes closed, her head tilted way back. "Gary, you little mischief, are you *trying* to make me come right here on the couch?"

For moments that seemed like hours, Buzz said nothing. What could he say? Certainly he had known that Gary was capable of killing. He knocked off criminals all the time. But those were vicious, savage monsters; psychopaths and ghouls; cold-blooded killers themselves; rabid animals that needed to be put down. The only difference between Gary's methods and those of any legitimate police force was that Gary didn't wait for the other man to draw a gun before delivering the killing shot. But, innocent people? Harmless civilians? Buzz had never known Gary to be anything but a devout and stoic protector of such people. It was hard to imagine him as a callous, unfeeling taker of defenseless life.

Then Gary began to do something that Buzz had never heard him do before. He began to cry.

"There was nothing good about who I was or what I did," he wept, covering his face with his trembling hands. "Not a damned thing. I was a monster. A monster, the same as those I fight everyday."

"Halleluiah!" Janet cheered, planting a sloppy kiss on Gary's cheek.

"That can't be right, Gary," said Buzz, softly, trying not to become too emotional himself. "You're a good man now, and you were a good man before. You were just...misled."

"No," Gary shook his head. "No, I knew what I was doing. I always knew what I was doing."

"The anguish you're experiencing is not uncommon for veterans of some form of combat," Buzz pressed on. "Soldiers returning home from war after participating in operations that incurred civilian casualties very often struggle with similar feelings, as do police officers who look back on the last perp they killed and agonize over and over about whether or not the use of lethal force was truly necessary."

"At least they can take solace in the knowledge that any innocent blood on their hands was the result of an accident," Gary continued to weep. "But I was cold; calculating; without mercy or remorse. My word, he was right. I tried hard not to believe him, but he was right."

"Who was right?"

"For two months I've been denying it. I've been telling myself over and over that he was a lunatic and that he didn't know what he was talking about. After all, he didn't know me well enough to make such pointed accusations. But now I see that I was just in denial. Now I see that he was right, and really, I must have known it all along."

"Gary, what are you talking about?"

"Shang Fear."

"Shang Fear?" Janet parroted. "Yes, I'm glad you brought him up, hon. You can't argue with him on this point, blind man. Gary really is a lot like that psycho Chink. In fact, lover, that's the reason I fucked him. I didn't really like him, but he reminded me so much of you. He was everything I loved about you, and more. Dark, solitary, ruthless, violent, tormented, with the added bonus of being completely crazy and not having any of those pesky problems with conscience that always made you push me away."

"Back in June, during our final fight, he accused me of being a mass murderer in crimefighter's clothing," said Gary. "He called me a bloodthirsty killer and said that I was just like him, the only difference being that I struggled to justify my violent behavior. And he was right. I've no choice but to finally throw up my hands and admit it. I *am* a stone cold butcher, just like he was!"

"Do you really believe that?" asked Buzz.

"Of course. It's the truth, isn't it? The only difference is that Fear was a psychopath and killed indiscrimantely, whereas I'm a sociopath and only go after the people whom I – I, in my infinite wisdom – deem deserving of such a violent end."

"A sociopath, Gary?" Buzz's brow furrowed.

"What else? I spend my days and nights killing, then when I finally get home, my leftovers are no less appetizing and sleep doesn't come any more fitfully. You're the psychologist, Buzz. If that's not the textbook definition of a sociopath, then what is?"

Buzz shook his head and pinched the bridge of his nose between his thumb and forefinger. "Take heart from an opinion that is both objective and professional, Gary," he said, at last. "I never said anything before, but, a few years ago, I had the opportunity to observe Shang Fear during the time of his incarceration at the Albany Institute for the Criminally Insane, and even a man with my particular handicap could see plainly that he suffered from borderline personality disorder, narcissism, authoritarian compulsions, and undifferentiated schizophrenia, to say the very least. You're not like him at all, my friend."

"Tell that to the families and friends of the people I murdered," Gary replied.

"You know, you don't hold the monopoly on self-pity," Buzz kept his even tone, but was beginning to lose patience. "I'm *blind*, Mr. Parker. From the day I was born I've lived in utter darkness. I've never seen anything for what it truly is – its shape, contours, colors – and even with all of society's self-soothing talk about blind people overcoming their disability and going on to live rich, fulfilling lives, the outlook can still be quite bleak from our side of the looking glass. Just imagine it, Gary. I've never seen colors, and there's no way you could ever describe them to me. You can tell me that the sky is blue, but I have absolutely no concept of what 'blue' is. And not once – not *once* – in all of our nineteen year marriage, did I ever lay eyes upon..."

Buzz stopped for a moment and took in a deep, quiet breath.

"A man is supposed to be able to protect his wife," he continued. "If he can't, then what sort of a man is he? My blindness rendered me incapable of protecting my wife from that mugger ten years ago, and so she was taken from me.You see, Gary, I was too weak to fend off the predator. But you're not. And if the truth be known, I've always been a little envious of your strength and ability to do that which is necessary. So don't hate yourself for it, because that's a stinging slap in the face to people like me."

Gary rubbed his fingers through his red eyes, and groaned again. "Fuck," he sighed. "I'm sorry, Buzz. Real sorry. I didn't mean to dredge up..."

"But there's still another part of your past that haunts you, isn't there?" said Buzz, reassuming the course. "Something unrelated to your government work. I think you know what I'm referring to."

"Allison and Samantha," Gary sighed, his head in his hand.

"Oh, no, not this," Janet groaned. "Don't get him started or he'll just whine, whine, whine for hours."

"I've heard you mention them only a couple of times over the past six years," said Buzz. "I gather they were very important to you. Would you like to tell me a bit about them?"

"My booze is gone," said Gary, dejectedly. "I was really hoping to have some on hand by the time we got to that."

"It's what turned you into an alcoholic in the first place, isn't it?"

"It's certainly what led me to discover I possessed the gene for alcoholism, yes."

"Tell me about them, Gary."

"You're not going to let me off the hook here, are you?"

"No."

"Well, maybe it's for the best. I haven't actually talked about it with anybody since it happened. All right, here goes." He took a deep breath, let it out, then leaned back, staring up at the ceiling. "Allison was the girl I lived with. Huh. Look at me. Already I'm not being honest. She was a lot more than that. She was the woman I loved."

"Bullshit," Janet hissed. "You wicked liar, *I* was the woman you loved! I was *always* the woman you loved!"

"Shut up!" Gary snapped. "I'm trying to have a breakthrough here!" He turned back to Buzz. "And I really did love her, y'know. Just because I wasn't in any great hurry to get married didn't mean I loved her any less."

"Was the idea of marriage a problem for you?"

"I was a little scared of it, yeah," Gary admitted. "It just seemed so... so permanent. And maybe I thought our relationship was fine just the way it was."

"But you've mentioned on previous occasions that she'd become your fiancée."

"That was after she got pregnant," Gary nodded. "I guess we got a little too comfortable, a little too careless after such a steady relationship. Or maybe she went off her pills deliberately, figuring – correctly, as it turned out – that a bun in the oven was just the nudge I needed. After recovering from the initial shock, I emerged completely ready and willing to commit. And I really got into this whole 'family' thing, Buzz. I got really enthusiastic about it."

"I'm sure you did," said Buzz.

"Gag me," Janet rolled her eyes again, and stuck her middle finger down the back of her throat.

"We were going to call her Samantha," Gary continued. "The baby, I mean. It was a girl, and we were going to call her Samantha."

"That's a nice name," said Buzz.

"But she never even had the chance to be born," Gary lamented. "It was...it was the Scotsman that did it." A pause as he rubbed the bridge of his nose and groaned the heavy groan of a man who had all but run out of raw emotion to vent. Then, "This is very hard for me, but I'm just going to come right out with it and get it over with. Y'see, there were these two crazy old Scotsmen living in an ancient stone castle in the Highlands. They were brothers, called Angus and Mengus, and neither one of them could have been a day under eighty-five. And they were absolutely stark, raving mad. They wore big, flamboyant kilts, they howled at the full moon, and it's my personal belief that they enjoyed the intimate company of sheep. The most heinous of their customs, however, was venturing down into the glens at night and actually hunting people as big game."

"I beg your pardon?" said Buzz.

"Yeah, with spears and arrows, mostly," said Gary. "Then, at the end of the night, they'd go back home with their kills and do an expert job of stuffing them. Pretty sick, right?"

"Sounds great to me," said Janet.

"And how did you come to be involved in this?" asked Buzz.

"Well, naturally a couple of crazy old blighters knocking off a few Scottish peasants wasn't exactly the government's top priority," said Gary, "but when a wealthy tourist family from London disappeared, a blind eye could no longer be turned. So they sent me up to resolve the situation.

"I'll say one thing for them. For octogenarians, they were remarkably fit. They fought like *Braveheart* extras, coming at me with everything from swords to maces to their own fists and feet, which packed way more of a wallop than you'd expect. And the creepy surroundings of the castle didn't exactly work to my advantage either. I mean, how was I supposed to stay focused with the glass eyes of human trophies staring at me from every corner?

"Finally I got the upper hand against Angus. I tore this bloody great shield down off the wall and smashed him over the head with it. He was a strong fighter, but his neck snapped like a dry twig. Mengus managed to escape, though, and, totally contrary to my usual nature, I actually dismissed it as being no big deal. After all, he was just one loony old geezer, right? So I went back to London, reported to my superiors, and went home. And...that was when I found Allison."

"Dead?" asked Buzz, gently.

"Mengus had found her," Gary nodded, somberly, "and he...he'd butchered her. With knives. Lots of them. The image..." a strangled sob, followed by fresh tears, "...the terrible image of it all still haunts me today!"

"It sounds absolutely horrific," said Buzz. "I can't believe you've been carrying this around all this time, pent up inside your head."

"I tracked down Mengus and killed him," said Gary. "Then I left the Service, came to New York, and lost myself at the bottom of a bottle. Eventually I found this; an untapped need for Machiavellian crimefighters, willing and able to use criminals' own perverted methods against them. Pouring my time and energy into that idea – the idea that

I could use my talents to finally become the crusader I'd always aspired to be – was what saved my sanity. It gave me a reason to go on living."

"It also meant that your terrible revenge against Mengus didn't have to end," Buzz pointed out. "It meant you could go on punishing him and his kind unto the very end of your days."

"Oh, shit!" Gary cried out suddenly, his hand flying to his mouth, his eyes widening in horror. "That woman! The one I saw out my window earlier today! She was in trouble, and I...I ignored it! I did nothing! I just stood there, and...fuck, I did it again!"

Gary shrieked like a tormented banshee as he leapt to his feet and clawed at his hair, wrestling with the agony that scraped at his insides, and Janet could see that she was losing him.

"Listen here, blind man, and listen good!" she hissed through set teeth, seizing Buzz by
the front of his bathrobe and hoisting him out of his chair. "No more talk! I've waited a long time to get Gary like this, and I won't have you ruining it for me!"

"Let him go, you bitch!" Gary grabbed her wrists with one hand and punched the side of her head with the other, then kicked her in the side, sending her somersaulting over the back of the couch. "I must've been really fucked up in the head to follow your lead on anything!" Then,
turning back to Buzz, "Thanks, old friend. I think the cobwebs are clearing. I mean, I'm far from
being all right, but I feel like the worst is behind me."

"You needed to talk," said Buzz. "Your demons needed an airing."

"I really appreciate it," said Gary. "But I have to go now."

"Go where?" asked Buzz.

"To see the very model of a modern Major General," said Gary, bolting with newfound energy towards the door. "Where else?"

"Gary, wait!" Janet cried out as she followed him out into the corridor, the pleading tone in her voice so unfamiliar as to stop him, however briefly, in his tracks. "You can't just run off like this! We...we were doing so well!"

Gary turned, looked into Janet's eyes – eyes that finally dared to betray the desperation and loneliness that had twisted her up inside for so long – exhaled heavily, and placed his hands gently on her bare shoulders.

"Perhaps there's no one with whom I'm better suited to spend my life," he said, "but you know just as well as I do that it's crazy."

"Think about this, Gary," Janet pleaded, grasping Gary's shoulders in turn. "Please think."

"There's nothing to think about."

"Remember the long, romantic evenings in London? Remember dancing till dawn on top of the Tower Bridge?"

"We weren't dancing, we were fighting."

"With people like us, it's the same thing."

"That's just it, Janet," said Gary, prying himself free of her grip. "I don't want to be 'people like us' anymore."

"But..."

"Good-bye, Janet," he said, turning away and striding quickly towards the elevator. "And good luck. Really, I mean that. Good luck."

Immediately after leaving Mr. Happy's, Peg had bundled the unconscious Vicki into a cab and gone straight home, where she had set the girl down in a tub full of cool water and had gently flicked some of it onto her face, and massaged her chest and limbs until she had begun to regain her senses. Almost instantly upon waking she had needed to throw up, so Peg had hurried her out of the tub and down onto her knees by the toilet, and had stood behind her and held back the girl's soft, beautiful hair while she vomited into the bowl.

After Vicki had thrown up what little had been inside her stomach and had finished with any dry heaves, Peg had walked the weak-kneed waif into her bedroom, where she had slipped an oversized t-shirt over her head and tucked her into bed. This was where they were now; Vicki still a little dopey, her head resting on the pillow like a lump of lead, just now beginning to understand who and where she was, and Peg coming back into the luxuriously dark room and sitting down in a chair beside the bed, a bowl of something hot and aromatic cradled in her hands.

"How are you feeling now, sweetie?" Peg asked, caressing Vicki's forehead, tenderly.

"Better...I guess," Vicki spoke for the first time, a feeble smile tugging at the corner of her mouth. "Hi, Peg."

"Hi yourself. I won't deny I'm really happy to see you again, but I wish you weren't so ill."

"Oh, I'm all right," Vicki sort of sighed. "I just haven't eaten much solid for a couple of days, and that drug that guy gave me..."

"I made you some soup," said Peg, showing Vicki the bowl. "Out of a can, of course. I'm not exactly what you might call a master chef. Would you like me to feed it to you?"

Vicki nodded, and Peg eased a spoonful of the broth into her mouth.

"I'm sorry it's just plain Tomato," Peg apologized, "but I'm afraid I haven't gone grocery shopping for a while. I don't even have any crackers."

"It tastes really good," said Vicki. "Thank you so much."

"I missed you, y'know," said Peg, giving Vicki another spoonful, which the girl swallowed gratefully. "What's it been? Two months? But I haven't stopped thinking about you."

"I missed you, too," said Vicki.

"So what the hell happened to you?" Peg finally posed the question she'd been dying to ask. "Otis said he found you with no money and no place to go. How did you end up in this predicament?"

"I ran away from home," Vicki answered. "About...three weeks ago, I think."

"But why? Your parents must be worried sick about you."

"My parents are dead. All I have is my aunt. It's her that I was running away from. She...she hurts me, Peg. She hurts me a lot."

Vicki went on to tell Peg everything about her abusive Aunt Millicent, from the frequent beatings to the forced slave labor to the dreaded wooden cane hanging in plain view on the living room wall, and, all throughout, Peg hung upon every word with the rapt fascination of one watching a graphically brutal horror movie.

"I knew I had to get away when she started seeing this new guy," Vicki went on. "A real sadistic freak. He liked...he liked to do things to me. He got a real hard-on from torturing me, and Aunt Milli let him do it. It was when he started cutting me that I knew I had to get away once and for all. But I had no place to go. So I've been trying to survive on the streets. Guess I haven't been doing a very good job so far, huh?"

"But why didn't you come here?" asked Peg. "I could have helped you. You could have stayed with me."

"I did come by once, but you weren't here. And I didn't come again after that because I...well, I wasn't totally sure you'd want me."

"Are you kidding? I can't remember the last time I've wanted someone more. I've been aching for you, you dumb little tart. Since we met, every person I've slept with has your face, and every time I touch myself, it's your name I'm whispering. I've been kicking myself for losing touch with you. And you've been eating out of trash cans and sleeping on top of heating vents for three weeks because you weren't sure I'd want you? Of course I want you, you stupid bitch!"

Vicki smiled, and a glow came into her eyes. "That's the nicest thing anyone's ever said to me," she said.

"Then it's settled," said Peg, laying it on the line. "You'll move in with me, as of right now. It'll be just like when Batman took in Robin, only we'll have nonstop sex."

"Will it be just you and me?" asked Vicki.

"Yes, honey, I promise. I'll be faithful to you. You're the one I want. As long as I have you, I don't need anyone else."

Vicki beamed.

"I have only a couple of stipulations," said Peg. "First of all, I get moody. And when I get moody, things get broken. I have my meds, but they'll just curb the storm. They won't stop it. So, when you see the hairs on the back of my neck start to stand up, the best thing you can do is stick on a Stanley Kubrick movie and hide all your breakables in a place I don't know about. Capiche?"

"Absolutely," Vicki nodded, readily.

"And secondly, I smoke. A lot. Two packs a day usually, and I'm not going to stop. But I'm sure we're not going to have any arguments about that, right?"

"No way," said Vicki.

"Fantastic," said Peg, maintaining an outward calm but dancing with excitement on the inside. "Consider yourself at home, starting now."

"There are some things I want to get from my aunt's house," said Vicki. "Not much, just a few things that are important to me and that I'd like to have. I'll get them tomorrow, then never look back."

"I'll go with you if you'd like," Peg offered.

"No, thanks. If I'm finally walking out on Millicent, I want to do it standing on my own two feet. Don't worry, I can face her. I feel so strong, now that I have you."

"Well, you're not strong at this very moment, anyway," said Peg, walking around to what would become her side of the bed, pulling back the single sheet and settling in beside her new roommate. "You need a good night's sleep. No fooling around tonight."

"Aww, not even a little?" Vicki grinned mischievously, letting her index and middle fingers 'walk' up the inside of Peg's thigh.

"No, not even a little," Peg insisted, removing Vicki's hand and turning over to face the wall. "Good night."

It took all of thirty seconds for the verdict to be reversed.

"Insatiable little tramp," Peg exhaled heavily, falling upon her.

The Red Cobras were prevalent throught the city, with pockets festering beneath the surface of every accessible neighborhood, but the gang's primary base of operations – the beating heart to which all arteries ran – was a former bowling alley on Allen Street on the Lower East Side. Closed down two years ago when Baron Striker's Twelve Lane Blitz moved into a larger building (and became Baron Striker's Twenty-Four Lane Blitz) in a better area, the defunct recreation center didn't have long to wait before the Cobras made it their new home, moving in and wasting no time in furnishing the place with their ill-gotten gains; pool tables, arcade video games, and skateboard ramps amused some of the Cobras, while others whiled away the hours of their misspent youths playing poker, brawling with their fellows, or having sex with young girls on the scattered couches.

Tash and Leon were sitting on a couch near where the snack bar had used to be. Tash had poured out a line of cocaine powder on the card table before them, and had chopped it finely with the edge of his switchblade, and now Leon took a dab on his fingertip and rubbed it over the middle of his tongue.

"Yeah, that's the good shit all right," he grinned.

"Ain't even cut with nothin' neither," said Tash, snorting half the line up into his right nostril through the hollowed-out shaft of a pen. "Call it a perk. A lotta major drug lords in big cities like this find out the easiest way to get their drugs on the street is by lettin' local gangs handle the customer service for 'em. We get the drugs in these big packs, see, then we split it all up into little bags, an' we sell it. Then we get our money and the drug lord gets his. Real sweet arrangement, dawg. Here, have a snort."

Tash handed the pen shaft to Leon, but, before the Cobra-in-training could take it, it was snatched away by the hand of a tall, shaven-headed thug with a scraggly goatee, a wooden toothpick in his mouth, and a Gorbachev-esque gash of a scar across the top of his bare scalp. This was Jag, the Cobras' leader for the past two years, and he crushed the pen shaft in his hand and scowled at Tash.

"Teachin' the newbie bad habbits," he said.

"Hey, what's up, nigga?" said Tash, dismayed. "Jus' partyin' a little."

"Not anymore," said Jag, sweeping the rest of the powder off the table and into the air, where it dispersed like so many dust particles. "From now on, any nigga who touches an ounce o' this stuff is a dead nigga. Got it? No more freebies."

"But..."

"Kwami here? Where is he?"

"He's over there," said Tash, pointing to the skinny, Rasta type who had just won a free ball on the Addams Family-themed pinball machine by the men's room. "But what..."

Before Tash could finish his inquiry concerning Jag's abrupt policy change, the Cobras' leader snapped his fingers and called loudly for the room's attention.

"Awright, listen up, ya losers," he said. "We all are gonna have a visitor in jus' a few moments, an' he's an important dude to everyone here, so try not to act like a bunch o' stupid animals right in front o' him, 'kay?"

"Who's comin'?" Leon whispered to Tash.

"I don't know shit 'bout anythin', dawg," Tash replied.

The assembled Cobras had only to wait but a few seconds before the front door flew open with a thunderous 'bang' and the identity of Jag's visitor was revealed; General Salvador Ramos, as finely dressed and stern-faced as ever, stormed into the room, trailed by the imposing Ron Grimace.

"Oh, motherfucker," Tash breathed.

"Ramos?" Leon exclaimed. "*He's* the dude who owns all that shit in the backroom?"

"There's only one reason why he'd come down here himself," said Tash. "Whatever you do, nigga, don't move."

"Thanks for comin', General," Jag greeted him.

"Shut up, boy," said Ramos, looking very angry. "Which one is it, then? Which one of these little black bastards has been stealing from me?"

"No one'll deny helpin' themselves to a little bit o' the stock free o' charge," said Jag, "but Kwami over there's been doin' most of it. He's been a real pig about it."

"What?" Kwami piped up, alarmed. "But I..."

"Gun, Grimace," said Ramos.

Once again Grimace took the AK-47 down from his shoulder and handed it to Ramos, who pointed it at the Cobra called Kwami and fired, splattering the young man's guts all over the Addams Family pinball machine. The electronic sign just above the picture of Uncle Fester with a lightbulb in his mouth read 'TILT'.

"So, we square now, right?" said Jag, while the other Cobras just stared. "I gave you the biggest sponge, so now the rest of us are okay."

"Don't let it happen again," Ramos warned, before disappearing through the door as abruptly as he had come.

"I think you should've done 'em all," said Grimace, once he and

Ramos were halfway across the empty, pothole-filled parking lot outside the former bowling alley.

"Time doesn't afford me the luxury of being heavy-handed," the General replied. "I need those punks more than they need me. I can only hope making an example of that one was enough."

"Oh, I think it was masterfully done," rasped Jack the Ripper, emerging from the shadows off to the right, clapping his hands slowly.

"What do you want?" asked Ramos, stopping to address the newcomer. "Have you reconsidered my offer?"

The Ripper laughed throatily, then thrust one gloved hand inside his coat, pulled out a manila folder stuffed with papers and bound with a rubber band, and tossed it to the General, who caught it.

"There's all the information on the Hellfighters that I've been able to amass," said the Ripper. "I should think there'd be something in there of use to you."

"My thanks," Ramos nodded. "No doubt our mutual enemy will soon be no more. Grimace, pay the man."

"No need," the Ripper held up a hand. "Money means very little to me."

"Then what do you wish in return?" asked Ramos.

"Just kill them," hissed the Ripper. "Kill them all."

To say that Leon had not been moved by the events at the Cobras' little Pleasure Island in the ghetto would be untrue. Though his perception of gang life had not been reversed, nor had it come away from the scene undamaged. Up until an hour ago he had been under the impression that comrades in this game abided by a certain code of honor; that they never, under any circumstances, ratted each other out. Yet Jag, whom Leon had idolized since their first meeting, had handed Kwami to General Ramos with a ribbon and bow attached, with absolutely no hesitation, nor consultation with fellow Cobras. Surely that couldn't be the usual state of affairs, could it? No, of course not. Not if the Cobras, like street gangs all across America, were to become a second family to its members; not if the Cobras were to become *his* second family.

In the manner of most adolescents who have encountered something unsettling, Leon decided not to dwell on it, and he pushed what few doubts he had to the back of his mind as he reached the top of the stairwell in the shabby, rundown, three-story tenement house in the Bronx neighborhood of Mott Haven. A large rat startled him as it skittered out in front of him on its way to a hole in the opposite wall, and he nearly fell backwards down the stairs. Fortunately the rickety banister didn't give way when he grabbed it, and he shook his head and composed himself before knocking on the left of a pair of doors. Seconds later, the door opened just wide enough for the apartment's unseen occupant to thrust out the biggest handgun Leon had ever seen.

"Who the fuck is it?" a gruff voice, tinged with nervousness, inquired.

"Uh...Jag sent me," stammered Leon, looking at the way the man's gun hand shook. "I've got your package."

Another quivering hand reached out and snatched the brown paper parcel from underneath Leon's right arm, then both hands shot back inside the apartment, and the door closed. Leon stood rooted to the spot for five seconds, then the door opened again, wider this time, and the boy could see a fierce, angry-looking man with long, dirty hair and fingernails, a woolly beard, and a pale, naked body pocked with needle tracks.

"So what're ya waitin' for, a tip?" he growled. "I don't owe nothin'! Get the fuck outta here!"

The door slammed again, and Leon thought it best to retreat as the man advised. On his way down the stairs, however, he heard a familiar voice emanating from one of the apartments on the second floor. The door in question was open, and, squinting through the weak, brown light provided by the room's only sixty watt bulb, Leon could see two men – one sitting on a battered, dusty couch, the other seated on an overturned egg crate – hunched over a game of checkers. He didn't recognize the elderly, prune-faced gentleman on the couch, but the musclebound guy on the crate was none other than Charlie, and the big man crowed boastfully as he took his opponent's last three pieces in one devastating sweep.

"You're slipping, old man," he chuckled, fingering the complete set of captured pieces like coins.

"I could take you anytime I wanted to if I had good eyesight," the old man replied, hoarsely.

"Want another Twinkie?" asked Charlie.

"No, thanks," said the old man, holding up a hand. "Could barely metabolize the last one, more's the pity."

"All right, I'll have yours then," said Charlie, peeling the wrapper off one of the yellow snack cakes and pushing the whole thing past his lips.

"Set up the board again," said the old man. "I'll get ya this time."

"It'd be the first time tonight," said Charlie. "You gotta quit sometime, pops."

"The only things I gotta do is stay black and die," said the old man. "You quit talkin' back and get them pieces set up again."

Charlie chuckled again, and raked in the pieces, then looked at the door and saw Leon.

"Hey, it's another one of my favorite folks!" he exclaimed. "Now it *is* a party. Come in, son, and have a Twinkie."

"What're you doin' here?" asked Leon, stepping inside.

"Now, is that nice?" said Charlie, turning back to the old man. "I don't ask *him* that, even though I'm sure his purposes are less noble than mine."

"Well, what *are* you doin' here?" Leon asked again. "This is a place for brothers who haven't changed their spots from black to white. This is the last place I figured to find you."

"It just so happens that I'm visiting an old friend of mine," said Charlie. "This here is Gus. Gus, this here is my girlfriend's boy."

Leon expected Gus to extend a reedy, arthritic hand in greeting, but he didn't. Instead the old man furrowed his brow and ran his eyes over the youngster's outfit.

"Red and black," he muttered, frowning. "He's a Cobra, Charlie; a dirty, stinkin' Cobra. You keep him outta my house."

"Hey!" Leon protested.

"Don't you 'hey' me, boy," Gus replied. "I can tell jus' by lookin' at you that you ain't good for nothin'. I don't want your kind 'round here. This hole in the wall may not look like much to you, but it's all I have, and it'd be jus' glorious by me if you and your fellow gang-bangers didn't come by and shoot it all up."

"Gus here was my parole officer when I was just a kid, not much older than you," said Charlie. "He helped to see me on the straight and narrow more 'an once, though I didn't always stay there for very long. He even helped me get into the Army."

"Yeah, and they threw you outta there too, ya bum," said Gus.

"Ol' Gus has always been a good friend to me," said Charlie, "although he plays just about the lousiest game of checkers you'll ever see."

"I want that no-account circus clown outta here," Gus continued to denounce Leon, his strained, raspy voice underlining his sincerity. "You know you're always welcome in my home, Charlie, but you can't bring that boy 'round. He's a thief an' a liar an' he's trouble."

"He comes from a good home, though," Charlie said, in Leon's defense.

"Home ain't got nothin' to do with it," said Gus. "Some's just born bad. If he was a fish, know what I'd say? Throw that one back!"

"Hey, just a minute, you old Grandpa Moses..." Leon had had just about enough.

"Throw that one back!" Gus reiterated.

"Who the fuck d'you think you are?"

"Oh, an' it cusses too," Gus observed. "So it's rotten *and* stupid."

"An' just what the fuck makes *you* so smart?"

"Spendin' all my bygone years dealin' with trash like you! 'Cause that's what y'are, boy, is trash! I seen 'em come an' I seen 'em go, an' none of y'all ever amount to nothin'!"

"It's okay, Gus, I'll take him home," said Charlie, getting to his feet.

"Hey, fuck you, man!" said Leon. "I don't need no babysitter to walk me home!"

"Boy, I saw a whole carload of Deer Hunters drive by this building just ten minutes ago," Charlie whispered to Leon. "What with those colors you're wearing, you should be thanking me for the escort."

"Why don't you get the fuck off my back?" the boy growled, as Charlie waved good-bye to Gus and began stomping down the creaky wooden stairs. "You might hit my mom's G-spot, but I don't need ya for nothin'! I already got a father!"

"I'm not trying to be your father," said Charlie, as he and Leon stepped out into the humid night air, "although it seems to me that you could stand to learn a few home truths that he never bothered to teach you."

"Yeah, you're one to talk," Leon rolled his eyes. "What do you know about anything? You're just a tamed house nigger anyway!"

Charlie's eyes flashed, and he raised his big hand, but he caught himself before he could go ahead and strike the boy.

"See, that's your problem right there," he said, glaring down at Leon. "You're a punk.

You're a punk, and what's worse is you're proud of it. You mope around all day, complaining about how the white man's down on you, but look at yourself. Wearing gang colors, carrying weapons, and talking like you got your English from a toilet bowl. You blow off school, you break laws, and you solve all your problems with violence. You bitch about the white man not respecting you, but how do you suppose all that looks to them?"

"I don't give a shit about what they think!"

"Well, I do! You're embarrassing me, boy! You're an embarrassment to all of us! We're a minority in this country, which means every single one of us represents our entire race! If white Mr. Smith gets attacked by another white guy, then he'll only hate that one individual. But if Mr. Smith gets attacked by a black guy, he'll wish all the millions of us would just go back to Africa! Now, that ain't necessarily Mr. Smith's fault, though it would be nice if he were a bit more broad-minded. That's just the way the human brain works. We identify things by the characteristics that make them unique. So the next time Mr. Smith sees a black guy – if he sees *me* – he'll cross over to the other side of the street. Now Mr. Smith hates all of us, all because some little punk like you decided to make his living by stealing wallets instead of staying in school and getting a job. You're helping to perpetuate a stereotype that makes everyone look down on us!"

"Fuck you, Oreo!" Leon, eyes dark with disdain, pushed past Charlie.

"I ain't finished yet!" Charlie grabbed Leon by the collar and slammed him back against a parked car. "You think I dunno what I'm talking about? I used to be just like you, kid! Dropped out of school, lived by stealing from others, ended up becoming a leg-breaker for a mobster. And y'know what color that mobster's skin was? He was as white as a trout's underbelly, and he had me under his thumb. 'Do this, nigger' and 'Do that, nigger' were the only words he ever needed to say to me, and I'd jump to it 'cause he was the boss. You kids think you'll be stronger if you drop out of the system, but does the life I used to have sound an awful lot like 'black power' to you?"

Leon might have said something here, but Charlie didn't pause long enough to allow him the chance.

"It took me a long time to realize that I had to take responsibility for my own destiny if I was gonna have any kind of a future, and I'm trying to save you years of trouble by sharing that wisdom with you now. I've got news for you, boy. The forty acres and a mule was bullshit. In this world you get what you work for, and there are plenty of people around to help you, your mother most of all. There's no one holding you down but you. If you spend the rest of your life in an' out of jail without a penny to your name, then it's not the fault of the white man, or your high school principal, or some slave trader who's been dead for three hundred years. It's *your* fault!"

"You..."

"And that n-word had better not be on the tip of your tongue," Charlie warned, cutting him off, "because if you call me that again, I'll slap you silly! To everyone else in the world, that word is just an anti-black slur, but to us it has layers of meaning. When I was a kid, the niggers were the trash; the shit at the bottom o' the barrel. By that definition, I was a nigger once, but I long ago earned the right not to be called that by anyone, least of all a little nigger like you!"

"I hate you!" Leon shouted.

"I'm not too crazy about you either!" Charlie fired back. "But I have very special feelings for your mother, so it looks like we're going to be stuck with each other for some time!"

"Fuck you *and* her!" Leon fumed, storming away down the street, turning around just long enough to flip Charlie the bird.

Charlie thought about going after him, then decided to let it rest for the night. The 'heart-to-heart' hadn't gone nearly as smoothly as he had hoped, and he doubted that sticking to each other like glue would do either of them any good for the time being.

How the hell do parents do this twenty-four hours a day? he marveled. *Next free moment I have, I'm definitely sending my mom a card.*

"I wasn't able to get all the details," said Sushi, the next morning, to the other Vigilantes assembled in the Rat Hole, "but thanks to our friends the fat Teddy Callahan and the late Edwin Bronson, Ramos has gotten his hands on no less than three tons of potassium cyanide."

"That stuff's the real thing," said Peg, having researched cyanide extensively in the past, for reasons both personal and professional. "Just a small dose will see you dead inside a few minutes. But why would he want such a staggering amount? The lethal dose for a healthy adult is only about three hundred milligrams."

"Three hundred milligrams," Carolyn mused, thoughtfully, rubbing her chin. "Will, get out your calculator. I want to try out a couple figures."

"If you think that's a kick," said Carla, "wait'll you hear what Zeke and I found out last night. Tell 'em, partner."

"Turns out ol' Ramos has himself a big ol' tumor in his brain," said Zeke, throwing down a stolen x-ray of the General's skull. "Of the inoperable variety. He ain't gonna live to see his next birthday."

"A brain tumor?" Peg marveled. "How could we have missed that?"

"It's only a recent development," said Carla, "and he's taken great pains to keep it quiet. Even those closest to him don't know."

"Um...Sushi? How much cyanide did you say Ramos had?" asked Carolyn, looking up from the figures she and William had been scratching out on a piece of scrap paper.

"Three tons."

"And, Peg, what did you say was the lethal dose?"

"Anywhere from two to three hundred milligrams, really."

"And the kind Ramos has is potassium cyanide?"

"Yes," said Sushi.

"The kind that comes in the form of a white powder, and could probably be cut into cocaine or heroin without anyone being the wiser?"

"Uh-oh," said Zeke.

"And approximately how many people live on this island of Manhattan, where Ramos has revitalized the drug market and cornered the supply?"

"Eight million, give or take," said Carla.

"Oh, shit," said Peg.

"Somebody call Gary," said Carolyn. "I don't care how crazy he is, just call him. Quickly."

The two-story building bordering a vacant lot on 126th Street, just a five-minute walk from the Harlem Institute of Fashion and the illustrious Black Fashion Museum, was an unassuming motel called The Plantation Inn, and Ron Grimace – having swapped his olive drab Army togs for a plain white t-shirt, a pair of blue jeans, and a heavy trenchcoat – strode confidently into the tiny lobby as if he owned the place. Other men might have been apprehensive at best, but two of Grimace's most defining attributes – his combat experience and his dark skin pigment – made him the ideal operative for this important mission.

"Good morning, sir," the neatly groomed desk clerk greeted him with a smile. "How may I help you?"

"I just came in to buy a watermelon," said Grimace.

"Ah," the clerk arched an eyebrow. "And why would you come in here to buy a watermelon?"

"Because the mean ol' overseer won't let me pick one of his," Grimace answered.

"I see," said the clerk, dropping a single silver key into Grimace's open palm and nodding his head in the direction of the inconspicuous door off to the left. "In that case, proceed unmolested, soul brother."

Grimace nodded his thanks, then advanced on the door, which he unlocked and pushed open to find what appeared to be an ordinary washroom. When he entered the third toilet stall, however, he found no toilet. Instead he took hold of a handle protruding from the wall just a few inches above the floor, then proceeded to peel the wall away like a garage door, revealing the interior of an elevator. Stepping inside, Grimace pulled the camouflaged door closed again, then pressed the button marked with a downward-pointing arrow. After a few seconds of jerking and rumbling, the elevator came to a stop and the door rattled open automatically to reveal just one of the numerous gray, concrete corridors making up the catacombs which the Harlem Hellfighters had renovated for their headquarters beneath the unsuspecting neighborhood.

Gotta hand it to 'em, thought Grimace, shedding his trenchcoat to allow himself unencumbered access to the guns, blades, and explosives he was carrying on his person. *They got the right idea. They have access to every corner of Harlem through these halls, and no one knows where to find 'em.*

Fully aware that he didn't have time to dwell on his surroundings, Grimace tore open the first air vent he could find and chucked two gas grenades into the ventilation shaft. As the grenades rolled, the noxious fumes spewed out of the canisters in thick, hazy clouds and spread out quickly, roiling down the shaft on their way to visiting every other vent in the complex. It was cyanogen chloride; a fast-acting, higly toxic blood agent that would cause immediate injury upon contact with the eyes or respiratory organs of its unfortunate victims. The way an underground bunker like this one depended upon the constant circulation of air, a little of the stuff would go a long way and nearly all of the Hellfighters would be choking on it very soon.

Securing his gas mask to his face – cyanogen chloride was known for its ability to penetrate the filters of gas masks, but Grimace didn't want to take the chance of dying before his mission was complete – the battle-scarred veteran took off running down the corridor, kicked open the first door he reached, and massacred the four surprised Hellfighters inside with a pair of AK-47s.

There'll be no joy in Mudville tonight, Grimace thought with a grin, turning to exit the blood-spattered room and resume his charge down the hallway.

By this time, other Hellfighters who had heard the abrupt shots were emerging from other rooms, and Grimace took a couple of bullets to the torso before stampeding into a hub area and kicking over a table, behind which he took adequate cover. He was wearing a Kevlar vest, but the bullets still stung like blazes.

While the onrushing tidal wave of Hellfighters screamed blue murder and fired their handguns, Grimace propped both his assault rifles on the edge of the table and held down the triggers, spraying the crowd with lead, shredding the men on the frontlines.

"You ain't nothin'!" he roared, his words muffled by his gas mask. "You ain't fuckin' nothin'!"

To see one man holding off so many was truly an awesome sight, but Grimace's maneuvers, as dictated by General Ramos, had been implemented perfectly. Grimace was behind cover and fortified with weapons, with his back to several different avenues of retreat, while his enemy was all lumped together. Even better, the cyanogen chloride had begun to affect those nearer the rear of the pack, and they were gasping and clawing at their throats as they fell to their knees.

When his rifles' magazines had been exhausted, and the Hellfighters' bullets had begun to chew through the table like metallic termites, Grimace pulled a grenade from his belt – an old-fashioned, exploding one this time – threw it into the mob's midst, and bolted for the nearest safe corridor as the handheld bomb blew away a third of the group's strength. A surviving Hellfighter managed to shoot Grimace in the right knee, but the devoted soldier kept moving anyway. Two more Hellfighters turned the corner in front of him and fired close to a dozen shots, some of which penetrated flesh and some of which bounced off the Kevlar, but even as Grimace crashed onto his back, he found his M16 in his hands, and he eviscerated the pair.

Groaning, crippled, and bleeding from several wounds, Grimace dragged himself onto his side and began pulling himself across the floor, clawing his way to the door at the end of the hall that had been his ultimate objective all along. Six Hellfighters from the previous group announced their pursuit, and they were coming up fast. Grimace peeled off his gas mask, stuck his Ka-Bar knife between his teeth, raised his M16 once again, and, leaning on his other arm for support, fired back at the killers. One fell, but the others kept coming, and they were on their weakened enemy in seconds. They punched and kicked him with a violence that would have killed a weaker man, but Grimace didn't even lose consciousness. Instead he stabbed his knife into the chest of one of the thugs and used the purchase to pull himself to his feet. Once standing again, albeit shakily, he yanked out the knife and slashed it across the throat of another man, then thrust the barrel of his M16 into the belly of a third and pulled the trigger, blasting a hole through his foe's midriff and sending him flying backwards against the wall.

One of the two remaining Hellfighters fired three bullets into the small of Grimace's back, one of which unmistakably penetrated the damaged vest, and blood flowed from Grimace's mouth as he tore one more grenade from his belt, pulled the pin, and dropped it to the floor. Three seconds later it exploded, dashing Grimace and his two foes like rag dolls against the wall. One of the Hellfighters was killed on impact with the wall as his neck broke, and Grimace, though severely burned and suffering from mortal injury himself – his left eye was gone, he couldn't move his right leg at all now, and he could tell that most of his ribs were broken and the organs they were supposed to protect were close to giving out – was more than capable of finishing off his final opponent, drawing his knife slowly, inexorably across the man's throat, cutting the soft flesh like butter.

Feeling woozy, losing cognizance, and tasting traces of the cyanogen chloride on his own tongue now, Grimace rolled over onto his belly and resumed crawling towards his objective, determined not to fail his leader in this monumental task entrusted to him. For several minutes he inched along the floor, leaving blood in his wake like a slug leaves a slime trail, until finally he reached the door, pushed it open, and beheld the hospital room. More bullets stung him like wasps, but he devoted what was surely his last reserve of strength to lurching in on bended knee and dispatching these last guards with a combination of clumsy but effective attacks with his knife and M16.

"Emerald," the dying soldier addressed the Hellfighters' leader, as always immobile and defenseless inside her shell, "General Ramos sends his regards."

One final slash with his knife was enough to sever the machine's vital cables, and the Emerald's eyes and mouth went wide as her lifeline flattened. Then Grimace joined her, collapsing facedown on the floor in a pool of his own blood.

General Ramos, standing tall in the center of an immense warehouse on 140th Street, looked at his gold pocket watch and smiled. By this time Grimace would have completed his mission. The Emerald would be slain, the Hellfighters would lie in ruin, and the gang's five tons of uncut cocaine would be his for the taking.

"It's here, just as Otis said," said Ramos. "All right, men, start loading it up. There's no one left to resist me now."

"A pity," said a voice from behind, near the building's wide entrance, as Ramos' minions began loading the big canisters onto a small fleet of flatbed trucks. "It's always an abomination when mania such as yours is allowed to run unchecked!"

Ramos turned to find Max Shepherd glaring at him, fairly trembling with anger, his countenance darker than the General had ever seen it. His right arm leaned on his ever present cane with seeming unsteadiness, and his left hand clutched a fat manila folder which he proceeded to dash at Ramos' feet, scattering papers across the concrete floor.

"I read it all!" he hissed, his face flushing crimson. "Every last word of this madness! No wonder you refused me full disclosure of our operations! This is, without a shadow of a doubt, the most reckless, irresponsible, self-destructive folly I've ever heard of! You're going to sink our entire empire – the business that *I* worked so hard to build while you were locked up in jail – just to satisfy your own petty, childish self-indulgences! Well, I'll not have it, Ramos! It stands to reason I'll not have it! I won't let you!"

Shepherd thrust his hand inside his jacket, but Ramos was much quicker, and after two loud retorts, Shepherd lay twitching and bleeding on the floor, twin holes in his chest.

"A woman scorned marks not the depth of hell's fury," said Ramos, coldly, advancing on his writhing, gulping lieutenant, "for the rage of a desperate man is far greater."

Shepherd gasped and coughed, and reached out to try and touch the cuff of Ramos' pant leg. Ramos just smirked, cruelly.

"I know," he sighed. "It's not fair, is it? But then, if life were fair, I wouldn't have a grapefruit inside my head."

The General allowed himself an arrogant chuckle, then turned back to face the legion of men that had halted in their work to observe the impromptu duel.

"Get back to work!" he barked. "The next man to pause will get what Shepherd got!"

Peg stepped off the elevator and onto the fourth floor of her apartment building, a brown paper sack of groceries cradled in one arm as she fished for her door key. After leaving the Rat Hole earlier that morning, she had stopped at the supermarket and picked up the fundamentals; bread, eggs, cheese, milk, fresh fruit, et cetera. Vicki had left the apartment even earlier than Peg had, and Peg was determined that the girl's first decent meal in weeks would be prepared and waiting for her when she returned to her new home.

Eleven-thirty, Peg consulted her wristwatch as she drew even with her door. *I'm no Betty Crocker, but I should have plenty of time to peel some fruit and fix some sandwiches.*

To Peg's surprise, the doorknob turned in her hand before she could insert her key. She was positive that she had locked the door when she had left hours ago, and she wondered briefly if she had become hostess to intruders. Then she remembered that she had given Vicki her own key to the place just last night, and she smiled to herself. Having a roommate would certainly take some getting used to.

"Hi, honey, I'm home," Peg announced herself as she entered. "I see you made it back all right. The wicked witch isn't so tough after all, eh?"

"Hi, Peg," said a weak, wounded voice emanating from the couch.

Peg gasped and put a hand to her mouth, and her groceries crashed to the floor as she took in the sight of Vicki, slouching there in the skirt and halter top she had borrowed from Peg's wardrobe, decked out with ugly bruises on her arms, legs, and face, a blacked left eye, and a deep, red gash festooning her forehead. There were tear streaks on her cheeks, but she wasn't crying now. She was just sitting, staring blankly at the wall, her hands folded in her lap.

"Vicki, what on earth?" Peg trilled with distress and concern as she rushed over to the couch and took the girl's face in her hands. "Did...did *she* do this to you?"

"I didn't want much," Vicki murmered, sounding very far away. "It was stupid to go back. I could have left everything behind. Really, I could have. I would've liked to have my snow globe, though."

"What?"

"My snow globe," Vicki sounded as if she was in a dream world. "My mother gave it to me for Christmas one year when I was little. It's nice. It has penguins in it."

"Honey, I think you're in shock," said Peg, picking up one of the girl's hands and holding it, firmly. "Come on, you know where you are. You know."

"She tried to kill me," said Vicki, her voice wavering from its monotone for the first time. "She actually tried to kill me. I mean, she always hurt me before, but this time she actually tried to kill me. I..."

Peg slipped both her arms around her younger lover and pulled her in close, patting her hair with one hand and rubbing her back with the other.

"It's all right, love," she whispered in her ear. "Everything's all right now. You're in a safe place now, with someone who's going to take really good care of you. It's all going to be just fine. Nothing like this will ever happen to you again."

Peg brushed Vicki's hair away from her face and kissed her softly on the lips, then pulled away and rose to her feet, smoothing her own skirt and top before marching determinedly towards the door.

"Wh-where are you going?" asked Vicki.

"To get your snow globe," Peg answered, closing the door behind her.

Ah, there he is, thought Sushi, perched atop a brownstone on East Seventh Street, wherefrom he could see clearly the bandaged, trenchcoated Jimmy Jay hunched over a garbage can on the cusp of Tompkins Square Park. *There's the little creep.*

Taking a flying leap from his three-story-high resting place, the ninja bounded across the street, using the roof of a parked station wagon as a springboard, and landed amidst the leafy boughs of a convenient tree, the branches of which provided shade for Jay as he recovered what appeared to be half a hamburger.

"Amazing, the food some people will just throw away," Sushi announced himself, swinging down from the tree, sticking a perfect landing just a few feet from his quarry.

"Leave me in peace, masked avenger," said the wretched Jay, parting his yellow lips and biting into the burger. "It's hard enough to eat as it is."

"I need to know where I can find Salvador Ramos," said Sushi. "Tell me."

"Fuck off."

"I need to find him as soon as possible, or countless lives could be at risk, though I don't suppose that matters to you."

"I said, fuck off!" roared Jay, turning on Sushi with a knife in his hand and lunging at the ninja.

Jay was good, but he might as well have been moving in slow motion as far as Sushi was concerned. The ninja didn't put one hair out of place in leapfrogging over Jay's back, seizing the collar of his coat, yanking the sickly assassin off his feet, and flipping him headfirst into the garbage can, which subsequently turned over and dumped him onto the ground.

"Give up, Jay," said Sushi, lifting the can off of the trash-covered thug. "You know you don't have anything left. You can't even get to your feet."

"How perceptive of you to notice," Jay scowled, his husky voice dripping with resentment.

"Tell me where I can find Ramos, Jay. You might as well. A man in your position gains no advantage from keeping secrets."

Jay groaned, as if finally shrugging the weight of the world from his shoulders and accepting the inevitable, then spoke in a strained, hoarse whisper of a voice.

"I know all about his tumor, y'know," he said. "He wouldn't tell anyone else, but he confided in me. I suppose it's because we ultimately share the same fate, and even the worst of us feel the need to talk about our deepest troubles." He paused to hack up a couple sprays of blood, then, "If I know his schedule, he should be in Chinatown this evening."

"Why would he be down there?"

"When you find him, you'll know," Jay wheezed, clutching his heaving chest. "But before you go, may I ask just one tiny favor?"

"What?"

"Kill me. Free me from this living hell. Take that sword of yours and run me through. I don't wish to live another minute trapped inside this body."

For several seconds Sushi regarded the pitiful man – sick, useless, and wracked with pain. Then he tore his dagger from its scabbard, twirled it once in his hand, and stabbed it into the soft earth next to Jay's left hip.

"Do it yourself," he said. "Perhaps a suicide will permit you to regain a shred or two of honor."

Jay looked into Sushi's eyes, his crestfallen countenance that of a man who has been left bereft of options, then wrapped his bandaged fingers slowly around the dagger's hilt and pulled the weapon out of the ground. Sushi turned his back on him and began walking as Jay directed the blade towards his own belly, and the ninja paid no attention to the final 'Hurk!' of agony sounding behind him as he detached his cell phone from his utility belt and dialed Carolyn's number.

"Have you gotten hold of Gary yet?" he asked. "Good. Tell him I know where he can find Ramos, come sunset."

Well, it doesn't exactly look like The Last House On the Left, thought Peg, standing in the driveway of the attractive, split-level Victorian home in Astoria, Queens. *Still, if I took any lesson away from the hot, steamy night I shared with that transsexual last month, it's that things aren't always what they seem.*

Determined to see it through, Peg stepped up to the front door and pressed the doorbell, which sounded out the first few chords of 'Amazing Grace'. The quality of the sound was melodious and pleasant; not tinny at all.

Down the rabbit hole, thought Peg.

Seconds later she could hear a series of audible clicks and clacks emanating from the other side of the door, as if several heavy locks were being thrown back, then the door opened, and Peg got an eyeful of a beautiful, willowy thirty-something with pale, creamy skin, an empowered bob of blond hair, and juicy, red lips that cried out to be kissed. She wore a pair of scarlet, open-toed heels, a provocatively short skirt, and a midriff-baring top that gave Peg a stellar view of a pierced naval and the playful 'Bitch' tattoo just below. It was all the stunned Vigilante could do to look the woman in the eye.

"Yeah? So, what is it?" asked the woman.

"Um...excuse me," Peg cleared her throat, "but is the lady of the house at home?"

"You're talking to her."

Now Peg was really astonished. While it was true that Vicki hadn't offered any physical description whatsoever of her aunt, Peg's mental picture had leaned towards an ugly, heavyset old woman who could have played tackle football with the men and enjoyed herself; a beefy, bulky, sneaker-wearing butch, possibly with false teeth and a disagreeable odor. Nothing had prepared Peg for the gorgeous creature who stood before her now.

"So...you're Millicent?"

"Yup."

"Well, hi, I'm Peg. I've come about your niece."

"Oh, really? That ungrateful little tramp? What about her?" Then her eyes darkened. "She hasn't been causing you any trouble, has she? I swear, I'll beat the living shit out of her if she's been making a pest of herself!"

"Oh, no, no, not at all!" Peg hastened to elaborate. "I just wanted to let you know that from now on...well, the fact of the matter is that from now on she'll be staying with me."

Millicent looked hard at Peg for several seconds, and the long silence made the Vigilante feel very uncomfortable before the other woman finally broke it with – of all things – a lilting, dismissive laugh.

"Boy, you had me worried for a moment there!" she chuckled. "I thought all this was about something important! Dearie, if you want her you can *have* her!"

"Really? Just like that?"

"Sure!" said Millicent, stepping back inside the house and beckoning for her visitor to follow. "Come on in. I'll make you a cup of tea if you'd like. I definitely need to get to know the person who's willing to take that little misery under their wing! Honey, you have no idea what you've let yourself in for, but it's too late now! No giving back!"

Not quite sure if this is the strangest afternoon I've ever spent, thought

Peg, stepping past the front door and into the living room, *but it's definitely in the top ten.*

"Um...you have a very lovely house," she said, aloud.

"Thank you," said Millicent. "Now, what did you say your name was? Really, it's a pleasure to meet you. Truth be told, I'm thrilled to pieces that someone is finally going to take that little whore off my hands. She's gotten to be far too much of a burden. Even with all her potential as free labor, she's just so much trouble. It's gotten to the point where she's just not worth the money I spend feeding her."

"It sounds as if you really don't care for her at all," said Peg.

"Oh, I promised my dear brother, as he lay dying in the hospital after that terrible car wreck, that I'd take care of her," said Millicent. "Geoffrey was always my weakness, God rest his soul. I'd do anything for him. So I've been putting a roof over her head and food in her stomach since she was twelve. And of course, she had her uses."

"Uses?"

"Well, I mentioned the free labor, didn't I? Not that she was ever very good at domestic chores, no matter how I motivated her. Still, better than spending money on a maid, right? Oh, and she was always a great little fluffer."

"Fluffer?"

"Yes, well, it can't have escaped your notice that Veronica is a very attractive girl," Millicent admitted, with all the grudging concession of a fairy tale stepmother. "I've certainly traded on her looks once or twice, but most often I'd have her fluff my dates. I'm sure you know how it is. Once a man gets even semi-erect, he wants to stick it in you. Well, that's not much fun for us, now, is it, dearie? So, before I'd even take my clothes off, I'd have the girl come in and use her mouth on him a bit. Y'know, sort of get him started for me. Get him all nice and hard."

Peg was speechless as Millicent continued.

"You'll find she's able to handle most tasks you throw at her," she said, as if negotiating the sale of a slave. "Mind you, you'll need to keep her under your thumb. Make sure she remembers who's boss. Me, I preferred to use corporal punishment."

"Yes, Vicki told me you beat her."

"As regularly as possible. Judge me as you will, but it always kept her in her place. The usual fare will do, if you care to adopt the method. Paddles and whips for spankings. Clothespins on her nipples. Buckets of water hanging from her shoulders. I strongly suggest you keep her chained up whenever possible, as she's prone to wander off. Oh, and I'm particularly fond of this."

Millicent walked over to the wall above the fireplace and took down the wooden cane.

"Made by Amish craftsmen," she smiled, caressing the cane lovingly. "Look, it even has her name inscribed here. Isn't that just too adorable? Here, hold it. Feel it."

"It's certainly a fine piece of work," said Peg, turning the smooth, polished cane over in her hands.

"Sturdy as hell," said Millicent, proudly. "She always knew she'd been a bad girl when she got six of the best from that. It has real sentimental value for me, but I think I could be persuaded to let you have it. After all, that's what it's for, isn't it? The thing you have to remember is to keep it on display in a place where she'll always be looking at it. Psychological, you see."

"No, I don't think that will be necessary," said Peg. "I can think of one or two better uses for it."

Before Millicent could ask, Peg spun on her heel, swinging the cane like a baseball bat, and dealt the other woman a vicious blow across the back of the head. Millicent screamed, and crashed to the floor, bleeding. Peg towered over her, raising the cane high into the air, a look of unbridled rage darkening her face.

"Is that how you hit her?" she snarled through set teeth, bringing the cane down hard on the small of Millicent's back. "Is that how? I mean, am I doing it right? Is this the proper technique?"

Another fierce blow with the cane, and Millicent screamed again.

"No, I don't think I've quite got the hang of this," said Peg. "I think I need a bit more practice!"

Peg clobbered her again as hard as she could, breaking skin and cracking bone as Millicent kept screaming and crying.

"Doesn't feel so divine when you're on the receiving end, does it?" said Peg, hammering away at the wicked woman's back as if it were an anvil. "You're not dealing with a scared little slip of a girl now! I'm a bitter, hardcore bitch with piss in my veins, scars on my wrists, and a different dick inside me each night of the week!"

Millicent shrieked as Peg smashed her with the cane one more time. Then the Vigilante dropped it on her and strode purposefully down the hall until she came to what had to be Vicki's bedroom.

All right, what did she say? Penguins, penguins...ah, here it is.

Peg tucked the snow globe safely under one arm, then marched back out into the living room, over to the helpless, sobbing woman on the floor. A satisfied smirk playing about her face, she knelt down to take

Millicent's tear-streaked, pain-contorted face in one hand, and tilted it upward so that she could look directly into her suffering eyes.

"And don't call the police," she cautioned, "or I'll come back and kill you. And believe me, lady, when I go off my meds I'm liable to do all kinds of crazy shit."

Millicent groaned as Peg patted her cheek and let her head fall to the floor, and by the time she'd gathered strength enough to lift it up again, she saw that her visitor had gone.

Nightfall in Chinatown, General Ramos mused to himself, gazing absentmindedly out the window of Auntie Ming's Herbal Emporium, watching the long shadows of twilight stretching out over Mott Street. *I grew up in a Mexican ghetto, and even I wouldn't care to linger here after dark.*

"Here you are, General, sir," said the elderly Auntie Ming, emerging from the backroom with a paper parcel tied up with hairy string. "Your usual order."

"Thank you," said Ramos, coolly, taking the parcel without making eye contact. "How much?"

"Two hundred dollars."

"What? My last order was only seventy-five!"

"You ordered more this time," said Ming, holding up a crooked finger. "Also, the stuff you have there is more potent than anything I usually sell. I had to order it special."

Ramos leered at her, then thrust his hand into his dress coat, pulled out his wallet, produced two one hundred dollar bills, and pushed them into Ming's bony hand.

"It's more than it's worth," he grumbled. "So far this rubbish hasn't helped at all."

"I never said ginseng was the magic bullet to cure all ills," Ming tutted, turning her back on him. "Good evening to you, sir."

Ramos was angry as he left the shop and began walking north. For the past two weeks he had been ingesting this muck; half a dozen Chinese herbs, the names of which he could neither remember nor pronounce. After being failed by Western medicine, he figured he had nothing to lose in trying something a little more folksy, but thus far he had been given no reason to believe the herbs were adding to his borrowed time. They weren't even much good against his persistent headaches.

Two hundred dollars for a bag of old roots, he thought, sourly.

"Hi, Ramos," said a sullen, familiar voice behind him.

Ramos turned to see Gary Parker standing ten yards away, his hands plunged into his pockets, the setting sun casting his long shadow out in front of him like the silhouette of a giant.

"You," the General hissed.

"Yeah, me," Gary replied. "Wanna fight about it?"

"You took away three years of my life," said the General. "I suppose you know about my...misfortune?"

Gary nodded.

"I was diagnosed in prison," said Ramos. "In prison, Parker, those with short sentences live for the day of their release. Imagine my dismay, sir, when I learned that my three years had been commuted to a death sentence."

"I'd like to say I sympathize, but I don't," said Gary, feeling rather like an emotional washcloth that had been wrung out completely. "You deserve to die."

"Perhaps," Ramos conceded. "But I am not ready."

"I know all about the cyanide," said Gary.

"Then I commend you on your excellent investigative skills," said Ramos.

"You're cutting it into your coke and heroin, aren't you?"

"Enough coke and heroin to satisfy this entire island," nodded Ramos. "It's all prepared, and ready to hit the streets within the week. Just one dose will kill any user almost instantly."

"So, all of this – the cornering of the drug market, and the reintroduction of casual drug use into mainstream society – it was never about the money or the power at all, was it?"

"Those things are useless to a dying man. All I have left is vengeance; vengeance against a world that wronged me."

"You're insane."

"I'm no more insane than the countless hordes who abuse their bodies and endanger their lives daily to slake their depraved addictions," said Ramos. "Look at them, Parker. See how cheaply they count their lives. What must a heroin addict have to live for? He poisons himself for a thrill, and does so until he has become a slave to his cravings. He runs out of money, his life lies in tatters, and he becomes so dependent upon the drug that he must dose himself just to gain the strength to stumble out of bed in the morning. Such a person does not appreciate this fragile gift that is life, Parker. What an insult it is to see otherwise healthy people behaving this way when *I* am condemned to die decades before my time! Well, if they want the ultimate designer drug, I'll give it to them! Soon, countless people all over this city – from homeless degenerates, to misguided children, to respected businessmen – will be falling down dead, as they rightly should have a long time ago!" Ramos fell silent for a moment, then chuckled in his throat as a thought came to him. "You know, every designer drug needs a name. I think I'll call this new concoction of mine 'the quality of life'. After all, that is what my innumerable customers will soon learn to appreciate, once they feel the cyanide corroding their insides and realize that death is coming for them right swiftly."

"You know I won't let you do it," said Gary.

"I invite you to try and stop me," said Ramos. "Shepherd put up rather a stink about it as well, so I had to shoot him. Knowing him, he was probably upset that I intended to kill off his entire customer base. All that money, you know. But I will not use a gun here, Parker. No, I'd much rather kill you with my bare hands. Come, then, and let us see if you still possess that which defeated me three years ago."

The two men closed the gap between them in an instant, leaping for each other's throats, and hitting the ground in an entanglement of muscular limbs. Gary was the first to draw blood, kneeling on Ramos' chest and cracking him a sound blow on the jaw, but the General rolled backwards and used his knees to kick the Vigilante off. Gary landed on all fours and sprang back to try and keep the General down, but Ramos used his powerful legs to propel himself to his feet, and caught his foe with a devastating uppercut to the chin.

"You can't win, Parker," Ramos smirked, as Gary landed flat on his back. "I'm the proverbial wounded beast. I'll fight to the last breath!"

Gary snarled, and kicked Ramos hard in the left knee. Ramos screamed in pain and dropped to the pavement once again while Gary charged forward and punched him in the face. Blood exploded from the General's nose, and Gary moved in for a kick to the solar plexus, but Ramos seized his ankle in mid-flight and twisted it hard, throwing Gary off balance and bringing him down again.

"I'll crush you, Parker!" he hissed, throwing himself down onto Gary and punching him twice in the face. "I'm a hero, after all!"

"You *were* a hero!" snarled Gary, catching the next punch in his hand and squeezing hard enough to make Ramos yell. "You left that behind a long time ago! Now you're just another bad guy!"

Gary kicked Ramos in the groin and threw him off, but the General was quick to recover, springing to his feet and catching the lunging Gary on the chin again, this time with the heel of his boot. Again, Gary fell back.

"Give up, you insolent punk!" said Ramos. "You can't beat an old military man!"

" 'Old' being the operative word! I'm younger than you, Ramos, and that means I'm *better!*"

With that final declaration of confidence, Gary threw himself headfirst like a torpedo into Ramos' midsection, propelling them both into the solid brick wall of Friendly Li's Bicycle Shoppe, and it was in this position – trapped between Gary and the wall – that Ramos slouched helplessly as his enemy rained down blow after blow upon him. Blood flowed, bells rang, and stars danced before his eyes as the fists kept flying in, showing no sign of relenting, and he couldn't move, even as his teeth broke out of his mouth, and his neck snapped from side to side as if boneless. At last he felt something explode inside his skull, and he cried out, holding up a trembling hand.

"Stop!" he lisped, frantically. "Please! No more! Don't you know how ill I am? I surrender! Just...please, don't hit me anymore!"

Gary, his eyes flashing wildly, his breath coming quickly and unevenly, stopped his fist in midair and regarded his vanquished foe, swooning like a disaster victim and pleading pitifully for mercy.

"No more," he continued to beg, quieter now, as his strength failed him. "I...don't want...to die. Please. I...give up. Just...don't kill me. Don't."

Gary looked at Ramos some more as he slowed his breathing and finally unclenched his fist. Then a gleam of enlightenment came into his eyes, and the corner of his mouth turned just slightly upwards.

"Know what, Ramos?" he said. "I'm *not* going to kill you. I'm going to let you have the rest of your worthless life, however brief it may be. Know why? It's not because I think you deserve another chance. It's because – and I want you to listen real well to this part, pal – I don't particularly *want* to kill you. Oh, sure, I'd kill you if I had to, but I don't have to. I've beaten you, and that's the end of it. And that proves that I'm not like all the psychos that I fight. Because, unlike them, I'm capable of mercy and restraint. So get on your feet, you old has-been, because I'm taking you back to jail."

Before Gary could extend a hand to help Ramos up, however, he heard five gunshots ring out from behind him in rapid succession, and he dove instinctively to the ground. Then he heard a guttural 'Urk!', followed by the long, drawn-out groan of a man who's breathed his last, and he looked up to see Ramos slumped like a sack of potatoes against the wall, dead, with five bloody holes in his broad chest.

"What the hell...?" Gary wondered, looking around for the shooter and finally laying eyes on an attractive young girl standing not twenty feet away, holding a smoking pistol in one hand.

"The bastard had it coming," said Tomboy, unemotionally. "It was his lousy heroin that killed my brother three years ago."

Without another word, Tomboy dropped the gun into a nearby garbage can, turned, and walked away into the night. Gary, still flat on his belly, was too astonished to stop her, or even to ask her who she was.

"Ah, *there's* my favorite lady!" exclaimed Dirty Otis, extending his arms and breaking out into a grin as he saw Peg, accompanied by Vicki, come in through the front door of Mr. Happy's Bar & Grill.

"Hi, Otis," said Peg, the squabble of the previous evening forgotten. "I've brought my new squeeze here for a drink to celebrate the christening of our sapphic love nest. Two mint juleps, if you please."

"Is she old enough to drink?" asked Otis.

"Do you really give a shit?" Peg replied, as she and Vicki climbed atop a pair of barstools.

"Nope," Otis produced two glasses and began mixing the cocktails.

"Cleans up nice, doesn't she?" Peg indicated Vicki, making the girl blush.

"She sure does," Otis whistled. "Hard to believe she and that little ragamuffin I was tying to a pole just twenty-four hours ago are one and the same."

"I'm sorry if I ruined your movie," said Vicki, looking shyly at the countertop.

"No harm done," said Otis, breezily. "In fact, an artist is often at his best when forced to improvise. It took me only a few minutes after you left to hit the nail on the head. I thought to myself, why kill just one character? Let's kill *everybody*! It's a truly spectacular scene! I'm tellin' you, girls, I can taste that award for Best Male-Female Orgy Longer Than Ten Minutes right now!"

"Good for you, Otis," Peg congratulated him. "You'll be sure to send me a copy of the final cut, won't you?"

"Absolutely," said Otis, topping off the drinks and pushing them across the bar to his customers. "After all, if you hadn't stolen my sacrificial virgin, the idea would never have materialized. Now, enjoy your drinks, my lovelies. I'd love to stay and chew the fat with you, but I've got to take a monkey wrench to that jukebox back there, or it's gonna be playing 'Material Girl' all night, and that isn't helping anybody."

"I thought he'd never leave us in peace," said Peg, once Otis was out of earshot.

"What'll we drink to?" asked Vicki.

"To soft skin and probing tongues," said Peg, clinking her glass against Vicki's. "And I don't want you to worry about your aunt anymore. I fixed it so she'll stay out of our hair forever."

"You...you didn't kill her, did you?"

"Why, Vicki! I'm surprised at you! What a naughty imagination you have! Of course I didn't kill her!" She paused to take a sip of her drink, then smiled. "I just made certain she'll never walk again."

Vicki stared at Peg for a long moment, trying to discern whether or not she was kidding, then decided it didn't matter, and laughed. To Peg, it was the tinkling of bells.

"Come on, sweetie," said Peg, downing the rest of her drink and rising from her stool. "Let's go shoot a game of pool. The loser has to go to bed with the winner."

Vicki laughed again, and followed happily. Otis, from his place at the foot of the jukebox (which had moved on to 'Piano Man'), watched them go.

"That Peg is a fine woman, Tove," he said to his bouncer, standing oak-like just a few feet away. "She's got looks, brains, and a sex drive that could take years off a man's life. I tell you, boy, if either one of us was the marrying type, I just might be able to see myself with her."

"Uhn?" said Tove.

"Yeah, that's what I like about you, buddy," said Otis, wistfully. "You always know exactly what to say."

Max Shepherd, clothed in a cotton gown that opened in the back, was sitting up in bed in a private room in New York Downtown Hospital, an IV tube stuck in his left arm and a TV remote in his right hand, and he scowled as he flipped continuously through the basic cable channels. There was nothing on. Just a lot of silly game shows, syndicated sitcoms, and procedural police dramas.

"A civilization may be judged by the uses it finds for its technology," he grumbled, turning off the TV in disgust.

"Oh, it's not so bad," said the attractive nurse taking stock of his vital signs. "I don't know what I'd do without *Days of Our Lives*."

Shepherd felt a twinge in his chest as he worked to suppress the rising bile, and looked to the tatty paperback – doubtless left behind by the room's prior occupant – on his bedside table for distraction, but it was just a pulp murder mystery. Puerile trash.

"Nurse, how long must I remain here?" he asked, impatiently.

"Sir, you came in with two bullets lodged in your chest," said the nurse. "The doctor will want you to stay for at least a few days."

Tell her that's unacceptable! barked the other man inside Shepherd's mind. *We can't afford to be laid up that long!*

"I must get back to work!" said Shepherd. "Those imbeciles can't be trusted to cope on their own! The ones who aren't incompetent are crooks!"

I'll not stay cooped up in here like some animal! the other man persisted. *The night belongs to* me! *You promised!*

"Shut up!" Shepherd growled, spittle forming at the corners of his mouth. "After your little stunt at the mansion last night, I'm not even speaking to you!"

Oh, no, you don't, you arrogant twit! You're not getting off the hook that easy!

"Sir, are you all right?" the nurse asked in alarm. "Your heart rate is hitting the ceiling!"

The hapless girl had time for just one scream as Shepherd's hands leapt to her throat. Moments later, a doctor and two orderlies rushed in to find the patient gone and the nurse lying dead on the floor, the heart monitor's cord tied tightly around her neck. A hastily scrawled note tucked into the collar of her uniform explained the situation.

They sure do like to scream, and no mistake. Damnedest thing I ever heard, all that screaming. Hardly touched her, and she still screamed to beat my giddy Aunt Sally. Why do they do it? Do they think it's attractive or something? Well, it doesn't do a thing for me, brothers.

From Hell.

"This is it, li'l dude," said Tash, leading Leon up the stairs to the rooftop of a four-story tenement building on 110th Street running through the heart of Spanish Harlem. "Baptism by fire. Do this next thing, and you're in."

"I'm ready, man," said Leon, his fists clenched in determination. "I'm so ready."

Tash smiled, opened the door to the roof, and led Leon out, where the younger boy saw two more Cobras standing over by the edge, flanking a Hispanic kid in contrasting colors. The kid was tied up, sitting on the ledge overlooking the street, and Leon could tell he was a Deer Hunter, not just by his blue bandanna, but also by his ethnicity; as the Cobras were predominantly black, the Hunters' membership was overwhelmingly Latino.

"Enrique here is in a heap o' trouble," Tash explained. "Three nights ago he fucked Kwami's sister in the ass. Now, jus' 'cause Kwami ain't with us no more don't mean the debt is forgot, so we're killin' two birds with one stone by bringin' you in on this fucker's retribution."

"Want me to kick him around a bit?" asked Leon.

"Hell no, brutha," said Tash. "I want you to kill him."

Leon did a double-take.

"You...you want me to *kill* him?"

"Nigga, what did you think you were gonna have to do when you met one o' these wetbacks?" asked Tash. "*Scare* him to death?"

"Well, no, but I..."

"I seen what you can do, kid," said Tash. "You ain't a sissy faggot like Jag thinks. You a bad motherfucker. When you get all wound up, even *I* wouldn't wanna fuck with you, dude. You deserve a place with the Cobras, but I can't give it to you until ya do this one last thing, so why don'tcha jus' give this sack o' shit a shove overboard an' we'll call it a night."

"He ain't gonna do it," the captive Deer Hunter sneered. "Look at him. Weak as faggot piss."

"He's dead anyway, brutha, 'cause if you don't do it, then I will," said Tash. "He's right there. Jus' reach out an' push him. C'mon, don't let me down now."

"What a little fag!" the Hunter derided him. "Man, I thought all you niggers were supposed to be all bad-ass! Or is that jus' an act y'all put on to keep whitey scared? I bet y'all don't even have big dicks or nothin'!"

"You're embarrassin' me, li'l dude," said Tash. "Do this fucker already."

"That shirt you're wearin' is made outta cotton," the Hunter continued his tirade. "Ya pick it yourself? Yeah, that's all any o' y'all are good for is work! That's why ya got brought over here, that's why ya had to rely on whitey to give ya your freedom, an' that's why you're still not worth shit even today!"

Leon's eyes darkened.

"Y'know why everyone calls you coons monkeys?" the Hunter laughed. "It ain't 'cause you come from the jungle. It's 'cause you're kinda like humans, only not as smart an' not as useful!"

"You're really startin' to piss me off, spick!" Leon snarled back.

"Whadda ya gonna do about it? Throw your shit at me like all the other monkeys do?"

"I'm warnin' you..."

"Tell ya what, li'l monkey. Let me go, an' I'll go get ya some o' the Colonel's chicken, an' a nice, ripe watermelon!"

"Shut up!"

"Then I'll show ya how you jigs can be useful! Know what I like to do in weather like this? I hang a couple o' niggers from a nice, shady tree, then tie 'em together at the ankles an' use 'em for a hammock!"

Leon lashed out, and the Hunter went over, somersaulting backwards for four stories and hitting the hard pavement below. Blood squirted out of the pulped body like water from a sponge, and a witness across the street screamed in horror.

"Yeah!" Tash hooted, triumphantly. "I knew ya had it in ya, dawg! I knew it! Welcome to the Red Cobras, my brutha!"

Tash handed Leon a red-and-black bandanna and a GLOCK 18 machine pistol, but Leon didn't really pay attention to the gifts.

One minority killin' off another one, he thought, somberly. *The joke's on us. Whitey must be laughin' his ass off.*

As he did every morning at about eleven o'clock, Skip clambered out of his cot, threw on his shabby clothes, picked up the money and duffel bags waiting for him outside his hut, crossed over to Eagle Pass on the go-fast boat, and walked half a mile to Tito's Eggs N' Things, where he took a seat in a booth by the window and ordered his usual fried eggs, bacon, hash browns, and black coffee. Jyro arrived soon afterwards, and the two colleagues discussed the state of the place in whispered tones as they tucked into their late breakfast.

"This is too fuckin' weird, man," said Skip, chewing nervously at his bottom lip. "I mean, this place is always crowded at this time. But look around. We're the only ones here. There's not another soul in the joint."

"Could you be any more paranoid?" asked Jyro, letting a cooler head prevail.

"It's not paranoia if people really *are* out to get you," argued Skip.

Jyro emptied three packets of Sweet 'N Low into his coffee, then took a sip. "I'm not prepared to hold a conversation with you until you achieve a more rational state of mind," he said, condescendingly.

"But look over by the kitchen!" said Skip. "Where's all the usual staff? Even our waiter was new!"

"Really, this is the limit," said Jyro, losing patience. "A quiet restaurant and a new waiter, and you're ready to believe the Martians have landed."

"There's something about him I don't trust," said Skip.

"The fellow was perfectly civil," said Jyro. "It made a nice change to be served by someone who could speak English."

"And that's another thing," said Skip. "What's a guy with a limey accent doing all the way down here?"

"I'm just this close to slapping you," threatened Jyro.

"You don't understand!" hissed Skip, leaning across his plate of scraps. "There are forces at work! Operations no one knows about! If we're not extra careful, we could end up...end up..."

"End up what?"

Skip's eyes started to glaze over, and his mouth fell wide open as he slumped down into his seat.

"Skip?" Jyro craned his neck to look down at him. "Skip, what's wrong? Are you all right?"

"The coffee," he groaned, quietly, just before crashing facedown onto the floor. "It was something...in the coffee."

Alarmed, Jyro shot a glance at his own coffee, and he could indeed see a white, milky substance bubbling slowly to the surface. Then he saw no more, as his eyelids fell like leaden weights and he too passed out where he sat.

"Well, that was fairly easy," said Gary, removing his apron and hairnet as he emerged from the kitchen. "A quick call to the police should see this pair off, and then I can get out of here."

"Going into business for yourself, Gary?" asked a familiar voice, as the bell above the diner's front door tinkled.

Gary whirled in surprise to see Carla standing inside the eatery's entrance. She smiled an amused little smile, and nodded towards Skip and Jyro.

"Your handiwork, I take it?" she said.

"I know what you're thinking, but it's just a sleeping drug," said Gary. "Scout's honor."

"What are you doing down here, anyway?" she asked.

"Just making sure that the fringes of Ramos' organization get clipped," he said. "My city is no longer his landfill."

"How exactly did you swing this little stunt?"

"In exchange for a handsome bribe, the owner of this place closed up for the morning and left me the key."

"Ah."

"And what are *you* doing here? How could you possibly have known where I was?"

Carla's smile grew, and her eyes warmed.

"I love you, Gary," she said. "I *always* know where you are."

Gary marveled at her, then shook his head and smiled himself. After all, what further explanation did he require, really?

"You're looking a lot healthier," Carla observed, brushing a hand against Gary's left cheek.

"I guess you could say I finally found what I was looking for," he said.

"Care to share with me what it was?" she asked.

Gary thought for a few seconds, then remembered something Ramos had said, and he chuckled.

"What?" asked Carla.

"The quality of life, I think," he said.

A sudden clap of thunder drew Gary and Carla's eyes to the window to see that the brilliant sun had disappeared behind a bank of dark, heavy clouds, and in the span of three seconds a torrent of rain began pouring down from the sky, sounding like nails clattering on the roof of the diner.

"Looks like this heat is finally going to break," said Carla. "I'm going to wash this awful sweat out of my hair. You coming?"

Gary's cell phone rang, and he took it out of his pocket. "You go ahead," he said. "I'll be with you in a second."

Carla nodded, and proceeded outside. Gary flipped open his phone and answered it.

"Hi, Janet," he said, for he knew 'twas her.

"I heard about what happened to Ramos," she said, "but I simply must get this from the horse's mouth. Is it true that he was killed by a five foot-nothing co-ed in pigtails?"

"Completely true," Gary affirmed.

"So, you didn't kill him yourself?"

"Nope. I didn't kill the bad guy this time. It was a terminal case of karma that did him in. They say you reap what you sow, and I guess they're right."

"I'm disappointed in you, Gary," she said. "I really thought you were ready this time. I really thought you were going to embrace the real you."

"You know the real me, Janet," he said. "He's someone you could never love."

The connection broke with a resounding 'click', and Gary smirked to himself, snapped the phone closed, slipped it back into his pocket, and headed for the door. He saw Carla luxuriating in the freshness of the cool, cleansing rain, and he waved to her.

Gary Parker, you are one of the strangest, saddest, craziest, most twisted fucks on this whole mudball planet, he told himself. *And may God bless you for it.*